# Putting it together

We do our best to find the best mix of the best books for Select Editions. This volume's lineup started with Michael Connelly. When one of his books arrives in the office, the editors push each other out of the way trying to read it first. Amy Reilly prevailed this time, and when she was done she proclaimed it "classic Connelly"—always a good thing.

Shortly after, we were pleased to see that one of our favorite writers, Belva Plain, was still at it. Once again Amy grabbed the book first, and in her review she called it "compelling and page-turning." That's high praise around here, and what better way to balance a legal thriller than with a fine family drama?

Tom Clemmons beat Amy to the latest from Karen Robards. In his summary of *Guilty,* a tale of romantic suspense, he wrote, "You get hooked and want to stay with it till you know just who—" Well, you can find out for yourself just who is doing what.

Amy was once again the first reader for the book we chose for our fourth selection. She found *Hannah's Dream,* a book about an elephant by a relative newcomer to publishing, to be "charming, with poignant scenes and gentle humor."

As for me, I was the second reader on all of these books, and I agreed with what the others had said about them. Now it's your turn. Enjoy.

Jim Menick
*Executive Editor*

## SELECT EDITIONS

### U.S. EDITORIAL

*Executive Editor:* James J. Menick

*Senior Editors:* Thomas S. Clemmons, Amy M. Reilly

*Art Director:* Robin Arzt

*Production Editor:* Lorraine Burton

*Production Assistant:* Joanna Luppino

### INTERNATIONAL EDITIONS

*Executive Editor:* Gary Q. Arpin

*Senior Editor:* Bonnie Grande

### RIGHTS AND PERMISSIONS

*Manager:* Carol Weiss Staudter

*Rights Associate:* Arlene Pasciolla

*Rights Administrator:* Ann Marie Belluscio

---

---

# SELECT EDITIONS

*Selected and Edited by Reader's Digest*

THE READER'S DIGEST ASSOCIATION, INC.

PLEASANTVILLE, NEW YORK • MONTREAL

# Inside
## SELECT EDITIONS

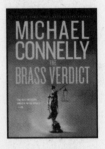

## THE BRASS VERDICT
*Michael Connelly*

Top-level legal intrigue proves once again that when Michael Connelly writes a book, you have no choice but to stop everything and read it.

**AFTERWORDS:** *The many ideas of Michael Connelly, plus some sleuthing and sightings.*

## CROSSROADS
*Belva Plain*

Two young women see in one another what they might want in themselves in a welcome return novel from a master storyteller.

**AFTERWORDS:** *Looking back with Belva Plain, with some corporate stepping up.*

## GUILTY
*Karen Robards*

Assistant DA Kate White has a past. And it catches up with her in this engaging thriller that doesn't let go until the very last page.

**AFTER WORDS:** *A conversation with Karen Robards, and an author's early submission.*

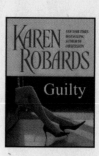

*page 288*

---

EXCITING NEW AUTHOR! ## HANNAH'S DREAM
*Diane Hammond*

What do you do with a lonely old elephant? That's the question posed in this charming novel about the main attraction at a private zoo on the decline.

**AFTER WORDS:** *All about Diane Hammond, the facts behind the fiction, and the real Sam.*

*page 442*

---

*page 167*

*page 286*

*page 440*

*page 573*

# MICHAEL CONNELLY

## THE BRASS VERDICT

# ONE

## 1992

EVERYBODY lies.

Cops lie. Lawyers lie. Witnesses lie. The victims lie.

A trial is a contest of lies. And everybody in the courtroom knows this. The judge knows this. Even the jury knows this. They come into the building knowing they will be lied to. They take their seats in the box and agree to be lied to.

The trick if you are sitting at the defense table

is to be patient. To wait. Not for any lie. But for the one you can grab onto and forge like hot iron into a sharpened blade. You then use that blade to rip the case open and spill its guts out on the floor.

That's my job, to forge the blade. To use it without mercy or conscience. To be the truth in a place where everybody lies.

I WAS in the fourth day of trial in department 109 in the downtown Criminal Courts Building when I got the lie that became the blade that ripped the case open. My client was riding two murder charges all the way to the steel gray room in San Quentin, where they serve you death juice direct through the arm.

Barnett Woodson was a twenty-seven-year-old drug dealer accused of robbing and killing two college students from Westwood. They had wanted to buy cocaine. He decided instead to take their money and kill them both with a sawed-off shotgun. Or so the prosecution said. It was a black-on-white crime, and that made things bad enough for Woodson—especially coming just four months after the riots that had torn the city apart. But what made his situation even worse was that the killer had weighed down the two bodies and dropped them into the Hollywood Reservoir. They stayed down for four days before popping to the surface. The idea of dead bodies moldering in a primary source of city drinking water caused a collective twist in the community's guts. When Woodson was linked by phone records to the dead men and arrested, the district attorney's office announced it would seek the death penalty.

The case against Woodson, however, was largely constructed of circumstantial evidence—the phone records—and the testimony of witnesses who were criminals themselves. And state's witness Ronald Torrance sat front and center in this group. He claimed that Woodson confessed the killings to him.

Torrance had been housed on the same floor of the Men's Central Jail as Woodson, in a high-power module whose sixteen single-prisoner cells opened onto a dayroom. Detainees had six a.m. to six p.m. access to the dayroom, where they ate and played cards at tables under the watchful eyes of guards in an overhead glass booth.

It was at one of these tables that Torrance claimed my client had confessed to killing the two Westwood boys.

On the fourth day of Woodson's trial, in direct testimony elicited by Jerry Vincent, the prosecutor, Torrance said Woodson not only confessed to the killings but furnished details that only the true killer would know.

During the testimony, Vincent kept Torrance on a tight leash with long questions designed to elicit short answers. Vincent finished his direct at eleven a.m., and I began my cross. I took a big, thick file with me to the lectern.

"Mr. Torrance, my name is Michael Haller. I work for the public defender's office and represent Barnett Woodson. You and Mr. Woodson, you two go back a long way, correct?"

Torrance gave an "aw shucks" smile. But I had done the due diligence on him, and I knew exactly who I was dealing with. He was thirty-two years old and had spent a third of his life in jails and prisons. Under the state's three-strike law, he was facing the lifetime achievement award if convicted of charges he robbed and pistol-whipped the female manager of a coin laundry. The crime had been committed during the rioting that ripped through the city after the not-guilty verdicts were announced in the trial of four police officers accused of beating Rodney King. In short, Torrance had good reason to help the state take down Barnett Woodson.

"Well, we go back a few months, is all," Torrance said. "To high-power module. In county."

"So you're talking about jail, correct?"

"That's right. We met for the first time in the jail."

"Let's do the math, Mr. Torrance. Barnett Woodson was transferred into the high-power module on the fifth of September, earlier this year. Do you remember that?"

"Yeah, I remember him coming in, yeah."

"And why were you there in high-power?"

"I got a count of assault and one of robbery."

"These alleged crimes took place during the riots, correct?"

"Yeah. I was out there like everybody else."

"And your response to the injustice of the Rodney King verdicts was to rob a sixty-two-year-old woman and knock her unconscious with a steel trash can. Is that correct?"

Torrance looked over at the prosecution table and then past Vincent to his own lawyer, sitting in the first row of the gallery. But his lawyers couldn't help Torrance now. He was on his own.

"I didn't do that," he finally said.

"You're innocent of the crime you are charged with?"

"That's right."

"What about looting during the riots?"

Torrance said, "I take the Fifth on that."

"All right, Mr. Torrance, let's get back to you and Mr. Woodson. You knew the details of this double murder before you met Mr. Woodson in lockup?"

"No, sir. I don't read no papers, and the module's TV been broke since I got there."

"According to the state's discovery material, you contacted the prosecution on October second to report Mr. Woodson's alleged confession. Does that sound right to you?"

"Yeah, that sounds right."

"Well, not to me, Mr. Torrance. You are telling this jury that a man facing the possible death penalty confessed to a man he had known for less than four weeks?"

Torrance shrugged before answering. "That's what happened."

"With your prior record and current charges, you are looking at fifteen years in prison if convicted, correct?"

"I don't know. I let my lawyer handle all that."

"I see. What have you asked the prosecutor for in exchange for your testimony?"

"Nothing. I don't want nothing."

"So you are testifying because you believe it is your duty as a citizen?" The sarcasm in my voice was unmistakable.

"That's right," Torrance responded indignantly.

I held up the thick file. "Do you recognize this file?"

"No, not that I recall."

"You don't remember seeing it in Mr. Woodson's cell?"

"Never been in his cell."

"My client had investigative documents relating to his prosecution in his cell. These contained several details you testified to this morning. You don't think that's suspicious?"

"No. All I know is that he sat there at the table and told me what he'd done. It ain't my fault people open up to me."

"Of course not, Mr. Torrance. Now can you tell the jury exactly what he said to you?"

"Well, we were sittin' the both of us by ourselves, and he just started talkin' about feelin' bad about what he'd done. I asked what'd you do, and he told me about that night he killed two fellas."

"Mr. Torrance, you are summarizing. Tell the jury the *exact* words Mr. Woodson said to you."

Torrance nodded as if he just realized what I was asking. "The first thing he said was, 'Man, I feel bad.' And I said, 'For what, my brother?' He said he kept thinking about those two guys. I didn't know what he was talking about, so I said, 'What two guys?' and he said, 'The two niggers I dumped in the reservoir.' I asked what it was all about, and he told me about blasting them with a shorty and wrappin' them up in chicken wire and such. He said, 'I made one bad mistake,' and I asked what it was. He said, 'I shoulda taken a knife and opened up their bellies so they wouldn't float up the way they did.' And that was what he told me."

I carefully moved in with the blade. "Did Mr. Woodson use that word? He called the victims 'niggers?' "

"Yeah, he said that."

I hesitated as I worked on the phrasing of the next question. I knew Vincent was waiting to object if I gave him the opening. I could not ask Torrance to interpret. I couldn't use the word "why" when it came to Woodson's meaning or motivation.

"Mr. Torrance, in the black community, the word 'nigger' could mean different things, could it not?"

"Yes."

"The defendant is African-American, as are you, correct, sir?"

Torrance started to laugh, "Since I was born," he said.

"When Mr. Woodson used that word, did it shock you?"

Torrance thought about the question. "Not really."

"Why weren't you shocked, Mr. Torrance?"

"I guess it's 'cause I hear it all a' time, man."

"From other black men?"

"That's right. I heard it from white folks, too."

"Okay, Mr. Torrance. Do you use that word on occasion?"

"I think I have."

"When you have used it, who were you referring to?"

Torrance shrugged. "Other fellas."

"Other black men?"

"That's right."

"Have you ever on occasion referred to white men as niggers?"

"No."

"Okay, so then what did you take the meaning to be when Barnett Woodson described the two men as niggers?"

Vincent moved in his seat, going through the body language of making an objection. But he must have known it would be useless.

"I took it that they were black and he killed 'em both."

I looked at the judge. "Your Honor, may I approach the witness?"

"You may," he said.

I walked to the stand and put the file down in front of Torrance. It was faded orange—a color code used by county jailers denoting private legal documents an inmate is authorized to possess. "Okay, Mr. Torrance, I have placed before you a file in which Mr. Woodson keeps discovery documents provided by his attorneys. I ask once again if you recognize it."

"I seen a lotta orange files in high-power. It don't mean I seen that one."

"You are saying you never saw Mr. Woodson with his file?"

"I don't rightly remember."

"Mr. Torrance, you were with Mr. Woodson in the same module for thirty-two days. You testified he confessed to you. Are you saying you never saw him with that file?"

I had backed him into a no-win corner. "What I'm saying is, I seen him with his file, but I never looked at what was in it."

Bang. I had him. "Then I'll ask you to open and inspect it."

The witness followed the instruction, and I went to the lectern.

"What do you see when you open the file, Mr. Torrance?"

"One side's got photos of two bodies on the ground. The other side is a bunch of documents and reports and such."

"Could you read from the first document on the right side?"

"No, I can't read. I didn't get the schooling."

"Can you read any of the words next to the boxes at the top?"

Torrance's eyebrows came together in concentration. I knew that his reading had been tested during his last stint in prison and determined to be below second-grade skills.

"Not really," he said. "I can't read."

I walked over to the defense table and grabbed another file and a Sharpie pen. I went back to the lectern and printed "CAUCASIAN" on the outside of the file in large block letters. I held up the file. "Mr. Torrance, this is one of the words checked on the summary. Can you read this word?"

Torrance was already shaking his head when Vincent objected to the demonstration without proper foundation. The judge sustained.

"Okay, Mr. Torrance," I said. "On the other side of the file, could you describe the bodies in the photos?"

"Um, two men. It looks like they opened up some chicken wire and some tarps and they're laying there."

"What race are the men on the tarps?"

"They're black."

"Have you ever seen those photographs before, Mr. Torrance?"

Vincent stood to object, but it was like holding up a hand to stop a bullet. The judge sternly told him he could take his seat. You put the liar on the stand, you take the fall with him.

"Mr. Torrance, have you seen those photographs before?"

"No, sir, not before right now."

"Would you agree that the picture portrays what you described earlier? That being the bodies of two slain black men?"

"That's what it looks like, but I ain't seen it before."

"Are you sure?"

"Something like these I wouldn't forget."

"You've told us Mr. Woodson confessed to killing two black men, but he is on trial for killing two white men. Wouldn't you agree that it appears he didn't confess to you at all?"

"No, he confessed. He told me he killed those two."

I looked up at the judge. "Your Honor, now might be a good time for the prosecutor to reacquaint his witness with the penalties for perjury."

It was a dramatic move made for the benefit of the jury. I was expecting I would have to continue with Torrance and eviscerate him with the blade of his own lie. But Vincent stood and asked the judge to recess the trial while he conferred with opposing counsel.

This told me I had just saved Barnett Woodson's life.

"The defense has no objection," I told the judge.

AFTER the jury filed out of the box, I returned to the defense table as the courtroom deputy was cuffing my client to take him back to the holding cell.

"That guy's a lying sack of crap," Woodson whispered to me. "I didn't kill two black guys. They were white."

My hope was that the deputy didn't hear that. "Why don't you shut up," I whispered back. "And next time you see that lying sack of crap in lockup, you shake his hand. Because of his lies, the prosecutor's about to come off of the death penalty and float a deal."

"Yeah, well, maybe I don't want no deal now. They put a damn liar on the stand, man. We can win this, Haller. Don't take no deal."

"Don't get greedy, Barnett. I'll be back with the news."

The deputy took him through the steel door. After the courtroom cleared, Vincent and I were left looking at each other.

"So," I said.

"First of all," Vincent said, "I want to make it clear that I obviously didn't know Torrance was lying."

"Sure."

"Why would I sabotage my own case like this?"

I waved him off. "Jerry, don't bother. I told you in pretrial that the guy had copped the discovery my client had in his cell."

"Haller, he was vetted by one of our best investigators, who told me the guy couldn't read."

"Jerry, I'm usually pretty reasonable. I try to get along with the D.A.'s office. But I gave you fair warning. So after the break, I'm going to gut him and you're going to sit there and watch. It's called rope a dope, but when I'm done, he's not the only one who's going to look like a dope. That jury's going to know you either knew this guy was a liar or you were too dumb to realize it."

Vincent calmly straightened his case files. He spoke in a quiet voice. "I don't want you going forward with the cross."

"Fine. Then cut the bull and give me a dispo I can—"

"I'll drop the death penalty. Twenty-five to life without."

"That's not going to do it. The last thing Woodson said before they took him back was he was willing to roll the dice. I'll go fifteen max. I think I can sell that."

"No way. They'll send me back to filing buy-busts if I give you that for two cold-blooded murders. My best offer is twenty-five with parole. Not bad for what he did, killing two kids like that."

I tried to read his face. I decided it was his best, and it wasn't a bad deal for what Barnett Woodson had done.

"I don't know," I said. "I think he'll say roll the dice."

"You have to sell it to him, Haller. I can't go lower, and if you continue the cross, then my career in the D.A.'s office is finished."

Now I hesitated. "Wait a minute. What are you saying, Jerry? That I have to clean your mess up for you?"

"I'm saying it's a fair offer to a man who is guilty as sin. Go work your magic, Mick. Convince him. We both know you're not long for the public defender's office. You might need a favor from me some-day out in the big world."

I just stared back at him, registering the quid pro quo of the of-fer. I help him, and somewhere down the line he helps me, and Bar-nett Woodson does an extra couple of years in stir.

"He'll be lucky to last five years in there, let alone twenty," Vincent said. "What's the difference to him? But you and I? We're going places, Mickey. We can help each other here."

I nodded slowly. Vincent was only a few years older than me but was trying to act like some kind of wise old sage.

"The thing is, Jerry, if I did what you suggest, then I'd never be able to look another client in the eye again."

I stood up and gathered my files. My plan was to go back and tell Barnett Woodson to roll the dice and let me see what I could do.

"I'll see you after the break," I said. And then I walked away.

# TWO

## 2007

IT WAS a little early in the week for Lorna Taylor to be calling me. Usually she waited until at least Thursday. Never Tuesday. I picked up the phone thinking it was more than a check-in call. "Lorna?"

"Mickey, where've you been? I've been calling all morning."

"I went for my run. I just got out of the shower. You okay?"

"I'm fine. Are you?"

"Sure. What is—"

"You got a forthwith from Judge Holder. She wants to see you—like an hour ago."

This gave me pause. "About what?"

"All I know is that first Michaela called, then the judge."

Michaela Gill was the judge's clerk. And Mary Townes Holder, chief judge of the Los Angeles Superior Court, didn't call lawyers without a good reason.

"What did you tell her?"

"I just said you didn't have court today and you might be out on the golf course."

"I don't play golf, Lorna."

"Look, I couldn't think of anything."

"It's all right. I'll call the judge. Give me the number."

"Mickey, the judge wants to *see* you in chambers. So just go."

"Okay, I'm going. I have to get dressed."

"Mickey? How are you really doing?"

I knew her code. I knew what she was really asking. She didn't want me appearing in front of a judge if I wasn't ready for it.

"You don't have to worry, Lorna. I'm fine. I'll be fine."

"Okay. Let me know what's going on as soon as you can."

I felt like I was being bossed around by my wife, not my ex-wife.

"Don't worry. I will."

AS THE chief judge of the Los Angeles Superior Court, Judge Mary Townes Holder did most of her work behind closed doors. Her courtroom was used on occasion, but her job largely pertained to the administration of the justice system in Los Angeles County. More than two hundred and fifty judgeships and forty courthouses fell under her purview. Every jury summons had her name on it, and every parking space in a courthouse garage had her approval. It was Judge Holder who decided whether a judge sat in Beverly Hills or Compton and whether they heard high-stakes financial cases in civil court or soul-draining divorce cases in family court.

I had dressed quickly in what I considered my lucky suit. It was an Italian import from Corneliani that I used to wear on verdict days. I had to take it out of a plastic bag hanging in the back of the closet. After that, I sped downtown, thinking that I might be headed toward some sort of verdict on myself. My mind raced over the cases and clients I had left behind a year earlier. As far as I knew, nothing had been left open. But maybe there had been a complaint; I entered Holder's courtroom with a lot of trepidation.

The courtroom was dark, and the clerk's pod was empty. I opened the gate and was heading toward the door to the back hallway when it opened and Michaela Gill ushered me in without delay.

I found the judge alone in her chambers, working at a massive desk made of dark wood. Her black robe was hanging on a hat rack.

She was dressed in a maroon suit and was attractive and neat, with a slim build and brown hair kept in a short no-nonsense style. I had never met her, but I knew she'd put twenty years in as a prosecutor.

"Mr. Haller, thank you for coming," she said. "I'm glad your secretary finally found you."

"She's not actually my secretary, Judge. But she found me. Sorry it took so long."

"Well, you're here. I don't believe we have met before, have we? I actually had a case with your father once. I was third chair, just out of USC Law, and I prepared a week for my one witness before your father destroyed the man on cross in ten minutes."

I nodded. Over the years I had met older lawyers who had Mickey Haller, Sr., stories. I had very few of my own.

"But that's not why I called you here," she said. "Did you know Jerry Vincent?"

I was immediately thrown by her use of the past tense. "Jerry? Yes, I know Jerry. What about him?"

"He's dead. Murdered."

"Dead? When?"

"Last night. I'm sorry. Were you close?"

It was a good question. "We had cases against each other when he was with the D.A. and I was at the PD. We both left for one-man shops around the same time, and over the years we worked some cases together, sort of covered for each other when it was needed."

I had a professional relationship with Jerry Vincent. Every now and then we clicked glasses at Four Green Fields, but for me to say we were close would have been an exaggeration. I knew little about him outside of the world of law. I had heard something about a divorce a while back but had never even asked him about it.

"You seem to forget, Mr. Haller, but I was with the D.A. back when Mr. Vincent was an up and comer. But then he lost a big case and his star faded. I seem to recall you were the defense attorney."

"Barnett Woodson. I got an acquittal on a double murder."

"Then why would Jerry ever work with you?"

"Because, Judge, a couple of years later he was making five times what he made with the D.A. He called me up and thanked me for showing him the light."

The judge nodded knowingly. "He wanted the money."

I shrugged like I was uncomfortable answering for a dead man. Then I tried to put the focus back on Jerry Vincent's murder.

"I can't believe this about Jerry. Do you know what happened?"

"He was found late last night shot to death in his car in the garage at his office. I am told the police are still at the crime scene and there have been no arrests. This comes from a *Times* reporter who called my chambers to make an inquiry about what will happen now with Mr. Vincent's clients—especially Walter Elliot."

I nodded. For the last twelve months I had been in a vacuum, but it wasn't so airtight that I hadn't heard about the movie mogul murder case, one of the high-profile cases Vincent had scored over the years. Walter Elliot was the chairman/owner of Archway Pictures and a powerful man in Hollywood. He had been charged with murdering his wife and her lover after discovering them together in a Malibu beach house. The case was drawing wide media attention.

The judge broke through my reverie. "Are you familiar with RPC two three hundred?"

I squinted my eyes at the question. "Uh . . . not exactly."

"Let me refresh your memory. It is the section of the California Bar's rules of professional conduct referring to the transfer or sale of a law practice. Mr. Vincent apparently named you his second in his standard contract of representation, but additionally he filed a motion ten years ago that allowed for the transfer of his practice to you should he become incapacitated or deceased."

I just stared at her. I knew about the clause in Vincent's standard contract. I had the same in mine naming him. But the judge was telling me that I now had Jerry's cases, Walter Elliot included. Each client would be free to move on to another attorney, but I would have first shot at them.

I hadn't had a client in a year, and the plan was to start back slow, not with a full caseload like the one I had apparently just inherited.

"However," the judge said, "I've checked with some of the

judges, and I'm aware that you have not been practicing law for almost a year. I have found no explanation for this. Before I issue the order appointing you replacement counsel, I need to be assured I'm not turning Mr. Vincent's clients over to the wrong man."

"Judge, you're right. I sort of took myself out of the game for a while. But I just started taking steps to get back in."

Her eyes held mine. "Why did you take yourself out?"

I spoke very carefully. "I had a case a couple years ago. The client's name was Louis Roulet—"

"I remember the case, Mr. Haller. You got shot. But I seem to remember news stories about you coming back to the job."

"Well," I said, "I came back too soon. I had been gut shot, and the next thing I knew, I started having pain, and the doctors said I had a hernia. So I had an operation, and there were complications, more pain, and . . . well, it knocked me down for a while. I decided the second time not to come back until I was sure I was ready."

The judge nodded sympathetically. I guessed I'd been right to leave out my addiction to pain pills and the stint in rehab.

"Money wasn't an issue," I said. "I got a settlement from the insurance company. I took my time coming back, but I'm ready."

"Then I guess inheriting an entire practice is quite convenient, isn't it?" she said in a smarmy tone.

"All I can tell you is that I'd take good care of Jerry's clients."

The judge nodded, but she didn't look at me. I knew the tell. She knew something that bothered her. Maybe she knew about rehab.

"According to bar records, you've been disciplined several times," she said.

"All of it ancient history, Judge. All technicalities. If you called the bar today, I'm sure you were told that I'm in good standing."

She dropped her eyes to the document in front of her on the desk. "Very well, then," she said.

She scribbled a signature on the last page. I felt the flutter of excitement begin to build in my chest.

"Here is an order transferring the practice to you," the judge said. "I'm going to be monitoring you. I want an updated inventory by the beginning of next week. The status of every case. After that, I want biweekly updates. Am I being clear?"

"Perfectly clear, Judge. How long do you want updates?"

Her face hardened. "Until I tell you to stop." She handed me the order. "If I were you, I'd get over to his office and protect my new clients from any unlawful search and seizure of their files by the police. If you have any problem, you can call me."

"Yes, Your Honor. Thank you."

"Good luck, Mr. Haller."

I stood up and headed out of the room. Once in the hallway, I read the document confirming that what had just happened was real.

It was. It granted me immediate access to the fallen attorney's office, files, and client bank accounts.

I pulled out my cell phone and called Lorna Taylor. I asked her to look up the address of Jerry Vincent's office. I told her to meet me there and pick up two sandwiches on her way.

"Why?" she asked.

"Because I haven't had lunch."

"No, why are we going to Jerry Vincent's office?"

"Because we're back in business."

I WAS in my Lincoln driving toward Jerry's office when I thought of something and called Lorna back. "I'm going to need an investigator. How would you feel if I called Cisco?"

Cisco was Dennis Wojciechowski, her significant other as of the last year. I was the one who had introduced them when I had used him on a case. Last I heard, they were now living together.

"Well, I have no problem working with Cisco. But I wish you would tell me what this is all about."

Lorna knew Jerry Vincent as a voice on the phone. I couldn't remember if they had ever met in person. I had wanted to tell her the news in person, but things were moving too quickly for that.

"Jerry Vincent is dead. He was murdered last night, and I'm getting first shot at all of his cases. Including Walter Elliot."

She was silent for a long moment before responding.

"My God . . . how? He was such a nice man."

"I couldn't remember if you had ever met him."

Lorna worked out of her condo in West Hollywood. All my calls and billing went through her. If there was a brick-and-mortar office for the law firm of Michael Haller and Associates, then her place was it. But there weren't any associates, and when I worked, my office was the backseat of my car. This left few occasions for Lorna to meet face to face with any of the people I associated with.

"He came to our wedding, don't you remember?"

"That's right. I forgot."

"Did he have a family?"

"I think he was divorced. I don't know if there were kids."

Lorna didn't say anything. We both had our own thoughts occupying us. "Let me go so I can call Cisco," I finally said.

"All right. What kind of sandwich do you want?"

"Stop at Dusty's and get me one of those turkey sandwiches with cranberry sauce. It's been almost a year since I've had one. And get something for Cisco in case he's hungry."

"All right."

I hung up and called Dennis Wojciechowski's cell phone. When he answered, I heard a mixture of wind and exhaust blast. He was on his bike, and even though his helmet was set up with an earpiece and mike, I had to yell. "It's Mickey Haller. Pull over."

I waited and heard him cut the engine on his '63 pan head.

"What's up, Mick? Haven't heard from you in a long time."

Wojciechowski was a freelance defense investigator I had used on a few cases before. That was how he had met Lorna, collecting his pay. I had known him before that because of his association with the Road Saints motorcycle club, a group for which I served as a de facto house counsel. There was already a Dennis in the membership, and his last name, Wojciechowski, was intolerably difficult to pronounce, so they called him the Cisco Kid, riffing off his dark looks and mustache. A big, imposing man, his mustache trimmed now and going gray, Cisco was a thorough and thoughtful investigator. And he could be physically intimidating when necessary, a useful attribute.

"You gotta put the baffles back in your pipes, man," I said. "Where are you? You on a case?"

"No, just a ride. Burbank. Why, you got something for me? You taking on a case finally?"

"A lot of cases. And I'm going to need an investigator."

I gave him the address of Vincent's office and told him to meet me there. I knew that Vincent would have used his own investigators and that there might be a loss of time as Cisco got up to speed on the cases, but I wanted an investigator I knew I could trust.

After closing the phone, I realized I had driven right by Vincent's office on Broadway. I wasted ten minutes working my way back, catching red lights, and resolved to hire a driver again as soon as possible so I could concentrate on cases instead of addresses.

Vincent's office was in a six-story structure simply called The Legal Center. Being so close to the main downtown courthouses meant it was a building full of trial lawyers. I saw the opening for the parking garage next door and pulled in.

As I was taking the ticket out of the machine, a uniformed police officer approached my car. "Sir, we are conducting a crime-scene investigation. There's no parking on the second level. They haven't cleared the scene."

I nodded and headed up the ramp. The second floor was empty of vehicles except for two patrol cars and a black BMW coupe being hauled onto the bed of a truck from the police garage. Jerry Vincent's car, I assumed. Two uniformed cops signaled for me to keep going up. I didn't find a space until I got to the fifth floor. One more reason I needed to get a driver again.

The office I was looking for was on the second floor at the front of the building. Its opaque glass door wasn't locked. I entered a reception area. Behind a counter sat a woman whose eyes were red from crying. "Are you with the police?" she asked.

"No, I'm not," I replied.

"Then I'm sorry, the office is closed today."

I pulled the court order from Judge Holder out of the inside pocket of my suit coat. "Not for me," I said.

She unfolded the document and stared at it. "What is this?"

"That's a court order," I said. "My name is Michael Haller, and Judge Holder has appointed me replacement counsel in regard to Jerry Vincent's clients. That means we'll be working together."

She shook her head as if warding off some invisible threat. "You can't do this. Mr. Vincent wouldn't want this."

I took the court papers out of her hand. "Actually, I can. The chief judge of Los Angeles Superior Court has directed me to do this. And if you look at the contracts of representation that Mr. Vincent had his clients sign, you will find my name already listed as associate counsel. I know this has been a very difficult day. I knew Jerry going back to his days at the D.A., so you have my sympathy."

I waited, but I wasn't getting a response. I pressed on.

"I'm going to need some things to get started. First of all, Jerry's calendar. I want to put together a list of active—"

Her eyes were staring blankly. "It's gone," she said abruptly.

"What's gone?"

"His laptop. The police told me whoever did this took his briefcase out of the car. He kept everything on his laptop."

"You mean, his calendar? He didn't keep a hard copy?"

"He kept it all on his laptop, and he kept a hard copy in the old portfolio he carried. But they're both gone."

I nodded. The missing calendar wasn't insurmountable.

"What about files? Did he have any in the briefcase?"

"I don't think so. He kept all the files here."

"Okay, good. I'll also need to see any books pertaining to the trust and operating accounts."

She looked up sharply. "You're not going to take his money."

"It's not— I apologize. Let's start over. What's your name?"

"Wren Williams."

"Okay, Wren, let me explain. It's not his money. It's his clients' money, and until they say otherwise, his clients are now my clients. Now I need you to decide if you are with me or against me, Wren. Because if you are with me, I need you to get me the things I ask for. If you are against me, then I need you to go home now."

"The detectives told me to stay until they were finished."

"What detectives? Only a couple uniforms are out there."

"The detectives in Mr. Vincent's office."

"You let—" I stepped around the counter, headed toward two doors on the back wall, and picked the one on the left.

Jerry Vincent's office was large and opulent and empty. I turned in a circle until I found myself staring into the eyes of a large fish mounted next to the door. The fish was a beautiful green, its body arched as if it had just jumped out of the water. Its mouth was open.

A brass plate said IF I'D KEPT MY MOUTH SHUT, I WOULDN'T BE HERE. Words to live by, I thought.

The sound of a metal drawer being banged closed spun me back around. On the other side of the room, a door was open about a foot and I could see light. I quickly pushed it all the way open. The file room was a windowless walk-in closet with rows of filing cabinets. Two men sat at the worktable against the back wall. One old, one young, they had their jackets draped over the chairs. I saw their guns and holsters and their badges clipped to their belts.

"What are you doing?" I asked gruffly.

The men looked up from their stack of files. The older detective's eyes momentarily widened in surprise when he saw me. "LAPD," he said. "And I guess I should ask you the same question."

"Those are my files, and you're going to have to put them down." I pulled the court order from my jacket again. "My name is—"

"I know who you are." The older man stood up. "But I still don't know what you're doing here."

I handed him the order. "I've been appointed by the chief judge of the Superior Court as replacement counsel to Jerry Vincent's clients. You have no right to be in here. It's a clear violation of my clients' rights to protection against unlawful search and seizure. These files contain privileged attorney-client information."

The detective flipped through the paperwork to the signature. He didn't seem impressed. "Vincent's been murdered," he said. "The identity of the killer could be in one of these files. We have to—"

"No, what *you* have to do is get out of this file room."

The detective didn't move a muscle. "I consider this part of a crime scene," he said. "It's you who has to leave."

"Read the order, Detective. I'm not going anywhere. Your crime scene is out in the garage, and no judge in L.A. would let you extend it to this office. It's time for you to leave."

"If I leave, I'm going to shut this place down and seal it."

I hated getting into pissing matches with cops, but sometimes there was no choice. "You do that and I'll have it unsealed in an hour. And you'll be standing in front of the chief judge explaining how you trampled on the rights of every one of Vincent's clients."

The detective smiled like he was mildly amused. "This gives you the entire practice? I guess that puts you on our list."

"What list?"

"Our suspect list."

"That's ridiculous. Why would I be on it?"

"You just told us why. Care to tell us where you were between eight and midnight last night?"

He grinned at me again without any warmth, giving me that practiced cop's smile of judgment. His brown eyes were so dark I couldn't see the line between iris and pupil. Like shark eyes, they didn't seem to carry any light.

"I'm not even going to begin to explain how ludicrous that is," I said. "I didn't even know I was in line for this."

"Don't worry, we'll be checking you out."

"Good. Now please leave or I make the call to the judge."

The detective took his jacket off the chair. He picked a file up off the table and shoved it into my chest. "Here's one of your new files, Counselor. Don't choke on it."

He stepped to the door, and his partner followed. I had a feeling it wouldn't be the last time I saw them.

"Look, Detectives, I'm sorry it's like this. I don't even know what I have here. Give me some time to—"

"We don't have time," the older man said. "We lose momentum and we lose the case. Do you understand what you're getting yourself into here, Counselor? Whoever killed Vincent in that garage was waiting for him. He was ambushed. I'd watch myself with those new clients of yours. Jerry Vincent knew his killer."

"Wait," I said. "You have a card? Give me a card."

The detectives turned back. The older one gave me a card out of his pocket. "That's got all my numbers."

"Let me just get the lay of the land here. There's got to be a way to cooperate and still not trample on anybody's rights." I looked down at the name on the card. Harry Bosch. "Look, Detective Bosch, good luck with the case. I hope you crack it."

Bosch nodded, and there was something familiar about the physical gesture. He turned to follow his partner out.

"Detective, did we ever cross paths on a case before?"

Bosch smiled glibly and shook his head. "No," he said. "If we'd been on a case, you'd remember me."

# THREE

AN HOUR later I was behind Jerry Vincent's desk with Lorna Taylor and Dennis Wojciechowski sitting across from me. We were eating our sandwiches, but nobody had much of an appetite, considering what had happened to the office's predecessor.

I had sent Wren Williams home. She had been unable to stop crying or objecting to my taking control of her dead boss's cases. She asked whether I was going to fire her, and I told her the jury was still out but to report for work as usual the next day.

With Jerry Vincent dead and Wren Williams gone, we were left stumbling around in the dark until Lorna figured out the filing system and started pulling the active case files. From calendar notations in each file, she was able to put together a master calendar—the key component in any trial lawyer's professional life. Once we had worked up a calendar, I began to breathe a little easier, and we broke for lunch and opened the sandwich cartons from Dusty's.

The calendar was light. A few case hearings here and there, but it was obvious Vincent was keeping things clear in advance of the Walter Elliot trial, which was scheduled to begin in nine days.

"So let's start," I said, my mouth still full with my last bite. "According to the calendar we've pieced together, I've got a sentencing in forty-five minutes. We could have a preliminary discussion; then I could leave you two here while I go to court. Then I'll come back after court to see how much further we've gotten before Cisco and I go out and start knocking on doors."

They both nodded, their mouths working on their sandwiches.

Lorna was as beautiful as ever. She was a stunner with blond hair and eyes that made you think you were the center of the universe. I had kept her on salary with my insurance settlement, not wanting to run the risk that she'd be working for another lawyer when it was time for me to come back.

"Let's start with the money," I said.

Lorna nodded. She had moved on from the active files to the bank books. "All right, good news and bad. He's got thirty-eight thousand in the operating account and a hundred twenty-nine thousand in the trust account."

I whistled. That was a lot of cash in the trust account. Money from clients goes into the trust account, and as work proceeds, it is transferred to the operating account. I always want more money in the operating account, because once it's moved from the trust account, the money's mine.

"There's a reason it's lopsided," Lorna said. "He just deposited a check on Friday for a hundred thousand dollars from Walter Elliot."

I tapped the makeshift calendar I'd drawn on a legal pad. "The Elliot trial starts Thursday next week. He took the hundred up front. As soon as we're done here, see if the check cleared."

"Got it."

"If a hundred's from Elliot, who's the rest for?"

Lorna opened one of the accounting books. Each dollar in a trust fund must be accounted in regard to which client it is being held for. An attorney must be able to determine how much of a client's advance has been transferred to the operating fund and used and how much is on reserve in trust. A hundred thousand of Vincent's trust account was earmarked for the Elliot trial. That left only twenty-nine thousand for the rest of the active cases. That wasn't a lot, considering the stack of active files we'd pulled together.

"That's the bad news," Lorna said. "It looks like there are only five or six other cases with trust deposits. With the rest of the active cases, the money's already been moved into operating, been spent, or the clients owe the firm. He's got two on pretrial payments, Samuels and Henson. They're both about five thousand behind."

I looked down at my notes. Both Samuels and Henson were on a sublist I had drawn up while reviewing the actives. It was a listing of cases I was going to cut loose if I could. This was based on my quick review of the facts of the cases. If there was something I didn't like about a case, then it went on the sublist.

"No problem," I said. "We'll cut 'em loose."

Samuels was a manslaughter DUI case, and Henson was a felony grand theft. Patrick Henson momentarily held my interest because Vincent was going to build a defense around the client's addiction to prescription painkillers in which the doctor was the one most responsible for the consequences of the addiction he created.

I was intimately familiar with this defense, because I had employed it repeatedly over the last two years to try to absolve myself of the many infractions I had committed as father, ex-husband, and friend. But I put Henson into what I called the dog pile because I knew at heart the defense didn't hold up—at least not for me.

Lorna nodded and made notes. "How many in the dog pile?"

"We came up with thirty-one active cases," I said. "Of those, I'm thinking only seven look like dogs."

"You think the judge is just going to let you drop those?"

"Nope. But I'll figure something out. Anything else?"

Lorna shook her head. "That's about it. When you're in court, I'll call the bank. You want us both to be signers on the accounts?"

"Yeah, just like with my accounts."

I hadn't considered the potential difficulty in getting my hands on the money that was in the Vincent accounts. That was what I had Lorna for. She was good on the business end in ways I wasn't.

My watch said I had ten minutes before I had to get going to court. "Cisco, whaddaya got?" I had told him earlier to work his contacts and to monitor Vincent's murder investigation as closely as possible.

"Not a lot," he said. "I called a guy I know in forensics, and they're still processing everything. Vincent was shot at least two times, and there were no shells at the scene. A contact in communications told me the first call came in at twelve forty-three."

"Is there a general idea of what happened?"

"It looks like Vincent worked late, which was apparently his routine every Monday, preparing for the week ahead. He packed his briefcase, locked up, went to his car in the garage, and got popped through the driver's-side window. When they found him, the car was in park, the ignition on. The window was down. He could've lowered it because he liked the chill or for somebody coming to the car."

"Somebody he knew." I thought about what Detective Bosch had said. "Nobody was working in the garage?"

"No. The attendant leaves at six. You have to put your money in the machine after that or use your monthly pass. There are license-plate cameras where you drive in and out, but there was nothing on tape that was useful."

"Who found Jerry?"

"The security guard hits the garage a couple times a night."

I nodded, thinking the killer knew the garage.

"Okay. Stay on it. What about the detective?"

"Harry Bosch. Supposedly he's one of the best. Retired a few years ago, and the police chief himself recruited him back. Full name is Hieronymus Bosch. Thirty-three years on the job, and you know what that means."

"No, what does it mean?"

"Well, under the LAPD's pension program, you max out at thirty years, so it makes no economic sense to stay."

"Unless you're a man on a mission. Wait a second," I said. "You said Hieronymus Bosch? Like the painter?"

"I don't know about any painter. But that's his name. Rhymes with anonymous, I was told. Weird, if you ask me."

"No weirder than Wojciechowski—if you ask me."

"I thought you didn't know him, Mickey," Lorna said.

"I never met him before, but the name . . . I know the name."

"You mean, from the paintings?"

I didn't want to get into a discussion of distant history. "Never mind. I've got to get going." I stood up and stepped around the desk. "I'll be in Judge Champagne's court. I'm taking a bunch of the active files to read while I'm waiting."

"I'll walk you out," Lorna said.

I saw her throw a look at Cisco. We walked to the reception area. I knew what she was going to say, but I let her say it. "Mickey, are you sure you're ready for this?"

"Absolutely."

"This wasn't the plan. You were going to come back slowly, take a couple cases. You're taking on an entire practice."

"I'm not practicing."

"Look, be serious."

"Don't you see this is better than the plan? The Elliot case is like having a billboard say 'I'm back' in big neon letters!"

"Yeah, and the Elliot case alone is so much pressure . . ."

"Lorna, I'm fine, I'm ready. I thought you'd be happy about this. We've got money coming in for the first time in a year."

"I don't care about that. I want to make sure you're okay."

"I'm more than okay. I'm excited. I feel like in one day I've got my mojo back. Don't drag me down. Okay?"

She stared at me, and I stared back, and finally a reluctant smile peeked through her stern face. "All right. Go get 'em."

"Don't worry. I will."

DESPITE the assurances I had given Lorna, thoughts about all the work to be done played in my mind as I walked to the bridge that linked the office building with the garage. I had forgotten I'd parked on the fifth level and walked up three ramps before I found the Lincoln. I popped the trunk and put a stack of files into my bag.

The bag was a hybrid I had picked up at Suitcase City while I was plotting my comeback. I could carry it as a backpack or a briefcase on the days I was strong. It also had two wheels and a telescoping handle so I could just roll it behind me on the days I was weak.

Lately the stronger days far outnumbered the weak, and I probably could make it with the traditional lawyer's leather briefcase. But the bag had a logo on it—a mountain ridgeline with SUITCASE CITY printed across it like the Hollywood sign. Skylights swept the horizon, completing the dream image of desire and hope. I think that was the real reason I liked the bag. Because I knew Suitcase City wasn't a store. It was a place. It was Los Angeles.

Los Angeles was the kind of place where everybody was from somewhere else. People drawn by the dream, people running from the nightmare. Figuratively, literally, metaphorically, everybody in L.A. keeps a bag packed. Just in case.

As I closed the trunk, I was startled to see a man next to my car. "Mr. Haller, I work for the *Times* and wonder if I could talk to you about Jerry Vincent."

I shook my head. "I don't know anything about the case."

"But you're taking over his clients, aren't you?"

"Who told you that?"

"Our court reporter got a copy of the order from Judge Holder. Why did Mr. Vincent pick you? Were you two good friends?"

I opened the car door. "Look, what's your name?"

"Jack McEvoy. I work the police beat."

"Good for you, Jack. But I can't talk about this right now. You want to give me a card, I'll call you when I can talk."

He made no move to give me a card. He just put his elbow on the roof of the car. "I was hoping we could make a deal," he said. "I've got the police department wired, and you've got the court-house wired. You tell me what you're hearing and I'll tell you. I have a feeling this is going to be a big case."

"You got a card?"

This time he took a card out of his pocket and handed it to me.

"Okay, deal."

I signaled him away and pulled the door closed, then started the engine. McEvoy called out to me just as I put the car in drive.

"Hey, Haller, love the plate."

I waved a hand out the window as I drove down the ramp. I tried to remember which of my Lincolns I was driving. I have a fleet of three Town Cars left over from my days when I carried a full case-load. In the last year, I'd put all three into a rotation to keep the dust out of the pipes. Part of my comeback strategy, I guess. The cars were exact duplicates, except for the license plates.

When I got to the booth and handed in my stub, I saw a video screen next to the cash register. It showed the view from a camera located behind my car. I could see my vanity plate: IWALKEM.

I smirked. I walk 'em all right. I was heading to court to meet one of Jerry Vincent's clients for the first time. I was going to shake his hand and then walk him right into prison.

JUDGE Judith Champagne was on the bench and hearing motions when I walked into her courtroom with five minutes to spare. There were eight other lawyers waiting their turn. I parked my roller bag against the rail and whispered to the courtroom deputy, explaining that I was there to handle the sentencing of Edgar Reese for Jerry Vincent. He told me the judge's motions calendar was running long but Reese would be first out for his sentencing. I asked if I could see Reese, and the deputy got up and led me to the holding cell.

"Edgar Reese?" I said.

A small, powerfully built white man came over to the bars.

"My name's Michael Haller. I'm filling in for your attorney. Did Jerry go over the sentence when you pled out?"

"Yeah, he told me. Five years in state, out in three if I behave."

It was more like four, but I wasn't going to mess with it.

"Okay, well, the judge is finishing some stuff up out there and then they'll bring you out. The prosecutor will read you a bunch of legalese, you answer yes that you understand it, and then the judge will enter the sentence. Fifteen minutes in and out."

"I don't care how long it takes. I ain't got nowhere to go."

I nodded and left him there. I tapped lightly on the metal door so the deputy—bailiffs in L.A. County are sheriff's deputies—in the courtroom would hear it. He let me out, and I sat in the first row of the gallery. I opened up my case and pulled out most of the files.

The top file was Edgar Reese. I had already reviewed this one in preparation for the sentencing. It was a garden-variety drug case.

The next file belonged to Patrick Henson, the painkiller case I had told Lorna I'd be dropping. I reconsidered and opened the file.

Henson was a twenty-four-year-old surfer from Malibu. He was a professional but with limited endorsements and winnings from the pro tour. In a competition on Maui he'd wiped out and crimped his shoulder. After surgery, the doctor prescribed oxycodone. Eighteen months later Henson was an addict, chasing pills to chase the pain. He lost his sponsors and hit bottom when he stole a necklace from a home in Malibu to which he'd been invited by a female friend. According to the sheriff's report, the necklace belonged to his friend's mother and contained eight diamonds. It was listed as worth twenty-five thousand dollars, but Henson hocked it for four hundred dollars and went to Mexico to buy two hundred tabs of oxy.

Henson was easy to connect to the caper, and film from a security camera showed him pawning the necklace. Because of its high value, he was hit with a full deck, dealing in stolen property and grand theft along with illegal drug possession.

When Vincent took Henson on, the surfer made the initial five-thousand-dollar advance payment in trade. Vincent took all twelve of his custom-made Trick Henson boards and sold them through his liquidator to collectors and on eBay. Henson was also placed on the thousand-a-month payment plan but had never made a payment, because he had gone into rehab the day after being bailed out of jail by his mother.

According to the file, Henson had successfully completed rehab and was working part-time at a surf camp for kids. He was barely making enough to live on.

The file was replete with motions to continue and other delay tactics while Vincent waited for Henson to come across with more cash. This was standard practice. There was a cell-phone number in the file. I could call him right now. The question was, Did I want to?

I looked up at the bench. There were still three lawyers waiting their turn at motions. I got up and whispered to the deputy, "I'm going out to the hallway to make a call."

He nodded. "Just turn that phone off before coming back in."

I walked out with the file, found a reasonably quiet spot, and called the number. It was answered after two rings. "This is Trick."

"Patrick Henson?"

"Yeah, who's this?"

"I'm your new lawyer. My name is Mi—"

"Whoah, wait a minute. What happened to my old lawyer? I gave that guy Vincent—"

"He's dead, Patrick. He passed away last night."

"Nooooo."

"Yes, Patrick. I'm sorry. My name is Michael Haller, and I'm taking over his cases. I've been reviewing your file and see you haven't made a payment on the schedule Mr. Vincent put you on."

"Ah, man, this is the deal. I've been concentrating on staying right, and I've got no money. Okay? I gave Vincent all my boards. He counted it as five grand, but I know those long boards were worth at least a grand apiece. He told me he got enough to get started, but all he's been doing is delaying."

"Are you staying right, Patrick? Are you clean?"

"As a whistle, man. Vincent told me it was the only way I'd have a shot at staying out of jail."

"Jerry was right, Patrick. You got a job?"

"Man, don't you guys see? No one's going to give a guy like me a job. I mean, I teach water babies part-time on the beach, but it don't pay me jack. I'm living out of my car, sleeping on the lifeguard stand at Sunset Beach."

"Yeah, I know, life sucks. You still have a driver's license?"

"That's about all I got left."

I made a quick decision.

"Okay. You know where Jerry Vincent's office is?"

"Yeah. I delivered the boards there. And my sixty-pound Tarpon, he was going to put it on the wall."

"Yeah, well, your fish is still there. Anyway, be at the office at nine sharp tomorrow morning and I'll interview you for a job."

"Doing what?"

"Driving me. I'll pay you fifteen bucks an hour to drive and another fifteen toward your fees. How's that?"

There was a moment of silence. "I can be there for that."

"Good. See you then. Just remember, Patrick. You gotta stay clean. If you're not, I'll know. Believe me, I'll know."

# FOUR

THE message from Lorna Taylor was short and to the point. I got it the moment I turned my phone on after leaving the courtroom and seeing Edgar Reese get his five years. She told me she'd been in touch with Judge Holder's clerk about obtaining a court order the bank was requiring before putting Lorna's and my names on the Vincent bank accounts. The judge had agreed to draw up the order, and I could walk down the hallway to her chambers to pick it up.

The courtroom was dark, but Michaela Gill was in her pod next to the bench. Judge Holder still had the order with her in chambers, and I asked if there was any chance I could talk to her for a few minutes. Michaela went behind her station, and when the door opened, I could see a man in a chair. I recognized him as Judge Holder's husband, a personal-injury attorney named Mitch Lester.

Michaela came out carrying the court order and told me I would be allowed back as soon as the judge finished up with her visitor, so I wandered the courtroom until I heard the bell tone sound.

When I took a seat in front of the judge, she asked, "What can I do for you, Mr. Haller? You got the order."

"Yes, Your Honor. Thank you for that. I wanted to update you a little bit and ask a question about something."

"Please go ahead, then."

"Well, on the update, things are going a bit slow because Vincent's laptop computer and hard-copy calendar were stolen. We had to build a new calendar, and in fact, I just came from a sentencing."

"How many active cases are we talking about?"

"It looks like there are thirty active cases. I've had a conversation with one client, and it looks like I will be continuing as his lawyer."

"Was that Walter Elliot?"

"Uh, no. I plan to talk to him later today. What I wanted to ask about was the police. When I got over to the office this morning, I found a couple of detectives going through the files. Jerry's receptionist was there, but she hadn't tried to stop it."

"I hope you did. Those officers should have known better."

"Yes, Your Honor. They backed off once I objected."

She nodded. "Then why are you here?"

"I'm wondering whether I should let them back in. The detective in charge said the evidence suggests Vincent knew his killer and probably allowed him to get close enough to shoot him. So they were looking for potential suspects when I walked in on them."

The judge waved her hands in a gesture of dismissal. "And trampling on clients' rights as they were doing it."

"They left behind a stack of files on the table. I looked them over, and there were threats in those files."

"Threats against Mr. Vincent?"

"Yes. Cases in which his clients weren't happy about the outcome. There were threats, and Vincent took each threat seriously enough to make a detailed record of what was said."

The judge leaned back. "You believe we are inhibiting the investigation by not allowing the police to do their job."

"I was wondering if there was a way to limit the harm to clients but let the police follow the investigation."

The judge considered this in silence, then sighed. "I wish my husband had stayed. I value his opinion greatly."

"Well, I have an idea."

"Of course you do. What is it?"

"I was thinking that I could vet the files myself and draw up a list for Detective Bosch and give the details of the threats as well. This way he's happy, I'm happy."

"Bosch is the lead detective?"

"Yes, Harry Bosch. He's with Robbery-Homicide."

"You have to understand, Mr. Haller, that even if you just give this man Bosch the names, you are still breaching client confidentiality. You could be disbarred for this."

"Well, I believe there's a way out. One of the mechanisms of relief from the client confidentiality bond is in the case of threat to safety. If I've been directly told by the lead detective on the case that it is highly likely that the identity of Jerry Vincent's killer is contained in files that are now mine, that information constitutes a threat to me. I feel I'm in some jeopardy here, Judge."

She reached over and drank from a glass of water by her computer. "All right, Mr. Haller. I believe that if you vet the files as you have suggested, then you will be acting in an acceptable manner. I would like you to file a motion that explains your actions and the feeling of threat you are under. I will sign it and seal it, and with any good luck, it will never see the light of day."

"Thank you, Your Honor."

"Anything else?"

"Yes, Your Honor. I saw your calendar from last week out there and saw that Jerry came in on the Elliot matter. Do you mind my asking what the hearing was about?"

The judge had to think for a moment to recall the hearing. "It was an emergency motion. Mr. Vincent came in because Judge Stanton had revoked bail and ordered Mr. Elliot remanded to custody. Mr. Elliot had traveled to a film festival in New York without getting permission. Mr. Vincent came to me for an emergency stay of his client's incarceration. I decided to give Mr. Elliot a second chance by making him wear an ankle monitor."

"I understand, Judge. Thank you."

I nodded and left the chambers. Harry Bosch's card was still in my pocket. I dug it out while I was going down on the elevator. I had parked in a pay lot right by Parker Center. I called Bosch's cell phone as I headed to the courthouse exit. "It's Mickey Haller."

There was a hesitation. "What can I do for you?" he asked.

"How's the investigation going?"

"It's going, but nothing I can talk to you about."

"Then I'll just get to the point. Are you in Parker Center now?"

"That's right. Why?"

"I'm heading over from the courthouse. Meet me out front. I think it will be worth your while."

I closed the phone before he could respond. It took me five minutes to get over to Parker Center. Bosch was standing next to the fountain that was part of the memorial for officers killed in the line of duty. I saw thin white wires leading from his ears to his jacket pocket. I walked up and pulled the ear buds out.

"Shutting out the world, Detective?"

"Helps me concentrate. Is there a purpose to this meeting?"

"After you left the office today, I looked at the files you'd stacked in the file room. I understand what you're trying to do. I want to help, but I want you to understand my position."

"I understand. You have to protect those files and the possible killer hiding in them, because those are the rules."

I shook my head. This guy didn't want to make it easy. "Tell you what, Detective Bosch. Come by the office at eight o'clock tomorrow morning and I'll give you what I can."

I think the offer surprised him. "I'll be there at eight."

"Okay, then." I was ready to walk away, but it looked like he wasn't. "What is it?"

"I was going to ask you if Vincent had any federal cases."

"I don't think so. He was like me, liked to stay in state court. The feds kind of like to stack the deck. They don't like to lose."

"Okay." He was putting something in place.

"That's it? That's all you wanted to ask?"

"That's it."

"Okay, Detective." I clumsily put out my hand, and when he shook it, he appeared to feel just as awkward about it. "Hey, there was something I was meaning to ask you, too."

"What's that?"

"I heard your full name is Hieronymus Bosch. Is that true?"

"What about it?"

"I was just wondering, where'd you get a name like that?"

"My mother gave it to me."

"Your mother? Well, what did your father think about it?"

"I never asked him, Counselor. Is there anything else?"

"No, that was it. I was just curious. See you at eight."

I left him and headed down the block, thinking about why he had asked if Vincent had federal cases. When I reached the corner, I glanced back and saw Bosch still standing by the fountain. He was watching me. He didn't look away, but I did, and I kept walking.

CISCO and Lorna were at work in Jerry Vincent's office when I got back. I handed over the court order and told Lorna about the early appointments I had set for the next day.

"I thought you put Henson into the dog pile," she said.

"I did. But now I moved him back."

She put her eyebrows together the way she did whenever I confounded her—which was a lot. I didn't want to explain things. I asked if anything new had developed.

"A couple things. The check from Walter Elliot cleared, and I found the contracts file. That hundred thousand deposited for trial was only a partial payment. Vincent took two-fifty up front, and that's all gone. But he was getting another two-fifty for the trial, nonrefundable. The rest is due on the first day of testimony."

I nodded with satisfaction. Vincent had made a great deal. I had never had a case with that kind of money involved. But I wondered how he had blown through the first two-fifty so quickly.

"Okay, all that's good—if we get Elliot. What else do we have?"

"We had visitors. One of Jerry's investigators came by, Bruce Carlin. Jerry hired him to work the Elliot case."

I nodded. Bruce Carlin was a former LAPD bull who had crossed to the dark side and did defense work now. A lot of attorneys used him because of his insider's knowledge of how things worked in the cop shop. I thought he was living off an undeserved reputation.

"Set up a time for him to come back in. I doubt his work is all in the files. Cisco can find out what he's got. Pay him for his time and then cut him loose when he's no longer useful."

"We also had a couple of clients drop by to ask for their files after they heard on the radio about Jerry's death."

"And?"

"We stalled them. I told them only you could turn over a file and that you'd get back to them within twenty-four hours. Those are the names. There's contact info, too."

One name was in the dog pile, but the other was a case I thought I could get dismissed. "I'll go see these two tonight. In fact, I want to hit the road with all the cases soon. Starting with Archway Pictures. I'm going to take Cisco. Gather up what you need, Lorna, and head on home. I don't want you here by yourself."

She nodded but then said, "Are you sure Cisco should go?" She was referring to his size and the tattoos, the boots and leather.

"Yeah. When I want to be subtle, he can just wait in the car."

Cisco nodded and seemed fine with the arrangement.

"Okay," I said. "I guess it's time for me to be a Lincoln lawyer again. Let's hit the road."

IN THE last decade, Archway Pictures had grown from a movie-industry fringe dweller to a major force. This was because of the one thing that had always ruled Hollywood. Money. As the cost of producing films grew exponentially, the major studios began to look for partners to share the cost and risk.

This is where Walter Elliot and Archway Pictures came in. On Melrose Avenue, just a few blocks from the behemoth Paramount Studios, Archway offered production facilities and sound stages when everything was booked at the big studios. It leased office space to would-be and has-been producers. It nurtured independent films. For a decade, it limped along until luck struck twice. In a space of only three years, two of the independent films became huge hits. Walter and his studio suddenly basked in success. Archway's cut from the two was over a hundred million dollars apiece.

With that newfound money, Walter Elliot cofinanced a number of productions in which the big studios were looking for partners. Over the next decade there were enough hits to double and triple his stake. He became a player, making regular appearances on the power 100 lists in industry minds and magazines. Elliot's personal wealth grew commensurately. He traded in his wife for a newer model, and together they started accumulating houses. They owned seven homes and two ranches in or around L.A.

Those top 100 lists came in handy when Elliot was charged with double murder. He pulled off something rarely accomplished in a murder case. He got bail. Set at twenty million dollars, he paid in real estate.

One of the properties was a waterfront weekender on a secluded cove in Malibu. It was there that thirty-nine-year-old Mitzi Elliot was murdered with her lover in a twelve-hundred-square-foot bedroom with a glass wall that looked out on the big blue Pacific.

The discovery file was replete with forensic reports and crime-scene photographs. The death room was completely white—walls, carpet, furniture, and bedding. Two naked bodies were sprawled on the bed and floor. Mitzi Elliot and Johan Rilz. The scene was red on white. Two bullet holes in the man's chest. Two in the woman's chest, and one in her forehead. Though the murder weapon was missing, slugs taken from the bodies had been identified as coming from a Smith & Wesson Model 29, a 44-magnum revolver.

Walter Elliot had been suspicious about his wife. She had announced her intentions to divorce him, and he believed there was another man involved. He told the sheriff's homicide investigators that he had gone to the beach house because he thought it was a lie when she told him she was going to meet with the interior designer. He timed his approach so that he could confront her with a paramour. He loved her and wanted her back. According to the statement, he found his wife and her lover naked and already dead. It turned out that the lover was in fact the interior designer, Johan Rilz, a German national that Elliot had always thought was gay.

Elliot called 911. After he gave investigators an account of his discovery of the two bodies, he was interviewed at the Malibu substation and at sheriff's headquarters, where in the crime lab, his hands and sleeves tested positive for high levels of gunshot residue.

I closed the file as Cisco pulled the Lincoln even with the guardhouse in front of Archway Studios. I lowered my window so I could speak to the uniformed man who stepped out.

"I'm Walter Elliot's attorney. I don't have an appointment, but I need to see him right away."

"Can I see your driver's license?"

I passed it through the window. "I'm handling this for Jerry Vincent."

The guard went into the booth, slid the door closed, and picked up the phone. He soon slid the door back open. "Mrs. Albrecht is Mr. Elliot's executive assistant. She wants to speak to you."

I took the extended phone. "Hello?"

"Mr. Haller, is it? What is this all about? Mr. Elliot has dealt exclusively with Mr. Vincent."

"I'd rather not talk at the front gate. Can I come see Mr. Elliot?"

"Can I place you on hold while I call Mr. Vincent?"

"Mrs. Albrecht, Jerry Vincent's dead. That's why I'm here."

I looked at Cisco in the rearview mirror and shrugged. The plan had been to finesse my way through the arch, then be the one to personally tell Elliot his lawyer was dead.

"Mr. Haller, did you say Mr. Vincent is . . . dead?"

"Yes. I'm his court-appointed replacement. Can I come in now?"

"Of course."

We were assigned to a prime parking space in the executive lot. I went in alone, carrying Vincent's two thick files on the case. One contained discovery materials turned over by the prosecution, including the investigative documents and interview transcripts, and the other contained work product generated by Vincent.

I followed a sidewalk across a beautifully manicured lawn to Walter Elliot's office in Bungalow One. Bungalows sounded small, but they were big in Hollywood. A Spanish-tiled entranceway led to a step-down living room with a fireplace and a mahogany wood bar. I stepped into the middle of the room and waited.

"Mr. Haller?"

I turned. Elliot's gatekeeper, Mrs. Albrecht, had stepped from some unseen entrance. Elegance was the word that came to mind. She was an aging beauty who appeared to take the process in stride. Gray streaked through her undyed hair, and tiny wrinkles seemed unchecked by injection or incision.

"Mr. Elliot will see you now."

I followed her down a short hall to Walter Elliot's office.

Elliot was an overly tanned man with more gray hair sprouting from his open shirt collar than from the top of his head. He sat behind a large glass worktable. No computer on it, though paperwork and scripts were spread across it. He had dark, piercing eyes.

"Mr. Elliot, this is Mr. Haller," Mrs. Albrecht said.

She signaled me to the chair across the table. Elliot made a dismissive gesture, and she left without another word. Over the years I had represented a couple dozen killers. They come in all sizes and shapes, rich and poor, humble and arrogant, regretful and cold to the bone. The percentages told me that it was most likely Elliot who had calmly dispatched his wife and her lover and arrogantly thought he could get away with it. But there was nothing on first meeting that told me for sure. And that's the way it always was.

"What happened to my lawyer?" he asked.

"Somebody killed him last night in his car."

"Where does that leave me, on trial for my life in a week?"

That was a slight exaggeration. The D.A.'s office had not announced it would seek the death penalty. But I didn't think it hurt to think in such terms. "That's why I'm here."

"And who are you? I've never heard of you."

"I make it a practice not to be heard of. Celebrity lawyers bring too much attention to their clients."

He pursed his lips. "You're taking over Vincent's practice?"

"Let me explain, Mr. Elliot. Jerry Vincent had a one-man shop. Just like I do. On occasion, each of us would need another attorney to fill in here and there. If you look at the contract of representation you signed, you'll find it allowed Jerry to discuss your case with me. In other words, Jerry trusted me. Earlier today the chief judge of the Superior Court issued an order placing me in custody of Jerry's cases. Of course, you ultimately choose who represents you at trial. I'm only here to tell you your options."

Elliot shook his head. "I really can't believe this. We were set for trial next week, and I'm not pushing it back. Do you have any idea what it is like for an innocent man to have to wait and wait for justice? To read all the innuendo in the media? Look at this!" He pulled his pant leg up to reveal the GPS monitor Judge Holder had ordered him to wear. "I want this over!"

I nodded in a consoling manner. "I've dealt with many clients wrongly accused," I lied. "The wait for justice can be almost intolerable. I spent the afternoon reviewing the files and evidence in your case. I'm confident you won't have to delay the trial, Mr. Elliot. I would be more than prepared to proceed. Another attorney, maybe not. But I'd be ready." There it was, my best pitch, most of it lies and exaggerations. "I've studied the trial strategy Mr. Vincent outlined. I wouldn't change it, but I believe I can improve on it."

Elliot nodded. "I have to think about this. I need to talk to some people and have you checked out. Like I had Vincent checked out."

I decided to gamble and try to force him into a quick decision. I didn't want him finding out I'd disappeared for a year. "It's a good idea," I said, "but the longer you wait, the greater the chance that the judge will find it necessary to push the trial back. In the absence of Mr. Vincent, he's probably already considering it. If you choose me, I will tell him we're good to go." I stood and handed him a card from my pocket. "Those are my numbers. Call any time."

Elliot took the card and studied it. Before I reached the office door, it opened and Mrs. Albrecht smiled warmly.

"I'm sure we will be in touch," she said.

I FOUND CISCO LEANING against the Lincoln smoking a cigarette. "That was fast," he said.

I got inside the car in case there were cameras in the parking lot and Elliot was watching me.

Cisco did the same. "Look at you with the encouraging word."

"I gave it my best shot. We'll probably know something soon."

Cisco backed out of the space and started heading toward the arch. It was hard to go from thinking about a quarter-million-dollar fee to some of Vincent's also-rans, but that was the job. I opened my bag and pulled out the other active files.

The address of each client was printed neatly on each file, and the woman charged with indecent exposure lived in Hollywood.

"Here we go," I said. "Head down Melrose to La Brea. After that stop, I'll ride in the front. Don't want you to feel like a chauffeur."

"Hey, Mick, I gotta tell you something," Cisco said. "Me and Lorna . . . we're gonna get married."

I had figured they were headed in that direction. Lorna and I had been friends for fifteen years before we were married for one. It had been a rebound marriage for me and as ill-advised as anything I had ever done. We realized the mistake and somehow managed to remain close. There was no one I trusted more in the world.

"That okay with you, Mick?"

I looked in the rearview. "I'm not part of the equation, Cisco."

"I know, but I want to know if it's *okay* with you."

I looked out the window, then looked back in the mirror.

"Yes, it's all right with me. But I'll tell you something, Cisco. She's one of the four most important people in my life. You have maybe seventy-five pounds on me, but if you hurt her, I'm going to find a way to hurt you back. That okay with you?"

He looked away to the road. "Yeah, Mick, I'm okay with that."

We were silent for a while after that. Cisco kept glancing at me in the mirror. "What?" I finally asked.

"Well, I got your daughter. That makes one. And then Lorna. I was wondering who the other two were."

Before I could answer, the electronic version of the William Tell

Overture started to play in my hand. My cell phone said PRIVATE CALLER on the screen. I opened it up. "Haller."

"Please hold for Walter Elliot," Mrs. Albrecht said.

Not much time went by before I heard, "Mr. Haller?"

"I'm here. What can I do for you?" I felt the stirring of anxiety in my gut. He had decided.

"Have you noticed something about my case, Mr. Haller?"

"How do you mean?"

"One lawyer. I have one lawyer, Mr. Haller. I not only must win this case in court, but in the court of public opinion."

"I see," I said, though I didn't quite understand the point.

"In the last ten years, I've picked a lot of winners. I know what people like, because I know what they're thinking. And I think the public believes the more guilty you are, the more lawyers you need. When I hired Mr. Vincent, I said, 'No dream team. Just you.' "

"I under—"

"I've decided, Mr. Haller. You impressed me when you were in here. I would like to engage your services for trial."

I calmed my voice. "I'm glad to hear that. Call me Mickey."

"And you can call me Walter. But I insist on one condition. We go to trial on schedule. I want to hear you say it."

I hesitated. I wanted a delay. But I wanted the case more. "We'll be ready to go next Thursday."

"Then welcome aboard. What do we do next?"

"Well, I could turn around and come back."

"I'm afraid I have meetings until seven and then a screening of our film for the awards season."

I would have thought that his trial would trump his meetings. "Okay, give me a fax number and I'll have my assistant send over a contract. It will have the same fee structure as Jerry Vincent's."

There was silence, and I waited. If he was going to knock down the fee, this is when he would do it. But instead he repeated a fax number I could hear Mrs. Albrecht giving him.

"What's tomorrow look like, Walter?"

"Tomorrow?"

"Yes, tomorrow. We need to talk and go over things."

I heard muffled voices as he conferred with Mrs. Albrecht. "I have a four o'clock open here at the bungalow."

"Okay. I'll be there. And Walter, I want to see the crime scene. Can I get into the house in Malibu before we meet?"

Again he covered the phone and I heard muffled conversation. Then he came back on the line. "How about eleven? I'll have someone there to let you in."

"That'll work. See you tomorrow, Walter."

I closed the phone and looked at Cisco. "We got him."

# FIVE

BOSCH arrived early the next morning. His peace offering was the extra cup of coffee he handed me. I don't drink coffee anymore—to avoid any addiction in my life—but I took it anyway, thinking maybe the smell would get me going. It was only seven forty-five, but I'd been in Jerry Vincent's office for more than two hours already.

I led Bosch back into the file room. He looked more tired than I felt, and I was pretty sure he was in the same suit he'd been wearing the day before. "Long night?" I asked.

"Oh, yeah."

I told him to have a seat, and I took the other chair.

"So," I said, picking up the yellow legal tablet on the table, "I met with Judge Holder and worked out a plan in which we can give you what you need without actually giving you the files."

Bosch shook his head. "You should've told me this at Parker Center. I wouldn't have wasted my time."

"I thought you'd appreciate this."

"It's not going to work. How many homicides have you investigated, Haller? And how many have you cleared?"

"All right, you're the homicide guy. But as a criminal defense attorney, I'm capable of discerning what constituted a threat to Jerry."

"Look, I'm the detective. No offense, but I'm in a position here where I have to take what an amateur is giving me. I don't trust the evidence unless I find it myself."

"Detective, you're lucky to get this much. Judge Holder wasn't interested in helping you out at all."

"So you're saying you went to bat for me?" He said it in a disbelieving, sarcastic tone, as if it were some sort of impossibility for a defense attorney to help a police detective.

"That's right," I said defiantly. "I went to bat for you. Jerry Vincent was a friend. I'd like to see you take down the person who took him down. Look, do you want the list or not?"

I held the legal pad up as if I were teasing a dog with a toy. He reached for it, and I pulled it back, then quickly handed it to him. It was an awkward exchange, like shaking hands the day before. "There are eleven names with a brief summary of each threat."

Bosch dropped his eyes to the page. "What else do you have?"

"What do you mean?"

"I'll run these names and see where these guys are at now. But these are dead cases. Most likely if these threats were legit, they would've been carried out long ago. I'm looking for something a little more current. Something from Vincent's open cases."

"Well, I can't help you there."

"Sure you can. I assume you're reviewing them. You're going to come across something that doesn't fit, maybe that scares you. That's when you call me. It might save you from . . ."

He didn't finish, but the message was clear. He was trying to scare me into cooperating more than Judge Holder was allowing.

"It's one thing sharing threat information from closed cases," I said. "It's another thing entirely to do it with active cases. And besides that, I know you are asking for more than just threats. You think Jerry stumbled across something that got him killed."

Bosch kept his eyes on me and slowly nodded.

"What about it being a two-way street, Detective? What do you know that you aren't telling me? What was in the laptop that was so important? What was in the portfolio?"

"I can't talk to you about an active investigation."

"You could yesterday when you asked about the FBI."

He squinted his dark eyes. "I didn't ask about the FBI."

"Come on, Detective. You asked if he had any federal cases. Why would you do that unless you have some sort of federal connection? I'm guessing it was the FBI."

Bosch hesitated. I had a feeling I'd guessed right and my mentioning the bureau made him think I knew something. He nodded.

"Okay. The killer took Jerry Vincent's cell phone. I got the call records. On the day he was killed, he got three calls from the bureau. Four days before that, there were two. He was talking to somebody over there. I can't tell who. All outgoing calls from there register on the main number. They were all short calls, none over a minute."

"Anybody there check in on the homicide investigation?"

"Not yet. It's not their style, if you know what I mean. Now your turn. What do you have that's federal?"

"Nothing. I confirmed that Vincent had no federal cases."

I watched Bosch do a slow burn as he realized I had played him.

"There's a rumor about a federal grand jury looking into state-court corruption. You know anything about that?"

I shook my head. "I've been on the shelf for a year."

"Thanks for the help."

"Look, Detective, I don't get this. Why can't you just call over there and ask who was calling your victim?"

Bosch smiled like he was dealing with a child. "If I call, they'll just shine me on. If this was part of a corruption probe, the chances of them talking to a local cop are between slim and none. If they're the ones who got him killed, make it none."

"How would they get him killed?"

"They kept calling. They were pressuring him. Maybe someone else knew about it and thought he was a risk."

"What about the laptop? Is that what this is all about, something in his computer?"

"You tell me."

"How can I tell you when I have no idea what was in it?"

Bosch nodded the point and walked out carrying the legal pad at his side. "Have a good day, Counselor."

LORNA and Cisco arrived together fifteen minutes after Bosch's departure, and we convened in Vincent's office. It was another scorekeeping session in which we went over what had been accomplished the night before and what still needed to be done.

With Cisco driving, I had visited eleven of Vincent's clients the night before, signing up eight of them and giving back files to the remaining three. And Walter Elliot's representation contract had already been signed and returned.

We next set the plan for the day. I told Lorna that I wanted her and Wren—if she showed up—to run down the remaining clients. I also wanted Lorna to continue building the calendar and familiarizing herself with Vincent's files and financial records.

I told Cisco to focus his attention on the Elliot case with emphasis on witness maintenance. This meant that he had to take the preliminary defense witness list, which had already been compiled by Jerry Vincent, and prepare subpoenas for the law-enforcement officers and other witnesses who might be considered hostile. For the paid expert witness and others who were willingly going to testify for the defense, he had to assure them that the trial was moving forward as scheduled, with me replacing Vincent.

"Got it," Cisco said. "What about the Vincent investigation? You still want me monitoring?"

"Yes. Keep tabs on that and let me know what you find out."

"I found out that they spent last night sweating somebody but kicked him loose this morning."

"Who?"

"I don't know yet. Whoever it was is cleared for now."

I nodded as I thought about this. No wonder Bosch looked like he had been up all night. Just then the office door swung open. Wren Williams stood tentatively in the doorway.

"Hello, Wren," I said. "Glad you're here. Lorna will be right out to work with you."

"No problem," she said. "One of the clients was waiting when I came in. Patrick Henson."

I looked at my watch. Five of nine—a good sign. "Send him in."

A young man walked in. Patrick Henson was smaller than I thought he would be. He had the requisite tan, but his hair was cropped short. No earrings, no tattoos that I could see. He wore black cargo pants and what probably was his best shirt. It had a collar.

"Patrick, we spoke on the phone. I'm Mickey Haller, and this is my case manager, Lorna. This big guy is Cisco, my investigator."

Patrick stepped to the desk and shook our hands, his grip firm.

"I'm glad you came in. Is that your fish back there?"

Henson looked at the fish on the wall. "Yeah. That's Betty."

"You gave a stuffed fish a name? Was it a pet?" Lorna asked.

Henson smiled to himself. "No, I caught it a long time ago, hung it by the front door. My roommates and me, we'd always say, 'Hel-looo Betty' when we came home. It was kind of stupid."

"Speaking of names, do we call you Trick?" I asked.

"Nah. That was just the name my agent came up with. I don't have him anymore. You can just call me Patrick."

"Okay. And you told me you had a valid driver's license?"

"Sure do." He reached into a front pocket, removed a thick nylon wallet, and pulled out his license. I studied it, then nodded.

"Okay, Patrick. I need a driver," I said. "I provide the car and gas and insurance, and you show up every morning at nine. I told you the pay schedule yesterday. Still interested?"

"I'm interested."

"Are you a safe driver?" Lorna asked.

"I've never had an accident," Patrick said.

I nodded my approval. "When can you start?"

He shrugged. "I don't have anything. . . . Whenever you want."

"How about we start right now? Today will be a test drive."

"Sounds good to me."

WE TOOK THE 10 OUT OF downtown and headed west toward Malibu. I sat in the back, opened my computer on the fold-down table, and waited for it to boot up.

"Patrick, my car is my office. I've got two other Lincolns just like this one. Each one's got a printer, a fax, and I've got a wireless slot card in my computer. There are more than forty courthouses in L.A. County. Being mobile is the best way to do business."

"I wouldn't want to be in an office either," Patrick said.

"Damn right. Too claustrophobic." My computer was ready, and I began to customize a pretrial motion. "I'm working on your case right now, Patrick."

He looked at me in the mirror. "What do you mean?"

"Well, I reviewed your file, and there's something Mr. Vincent hadn't done that I think we need to do that may help."

"What's that?"

"Get an independent appraisal of the necklace you took. They list the value as twenty-five thousand. That bumps you up to a felony."

"You mean, like if the diamonds are bogus, there's no felony?"

"It could work out like that, but I was thinking of something else." I pulled out his file to check a name. "Let me ask a question. What were you doing in the house where you took the necklace?"

He shrugged his shoulders. "I was dating the old lady's youngest daughter. I met her on the beach and was sort of teaching her to surf. There was a birthday party at the house, and I was invited, and the mother was given the necklace."

"That's when you learned its value."

"Yeah. The father said they were diamonds."

"So then the next time you were there you stole it."

He didn't respond.

"Patrick, I'm your lawyer now, and we need to discuss the facts of the case. You stole the necklace. Tell me about it."

"We were there alone using the pool, and I said I had to go to the can, only I really wanted to check the medicine cabinet for pills. I was hurting. There weren't any downstairs, so I went upstairs and looked around. I saw the necklace and just took it."

He shook his head, and I knew why. He was thoroughly embarrassed and defeated by his addiction.

"It's okay, Patrick. What did the guy say when you pawned it?"

"He said he'd only give me four bills because the chain was gold, but he didn't think the diamonds were legit. I took the money. I was so messed up on the stuff I didn't care."

"Have you talked to the girl since you were arrested?"

"No, man. We're done." Now the eyes in the mirror looked sad and humiliated. "The whole thing was stupid."

I reached into my jacket pocket and pulled out a photograph. I tapped Patrick on the shoulder with it. "Take a look at that."

He held it on top of the steering wheel. "What happened?"

"I tripped over a curb. Broke a tooth, my nose, opened up my forehead. They took that in the ER as a reminder."

"Of what?"

"I had just gotten out of my car after driving my eleven-year-old home to her mother. By then I was up to three-hundred-twenty milligrams of oxycontin a day." I let him register that for a moment. "You think what you did was stupid? I was driving my little girl around on three-hundred-twenty migs of hillbilly heroin."

He was staring directly at me in the mirror.

"There's nothing you can do about the past, Patrick. Except keep it there. I'm going to help you get through the legal stuff, but it's up to you to do the hard part."

He nodded.

"Anyway, I see something Jerry Vincent didn't see. The victim's husband's a big supporter of elected people in the county. And if the diamonds are phony, he's not going to want that coming up in court if his wife doesn't know."

"But how's he gonna stop it?"

"Patrick, his contributions helped elect at least four supervisors. Their board controls the district attorney's budget. The D.A. is prosecuting you. It's a food chain. If the husband wants to send a message, believe me, it will be sent. The motion I'm filing requests that we be allowed to independently appraise the evidence."

"That's cool! Thanks, Mr. Haller."

"You're welcome, Patrick. Can I have my picture back now?"

He handed it over, and I took a look. The eyes were the toughest part. Dazed and lost, staring unsteadily at the camera. Me at my lowest point. I put it back in my pocket for safekeeping.

We drove in silence while I finished the motion, went online, and sent it in. The Lincoln lawyer was back on the beat.

I made sure I looked up when we hit the tunnel that dumps the freeway out onto the Pacific Coast Highway. I lowered the window. I always loved the feeling I got when I'd swing out of the tunnel and see and smell the ocean.

I started seeing surfers on the swells and saw Patrick taking glances toward the water. "It said in the file you did rehab," I said.

"Yeah. It worked. Did you do rehab?"

"Yeah, in Laurel Canyon. You thinking about going back into surfing?"

"I don't think so. Not on a professional level. I lost my move getting up. Besides, I'm taking things one day at a time. They taught you that in Laurel Canyon, didn't they?"

"They did. But surfing's a one-wave-at-a-time thing, isn't it?"

He nodded, and I watched his eyes trip to the mirror.

"What do you want to ask me, Patrick?"

"Um, yeah, you know how Vincent kept my fish on the wall? I was wondering if he kept any of my boards."

I opened his file and looked through it. "You gave him twelve boards, right?"

"Yeah. All of them."

"Well, he gave them to the liquidator he used when he took assets from clients. The guy sold all twelve, took twenty percent, and gave Vincent forty-eight hundred dollars."

Patrick didn't say anything. I remembered he'd said the two long boards were the most valuable. On the inventory there were two boards ten feet long. One sold for twelve hundred dollars to a collector and the other for four hundred dollars on eBay. The disparity made me think the eBay sale was bogus. The liquidator had probably sold the board to himself cheap. He would then turn around and sell it at a profit he'd keep for himself. Everybody's got an angle. Including me. I knew that if he hadn't resold the board yet, then I still had a shot at it.

"What if I could get you one of the long boards back?" I asked.

"That would be awesome! I just wish I had kept one, you know?"

"No promises. But I'll see what I can do."

In another twenty minutes, we pulled into the driveway of Walter Elliot's house. It was of Moorish design, with white stone, dark brown shutters, and a central façade tower. A silver midlevel Mercedes was parked on the cobblestone pavers.

"You want me to wait here?" Patrick asked.

"Yeah. I don't think I'll take long. Pop the trunk for me."

I got out, went to the back to retrieve my digital camera, and took a quick shot in front of the house. Then I walked to the entrance. The door opened, and Mrs. Albrecht stood there, looking lovely.

When Walter Elliot had told me he would have someone meet me in Malibu, I hadn't expected it to be his executive assistant.

"Mrs. Albrecht, how are you today?"

"Very well. Come in, please. This way." I followed her into the great room, which was larger than my entire home. It was a complete entertainment area, with a glass wall on the western exposure that brought the Pacific right into the house.

"Beautiful," I said.

"It is indeed. Do you want to see the bedroom?"

Ignoring the question, I turned the camera on and took a few shots of the living room and its view.

"Do you know who has been in here since the sheriff's department relinquished control of it?" I asked.

"Very few people. I don't believe Mr. Elliot has been out here. Mr. Vincent came once, and his investigator came twice."

"Then let's go up."

As we went up a winding white staircase with an ocean-blue banister, I asked Mrs. Albrecht what her first name was.

"My name is Nina. You can call me that if you want."

"Good. And you can call me Mickey."

The stairs led to a door that opened into a bedroom suite the size of some courtrooms. It had twin fireplaces, a sitting area, a sleeping area, and his-and-her bathrooms. Nina Albrecht pushed a button, and the curtains split to reveal a wall of glass looking out on the sea.

The custom-made bed was double the size of a regular king. It had been stripped of the top mattress. Next to the door, a six-foot square segment of carpet had been cut out, and on the wall-blood, spatter marks had been circled and marked with letter codes.

The investigative summary in the file suggested that the naked couple had heard an intruder in the house. Rilz went to the bed-room door and opened it, only to be immediately shot down. The killer stepped over his body, and Mitzi Elliot jumped up from the bed, clutching a pillow in front of her body. She was shot twice through the pillow and knocked back onto the bed. The killer pressed the barrel of the gun against her forehead for the kill shot.

I walked over to the glass doors that led out to a deck overlook-ing the Pacific. I opened them and stepped onto the deck. The surf was washing right up to the piers on which the house was built.

I walked back inside, and as soon as I closed the doors, I realized my phone was ringing. It said PRIVATE CALLER on the screen.

"Nina, I have to take this. Do you mind waiting downstairs?"

"No problem."

"Thank you." I took the call. "Hello?"

"It's me. I'm just checking to see when you're coming by."

"Me" was my first ex-wife, Maggie McPherson. Under a re-vamped agreement, I got to be with my daughter on Wednesday nights and every other weekend. It was a long way from the shared custody we'd once had, but I had blown that. "Probably around seven thirty. I have a meeting, and it might run a little late."

There was silence, and I sensed I'd given the wrong answer. "What, you've got a date? What time you want me there?"

"I'm supposed to leave at seven thirty."

"Then I'll be there before then. Who's the lucky guy?"

"That wouldn't be any of your business. But speaking of lucky, I heard you got Jerry Vincent's practice." As a deputy district attorney assigned to the Van Nuys courthouse, my ex-wife was in a position to hear things about me.

"I'm his replacement. I don't know how lucky that makes me."

"You should get a good ride on the Elliot case," she said with a prosecutor's sneer. "If anyone can get him off, it's certainly you."

"I guess I won't respond to that."

"One other thing. You're not having company tonight, are you?"

"What are you talking about?"

"Hayley said a woman was there two weeks ago. I believe her name was Lanie? She felt very awkward about it."

"Don't worry, she won't be there. She's just a friend and she used the guest room. But for the record, I can have anybody I want over because it's *my* house. You're free to do the same."

"And I'm also free to go to the judge and say you're exposing our daughter to people who are drug addicts."

I took a deep breath. "How would you know?"

"Because your daughter isn't stupid and her hearing is perfect. It was easy to figure out that your . . . friend is from rehab."

"And so that's a crime, consorting with people from rehab?"

"It's not a crime, Michael. I just don't think it's best for Hayley."

"I guess the one addict you're most concerned with is me."

"Well, if the shoe fits . . ."

I almost lost it, but I knew that showing anger would only hurt me. "This is our daughter we're talking about. Don't hurt her by trying to hurt me. She needs her father, and I need my daughter."

"And that's my point. You are doing well. Hooking up with an addict is not a good idea."

I squeezed my phone so hard I thought it might break. My words came out strangled by my own failures. "I have to go."

"And so do I. I'll tell Hayley you'll be there by seven thirty."

# SIX

AT ARCHWAY Studios, we made it through the security checkpoint without any of the delay of the day before. It helped that Nina Albrecht was in the car in front of us and had smoothed the way. The studio was emptying out for the day, and Patrick got a parking spot in front of Elliot's bungalow.

As I followed Nina in, she said she was taking me to the executive boardroom and I could set up there while she went to get her boss. It was a big room with black leather chairs around an oval table. I took a seat, and twenty-five minutes later Elliot walked in.

Nina trailed him into the room to see what she could get us for refreshment. "Nothing, Nina," I said before Elliot could respond. "We need to get started."

Elliot nodded, and she left, closing the double doors behind her.

I looked across the table at my client. "Walter, when we set a meeting, let's be on time for it. There's a lot of ground to cover. For the next two weeks, you have one priority. This case."

It may have been the first time in his life he had been chided for being late, then told what to do. Finally, he nodded. "Fair enough."

"Good," I said. "Now let's get to work." I opened the defense file and looked at my notes on the inside flap. "I think we're set in terms of witnesses and strategy when it comes to the state's case. What I haven't found is a strategy for putting forth your defense."

"What do you mean? Jerry told me we were ready."

"Maybe not. I know it's not something you want to see, but I found this in the file." I slid a document across to him.

He glanced at it. "What is it?"

"A motion for a continuance. Jerry hadn't filed it, but it seems he wanted to delay the trial. The coding indicates he printed it Monday, just hours before he was killed."

Elliot shoved the document back. "No. We talked about it, and he agreed to move forward on schedule."

"That was Monday?"

"Yes, Monday. The last time I talked to him."

I nodded. I had noted that Vincent had billed an hour on the day of his murder. "Was that a conference at his office or yours?"

"It was a phone call. Nina can get you the exact time."

"He has it down at three. Why did he want a continuance?"

"He wanted more time to prepare and maybe pad his bill. I told him we were ready, like I'm telling you. We are ready!"

I sort of laughed. "The thing is, you're not the lawyer, Walter. I am. And I'm not seeing much in terms of a defense strategy. I think that's why Jerry wanted to delay the trial. He didn't have a case."

"No, it's the prosecution that doesn't have the case."

"Let me explain how this works," I said wearily. "The prosecutor goes first, and he lays out his case. We get a chance to attack it as he goes. Then we get our shot, and that's when we put up our evidence and alternate theories of the crime."

"Okay."

"And what I can tell from the files is that Jerry has counter witnesses and cross-examination plans ready for everything the prosecution is going to put forward. But on the defense side, we've got no alibi, no alternate suspects, no alternate theories, nothing. Did he ever discuss with you how he planned to roll out the defense?"

"No. We were going to have that conversation, but he got killed. He said he had the magic bullet and the less I knew the better."

I knew the term. The magic bullet was the witness or piece of evidence that you had in your back pocket that was going to either knock all the evidence down like dominoes or permanently fix reasonable doubt in the mind of every juror on the panel.

"You have no idea what this magic bullet was?"

"Just what he told me, that he found something that was going to blow the state out of the water."

"That doesn't make sense if on Monday he was talking about delaying the trial," I said, but my mind was on Vincent's missing laptop. Was the magic bullet there? Was it the reason for his murder?

I decided to move on.

"Well, Walter, I don't have the magic bullet. But if Jerry could find it, so can I. Let's talk about an alternate theory."

"Okay. Meaning what?"

"Meaning that the state has its theory and we should have ours. The state's theory is that you were upset over your wife's infidelity and what it would cost to divorce her. So you went to Malibu and killed her and her lover. You then hid the murder weapon or threw it into the ocean and called nine one one. But to back it up, they have the GSR—the gunshot residue—and almost nothing else."

"That test was a false positive! I never shot any weapon. And Jerry told me he was bringing in the top expert in the country to testify that the procedures were sloppy."

I nodded. "Yes, but the prosecution will counter with their own expert saying the opposite. At best, the GSR will be a wash. The prosecution will lean heavily on motive and opportunity. They'll say you knew Rilz was your wife's lover and trot out evidence indicating a divorce would cost you a hundred million dollars."

"And it's all bull."

"A lot of their positives can be turned into negatives. It will be a dance, Walter. We'll trade punches. We'll try to distort and destroy, but ultimately they'll land more punches than we can block and that's why it's always good for the defense to float an alternative theory. We throw suspicion away from you and at somebody else. The prosecutor, Jeffrey Golantz, is a seasoned pro. He's never lost at trial. Something like twenty-seven and oh."

Elliot nodded thoughtfully as he looked at the polished tabletop.

I checked my watch. Time had passed quickly, and I needed to keep things moving if I was going to pick my daughter up on time.

"Okay," I said. "There are other things we need to cover. I want to add a couple people to the defense team. A jury selection consultant and somebody to work with you on image and testimony."

He shook his head. "No jury consultant. Makes it look like you're trying to rig things."

"Look, the person I want to hire will sit out in the gallery. No one will notice. She just reads people's faces and looks for giveaways."

"No. I won't pay for that mumbo jumbo."

"Are you sure, Walter?"

I spent five minutes trying to convince him, stressing that in circumstantial cases the priority had to be in picking jurors with open minds. At the end of my plea, Elliot simply shook his head.

"Mumbo jumbo. I will trust your skills."

BY THE time I dropped Patrick back at his car downtown in heavy traffic, I knew I was going to be late and I was heading toward another confrontation with my ex-wife. I called, but she didn't pick up. When I got to her apartment in Sherman Oaks, it was almost seven forty, and I found mother and daughter out at the curb waiting. Hayley had her head down and was looking at the sidewalk.

I popped the locks as I pulled to a stop and Maggie helped Hayley in with her school backpack and overnight bag.

"Thanks for being on time," Maggie said in a flat voice.

"No problem," I said, just to see if it would put the flares in her eyes. "Must be a hot date if you're waiting out here."

"No, not really. Parent-teacher conference at the school."

That got through my defenses. "You should've told me. We could've gotten a babysitter and gone together."

"We tried that," Maggie said. "Remember? You jumped on the teacher so badly about Hayley's math grade—which you knew nothing about—you were asked not to come back."

The incident sounded only vaguely familiar, locked away in my oxycodone-corrupted memory banks. I didn't have a comeback.

"I have to go," Maggie said quickly. "Hayley, I love you. Be good for your father and I'll see you tomorrow."

"Okay, Mom."

We drove silently down Ventura Boulevard and stopped at DuPar's, my daughter's favorite place to eat dinner because I always let her order pancakes.

I ordered a BLT. We did her homework together; then I asked

her what she wanted to do. I was willing to do a movie, the mall, whatever, but I was hoping she'd just want to go home to my place, maybe pull out some old family scrapbooks and look at the photos.

She hesitated, and I thought I knew why. "There's nobody at my place, Hay. Lanie doesn't visit anymore."

"You mean, like, she's not your girlfriend anymore?"

"She never was my girlfriend. Remember when I stayed in the hospital last year? We became friends, and we tried to watch out for each other."

It was the shaded truth. Lanie Ross and I had met in rehab. We continued the relationship after leaving the program but never consummated it as a romance, because we were emotionally incapable of it. Once we were in the real world, I instinctively knew she wasn't going to go the distance, and I couldn't make the journey to relapse with her. We went our separate ways.

"I think I just want to go home and watch TV, then."

"Good. That's what I want to do."

We packed up her schoolbooks, and I paid the bill. On the drive over the hill, she said her mother had told her I had gotten an important new job. "She said you had a big case and everybody would be jealous but you would do real good."

"Your mom said that?" I was surprised but happy.

"Yeah."

I drove for a while thinking about that. Maybe I hadn't entirely blown things with Maggie. She still respected me on some level.

"Um . . ." Hayley was looking away from me.

Children are so easy to read sometimes. If only grown-ups were the same. "What's up, Hay?"

"Um, I was just wondering why you can't do what mom does."

"What do you mean?"

"Like putting bad people in jail. She said your case is with a man who killed two people. It's like you always work for the bad guys."

I was quiet for a moment. "The man I am defending is accused of killing two people. Nobody has proved he did anything wrong. Right now he's not guilty of anything."

She didn't respond, and her skepticism was almost palpable.

"Hayley, when somebody is accused of a crime in our country, they are entitled to defend themselves. What if at school you were accused of cheating and you knew that you didn't cheat? Wouldn't you want to be able to explain?"

"I think so."

"I think so, too. It's like that with the courts. If you get accused of a crime, you can have a lawyer like me help you. It's part of the system. An important part."

On an intellectual level, I believed the argument, but on a father-daughter level, it felt hollow. How could I get her to believe it when I wasn't sure I believed it anymore myself?

"Have you helped any innocent people?" my daughter asked.

"A few, yes." It was the best I could honestly say. I turned the radio on to the Disney music station.

Maybe grown-ups were just as easy to read as their children.

# SEVEN

AFTER dropping my daughter off at school Thursday morning, I drove directly to Jerry Vincent's offices. It was still early, and when I got to the garage, I almost had my pick of the place. I parked on the second level, and as I walked to the bridge, I noticed a parked Subaru station wagon with surfboard racks on the roof.

The back windows on the wagon were tinted, and I looked in through the driver's-side window. The backseat had been folded flat, and half the rear area was cluttered with boxes full of clothes. The other half served as a bed for Patrick Henson, lying asleep in a sleeping bag. It was only then I remembered that he'd told me he was living out of his car and sleeping in a lifeguard stand.

I wouldn't need him until later in the morning. There was no need to roust him. I crossed into the office complex and headed down the hallway. Standing in front of Jerry Vincent's door was Detective Bosch. He was listening to his music, hands in his pockets, looking pensive. He pulled out the ear buds as I approached.

"What, no coffee?" I said by way of a greeting.

"Not today. I could tell you didn't want it yesterday." He stepped aside so I could use a key to open the door.

"Can I ask you something?" I said.

"If I said no, you'd ask anyway."

"You're probably right." I opened the door.

"So then just ask the question."

"All right. Well, you don't seem like an iPod sort of guy to me. Who were you listening to there?"

"Somebody I am sure you never heard of. Frank Morgan."

"The saxophone player? Yeah, I know Frank."

"You know him," Bosch said in a disbelieving tone.

"Yeah. I usually drop by and say hello when he plays at the Catalina or the Jazz Bakery. Back in the sixties, my father was Frank's lawyer. Before he got straight, Frank played in San Quentin with Art Pepper—you've heard of him, right?"

It took Bosch a moment to recover from my surprise knowledge of Frank Morgan, the obscure heir to Charlie Parker. We crossed the reception area and went into the main office.

"So how's the case going?" I asked.

"It's going," he said.

"I heard that you spent yesterday in Parker Center sweating a suspect. No arrest, though?"

I sat behind Vincent's desk, and Bosch stayed standing. "Who told you that?" he asked.

"I don't know," I said. "I must've heard it somewhere. Maybe a reporter. Who was the suspect?"

"That's none of your business."

"What's my business with you, Detective? Why are you here?"

"I came to see if you had any more names for me."

"What happened to the names I gave you yesterday?"

"They've checked out."

"How could you check them all out already?"

He leaned down and put both hands on the desk. "Because I'm not working this case alone. Every one of them is either in jail, dead, or was not worried about Jerry Vincent anymore. It's a dead end."

I felt disappointed and realized maybe I'd put too much hope into the possibility of one of those names belonging to the killer.

"Well, what can I tell you, Detective. I can't reveal anything about active cases, but here's the deal: There's nothing to reveal."

He shook his head in disbelief.

"I mean it. There is nothing in any of them that constitutes a threat, nothing that connects to the FBI. And he had only one murder case—Walter Elliot—and there isn't anything there. Believe me, I've looked."

I wasn't so sure I believed it as I said it, but Bosch didn't seem to notice. He finally sat down on the edge of a chair. There was an almost desperate look to his face.

"Jerry was divorced," I offered. "Check out the ex-wife."

"She's happily remarried and seven months pregnant."

"Any other relatives? Girlfriend?"

"He was banging his secretary, but there was nothing serious there. And she was also banging his investigator. And that night, they were together with friends at a screening at Archway. That bigshot client of yours got them the invitation."

I nodded and took an educated guess. "The guy you sweated that first night was the investigator, Bruce Carlin."

"Who told you that?"

"You just did. You had a classic love triangle. It would've been the place to start."

"Smart lawyer. Tell me about the money."

He'd thrown a zinger right back at me. "What money?"

"The money in the business accounts."

"Actually, my case manager tells me they're clean. Every penny Jerry took in is accounted for. I think Jerry probably paid himself a little too quickly, but there's nothing technically wrong."

I saw Bosch's eyes light. "He paid himself too quickly?"

"The way it works is you take on a client and you receive an advance that goes into the client trust account. It's their money, but as you prepare the case, you move your fees to the operating account."

"Okay, so how did Vincent pay himself too quickly?"

"Well, he liked to keep a low balance in operating. He happened to have had a franchise client who paid a large advance, and that money went through the accounts pretty quickly. After costs, the rest went to Vincent in salary."

Bosch leaned toward me. "Walter Elliot, was he the franchise?"

"I can't give out that information but it's an easy guess to make."

Bosch nodded. I waited, and he said nothing.

"Look," I said, "we both have rules we have to follow. We're flip sides of the same coin. I'm just doing my job. If there is nothing else I can help you with, I'll get back to it."

He stared at me. "Who did Vincent bribe on the Elliot case?"

The question came out of left field, but I realized it was the question he'd come to ask. Everything else was window dressing.

"What, is that from the FBI?"

"I haven't talked to the FBI. I'm talking about a payoff."

I smiled. "I told you, the books are clean. There's—"

"If you were going to bribe someone with a hundred thousand dollars, would you put it in your books?"

""I guess you're right," I said to Bosch. "I wouldn't do it that way. So what aren't you telling me?"

"This is in confidence, Counselor. But I need your help, and I think you need to know this in order to help me."

"Okay."

"Then say it."

"Say what?"

"That you will treat this information in confidence."

"I thought I did. Fine. I will."

"I have Vincent's private accounts. Five months ago he accumulated a hundred grand in a personal investment account and a week later told his broker he was cashing out."

"A hundred thousand in cash? What happened to it?"

"I don't know. But his broker asked a lot of questions to make sure there wasn't a security issue. Vincent said he needed the money to buy a boat and he'd get the best deal in cash."

"So where's the boat?"

"There is no boat. We've checked all state transactions and asked questions all over Marina del Rey and San Pedro. We've searched his home twice and reviewed his credit card purchases. No Coast Guard registration. He bought something else, and Walter Elliot probably knows what it was."

I tracked his logic and could see it coming to Walter Elliot's door. But I wasn't going to open it with Bosch looking over my shoulder. "I think you've got it wrong, Detective."

"I don't think so, Counselor."

"Well, I have no idea about this, and my client's off limits. He's not talking to you about this or anything else."

Bosch shook his head. "I wouldn't waste my time trying to talk to him. He used his lawyer as cover. But you should take it as a warning, Counselor. Remember, that little trickle down your spine from the back of your neck—that's the feeling you get when you know you're in danger."

I smiled. "Oh, is that what that is? You've been running a game on me for two days, Detective, and it's been a waste of my time."

I extended a hand toward the door. Bosch stood up. "Don't kid yourself, Haller. Don't make a mistake." He pulled a photograph from his pocket and put it on the desk. "You recognize that man?"

It was a grainy still taken off a surveillance video. It showed a man pushing out through the front door of a building. "This is the Legal Center entrance, isn't it?"

"Do you recognize him?"

The shot was taken at a distance. The man looked to be of Latin origin. He had dark skin and hair and a Pancho Villa mustache. He wore a panama hat and an open-collared shirt beneath a leather sport coat that had pulled open as he'd pushed the glass door. I could see what looked like the top of a pistol tucked into his pants.

"Is that a gun? Is this the killer?"

"Do you recognize this man? That's all I want to know."

"No, I don't, Detective. Happy? But that's not a great photo you've got there. Where's it from?"

"A camera on Broadway and Second. It sweeps the street, and we only got this guy for a few seconds."

I knew that the city had been quietly installing street cameras on main arteries. "Well, it's better than nothing. You think the hair and the mustache are a disguise?"

"Let me ask the questions. Could this guy be a client?"

"I don't know. I haven't met them all. Leave me the photo, and I'll show it to Wren Williams."

Bosch reached down and took the photo back. "It's my only copy. When will she be in?"

"In about an hour."

"I'll come later. Meantime, Counselor, watch yourself."

He pointed a finger at me like it was a gun, then turned and walked out, closing the door behind him.

I got up from the desk and started to pace the office, hands in my pockets, trying to evaluate what the information from Bosch meant.

According to Bosch, Jerry Vincent had paid a sizable bribe to a person or persons unknown. I considered the timing of Vincent's transaction. Bosch said the money transfer had gone down five months ago. Vincent's murder was just three nights ago. The distance between the two seemed to strain any possibility of a link.

But still, I could not push the two apart, and the reason for this was Walter Elliot. Through the filter of Bosch's information, I now began to view my client—and myself—differently. I now saw Elliot's confidence in his acquittal coming possibly from his belief that it had been bought and paid for. I now saw his unwillingness to delay the trial as a timing issue relating to the bribe. And his quick willingness to allow me to carry the torch for Vincent as a move made to get to the trial without delay. It had nothing to do with my skills and tenacity. In fact, I was perfect. Pulled out of the lost-and-found bin, dusted off and suited up and sent in, no questions asked.

Money had been paid for a specific fix, and that fix was tied to the trial staying on schedule. Why must the trial take place as scheduled?

I continued my pacing. The next thing I needed to consider was the photograph Bosch showed me. Early indications were that Vincent had known the person who killed him, but the man in the photograph appeared to be in disguise. The calls from the FBI were also part of the equation. What did the bureau know, and why had no agent come forward to Bosch? And the last unknown was Vincent's murder itself. He'd paid the bribe and was ready for trial. His murder certainly threatened the timetable. Why was he killed?

There were many unknowns, but there was one conclusion that seemed clear: I was being mushroomed by my client. Elliot was keeping me in the dark about the interior machinations of the case.

But that could work both ways. I decided I would do exactly what Bosch asked; I would not question Walter Elliot. I'd keep my head above the dark waters of the case, my eyes wide open.

I shifted focus from my thoughts to what was directly in front of me. I was looking at the gaping mouth of Patrick Henson's fish.

The door opened, and Lorna entered the office to find me staring at the tarpon. "What are you doing?" she asked.

"Thinking."

"Well, Cisco's here and we've got to go. You have a busy court schedule today, and I don't want to make you late."

"Then let's go. I'm starved."

I followed her out but not before glancing back at the big beautiful fish hanging on the wall. I thought I knew exactly how he felt.

I HAD Patrick drive us over to the Pacific Dining Car. Cisco and I ordered steak and eggs; Lorna had tea and honey. The Dining Car was a place where downtown power brokers gathered before a day of fighting it out in the nearby glass towers. The food was overpriced but good. It made the downtown warrior feel like a heavy hitter.

As soon as the waiter took our order, Lorna put her silverware to the side and opened a spiral-bound At-A-Glance calendar on the table. "Eat fast," she said. "You have a busy day."

"Tell me."

"All right, the easy stuff first."

She flipped pages back and forth. "You have a ten a.m. in chambers with Judge Holder. She wants an updated client inventory."

"She told me I had a week," I protested. "Today's Thursday."

"Michaela called. I think the judge saw in the paper that you are continuing on as Elliot's lawyer and she's afraid you're spending all your time on him. Don't worry, I have a hard-copy inventory—who you've met, who you signed up, and calendars on all of them."

I smiled. "Great. What else?"

"At eleven, you have an in-chambers with Judge Stanton. He wants to know if you'll be able to go next Thursday."

"No, but Elliot won't have it any other way."

"Well, the judge is requiring the defendant's presence."

That was unusual. "Did you let Elliot know? He may—"

"He knows, and he'll be there. I talked to his assistant."

"Good," I said. "That it?" I wanted to get to Cisco.

"Not by a long shot. Now we get to the mystery case. Yesterday afternoon Judge Friedman's clerk called Vincent's office blind to see if there was anyone aware of the hearing scheduled today at two. So you have a hearing for a case we not only don't have on calendar but don't have a file for either."

"What's the client's name?"

"Eli Wyms."

It meant nothing to me. "Did Wren know the name?"

Lorna shook her head in a dismissive way.

"Did you check the dead cases? Maybe it was just misfiled."

"We checked. There's no file in the office. Wyms is charged with attempted murder of a peace officer and other weapons-related charges. He was arrested May second at a county park in Calabasas. He was arraigned and sent out to Camarillo. He must've been found competent because the hearing is to set a trial date."

I nodded. From the shorthand, I could read between the lines. Wyms had gotten into a weapons-related confrontation with the sheriff's department, which provided law-enforcement services in the unincorporated area known as Calabasas. He was sent to the state's mental evaluation center in Camarillo. The docs determined he was competent. There would be more detail in the file, but we had no file.

"No reference in the trust-account deposits, I assume. Maybe Jerry took him on pro bono."

"You know what I was thinking?" Lorna said. "That Jerry had the file in his briefcase when he left Monday night."

It made sense. He was preparing for the week and had a hearing Thursday on Wyms. "Who's the prosecutor?"

"Joanne Giorgetti, and I'm way ahead of you. I called her yesterday and explained our situation and asked if she wouldn't mind copying the discovery for us. She said no problem. You can pick it up after your eleven with Judge Stanton and then have a couple hours to familiarize yourself with it before the hearing at two."

"You think of everything, Lorna. Why don't you just take over Vincent's practice and run with it? You don't need me."

She smiled. "I like working in the background. I'll leave center stage for you."

Our plates were served, and I spread a liberal dose of Tabasco sauce on both my steak and the eggs. Cisco dug into his meal, and I knew better than to keep him from his food, so I asked Lorna how things were working out with Wren Williams.

"She's not a lot of help, Mickey. She seems to have no idea of how the office worked or where Jerry put things. If you ask me, she was working here for some other reason."

I could have told her the reason, but I didn't want to distract Lorna with gossip. I saw Cisco was mopping up his steak juice with a piece of toast. "What do you have going, Cisco?"

"I'm working on Rilz and his side of the equation. There'll be a couple things you can use. Want to hear about it?"

"Not yet. I'll ask when I need it." I didn't want information I might have to turn over in discovery.

"I also have the Bruce Carlin debriefing this afternoon."

"He wants two hundred an hour," Lorna said. "Highway robbery, if you ask me."

I waved off her protest. "It's a one-time expense, and he probably has information we can use, and that might save Cisco some time."

"Don't worry, we're paying him. I'm just not happy about it. He's gouging us because he knows he can," Lorna said.

"Technically, he's gouging Elliot, and I don't think he cares."

I turned back to my investigator. "Cisco, you have anything new on the Vincent case?"

Cisco updated me with what he had, mostly forensic details. He said Vincent had been shot twice in the area of the left temple. Powder burns on the skin and hair indicated the weapon was nine to twelve inches away and the killer was able to cluster the impacts. Additionally, the slugs were recovered during the autopsy.

"They were twenty-fives," Cisco said.

"They know the exact weapon yet?"

"A Beretta Bobcat. You could almost hide it in your hand."

A completely different weapon than the one used to kill Mitzi Elliot and Johan Rilz. "So what's all of this tell us?"

"It's a gun you take when it's going to be a head shot."

"So this was planned. Okay, what about the suspect?"

"The guy they sweated the first night?"

"No. That was Carlin they cut loose."

Cisco looked surprised. "How'd you find out it was Carlin?"

"Bosch told me this morning."

"Are you saying they have another suspect?"

"He didn't have a name. He showed me a photo of a guy coming out of the building at the time of the shooting. He had a gun and was wearing an obvious disguise."

I saw Cisco's eyes flare. It was a point of professional pride that he provide me information like that. If I'd told him about the FBI calls, he'd probably have picked the table up and thrown it through the window. "I'll see what I can find out."

We were finished. I pulled out my cell phone to call Patrick, which reminded me of something. "Cisco, one other thing. Go to Vincent's liquidator and see if he's sitting on one of Patrick's surfboards. If he is, I want it back."

Cisco nodded. "I can do that. No problem."

WAYLAID BY THE SLOW ELEVATORS in the Criminal Courts Building, I was four minutes late when I walked into Judge Holder's courtroom and hustled through the clerk's corral to her chambers.

She was behind her desk, and her black robe told me she probably had a hearing scheduled soon in open court. "Mr. Haller, our meeting was set for ten o'clock. I believe you were given proper notice."

"Your Honor, I'm sorry. The elevators in this building—"

"All lawyers take the same elevators, and most seem on time for meetings. Did you bring your checkbook?"

"Yes, Your Honor. I think so, yes."

"Well, we can do this one of two ways. I can hold you in contempt, fine you, and let you explain yourself to the California Bar, or you can make a donation to the Make-A-Wish Foundation. It's my favorite charity. They do good things for sick children."

I was being fined for being four minutes late. The arrogance of some judges was amazing. "I like the idea of helping out sick children," I said. "How much do I make it out for?"

"As much as you want. And I will even send it in for you."

I found my checkbook, and I wrote a check for two hundred and fifty dollars. The judge nodded approvingly, and I knew I was all right.

"Thank you, Mr. Haller." She put it on top of two others. "They'll be sending you a receipt in the mail."

"Like you said, they do good work."

"Yes, they do. Now let me ask you a question. Do you know if the police are making any headway on Mr. Vincent's death?"

I wondered what I should tell the chief judge of the superior court. "I'm not really in the loop on that. But I was shown a surveillance shot of a man I assume they're looking at as a suspect. The guy might be disguised, and it looks like he has a gun. Detective Bosch came to the office with it this morning."

The judge nodded. We were quiet for a moment, and then I took from my bag the scorecard Lorna had prepared for me.

Judge Holder kept me for the next hour while I went over every case. By the time she let me go, I was late for my eleven-o'clock hearing. I hit the stairs and charged up two flights, wondering if it was going to cost me another donation to another favorite charity.

The courtroom was empty, but Stanton's clerk was in her corral. She pointed with a pen to the open door. I quickly moved to the chambers and saw the judge behind his desk. To his left was a stenographer, and across from him were three chairs. Walter Elliot was sitting in the chair to the right, the middle chair was empty, and Jeffrey Golantz was in the third. I had never met the prosecutor before, but he was recognizable because I had seen his face on TV and in the newspapers. In the last few years, he had successfully handled a series of high-profile cases and was making a name for himself. He was the undefeated up-and-comer in the D.A.'s office.

I loved going up against undefeated prosecutors. Their confidence often betrayed them.

"Sorry I'm late, Your Honor." I slid into the empty seat.

"Let's go on the record now," Stanton said, and the stenographer put her fingers on the keys of her machine.

"In the matter of California versus Walter Elliot . . . we are in chambers today for a status conference. Present is the defendant, along with Mr. Golantz for the state and Mr. Haller, who is here in the late Mr. Vincent's stead." The judge gave the spellings of the names. "We're scheduled for voir dire next Thursday—a week from today. Mr. Haller, I have received no motion from you to continue the matter while you get up to speed on the case."

"Your Honor," I said. "I have spent the week getting up to speed and will be prepared to begin jury selection next Thursday."

The judged squinted his eyes at me. "You sure, Mr. Haller?"

"Absolutely. Mr. Vincent kept thorough records. I understand the strategy he built, and the case has my full attention."

The judge looked at Elliot. "Mr. Elliot, I'd like to hear that you are in full agreement and understand the risk you run in bringing in a fresh lawyer so close to trial. It's your freedom at stake here, sir."

"Judge," Elliot said. "I am being persecuted for something I did not do. I loved my wife. I didn't kill her, and it pierces my heart hearing people saying vile things about me on TV. The sooner Mr. Haller gets to prove my innocence, the better."

It was OJ 101, but the judge nodded thoughtfully. "Mr. Golantz? What is the state's view of this?"

The telegenic deputy district attorney was handsome and dark, and his eyes seemed to carry the very wrath of justice. "Your Honor, the state is prepared for trial on schedule. But I would ask that if Mr. Elliot is so sure about proceeding, he formally waive any appellate redress should things not go as he predicts."

The judge swiveled his chair. "What about that, Mr. Haller?"

"Your Honor, I don't think it's necessary for my client to waive any protections afforded to him," I said, then argued that Elliot shouldn't have to give away his right to appellate review just because he wanted the speedy trial he was entitled to. Judge Stanton sided with Golantz, but that was okay with me. Under the Byzantine rules of law, almost nothing was safe from appeal.

Next the judge gave us until Monday for submitting final discovery. The witness lists were due the day after that. This was not going to be a problem from the defense's side of the aisle. Vincent had already made two previous discovery filings, and my plan was to give Golantz a witness list naming every law officer and forensic tech mentioned in the sheriff's reports. He'd have to puzzle over who I really would call to testify.

"All right," Stanton said. "Are we clear on everything?"

Golantz and I nodded our heads.

"Okay, then," the judge said. "We can talk about ground rules Thursday morning. I'm going to run this trial like a well-oiled machine. No surprises, no shenanigans. Are we clear?"

Golantz and I both agreed, but the judge squinted at me in suspicion. "I'm going to hold you to that," he said.

How come, I wondered, it's always the defense attorney who gets the judicial squint?

# EIGHT

I GOT to Joanne Giorgetti's office a minute before the noon break. I knew the D.A.'s offices literally emptied during the lunch hour. Giorgetti had a small office, with most of the floor space taken up by cardboard file boxes. She handed me the Wyms file with a thick stack of documents and told me she wouldn't oppose a continuance, considering what happened with Jerry Vincent.

"What do you think happened to Jerry's file?" she asked.

"I think maybe it was in his briefcase, which the killer took."

She made a cringing face.

"Weird. Why would the killer take this file?"

"Probably unintended. Jerry's laptop was in the briefcase. The killer just took the whole thing."

"Hmmm."

"Well, is there anything unusual about this case? Anything that would have made Jerry a target?"

"I don't think so. Just your usual everyday crazy-with-a-gun sort of thing."

I nodded, and thanked her again for the file.

I left the D.A.'s office and waited ten minutes to get on an elevator with the lunch crowd. When I stepped out and came through the front doors, I could see the Lincoln at the curb waiting. I got in the back—I tell my drivers never to open the door for me—and Patrick dropped me over at Chinese Friends on Hill Street.

Wanting to get right to work, I ordered a plate of the fried pork chops. They were paper thin and delicious, and I could eat them with my fingers without taking my eyes off the Wyms file. It contained copies of what the prosecutor had turned over under the rules of discovery—primarily sheriff's documents relating to the incident, arrest, and follow-up investigation.

The natural starting point was the arrest report, which started with 911 calls. Multiple reports of gunfire came in from a neighborhood next to a park in Calabasas, in an unincorporated area north of Malibu. The first deputy to respond, Todd Stallworth, had been dispatched at ten twenty-one p.m. to Malibu Creek State Park, where he heard the shots, called for backup, and drove in to investigate.

There were no lights in the park. As Stallworth's headlights picked up a reflection from a vehicle parked in a clearing, he put his spotlight on a pickup truck with a pyramid of beer cans on its tailgate and what looked like a gun bag with several rifles.

Stallworth stopped his patrol car and was on the radio to the Malibu station describing the truck, when suddenly there was a gunshot and the searchlight exploded. Stallworth killed the rest of the car's lights and crawled into some bushes using his handheld radio to call for the special weapons and tactics team.

A three-hour standoff ensued. Hidden in wooded terrain near the clearing, the gunman fired his weapon repeatedly, but apparently his aim was at the sky. Finally a deputy in black SWAT gear worked his way close enough to read the license plate, which led to the name Eli Wyms and a cell-phone number. The shooter answered on the first ring, and a SWAT team negotiator began a conversation.

The shooter was indeed Eli Wyms, a 44-year-old housepainter. He was characterized in the arrest report as drunk, angry, and suicidal. Earlier in the day he had been kicked out of his home by his wife, who had informed him she was in love with another man.

Wyms told the negotiator that he heard noises in the dark and believed he was shooting at rabid coyotes that wanted to eat him. He said he was afraid the spotlight would give his position away. He said he'd qualified as an expert marksman during the first war in Iraq. Investigators eventually collected ninety-four spent bullet casings.

Wyms did not surrender that night until he ran out of beer and told the negotiator he'd trade one rifle for a six-pack. He was turned down. He then announced that he was going to kill himself and literally go out with a bang. The negotiator tried to talk him out of it while a two-man SWAT unit moved toward his position, but soon he heard snoring on the cell line. Wyms had passed out. He was captured and taken in Stallworth's squad car to Malibu and jailed.

Other documents in the file continued the saga. At his arraignment, Wyms was declared indigent and assigned a public defender. The case moved slowly in the system, but then Vincent stepped in and offered his services pro bono. His first move was to ask for a competency evaluation. Wyms was carted off to the state hospital in Camarillo for a ninety-day psych evaluation. All the doctors agreed that he was competent and ready to stand trial.

In the hearing scheduled before Judge Friedman at two, a trial date would be set. To me it was a formality. One read of the case and I knew there would be no trial. What the day's hearing would do is set the time period I would have to negotiate a plea agreement.

It was a cut-and-dried case. Wyms would enter a plea and probably face a year or two of incarceration and mental-health counseling. The only question I had was why Vincent had taken the case in the first place. It didn't fall into line with the kind of cases he usually handled, with paying or higher-profile clients. My immediate thought was to suspect that there was a connection to the Elliot case. Vincent had found some sort of link.

But on first read, I couldn't nail it down. There were two general connections in that the Wyms incident had happened less than twelve hours before the beach house murders and both crimes occurred in the sheriff's department's Malibu district. But those connections didn't hold up to further scrutiny. As far as I could recall, none of the names in the Wyms file were mentioned in the Elliot materials I had reviewed. The Wyms incident happened on the night shift, the Elliot murders on the day shift.

With frustration, I closed the file with the question unanswered. I checked my watch and saw I had to get back to the CCB if I wanted time to meet my client in lockup before the hearing.

I called Patrick, paid for lunch, and stepped out to the curb. I was on my cell talking with Lorna when the Lincoln pulled up.

"Has Cisco met with Carlin yet?" I jumped in the back.

"No. That's at two."

"Have Cisco ask him about the Wyms case, too. Ask him why Vincent even took it."

"You think they're connected? Elliot and Wyms?"

"I think it, but I don't see it."

"Okay, I'll tell him."

"Anything else going on?"

"One thing. The landlord for the building wants to know if we're going to keep the office."

I looked out the window of the Lincoln as we cruised across the 101 overpass back to the civic center area. I could see the newly built Catholic cathedral and the waving steel skin of the Disney music center. "I don't know, Lorna. I like working from here. It's never boring. What do you think?"

"I'm not fond of putting on makeup every morning."

As usual, we were on the same page.

ELI Wyms was still doped up from the three months he'd spent in Camarillo. He'd been sent back to county with a drug prescription that wasn't going to help me defend him, let alone help him answer any questions about Vincent. It took me less than two minutes in courtside lockup to decide to submit a motion requesting that all drug therapy be halted. I went back to the courtroom and found Joanne Giorgetti at the prosecution table. The hearing was scheduled to start in five minutes.

"You want a continuance, don't you?" she said.

"And a cease and desist on the drugs. The guy's a zombie."

"I'm not sure I object to his being in that condition. Your client shot at an occupied sheriff's car. The state is interested in sending a message on this one."

"I would argue that my client, panicked as he was by the coyotes, was shooting at the light, not into the car. Your own documents say he was an expert marksman."

"Well, that's an argument you could make to the jury."

I wheeled over one of the chairs from the defense table and sat down. "Sure, but it is probably in the state's best interest to bring this case to a close and get Mr. Wyms into some sort of therapy that will help prevent this from ever happening again. So what do you say? Should we go off into a corner someplace and work this out?"

"As long as I get to pick the corner."

"That's fine with me." I got up to push the chair back. "Let me ask you something. Why did Jerry Vincent take on this case?"

She shrugged and shook her head. "I don't know."

"Well, did it surprise you?"

"Sure. It was kind of strange, him showing up. I knew him from way back when, you know? From when he was a prosecutor."

"Yeah, so what happened?"

"One day—a few months ago—I got notice of a competency motion on Wyms and Jerry's name was on it. I called him up and said what the hell, you know? You don't even call to say I'm taking over the case? He said he wanted to get some pro bono in and had asked the PD for a case. But I know Angel Romero, the PD who had the case originally. One day I ran into him and he asked me what was happening on Wyms. He told me that Jerry didn't just come asking for a pro bono referral. He went to Wyms in men's central, signed him up, and then came and told Angel to turn over the file."

"Why do you think he took the case?"

I've learned over the years that sometimes if you ask the same question more than once, you get different responses.

"I don't know. I asked him that, and he changed the subject and it was all kind of awkward."

The case was getting more mysterious. "Joanne, what do you—"

I was interrupted by the clerk, who called court into session, and I looked up to see Judge Friedman taking the bench.

"Eenie, meenie, minie, moe, catch a killer by the toe. If 'is lawyer's Haller let him go. Eenie, meenie, minie, moe. Hey bro."

Angel Romero was smiling. I'd been waiting for him in the hallway outside Judge Champagne's courtroom. I hadn't heard that homespun jingle since he'd made it up after the not-guilty verdict in the Barnett Woodson case.

We bumped fists. "What's up?" Romero asked. A former gang-banger, he'd grown up hard on the streets of East L.A.

"I'll tell you what's up, Angel. I want to ask you about a client you had earlier this year. Eli Wyms."

Romero immediately recognized the case. "Yeah. Vincent took that one off me. You got it now with him being dead?"

"I got all Vincent's cases. I just found out about Wyms."

"Well, good luck with them, bro. What do you need to know?"

"I got a handle on the case. What I'm curious about is according to Joanne Giorgetti, Vincent went after it. Is that right?"

Romero rubbed his chin as he checked the memory banks. I could see faint scars across his knuckles from where he'd had tattoos removed. "Yeah, he went down to the jail and talked Wyms into it, got a signed discharge letter."

"Did he say why he wanted the case? Did he know Wyms?"

"Not that I know of. He just gave me the big wink, you know?"

"No." I moved in closer. "What's the big wink?"

"I asked him why he was taking on a homeboy who shot the place up in white-people country. I thought he had some racial angle, but he just gave me the wink, like there was something else."

"Did you ask him what?"

"Yeah, man, but he wouldn't tell me. He just said that Wyms had fired the magic bullet. I didn't know what the hell he meant."

The magic bullet. There it was again. I could feel the blood in my veins start to move with high velocity.

I ENTERED the office and blew right by Lorna and Cisco, who were at the reception desk looking at the computer. I spoke without stopping on my way to the inner sanctum. "If you two have any updates or anything, come in now. I'm about to go into lockdown."

"And hello to you, too," Lorna called after me.

But Lorna knew well what was about to happen. Lockdown was when I closed all the doors and windows, drew the curtains and killed the phones, and went to work with total absorption. There was no getting me out until I'd found what I was looking for.

I moved around Vincent's desk and dropped into the seat. I opened my bag and started pulling out the files. I viewed it as me against them. Somewhere in the files I would find the key to Jerry Vincent's last secret. I would find the magic bullet.

Lorna and Cisco came into the office soon after I was settled.

"I didn't see Wren out there," I said before either could speak.

"And you never will again," Lorna said. "She quit. She went out to lunch and never came back."

"That was kind of abrupt. Did she call?"

"Yeah. She's going to be Bruce Carlin's secretary now."

I nodded. That seemed to make a certain amount of sense.

Lorna sat down in one of the chairs. Cisco stayed standing, more like pacing, behind her.

"One thing," Lorna said. "You must've touched a nerve with that motion you filed on the evidence in Patrick's case. The prosecutor's called three times today."

I smiled. It looked like I might be able to help Patrick.

"You didn't tell me you filed motions," Lorna said.

"From the car yesterday. I think the wife got phony diamonds for her birthday. Now to make sure she never knows it, they're going to float a deal to Patrick if I withdraw my request."

"Good. I think I like Patrick."

"I hope he gets the break. What's next?"

Lorna looked at the notes on her steno book. I knew she didn't like to be rushed, but I was rushing her.

"You're still getting a lot of calls from the local media. About Jerry Vincent or Walter Elliot or both. You want to go over them?"

"No. I don't have the time for any media calls."

I looked over Lorna's shoulder at Cisco, who was still standing.

"Okay, Cisco, your turn. What've you got?"

"I got with my source on Vincent, and he didn't know anything about a suspect or this photo Bosch showed you."

"Nothing? What do you think? Does Bosch know your guy's the leak and is shutting him out?"

"I don't know. But this photo was news to him."

"Did Bosch ever come show Wren the photo this morning?"

"No," Lorna said. "I was with her. Bosch never came in."

I wasn't sure what any of this meant. "Anything else?"

"Yeah. Vincent's liquidator has one of Patrick's long boards."

I raised my eyebrows. "What's he want for it?"

"Nothing. Let's just say he'd like to do you the favor. I think he's hoping you'll use him for future liquidations. Somebody's supposed to bring it in to him this afternoon."

"Thanks, Cisco. Get me an address and I'll have Patrick pick it up. Did you debrief Bruce Carlin?"

Cisco and Lorna looked at each other.

"What's wrong?" I asked.

"Carlin's messing with us," Lorna said. "He must've put his thinking cap on. He called at two o'clock—right after Wren called and quit—and said he wanted a flat fee or we could figure out things on our own."

I shook my head in annoyance. "Like how much does he want?"

"Ten thousand dollars."

"You gotta be kidding me." I looked at Cisco. "This is extortion. Isn't there a state agency that regulates you guys?"

Cisco shook his head. "There are all kinds of regulatory agencies, but he had no deal with Vincent. We can't find any contract, so it's probably legal. I mean, you're the lawyer. You tell me."

I thought about it for a few moments, then tried to push it aside. I was still riding on the adrenaline charge I'd picked up in the court-house. "All right, I'll ask Elliot if he wants to pay it. Meantime, I'm going to hit the files, and if I get lucky, we won't need him. Thank you both for all you've been doing. Go out and have a good night."

Lorna looked at me curiously. "You're sending us home?"

I checked my watch. "Why not? It's almost four thirty."

"You're going to work here alone tonight?" Cisco asked.

"I'll lock the door. I won't let anybody in even if I know him."

I smiled. Lorna and Cisco didn't. I pointed to the open door to the office. It had a slide bolt at the top of the door frame and gave the idea of lockdown new meaning.

"I'll be fine. Patrick should be out there. Tell him to keep hanging. I might have something to tell him after I make that call."

I OPENED the Patrick Henson file on my desk and looked up the prosecutor's number. I wanted to get this out of the way.

The prosecutor was Dwight Posey, a guy I had dealt with before and never liked. Some prosecutors deal with defense attorneys as if they are only one step removed from their clients, and unfortunately, Posey was one of them.

"So, Haller," he said, "they've got you walking in a dead man's shoes, don't they?"

"Yeah, something like that. Anyway, Dwight, I'm returning your call. Actually, your three calls. What's up?"

"I got the motion. It's sitting right here on my desk."

"And?"

"And, uh, well, we're not going to do that, Mick. Put our evidence out there for examination."

"Dwight, that's the beauty of the system. You don't make that decision. A judge does. That's why I put it in a motion."

"No, actually, we're going to drop the theft charge and just proceed with the drug charge."

I smiled and nodded. "Only problem with that is the drug charge came out of the theft investigation, so you don't have one without the other. That won't fly in any court I've ever been in."

"Then maybe we can just talk about a disposition on the matter."

"I'm open to it, Dwight. You should know that my client has voluntarily completed rehab, has full-time employment, and has been clean for four months. He'll give his piss anytime to prove it."

"That's really good to hear. The D.A.'s office looks favorably on voluntary rehabilitation. Tell you what, let's make it go away. Maybe Patrick can use this opportunity to move ahead."

"Sounds like a plan, Dwight. You're making my day."

"Okay, get me his rehab records. We'll put it in a package."

Posey was talking about making it a pretrial intervention case. If Patrick kept clean, the case would go away in six months.

He'd have an arrest on his record but no conviction. Unless . . .

"You willing to expunge his record?" I asked.

"Uh . . . that's asking a lot, Mickey. He did, after all, break in and steal the diamonds."

"He didn't break in, Dwight. He was invited in. And the alleged diamonds are what this is all about, right?"

"All right, fine. We'll put it into the package."

"You're a good man, Dwight."

When I hung up the phone, Cisco came in carrying a Post-it and a gun in a leather holster. He walked around the desk, put the Post-it down in front of me, then opened a drawer and put the weapon in it.

"I thought you were sent home," I said. "What are you doing? You can't give me a gun."

"It's totally legal and registered to me. I'm just storing it here."

"I think you're overreacting."

"Better than underreacting. See you tomorrow."

"Thank you. Will you send Patrick in before you go?"

"You got it."

He left the room, and Patrick soon came in.

"Patrick, Vincent's liquidator still has one of your long boards." I handed him the Post-it. "You can go by and pick it up. Just tell him you're picking it up for me."

"Oh, man, thank you!"

"Yeah, well, I've got even better news than that on your case." I went over the phone call I'd just had with Dwight Posey. I watched Patrick's eyes gain a little light.

"I have to call my mom," he said. "She's gonna be so happy."

"Yeah, well, I hope you are, too."

"I am, I am."

"Now, the way I figure it, you owe me a couple thousand for my work on this. That's about two and a half weeks of driving. If you want, you can stick with me until it's paid off. After that, we can see where we're at."

"That sounds good. I like the job." Patrick smiled broadly.

"Good. Then it's a deal. One other thing. I saw you sleeping in your car in the garage this morning."

He looked down at the floor. "Sorry. I'll find another spot."

"No, *I'm* sorry," I said. "I forgot you were sleeping in your car or on a lifeguard stand. I just don't know how safe it is to be sleeping in the same garage where a guy got shot. If I give you an advance on your pay, would that help you get a motel room or something?"

"Um, I guess."

I knew living out of a motel was almost as depressing as living out of a car. "I'll tell you what. If you want, you could stay with me for a couple weeks. Until you get a better plan going. I've got a house, and you'd have your own room. But on Wednesday nights and every other weekend, it would be better if you stayed with a friend. That's when I have my daughter."

He thought about it and nodded. "Yeah, I could do that."

I reached across the desk and signaled him to give me back the Post-it. I wrote my own address on it. "Why don't you go pick up your board and then head over to my place. Fareholm is right off Laurel Canyon. You go up the stairs to the front porch and there's a table and chairs and an extra key under the ashtray. The guest bedroom is next to the kitchen. Just make yourself at home."

"Thanks." He took the Post-it and looked at the addresses.

"Look, we're only talking about a few weeks. Meantime, maybe we can help each other out. You know, like if one of us starts to feel the pull, maybe the other one will be there to talk about it."

"Okay."

We were quiet for a moment. I didn't tell Patrick that he might end up helping me more than I'd help him. In the past forty-eight hours, the pressure had begun to weigh on me. I could feel myself being pulled back, the desire to go to the cotton-wrapped world the pills could give me. Up front and deep down I knew I didn't want that again, and maybe Patrick could help me avoid it.

"Thanks, Mr. Haller."

"Call me Mickey. And I should be the one saying thanks."

"Why are you doing all of this for me?"

I looked at the big fish on the wall behind him. "I'm not sure, but I'm hoping that if I help you then I'll be helping myself. Make sure you remember to call your mother."

# NINE

AFTER I was finally alone, I started the process the way I always do, with clean pages and sharp points. From the supply closet, I retrieved two fresh legal pads and four Black Warrior pencils and got down to work.

Vincent had broken the Elliot case into two files. One file contained the state's case, and the second the defense case. The defense file was thin, as by the rules of discovery anything that went into it went to the prosecutor. I began with the prosecution's file and read straight through, every word. I took notes on one legal pad and drew a time and action flowchart on the other. From there, I moved on to the defense file and again read every word on every page.

When I was finished with the Elliot files, I opened the Wyms case and read every document. Because Wyms was arrested following a public incident involving uniform and SWAT deputies, this file was thick with reports—transcriptions of conversations, ballistics reports, evidence inventory, witness statements, dispatch records, and patrol deployment reports. I checked every name against the list of names from the Elliot files. I cross-referenced every address.

I found what I was looking for an hour into my second run at the files. It had been there in front of me the whole time. First in Elliot's arrest report and then on the time and action chart I had drawn myself. I called the chart the Christmas tree. It always started basic and unadorned. Just the bare-bones facts of the case. Then, as I studied the case, I started hanging lights and ornaments on it. Witness statements, evidence, lab results. Soon the tree was lit up and bright. Everything about the case was there for me to see.

Walter Elliot was the trunk, and all branches came from him. I had his movements, statements, and actions noted by time. On the second go-round, I started adding decorations.

12:40 p.m.—WE arrives at house; front door unlocked
12:50 p.m.—WE discovers bodies; balcony door open
1:05 p.m.—WE calls 911, waits outside
1:24 p.m.—WE calls 911 again; what's the hold up?
1:28 p.m.—Deputies arrive on scene; Murray (4-alpha-1) and Harber (4-alpha-2)
1:30 p.m.—WE secured (placed in patrol car); Murray/Harber search house
2:15 p.m.—Homicide arrives—first team: Kinder and Ericsson; second team: Joshua and Toles
2:30 p.m.—WE taken inside house, describes discovery
2:40 p.m.—WE taken to Malibu by Joshua and Toles
4:55 p.m.—WE interviewed; Kinder takes lead in interview
5:40 p.m.—WE transported to Whittier (Joshua/Toles)
7:00 p.m.—GSR testing
8:00 p.m.—Second interview attempt, Ericsson in lead; WE declines
8:40 p.m.—WE taken to Men's Central (Joshua/Toles)

As I constructed the Christmas tree, I kept a separate list of every person mentioned in the sheriff's reports. This would become the witness list I would turn over to the prosecution. From the list and the tree, I could infer what witnesses the prosecution was avoiding and possibly why. It was while I was thinking in these terms that I felt the cold finger of revelation go down my spine. Everything became clear, and I found Jerry Vincent's magic bullet.

Walter Elliot had been taken from the crime scene to the Malibu station so he would be out of the way and secured while the lead detectives continued their on-site investigation. One short interview was conducted. He was then transported to sheriff's headquarters in Whittier where his hands tested positive for nitrates associated with gunpowder. After Kinder and Ericsson took another shot at interviewing their suspect, he was formally placed under arrest.

Elliot was handled solely by the homicide detectives as he was moved from crime scene to headquarters to jail. But it was how he was handled previous to their arrival that caught my eye. The uniform deputies who first responded to the call had the designations 4-alpha-1 and 4-alpha-2 after their names. And I had seen at least one of those designations in the Wyms file.

I quickly scanned the Wyms arrest report until my eyes came to the first 4-alpha-1 designation. Deputy Todd Stallworth, who drove the car Wyms fired upon and took him to jail, had the designation written after his name.

I realized that 4-alpha-1 did not refer to a specific deputy, and as the Malibu district covered huge areas, I assumed that this was the fourth district for a patrol zone and alpha was the designation for a specific patrol car. It seemed the only way to explain why deputies who worked different shifts would share the same designation.

Adrenaline crashed into my veins as I realized what Vincent had been up to. I didn't need his laptop or his investigator. I knew exactly what the defense strategy was.

I pulled my cell phone and called Cisco. "Cisco, any sheriff's deputies you know work out of the Malibu station?"

"Uh, I know one guy who used to."

"Can you call him tonight? I need to know what the patrol designation four-alpha-one means."

"Shouldn't be a problem. Hold on. Lorna wants you."

I waited while she was given the phone. I could hear TV noise in the background. I had interrupted a scene of domestic bliss.

"Mickey, are you still there at the office?"

"I'm here."

"It's eight thirty. I think you should go home."

"I think I should, too. I'll wait to hear back from Cisco, then go over to Dan Tana's to have steak and spaghetti."

She knew I went to Dan Tana's when I had something to celebrate. Usually a good verdict. "You had steak for breakfast."

"Then I guess this will make it a perfect day."

"Things went well tonight?"

"I think so. Real well. I'll see you tomorrow, Lorna."

"Okay, Mickey. Have fun."

I hung up and waited, thinking it all through again. Vincent had not taken on the Wyms case out of any obligation to the poor; he was using Wyms as camouflage. Stashing him out at Camarillo, keeping the case active. Meantime, he gathered information under the flag of the Wyms defense that he'd use in the Elliot case. Technically, he was probably acting within bounds, but ethically it was underhanded. Elliot got the magic bullet, while Wyms got the zombie cocktail.

It didn't take too long before Cisco called back.

"Four-alpha is Malibu's lead car. Four for the Malibu station and alpha for . . . alpha. Priority calls go to the alpha car. Four-alpha-one would be the driver. The partner would be four-alpha-two."

"So the alpha car covers the whole fourth district?"

"That's what he told me. Does that help, Mick?"

A double murder and shots near a residential neighborhood would certainly be alpha car calls. "It does, Cisco. But it also means more work for you. Find out everything you can about the night Eli Wyms was arrested. Get me details."

"That's what I'm here for."

THE night's discovery pushed the case off the paper and into my imagination. I was starting to get courtroom images in my head. Scenes of examinations and cross-examinations. I was laying out the suits I would wear. The case was coming alive inside, and this was a good thing, a momentum thing. You time it right and you go into trial with the inescapable conviction that you will not lose.

My plan was to sit in a corner booth at Dan Tana's and sketch out some of the key witness examinations, listing the baseline questions and probable answers for each. I was excited about getting to it.

After quickly repacking the files, I killed the lights, locked the office door, and headed down the hallway across the bridge. Just as I was entering the garage, I saw a man walk up the ramp from the first floor. He was the man in Bosch's photograph.

My blood froze. I knew the man coming toward me was the killer and that he had a gun. I swung around and started to run.

"Hey!" a voice called from behind me.

I kept running. I moved back across the bridge to the glass doors. One single thought fired through every synapse. I had to get to Cisco's gun. I shot my hand into my pocket in search of the keys, then jerked it out, bills, coins, and wallet flying out with it. As I jammed the key into the lock, I could hear steps behind me. *The gun! Get the gun!*

I finally yanked the door open and bolted toward the office. I glanced behind me and saw the man catch the door.

Keys still in my hand, I reached the office door and fumbled the key in the lock. I could feel the killer closing. Finally I entered, slammed the door, and threw the lock. I hit the light switch, then charged into Vincent's office.

The gun was there in the drawer. I yanked it out of its holster and went out to the reception area. Across the room, I could see the killer's shape through the frosted glass. He was trying to open the door. I pointed the gun high and fired two shots into the ceiling. The sound was deafening. "That's right!" I yelled. "Come on in!"

The image on the other side of the glass disappeared. I heard footsteps move away, then the door to the bridge open and close. I stood stock-still, listening. There was no sound. I stepped over to the reception desk and called 911, but a recording told me I needed to hold on for the next available dispatcher.

Shaking, I checked my pockets and found I hadn't lost my cell phone. Harry Bosch answered on the first ring.

"Bosch! That guy you showed me was just here!"

"Haller? What are you talking about? Who?"

"The guy in the photo you showed me today! With the gun!"

"All right, calm down. Where is he? Where are you?"

"I was leaving Vincent's office, and I saw him in the garage. I ran back in, and he ran after me. I fired a couple of shots—"

"You have a gun?"

"Damn right I do."

"I suggest you put it away before somebody gets hurt."

"He'll be the one getting hurt. Who the hell is he?"

There was a pause. "I don't know yet. Look, I was just heading home myself. Sit tight and I'll be there in five minutes. Don't shoot me when I get there. What did he want?"

"That's a damn good question. I don't have the answer."

"Haller, stop messing around and tell me!"

"I'm telling you! Now get over here!" I yelled, involuntarily squeezing my hands into fists and putting a shot in the floor. I jumped as though I'd been shot.

"Haller!" Bosch yelled. "What the hell was that?"

I pulled in a deep breath. "Get over here and find out."

"Did you hit him? Did you put him down?"

Without answering, I closed the phone.

BOSCH made it in six minutes, but it felt like an hour. He knocked sharply. "Haller, it's me, Bosch."

Carrying the gun at my side, I unlocked the door and let him in.

"Anything since we were on the phone?" he asked.

"Haven't seen or heard him. I guess I scared him away."

Bosch threw me a look. "What was that last shot?"

"An accident." I pointed to the hole in the floor.

"Give me that gun before you get yourself killed."

I handed it over. "My investigator leaves it here at night."

Bosch looked up, and his eyes found the two holes in the ceiling. He shook his head, then went over to the blinds and looked out on the street. Broadway was dead out there this time of night.

"Okay," he said. "Let's sit in your office to talk about this."

I took a seat behind the desk. Bosch sat across from me.

"First of all, here's your stuff. I found it out there on the bridge." From the pocket of his jacket he pulled my wallet and loose bills. He put it all on the desk.

I put my property back in my pocket. "Okay, now what?"

"Now we talk. First off, do you want to file a report?"

"It's your case. Why don't you know who this guy is?"

"We're working on it."

"That's not good enough, Bosch! Why can't you ID him?"

"Because we think he's a hitter brought in from out of town."

"How totally fantastic! Why did he come back here?"

"Obviously, because of you. You've been in here for three days. You must know something that makes you a danger to him."

"Me? I don't know anything. I can't think of a single—"

"Come on, Haller!" Bosch barked at me. "Your life is threatened here! Don't you get it? What've you got?"

"I told you!"

"Who did Vincent bribe?"

"I don't know and I couldn't tell you if I did."

"What did the FBI want with him?"

"I don't know, that either!"

He started pointing at me. "You hypocrite. You're hiding behind the law while the killer is out there. Tell me what you've got!"

"Don't point your finger at me. This isn't my job. It's your job."

"But you had him right here. Right here! He came to either kill you or to get something from you. Something in this office that could lead to his identity."

"All I can tell you is that I have had my case manager in here since Tuesday. I've had my investigator and Jerry Vincent's own receptionist in here. And none of us, Detective, *none of us,* has found the smoking gun you're so sure is here. You tell me that Vincent paid somebody a bribe. But I spent the last three hours in here looking at the Elliot file. I saw no indication he paid anybody off. In fact, I found out that he didn't *need* to. Vincent had a shot at winning the case fair and square."

"What about the FBI?"

"Same answer. Nothing."

Bosch didn't respond. I saw true disappointment cloud his face. He abruptly stood up and put Cisco's gun down on the desk. "Keep it loaded. And if I were you, I'd stop working at night." He headed toward the door.

"That's it?" I called after him.

He spun in his tracks. "What else do you want?"

"You want information I can't give, but you give nothing back. And I'm scared as hell that's half the reason I'm in danger."

Bosch looked like he might be about to jump over the desk at me. But then I saw him calm himself. All except for the palpitation high on his left cheek. That was his tell, and it was a tell that once again gave me a sense of familiarity.

"Damn it," he finally said. "What do you want to know, Counselor? Go ahead. Ask me a question and I'll answer it."

"I want to know about the bribe. Where did the money go?"

Bosch laughed in a false way. "I give you a free shot and you ask me that? You think if I knew where the money went that I'd be here right now? Uh-uh, Haller. I'd be booking a killer."

"But the bribe—if there was a bribe—went down five months ago. Why was Jerry killed now? Why's the FBI calling?"

"Good questions. Let me know if you come up with answers. Anything else I can do for you? I was heading home when you called."

"Yeah, there is. I was on my way out, too."

He looked at me. "What, you want me to hold your hand on the way to the garage? Fine, let's go."

I closed the office again, and we proceeded down the hall to the bridge. The silence was nerve-racking. I finally broke it.

"I was going to go have a steak. You want to come? Maybe we'll solve the world's problems over some red meat."

"Where, Musso's?"

"I was thinking Dan Tana's."

Bosch nodded. "If you can get us in."

"Don't worry. I know a guy."

Bosch followed me, but when I slowed on Santa Monica Boulevard to pull into the valet stop in front of the restaurant, he kept going. I went in by myself, and Craig, who worked the door, sat me in one of the cherished corner booths.

Ten minutes later Bosch finally appeared and Craig led him to me. "Get lost?" I asked as he squeezed into the booth.

"I couldn't find a parking space."

"I guess they don't pay you enough for valet."

"No. Valet's a beautiful thing. But I can't give my city car to a valet. Against the rules."

I guessed that he probably packed a shotgun in the trunk.

When the waiter came, we both ordered the Steak Helen with spaghetti and red sauce on the side. Bosch ordered a beer.

"So," I said, "where's your partner been lately?"

"He's working on other aspects of the investigation."

"Well, I guess it's good to hear there are other aspects."

Bosch studied me. "Is that supposed to be a crack?"

"Just an observation. Doesn't seem to be much happening."

"Maybe that's because your source dried up and blew away."

"My source? I don't have any source."

"Not anymore. I figured out who was feeding your guy."

"I know you won't believe me, but I have no idea who or what you are talking about. I get information from my investigator. I don't ask him how he gets it."

Bosch nodded. "That's the best way to do it, right? Insulate yourself and then you don't get any blowback. In the meantime, if a police captain loses his job and pension, those are the breaks."

I hadn't realized Cisco's source was so highly placed.

The waiter brought our drinks and a basket of bread. I drank some water as I contemplated what to say next. Bosch raised his eyebrows like he was expecting something.

"How'd you know when I was leaving the office tonight?"

He looked puzzled. "What do you mean?"

"I figure it was the lights. You were out there on Broadway, and when I killed the lights, you sent your guy in."

"I don't know what you are talking about."

"Sure you do. The photo of the guy with the gun. It was a phony. You set it up to smoke out your leak, then tried to scam me with it."

Bosch shook his head and looked out of the booth.

"You know what your mistake was? Not coming back like you said to show the photo to Vincent's secretary."

Bosch looked toward the bar's overhead TV. It was showing sports highlights. I leaned across the table.

"So who's the guy with the stick-on mustache? Some clown from vice? Don't you have better things to do than run a game on me?"

Finally he looked at me. "Okay, I guess that makes you one smart lawyer, Haller. Just like the old man. I wonder why you're wasting it defending scumbags."

I smiled. "Is that it? You get caught, so you respond by accusing the other guy?"

Bosch laughed, his face turning red as he turned away, and his mention of my father brought a vague memory of him laughing uneasily and looking away as my mother accused him of something I was too young to understand.

Bosch put both arms on the table. "You've heard of the first forty-eight, right? The chances of clearing a homicide diminish by almost half each day if you don't solve it in forty-eight hours. I'm coming up on seventy-two hours, and I've got nothing. I was hoping I might scare you out of something."

I sat there staring at him. "You actually thought I knew who killed Jerry and wasn't telling?"

"It was a possibility I had to consider."

"Damn you, Bosch."

Just then the waiter came with our steaks. As the plates were put down, Bosch stared at me with what looked like a knowing smile.

"You're an arrogant son of a bitch," I said.

Bosch cut into his steak left-handed. He put a chunk of meat into his mouth and rested his fists on either side of his plate, fork and knife in his grips, as if guarding the food from poachers. A lot of my prison clients ate the same way.

"Why don't you take it easy there, Counselor," he said. "I'm not used to being on your side of the line, okay? Defense attorneys have tried to portray me as stupid, corrupt, bigoted—you name it—so yes, I tried to run a game on you to solve a murder. I apologize. If you want, I will have them wrap up my steak and I'll take it to go."

I shook my head. Bosch had a talent for trying to make me feel guilty for his transgressions. "Maybe now you should be the one who takes it easy," I said. "I've acted openly and honestly with you. I've told you what I could tell you. You're damn lucky I didn't put a bullet in your man's chest at the office door."

"You weren't supposed to have a gun. I checked." Bosch kept his head down as he worked on the steak. "So now that we have that out of the way, will you help me?"

I blew out my breath in a laugh. "Are you kidding? Have you heard a single thing I've said?"

"Yeah. When all is said and done, I could still use your help."

I started cutting my steak. I took my time, savoring the first bite. "What kind of help?"

"We draw out the killer."

"Great. How dangerous will it be?"

"Depends. It could get dangerous. I need you to shake things up, make whoever's out there think you might be dangerous to them."

"How do we shake things up?"

"I was thinking a newspaper story. I assume you've been getting calls from the reporters. We pick one and give them an exclusive, and we plant something in there that gets the killer thinking."

"There's a guy at the *Times*," I said. "I kind of made a deal with him to get him off my back. I told him when I was ready to talk I would talk to him."

"That's a perfect setup. We'll use him. So are you in?"

I cut into the steak again. Blood ran onto the plate.

"Yeah," I said. "I'm in."

# TEN

EVERYBODY lies.

Cops lie. Lawyers lie. Clients lie. Even jurors lie.

There is a school of belief in criminal law that every trial is won or lost in the choosing of the jury. I do know there is probably no phase in a murder trial more important than the selection of the twelve citizens who decide your client's fate. It is also the part of the trial most reliant on the whims of fate and luck and being able to ask the right question at the right time to the right person.

Jury selection in *California v. Elliot* began on schedule in Judge James P. Stanton's courtroom at ten a.m. Thursday. The courtroom was packed, half filled with the venire—the eighty potential jurors called randomly from the jury pool on the third floor of the Criminal Courts Building—and half filled with media, well-wishers, and just plain gawkers.

I sat at the defense table alone with my client. Spread in front of me were three colored markers, a Post-it pad, and an open empty manila file. Back at the office, I had prepared the file by drawing a grid across it. There were twelve blocks, each the size of a Post-it. Each block was for one of the twelve jurors. Some lawyers use computers to track potential jurors. They even have software that can filter information through a socio-political pattern recognition program and spit out recommendations. I had been using the old-school grid system since I had been a baby lawyer in the public defender's office. A computer can't hear how someone gives an answer. It can't see someone's eyes when they lie.

The way it worked was that the judge had a computer-generated list from which he called the first twelve citizens from the venire and they took seats in the jury box. But they only got to keep their seats if they survived *voir dire*—the questioning of their background and views and understanding of the law. The judge asked them a series of basic questions, and then the lawyers followed up.

Jurors could be removed in two ways. They could be rejected for cause if they showed through their answers or demeanor or even their life's circumstances that they could not be fair or hear the case with an open mind. There was no limit to the number of challenges for cause at the disposal of the attorneys. The second method of removal was the preemptory challenge, and because this trial involved murder, the prosecution and defense would have up to twenty preemptory challenges each. A preemptory challenge let the attorney strike a juror for no reason other than instinctual dislike.

The rules of voir dire were designed to remove bias and deception from the jury. The term itself came from the French phrase "to speak the truth." But this of course was contradictory to each side's bottom line. I wanted a jury biased against the state and the police. I wanted them predisposed to be on my side or easily pushed there. And, of course, the man sitting four feet from me in the courtroom wanted a diametrically opposite result.

By ten fifteen the efficient Judge Stanton had welcomed the randomly selected first twelve candidates to the jury box—six men and six women. We knew where they were from and what they did, but we didn't know their names. The judge had been adamant about protecting the jurors from public scrutiny. He had ordered that the Court TV camera be mounted on the wall over the jury box so that the jurors would not be seen. He had also ruled that the identities of all prospective jurors be withheld.

The process began with the judge asking the prospective jurors questions about what they did for a living and where they lived. He then moved on to questions about whether they had been victims of crime, had relatives in prison, or were related to any police officers or prosecutors. He asked who had prior jury experience. The judge excused three for cause and agreed with a fourth's plea for a hardship dismissal. The four were quickly replaced with four more random selections from the venire. And so it went. By noon I had used two of my preemptories, while Golantz was holding fast.

Elliot had insisted that he be allowed to sign off on each of my preemptory challenges. It took extra time to explain to him, but each time, he ultimately nodded his approval. Shortly after noon, the judge broke for lunch. It being technically the first day of my first trial in over a year, Lorna Taylor had come to court to show her support. The plan was to go to lunch together, and then she would go back to the office and start packing it up.

As we entered the hallway outside the courtroom, I asked Elliot if he wanted to join us, but he said he had to make a quick run to the studio. Lorna and I hung back and let the prospective jurors crowd onto the elevators. I didn't want to ride down with them. Inevitably one of them asks something improper and you then have to go through the motions of reporting it to the judge.

When one of the elevators opened, I saw the reporter Jack McEvoy push his way out past the jurors, scan the hallway, and zero in on me. He walked directly toward me.

"Great," I said. "Here comes trouble. What do you want?"

"To explain."

"What, you mean explain why you're a liar?"

"No, look, when I told you it was going to run Sunday, I meant it. That's what I was told."

"And here it is Thursday and no story in the paper, and when I've tried to call you about it, you don't call me back. I've got other reporters interested, McEvoy. I don't need the *Times*."

"Look, I understand. But they decided to hold it so it would run closer to the trial. They're running it out front this coming Sunday."

"The front page on Sunday. I'll believe it when I see it."

I took Lorna by the arm and started leading her toward the elevators. I pushed past the reporter.

"So we're okay?" McEvoy said. "You'll hold off on giving away the exclusive."

"Whatever."

I left him hanging and got on an elevator. When Lorna and I got out of the building, we walked a block over to city hall, and I had Patrick pick us up there. I didn't want any prospective jurors to see me getting into the back of a chauffeured Lincoln. I told Patrick to take us over to the French Garden on 7th Street.

"Listen," I told Lorna, "when you go back to the office, call Julie Favreau and see if she can come tomorrow."

"I thought Elliot didn't want a jury consultant."

"He doesn't have to know we're using her. Take it out of general operating. I already burned through two strikes. Just tell her the bailiff will have her name and will make sure she gets a seat."

"Okay, I'll call her. Are you doing all right, Mick?"

I must've been talking too fast or sweating. I was feeling shaky, and I didn't know if it was because of the growing realization that what I'd been working toward for a year would soon be upon me.

"I'm fine, just hungry. You know how I get when I'm hungry."

"Sure," she said. "I understand."

The truth was, I wasn't hungry. I was feeling the weight on me. The burden of a man's future.

And it wasn't my client's future. It was my own.

BY THREE o'clock on the second day, Golantz and I had traded preemptory and cause challenges for more than ten hours of court time. It had been a battle. We had quietly identified each other's must-have jurors and struck them without care or conscience. We had gone through almost the entire venire, and my jury seating chart was covered with as many as five layers of Post-its. I had two preemptory challenges left. Golantz was down to his final one.

The panel now included an attorney, a computer programmer, two postal service employees, and four retirees, as well as a male nurse, a tree trimmer, an engineer, and an artist. From the original 12, the engineer in seat 7 and one of the retirees, in seat 12, had somehow gone the distance. Both were white males, and on my chart I had written notes about both in blue ink—my code for being cold to the defense. But their leanings were so slight that I still had not used a precious challenge on either.

The latest addition to the box was the artist. During the general questioning of Judge Stanton, I had taken notes about her in red and grew happier and happier with her on my jury. When it was the lawyers' turn, Golantz asked questions he hoped would draw out a bias, but the woman held her own, appearing very open-minded.

Four questions into the prosecutor's effort, I felt a vibration in my pocket and reached in for my cell. I held it down below the defense table. Julie Favreau had been texting me all day from the gallery.

SHE'S A KEEPER. DON'T LIKE 8. HAVEN'T HEARD ENOUGH FROM 10. KICK 7 IF YOU HAVE TO.

Juror 8 was the tree trimmer. I had him in blue because of answers he gave about the police. I also thought he was anxious to be on the jury, a flag in a murder case. It signaled strong feelings about law and order and lack of hesitation about sitting in judgment.

Judge Stanton was allowing us a lot of leeway. When it was my turn to question the artist, I accepted her without further questioning. I was allowed instead to make further inquiries of juror 8. I found him deceptive and decided Favreau was right. He had to go.

When the judge asked if the prosecution and defense accepted the panel as composed, Golantz used his last preemptory to remove the artist. I used my second to last to remove the tree trimmer.

Two more names were called from the venire, and a real estate agent and one more retiree took seats 8 and 11 in the box. Their answers to the questions from the judge put them right down the middle of the road.

The bottom line was that I had one preemptory left to use on juror 7 or juror 10. The engineer or the retiree.

I asked the judge for a moment to confer with my client and slid my chart in front of Elliot. "Walter, what do you think? We need to get rid of seven and ten but can only get rid of one."

Elliot tapped a finger on the block for juror 10, a retired technical writer for a toy manufacturer. "Get rid of him."

I looked at the grid. There was a lot of blue on block 10, but there was an equal amount on block 7. The engineer.

I had a hunch that the technical writer, like the tree trimmer, wanted badly to be on the jury but probably as research for a book, as he had acknowledged during voir dire that in retirement he was trying to write fiction. Juror 7 was blue for another reason. He was listed as an aerospace engineer. In general, engineers were conservative politically and religiously, two blue attributes, and they worked for companies that relied on huge government contracts. A vote for the defense was a vote against the government. Lastly, engineers exist in a world of logic and absolutes often not applicable to a crime scene or even to the criminal justice system as a whole.

"I don't know," I said. "I think the engineer should go."

"No, I like him. I've liked him since the beginning. He's given me good eye contact. I want him to stay."

"Mr. Haller," Judge Stanton said. "Do you wish to use your last challenge or accept the jury as it is now composed? I remind you, it is getting late in the day."

My phone was buzzing. "One more moment, Your Honor."

I leaned into Elliot and whispered, "Are you sure, Walter?" But what I was really doing was pulling my phone.

"Look, I make my living reading people," Elliot whispered.

I nodded and looked down. It was a text from Favreau.

KICK 10. 7 FITS PROSECUTION PROFILE BUT OPEN FACE. HE'S INTERESTED IN YOUR STORY. HE LIKES YOUR CLIENT.

That settled it. I slipped the phone back into my pocket and stood up. "Your Honor, the defense would like to thank and excuse juror ten at this time."

# WALKING IN A DEAD MAN'S SHOES
## Attorney Takes Over for Murdered Colleague
## First Case: The Trial of the Decade
by Jack McEvoy, *Times* Staff Writer

It wasn't the 31 cases dropped in his lap that were the difficulty. It was the big one with the big client and high stakes. Defense attorney Michael Haller stepped into the shoes of the murdered Jerry Vincent two weeks ago and now finds himself at the center of this year's so-called Trial of the Decade.

Today testimony is scheduled to begin in the trial of Walter Elliot, the 54-year-old chairman of Archway Studios, charged with murdering his wife and her alleged lover six months ago in Malibu. Haller stepped into the case after Vincent, 45, was found shot to death in his car in downtown Los Angeles.

Vincent had made legal provisions that allowed Haller to step into his practice in the event of his death. Haller, who had been at the end of a yearlong sabbatical from practicing law, is the 42-year-old son of the late Michael Haller, Sr., one of Los Angeles's storied defense attorneys in the '50s and '60s.

The investigation of Vincent's murder is ongoing. Detectives say there are no suspects. He was shot twice in the head while sitting in his car in the garage next to the building where he kept his office, in the 200 block of Broadway.

Following his death, the fallen attorney's entire law practice was turned over to Haller. His job was to cooperate with investigators within the bounds of attorney-client protections, inform all active clients of Vincent's death, and give them the option of hiring a new lawyer. The majority of cases remained with Haller. By far the biggest of these is the "Murder in Malibu" case.

The case came with one big condition. Elliot would agree to keep Haller only if Haller agreed not to delay the trial.

"Walter has insisted on his innocence since day one," Haller told the *Times* in his first interview since taking on the case. "There were early delays, and he has waited six months for his day in court. We've been working around the clock to be ready, and I think we are."

It wasn't easy to be ready. Whoever killed Vincent also stole his briefcase from his car. It contained Vincent's laptop computer. "It was the central storage point for case information and strategy," Haller said. "The hard files in the office were incomplete, and at first I thought we were dead in the water."

But then Haller found out that Vincent backed his computer up on a digital flash drive attached to his keychain. When the testimony begins today, he will be fully prepared. Legal experts expect the defense to attack the handling of evidence in the investigation and the testing procedures that determined that Elliot had fired a gun.

Deputy district attorney Jeffrey Golantz, who is prosecuting the case, declined comment for this story.

# ELEVEN

THE jury came out in a single-file line like the Lakers taking the basketball court. The same feeling of anticipation was in the air. They split into two lines, moved down the two rows of the jury box, and took the same seats where they were sworn in.

It was almost ten a.m. Monday. Judge Stanton had had the lawyers and the defendant back in chambers for almost forty minutes while he went over last-minute ground rules and took the time to give me the squint and to express his displeasure over the story on the front page of the morning's *Los Angeles Times*.

I turned and looked back at the gallery. The courtroom once again was packed with members of the media and the public, as well as those with a blood link to the case. Directly behind the prosecution's table, Golantz had positioned Mitzi Elliot's mother. Next to her sat Johan Rilz's father and two brothers who had traveled all the way from Berlin. In the first row behind me were Lorna, Cisco, Patrick, and Julie Favreau—who I'd hired to ride through the trial and observe the jury for me.

An empty fifth seat had been reserved for my daughter. My hope had been that I'd convince my ex-wife to allow Hayley to go to court with me for the day. She had never seen me at work, and I thought opening statements would be the perfect time. I had even employed the Mark Twain line about taking her out of school so that she could get an education. But my ex-wife refused to allow it.

Walter Elliot had no one in the gallery. He had no children and no relatives he was close to. Because Nina Albrecht was listed on both the prosecution and defense witness lists, she was excluded from the gallery until her testimony was completed. My client had plenty of associates and hangers on that wanted to be there for him, even A-list movie actors. But I told him a Hollywood entourage would broadcast the wrong image. It is all about the jury, I told him. Every move that is made is in deference to the jury.

Judge Stanton began the proceedings by asking if any jurors had seen the *Times* story. None raised their hands, and Stanton repeated an earlier reminder about not reading or watching reports on the trial. He said the trial would begin with opening statements from the opposing attorneys.

"Ladies and gentlemen, remember," he said. "These are statements. It's up to each side to present the evidence that backs them up. And you will be the ones at the end of the trial who decide if they have done that."

Gesturing to Golantz, he said the prosecution would go first.

Impressive-looking in a black suit, white shirt, and maroon tie, Golantz stood, introduced himself, and got down to it.

"Ladies and gentlemen, we are here today because of unchecked greed and anger. Plain and simple. The defendant, Walter Elliot, is a man of great power, money, and standing. But that was not enough for him. He did not want to divide his money and power. He did not want to turn the cheek on betrayal. Instead, he lashed out in the most extreme way possible. In a moment of high anger and humiliation, he raised a gun and killed both his wife, Mitzi Elliot, and Johan Rilz. He believed his money and power would save him from punishment for these heinous crimes. But the state will prove to you beyond any reasonable doubt that Walter Elliot pulled the trigger and is responsible for the deaths of two innocent human beings."

I was turned in my seat, half to obscure the jury's view of my client and half to keep a view of Golantz and the gallery rows behind him. Before his first paragraph was completed, the tears were flowing from Mitzi Elliot's mother. The theatrics were prejudicial, and I would need to ask the judge to move her. I saw hard grimaces on the faces of the men from Germany. I was very interested in how they would appear to the jury, and I knew I was off to a good start. They looked angry and mean.

Golantz laid his case out to the jurors, telling them what he'd be presenting in testimony and evidence and what he believed it meant. There were no surprises.

At one point I got a one-line text message from Favreau: THEY ARE EATING THIS UP. YOU BETTER BE GOOD.

Right, I thought. Tell me something I don't know.

There was always an unfair advantage to the prosecution built into every trial. The state has the power and the might on its side. It comes with an assumption of honesty and integrity and fairness. And anybody who has ever stepped foot into a courtroom knows that presumed innocence is just one of the idealistic notions they teach in law school. There was no doubt in my mind that I started this trial with a defendant who was presumed guilty.

Golantz lasted his entire allotted hour, leaving no secrets about his case hidden. It was typical prosecutorial arrogance; put it all out there and dare the defense to try to contradict it.

The judge had told us in the pretrial session that we would be required while addressing witnesses to remain at our tables or to use the lectern placed between them, but during opening statements and closing arguments, we were free to use the space directly in front of the jury box—a spot called the proving grounds. Golantz finally moved to the proving grounds when it was time for his big finish and held his hands wide, like a preacher in front of his flock.

"In closing," he said, "I urge you to take great care as you listen to the evidence and the testimony. Common sense will lead you. Remember, two people had their lives stolen from them. That is why we are here today. For them. Thank you very much."

It was a solid beginning, if too long. I was going to get in and get out, make a few points, raise a few questions. I was going to make them like me. If they liked me, they would like my case.

Once the judge gave me the nod, I immediately moved to the proving grounds. I wanted nothing between me and the jury.

"Ladies and gentlemen, I know the judge already introduced me, but I would like to introduce myself and my client. I am Michael Haller, the attorney representing Walter Elliot, who you see here sitting at the table by himself."

I pointed to Elliot, and by prior design he nodded somberly.

"Now, I am not going to take a lot of time, because I want to get to the testimony and the evidence. Mr. Golantz wove a big and complicated picture, but I am here to tell you this is not complicated. What the prosecution's case amounts to is a labyrinth of smoke and mirrors. And when we blow away the smoke and get through the labyrinth, you will find that there is no fire—that there is more than reasonable doubt here. And outrage that this case was ever brought against Walter Elliot in the first place."

Again I turned and pointed to my client. He sat with his eyes cast downward, writing notes, actively involved in his own defense.

I turned back to the jury. "I counted six times that Mr. Golantz mentioned the word 'gun' in his speech. Six times he said Walter took a gun and blew away the woman he loved and an innocent bystander. Six times. But what he didn't tell you is that the sheriff's department has no gun. Mr. Golantz told you that he will introduce indisputable evidence that Walter fired a gun, but let me tell you to hold on to your hats. Let's see whether that so-called evidence is indisputable. Let's just see if it is even left standing."

As I spoke, my eyes washed back and forth across the jurors like the spotlights sweeping the Hollywood sky. I felt a calm rhythm in my thoughts, and I instinctively knew I was holding the jury.

"In our society, we want our law-enforcement officers to be professional and thorough. We see crime on the news and in the streets, and we know that these men and women are the thin line between order and disorder. We want our cops to step in and save the day. But that's not what happened here. The state's own evidence and testimony will show that from the start investigators focused on Walter Elliot. All other avenues of investigation were halted or never pursued. They had a suspect, and they never looked back."

I stepped forward in front of juror number one. I slowly walked along the front of the box, hand sliding along the railing.

"Ladies and gentlemen, this case is about tunnel vision. The focus on one suspect and the complete lack of focus on anything else. And I promise you, that when you come out of the prosecution's tunnel, you're going to be looking at each other and squinting your eyes against the bright light, wondering where the hell their case is. Thank you very much."

ONCE more, my client eschewed lunch with me so he could get back to the studio and make his business-as-usual appearance. I was beginning to think the trial simply wasn't a priority. That left me with my entourage from the first row, and we went over to Traxx in Union Station, far enough away to avoid our ending up in the same place as the jurors. I had Patrick valet the Lincoln and join us so that he would feel like part of the team.

They gave us a table next to a window that looked out on the train station's huge and wonderful waiting room. Lorna made the seating arrangements, and I ended up next to Julie Favreau. Ever since Lorna had hooked up with Cisco, she had endeavored to be something of a matchmaker. But my addiction had left me with an emotional distance from people, and I was only now beginning to make it a priority to reconnect with my daughter.

Romance aside, Julie Favreau was wonderful to work with. "So," I said as I spread a napkin on my lap, "how is my jury doing?"

"I think it's a good jury," she said. "Overall, I see them willing to listen to your case. They haven't shut the door on anything."

"Any change from Friday? I still present to number three?"

"I think he's still good. I like eleven and twelve, too. Retirees sitting next to each other. I have a feeling they're going to bond when it gets to deliberations. You win one over and you win them both."

"What about juror seven?" I asked. "During selection, he was all eyes. Now he won't look at me."

Julie nodded. "Eye contact has dropped off the chart. Like something changed since Friday. I would have to say at this point he's in the prosecution's camp."

"So much for listening to my client," I said under my breath.

We ordered lunch. While we waited, I checked with Cisco on our witnesses, and he said we were good to go. I was halfway through my grilled chicken salad when I glanced through the window into the waiting room. A grand mixture of architectural designs with an art-deco vibe, it had rows of big leather chairs and huge chandeliers. I saw people sitting with their suitcases gathered around them.

And then I saw Bosch. He was sitting alone in the third row. He had his earphones in. Our eyes held for a moment, and then he looked away. I put my fork down, put five twenties on the table, and told the others to finish eating while I stepped out to make a call.

I left the restaurant and called Bosch's cell. He pulled his plugs and answered as I was approaching the seats.

"What?" he said by way of a greeting.

"Frank Morgan again?"

"Actually, Ron Carter. Why are you calling me?"

"What did you think of the story?"

I sat in the open seat across from him, gave him a glance, but acted like I was talking to someone far away from me.

"This is kind of stupid," Bosch said.

"Well, I didn't know whether you wanted to stay undercover—"

"Just hang up."

We closed our phones and looked at each other.

"Well?" I asked. "Are we in play?"

"I think the story did what we wanted it to do. Now we wait. We won't know we're in play until we're in play."

I nodded. "Is it just you here? Watching me by yourself?"

"Don't worry. You have people around you that you'll never see. I've got people on your office whether you are there or not."

And cameras. They had been installed ten days earlier.

"Yeah, good, but we won't be there for long."

"I noticed. Where are you moving to?"

"Nowhere. I work out of my car."

"Sounds like fun."

I studied him a moment. He had been sarcastic in his tone, as usual. He was an annoying guy, but somehow he had gotten me to trust my safety to him. "Well, I've got to get to court. Any particular way you want me to act or anything I should be doing?"

"Just do what you always do. But there is one thing. Keeping an eye on you in motion takes a lot of people. So at the end of the day, when you are home for the night, call me and tell me so I can release some people."

"Okay. But you'll still have somebody watching, right?"

"Don't worry. You'll be covered twenty-four seven. Oh, and one other thing. Don't ever approach me again like this."

"Got it." I stood up without looking at him. "See ya, Detective."

AFTER lunch, Golantz began to present his case. He started at the very beginning, proceeding in linear fashion. The first witness was an emergency operator used to introduce the tape recordings of Walter Elliot's calls for help. I had sought in a pretrial motion to thwart the playing of the two tapes, arguing that printed transcripts would be clearer, but the judge had ruled in the prosecution's favor.

The tapes were prejudicial to my client. When in the first call Elliot had calmly reported that his wife and another person had been murdered, there was room for an interpretation of calculated coldness that I didn't want the jury to make. The second tape was worse. Elliot sounded annoyed and indicated with almost a sneer that he knew and disliked the man who'd been killed with his wife.

Dispatcher: Nine one one, what is your emergency?

Walter Elliot: Yeah, I called before. Where is everybody?

Dispatcher: You called nine one one?

Walter Elliot: Yeah, my wife's shot. So's the German. Where is everybody?

Dispatcher: Is this the call on Crescent Cove Road?

Walter Elliot: Yeah, that's me. I called at least fifteen minutes ago and nobody's here.

There was nothing to be gained for the defense, and I passed on questioning the dispatcher. Next up was sheriff's deputy Brendan Murray, who was driving the alpha car that responded to the 911 call. Golantz led the deputy through discovery of the bodies in minute detail. According to Murray, the defendant showed no emotions when leading them to the bedroom. He calmly stepped over the legs of the dead man, pointed to the naked body on the bed, and said, "That's my wife. I'm pretty sure she's dead." Murray also testified that Elliot said at least three times he had not killed them.

"Well, was that unusual?" Golantz asked.

"Well, we're not supposed to get involved in murder investigations," Murray said. "So I never asked Mr. Elliot if he did it."

I had no questions for Murray either. I waited for the next witness, Christopher Harber, Murray's rookie partner. I thought that if either of the deputies were to make a mistake, it would be him. Harber's short testimony was used primarily to confirm his partner's testimony. "Just a few questions, Your Honor," I said.

While Golantz had conducted his direct examination from the lectern, I remained at the defense table. I wanted the prosecutor to think I was just going through the motions. The truth was I was about to plant a key point in the defense's case.

"Now, Deputy Harber, when you and your partner arrived at the Elliot house, you said you saw my client out front, correct?"

"That is correct."

"Okay, what was he doing?"

"Just standing there. He had been told to wait there for us."

"Okay, now what did you know about the situation when the alpha car pulled in there?"

"Dispatch told us a man named Walter Elliot called from the house and said two people had been shot dead inside."

"Had you ever had a call like that before?"

"No."

"Were you scared, nervous, what?"

"The adrenaline was flowing, but we were pretty calm."

"Did you draw your weapon when you got out of your car?"

"Yes, I did. I carried it at my side."

"Did your partner draw his weapon?"

"I believe so."

"Did he point it at Mr. Elliot?"

He hesitated. I always liked it when witnesses for the prosecution hesitated. "I don't recall. I looked at the defendant."

I nodded. "To be safe, correct? You didn't know this guy."

"That's right."

"Is it correct to say you approached Mr. Elliot cautiously?"

"That's right."

"When did you put your weapon away?"

"After we had searched and secured the premises."

"Okay. When you were doing this, was Mr. Elliot with you?"

"Yes. We needed him to show us where the bodies were."

"Now was he under arrest?"

"No, he was not. He volunteered to show us."

"But you handcuffed him, didn't you?"

Harber's second hesitation followed. He was in uncharted water. "He had voluntarily agreed to be handcuffed. We explained that we were not arresting him but that it would be best for his safety and ours until we secured the premises."

"Were his hands cuffed behind his back or in the front?"

"In the back, according to procedure."

"I know you are new on the job, but how often have you hand-cuffed someone who was not under arrest?"

"It happens on occasion. I don't recall the number of times."

"Now, your partner testified and you have testified that Mr. Elliot on three occasions told you both that he was not responsible for the killings in that house. Right?"

"Right."

"Was that when you were outside or inside or where?"

"That was inside, when we were up in the bedroom."

"So that means that he made these supposedly uninvited protes-tations of his innocence while he was handcuffed with his arms be-hind his back and you and your partner had your weapons drawn and ready. Is that correct?"

The third hesitation. "Yes, I believe that would be so."

"Okay, so what happened after you and your partner determined that there was no one else in the house?"

"We took Mr. Elliot back outside, we sealed the house, and we called detective services for a homicide call-out."

"Good. Now, Deputy Harber, did you take the handcuffs off Mr. Elliot then, since he was not under arrest?"

"No, sir. It is against procedure to place a subject in the back of a sheriff's car without handcuffs."

"Okay, how long was he in the backseat of that car?"

"Approximately one half hour while we waited for homicide."

"And what happened when the homicide team arrived?"

"They looked in the house first. Then they came out and took custody of Mr. Elliot. I mean, took him out of the car."

"He was in custody at that time?"

"No. I made a mistake there. He voluntarily agreed to wait."

"You are saying he voluntarily agreed to be handcuffed in the back of a patrol car?"

"Yes."

"When did the handcuffs finally come off Mr. Elliot?"

"When the detectives removed him from the car."

"Okay." I nodded like I was finished, and flipped a few pages on my pad. "Oh, one last thing. The first call to nine one one went out at one oh five according to the dispatch log. Mr. Elliot had to call again nineteen minutes later, and then you and your partner finally arrived four minutes after that." I looked up. "Deputy, why did it take so long to respond to what must've been a priority call?"

"The Malibu district is our largest. We had to come all the way over the mountain from another call."

"Wasn't there another patrol car that was closer?"

"My partner and I were in the alpha car. We handle the priority calls, and we accepted this one when it came in."

"Okay, deputy, I have nothing further."

The judge adjourned for the afternoon break. As soon as the jury had cleared the courtroom, I heard a whispered voice call my name. I turned around and saw Lorna, who pointed toward the back of the courtroom. There was my daughter and her mother squeezed into the back row. My daughter waved to me, and I smiled back.

# TWELVE

I MET them in the hallway outside the courtroom. Hayley hugged me, and I was overwhelmed that she had come. I saw an empty wooden bench, and we sat down.

"How long were you guys there?" I asked. "I didn't see you."

"Unfortunately, not that long," Maggie said. "Her last school period was PE, so I decided to pull her out early. We saw most of your cross with the deputy."

I looked from Maggie to our daughter, sitting between us. She had her mother's looks: dark hair and eyes, skin that held a tan long into the winter. "What did you think, Hay?"

"Um, I thought it was really interesting. You asked him a lot of questions. He looked like he was getting mad."

"Don't worry, he'll get over it."

I looked over her head at my ex-wife and nodded my thanks. She had put aside any anger for me and put our daughter first.

"Do you go back in there?" Hayley asked.

"Yes. This is just a little break so people can get something to drink or use the bathroom. We have one more session."

She nodded toward the courtroom door. People were starting to go back in. "Um, Daddy? Did that man kill somebody?"

"Well, honey, we don't know. He is accused of that, yes, and a lot of people think he did. But nothing has been proven yet. Remember how I explained that?"

"I remember."

"Mick, is this your family?"

I looked over my shoulder and froze. Walter Elliot was smiling warmly, expecting an introduction.

"Uh, hi, Walter. This is my daughter, Hayley, and this is her mom, Maggie McPherson."

"Hi," Hayley said.

Maggie nodded and looked uncomfortable. Walter made the mistake of thrusting his hand out to her. She shook it once quickly. When his hand moved toward Hayley, Maggie jumped up and pulled her from the bench. "Hayley, let's go to the restroom before court starts again."

She hustled Hayley off, and Walter watched them go. I stood up. "Sorry, Walter, my ex-wife's a prosecutor. She works for the D.A."

His eyebrows climbed his forehead. "Then I guess I understand why she's an ex-wife."

I told him to go on back into the courtroom and walked to the restrooms. Maggie and Hayley were coming out.

"We're going to head home," Maggie said. "She's got a lot of homework, and I think she's seen enough for today."

I could've argued, but I let it go. "Okay. Hayley, thanks for coming. It means a lot to me."

"Okay."

I bent down and kissed her on the top of the head, then pulled her in close for a hug. "Thanks for bringing her."

Maggie nodded. "For what it's worth, you're doing good in there."

"It's worth a lot. Thank you."

She shrugged and let a small smile slip out. That was nice.

I watched them walk to the elevators, knowing they weren't going home to my house and wondering how I messed up my life so badly. "Hayley!" I called after them.

My daughter looked back at me.

"See you Wednesday. Pancakes!"

She was smiling as an elevator opened. My former wife was smiling, too. I pointed at her. "You can come, too."

She nodded. "We'll see," she said.

IN ANY murder trial, the main witness for the prosecution is the lead investigator. Because there are no living victims to tell the jury what happened, it falls on the lead to speak for the dead. The lead investigator puts everything together, makes it clear and sympathetic. His job is to sell the case, and like any transaction, it is often as much about the salesman as it is about the goods being sold.

Golantz called the case's lead investigator to the stand after the afternoon break. It was a stroke of genius and master planning. John Kinder would hold center stage until the jurors went home with his words to consider over dinner and into the night.

Kinder was a large, affable black man who spoke with a fatherly baritone. He slipped reading glasses onto the end of his nose when referring to the binder he carried. Between questions, he would look over the rims at Golantz or the jury. His eyes seemed kind and wise.

With Golantz's precise questioning and a series of blowups of crime-scene photos, Kinder led the jury on a tour of the murder scene. It was purely clinical, but with his authoritative voice, he came off as something akin to a professor teaching Homicide 101.

I objected here and there when I could in an effort to break the Golantz/Kinder rhythm. My client, it appeared, was barely paying attention. He was writing notes on a legal pad, but I saw the heading "Foreign Distribution." I whispered, "This guy's killing us up there."

A humorless smile bent his lips, and Elliot whispered back, "I think we're doing fine. You've had a good day."

I shook my head. He was well aware I had the magic bullet in my gun, but nothing is a sure thing when you go to trial. And a murder trial is the biggest gamble of them all.

After the crime-scene investigation was covered, Golantz moved to Elliot, basically confirming Murray's testimony. Finally he asked, "Where did Elliot lead you in the house, Detective Kinder?"

"He walked us straight upstairs to the bedroom. I asked if he'd been anywhere else in the house, and he said no."

"Did that seem unusual or inconsistent to you?"

"Well, I thought it was odd that he'd gone directly up to the bedroom without looking around the first level. It also didn't jibe with what he told us when we got back outside. He pointed at his wife's car parked out front and said that was how he knew she had somebody with her in the house. He said they had stored a bunch of furniture in the garage and that left only one space and the German had hidden his Porsche in there."

"And what was the significance of that to you?"

"It showed deception. He'd told us he hadn't been anywhere but the bedroom, but it was pretty clear he'd looked in the garage."

Golantz nodded emphatically, driving home the point. The prosecutor continued to lead Kinder through the investigation up until he cleared the crime scene and interviewed Elliot at the Malibu station. This set up the introduction of a videotape I knew was unremarkable in terms of content. But Elliot appeared as calm as a summer sunset, and that made him look like an ice-cold killer.

A video screen was set up in front of the jury box, and Golantz played the ten-minute tape. There were no hard questions, and the interview ended with Kinder presenting the search warrant that granted the sheriff's department access to test Elliot's hands, arms, and clothing for gunshot residue.

Elliot smiled slightly as he replied. "Have at it, gentlemen. Do what you have to do."

Golantz used a remote to freeze the image of Elliot's catch-me-if-you-can smile on the screen. "Your Honor," he said. "I think now would be a good time to break for the day. I will be moving with Deputy Kinder in a new direction after this."

The judge agreed, adjourning court after once more admonishing the jurors to avoid all media reports on the trial.

I stood at the defense table and watched the jurors file out. "Walter, what do you have going tonight?" I asked.

"A small dinner party, then the first cut of a film my studio is producing, with Johnny Depp playing a detective."

"Well, call and cancel it all. You're having dinner with me."

"I don't understand."

"Yes, you do. You've been ducking me, and that was okay because I didn't want to know what I didn't need to know. Now we're in trial, and I need to know everything, Walter. We're going to talk tonight or you're going to hire another lawyer."

I saw his face grow tight with anger. In that moment, I knew he could be a killer, or at least someone who could order it done.

"You wouldn't dare," he said.

"Make your calls," I said. "We'll take my car."

WITH a thirty-second phone call, Elliot got us a private booth at the Water Grill over by the Biltmore and had a martini waiting on the table for him when we got there. As we sat down, I asked for a bottle of flat water and some sliced lemons.

I sat across from Elliot and watched him study the menu. "You called it a dinner meeting," he said. "Aren't you going to look?"

"I'm having what you're having, Walter."

He put the menu to the side. "Filet of sole."

He signaled a waiter and ordered for us both, adding a bottle of chardonnay to come with the fish. He then clasped his hands on the table and looked expectantly at me. "This better be good."

"Walter, this *is* going to be good. This is going to be where you stop hiding from me. If I know what you know, I'm not going to get sandbagged. I'm going to know what moves Golantz is going to make before he makes them."

Elliot nodded as though he agreed. "I did not kill my wife or her Nazi friend," he said. "I have told you that from day one."

"That's not good enough. I said I want to know what really happened, Walter, or I'm going to be moving on."

"Don't be ridiculous. No judge is going to let you walk away in the middle of a trial."

"You want to bet your freedom on that, Walter? If I want off this case, I will find a way off it."

He hesitated. "You should be careful of what you ask for. Guilty knowledge could be a dangerous thing."

I leaned across the table to him. "Walter, I'm your lawyer. You can tell me what you've done and it stays with me."

Before he could speak, the waiter brought a bottle of European water and a plate of sliced lemons. Elliot waited until he had filled my glass and moved away. "What is going on is that you have done an excellent job preparing my defense, and all in two weeks. Astonishing!"

"Drop the bull!"

I said it too loud. Elliot looked outside the booth and stared down a woman at a nearby table who had heard me.

"You'll have to keep your voice down," he said. "The bond of attorney-client confidentiality ends at this table."

I looked at him. I knew he was reminding me of what I had already assured him of, that what was said here stayed here. Was it a signal that he was willing to finally talk? I played the only ace I had. "Tell me about the bribe Jerry Vincent paid."

I detected shock in his eyes, then a knowing look as the wheels turned inside. Then I saw a flash of regret. I wished Julie Favreau had been sitting next to me. She could have read him better.

"That is a very dangerous piece of information to be in possession of," he said. "How did you get it?"

I obviously couldn't tell him I got it from a detective. "You could say it came with the case. I have all Vincent's records. It wasn't hard to figure out that he funneled a hundred thousand of your advance to an unknown party. Is the bribe what got him killed?"

Elliot raised his martini glass with two fingers clenching the delicate stem and drank what was left in it. He then nodded to someone unseen over my shoulder. "I think it is safe to say a confluence of events led to Jerry Vincent's death."

"Walter, I need to defend you. And to protect myself."

He nodded. "I think you may have found the reason for his death. It was in the file. You even mentioned it to me."

"I don't understand. What did I mention?"

"He planned to delay the trial. You found the motion. He was killed before he could file it."

I tried to put it together. "That got him killed? Why?"

Elliot leaned toward me. He spoke in a tone just above a whisper. "Okay, you asked for it and I'll tell you. Yes, there was a bribe. He paid it, and the trial was scheduled, and all we had to do was be ready to go. But then he changed his mind and wanted to delay."

"Why?"

"I think he actually thought he could win without the fix."

It appeared that Elliot didn't know about the FBI's phone calls and apparent interest in Vincent. If he did know, now would have been the time to mention it. The FBI's focus on Vincent would have been as good a reason as any to delay a trial involving a bribery scheme.

"So delaying the trial got him killed?"

"That's my guess, yes."

"Did you kill him, Walter?"

"I don't kill people."

"You had him killed."

Elliot shook his head. "I don't *have* people killed either."

A waiter moved up to the booth with a tray and a stand. He deboned our fish, plated them, and put them on the table along with a fresh martini. He uncorked the wine and asked if Elliot wanted to taste it. Elliot shook his head.

"Okay," I said when we were left alone. "Who was bribed?"

Elliot downed half his new martini in one gulp. "That should be obvious, when you think about it. A trial cannot be delayed. Why?"

My eyes stayed on him, but I was no longer looking at him. I went inside to work the riddle. Ticking off the possibilities—judge, prosecutor, cops, witnesses, jury—I realized that there was only one place where a bribe and an unmovable trial intersected. "There's a sleeper on the jury," I said. "You got to somebody."

Elliot let me run with it, and my mind swept along the faces in the jury box. "Number seven. You wanted him. Who is he?"

Elliot gave me that half smile and took his first bite of fish before answering. "I have no idea and don't really care to know. But he's ours. And he's no sleeper. He's a persuader. When it gets to deliberations, he will go in there and turn the tide. With the case Vincent built and you're delivering, it probably won't take more than a little push. They will never convict me, Mickey. Never."

I pushed my plate aside. I couldn't eat. "Walter, no more riddles. Tell me how this went down."

Elliot poured himself a glass of wine. "This is a long story, Mickey. Would you like wine to go with it?" He held up the bottle.

I shook my head. "No, Walter. I don't drink."

"I'm not sure I can trust someone who doesn't take a drink from time to time." Chuckling, he drank heavily and began his story.

"When you come to Hollywood, it doesn't matter who you are as long as you've got money. I came twenty-five years ago, but it wasn't my money."

"I thought the story was that you came from a family that owned a phosphate shipping operation in Florida."

He nodded emphatically. "All true, but it depends on your definition of family."

It slowly came to me. "Are you talking about the mob?"

"I'm talking about an organization with a tremendous cash flow that needed legitimate businesses to move it through and legitimate front men to operate those businesses. I was an accountant. I was one of those men."

It was easy to put together. Florida twenty-five years ago. The heyday of the uninhibited flow of cocaine and money.

"I was sent west," Elliot said. "I had a story, and I had suitcases full of money. And I loved movies. I knew how to pick 'em and put 'em together. I took Archway and turned it into a billion-dollar enterprise. And then my wife . . ."

A look of sad regret crossed his face.

"What, Walter?"

"The day after our twelfth anniversary—after our prenuptial agreement was vested—she told me she was getting a divorce."

I nodded. With the prenup vested, Mitzi Elliot would be entitled to half of Elliot's holdings, only his holdings actually belonged to the organization. And it wasn't the type of organization that would allow half its investment to walk out the door in a skirt.

"I tried to change her mind," Elliot said. "She was in love with that Nazi bastard and thought he could protect her."

"The organization had her killed."

"I wasn't supposed to be there that day," Elliot said. "I was told to stay away, to make sure I had a rock-solid alibi."

"Why'd you go, then?"

His eyes held on mine. "I still loved her in some way. I went out there to try to stop it, maybe be the hero, win her back. I don't know. But I was too late. They were both dead when I got there."

"Then came Jerry Vincent," I said. "Tell me about the bribe."

"I don't have a lot to tell. My corporate attorney hooked me up with Jerry, and he was fine. We worked out the fee arrangement, and then he came to me—this was early on—and said he had been approached by someone who could salt the jury. You know, put someone on the jury who would be for us. He would be a skilled persuader—a con man. The catch was that the trial would have to stay on schedule so that this person would end up on my jury."

"And you and Jerry took the offer."

"We took it. This was five months ago. At the time, I didn't have much of a defense. I didn't kill my wife, but it seemed the odds were stacked against me. We had no magic bullet . . . and I was scared."

"How much?"

"A hundred thousand up front. Jerry inflated his fee, and I paid him, and then he paid for the juror. Then it was going to be another hundred for a hung jury and two-fifty for an acquittal. These people had done it before."

I thought of the FBI. "Were Jerry's trials fixed before?"

"He didn't say, and I didn't ask. But then the Monday before he was killed, he told me he was going to delay the trial. He said he had the magic bullet and was going to win without the sleeper."

"And that got him killed."

"It had to be. I don't think these kind of people just let you change your mind and pull out of something like this."

"Did you tell anyone Jerry was going to delay the case?"

"No."

"Then who did Jerry tell?"

"I don't know. He wouldn't say who he made the deal with."

I had to end this and get away by myself to think. I glanced at my untouched fish and wondered if I should take it to go for Patrick.

"You know," Elliot said, "not to put any more pressure on you, but if I get convicted, I'm dead."

I looked at him. "The organization?"

He nodded. "A guy gets busted, and normally they wipe him out before he even gets to court. But they wipe me out and they lose Archway, the real estate, everything, so they're hanging back and watching." He drained his glass. "Mick, the things I've told you could get you killed in a heartbeat. Just like Jerry. Remember that."

He waved down a waiter and asked for the check.

I was thankful my client liked his martinis before dinner and his chardonnay during and after. I wasn't sure I'd have gotten what I got from Elliot without the alcohol loosening his tongue. But afterward I didn't want him pulled over on a DUI in the middle of a murder trial. I drove him home while Patrick followed.

"Walter," I said to him, "despite everything you told me tonight, I'm going to do my best for you."

"Then you believe I'm innocent."

I hesitated. "I believe you didn't shoot your wife and Rilz. I'm not sure that makes you innocent, but that's all I need."

Elliot lived in Beverly Hills in a gated estate in the flats south of Sunset. He pushed a button on his car's ceiling, and we slipped through the steel entry gate, Patrick coming in right behind in the Lincoln. We got out, and I gave Elliot his keys and said goodnight.

The internal gears were working all the way to my house. I sat gazing out the back window. It wasn't hard to figure out how Jerry Vincent's deal was done. The question was who did it.

Elliot had admitted several crimes over dinner, but these admissions would remain confidential under the bonds of the attorney-client relationship. The exception to this rule was if I was endangered by my knowledge or had knowledge of a crime that had not yet occurred. The bribe had occurred, but the jury tampering wouldn't take place until deliberations, so I was duty-bound to report it, even though Elliot apparently was convinced that the threat of my meeting the same end as Jerry would keep me in check.

I thought about all this, then realized I wouldn't have to report the intended crime if I were to stop it from happening.

I looked around. We were on Sunset coming into West Holly-wood, and I saw a familiar sign. "Patrick, pull over in front of Book Soup. I want to run in for a minute."

Patrick pulled the Lincoln to the curb, and I jumped out. I went in the door and back into the stacks, found an empty alcove, and called my investigator.

"Cisco, it's me. Where are you?"

"At home. What's up?"

"Lorna there?"

"No. She went to a chick flick with her sister."

"I want you to do something you may not want to do. If you don't, I understand. Either way, I don't want you to talk about it with anybody. Including Lorna."

There was a hesitation before he answered. "Who do I kill?"

We both laughed, and it relieved some of the night's tension. "We can talk about that later, but this might be just as dicey. I want you to shadow juror number seven."

BY THE time Patrick pulled the car into the garage below my house, it was almost ten o'clock. We walked up the stairs to the front deck. I was beat after a fourteen-hour day, but my adrenaline kicked in when I saw a man in one of the deck chairs. I put my arm out to stop Patrick the way a parent would stop a child from step-ping into the street.

"Hello, Counselor."

Bosch. I relaxed. We stepped up onto the porch, and I unlocked the door to let Patrick in, then closed the door and turned to Bosch.

"Nice view," he said. "Defending scumbags get you this place?"

I was too tired to do the dance with him. "What are you doing here, Detective?"

"I figured you might be heading home after the bookstore."

"Well, I'm done for the night. You can give your team the word, if there really is a team."

"After court, you had dinner with your client at Water Grill. You both had the filet of sole and your client drank liberally, which resulted in you driving him home in his car. On your way back, you stopped into Book Soup and made a phone call you obviously didn't want your driver to hear."

I was impressed. "Okay, then never mind that. I get it. They're out there. What do you want, Bosch? What's going on?"

Bosch stood up and approached me.

"I was going to ask you the same thing," he said. "What was Walter Elliot so hot and bothered about tonight at dinner? And who'd you call in the back of the bookstore?"

# THIRTEEN

MY TURN at Detective Kinder did not come until late on Tuesday, after the prosecutor had spent several hours delving into the defendant's marriage, the discovery of the recently vested prenuptial agreement, and Elliot's efforts before the murders to determine how much money and control of Archway Studios he would lose in a divorce. Kinder had also established that Elliot had no credible alibi for the estimated time of the murders. And he described the many unfounded leads that were called in and dutifully checked out.

These details worked in my favor. I thought the jury—and Julie Favreau confirmed this by text message—was bored by the minutiae. But all in all, Golantz and Kinder appeared to have done a thorough job of nailing my client to the murders, and by mid-afternoon the young prosecutor was satisfied enough to say, "No more questions, Your Honor."

It was now finally my turn, and I moved to the lectern.

"Detective Kinder, I know we'll hear from the medical examiner later, but you testified that you were informed after the autopsy that the time of death of Mrs. Elliot and Mr. Rilz was estimated to be between eleven a.m. and noon."

"That is correct."

"Was it closer to eleven or closer to noon?"

"It's impossible to tell. That's just the time frame."

"Once you had that frame, you proceeded to make sure the man you had already arrested had no alibi, correct?"

"I wouldn't put it that way, no. I would say it was my obligation to continue to investigate the case. In carrying out that obligation, I determined according to multiple interviews as well as gate records that Mr. Elliot left Archway Studios, driving by himself, at ten forty that morning. This gave him plenty—"

"Thank you, Detective. You've answered the question."

Golantz stood and asked if the witness could finish his answer, and Stanton allowed it. Kinder continued his Homicide 101 tone. "This gave Mr. Elliot plenty of time to get to the house within the estimated time of death."

"Did you say plenty of time to get there?"

"Enough time."

"Earlier you described making the drive yourself several times. When was that?"

"The first time was one week after the murders. I left Archway at ten forty and arrived at the Malibu house at eleven forty-two."

"Did you know you were taking the same route as Mr. Elliot?"

"I didn't. I just took what I considered the most obvious and quickest route that somebody would take."

"Traffic in Los Angeles can be very unpredictable, can it not?"

"Yes."

"Is that why you drove the route several times?"

"One reason, yes."

"Detective, you testified you drove the route five times and got to the Malibu house each time before your so-called murder window closed, right?"

"Correct."

"Please, tell the jury how many times you began the route but broke off when you knew you weren't going to make it before that window closed."

"That never happened."

But there had been a slight hesitation in Kinder's response. I was sure the jury picked up on it. "Detective, if I were to produce records that showed you started at the Archway gate at ten forty in the morning seven times and not five, would those records be false?"

"No, but I didn't—"

"Thank you. Detective, tell us how many of these test drives you broke off before reaching the house in Malibu."

"There were two."

"Which ones?"

"The second time and the last time—the seventh."

"You stopped these because you knew you'd never make it to the house within the murder window, correct?"

"No. One time I was called back to the office to conduct an interview, and the other time I heard a radio call and diverted to back up a deputy."

"Why didn't you document these in your driving-time report?"

"They were incomplete tests. I didn't think they were germane."

"So we only have your word about what caused you to stop them before reaching the Elliot house, correct?"

"That would be correct."

I had flogged him enough on this front. But I hoped I had raised at least a question of trust. I decided to hit Kinder with a punch he wouldn't see coming.

I asked the judge for a moment and went to the defense table. I bent down to my client's ear. "Just nod like I am telling you something really important," I whispered.

Elliot did as instructed, and then I picked up a file, went to the lectern, and opened it. "Detective, at what point did you determine that Johan Rilz was the primary target of this double murder?"

Kinder opened his mouth to respond, then sat back and thought for a moment. "At no point did I ever determine that."

"He was at no point front and center in your investigation?"

"Well, he was the victim of a homicide. That made him front and center in my book."

"Then him being front and center explains why you went to Germany to investigate his background, correct?"

"I did not go to Germany."

"What about France? His passport indicated he lived there before coming to the United States."

"We didn't believe it was necessary. We'd asked Interpol for a background check, and it came back clean."

"What is Interpol?"

"It stands for International Criminal Police Organization. It links the police in more than a hundred countries."

"Did you directly check with police in Paris, where Rilz lived five years ago?"

"No. We relied on our Interpol contacts for background."

"The Interpol check was for a criminal arrest record, correct?"

"That was included, yes. I'm not sure what else."

"If Mr. Rilz had worked for the Paris police as an informant on a drug case, would Interpol have given you this information?"

Kinder's eyes widened for a split second. "I don't know."

"Law-enforcement agencies usually don't give out the names of their confidential informants willy nilly, do they?"

"No, they don't. It might put the informants in danger."

"So being an informant in a criminal case can be dangerous?"

"On occasion, yes."

"Detective, have you ever investigated the murder of a confidential informant?"

Golantz stood up and asked for a sidebar conference. The judge signaled us up, and we huddled.

"Mr. Golantz?" the judge prompted.

"Judge, nothing in any of the defense's discovery even hints at what Mr. Haller is asking the witness about."

The judge swiveled in his chair. "Mr. Haller?"

"Judge, this was a sloppy investigation that—"

"Save it for the jury. Whaddaya got?"

I put a computer printout from the file in front of the judge, positioning it so it was upside down to Golantz. "A story in *Le*

*Parisien* four and half years ago. It names Johan Rilz as a witness for the prosecution in a major drug case. He was used by the Direction de la Police Judiciare to make buys and get inside knowledge of the drug ring. And these guys over here never even—"

"Mr. Haller, this is in French. Do you have the translation?"

"Sorry, Your Honor." I put a second sheet down.

Golantz twisted his head as he tried to read it. "How do we know this is the same Johan Rilz? This isn't an official document."

I put a last sheet down. "This is a photocopy of a page from Rilz's passport from the state's own discovery. It shows Rilz left France for the United States one month after this story. Plus, the article has his age right and says he was making drug buys for the cops out of his business as an interior decorator. It obviously is him, Your Honor. He put a lot of people over there in jail."

Golantz shook his head in a desperate sort of way. "This is a violation of the rules of discovery. You can't sit on this, then sucker punch the state with it."

The judge swiveled his view and gave me the squint.

"Your Honor, if anybody sat on anything, it was the state. I think the witness did know about this and *he* sat on it."

"That is a serious accusation, Mr. Haller," the judge intoned. "Do you have evidence of that?"

"Judge, the reason I know about this at all is by accident. On Sunday, I noticed my investigator had run all the names associated with this case through the LexisNexis search engine using the computer I'd inherited with Vincent's law practice. The default setting was for English-language search only. Having looked at the photocopy of Rilz's passport in the discovery file, I did the search including French and German and came up with this article in about two minutes. I find it hard to believe I found something the entire sheriff's department, the prosecution, and Interpol didn't know about. Judge, the defense is certainly feeling like the damaged party here."

I couldn't believe it. The judge swiveled to Golantz and gave him the squint. The first time ever. I shifted to my right so that a good part of the jury had an angle on it.

"What about that, Mr. Golantz?" the judge asked.

"It's absurd. Anything we've found has gone into the discovery file. I'd like to ask why Mr. Haller didn't alert us to this yesterday."

I stared deadpan at Golantz. "If I'd known you were fluent in French, I'd have given it to you, Jeff. I was handed that translation ten minutes before I started my cross."

"All right," the judge said. "What are you going to do about verifying this information, Mr. Haller?"

"I'm going to put my investigator on it to do the job the sheriff's department should have done six months ago."

"We're obviously going to verify it as well," Golantz added.

The judge held up a hand. "Okay," he said. "Mr. Haller, I'll allow you to lay the foundation for this during the presentation of the defense if you can verify the report and the identity. I think we are done here, gentlemen."

The judge rolled back into position, and the lawyers returned to theirs. I noticed the courtroom clock said ten minutes until five.

I stood at the lectern. "Judge, I look forward to exploring Mr. Rilz's activities in France during the defense phase of the trial. Until then, I have no further questions for Detective Kinder."

I sat down. The judge announced that court was recessed.

I watched the jury file out, then glanced to the gallery. All three Rilz men were staring at me with hardened, dead eyes.

CISCO called me at home at ten o'clock. He said he was nearby in Hollywood and that he could come right over. He said he already had some news about juror number seven.

After hanging up, I told Patrick that I was going out on the deck to meet privately with Cisco. I put on a sweater, grabbed the file I'd used in court earlier, and went out to wait for my investigator.

The Sunset Strip glowed like a blast furnace over the hills. I'd bought the house in a flush year because of the view the deck offered of the city. It never ceased to entrance me, day or night.

"Hey, Boss."

I jumped. Cisco had climbed the stairs and come up behind me without my even hearing him. He must've come up the hill on Fairfax, killed the engine, and freewheeled down to my house.

I pointed him to the small table and chairs under the roof's eave. He sat down and looked through the living room. The television was on, and Patrick was in there watching the extreme sports channel on cable. People were doing flips on snowmobiles.

"Is that a sport?" Cisco asked.

"To Patrick, I guess."

"How's it working out with him?"

"It's working. He's only staying a couple weeks. Tell me about number seven."

"Down to business. Okay." He reached behind him and pulled a small journal out of his back pocket. "His name is David McSweeney, and almost everything he put on his J sheet is false."

The J sheet, filled out as part of the voir dire process, carried the prospective juror's name, profession, and area of residence by Zip code as well as a checklist of basic questions. In this trial, the name would've been excised.

"Give me some examples."

"Well, according to the Zip, he lives down in Palos Verde. Not true. I followed him directly to an apartment off Beverly, over behind CBS." Cisco pointed south in the direction of the CBS television studio. "I had a friend run the plate on the pickup—David McSweeney, same address I saw him go into. Then run his DL and shoot me over the photo. McSweeney is our guy."

"Cisco, your prints are going to be all over this."

"Chill, man. My guy doesn't use his terminal, and he cadged an old lieutenant's password. So we're safe on this, okay?"

Cops stealing from cops. Why didn't that surprise me?

"All right," I said. "What else?"

"Well, he checked the box that said he'd never been popped before. ADW in ninety-seven and conspiracy to commit fraud in ninety-nine. No convictions is all I know right now."

I wanted to know how arrests for fraud and assault with a deadly weapon could result in no convictions, but if Cisco pulled records, he'd have to show ID. "Let it go for now. You got anything else?"

"Yeah. I'm telling you, I think it's all phony. He says he's an engineer with Lockheed, and they don't have a David McSweeney in the Lockheed phone directory." He raised his hands palm up. "So what's going on? Don't tell me that scumbag prosecutor put a sleeper on the jury."

"It's better if I don't tell you. Did you see this guy with anybody?"

"Not so far. I've only been with the guy since five."

"Okay, Cisco, you did good. You can drop it and go back to this." I slid the file across to him.

He smiled slyly. "What did you tell the judge at the sidebar?"

I had forgotten he had been in the courtroom. "I told him I redid the search to include French. I even printed the story out again Sunday so I would have a fresh date on it. Where's the translator you used on the printout?"

"Probably in her dorm over in Westwood. She's an exchange student I came up with on the Net."

"Well, call her and pick her up, because you're going to need her tonight to translate. They're—what, nine hours ahead over there in Paris? At midnight, start calling all the gendarmes who worked that drug case and get one of them on a plane over here. Spend whatever needs to be spent. Just get him here as soon as possible."

"You want me to call you tonight when I have it set up?"

"No. I need my beauty rest. Just call me in the morning."

# FOURTEEN

ON MONDAY morning I had my Corneliani suit on. I was sitting next to my client ready to begin to present his defense. Jeffrey Golantz sat at his table ready to thwart my efforts. And the gallery behind us was maxed out once again. But the bench in front of us was empty. The judge was sequestered in his chambers and running almost an hour behind. Something had come up, but we had not yet been informed. We had seen sheriff's deputies escort a man I didn't recognize into chambers and then out again.

"Jeff, what do you think?" I finally asked across the aisle.

Golantz looked over at me. He was wearing his nice black suit, but he had been wearing it every day and it wasn't as impressive anymore. He shrugged. "No idea."

The prosecution's case had strung out through the entire previous week. I had helped with a couple of protracted cross-examinations, but for the most part it had been Golantz engaging in overkill. He kept the medical examiner on the stand for nearly an entire day explaining in excruciating detail how and when the victims died. He kept Walter Elliot's accountant for half a day explaining how much Walter stood to lose in a divorce. And he kept the sheriff's forensic tech on for nearly as long, explaining his finding of high levels of gunshot residue on the defendant's hands and clothes.

In between, he conducted shorter examinations of lesser witnesses and then finished Friday afternoon with a tearjerker. Mitzi Elliot's lifelong best friend testified about Mitzi confiding her divorce plans, the fight that followed between husband and wife, and the bruises on Mitzi's arms the next day. She never stopped crying.

The trial would move to the defense phase the following Monday. I spent the weekend strategizing and preparing my two anchor witnesses, my gunshot-residue expert and a jetlagged French police captain. Now I was ready to go, but there was no judge on the bench.

"What's going on?" Elliot whispered.

I shrugged. "Your guess is as good as mine."

A deep furrow had settled into Elliot's brow. He knew something was up. I looked back into the gallery and noticed that behind the prosecution table, there was a gap in the spectators. No Germans. I was about to ask Golantz where Rilz's family members were when a uniformed sheriff's deputy walked up to the rail and beckoned him with a document.

"Excuse me, are you the prosecutor?" the deputy said. "Who do I talk to about this?"

Golantz got up and walked over to take a look at the document. "It's a defense subpoena. Are you Deputy Stallworth?"

"That's right."

"Then you're in the right spot."

"No, I'm not. I didn't have anything to do with this case."

"You weren't at the house? What about the perimeter or traffic control?" I could see the wheels begin turning, but it was going to be too late when he figured things out.

"I was home asleep. I work midnight shift."

"Hold it a second." Golantz went back to his desk and checked my final witness list. "What is this, Haller?"

"What's what? He's on there. He's been on there for two weeks." I got up and went to the rail. "Deputy Stallworth, I'm Michael Haller, the one who summoned you. If you wait out in the hall, I'll try to get you in and out as soon as court starts."

The deputy looked over at Golantz for help, but the prosecutor was whispering into a cell phone. "Look," I said, "just go out into the hall and I'll—"

The clerk was signaling us to the judge's chambers. Golantz ended his call and got up, and I followed him.

The judge sat behind his desk in his black robe. "Gentlemen," he said. "Have a seat and I'll tell you what's going on."

Golantz and I sat side by side. Stanton clasped his hands on top of a folded piece of paper in front of him. "We have an unusual situation involving juror misconduct," he said. "My office received a letter Thursday addressed to me that I didn't get a chance to open until after court on Friday. The letter said—well, here is the letter. I've already handled it, but don't either of you touch it."

He unfolded the piece of paper and allowed us to read it.

> Judge Stanton, you should know that juror number seven is not who he says he is. Check Lockheed and check his prints. He's got an arrest record.

The letter looked like it had come out of a laser printer. "Did you keep the envelope it came in?" I asked.

"The postmark is Hollywood. I didn't talk to number seven. I conferred with a few other judges on the matter and was fully prepared to bring it up with counsel this morning. The only problem is, juror seven didn't show up today."

That brought a pause to both Golantz and myself.

"He's not here?" Golantz said. "Did you send deputies to—"

"Yes, I sent court deputies to his home, and his wife told them that he was at work. They went over to Lockheed and found the man and brought him here. He was not juror number seven. We had seven in the computer as Rodney L. Banglund, but the man who has been sitting for two weeks is not Rodney Banglund. We don't know who he was, and now he's missing."

"What does this do?" I asked. "Do we have a mistrial?"

"I don't think so. I think we bring the jury out, we explain that number seven's been excused, and we drop in the first alternate. Meantime, the sheriff's department makes damn sure everybody else in that box is who they're supposed to be. Mr. Golantz?"

"I think the state would be prepared to continue."

"Mr. Haller?"

I nodded approval. The session had gone as I'd hoped. "I've got witnesses from Paris. My client doesn't want a mistrial."

"Okay. Go on back out and we'll get going in ten minutes."

Elliot was all over me when I got to the defense table. "What happened? What's going on?"

"Juror seven didn't show up, and the judge found out he was a phony," I whispered.

Elliot stiffened. "My God, what does this mean?"

"The trial continues with an alternate juror, but there will be an investigation of who number seven was. Hopefully, Walter, it doesn't come to your door."

"But we can't go on now. You have to get a mistrial."

I saw the pleading look on my client's face and realized he'd never had any faith in his defense. "The judge said no on a mistrial. Don't worry, Walter. We're going to win fair and square."

The clerk called the courtroom to order, and the judge bounded up the steps to the bench. "Back on the record with California versus Elliot," he said. "Let's bring in our jury."

THE first witness for the defense was Julio Muniz, a freelance videographer from Topanga Canyon who got the jump on the rest of the media on the day of the murders. I quickly established through my questions how Muniz listened to police scanners in his home and car, picked up addresses for crime scenes, and took film he then sold to local news broadcasts.

"Mr. Muniz, what did you do when you arrived at the Elliot house?" I asked.

"Well, I noticed they had some suspect in the patrol car, so I got my camera out."

I introduced the digital videocassette Muniz used that day as the first defense exhibit, spooled to begin at the point that Muniz began shooting Elliot. Using a remote, I froze the image. Elliot was in the rear passenger side seat. He was leaning forward because his hands were cuffed behind his body and it made sitting awkward.

"Okay, Mr. Muniz, let me draw your attention to the roof of the patrol car. What do you see painted there?"

"I see the car's designation. It is four-A or four-alpha."

"Did you recognize that designation? Had you seen it before?"

"Well, I had actually seen the four-alpha car earlier that day."

"And what were the circumstances of that?"

"I had heard on the scanner about a hostage situation in Malibu Creek State Park. I shot that about two a.m."

"So about twelve hours before you were videoing the activities at the Elliot house, you shot this hostage situation?"

"That's correct."

"And the four-alpha car was involved in this incident?"

"Yes. When the suspect was finally captured around five a.m., he was transported in four-alpha. The same car. That footage comes earlier on the same tape."

"Then let's see," I said.

Golantz immediately stood, objected, and asked for a sidebar. The judge waved us up, and I brought the witness list.

"Your Honor," Golantz said angrily. "The defense is sandbagging. There's been no indication in discovery or otherwise of intent to explore some other crime with this witness."

I calmly slid the list in front of the judge. "It clearly says Muniz would testify about video he shot on May second, the day of the murders. The video at the park was shot on May two. Mr. Golantz could have checked out his videos."

The judge studied the list for a moment and nodded. "Objection overruled. You may proceed, Mr. Haller."

I went back and reversed the video and started to play it. It was a night shoot, and the images were grainy. Finally it came to footage showing a man with his hands cuffed behind his back being placed into a patrol car. A deputy closed the door. As the car drove by the camera, I froze the image. The light of the camera illuminated the roof of the car as well as the man in the backseat.

"Mr. Muniz, what's the designation on the roof of that car?"

"Again, it's four-A or four-alpha."

"And the man being transported—where is he sitting?"

"In the rear right passenger seat."

"Is he handcuffed?"

"His hands were cuffed behind his back. I shot it."

"Now is he in the same position in the patrol car that Mr. Elliot was in when you videotaped him eight hours later?"

"Yes, he is. Exact same position and seat."

"Thank you, Mr. Muniz. No further questions."

Golantz passed on cross examination. There was nothing that could be attacked. Muniz stepped down, and I called Deputy Todd Stallworth to the stand.

Stallworth looked beat as he came into the courtroom. I quickly established that he was driving the alpha car in the Malibu district during the first shift on the day of the murders. Golantz once more objected and asked for a sidebar, palms raised up in a "What's this?" gesture. His style was getting old with me.

This time I slapped the list down in front of the judge and ran my finger down the names until I reached Todd Stallworth. "Judge, he's clearly listed under law-enforcement personnel. The explanation, as before, says he'll testify about his activities on May second. That's all I put down, because I never talked to him."

Golantz tried to maintain his composure. "Judge, from the start of this trial, the defense has relied on trickery and deception to—"

"Mr. Golantz," the judge interrupted. "Don't say something you can't back up. This witness, just like the first one, is right there on this list in black and white. You better watch yourself."

Golantz stood with his head bowed. "Your Honor, the state requests a brief recess," he said in a quiet voice.

"Your Honor," I cut in. "I object to any recess. He just wants to grab my witness and turn his testimony."

"Now *that* I object to," Golantz said.

"No recess," the judge said. "Objection overruled."

We returned to our places, and I played the cut showing the handcuffed man being placed in the back of the 4 Alpha car at Malibu Creek State Park. I froze the image as before. "Deputy Stallworth, is that you driving that car?"

"Yes, it is."

"Who is the man in the backseat?"

"His name is Eli Wyms."

"Was he handcuffed because he was under arrest?"

"Yes. He was arrested for trying to kill me, for one. And for unlawful discharge of a weapon."

"How many counts of unlawful discharge of a weapon?"

"I can't recall the exact number."

"How about ninety-four?"

"That sounds about right. He shot the place up."

"So you took him to the nearby Malibu station?"

"No. I transported him to the county jail downtown."

"How long did that take? The drive, I mean."

"About an hour."

"And then you drove back to Malibu?"

"No. First I had four-alpha repaired. Wyms had taken out the side lamp. While I was downtown, I went to the motor pool. They only have a couple guys work midnight watch, so that took up the rest of my shift."

"So when did the car return to Malibu?"

"At shift change. I turned it over to the day-watch guys."

I looked down at my notes. "Deputies Murray and Harber?"

"That's right."

"Deputy, when you turn the car over from shift to shift, do you clean it out or disinfect the car in any way?"

"You're supposed to. Realistically, unless you've got puke in the backseat, nobody does that. Cars get taken out of rotation once or twice a week, and the motor guys clean them up."

"Did Eli Wyms puke in your car?"

"No. I would've known."

"Okay, Deputy Stallworth. Eli Wyms was arrested, his hands were cuffed behind his back, and he was transported by you downtown. In the video, Mr. Wyms can be seen in the rear passenger side seat. Did he stay there for the hour-long ride downtown?"

"Yes, he did. I had him belted in."

"Deputy, I noticed on the tape that you did not place Mr. Wyms's hands in plastic bags. Why is that?"

"Didn't think it was necessary. The evidence was overwhelming that he had fired the weapons in his possession." Stallworth yawned. "We weren't worried about gunshot residue."

"Thank you, Deputy. I hope you get some sleep."

I sat down and left the witness for Golantz, but there was little he could do to stop me now. He passed on another round, and the judge adjourned for lunch.

DR. SHAMIRAM Arslanian was a surprise witness. Not in terms of her presence at trial, but in terms of her physical appearance and personality. Her name and pedigree in forensics conjured an image of a woman deep, dark, and scientific. A white lab coat and hair ironed back in a knot. But she was a vivacious, blue-eyed blonde with an easy smile. She was telegenic, articulate, and confident but never arrogant. The one-word description for her was likable.

I had spent most of the weekend with Shami, as she preferred to be called. We had gone over the evidence, her testimony for the defense, and her expected cross examination late in the game to avoid discovery issues. So she was kept in the dark about the magic bullet until the last possible moment.

There was no doubt that she was a celebrity gun for hire. Once hosting a show on Court TV, she charged a celebrity level fee as well. For four days in Los Angeles to study, prepare, and testify, a flat rate of ten thousand dollars plus expenses. I knew after spending ten minutes with her that she was worth every penny. Her personality was going to win over the jury, and her facts were going to seal the deal.

I heard the low hum of recognition in the courtroom as my witness made her entrance from the back, holding all eyes as she walked to the witness stand. She wore a navy-blue suit that fit her curves snugly and accentuated her cascade of blond curls.

After she took the oath, I went to the lectern with my legal pad. "Good afternoon, Dr. Arslanian. How are you?"

"I'm doin' just fine. Thanks for asking."

"You are a paid consultant to the defense, is that correct?"

"I'm paid to be here, not paid to testify to anything other than my own opinion. That's my deal, and I never change it."

"Okay, tell us where you are from, Doctor."

"I live in Ossining, New York, right now. I was born and raised in Florida and spent a lot of years in the Boston area."

"Shamiram Arslanian doesn't sound like a Florida name."

She smiled brilliantly. "My father is one hundred percent Armenian. That makes me half Armenian and half Floridian. My father said I was Armageddian when I was a girl."

Many in the courtroom chuckled politely.

"What is your background in forensic sciences?" I asked.

"Well, I got my masters at the Massachusetts Institute of Technology in chemical engineering, then a Ph.D. in criminology awarded from John Jay College."

"When you say awarded, does that mean it's honorary?"

"Hell, no," she said forcefully. "I worked my butt off."

This time laughter broke out across the courtroom, and even the judge smiled before politely tapping his gavel. I checked the jury and saw all twenty-four eyes rapt with attention.

"What are your undergraduate degrees?"

"I got one from Harvard in engineering and one from the Berklee College of Music at the same time."

"You have a music degree?" I said with feigned surprise.

"I like to sing."

More laughter. The hits kept coming one after another.

Golantz finally stood. "Your Honor, the state would ask that the witness provide testimony regarding forensics, not music or things not germane to this trial."

Stanton grudgingly asked me to keep my examination on point. Golantz won, but everybody now viewed him as a spoilsport.

I asked a few questions that revealed that Dr. Arslanian currently worked as a teacher and researcher at John Jay, then finally brought her testimony to her study of the gunshot residue found on Walter Elliot's body and clothing on the day of the murders in Malibu.

"Now, Dr. Arslanian, the state's forensic witness testified that tabs wiped on Mr. Elliot's hands, sleeves, and jacket tested positive for certain elements associated with gunshot residue. Do you agree?"

"Yes. For elevated levels of barium, antimony, and lead."

"What does elevated levels mean?"

"That you'd find some of these materials on a person whether they'd fired a weapon or not. From everyday life."

"So are elevated levels of all three materials required for a positive result in gunshot-residue testing?"

"Yes. That and concentration patterns."

"Can you explain what you mean by concentration patterns?"

"Sure. When a gun discharges, there is an explosion in the chamber that sends gases out the barrel as well as any little crack and opening. The escaping gases propel microscopic elements backward onto the shooter."

"And that's what happened in this case, correct?"

"Based on the totality of my investigation, I can't say that."

I raised my eyebrows in surprise. "But Doctor, you said you agreed with the state's conclusion that there was gunshot residue on the defendant's hands and sleeves."

"I do agree. But that wasn't the question you asked."

I took a moment as if to retrace my question. "Dr. Arslanian, are you saying that there could be an alternate explanation for the gunshot residue on Mr. Elliot?"

"Yes, I am."

We were there. It was time to shoot the magic bullet. "Did your studies of the materials provided by the defense lead you to an alternate explanation?"

"Yes, they did. It is very highly likely, in my opinion, that the residue was transferred there inadvertently by contact."

"What does transfer by contact mean?"

"It means the material alights on a surface after it's discharged from the gun. If that surface comes into contact with another, some of the material will transfer. This is why suspects in gun crimes often have their clothes removed for preservation and study."

"Can this material be transferred more than once?"

"Yes, it can, with depreciating levels. This is a solid material. It has to be someplace at the end of the day. I have conducted numerous studies and found that transference can repeat and repeat. It's all a matter of how much you start with."

I nodded. "Okay, Doctor, with these theories in mind, can you tell us what happened in the Elliot case?"

"I can. When Mr. Elliot was handcuffed and placed in the back of the four-alpha patrol car, his hands, arms, and clothing were in direct contact with gunshot residue from another case. Transfer would have been inevitable."

Golantz quickly objected, saying I had not laid the groundwork for such an answer. I told the judge I intended to do that now and asked to set up the video equipment again.

Dr. Arslanian had edited the video shot by Julio Muniz into one demonstration video. Using it as a visual aid, I carefully walked my witness through the defense's theory of transference.

"A man who had fired weapons at least ninety-four times was placed in that seat," she said. "Ninety-four times! He would have literally been reeking of gunshot residue."

Then it was time to bring in the big prop to drive Dr. Arslanian's testimony home. "Doctor, did you draw any other conclusions from your analysis of the GSR evidence that supported the theory of transference?"

"Yes, I did. Can I use my mannequin to demonstrate?"

The judge granted permission without objection from Golantz, and I wheeled Dr. Arslanian's mannequin in front of the jury. A full-body model with manipulating limbs, hands, and fingers, it was made of white plastic and was dressed in blue jeans and a dark blue collared shirt beneath a University of Florida football Windbreaker.

Handing a wooden gun and collapsing pointer to Dr. Arslanian, I went back to the lectern. "Okay, what do we have here, Doctor?"

"This is Manny, my demo mannequin. Manny, this is the jury."

There was a bit of laughter, and the lawyer even nodded hello.

"Manny's a Florida Gator fan?"

"Uh, he is today. His clothes are exact duplicates of what Mr. Elliot was wearing."

"Why do we need Manny here, Doctor?"

"Because an analysis of the SEMS tabs collected by the sheriff's forensic expert can show us why the gunshot residue on Mr. Elliot did not come from his firing of a weapon."

"The state's expert explained these procedures last week, but I'd like you to refresh us. What is a SEMS tab?"

"The GSR test is conducted with round tabs that have a sticky side that is patted on the test area to collect all the surface microscopic material. The tab then goes into a scanning electron microscope or SEMS and we see or don't see the barium, antimony, and lead."

"Okay, then do you have a demonstration for the jury?"

"Yes, I do." Dr. Arslanian extended her pointer. "Mr. Guilfoyle, the sheriff's forensic expert, took eight different coded samples from Mr. Elliot's body and clothes." She pointed to the locations of the samples. "Tab A was the top of the right hand, Tab B the top of the left. Tab C was the right sleeve of Mr. Elliot's Windbreaker, and D was the left sleeve. Then we have tabs E and F being the right and left front panels of the jacket, and G and H being the chest and torso portions of the shirt."

"Okay, what did you learn from your analysis of the tabs?"

"I learned the levels of gunshot residue greatly differed."

"How so?"

"Well, tabs A and B from Mr. Elliot's hands were where the highest levels of GSR were found. From there we get a steep drop-off—tabs C, D, E, and F with much lower levels, and no GSR reading on tabs G and H."

"What did that tell you, Doctor?"

"First, comparable readings coming from both hands indicates that the weapon was fired in a two-handed grip." She pulled the mannequin's hands together out front around the wooden gun. "But a two-handed grip would also result in higher levels on the sleeves of the jacket in particular, and the rest of the clothes as well. The tabs processed by the sheriff's department show the opposite."

"So in your expert opinion, what does it mean?"

"A compound transfer exposure. The first exposure occurred when he was placed with his hands and arms behind his back in the four-alpha car. After that, the material was on his hands and arms and some of it was transferred onto the front panels of his jacket during normal hand and arm movement."

"In your expert opinion, Doctor, is there any way he could have gotten this pattern of GSR by discharging a firearm?"

"No, there is not."

"Thank you, Doctor Arslanian. No further questions."

I returned to my seat, and Walter Elliot whispered, "The best ten thousand dollars I've ever spent."

I didn't think I'd done so bad myself. Golantz asked the judge for the afternoon break. I couldn't imagine he had much in his arsenal or he'd have gotten up and charged right after my witness.

After the jury and the judge had vacated the courtroom, I saun-tered over to the prosecutor's table. Golantz was writing out ques-tions on a legal pad. "What?" he said.

"The answer's no."

"To what question?"

"The one you were going to ask about a plea agreement."

Golantz smirked. "You're funny, Haller. So what, you've got an impressive witness. The trial's a long way from over."

"And I've got a French police captain who's going to testify to-morrow that Rilz ratted out seven of the most dangerous, vindic-tive men he's ever investigated. Two of them happened to get out of prison last year."

Golantz put his pen down. "Yeah, I talked to your Inspector Clouseau yesterday."

"So where are the Germans?" I asked.

"I told them that they had to be prepared for your building a de-fense by crapping all over the memory of their son and brother, us-ing Johan's problems in France to try to get his killer off and depicting him as a German gigolo who seduced rich men and women all over Malibu. You know what the father said?"

"No, but you'll tell me."

"He said that they'd had enough of American justice and were going back home."

I tried to retort with a clever comeback. I came up empty.

"Don't worry," Golantz said. "I'll tell them the verdict."

I went out to the hallway and saw my client in the center of a ring of reporters. He was working the big jury—public opinion.

"All this time they've concentrated on coming after me, the real killer's been out there running around free!" he said.

I was about to grab him when Cisco intercepted me first. "Come with me," he said.

We walked down the hallway away from the crowd.

"What's up, Cisco? I was wondering where you've been."

"I got the report from Florida. Do you want to hear it?"

I had told him what Elliot had told me about fronting for the so-called organization. Elliot's story had seemed sincere enough, but in the light of day, I reminded myself of a simple truism—everybody lies—and told Cisco to see what he could do about confirming it.

"Give it to me," I said.

"I used a PI in Fort Lauderdale. I wanted to go with a guy I trusted. Elliot's grandfather founded a phosphate shipping operation seventy-eight years ago; then Elliot's father worked it. Elliot didn't like getting his hands dirty and sold it a year after his father died. Newspaper articles put the sale at about thirty-two million."

"What about organized crime?"

"My guy couldn't find a whiff of it. The man's lying."

I nodded. "Okay, thanks, Cisco. I'll talk to you."

He headed off to the elevators, and I was left to stare at my client holding forth with the reporters. A slow burn started in me. "Okay, that's all, people," I said. "No further comment."

I walked Elliot down the hall, shooing away reporters. Smiling gleefully, he pumped a fist into the air. "Mick, it's in the bag. She was outstanding in there. I mean, I want to marry her!"

"Yeah, that's nice, but let's see how she does on cross. Listen, Walter, we need to talk. I had a private investigator check out your Florida story, and I just found out it was bull. You lied to me, Walter, and I told you never to lie to me."

He looked annoyed at my taking the wind out of his sails.

"Why did you lie to me, Walter? Why'd you spin that story?"

He shrugged. "The story? I read it in a script once, actually."

"But I'm your lawyer. You can tell me anything. I asked you to tell me the truth, and you lied to me. Why?"

He finally looked me in the eyes. "I knew I had to light a fire under you. Come on, Mickey. Let's not get—"

He was turning to go into the courtroom, but I grabbed him roughly by the arm. "What fire did you light?"

"You're hurting my arm."

I relaxed my grip but didn't let go. He put an "aw shucks" grin on his face. "Look," he said. "I needed you to believe I didn't do it. It was the only way to know you would bring your best game."

The smile became a look of pride. "I told you I could read people, Mick. I knew you needed something to believe in. If I was a little guilty but not guilty of the big crime, it would give you your fire back."

They say the best actors in Hollywood are on the wrong side of the camera. At that moment, I knew that was true. I knew that Elliot had killed his wife and her lover and was even proud of it.

"Where'd you get the gun?"

"I had it. Bought it under the table at a flea market in the seventies. I kept a forty-four mag at the beach house for protection."

"What really happened in that house, Walter?"

"I went out there to confront her and whoever she was with like clockwork every Monday. But when I got there, I realized it was Rilz. She'd passed him off as gay, had him to dinners and parties with us, and they probably laughed about it later. It got me mad. Enraged. You should have seen them when they saw that big gun."

I stared at him for a long moment. I'd had clients confess before, but Walter Elliot was cold to the bone. "How'd you get rid of it?"

"I had somebody with me, and she took the gun, the rubber gloves, and my first set of clothes down the beach, walked to the Pacific Coast Highway, and caught a cab."

I had a flash vision of Nina Albrecht easily unlocking the door to the deck when I couldn't figure it out. It showed a familiarity with her boss's bedroom that struck me the moment I saw it.

"I never counted on the transference. I thought I was clean and that would be the end of it." He shook his head at such a close call.

I looked down at the floor, scuffed by a million people who had trod a million miles for justice. "Did you kill Jerry Vincent?"

"No. But it was a lucky break, because I ended up with a better lawyer. Thank God for lawyers like you."

# FIFTEEN

THAT night, I sent Patrick to the movies because I wanted the house to myself. I wanted no interruption. It was not so that I could prepare for what likely would be the last day of the trial. I had the French police captain primed for that. But I was feeling bruised because I'd been used. And because I'd forgotten everybody lies.

I was feeling bruised, too, because I could not stop thinking about Rilz's father and brothers not waiting to see their dead loved one dragged through the sewers of the American justice system. I didn't feel very good about myself or the work I would perform the next day.

It was in these moments that I felt the strongest desire to find that distance again. To take the pill for the physical pain that I knew would numb me to the internal pain. It was in these moments that I realized that I had my own jury to face and that the coming verdict was guilty, that there would be no more cases after this one.

I went out to the deck. The night was cool and clear. Los Angeles spread out in a carpet of lights, each one a verdict on a dream somewhere. Some people lived the dream and some didn't. Some people cashed in their dreams a dime on the dollar, and some kept them close and as sacred as the night. I had only sins to confess.

After a while, a memory washed through me, and somehow I smiled. It was one of my last memories of my father. An antique glass ball passed down through my mother's family had been found broken beneath the Christmas tree. My mother brought me to view the damage and to give me the chance to confess. By then my father was sick and wasn't going to get better. He had moved his work—what was left of it—home to the study next to the living room. Through the open door, I heard his voice in a singsong rhyme.

*"In a pickle, take the nickel . . ."*

I knew what it meant. Even at five years old, I was my father's son in blood and the law. I refused to answer my mother's questions. I refused to incriminate myself.

Now I laughed out loud as I looked out at the city of dreams. I leaned down, elbows on the railing, and bowed my head.

"I can't do this anymore," I whispered to myself.

The song of the Lone Ranger suddenly burst from the open door behind me. I stepped inside and looked at the cell phone on the table. It said PRIVATE NUMBER. At the last moment, I took it.

"Is this Michael Haller, the lawyer?"

"Yes. Who is this?"

"This is Los Angeles police officer Randall Morris. Do you know an individual named Elaine Ross, sir?"

I felt a fist grip my guts. "Lanie? What's wrong?"

"Uh, sir, I have Miss Ross up here on Mulholland Drive, and she shouldn't be driving. In fact, she sort of passed out after she handed me your card."

Lanie Ross. She had fallen back. An arrest would put her back into the system and probably cost another stay in jail and rehab.

"Which jail are you taking her to?"

"I gotta be honest. I'm code seven in twenty minutes. If I take her down to book her, I'm looking at two more hours. If you send somebody for her, I'm willing to give her the break."

"Thank you, Officer. I'll come if you give me the address."

"You know where the overlook is above Fryman Canyon? We're right here. Make it quick."

Fryman Canyon was only a few blocks from a friend's converted garage guesthouse where Lanie lived rent free. I could get her home and walk back to retrieve her car. I left the house and drove Laurel Canyon up the hill to the top and took a left on Mulholland, then followed the serpentine road west half a mile.

My cell phone buzzed as I'd been expecting it to. "What took you so long to call, Bosch?" I said by way of a greeting.

"I've been calling, but there's no cell coverage in the canyon,"

Bosch said. "Is this some kind of test? Where the hell are you going? You called and said you were done for the night."

"I got a call. A . . . client of mine got busted on a deuce up here at the Fryman Canyon overlook. The cop's giving her a break if I drive her home."

"Who was the cop?"

"Randall Morris."

"Okay. Pull over until I can check it out."

"Pull over? I'm already here."

The overlook was on the Valley side. I took a right to turn in and drove by the sign. I didn't see Lanie's car or a police cruiser. The parking area was empty. "Damn!"

"What?" Bosch asked.

I hit the heel of my palm on the steering wheel. Morris hadn't waited. "She's not here. He took her to jail." I would now have to figure out which station Lanie had been transported to and probably spend the night arranging bail and getting her home.

I put the car in park and got out and looked around. The lights of the Valley spread out below the precipice for miles and miles.

"Bosch, I gotta go. I have to try to find—"

I saw movement to the left. I turned and saw a crouching figure coming out of the brush. He was dressed in black, and a ski mask was pulled down over his face. As he straightened, he raised a gun.

"Wait a minute," I said. "What is—"

"Drop the phone!"

I dropped it and raised my hands. "Are you with Bosch?"

The man moved quickly toward me and shoved me. I stumbled to the ground and felt him grab the back of my jacket collar. "Get up! Now!" He started pulling me up.

"Okay, I'm up." The moment I was on my feet, I was shoved forward across my car lights. "Where are we going? What is—"

I was shoved again. "You ask too many questions, lawyer."

He shoved me toward the precipice. I knew it was almost a sheer drop-off. I tried to dig my heels in, but the man shoved harder. He was going to run me off the edge into the blackness of the abyss.

"You can't—"

Suddenly there was a shot. The man yelped and fell into the brush. Then came voices and shouting.

I dove facedown into the dirt and put my hands over my head. I heard more yelling, the sound of running, vehicles roaring across the gravel. When I opened my eyes, I saw blue lights flashing.

"Counselor," a voice above me said, "you can get up now."

I craned my neck to look up. It was Bosch, his shadowed face silhouetted by the stars above him.

"You cut that one pretty close," he said.

THE man in the mask yelped in pain as they handcuffed him. "My hand! My hand is broken!"

I climbed to my feet and saw men in black Windbreakers moving about like ants on a hill. Some raid jackets said LAPD, but most had FBI across the back. Soon a helicopter came overhead and lit the clearing with a spotlight.

Bosch stepped over to the FBI agents huddling over the man in the mask. "Was he hit?" he asked.

"No. The round hit the gun," an agent said. "We're still looking for it." They pulled the man up into a standing position.

"Let's see who we've got," Bosch said.

The ski mask was unceremoniously yanked off. Bosch turned and looked back at me.

"Juror number seven," I said. "He didn't show up today, and the sheriff's department was looking for him."

Bosch turned back. "Hold him right there."

Signaling me to follow him, he walked out to my car. I got my question in first. "What just happened?"

"What happened was we just saved your life."

"I know that, but where did all these cops come from? You said you'd let people go at night. What's the FBI doing here?"

"Things were different tonight. Let's talk about juror number seven. Why didn't he show up today?"

"You should probably ask him that. All I can tell you is that this morning the judge said he got an anonymous letter saying he was a phony. And he lied about having a record."

"Why did he want to kill you?" Bosch asked.

I raised my empty hands. "I don't know. Maybe because of the story we planted. Wasn't that the plan, to draw him out?"

"I think you're holding out on me, Haller."

"You're the one holding out. What's the FBI doing here?"

"They've been in it from the start."

"Right, and you just forgot to tell me."

"I told you what you needed to know."

"Well, I need to know it all or my cooperation with you ends now. That includes being any sort of witness."

He smiled in frustration. "Come on, man, cool your jets. Don't be throwing empty threats around."

"We'll see how empty it is when I start stringing out the federal grand jury subpoena. I can argue client confidentiality all the way to the Supreme Court. Your pals in the bureau are going to wish you'd come clean when you had the chance."

Bosch thought a moment and pulled me by the arm. "All right, tough guy, come over here."

We walked to a spot in the parking area even farther from the law-enforcement anthill. Bosch started to talk.

"The bureau contacted me after the Vincent murder and said he'd been a person of interest. That's all. A person of interest. One of the lawyers whose name came up in their look at the state courts. Things he had supposedly told clients he could get done, connections he claimed to have. They invited him in as a cooperating witness, and he declined. They were increasing the pressure on him when he got hit."

"So you joined forces. Isn't that wonderful?"

"Like I said, you didn't need to know. Counselor, if it wasn't for the bureau, right now you could be lying down there at the bottom of the mountain."

I tried to accept that reality. And the reality that I had been used as a pawn from the beginning—by my client and Bosch and the FBI. Bosch signaled over an agent who was now standing nearby.

"This is Agent Armstead. He's been running the bureau's side of things, and he's got some questions for you."

"Why not?" I said. "Nobody answers mine. I might as well answer yours."

Armstead was young, with a precision military haircut. "Mr. Haller, your cooperation will be greatly appreciated. Is juror number seven the man Vincent paid the bribe to?"

I looked at Bosch with a "who is this guy?" expression.

"Man, how would I know that? I wasn't part of this thing. You want an answer to that, go ask him."

"Don't worry. We will. What were you doing here, Mr. Haller?"

"I told you people. I told Bosch. I got a call from somebody who said he was a cop. He said he had a woman I know personally up here and she was under the influence and that I could come up and drive her home and save her from getting booked on a deuce."

"We checked that name you gave me on the phone," Bosch said. "Randall Morris is on gang detail in South Bureau."

I nodded. "Yeah, well, I think it's pretty clear that it was a fake call, but he knew my friend's name, and he had my cell."

"How did he get the woman's name?" Armstead asked.

"Good question. I don't know. Go ask McSweeney."

I immediately realized I had slipped up. I wouldn't know that name unless I had been investigating juror number seven. Bosch looked at me curiously. I was saved by someone yelling from the brush, "I've got the gun!"

Bosch pointed a finger at my chest. "Stay right here."

I watched Bosch and Armstead trot over and join a few of the others as they bent down to study the found weapon under a flashlight. Then the William Tell Overture started to play behind me, and I saw my phone on the gravel, its tiny screen glowing like a beacon. I went over and took the call.

"Cisco, I gotta call you back."

"Make it quick. I've got some good stuff."

I closed the phone and watched Bosch step over to McSweeney and whisper something into his ear. He didn't wait for a response.

He just walked back toward me. I could tell even in the dim moonlight that he was excited. Armstead was following behind him.

"The gun's a Beretta Bobcat like we were looking for on Vincent," he said. "Put this together for me, Haller. If the ballistics match, why'd he want to kill you, too?"

"I don't know."

"How did he know your friend's name on the phone?"

"I don't know that either."

"Then what good are you?" Bosch asked.

It was a good question. "Look, Detective, I—"

"Don't bother, man. Why don't you just get in your car and get the hell out of here? We'll take it from here."

He started walking away, and Armstead followed. I hesitated and then called out. Bosch came back alone.

"No bull," he said impatiently. "I don't have the time."

"Okay, this is the thing," I said. "I think he was going to make it look like I jumped. Like a suicide."

Bosch considered this and then shook his head.

"You've got the case of the decade, man. You're hot. You're on TV. And you've got a kid to worry about. Suicide wouldn't sell."

I nodded. "Yes, it would."

He looked at me and said nothing, waiting for me to explain.

"I'm a recovering addict, Bosch. The story would go that I couldn't take the pressure of the case and the attention and I jumped. It makes me think that . . ."

"What?"

I pointed across the clearing toward juror number seven.

"That he and whoever he was doing this for know a lot about me. They did a deep background. They came up with my addiction and Lanie's name; then they came up with a solid plan for getting rid of me. I guess they think I know too much."

"Do you?"

Before I could answer, McSweeney started yelling. "Hey! Over there! I want to make a deal."

"My tip?" I said. "Strike while the iron's hot. Before he remembers he's entitled to a lawyer. But before you go, you owe me one answer. You were supposed to cut the surveillance down to one car for the night. But this is the whole enchilada. What changed your mind?"

Bosch signaled Armstead to go to McSweeney. "You really haven't heard, have you?"

"Heard what?"

"You get to sleep late tomorrow, Counselor. There's no trial anymore. Your client's dead. Somebody took Elliot and his girlfriend out when they came home from dinner. His electric gate wouldn't open, and when he got out to push it, somebody put a bullet in the back of his head. He hit Nina Albrecht in the car."

I took a half step back in shock.

"I got tipped from a friend at the medical examiner's and figured somebody might be cleaning the slate tonight. I figured I ought to call the team back. Lucky for you I did."

I stared right through Bosch. "Yeah," I said. "Lucky for me."

THERE was no longer a trial, but I went to court Tuesday. I took my place next to the empty seat Walter Elliot had occupied for the past two weeks. The photographers allowed in the courtroom seemed to like that empty chair. They took a lot of photos of it.

Jeffrey Golantz sat across the aisle. He was the luckiest prosecutor on earth. He had left court one day thinking he was facing a career-hobbling loss and came back the next with his perfect record intact. He had nothing to say to me as we waited for the judge.

But there was a lot of talk in the gallery. People were buzzing with news of the murders of Walter Elliot and Nina Albrecht. No one made mention of the attempt on my life. Bosch and Armstead had asked me to keep quiet so they could move slowly with their cooperating suspect. I was happy to cooperate. To a point.

Judge Stanton took the bench promptly at nine. His eyes were puffy, and he looked like he'd had very little sleep. The jury was brought in, and if any of them knew what had happened, they weren't showing it. Several checked out the empty seat beside me as they took their own.

"Ladies and gentlemen, good morning," Stanton said. "At this time, I am going to discharge you from service in this trial. The defendant was the victim of a homicide last night."

Half the jurors' mouths dropped open in unison.

"I know that to all of you this is rather shocking news," Stanton told the jurors. "Be assured that the authorities hopefully will soon bring the individual or individuals responsible to justice. You'll learn all about it when you read the paper or watch the news. I want to thank you for your service. You are excused."

We stood one last time for the jury. After they filed through the doorway, the judge thanked Golantz and me for our professional demeanor during trial and quickly adjourned court. I stood motionless for the longest time after he left the courtroom. Golantz approached me with his hand out, and without thinking, I shook it.

"No hard feelings, Mickey. You're a damn good lawyer."

*Was,* I thought. "Yeah," I said. "No hard feelings."

"Take care of yourself." He clapped me on the shoulder and pushed through the gate. I was sure there would be a throng of media out in the hall and he'd tell them that in some strange way, justice had been served. Live by the gun, die by the gun.

I gave him a good lead and then followed. The reporters were surrounding him, and I was able to hug the wall and escape notice. I went down three landings into the hallway on eleven, then walked to Judge Holder's courtroom and entered.

Michaela Gill was in the clerk's pod. I asked if I could see the judge about the Vincent files, and she picked up the phone and gave my request, then told me I could go right to her chambers.

The judge was behind her desk. "Well, Mr. Haller," she said. "It's certainly been an eventful day. Have a seat."

I sat in the familiar chair. "Thank you for seeing me, Judge."

"What can I do for you?" She started scribbling signatures on a series of documents.

"I just wanted you to know I will be resigning as counsel on the rest of the Vincent cases."

She put her pen down and looked at me. "What?"

"I'm resigning. I came back too soon or probably should have never come back at all. But I'm finished."

"That's absurd. Your defense of Mr. Elliot has been the talk of this courthouse. I watched parts of it on television. I don't think many observers would have bet against an acquittal."

I waved the compliments away.

"Anyway, it's not really why I'm here. I want you to know that I know. And soon everybody else will as well."

"What are you talking about? What do you know, Mr. Haller?"

"That you are for sale and that you tried to have me killed."

She barked out a laugh. "Is this some kind of joke?"

"No, it's no joke."

"Then, Mr. Haller, I suggest you compose yourself. If you go around this courthouse making outlandish accusations, there will be severe consequences. Maybe you're right. You're feeling the stress of coming back too soon from rehab."

I smiled. I could tell by her face she realized her mistake.

"How'd you know I was in rehab, Judge? Better yet, how did juror number seven know how to lure me from home last night? You had me backgrounded, set me up, and sent McSweeney to kill me. Last time I saw him, he was playing Let's Make a Deal with the federal government."

It hit her like a punch in the gut. I knew it wasn't going to endear me to Bosch or Armstead, but I didn't care.

"My investigator traced McSweeney," I said. "Nine years ago he was arrested for an ADW, and who was his attorney? Mitch Lester, your husband. The next year, he was popped again for fraud, and Mitch was on the case. There's the connection. It makes a nice little triangle, doesn't it? You planted the sleeper on my jury. Jerry Vincent paid you but changed his mind after the FBI came around. You couldn't run the risk that Jerry might try to deal a judge to them, so you sent McSweeney. Then, when it all turned to crap yesterday, you sent McSweeney after Elliot and Albrecht, then me. How am I doing, Judge? I miss anything so far?"

She stood up. "This is absurd. Get out of my chambers."

"The whole house is going to fall. The FBI has McSweeney. You're about to trade that black robe for an orange jumpsuit."

"Get out or I will call security and have you arrested!"

She pointed to the door. I calmly stood up. "Sure, I'll go. And I may never practice law again in this courthouse, but I'll come back to watch you prosecuted. You and your husband."

The judge stared at me, the anger in her eyes slowly changing to fear. Her arm dropped. I left her standing there.

I took the stairs all the way down. Eleven flights. At the bottom I pushed through the doors, pulled out my phone, and told Patrick to bring the car around. Then I called Bosch.

"I didn't want to wait around a year and a half while the bureau made its case. Sometimes justice can't wait, Detective."

"What did you do, Haller?"

"I had a conversation with Judge Holder—yes, I figured it out. If I were you, I'd hurry up your case and keep tabs on her. She doesn't seem like a runner, but you never know. Have a good day."

I closed the phone. It felt good to turn the tables on him, make him and the FBI do the dancing at the end of the string.

# SIXTEEN

BOSCH knocked on my door early Thursday morning. He looked like he had pulled an all-nighter. "I wake you?" he asked.

I shook my head. "I have to get my kid ready for school. What's up, Detective?"

"I thought you'd be interested in knowing where things stand."

"Sure. Let's sit out here. I don't want her hearing this."

"I don't want to sit," Bosch said. "I don't have a lot of time." He leaned his elbows down on the railing.

I changed directions and did the same thing right next to him. "I don't like to sit when I'm out here either."

"I have the same sort of view at my place," he said. "Only it's on the other side."

"I guess that makes us flip sides of the same mountain."

He turned his eyes from the view to me for a moment. "Something like that," he said.

"What's happening? I thought you'd be too angry to tell me."

"Truth is, I think the bureau moves too slowly myself. They didn't like what you did very much, but it got things rolling." Bosch straightened up and leaned back on the railing, the city behind him. "The grand jury came back with indictments last night. Holder, Lester, Carlin, McSweeney, and a supervisor in the jury office who gave them computer access. We're taking them all down this morning, so keep it under your hat."

It was nice he trusted me enough to tell me before the arrests. I thought it might be even nicer to go down to the CCB and watch them take Holder out in handcuffs. "Is it solid?" I asked. "Holder *is* a judge. You better have it nailed down."

"McSweeney gave it all up. We've got phone records, money transfers. He even taped her husband's conversations."

I nodded. "I didn't know Carlin was hooked up in this."

"He goes way back with the judge, and she used him to approach Vincent. Vincent used him to deliver the money. Then when Vincent got cold feet, Carlin got wind of it and told the judge."

"Got wind of it how? Wren Williams?"

"Yeah. We think he got close to her to keep tabs on Vincent."

"What about McSweeney? He just did what he was told?"

"McSweeney was a con man before he was a killer. I don't for a minute think we're getting the whole truth, but he says the judge explained that either Vincent went down or they all did. Besides, she promised to increase his cut."

I nodded. "So what are the indictments?"

"Conspiracy to commit murder, corruption. More down the road. McSweeney's been on four juries in seven years. Two acquittals and two hangers. Three courthouses."

I whistled. "This is going to be huge."

"Biggest one I've ever had." He glanced over his shoulder. "You've got the Sunset Strip, and I've got Universal," he said.

I heard the door open and looked back to see Hayley peeking out. "Dad? Is everything all right?"

"Everything's fine. Hayley, this is Detective Bosch. He's a policeman."

"Hello, Hayley," Bosch said. I think it was the only time I had ever seen him put a real smile on his face.

"Hi," my daughter said.

"Hay, did you eat your cereal?" I asked.

"Yes."

"Okay. Then you can watch TV until it's time to go."

She disappeared inside and closed the door.

"She's a cute kid," Bosch said.

I nodded.

"I gotta ask you a question," he said. "You sent that anonymous letter to the judge, didn't you?"

"If I say yes, am I going to become a witness?"

"No. I just want to know if you did the right thing."

Ultimately I wanted him to know. "Yeah, that was me. I didn't expect Judge Stanton to consult other judges."

"He called up the chief judge and asked her advice."

"It's gotta be what happened," I said, shaking my head. My own actions had almost brought about my own demise in the form of a three-hundred-foot dive off Mulholland. "I guess I was stupid."

"You're still standing. After today, none of them will be."

"There's that. What kind of deal did McSweeney cut?"

"No death penalty, and consideration. If everybody goes down, he'll probably get fifteen and do thirteen."

"Pretty good deal for three murders," I said.

"One murder," Bosch corrected. "He didn't kill Elliot and Albrecht. Those two didn't match up."

"What are you talking about?"

"It was a different weapon."

I was stunned silent. "Does Beverly Hills have any ideas?"

"Yeah. They're pretty sure, but they'll never make a case."

The hits kept coming one after another. "Who?"

"The family of Johan Rilz. They took care of it."

"How do they know that?"

"Lands and grooves. The bullets were nine-millimeter Parabellums. Brass jacket and casing and manufactured in Germany. BHPD took the bullet profile and matched them to a C ninety-six Mauser, also manufactured in Germany. They're thinking it's almost like somebody was sending a message."

"A message from Germany. What will happen now?"

Bosch shrugged. "I know a couple of detectives who'll get a nice trip to Germany out of it. They'll go through the motions and the due diligence. But if the hit was done right, nothing will happen."

"How'd they get the gun over here?"

"It could be done. Through Canada or *Der* Fedex if it absolutely, positively has to be there on time."

I didn't smile. I was thinking about Elliot and the equilibrium of justice. Somehow Bosch seemed to know what I was thinking.

"Remember what you said when you told me you had told Judge Holder you knew she was behind all of this?"

I shrugged. "What did I say?"

"You said sometimes justice can't wait."

"And?"

"And you were right. Sometimes it doesn't wait. In that trial, Elliot looked like he was going to walk. So somebody decided to deliver his own verdict. Back when I was riding patrol, you know what we called a killing that came down to simple street justice?"

"What?"

"The brass verdict."

I understood. We were both silent for a long moment.

"Anyway, that's all I know." Bosch pushed his weight off the railing. "I gotta go put people in jail. It's going to be a good day."

"It's funny you coming here today," I said. "Last night I decided I was going to ask you something the next time I saw you."

"Yeah? What's that?"

I thought a moment, then nodded. It was the right thing to do. "Flip sides of the same mountain . . . Do you know you look a lot like your father?"

He said nothing. He just nodded and turned to cast his gaze at the city. "When did you put that together?"

"Technically, last night when I was looking at old photos and scrapbooks with my daughter. But I think on some level I've known it for a long time. We were looking at photos of my father. They kept reminding me of somebody, and then I realized it was you. Once I saw it, it seemed obvious." I walked to the railing and looked out at the city with him.

"Most of what I know about him came from books," I said. "A lot of different cases, a lot of different women. But there are a few memories that aren't in books and are just mine. I remember coming into the office he set up at home when he got sick. There was a painting framed on the wall—a print, actually. The Garden of Earthly Delights. Weird, scary stuff for a seven-year-old . . . He held me on his lap and made me look at it and told me that it wasn't scary. That it was beautiful. He tried to teach me the painter's name. Hieronymus Bosch. Rhymes with anonymous, he told me."

I wasn't seeing the city out there. I was seeing the memory. I was quiet for a while after that. It was my half brother's turn. Eventually, he leaned his elbows down on the railing and spoke.

"I remember that house," he said. "I visited him once. Introduced myself. He was on the bed. He was dying."

"What did you say to him?"

"I just told him I'd made it through. That's all. There wasn't really anything else to say."

Like right now, I thought. What was there to say?

"You've known all these years. Why didn't you ever make contact? I have another half brother and three half sisters. They're yours, too."

Bosch gave an answer I guessed he'd been telling himself for a few decades. "I don't know. I didn't want to rock anybody's boat. Most of the time people don't like surprises. Not like this."

For a moment, I wondered what my life would be like if I had known about Bosch. Maybe I would've been a cop instead of a lawyer. "I'm quitting, you know."

"Quitting what?"

I wasn't sure why I had said it. "My job. The law. You could say the brass verdict was my last verdict."

"I quit once. It didn't take. I came back."

"We'll see."

Bosch glanced at me and then put his eyes back out on the city. It was a beautiful day with low-flying clouds, and a cold air front had compressed the smog to a thin amber band. The sun had just crested the mountains and was throwing light out on the Pacific. We could see all the way to Catalina.

"I came to the hospital that time you got shot," he said. "I wasn't sure why. I saw on the news that it was a gut shot, and I knew those could go either way. I thought maybe if they needed blood or something, I could . . . I figured we matched, you know? Anyway, there were all these reporters and cameras. I ended up leaving."

I smiled, and then I started to laugh. I couldn't help it.

"What's so funny?"

"You, a cop, volunteering to give blood to a defense attorney. I don't think they'd let you back in the clubhouse if they knew."

Now Bosch smiled. "I guess I didn't think about that."

And just like that, both our smiles disappeared and the awkwardness of being strangers returned. Eventually, Bosch checked his watch. "The warrant teams meet in twenty minutes. I gotta roll."

"Okay."

"I'll see you around, Counselor."

"I'll see you around, Detective."

He went down the steps, and I stayed where I was.

I STAYED out on the deck after that and looked out at the city as the light moved across it. Many different thoughts filtered through my head and flew off into the sky, like the clouds up there. Remotely beautiful and untouchable. Distant. I was left feeling that I would never see Bosch again. That he would have his side of the mountain and I would have mine and that's all there would be.

After a while, I heard the door open and footsteps on the deck. I felt my daughter by my side, and I put my hand on her shoulder.

"What are you doing, Dad? Are you all right?"

"I'm fine. Just looking."

"What did that policeman want?"

"Just to talk. He's a friend of mine."

We were silent a moment before she moved on. "I wish Mom had stayed with us last night," she said.

I squeezed the back of her neck. "One thing at a time, Hay. We got her to have pancakes with us, didn't we?"

She thought about it and gave me the nod. She agreed. Pancakes were a start.

"I'm going to be late if we don't go," she said. "One more time and I'll get a conduct slip."

I nodded. "Too bad. The sun's just about to hit the ocean."

"Come on, Dad. That happens every day."

"Somewhere, at least."

I went in for the keys, locked up, and we went down the steps to the garage. By the time I backed the Lincoln out and had it pointed down the hill, I could see the sun was spinning gold on the Pacific.

# The Many Ideas of
## *Michael Connelly*

FOR Michael Connelly fans, *The Brass Verdict* is a dream come true, because it features *two* of Connelly's finest characters—defense attorney Mickey Haller and LAPD detective Harry Bosch.

Harry Bosch has appeared in several Connelly books, debuting in the author's first novel, *The Black Echo,* in 1992. Mickey Haller was introduced in *The Lincoln Lawyer* (2005), which quickly became a bestseller and immediately established Haller's appeal.

Generally, Connelly tries to alternate between Harry Bosch books and stand-alone thrillers. But this time around, he decided on a hybrid of sorts. The tiniest seed for *The Brass Verdict* was sown many years ago, in an early Connelly novel called *The Black Ice* (1993). In this tale, a young Harry Bosch reminisces about having observed the funeral of his

## Vital Stats

**BORN:** Philadelphia, PA, 1956
**RESIDENCE:** Tampa, FL
**FAMILY:** Wife; one daughter
**FAVORITE AUTHORS:** Raymond Chandler, George Pelecanos, Charles Willeford, Joseph Wambaugh
**FAVORITE MUSIC:** Jazz
**WEBSITE:** www.MichaelConnelly.com

father, whom he never knew. (Bosch's mother was a prostitute who was murdered when he was a child.) Bosch stands on a hillside away from the grave site and watches the burial of famous L.A. attorney Mickey Haller, Sr. Bosch sees Haller's family, which includes several children, one of whom is Mickey Haller, Jr. And voilà—a future Connelly character was born. Mickey Haller, Jr., grows up to become Connelly's Lincoln Lawyer, so named because he works out of the back of a Lincoln Town Car.

Although it might sound like a grand scheme to have these half brothers come together in a novel years later, Connelly says it wasn't his plan. He was stumped for a new book idea and dug back into his old stories looking for a new angle to develop. He remembered he'd given Bosch a half brother, and then the ideas started to roll.

Connelly first got the idea for Mickey Haller, Jr.'s personality after attending a Los Angeles Dodgers baseball game with a group of friends. He sat next to someone he'd never met, and they got to talking.

The man was a criminal defense attorney, and Connelly asked him in which area of the county he worked. The lawyer replied, "Have case, will travel." He explained that he essentially worked out of his car because he took cases from courthouses spread throughout the county. He had a driver (a client working off legal fees, à la *The Brass Verdict*), and his car was equipped with a computer, a printer, a wireless fax, a phone, and a fold-down desktop. Connelly says, "I ended up spending more time talking to him than I did watching the game, and

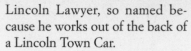

## California Sleuthin'

For some reason, California is fertile ground for writers and their sleuths. Along with Michael Connelly, some biggies include:

- Ross Macdonald: Hero Lew Archer was so closely identified with Los Angeles that he even shared the town's initials.
- Sue Grafton: Her character Kinsey Milhone lives in fictional Santa Teresa, CA.
- Raymond Chandler: Tough-talking gumshoe Philip Marlowe eloquently describes the scruffiness of 1950s Los Angeles.
- Dashiell Hammett: Sam Spade of *The Maltese Falcon* maintains a shabby office in San Francisco.

## Bosch Sightings

Mystery authors might spend their days penning dark tales of murder and mayhem, but they know how to have a little fun, too. Slipping sightings of colleagues' sleuths into their own books has become a small but growing trend—and Harry Bosch appearances are the favorite.

In *Strange Bedfellows* (2006) by Paula L. Woods, series cop Charlotte Justice spots "a curly-haired mustachioed guy" in conversation with her boss in front of LAPD headquarters. Charlotte instantly knows it's the legendary Harry Bosch. Writer Joe Gores had his fictional cops "talking to Harry Bosch down at the Hollywood station" in *Cons, Scams, and Grifts* (2002).

Perhaps the most elaborate scheme was in 2003, when Connelly and Robert Crais planted sightings of each other's heroes in their books. In *Lost Light,* Connelly had Bosch stop at a red light, and in the car next to him was Elvis Cole, Crais's private eye, in his signature yellow Corvette. In *The Last Detective,* Crais returned the favor by having Elvis Cole run into an LAPD detective acquaintance, a Vietnam veteran whom fans will easily recognize as Harry Bosch.

when I went home, I had an idea for a new character."

Creating new characters is just one example of how Connelly stays ahead of the mystery-writing pack. Another is his ability to write concisely. He attributes this skill to his background as a reporter. Journalists never get enough space to say what they want to say. "You learn to make every sentence count," he explains. "You try to have every quote carry information the reader needs. It creates a certain velocity to the story. I have tried to carry that over to my fiction."

While most writers hesitate to name the favorite book they have published, Connelly admits that he has a soft spot for his fourth book, *The Last Coyote* (1995). This is because it was the first book he wrote as a full-time writer, after he quit his day job in journalism. Additionally, Connelly says *Coyote* is really Bosch's core story. "It's about what makes him tick both as a cop and as a man."

Despite his special affection for that novel, Connelly says he hopes his best is still yet to come—and he is already at work on his next book. Fans rejoice! ∎

# BELVA PLAIN

# CROSSROADS

A NOVEL

# CHAPTER 1

IF THE gray clouds in the sky had not suddenly split apart and released an explosion of rain, Jewel Fairchild would have chosen to walk back to the train station on the shady road between two walls of green shrubs and trees. It was really amazing that such peace and quiet could exist not many miles from the crowded streets where she lived and worked. But had this entire day not been amazing?

Cassandra Wright, the owner and CEO of

Wright Glassworks, had been riding her horse and, having come too close to a fence post, had hurt her leg. She would have to stay at home for a few days—an unheard-of occurrence at the glassworks, where her dawn-to-dusk work ethic was legendary. Her efficient secretary had spent most of the day on the phone, as Mrs. Wright was directing the business from her home. When it was discovered late in the afternoon that an important paper required the CEO's signature, Jewel, who was a receptionist at the glassworks, had been summoned by her supervisor and told to hand-deliver the document to Mrs. Wright's home. Although to call the place a "home" was to understate so totally the grandeur, the dreamlike otherworldliness of it, it was almost funny.

Of course, Jewel had known that Mrs. Wright and her family wouldn't live in a hut, but she'd never seen anything like what she'd seen today. Now, as she leaned her head back on the seat of the car in which the Wright family gardener was driving her back to town, she went back over every moment of the last few hours, trying to fix them in her memory forever.

First there had been the train trip out of Wrightstown, the busy city that was named for the glassworks that gave it its reason for being. Cassandra Wright didn't live near her business—of course not. She lived out in the country, where the air was pure and the nights were quiet. A special spur off the main train line serviced the area. Jewel had walked from the station—it hadn't started raining yet—and after about fifteen minutes, she'd approached a big white house gleaming in the gray gloom of the day.

Inside the house, everything gleamed, too. The housekeeper had answered the door and led Jewel into the foyer, where she had a quick impression of glossy furniture, silk, crystal, and photographs in silver frames. Light sparkled from a chandelier above her. The housekeeper led her through a series of hallways and rooms. In the main hall, a clock chimed like music.

At first, Jewel was too overwhelmed to do more than stare. But slowly, a need started to grow inside her to touch what she was seeing. As the housekeeper hurried her along, she dug a foot into the carpet to feel the depth of the silky nap; she allowed a finger to trace the back of a richly brocaded chair. Jewel would have done anything to take all this gleaming beauty inside herself, to own it, just for one second.

There was only one object in the place that did not seem to gleam. Actually, she wasn't an object; she was a young girl, and she was sitting on a sofa reading a book. She was in the library, which was where the housekeeper had brought Jewel.

"Oh, I'm sorry to disturb you, Miss Gwen. I didn't see you there," the housekeeper said. The girl didn't seem surprised that she'd been overlooked. "This is a person from the glassworks come to give your mother a paper to sign," she went on. "I'll put her in the sitting room."

"It's all right," the girl said. "Let her stay." Her voice was light, and there was a trace of something in it that Jewel wanted to say was snooty. She looked at the girl; this was Gwendolyn Wright, Cassandra Wright's daughter—her adopted daughter. In Wrightstown, the fact that Queen Cassandra had adopted this girl made her something of a celebrity, or at the very least an object of curiosity.

It took Jewel only a second to pass judgment on her. "Miss Gwen," she decided, was dull. Her face wasn't exactly homely, but it was just like the faces that you see on the street and would not recognize if you were to see them again. Her hair was red but not a vibrant shade; it was rather washed out. Her eyes were a nondescript brown. The only bright things about her were the gold bracelet glinting on one arm and the gold wristwatch on the other. She looked down at her hands, which were folded in her lap. And there her gaze stayed, while the silence in the room grew from being merely uncomfortable to downright insulting.

*She's shy,* Jewel thought. *I guess it's up to me to help us out.* Jewel smiled her own wide, welcoming smile. She had a beautiful mouth and perfect teeth, and she knew how to use them. Unlike Gwen Wright's drab tresses, her own hair was a shimmering mass of ebony waves. Her wide blue eyes—really they were closer to violet—were fringed with thick lashes, her complexion was porcelain white, her nose was as beautiful as her mouth, and as for her figure . . . well, let's just say she'd never had any trouble attracting boys.

"What are you reading?" Jewel asked to break the ice.

"*Le Petit Prince* by Saint Exupéry."

"That's French, isn't it?"

Gwen nodded.

"Do you speak it?"

Another nod. "I'm going to Paris, you see, so I need to bone up on my French. Hence Exupéry."

Her lack of enthusiasm made Jewel annoyed. *I've never been anywhere, not even to Boston or New York. She's going to Paris, and she looks miserable about it.*

"I know I should be excited," Gwen said, seeming to read her mind. "But the thing is, I'm going with Mother."

And that did explain some of Gwen's attitude. Jewel had a brief but vivid vision of the formidable Mrs. Wright, who had been married twice but still retained her maiden name of Wright, because that was the name of her forefathers and her business. Mrs. Wright, whose every instruction was carried out with every *t* crossed and every *i* dotted. The instructions were always graciously given, but they were obeyed in record time, because no one could imagine what might happen if they weren't. Mrs. Wright was a stickler for order at home, too, as everyone knew from her servants' gossip. Jewel tried to imagine what it would be like to take a trip with a woman who insisted that her mail must be sorted in a tray by the time she walked in the door from work, whose Christmas presents were wrapped and ready to be delivered by December first. No, Cassandra Wright would not be an easy traveling companion.

"I'm sure you'll have a wonderful time," Jewel said politely. "Paris should be very . . . interesting."

"Oh yes," Gwen said. "The trip will definitely be interesting." And for the first time, Jewel thought she saw a spark of humor in the nondescript brown eyes. It vanished the next moment, when Mrs. Wright entered the room.

Jewel had seen the woman at the glassworks, of course. She

passed Jewel at the receptionist's desk every morning on her way to her own office and always threw a "Good morning, Jewel" over her shoulder as she went by. "Purposeful" was a good word for her; "regal" was another.

Seeing her here at home, Jewel thought she was still regal, but there were differences, too. First there were the dogs that bounded in at her side. One was a collie she called Missy and the other an exuberant mutt named Hank. Mrs. Wright made them both sit and then cooed "good dogs" in a tone of voice Jewel couldn't have imagined her using. Then there was the way she was dressed. At work, she wore structured pastel suits that were always in the latest style; the tweed skirt and gray turtleneck she was wearing at home had been softened by wear, and she seemed softer, too. Her graying brown hair was tucked into her signature chignon, but a few tendrils had escaped around her face. Her high cheekbones and deep-set, intelligent eyes all seemed gentler somehow.

The documents were produced and whisked away by the housekeeper to be signed at Mrs. Wright's leisure. Jewel was thanked for coming out in such inclement weather. Then it was over, and Mrs. Wright was saying, "I'll ask our gardener, Albert, to take you back to your home. It's too late for you to go back to work today. Albert is a very nice man, and we've known him forever."

As HE drove Jewel home, Albert proved to be not only a nice man, but also a talkative one. He pointed out the stable where Mrs. Wright boarded her beloved horses and told several stories about her prowess as a rider.

"You know Mrs. Wright very well," Jewel said to say something.

"I've been with the Wright family for twenty years," was the proud reply. "Mrs. Wright is the salt of the earth, let me tell you." He looked at Jewel in his rearview mirror, as if he was waiting for her to chime in. But Jewel was thinking about the beautiful white house that was receding behind them. The sense of well-being and pleasure she'd felt while she was inside it was receding, too—in spite of her efforts to recapture it. Tomorrow she would go back to her dreary job and smile and be sweet, because no one must ever know how much she hated it. And behind her in the white house was a girl who complained about going to Paris.

Albert broke into her reverie. "Did you see that mutt—Hank? Mrs. Wright took him in even though she has Missy—that's her collie that wins all the awards," he said. "Mrs. Wright can't stand to see any animal in trouble. That little stray showed up at the back door loaded with mange. Anyone but Mrs. Wright would have had the dog put down, but she told the vet to do whatever he had to to save it. That's the kind of person she is." He paused, and once again, Jewel knew that was her cue to respond.

"Mmmm," she said.

That wasn't good enough for Albert. "Look at the way Mrs. Wright took in Gwen when she was just a baby. That poor little thing was all alone in the world."

"Oh for Pete's sake!" she said. "You feel sorry for Gwen Wright? Have you looked at the bracelet she has on her arm?"

"Mrs. Wright gave it to her for her eighteenth birthday. That's my point; she's so good to Gwen . . . after everything that—" Suddenly he stopped short.

"After what?" Jewel asked, her bad mood replaced by curiosity.

"Nothing. Just . . . Mrs. Wright is a good woman, that's all."

"Because she wanted a baby and she adopted one? There's nothing wonderful about that! People do it every day."

"But Mrs. Wright didn't want this baby—she couldn't have!"

The words had slipped out; Jewel could tell. There was no way she was going to let him clam up. "What are you talking about?"

"It's not important."

"What do you know about Mrs. Wright and Gwen?"

"Nothing. That is . . . I don't really know . . ."

"But there's something you *think* you know. Something bad . . ."

"It's not bad! Just drop it!" The man was really upset now.

"Okay. But if you won't tell me, I'll start asking around. It would probably be better if I heard it from you instead of digging up a lot of old dirt."

He seemed to realize the sense of that. She saw him gather his thoughts for a second; then he plunged in. "Mrs. Wright has had her own share of troubles. Life hasn't been as easy for her as everyone thinks. Her first husband died in a car accident. . . ."

"Yes, I know about that. He was on a business trip in New Orleans. Checking on an outlet down there."

"It wasn't like that, not quite." Al paused. "The truth is, that man was no good. Most people didn't know it, because he was so friendly and likeable, but some of us who saw him up close . . . we had his number." He paused again. "Do you remember what he looked like?" he asked.

"I was only four when he died," she said.

"He had red hair. Not bright red, kind of dull. Like Gwen's."

It took Jewel a moment to grasp his meaning. *Oh my God!* she thought . . . as icy prickles ran down her spine. "Are you saying?"

"I'm saying I don't know for sure. But all the servants in the house knew that man cheated on Mrs. Wright. And the outlet in New Orleans was his idea, and it never made any money. . . ."

"So she found out about the baby after his death." Jewel's mind was reeling.

"And she took her in. Her husband's illegitimate child."

"And she never told anyone."

"Just Gwen's nursemaid, Mavis, and Mavis told me in strict confidence. Mrs. Wright wanted to protect Gwen from humiliation."

"Does Gwen know?" Jewel asked Albert. "About her father?"

"Of course not. And you can't say a word about any of this. Like I said, I'm the only one Mavis told and . . ."

She gave him an injured look. "I'm not that kind of person."

He seemed reassured. "I wouldn't want anything to hurt Gwen."

"Of course not."

"You see, she's a good kid. But she's . . . well, she's different."

*DIFFERENT.* The word kept repeating itself in Jewel's head for the rest of the ride home. *Yes, Gwen Wright is different. From me, anyway. She's eighteen, and I'm twenty-two. Her mother was a tramp who slept with a married man, and mine was a decent woman who got married and took care of five kids until she was so worn out she died. Now the tramp's daughter has everything a person could ever want, and I have to scrape by.*

"Duffy Street—is this the place?" Albert asked. She'd been so busy with her thoughts she hadn't noticed they'd reached the city.

"Yes, here. In front of the delicatessen. I live on the third floor."

"Then here you go."

"Thank you. Good night, Albert."

"Uh . . . Jewel?"

"Mum's the word, Albert. I promise."

"Well, then, good night."

Jewel got out of the gardener's car and watched as the last vestige of her visit to paradise drove off. *Now you're back in your world, Jewel,* she told herself. *Here it is in all its glory—two rooms and a kitchenette. Still, you will never forget the home where Gwen Wright lives, not until the day you die.*

There was a rocking chair in Jewel's living room, the one new piece of furniture she'd bought for herself. She sat in it now, closed her eyes, and tried to let the back-and-forth motion soothe her. But it didn't work. Not tonight. She looked around her room in the darkness. She'd been so pleased with herself when she'd moved to Wrightstown; she'd been sure she'd been moving up in the world.

Wrightstown had been built on a river, like so many New England towns were. It was because of the glassworks that the township had grown and remained vibrant while other small communities had withered away. There were jobs to be had in Wrightstown, and because of that, other smaller businesses flourished there, too. There were restaurants and movie theaters and a shiny new mall just a few miles away.

Jewel had not come from Wrightstown. Her home was farther up the river, a smaller community that had once surrounded a textile mill. Jewel's father had come there from his family's failing dairy farm. The only work he'd been able to find in the dying textile town had been with a cabinetmaker. He came home at night smelling of wood, sweat, and machine oil. Jewel couldn't remember seeing him without sawdust in his hair, not even on Sunday.

Her mother had not been as smart as her father, but she had been a beauty. It was from her ma that Jewel had gotten her spectacular eyes, mouth, and hair. As a child, Jewel had watched her mother's beauty disappear as lines brought on by stress etched themselves on her lovely face. It was money, or the lack of it, that had robbed Ma of her youth and her smile. Money made all the difference—always.

One bright day, when she was eighteen, Jewel went walking alone beyond the town. She kept on going until she reached the farm country, where cornfields bordered the road on either side. Clouds overhead clove the blue. She had heard in school the words "lapis lazuli." Was this it? And suddenly, before her eyes, Jewel saw how the ocean must look as the sky arches over it. Everything was alive, from the ocean to the growing corn, to the birds that passed high overhead, all moving things going somewhere. Somewhere!

Jewel stopped rocking. Now she was no longer eighteen, and she was going nowhere. Her life was empty, and she had no idea how to fill it. Of course, a man would be a solution, and she'd met quite a few men who were attracted to her. But she hadn't loved any of them, because they were in the same predicament she was: working hard and not having enough to show for it. And she wasn't going to risk winding up like Ma.

She got up to pull down the shade. The rain and wind were bending back a scrawny tree that was outside her window. Beyond the tree was the endless dark. She turned away. She was going to bed. One way to get rid of the pictures in her mind was to sleep.

But sleep was coming slowly. Jewel twisted and turned in the bedsheets. The pictures kept on coming. Now she was back to that wonderful house. Then she was in the car with Albert, and he was telling her about Cassandra Wright's secret. A thought joined the pictures racketing around in Jewel's brain. *I wonder what would happen if Gwen were to find out.* She tried to push the thought aside, but like the pictures, it just kept coming back.

# CHAPTER 2

THE morning after the rainstorm dawned clear and achingly beautiful. But that was not the reason why Gwen awoke and knew she couldn't stay inside. The encounter with the girl who worked at the glassworks had upset her—sent her back to a place she thought she'd left behind. It was a gray place, full of foggy emotions that could engulf her if she wasn't careful.

When Jewel Fairchild had appeared in the library, Gwen had to keep herself from gasping. *She's so beautiful!* Gwen had thought. *Like a tropical flower, with that white skin and those blue eyes and that red, perfect mouth.* And a stab of an emotion Gwen had recognized as her old nemesis, envy, had shot through her. And once again, she'd been a child of five, and it was her birthday.

She went to her closet and reached for her clothes. She was not going to remember her fifth birthday, not today, she told herself. But after a moment, it was clear that blotting it out was going to be easier said than done. That fifth birthday still seemed to encompass everything Gwen had been as a child—all her doubts and angers.

SHE had known that her party was not going to be an elaborate affair; Cassandra didn't believe in conspicuous displays, and Gwen was fine with that. But she had expected that on her special day, she would be the prettiest girl in the room. She was relying on her new dress to accomplish this feat for her—from an early age, she had known she was not pretty. But her party dress was beautiful. Gwen had chosen it herself on a trip to Wrightstown's most expensive department store. She'd been attracted by the magic of the fabric—an iridescent silvery taffeta that shimmered with different undertones. Gwen had known instantly that she wanted it. On the day of the party, she had put it on confidently, knowing that she would be prettier than all the other girls . . . until the moment that a late-comer named Carol Anne Jenkins had walked in.

Carol Anne had blond hair that fell into long shiny curls and large blue eyes. Adults loved her, and through sheer personal charisma, she managed to be popular with her peers in spite of it.

Carol Anne was wearing a pink tulle dress. "Mama made it for me," she announced proudly. "And the petticoats, too." There were three of them, liberally trimmed with ruffles. Fake pink roses tied with pink satin bows were buried among the tiers, and more roses and lace edged the bodice and the sleeves.

At that moment, Gwen knew that Carol Anne Jenkins had stolen her day. If Gwen had been asked what she was feeling, she would have said, "I'm not enough." She hated feeling that. She watched as the other girls flocked around the thief, gushing over the roses and the ruffles. Finally she couldn't stand it anymore. She inched her way through the admiring throng until she was at Carol Anne's side, then reached out and yanked one of the golden curls as hard as she could.

Carol Anne began to cry. Cassandra came rushing in, and by the time the adults had sorted out the different versions of the incident offered by the witnessing children, Gwen was already regretting what she'd done. She probably would have said she was sorry on her own if Cassandra hadn't said, "Gwen, I'm ashamed of you. Apologize to Carol Anne immediately."

All Gwen's grievances came back to her, and iron entered her soul. She raised her head to look her mother in the eye and shook her head. "No," she whispered.

Cassandra was stunned. She couldn't believe she was being de-fied. Gwen had been sent to her room while the other children were served cake and ice cream and sent quickly on their way. After they were gone, Cassandra had come upstairs to see her. With stubborn pride, Gwen had refused to explain herself. But Cassandra had seen into Gwen's mind and understood what had motivated her.

"Jealousy is a particularly ugly emotion," she'd said. "Especially for someone in your position, who has so much. Giving in to it is nothing more than self-indulgence."

But Gwen still couldn't choke out the words "I'm sorry."

There was no way to tell her mother why. Perhaps at that age she didn't know all the reasons herself. Years later, she would understand that it hadn't just been that one party where she'd felt like she was "not enough." She'd been feeling that all her life—and the person who made her feel that way was Cassandra.

GWEN had finished dressing. She was wearing her favorite outfit for early autumn—a flared corduroy skirt and a light sweater with a flannel shirt tossed over it, in case there was a nip in the air.

Obviously, she was as capable of jealousy today as she had been when she was five. And she didn't want to be. The sad part was, she knew why she was so vulnerable.

It had started when she was an infant. She couldn't remember that time, of course, but she knew that was when she'd gotten the message that she was "not enough." That her mother, the most important figure in her life, had found her lacking in some way. How she had gotten that feeling Gwen couldn't have said.

Was it the fact that her mother did not do the daily chores of caring for her, as other mothers did? It was impossible to imagine her changing a diaper or patiently feeding spoonful after spoonful of sloppy baby food into a tiny resisting mouth. Servants did such things for her and had since she herself was a child.

Gwen also understood that her mother was not one for overt gestures of affection; she did not expect Cassandra to throw her arms around her, to shower her with kisses, or to coo over her. So why did she feel that in some profound way she was a disappointment? Why did she feel that there was a barrier that sometimes descended when her mother was with her? It wasn't there all the time, but when it came, she could feel her mother withdraw in a subtle way.

She'd always known she was adopted. Cassandra had told her when she was very young. "You probably weren't old enough to understand, " Cassandra said later—Gwen was seven at the time, and they'd been talking about it. "It probably would have been better if I had waited until you were more mature. But too many people around here know about it, and I didn't want you to hear it from anyone but me." She paused. "Of course, I was sure if you had questions, you would have asked me."

*But I did have questions. I just never felt like I could ask them.*

And then, because hope springs eternal, Gwen asked her biggest question. "Why did you pick me?"

And, still clinging to hope, she waited for her mother to say, *Because I fell in love with you the second I saw you. Because I couldn't imagine my life without you.*

"I had wanted children throughout my first marriage," Cassandra said. "And after he . . . my husband . . . died, and I saw you . . . it seemed like a golden opportunity. . . ."

Her mother, who always knew what to say, was stumbling. And hope died. "But it wasn't a golden opportunity," Gwen said slowly. "You made a mistake."

Her mother gave a little gasp. "No, Gwen!"

"You thought you wanted a child, but you really didn't. It's okay, Mother. Everyone makes mistakes." She was trying to sound like a grown-up girl, but then she spoiled everything by starting to cry.

Cassandra got down on her knees to look Gwen in the eye. "Gwen, I've never regretted it!" she said. And then she added something that Gwen would ponder for years. "No matter how it started out, I am so glad I did it. Always remember that."

GWEN realized that not all her difficulties could be attributed to her mother's strange shifts in mood. From the very beginning, Gwen had been . . . unusual. Ordinary experiences could trigger ideas and fantasies in her that didn't occur to other more . . . well, usual children. A case in point had been the Face in the Window Incident.

When she was quite small, Gwen had seen her own reflection in a window. When she'd moved in a certain way, the vision of her face had vanished altogether. When she moved again, it reappeared, but it was distorted. This had brought up thoughts that were disturbing but also fascinating. She'd tried them out on her nursemaid.

"How do I know I'm real?" she asked the woman. "How do I know I'm really here?"

"What silly questions. You're a real little girl, and you're right here. Where else would you be? Now eat your lunch."

Later, Gwen overheard the nursemaid telling the cook about it. "She's an odd duck," the nursemaid said.

There were other indications of Gwen's oddness. For a while, she had become obsessed with words. "Why do we say it's a plate?" she demanded. "Why don't we call it spinach? Or a mud pie?"

"Because it's a plate; that's its name," her nursemaid had replied.

"But what if the name is wrong? Or what if words don't mean anything? What if nothing means anything?"

"Odd duck," said the nursemaid to the cook. "Just odd."

GWEN left the bedroom and walked quickly down the long hallway to the wide curving staircase. At the bottom of the stairs, she was met by undulating fur as Missy and Hank surrounded her. Having recognized her outfit as the one she wore when she was going outdoors, they tried to follow her. But Gwen held them back.

"Not this time, babies," she said. "I'd take you, but I'm going up the hill, and you know what you did the last time you came with me. I won't have you bothering my little guys, you know."

So she left the dogs behind her and walked outside.

# CHAPTER 3

THE land on which Cassandra's home sat was well maintained but not manicured. There was a long lawn in the front of the house, a row of red maples that protected it from the road, and flower beds lining the front path, in which daffodils, iris, and peonies bloomed in the spring. In back of the house, the lawn was smaller, and it gave way to the surrounding forest of the area.

Behind the back lawn, there was a hill. Halfway up it, beneath the oaks, the pines, and the thread of sunshine that seeped through the undergrowth, there was a flat stump that provided a seat where one could comfortably settle down. This was Gwen's destination—her special place where, as everyone in the house knew, she was not to be disturbed. She'd been coming here since she was a child. Sometimes she came to read. Sometimes she merely sat quietly and watched the small creatures who lived there: the squirrels that barely disturbed the silence when they buried nuts or the chipmunks that scurried in and out of their three-room "apartments." It was because of these little creatures that she would not take Missy and Hank with her to her retreat on the hill—the dogs frightened them away.

Gwen sat on the stump and prepared to enjoy the silence and the companionship of the squirrels. Instead, another memory flooded back. But this was one she welcomed. She never tired of reliving it.

IT HAD happened when she was sitting on this very stump, on this very hill—she had been six years old. A man had climbed up the hill to talk to her. His name was Walter Amburn, and Gwen would always believe that he had changed her life.

Gwen had seen him before that day. For several months, he had been coming to the house, mostly in the evenings, to escort her mother to various events. He wasn't exactly handsome. His best feature was his hair, light brown and curly, but his nose was a bit too big for good looks, and his eyes were too deep-set. But there was something about his face—something kind and humorous—that Gwen liked.

She always knew when he was coming, because Cassandra's eyes would flash in a way they never had before. Sometimes, when she was getting dressed to go out with him, she would look at herself in the mirror, and she wouldn't like the dress she had chosen or the earrings, and she would change them at the last second—a phenomenon totally out of character for one as decisive as she. Then she would have to rush down the stairs in a clatter of high heels so she would not be late when Walter arrived.

There were times when Walter and her mother did not leave the house right away, when they only had plans for dinner in a local restaurant or at the home of friends. Then Walter would take off his coat and Cassandra would lead him to the living room, where they would have drinks in front of the fireplace. The sound of them, of their laughter and talk, would echo down the halls of the house.

Gwen had been introduced to Walter during one of these interludes. But she hadn't really talked to him until the day under the trees. When he appeared there in her refuge, Gwen had looked at him, seeing the kindness in his face and the warmth in his smile. Now he was bending over so that Gwen and he were eye to eye.

"I hope I'm not intruding," he'd said gently. "Your nursemaid said I might find you here. I understand this is your special spot."

Shy, Gwen had nodded silently.

Walter had looked appreciatively at the canopy of green branches overhead. "I can see why," he'd said. "May I sit down?"

Gwen had nodded again, and he had settled himself next to her on the ground. He began talking to her, but not in the silly way that adults usually talked to children. Walter told her how the moss that carpeted the ground under them had grown, and he showed her how to tell how old a tree was. And before Gwen knew how it had happened, she was telling him about the squirrels and the chipmunks she watched.

Then she asked him why he had come to sit under her trees, because it wasn't something adults usually did.

"I thought we should get to know each other," he'd said. "Because I'm going to be in your life for a long time. I'm going to be marrying your mother. I hope that meets with your approval."

And Gwen had thought about the shine in Cassandra's eyes and the way she ran down the stairs to meet him. And she'd said, "Yes. I think that will be fine."

"Thank you," he'd said gravely. "That's a big relief to me."

IT HAD been better than fine. The advent of Walter had been the beginning of a new relationship between Gwen and Cassandra. The chill Gwen had always felt had begun to warm; the distance had been lessened. Her mother was a happier person now, and the happiness poured over everything and everyone around her.

Of course, Gwen still had her scar tissue, and there were times when she was angry—usually when she realized, once again, that she would never fit in with other youngsters her age.

"Yes, you're different," Walter said one day when they were having iced tea in his studio. Walter was an artist, very much in demand as a portrait painter. Gwen thought it was because he always seemed to find whatever it was that made his subject special, and somehow he managed to put that on the canvas. "I know being different isn't fun now, but you have to look at the bigger picture. Most of the world's great ones were odd ducks, as you call yourself. They couldn't fit in, so they had to discover something else to get them through, some great passion. They became our geniuses, our poets and composers, our philosophers and scientists. I believe passion is what brings joy." He'd paused for a second, and then he'd smiled his warm smile. "In any event, that's what this odd duck keeps telling himself."

When Walter said things like that to Gwen, it didn't make up for snubs on the playground or other children giggling when she said something they thought was weird. But it helped.

THERE was a big bay window in the back of the living room. Cassandra liked to take her early morning coffee there, where she could watch the hill behind the house as it slowly came alive. So she had seen Gwen make her solitary journey to the place beneath the trees that had been her refuge since she was a child.

*And in so many ways she still is a child. She is so vulnerable. She will let herself be intimidated by that Jewel Fairchild from the glassworks. She felt uncomfortable around her, because Jewel is pretty and has confidence. The kind of mindless confidence Gwen will never have, because she's too smart and sensitive. Even when she was ten months old, the first time I saw her . . .*

Cassandra turned away from the bay window. She didn't like to live in the past, but there were times when her mind went back. Back to her first marriage and her first husband. Back to the carnage she could still imagine after all these years . . . and to the opening sentence of the headline story in a New Orleans newspaper: *After a horrendous collision between a car and a truck, a man and a woman are dead tonight.*

The news had flown quickly from Louisiana to Cassandra Wright. Her husband was dead. He'd been in New Orleans troubleshooting for the outlet he'd opened there, and at the time of the accident, he'd been giving one of the outlet employees a lift home.

Her husband's name was Bradford Curtis Greeley. Cassandra had married him for a variety of reasons. Several of them, she had realized later, had not been good ones. But she was a woman who stood by her commitments, and at the time of his death, they had been together for ten years.

Originally she had married him because she loved him. But love for her had not been a simple thing. From the time she had reached puberty, her father had warned her against fortune hunters.

"You will be prey to them, Cassie," he'd said. "Your private assets are considerable—but it is the glassworks that is the rich prize. There are many unscrupulous men who would do anything to gain control of it."

Father's warnings about fortune hunters had borne fruit. He hadn't trusted Bradford—even though he had hired the young man to head up the woefully dated sales division at Wright Glassworks. "A bit too slick for my taste," he'd said of his new employee. "A bit too much of the snake-oil salesman."

But sales were down, and Bradford, who had a marketing degree from Harvard, had been highly recommended by several of Father's friends. Father had signed him on—reluctantly. And Cassandra had fallen in love.

Cassandra sipped her coffee and leaned back in her chair.

*How could I have loved Bradford? Yes, he was interesting. But he'd mentioned a trust fund—I thought a man who was independently wealthy wouldn't need to marry me for the glassworks. I fell in love*

*with Bradford because I thought he was interested in me for myself.
And because after Father was gone, there was no one to run the glassworks, and I thought I needed a man to do it.*

Maybe not the best reasons in the world, but she'd built a marriage on them. And then Bradford had died. As Cassandra was
preparing to fly to Louisiana to bring the body home, she'd had a
phone call from a lawyer she'd never heard of whose office was in
New Orleans. The man said he had handled Brad's affairs in New
Orleans. They had scheduled a meeting for the next day.

And there she was, dressed in mournful black, sitting across a
desk from a middle-aged lawyer, whose voice was low and whose
expression was very kind.

"You know," he said, "your husband came to this city often."

"Yes, on business." There was something about the way the man
was looking at her that made her uncomfortable.

There followed a silence that she had never forgotten. Speaking
with obvious difficulty, the lawyer, Mr. Robichaud, said, "Life is not
always what we expect, is it? Every one of us has to learn that in
some way, sooner or later."

She drew in a breath. "Please, Mr. Robichaud, tell me what it is
that I have not expected."

"That woman—the woman in the car—she was not . . ." He
trailed off, his face reddening. And then she saw it. She knew.

The lawyer continued. "She worked in the bar at the hotel where
he stayed . . . and she . . ." He was stumbling, trying to make this
easier for Cassandra, but he knew he was making it worse.

"Tell me," Cassandra commanded.

And the man with the kind expression looked to the floor. "Your
husband had a child. A baby girl. Ten months old now."

When he looked up at her, their eyes met.

"A child?" She couldn't get her brain to take it in. She had
wanted to have children; he always said he didn't. "A baby? His?"

"Yes," said the lawyer. "The DNA . . . in anticipation of your arrival, I had it done. . . . I'm afraid there's no mistake."

*I've known—deep down—for a long time that Bradford did*

*marry me for the business, just the way Father said someone would. But I told myself he wanted me, too. I backed him. When there was criticism of his policies at the glassworks, I refused to listen. I told the men who had been with my father for decades that my husband was in charge. I said they must obey him. And this is how he repaid me.*

Then the lawyer had said, "Your husband's child has no one. None of our local agencies have been able to trace her mother's people . . . and as for your husband . . . I'm afraid you are as close to family as this baby has."

How did a person walk away from a responsibility like that? Cassandra hadn't planned to see the baby, but she had to admit that a part of her was curious. In a sad, angry way that she wasn't proud of, she wanted to see the baby her husband—who wouldn't have a baby with her—had had with someone else.

"I have some time tomorrow," she told the lawyer.

"I'll drive you to her home."

SHE wasn't a pretty child. She was small for her age, and her features were weak—a pinched little nose and thin lips. She hadn't gotten those from Bradford. And those brown eyes weren't his—the unknown woman was responsible for them, too. But there was no question that she was her father's daughter. She had his square jaw, his chin, and, most important, that unmistakable red-brown hair. Cassandra just stood there, looking.

The child was very still. "Is she always this quiet?" Cassandra asked the woman who had been hired to help care for the baby since she was born.

"She's good as gold," said the woman, looking down at the child who was sitting in her lap. The little girl was afraid, that was clear, but she wasn't cowering. She stared at Cassandra from behind the nanny's fleshy arm.

*Good for her!* The thought flashed through Cassandra's mind. *She doesn't want to show she's afraid.*

"Lotta has been staying here in the house with the baby. She's been paid through to the end of the month," the lawyer said. "After that . . ." He let the sentence dangle.

*The poor little thing has been through so much already. And if someone doesn't do something for her . . . But there is that red hair . . . his red hair . . . Do I want to see it every day of my life?*

"What will happen to her?" Cassandra asked.

"If you don't intervene? The state will take her."

"And they'll find parents for her. A good family. Right?"

"They'll try. But she's ten months old, and most people want to adopt an infant. It's more than likely she'll wind up in foster care."

So there they were. A man and a woman had had some pleasure, and the result was a human being who didn't ask to be born, but she had been, anyway. She had a right to grow and find her place in the world. And there was no one to help her except Cassie Wright.

MR. ROBICHAUD said he'd take care of the adoption. The only thing left to do was shut down the little girl's life in New Orleans. But that was a revelation. It seemed that the house in which she lived, the nanny who cared for her, and the bank account that had been opened in her name had all been charged to Wright Glassworks. *Clearly, I'll have to call for an audit of the company now that Bradford is gone,* Cassie thought. It was her first inkling of what was to come.

Cassandra arrived in Wrightsville with the solemn-eyed baby she had named Gwendolyn, and she hired a nursemaid to take care of her. And if the child was frightened or unhappy she didn't give any indication of it. She ate her food, she took her naps, and she never cried herself to sleep at night. But she didn't smile, either.

Meanwhile, Cassandra was facing disaster as one by one, the heads of departments at Wright Glassworks came to report to her.

"I'm afraid we're behind the rest of the industry when it comes to research and development," said one of the managers. "Mr. Greeley put more of an emphasis on selling than production. . . ."

"We're pretty much shut out of the fiber-optic field," said her father's trusted vice president. "I felt we ought to get into it, but Mr. Greeley didn't agree. Now it's too late."

"He said our high-end glassware was the jewel in our crown, but that is not where our money is made."

And then came reports that sent ice water down Cassie's veins.

"I tried to warn your husband that we were overextended. . . ."

"I'm afraid we haven't paid the taxes. . . ."

"We're late with the bank loans. . . ."

"Good God, what a mess," said the outside accountant Cassandra finally brought in to try to make some sense out of the books that seemed to be bleeding with red ink. "Your best bet is to declare bankruptcy and get out now."

*I'm going to be the one who loses Wright Glassworks? My family's company is going to go under on my watch? No! Never!*

So she started fighting. It took her three years. During those years, there were times when she was exhausted and frightened and she'd see his child with his red hair playing in her playpen or sitting in her high chair. And Cassie would have to turn away. She'd feel herself pulling back emotionally from Gwen; she couldn't help it. All she could do was hope that the little girl didn't sense it.

But she had turned the business around. Wright Glassworks had become a major provider of the specialized polymer products used in biotechnology. They were a top producer of high-performance glass for computers. On the retail side, their handcrafted, one-of-a-kind glassware was still the jewel in their crown, but a much more durable and reasonably priced line of tableware went on the store shelves.

And Cassandra Wright became the woman she now was. A formidable woman, some said. A woman whose slightest command was followed instantly. A woman who had survived fear and doubt and betrayal. And for a long time, she was a woman who thought she was going to spend the rest of her life without a man.

THERE was a footstep behind Cassandra, one she knew very well. She started to turn away from the window but was caught by a kiss on the side of her neck. "Hi," she said.

"Good morning," Walter said. Walter, her husband. And, oh, how good that word sounded—even after all these years.

"Gwen's gone off to her Never Never Land?" Walter asked as he moved to the sideboard to pour himself a cup of coffee.

"She ran out there without any breakfast, not even a piece of toast. I do wish—" She stopped short.

Walter laced the coffee liberally with cream and sugar. "She'll be all right, you know," he said with a smile.

"You think so? Look at the choices she's made! She's so bright; she got into Yale on early admission, and instead she's going to a little local college."

"She can always transfer if she wants," Walter said.

"That's just it—she doesn't know what she wants! She doesn't know her own worth. Do you know why she's up in her Never Never Land, as you call it? Because yesterday that ridiculous Jewel Fairchild came here on an errand, and she ran into Gwen in the library. By the time I got there, Gwen was wilting in front of her just because the girl is pretty in a cheap way and she—"

"Excuse me, who is Jewel Fairchild?"

"The receptionist at the glassworks! You met her at the company Christmas party last year. She was the one who started everyone singing the carols."

"Oh yes. She is very pretty."

"She's breathtaking. And Gwen is worth ten of her."

"Gwen will figure that out eventually."

"I'm not so sure. In the beginning," she said softly, "when I first brought her home, it was a bad time. . . . I wasn't always . . ."

"The perfect mother? I wonder how many women are."

"But Gwen deserved better. And now I don't know how to . . . well, to fix it."

"I think you know how to fix it," he said.

"I should tell Gwen about her father."

"She'd be able to understand a lot of things she can't now—"

"I know." She cut him off. "You've told me all that."

"Yes," he said gently. "Repeatedly."

She drew in a deep breath. "I'm sorry for snapping. The truth is, I know I have to tell Gwen—all of it. I've decided I'll do it when we're in Paris. It'll just be the two of us—no interruptions." She paused. "All those years when I kept it from her—the truth about her father—I was trying to do what was best for her."

"I know."

"As long as she's happy, I really don't care about anything else."

But that wasn't altogether true. There was a picture in Cassandra's mind that was too private even to share with Walter—a picture of Gwen taking her place someday as the owner of the glassworks. She could see Gwen as the mistress of this house, see her following the path that the Wrights had laid out for their own for generations. With her fine mind, Gwen would be a worthy heir to follow Father and Grandfather. If only Gwen could just . . .

"I want Gwen to believe in herself," she cried. "Is that wrong?"

"Did you believe in yourself when you were her age?"

"No. And I paid for that."

"And look at you now," he said.

She knew what he was saying. Gwen would have to find her own way, as everyone does. She would make her own mistakes, no matter how much her mother wanted to spare her. And yet . . . Cassandra looked out the window, up at the hill where her smart, sensitive, insecure, shy daughter was hiding.

"Why didn't I ask them to send my secretary out here with those papers instead of Jewel?" She let out a sigh of frustration. "That darned Jewel Fairchild."

# CHAPTER 4

THE Algonquin Mall was the pride and joy of Wrightstown. All the expensive shops could be found there. And it was to the Algonquin Mall that Jewel went every other Saturday to treat herself to a manicure. While her nails were drying, she liked to look through a weekly local magazine called the *Wrightstown Gazette.* It listed all the events that were going on in the area. This week the society editor had decided that Cassandra Wright's upcoming trip to Paris with her daughter was newsworthy.

Jewel asked the nail tech if she could take the magazine with her, and when she passed the food court, she bought herself a cup of coffee and settled down to read.

"I'm looking forward to this adventure with my daughter," Mrs. Wright was quoted as saying. "I went to France with my father when I was Gwen's age. It was a bonding time for both of us, and it gave us cherished memories to share."

*Well, that's interesting, because I had a bonding experience with my father when I was Gwen's age. We watched my mother die together.* Jewel threw the magazine down. *That's enough!* she told herself. *You've got to stop thinking about Gwen and Cassandra Wright.*

Jewel stood up, tossed the magazine and her Styrofoam coffee cup into a trash barrel, left the food court, and started walking fast. She was headed toward the one place where she knew she could jolt herself out of her funk—a dress shop named Sofia's. This store, owned by a stylish émigré from Milan, was the most expensive shop in Wrightstown. And it was Jewel's favorite. Of course, it was ridiculous for her to even walk in the door, because there was nothing in the place she could afford—the smallest silk scarf would have cost two weeks of her salary.

But there was a salesgirl who worked in the store on the weekends who had become a friend. Edie was about the same age as Jewel, and she understood what it was like to be broke and pretty and hungry to dress like a movie or TV star. So if there weren't any customers, Edie would let Jewel try on Sofia's most gorgeous selections. An early Saturday morning visit to Sofia's was the best antidote Jewel knew for depression.

But as Jewel walked into the shop, Edie hurried up and whispered, "Not today. Sofia is here. We've got a VIP in the store, and she's waiting on her personally."

And somehow Jewel knew even before she looked in the direction where Edie was pointing who the VIP was.

"I think you'll be happy with the blue, Miss Wright," Sofia said as she closed a glossy box with the store's logo on the top.

"Thank you for suggesting it. I wouldn't have picked it out myself," Gwen said. "I'm afraid I'm not much for shopping, but Mother wanted me to have new clothes to wear on our trip." A stack of additional glossy boxes sitting on the counter next to the cash register bore testimony to a big spree.

Jewel looked from the bags and boxes to Gwen's unhappy face, and the anger she'd been trying so hard to shake started boiling inside her. *I come into this store to pretend for a few minutes that I can afford more than discount outlets. This morning I didn't even get to do that because this spoiled brat was buying out the place.*

She had to get out of the store before she said something she would regret. She started for the door, and she would have made it if a soft, slightly snooty voice hadn't called out, "Jewel. Hello." And she had to turn and give Gwen Wright a big, friendly smile.

GWEN hadn't wanted to call out to Jewel; she'd done it because she felt she had to. It seemed to her that every time she turned around these days, she was tripping over Jewel Fairchild. And every time Gwen saw her, she looked prettier than she had before.

*I'm jealous of her, plain and simple,* Gwen thought. *And I should be ashamed of myself.*

And that was why she heard herself call out to Jewel. And when Jewel turned and smiled her big wide smile, instead of giving in to the green-eyed monster that was telling her to just get away from Jewel, Gwen invited her to have lunch. And Jewel accepted.

YEARS later, when she looked back on that Saturday lunch with Gwen, Jewel would think that what had taken place was inevitable. It was as if fate had stoked the flames of her anger until the only thing that could happen did. And she could trace everything else—the good and the bad of her life—back to that meal. It had been a true crossroads for her.

The Villa Tuscany prided itself on its authentic northern Italian cuisine and its pricey menu. Gwen had suggested it to Jewel when they left Sofia's. "I've eaten there with Mother," she said. "I'm afraid I don't know any other restaurants in the mall."

"Villa Tuscany will be great," Jewel said. And the anger grew.

The final straw came when they were seated. Gwen ordered a salad. Jewel had decided on the lobster ravioli, which sounded very exotic. But as she was about to order, she saw the price. "Oh, it's so expensive," she'd blurted out.

"Please, have whatever you want," Gwen said with a wave of her hand. It was that casual, dismissive gesture that did it. Suddenly Jewel knew the pasta that cost thirty dollars a serving was going to choke her. She asked for a salad. After they'd ordered and Gwen had nothing to say—as usual—she started talking about families.

She told a few anecdotes about her own clan. She was a good storyteller, and she could make a tale of five children all getting the flu at the same time sound very funny. From talking about the whole family, it was a natural progression to her father.

"My pop was a hard worker," she said. "Not as successful as your father, of course, but then he never finished college."

Later, she would swear that the fatal words just slipped out. But no matter what her intentions, the effect on Gwen was immediate.

"My father?" she repeated. "I don't have a father. Walter is my stepfather."

And this was where all Jewel's later denials would break down. Because at that moment, as Gwen was staring at her, all she had to do was laugh a little and say, *Oh, of course!* Stepfather *was what I meant to say.* Instead she said, "Yes, I know Mr. Amburn is your stepfather. I was talking about your birth father."

The effect on Gwen this time was electric. "No one knows who he was. When Mother adopted me, the files were closed."

There was still time to back off and to say something soothing and reassuring. What Jewel said was "Oh." One syllable. Loaded with all the cynicism she could muster. And then she added, "Well, I'm sure if that's what your mother told you, it must be true." But she might as well have been saying, "Your mother is a liar."

"You don't believe that," Gwen said. "You know something."

Now the game was easy. "It's just . . ." Jewel stammered for effect. "Look, I'm sorry I ever said anything. Why don't we change the subject?"

She let Gwen beg, cajole, and demand for another three minutes before she finally laid out the whole sordid story of the womanizing husband and the mistress in New Orleans. Just for good measure, she mentioned twice the fact that Bradford Greeley's hair was a distinctive shade of red-brown. And she waited for it to sink in.

*Now who's so high and mighty?* But as she looked across the table at Gwen, she was a little surprised. The only sign of distress was a face that had gone very white.

THERE was a look of triumph on Jewel's face. Gwen caught it even as she was trying to absorb the blow Jewel had just delivered.

*She's enjoying this,* Gwen thought. *No matter how much she says she's sorry, this wasn't an accident. She wanted to tell me this.*

"Are you all right?" Jewel asked.

"Oh yes," Gwen said, and she smiled brightly. "I'm not going to say that what you've just told me isn't a surprise. Obviously, I hadn't heard it before. But I have always known that I was adopted. So it's not a total shock."

*And I'll be damned if I'll let you see me cry. I'm still my mother's daughter—in this if nothing else.*

Gwen would never remember how she got through the rest of her lunch with Jewel, but somehow she'd done it without breaking down. She waited until she was home; then she raced out to the flat stump under the oak trees and sat down in the place where she'd come to cry her heart out so many times before. But once she was there, she stayed dry-eyed. Thoughts raced through her aching mind. And they always came back to the same person—her mother.

*Why didn't she tell me about my father? Because she didn't want to dwell on something that was painful? I want to ask her, but I don't have the courage.*

*So next week we'll go to Paris together, and I won't say a word.
I'll be a good dutiful daughter who never questions her mother.*
And she still couldn't cry.

"WE MUST remember," Cassandra said, "that the fork goes in the left hand." They were sitting in one of the cafés that seemed to be in endless supply in Paris. It was one of Cassandra's favorites.

"What difference does it make how you hold your fork?" Gwen mumbled. "It's a lot of nonsense, all this stuff about manners and ceremonies!" She slouched low in her chair.

"It can be, but when you think carefully, you see it's not *all* nonsense. Manners keep things in order; they oil the wheels."

Cassandra watched Gwen slouch down until she looked like she was going to slide onto the floor. Where were the days when her daughter, eager to please, sat straight and tall at the table, as she she'd been taught? *I'm trying to understand her, but I just can't,* Cassandra thought. *Ever since we got to Paris, she's been sullen and rude.*

At that second, Gwen looked up and there was something in her eyes, something that was almost like a plea. Cassandra sighed.

She made herself smile at her daughter, who was now picking at her éclair. "I bought you a little present," she said cheerfully as she reached into the bag she'd been carrying and pulled out a book. "I thought since we're going to be seeing the Petit Trianon at Versailles, we should read up on Madame de Pompadour. Most people think of Marie Antoinette when they think of the Petit Trianon, but it was actually de Pompadour who inspired it, when she was the mistress of Louis the Fifteenth."

"Thanks, I'll pass," Gwen broke in.

"We wouldn't have to read the entire book, just skim it—"

Suddenly the slumping figure across the table sat up, her eyes glaring. "I'm not interested in reading about Louis the Fifteenth's mistress."

"She was fascinating, a courtesan in the grand tradition—"

"I don't want to hear about kept women or great courtesans or any other euphemism you've got for them. I don't want to hear about their illegitimate children. Or, if you want to be vulgar—their bastards. It hits a little too close to home for me. I should think you'd feel the same way."

"What on earth are you—"

"My mother! She was my father's mistress, right? And my father was your husband. And I'm his . . . How should we say it? Love child?"

And there it was. The secret Cassandra had kept at so much cost for so many years. The secret that was hers and hers alone to tell.

"Who told you?" she heard herself ask through the mists of shock and rage.

"What difference does it make? At least someone finally did. You've been lying to me for my whole life."

It was the disgust in Gwen's voice that got to her. She wanted to tell her daughter to drop that tone instantly. She wanted to demand an apology. But Gwen was right. Partially right.

"It was a complicated situation, Gwen, and I—"

"Other people knew about it! Didn't you realize someone would tell me someday? Did you think about what that was going to be like for me? To sit at lunch with my mother's receptionist and have her tell me what I should have known already?"

*It was Jewel Fairchild!* For some reason, Cassandra wasn't surprised. "I did what I thought was best . . ." she started to say.

"You did what was easiest for you. You weren't thinking of me."

"Gwen, if you'll let me explain—"

"I don't want to hear it. I don't want to hear that you lied to me for my own good."

Later, when Cassandra was full of regret, she would realize that Gwen had touched all her most vulnerable points—her dislike of being wrong, her pride, and most of all her sense of herself as a decent person. No one had ever attacked her like this. No one had ever called her a liar. When she looked across the table, all she could see was that red-brown hair. And something inside her snapped.

"Perhaps you're right," she said in a frigid voice. "Perhaps I didn't want to remember that I had the bad judgment to choose an adulterer who married me for my business and my money, then proceeded to destroy the first and squander the second on a barmaid he picked up while he was slumming. Perhaps I was embarrassed to admit to you just how arrogant and shallow he was. However, if you'd like all the squalid details, I'll do my best to oblige you."

"You hated him." Gwen shot the accusation across the table.

"Do you blame me?"

That was when Gwen started to sob. And then she started to run.

GWEN ran through the streets of Paris until she reached their hotel. Then she ran through the lobby and into the elevator, and into her room in the suite she shared with her mother. And she kept on crying. *I knew I shouldn't have told her I know about my father.*

Her mother had entered the other room—Had she run through the streets? No, Cassandra would have found a taxi—and now she was opening the door that separated the two bedrooms. "Gwen, I shouldn't have said all that." Cassandra was searching for words. "Your father was very charming . . . and he could be witty . . . people liked him . . ."

"And you hated him."

"Hate is a strong word," she said.

*But it was what you felt. You still do. When I did something that reminded you of him, did you hate me?*

"It doesn't matter what your father was," her mother went on. "That has nothing to do with who you are."

*But it does, because I am part of him. And I am part of the barmaid, too. I had a right to know about them years ago.*

And her mother seemed to be thinking the same thing, because she said, "This is not the way I wanted you to find out. I was going to tell you myself, while we were here in Paris." Cassandra was trying to regain control now, and Gwen didn't stop her. "I think perhaps we should put it aside for now and talk about it again when we are less . . . heated."

*That means we never will,* Gwen thought. But because they were civilized, and because Cassandra was a Wright, and Gwen—in spite of everything—was her daughter, they put it aside. They patched up their—what should it be called? Quarrel? Gwen had a vision of a piece of fragile silk cloth, thin as a membrane, being stretched until it ripped, and then it was darned. The darning thread would always show; there would always be wrinkles where the fabric had been pulled together to mend the tear—but it was patched up.

ON THE plane going home, Cassandra said, "I'm going to fire Jewel Fairchild. I just wanted you to know."

Jewel's beautiful face with the ruby red lips and the extraordinary blue eyes floated in front of Gwen, and in those eyes she saw once again the little gleam of triumph as Jewel told Gwen the devastating news. For a moment, Gwen wanted to cheer her mother on. But then she looked at Cassandra sitting next to her, serene in her conviction that punishing Jewel would make everything all right.

"Why do you want to do that?" she demanded. "All Jewel did was tell me the truth."

There was a certain kind of tear that could never be patched up. Not really.

## CHAPTER 5

PAST Times ("We sell gently used vintage couture," said the ad in the phone book) was located in a small shopping center about a quarter mile north of the Algonquin Mall. The rent in the Plaza Shopping Center wasn't as high as it was in the Algonquin, but it was close enough to attract the overflow from its fancier neighbor. At least that was what Past Times's owner, Patsy Allen, believed.

"We appeal to the woman who isn't impressed by the trendy clothes at Sofia," she liked to say. "She leaves the Algonquin Mall unsatisfied, and here we are, practically next door, ready to show her the unique classic pieces she's been craving."

Jewel could still remember the day, six months ago, when her supervisor at Wright Glassworks had told her she was fired. The order had come from Mrs. Wright personally—it was the first thing she had done when she came back from her vacation in Paris. Jewel's punishment for a few seconds of satisfaction had been the loss of her weekly paycheck, followed by three months of panic while she tried to find work and her meager savings ran out.

By the time she'd landed the job as salesgirl at Past Times, her landlord was threatening to evict her. So even though the pay was less than she'd made at the glassworks, and she had to spend eight hours a day on her feet, she wasn't going to make waves. No, sir.

"Now, this one is absolutely divine!" Patsy said as she pulled a white lace dress out of the tissue paper in which it had been lovingly packed. She'd just come back from a buying trip, and she liked to show Jewel her "finds."

Jewel nodded reverently and said, "I love the bolero jacket. You're amazing, the way you uncover these treasures."

Privately, she thought she wouldn't be caught dead in a dress that looked like something your grandmother would wear.

"Whoo, it's warm!" Patsy said. It was going to be a scorcher of a day, and they were unpacking the clothes in the back workroom, where the air-conditioning did not penetrate. "Let's go out front for a minute and sit." She started out of the workroom. "Don't bring the white lace out," she said over her shoulder. "Hang it here in the back. We'll show it when we have the right buyer."

It took her a few seconds to find one of the special padded hangers they used for their fragile clothes, and by the time Jewel left the workroom, Patsy was already perched on one of the stools next to the counter in front of the cash register. She'd been leafing through the *Wrightstown Gazette,* and now she handed it to Jewel.

"I'd kill to be invited to that party," she said as she indicated the lead story on the page. "I'd wear the Armani—you know, the purple satin from the spring collection in '82—and I swear, it wouldn't take me more than twenty minutes to have all those fancy women dying to come here to do their shopping. . . ."

But Jewel had stopped listening. Because there was a picture accompanying the magazine story, and Jewel had recognized the subject. It was Gwen Wright, looking as dull as ever. She began skimming the story, which was all about the party Cassandra Wright was throwing for her daughter's birthday.

The party was scheduled for that evening, and, according to the newspaper, it was going to be huge, with tents on the front lawn and a lighting system installed especially for the occasion. The governor had been invited, and he had accepted, as had two state senators—and, Jewel had no doubt, all the eligible young men Cassandra Wright had rounded up to meet her daughter. That was the way the parents of rich girls made sure their daughters stayed rich—by introducing them to the sons of the rich. No matter how many women became lawyers or doctors or heads of companies, the best bet for a girl was still to marry a rich man.

ACCORDING to the thermometer, it was ninety degrees in the shade. Gwen looked out through the kitchen window, where a man was hanging electrified lanterns on the new posts that had just been installed between the house and the hill. Along with the lanterns, there was a large white tent at one end of the back lawn and round tables covered with white cloths dotting the other end.

Gwen was wondering, as she often did, what someone who wasn't a part of her social world—say, someone like the young workman who was stringing up lights—might be thinking about all these elaborate preparations.

He was interesting-looking rather than classically handsome, she decided. His dark hair was a little too long, so it kept falling in his eyes and he had to push it aside. His features were strong, and his eyes were brown. Gwen thought they looked light, almost hazel. But that could have been a trick of the sunlight. He moved easily— the way people who do physical jobs tend to move—and there was a surety in the way he worked. He knew what he was doing.

Right now, he had stooped to pick up a bottle of water, but apparently finding it empty, had laid it down again on the grass. Gwen scanned the lawn. The workmen who had just finished putting up the tent had taken a break for lunch, and the place was deserted. Wouldn't it be nice to give the young man with the unruly hair some of the lemonade that she had just taken out of the refrigerator? She filled a small pitcher, placed it on a tray with a glass, and went outside with it.

"I thought you must be thirsty in this heat," she said.

"Oh, this is so nice of you!" His eyes *were* hazel; it hadn't been the sunshine.

She saw that he was slightly unsure whether he ought to stand up in the blazing sun while he drank or move under the trees, where there were lacy iron chairs in the shade just a few feet away. Gwen walked over to them and so did he. But then after they'd both sat down, neither one of them seemed to know what to say. The only thoughts that came to her mind were the kind of shallow questions people asked at social gatherings when they didn't care about the answers. She didn't want him to think she was like that.

"Do you live here in town?" she finally asked.

"I do now. I was planning to go to New York to work with a cousin, but I've changed my mind."

"It would've been nice to work with your cousin, wouldn't it?"

*Shallow,* she thought. *Shallow chitchat.* But he looked like he was considering the question seriously.

"Well, that depends. We had a falling out. He put a big dent in somebody's car in a parking lot, and I told him to leave a note with his name and telephone number, but he wouldn't do it. He has a head for business, you see, and thank goodness, I really have not. At least for that kind of business. Anyway, now that I'm through with school, this is better than doing nothing."

"What school?"

"Trade school. What about you?"

"It's vacation time. In the fall, I'll be going to the college here in town to learn how to teach nursery school."

"Didn't I hear somewhere that you were going to a big place, some Ivy League university?"

*It just shows how people talk, especially in this town.*

"I was accepted at Yale."

"You don't want to go there?"

"No, I don't," she said firmly.

"That's unusual. Most people would give their eyeteeth for a chance like that."

"Would you?"

"Well, I had a chance, but I didn't take it. I had a partial scholarship. Not to an Ivy League university—it was in Chicago."

"So why didn't you take it?"

"Because I like what I'm doing. If it weren't for electricians—for power—we'd be stuck in the seventeenth century. We can thank Ben Franklin for what we've got. Without his tricks with lightning, we'd have no cars, no vacuum cleaners, and the dentist wouldn't be able to clean your teeth properly." He laughed.

He had a lively smile. It filled his face and crinkled around his hazel eyes, eyes that now were regarding her with frank curiosity.

"I would have imagined you differently, Gwen, if the subject had ever come up."

"How differently? And how do you know my name is Gwen?"

"The newspaper. There was an article about the party tonight, and your name was in it." He looked down at his glass for a second, then looked up. "And I guess I thought you'd be a young version of Mrs. Wright, sort of a grande dame."

"I'm not a grande dame," she said. "And since you know my name, what's yours?"

"Stanley. Stanley Girard. It's French. My great-great—or maybe it's three greats—came from there. I've always wanted to see it."

"I've been to France. It's beautiful. The museums, the gardens, especially at Versailles . . ." But then she stopped. Because the mention of Versailles brought up another image—of Cassandra's eyes when she had to admit that she had lied for so many years.

He was frowning. "But you didn't like it," he said. He'd picked up on her negative feelings; he was very observant. It would be hard to have secrets with him around. Or lies.

"Versailles was fantastic. It was just . . . There are some things it's better to see on your own." That was partially true, at least.

Suddenly there seemed to be nothing more to say. Locusts were buzzing through the silence, which was becoming embarrassing. Finally, this time it was he who broke it.

"I've finished hanging the lanterns," he said. "I'll come back tonight about half an hour before the party starts and turn them on. They're on a special circuit, so they can be tricky." He handed her his empty glass. "Thank you for the lemonade."

He stood up and started walking. He was going to leave. But then she heard herself call his name. "Stanley," she said. He turned. "You said . . ." She paused. She could feel her face getting red. "You said I wasn't what you imagined." He nodded. She tried to come up with a smile and failed. "So what am I?" she asked.

He had that considering look in his eyes. "Old-fashioned," he said slowly. "There's something about you that's kind of . . . quaint."

"I think I like that," she said after a minute.

He nodded and then he turned and left.

GWEN brought the tray and the lemonade pitcher back into the kitchen. She looked up at the clock. It was a little after noon. Stanley Girard would be coming back to the house in six hours.

She left the kitchen and started upstairs. She walked into her bedroom, and there hanging on the closet door was the dress she and Cassie had chosen for the party. It was green, and it was the absolute latest style. Nothing about it was old-fashioned or quaint.

Gwen started to run. She ran out of her bedroom, down the stairs, and into the foyer, where she grabbed her car keys and ran out the front door. She got into her car, and she began to drive.

There was a shop she'd seen advertised, although she'd never been inside it. According to the advertisement, the place, Past Times, sold vintage clothes.

GWEN Wright had come to Past Times to shop! On the day of her big birthday party, no less. Jewel couldn't believe it. The only consolation was that Gwen had been as surprised—and dismayed—to see Jewel as Jewel was to see her.

"Oh my . . . Jewel! I didn't expect . . . that is, I didn't know . . ." she'd stammered.

"Yes, I work here now," Jewel said. "Since your mother fired me."

They stood facing each other. Jewel was pretty sure the smile on her face was as sick as the one on Gwen's. That was when, thank God, Patsy came in from the back room. She recognized Gwen and fluttered around for a few seconds, welcoming her into the shop. Then she said, "Now, Miss Wright, how can I help you?"

THE white lace dress was exactly what Gwen had been looking for. Gwen tried it on, and now she stood in front of the mirror seeing herself as if for the first time. The bodice had a square neckline that framed her face, and the delicate lace fell gracefully to her ankles. She looked like a heroine from a Jane Austen novel—almost.

"My hair . . ." Gwen moaned.

"An upsweep," Patsy decreed. "Not too period—but it must be off your face."

"I don't know how to make it do that. And I think it's too late to get an appointment at the beauty salon."

Gwen looked as if she was going to cry. It almost made Jewel feel sorry for her.

*What the hell,* Jewel thought. "I can do your hair," she said.

Gwen looked terrified.

"If you don't like it, you can always take it down," Jewel added briskly. And before Gwen could protest, Jewel was seating her on a stool in front of the counter.

Jewel worked fast and with assurance. Her fingers smoothed, twisted, and pinned Gwen's curly mass into place. A narrow silk ribbon was threaded through the curls at the back of Gwen's head and tied in a tiny bow that perched behind one ear. Only after Jewel was completely satisfied with the final effect was Gwen allowed to stand once again in front of the mirror and see herself.

"Oh," she breathed.

"Just right." Patsy studied her critically. "The hair and the dress are perfect."

*And I did it,* Jewel thought. And then a really pleasant feeling came over her. *I just did Princess Gwen a favor. Now she owes me one. Little old me.*

Gwen turned away from the vision of herself in the mirror and said to Jewel and Patsy, "I don't know how to thank you."

Then she picked up one of the gift cards on the counter and scribbled something on it. "I know it's short notice, and I hope you're not offended, but would the two of you like to come to my party tonight? If you give them this at the front door, they'll know you're my guests."

Patsy fell all over herself thanking Gwen, but Jewel thought, *She couldn't stand it when she had to thank me! Now she's got to even the score by throwing me a crust and inviting me to her big shindig— at the last minute. It's insulting.*

For a second, Jewel thought about turning down the offer and not letting Gwen get the upper hand again. But the party would be a chance at the magical inner circle—the one where a girl could meet the right man and change her life.

"Thank you," she said. And she took the invitation Gwen had scribbled out.

IT WAS almost dark when Gwen seated herself in a rocker on the front porch of her home to wait until Stanley showed up to turn on the lanterns. So far, there was no sign of his truck coming up the driveway. Behind her, the house was brightly lit; the hired waiters and bartenders were rushing around taking care of last-minute details. And the daughter of the house, for whom all the fuss was being made, was sitting outside, wearing a white lace dress and trying to pretend she hadn't bought it for a man she'd talked to for ten minutes that afternoon. *You're a fool, Gwen Wright,* she told herself. But nothing on earth could have dragged her inside.

Two minutes later, she had her reward when she heard the sound of gravel crunching under truck tires. The door of the truck opened, and Stanley got out. He was carrying something—was it a tool kit of some sort? But he must have seen her, because after a second, he dropped it and came toward her.

STANLEY knew right away who it was sitting on the front porch, looking exactly the way he'd imagined she would. The way she was meant to look. He knew that all of it—the hair, and the dress, and the nonchalant pose in the rocking chair—had been done for him. And something in his heart turned over. There was something so . . . vulnerable and . . . young about the way she was sitting there waiting for him. He wasn't sure what to do. If he told her she looked lovely, she might blush with that fiery red spreading over her cheeks. And besides, she wasn't really lovely in the classic sense of the word. To him, what she had was better than mere loveliness—she was unique.

GWEN walked to the edge of the porch as Stanley came up to the railing. She said the only thing she could think of.

"It's cooled down since this afternoon."

At the same moment, he said, "I like your dress."

And then they were staring at each other. Through the open window of the house, she heard someone say, "No, no, the champagne flutes go on the tables."

And someone else was asking, "When will the band set up?"

And that broke the spell. In the darkness, Stanley frowned. "I'd better see about those lanterns," he said, and started to move away.

And she was going to cry. She didn't know what she had expected from Stanley, but it was more than just "I like your dress" and walking away. But then he stopped. And came back to her.

"There's a little movie house over in Tyler," he said. "Art movies, you know, the kind of foreign pictures with subtitles. They're really great, most of them."

"I saw one there, too, an Italian one," she said, and then before she could stop herself, "Would you like to go again with me?"

When he said yes, he smiled at her, and she was glad she hadn't stopped herself.

THE PARTY WAS IN FULL SWING. And Gwen was floating somewhere above all the chatter and the music from the band. Nothing could get to her, not even a scolding from Cassie—which had occurred a few minutes earlier, when Jewel Fairchild and Patsy Allen had walked in and handed the butler Gwen's handwritten invitation.

"What possessed you?" Cassie had demanded.

"I ran into her and thought it would be polite," Gwen said.

"She's a horrible person."

And because Cassie was so adamant about it, Gwen heard herself say, "She's not all that bad. She did my hair for tonight."

"She did what? How? Sometimes I don't understand you . . . And why did you decide to change your dress after we spent so much time picking out the green one?"

"I thought this looked nice."

"I'm not saying it doesn't, but . . . Good Lord, is that woman giving out business cards?" And sure enough, Patsy Allen was handing a Past Times card to a woman in a gown with huge puffed sleeves. Cassie drew in a deep breath, and Gwen prepared herself for a lecture, but fortunately a woman broke in to say, "Cassie, dear, there's someone I want you to meet."

"Go ahead, Mother, " Gwen said heartily.

Cassie murmured, "Later, Gwendolyn." Then she allowed herself to be led away.

THE party—Jewel's chance to break into the magic circle of the rich—was not turning out to be very magical after all. She kept her wide, friendly smile plastered on her face, but she was getting discouraged. Oh, she was getting plenty of interest—she always did. But she'd been around long enough to know the right kind of interest from the kind that never produced anything more than a minor piece of jewelry.

Then she saw the latecomer. His long face was becomingly tanned, although he was certainly not handsome. He was older than she but not "old-old." His striped tie was of the sort called "regimental." And at a party where most of the men were wearing light-colored suits or pastel blazers, that tie and his navy blue jacket made him stand out. But while he was definitely upper class, he was different from the others in some way Jewel couldn't quite describe. She watched him as he walked onto the patio and stood scanning the scene in front of him. He slid his hands into his pockets and leaned up against the back wall of the house. But for all the casualness of his pose, there was something coiled and slightly dangerous about him. She was wondering if she wanted to try to work her way over to him when Walter Amburn came up to greet him and led him to Cassie and Gwen.

"GWEN, Cassie, this is Jeff Henry." Walter introduced the man who had come more than fashionably late to the party.

Cassie held out her hand. "Glad you could make it, Mr. Henry."

"So am I, Mrs. Wright," he said cheerfully, and went on to wish Gwen a happy birthday.

*There's something about him,* Gwen thought as she thanked him. *He's like a pirate. There's something a little uncivilized about him.*

"Jeff is interested in buying my painting of the girl on the rooftop," Walter said.

That was a surprise. Walter had made his reputation with the portraits he did on commission, but he also painted his own works—many of museum quality. The painting he was talking about was a delicate, shadowy piece, a picture of a child sitting on the roof of one of the run-down bungalows near the river, with storm clouds above her and gray water behind her. Gwen couldn't imagine it appealing to the swashbuckler standing in front of her. Clearly, there was more to Mr. Jeff Henry than one saw at first glance.

And then she realized that she and her mother and Walter no longer had Jeff Henry's undivided attention. Something had caught his eye. Gwen looked in the direction of his gaze. Jewel was standing under a lantern—one of the lanterns Stanley had strung up earlier that day. Gwen felt herself smiling. And a few minutes later, when Jeff excused himself, she really wasn't irritated when she saw him making his way toward Jewel.

JEWEL LOOKED LONGINGLY TOWARD the front of the house, where an attendant was waiting to retrieve the guests' cars for them. She just wanted to go home and sleep for a month. Unfortunately, she was going to have to wait a while longer, because Patsy wasn't ready to leave yet. Patsy was her ride for the night, because Jewel's clunker was in the shop. Again.

Jewel walked to the side of the lawn, where there were two iron chairs, and wiped the seat of one before she sat. Her violet blue dress was on loan from Past Times, and Patsy would be upset if she got a smudge on it. She lowered herself into the chair and closed her eyes.

"Mind if I join you?" asked a masculine voice. She looked up to see the man in the navy blue jacket.

If she hadn't been so tired, she might have tried to flirt. But she'd finished with that for the night. "No, I don't mind," she said. He sat next to her, and they looked out at the party in silence.

"Forgive me if I'm presuming," he said finally. "But I don't think you're having a very good time."

"I don't belong here," she said. The words just slipped out, and after they did, she could have kicked herself.

"I know what you mean," he said. "I don't belong, either."

"Of course you do!" The words slipped out again. "You're one of them."

"No," he said, looking thoughtfully out at the partygoers. "I'm not in this league." Then he added softly, "Not yet, anyway."

There was something about the way he said it that piqued her curiosity. She sat up to look at him. "You dress the right way, you speak the right way . . . What are you talking about?"

He turned to her with a slightly twisted little smile. "Money. I'm talking about money, of course. What else?"

WHY *the hell am I telling her this?* Jeff wondered to himself. But he knew why. There was something electric about this girl; even now, when she was obviously down about something, he could feel the energy in her. So many women held no surprises, but every instinct he had said this one was different.

And then she proved it again. "Are you saying you're poor?" she demanded. "Because I don't believe it."

He laughed at that. "I guess 'poor' is a relative term," he said. "If you're talking about the Wright family, and most of the people here tonight, I'm barely getting by. If you're talking about the people I grew up with, I'm doing fine." He paused. "I think I'm going to be all right with it, but then I come to a house like this and . . ."

"You come to a house like this and . . . what?" she prompted.

*What am I doing?* he thought. *I don't talk this way to friends, and I don't even know her.* But she was so pretty. And so different.

"I want," he confessed. "Want everything. It's embarrassing to admit."

"So what are you going to do about that?"

"Funny you should ask," he said, but then he stopped himself. Because now he really was going too far into private matters with a total stranger. "What about you?" he asked. "Where do you live?"

"In a dump of an apartment over a deli. But don't change the subject; what are you going to do?"

He shouldn't tell her. But then she smiled. "I'm kind of at a crossroads," he said. "There's a business I've been thinking about getting into."

"Could you make lot of money doing it?"

"Yes. But there's risk involved. Nothing I can't handle, but still . . . it's going to mean dealing with some tough players."

"Can't you be tough, too?"

"Yes." And in spite of himself, he added, "But I'm not sure I like that in myself."

"Get over that," she said. Her pretty face was so earnest that he couldn't take offense at the abruptness of the command. "I mean it. Because you won't be happy unless you try."

"How do you know that?"

"Because I know about wanting."

Across the lawn, a woman was beckoning to her. She stood up. "My ride is waiting for me," she said. She held out her hand. "I expect to see your picture in the paper when you make your first million." She shook his hand and walked away. It wasn't until after she was out of sight that he realized they hadn't exchanged names.

I'M KIND *of at a crossroads.* That was what the nameless man in the navy blue jacket had said. *So am I,* Jewel thought as she and Patsy waited for the parking attendant to bring the car to them. *That's the exact word for where I am—a crossroads.*

"Who was that man you were talking with?" Patsy asked.

"Nobody," Jewel said; then she added, "I think he could be someone. A really big someone. If he doesn't think too much and get in his own way."

# CHAPTER 6

UNCOUNTED millions of written pages in every possible language have described the discovery of mutual love. What was it, Stan often asked himself, that had led him to Gwen and led her to him?

She was not really very beautiful; he'd decided that early on—and had also known that it didn't matter to him. She was not easy to know—at least at first. Yet there was something about her that led him to call her the day after the party and ask her to go to a movie with him.

Tyler, the town where the movie house was, was a perfect place to take a girl for a night out. The little community had a number of lovely public buildings and gracious private homes built on an exceptionally pretty stretch of the river. The old homes were refurbished as charming bed-and-breakfasts, and a newly built river walk became a magnet for dozens of delightful shops and food stalls.

So it was that after the movie and a very good supper in a little bistro near the docks, Stan and Gwen found themselves strolling by the river, eating peppermint ice cream in handmade cones. In the sky above, the clouds framed clusters of stars, and the river spread silent and silver underneath it. Stan knew he would remember for the rest of his life the sharp sweet taste of peppermint and the far-away expression Gwen wore when she was thinking about something that mattered to her.

"I liked that movie," she said. "Especially the ending—it must have been a big temptation for the screenwriter to just wrap up all the loose ends in a nice big bow, but he didn't do that."

"You don't like happy endings?" he asked.

"Not when I can tell that they've just been tacked on to a story to sell tickets," she said firmly. The firmness was a surprise. Most of the time she was tentative when he asked her opinion about something. But now she was very sure of herself. "Sometimes, if it's light entertainment, it's all right to work the plot around until you have a happy ending, even if it isn't totally believable," she went on eagerly. "But with a movie like the one we saw tonight, where all the characters are so real and the situation is so true, you have to stay honest. Even if your audience feels a little sad at the end."

"Do you always analyze movies like this?" he asked. He loved this new intensity in her.

"Actually, now that I think about it, it's storytelling in general that interests me," she said slowly. "I've always wondered why one book touches your heart and another one with a similar plot leaves you cold. It must be in the telling, you know?"

"I'm afraid that's something I haven't thought about very much."

"I guess when you read all the time the way I do, you can't help wondering what makes it all come together. Do you like to read?"

"Yes. But not a lot of fiction. Mostly biographies."

"Of people like Benjamin Franklin? I ordered a biography of him the other day after you mentioned him."

He told himself it was ridiculous to be so pleased that she was following up on a name he had dropped.

OVER the weeks, Stan continued his careful courtship. Finally, he felt the time was right to show her his electrician's shop in Wrightstown's commercial district. The shop was his pride and joy.

He'd only been in business for two years, but he was already turning a profit. A profit that was big enough to allow him to leave his cramped studio apartment and move to one with two bedrooms and an eat-in kitchen in a new building that had all the amenities.

Still, he had hesitated about letting Gwen see Stan's Electronics. A girl who'd grown up around a multimillion-dollar enterprise like the glassworks might not understand what an accomplishment his fledgling business represented.

He brought her to the shop, showed her around, offered her some iced tea from the small refrigerator in his small office, and braced himself for her response.

He need not have worried. "You do everything!" Gwen exclaimed. "You can install a new electrical system for a business complex, and you can maintain it, too! And you also create your own advertising, and you keep your own books. At the glassworks, there are separate departments for all those things."

"With a small operation like this, I have to be a one-man band," he'd protested. But he'd been foolishly, childishly pleased.

"But I think if your company was as big as Mother's, you'd still want to be hands-on. Mother is. She learned her lesson, you see, because she almost lost everything when she didn't do that, when she turned it all over to my . . ." But then she stopped short.

Gwen felt her face get red. She'd almost spilled the secret of her birth parents! The secret that could not be told because that would be disloyal to Cassie. And yet it was Gwen's secret, too. Should it always be off-limits? With everyone? Gwen looked at Stan. He had brought her here to his little shop and shared it with her because he wanted her to know him better. Wasn't it time to return the favor?

She sat down on a workbench and motioned to him to sit next to her. She said, "I have something I'd like you to know about me." And she told him about her father and the woman who had been her birth mother. When it was over, she turned to Stan. And she realized that without meaning to, she'd given him a test. There were so many things he could say that would be wrong. If he said, *Cassandra Wright was good to take you in,* that would be the worst.

He looked at her for what seemed like an eternity, and then he said, "I'm sorry your mother didn't tell you the truth years ago. It's something you should have known."

He was perfect! She threw her arms around him, and she hugged him. And for a second, he hugged her back, but then she felt something in him change, and then he was pulling her to him as if he couldn't let her go. When he took her face in his hands and brushed her hair aside with his fingertips, she knew what was coming. She didn't have time to think or talk, because her body was melting into his, and her mouth was joining his.

Stan pulled back from the kiss. He didn't want to go too fast. This was too serious to rush.

"I'll drive you home," he said softly, and was happier than he'd ever thought he could be when she looked disappointed.

EVENING coffee in the den was a ritual that Cassie always welcomed. This night, however, was different. Neither the coffee nor the plate of cookies had been touched, and the atmosphere between mother and daughter was heated.

"You used to complain because I had no dates," Gwen said. "Now I have somebody who likes me, and you don't approve."

"I never said that, not exactly . . ."

"You didn't have to. You don't approve because he has none of what you call 'status'! You think he's nobody."

"That's unfair. I am not a snob. And I'm not so trivial that I would object to a good man just because of his position in life."

"What is it that you have against Stan?"

"I'm not 'against' the man," Cassie said. "I simply feel that you are spending too much time with him. You're only nineteen, and, frankly, you're very naïve, even for nineteen. And he's naïve, too."

"How can you say that? Stan has his own business, for heaven's sake! He built it himself from nothing."

"As admirable as that is, I'm not talking about his ability to earn a living."

"If you think I'm the first girlfriend he's ever had, think again."

There was a pause. Cassie was choosing her words carefully now. "Gwen, I'd be stunned to hear that Stanley Girard hasn't had many other 'girlfriends' in his career. But I would be willing to guess that you are the first one of your—as you put it—status."

"Which means 'class.' "

Cassie shook her head. "All right, if you must, yes. It is a question of class, but not in the way you mean. He has nothing to offer you. He wants to install air conditioners and refrigerators for a living. There's nothing wrong in that, but you were raised for more. You and Stan are not equals. And if there is one thing I've learned in this life, it is that the man you choose must be your equal."

But now it was Gwen's turn to shake her head. "I can't believe you're saying this. You're supposed to be a good person. That means you keep an open mind about people."

"I have standards, and I'm proud of it. But they are based on character traits, like discipline, a strong work ethic, and, yes, a healthy ambition."

"I'm not going to stop seeing him. And you can't drive him away. He's much too strong to allow himself to be scared off."

"I don't intend to meddle, Gwen. It's not my way," Cassandra continued. "Think about what I've said, for his sake as well as for yours. He's in over his head. " She closed her eyes. "I've often wondered about your father—would he have done the things he did if he had married someone . . . at his own level? Maybe if he hadn't had to prove himself, he would have been different."

"Stan would never feel he had to prove anything," Gwen said.

Cassandra opened her eyes and looked directly into Gwen's. "I thought that, too—once."

There was no way to answer that, nothing more to be said. Gwen opened the door and walked out.

"THE Wright Glass Museum is celebrating its fiftieth anniversary today, and there's going to be a big shindig," Gwen told Stan during the phone call that had become a daily occurrence for them. It was now several days after her futile confrontation with Cassie.

"The museum was built by Mother's father to showcase the Wright Studio Glass line," she went on. "That's the handmade division. It's considered one of the great producers of glass artwork. . . ."

*Get on with it, Gwen.*

"Anyway, Mother and Walter will be gone for hours, so I was wondering . . ." She drew a big breath. "I was wondering if you would like to come out here to the house to have lunch with me today." She waited for his answer and realized she was now holding her breath. She wanted him to say yes so very much.

"What time would you like me to show up?" he asked.

It was amazing the way he never ever failed her.

"SOMETIMES I almost don't like Cassie at all," Gwen told Stan. They had just finished lunch—sandwiches that Gwen, not the maid, had made and served. She'd brought them outside to him, and they'd sat at one of the round tables with the big flowered umbrellas. "I know it's wrong of me to feel the way I do about Mother, because she's such a *good* person. But sometimes I want more . . . well, just more." Gwen faltered. "When I was in high school, Mother decreed that for one evening a week, we had to speak French during dinner."

"What was the reason?" Stan asked.

"It was me, so I could get into intermediate French right away when I went to college. And the thing is, I don't want to go."

"Not even to the local college? I thought Yale was the problem."

Gwen shook her head. "I just don't want to put off my life for another four years." Stan was looking at her intently. "I'll always learn what I want to learn; that's the way I'm made. So what's the point of going to classes I'll never remember?"

"There's no point," he said slowly. "But you need a degree to be a teacher. I thought that was what you wanted to do."

She shrugged. "I had to pick something, and I love children. But taking on the responsibility for teaching them—I'm afraid I won't be much good at that."

"Then what will you do with your life?"

"Sometimes I think I'd like to write something."

"Well, go ahead. Do it."

"The trouble is, I don't know what I'd like to write." She threw down her napkin. "The truth is, I don't know what I want."

Stan laughed. "You can always marry me."

Then he stopped laughing. For a second, his words hung in the air. There was a funny little smile on his face.

*Did you mean that?* she wanted to ask. Because as he sat there smiling in that strange way, she couldn't read him. And she always had been able to. With him, what you saw was what you got. But now when it was so important, she didn't know what was going through his mind. She wanted to scream, *What are you thinking?*

*WHAT am I thinking?* Stan thought. *I just asked her to marry me. I'll be lucky if she doesn't throw me out.*

"But if you don't want to marry me, and you probably don't," he heard himself say, "maybe we could see that favorite place of yours that you've been telling me about."

Her face flushed crimson. "This way," she said. She indicated a hill behind them and started marching toward it at a brisk pace. He had to walk fast to catch up with her.

Walking up the hill, they were soon in the depths of a forest. Over Stan's head was a canopy of branches. And everything was still—the only other sounds were the calls of birds and the rustling of small creatures. Stan wasn't much of an outdoorsman—city apartments and small spaces were what he had known most of his life—but even he could appreciate the beauty of this place.

Ahead of him, Gwen led the way upward, going deeper into the woods until all of a sudden they were in a small clearing. She stopped abruptly, and Stan looked around. In spots where sunlight came through the heavy leafage, the grass lay green and as soft as a couch. A stump, aged to silvery gray, sat in the middle of the space, and Gwen started to move to it, but he reached out his hand and stopped her. And then, and he was never quite sure how it happened, they were lying down together on that soft sweet grass, with the ribbons of sunlight playing over them.

GWEN KNEW THAT SHE WOULD never again experience a closeness like this, a feeling of being joined so totally and blissfully. And after they had reached the moment of release, Stan folded his body into hers and held her, and she truly thought that there was nothing more she could ever want from life.

AS IF in a state of shock, Cassie lay back in her chair. She had read Gwen's letter over and over; she had even examined the envelope, postmarked PARIS, as if there could have been some hidden meaning there that she had failed to see. *Foolish, foolish child!* she thought. *Why couldn't she just have had an affair? Why on earth did Gwen have to marry him?*

Cassie's head throbbed. From the library, where she was sitting, she looked out at the back lawn and the depressing rain that dripped out of the trees and from the pretty lanterns, which had been installed by the man who had caused this headache. Stanley Girard wasn't worthy of the sacrifices Gwen was making for him.

"I thought I'd find you in here," Walter's voice said behind her. She hadn't heard him come in. "You're going to wear a hole in that letter," he said as he sat in the chair next to hers.

"She's doomed herself to a dreary existence with a man who doesn't know which side is up. And she'll have a house full of children whether they can afford them or not. They better not turn to me for help."

"You don't mean that. Besides, my sense of your new son-in-law is that he'd rather be boiled in oil than take help from anyone." He looked at her thoughtfully. "I think your real problem with Stanley Girard is that he's such a worthy opponent."

"He's a half-educated man without strength or ambition."

"He has plenty of ambition, and more than enough strength to challenge your hold on Gwen. That's what disturbs you so."

He got up and came over to stroke her cheek. "Cassie, my darling, you can't undo the marriage. So try to give it a chance. That's all anybody can do. If it's going to fall apart, it will do so without anybody's help."

PATSY ALLEN HAD PROVED TO BE a far better businesswoman than Jewel had given her credit for. It had been two years since Gwen Wright's birthday party, when Patsy had embarrassed Jewel by handing out her business cards and turning herself into a walking advertisement for Past Times. Jewel had to admit that the ploy had worked. The shop had done so well that Patsy was ready to expand her operation. "We're going to move to the Algonquin Mall," she told Jewel excitedly. It was early morning, and Jewel and Patsy were in the back drinking coffee. "We'll be doubling our space and hiring two more salesgirls," Patsy went on. "And here's the best part—I'm going to promote you. You're my new manager, Jewel!" She stared expectantly at Jewel, waiting for squeals of delight—or possibly tears of joy.

Jewel wanted to weep, but not from happiness. She'd never felt so frustrated and trapped in her life. The big promotion Patsy was promising her would mean a raise, but it wouldn't be big enough to get Jewel out of her little apartment over the deli or to buy her a car that actually ran. *Two years,* she thought hopelessly. *I thought I'd be on my way by now.*

Jewel forced a smile. She threw her arms around the woman who wrote out her paycheck. "Oh, Patsy!" she managed to squeal. "This is fabulous! I'm so happy; I don't know how to thank you."

Fortunately, at that moment, three customers walked in and she didn't have to keep on pretending. Patsy gulped down her coffee, whispered, "Showtime!" and headed for the front of the store.

As Patsy hustled out to greet the girls, Jewel tried to make her mind a blank. But of course the thought that popped into her head was of Gwen Wright.

Surprising as it might seem, Jewel often thought about Gwen. During the past two years, the only thought that had been comforting to Jewel was the reflection that no matter what kind of mess she'd made of her life, Gwen had done worse. Jewel could still remember when she'd opened the *Wrightstown Gazette* and read that Ms. Gwendolyn Wright had gotten married to a plumber. Or maybe an electrician. Jewel had been too stunned to pay attention. *I wish I'd been a fly on the wall when Queen Cassie heard that!*

Jewel thought now. She tried to picture the fit the woman must have thrown. But trying to imagine Cassie's reaction didn't make Jewel feel better. She was too busy focusing on her own situation.

She was in her midtwenties—nearer thirty than twenty. It wasn't as if she hadn't tried to find the right man. Jewel had screened her potential suitors carefully—so carefully, in fact, that there had only been two of them in the past two years. But she was no closer to marriage than she had been on that rainy day so long ago when she'd taken the train to the country and seen paradise in Cassandra Wright's gleaming white house. The clock was ticking. She just didn't know what to do about it.

"JEFF Henry," said Patsy. "Isn't he that man you talked to at Gwen Wright's birthday party?" She and Jewel had taken the afternoon off to go to the bank so Patsy could sign the paperwork for the loan she needed to build her new store. Now she and Jewel were in the lobby of the Amber, the glitziest high-rise in Wrightstown. Patsy had been scanning the directory in the lobby to find the loan offices of the Penobscot National Bank. Now she was pointing to the directory, which indicated that the two top floors of the Amber were occupied by a company called JeffSon. The owner of the company was listed as Jeff Henry. Although Jewel hadn't learned directly the name of the man in the navy blue blazer, she'd caught an interview he'd given on a Sunday morning television show, and she had recognized him.

"Yes," she said. "Jeff Henry is the man I talked to."

"Rents in the Amber don't come cheap," Patsy said. "It's obvious that your Mr. Henry is doing very well for himself."

"He's not my Mr. Henry," Jewel said automatically. But when she thought about it, he'd been attracted to her that night two years ago. And it hadn't been a surfacey flirtation. He'd told her things about himself. Personal things. She had a feeling he didn't do that with everyone. Jewel looked at the directory. It would be so easy to find out if he was in the building today. She'd just run out to the parking garage, where she'd noticed that the premium spaces had names on them, and see if there was a car in his spot. What did she have to lose? She opened her purse and started fishing around.

"Oh no," she moaned. "I can't find my credit card case. Patsy, I've got to go back to the car and see if I left it there. I'll catch up with you."

ACCORDING to the parking attendant, Jeff Henry did have one of the VIP parking slots, and his car had been there, but he'd driven it out earlier. He often did that on Wednesdays, said the attendant, and he would probably be back in about three hours. Whenever Mr. Henry took off on a Wednesday, his car was always back in three hours. Jewel gave the attendant her most dazzling smile when she thanked him.

It was just as well that Jeff Henry wasn't in the building, she thought as she hurried off to find the bank and the waiting Patsy. Jewel needed time to think through her strategy. She didn't want to make any mistakes with Jeff Henry.

HORACEVILLE was only twenty miles north of Wrightstown, but it couldn't have been more different. For one thing, it was a much smaller town, and unlike bustling busy Wrightstown, it seemed to be preserved in a time gone by. Main Street ran through its heart. Oak and chestnut trees shaded the town hall. The police and fire departments were brick with white trim, in pseudo-colonial style.

Jeff pulled his Lamborghini into the driveway next to a modest frame house in a neighborhood that had been recently rezoned as both commercial and residential. That was different from the days when Jeff had grown up here. Back then, his street—this street— had been lined with the homes of families who considered themselves upper middle class. Now, several of the houses had two or more mailboxes on the front porch, suggesting that whoever owned them was renting out unused rooms to bring in extra income. To put it simply, the area was going downhill—an argument Jeff was going to try to make. Once again. He turned off the purring automobile that was the most beloved of all his toys and sat for a few seconds trying to put together his thoughts before he went into the house. He would need to be at his most forceful, he knew.

"JEFFIE, I don't know how many ways I have to tell you that I don't want to leave my home," said Jeff's father. "Besides, where would you have me go? That 'assisted living facility' into which you are trying to push me has no space for my library or my prints!" Father's library consisted of the books that filled the shelves on two walls of the room he called his den. They were in that room right now. When Jeff's mother had decorated it some forty years ago, she'd had the room paneled with a dark wainscoting and painted a dark green. The rest of the house was furnished in the same way, with dark antiques. Mother and Father had adored it.

"We are simple academics," his father liked to say. "We don't need the trappings of success, just a few old treasures—our books, our antiques, our prints, and of course our music." And Mother would nod and smile. His parents were so proud of their status as intellectuals. Father was a professor of art history at Wrightstown College. One of his prouder accomplishments was the fact that one of his prize students, a man named Edward Lawrence, had become the curator of the Wright Glass Museum. Edward still held the position after twenty years.

Then four years ago, Mother had become ill and Father had taken early retirement to care for her until she died two years later. Since that time, Father had continued living in the house he could no longer maintain in a neighborhood that was quietly slipping.

The old man turned away from his shelves crammed with books to glare at Jeff. "Well, son?" he demanded. "Could I take all my treasures to that warehouse for the ancient you selected for me?"

"Dad, I've already told you, if you don't like the idea of Shady Manor, you can build a house near me. There's a new development going up outside of town."

"And how will I pay for this brand-new house?" Father asked.

"As I've said, I'll pay for it. God knows I don't expect you to do it!" But then Jeff looked at the man. And Jeff saw how alone and how frightened he was. "Father, please," he said more gently. "Let me do this for you. I can afford it."

His father sat wearily in a crumbling wing chair. "Tell me again what this business of yours is, Jeffie," he said. "I never seem to be able to understand it."

Jeff sat across from him. "JeffSon is one of the major distributors of electricity and natural gas in the United States. We're involved in the development as well as the building and the daily running of power plants and pipelines."

"And how did my son, the philosophy major, get into such a business?"

"Dad, you know I dropped my philosophy major in my sophomore year and went into business administration. I'm very happy with my choice. I'm sorry if you're not."

His father sighed. "I'd like to know how a man working for a small brokerage house in Wrightstown becomes owner of a multi-million-dollar corporation that sells natural gas and electricity."

The question he asked was astute. And the answer was that there had been a series of mergers, some of which were frankly questionable, followed by takeovers of small companies by larger holding companies that had skated perilously close to violating several FTC regulations. When all the smoke cleared, Jeff had emerged as the CEO of the newly formed company now called JeffSon.

"The ways in which companies acquire assets are very complicated, Father."

"And what do you know about these commodities you sell?"

"I don't sell them exactly; I distribute them. And I don't have to know the details. I hire people for that. I oversee the financial end, and of course I decide where and how we should expand next."

"Expand? Aren't you big enough, Jeffie?"

And that was a good question, one that both scared and excited Jeff. Because it was Jeff's belief that you had to grow in order to survive. If you lost your nerve and stopped growing, the sharks in the water around you would smell blood. Besides, when you came from a home where the standards for excellence were Plato, Shakespeare, and Mozart, it was a heady feeling to find yourself hailed as a wunderkind. So it was worth it to fly blind and risk falling.

"There's no such thing as being too big," he told his father cheerfully. "But I came here to talk about you. Now, since Shady Manor is out, I'm assuming you'll move to Wrightstown. You can stay with me until I have your new place built."

"You know, son, I'd rather stay put," was the infuriating reply.

Jeff exploded. "Why do you want to live in an old dump in a lousy neighborhood when you could have the best of everything?"

His father's answer surprised him. "I'm afraid I don't trust the business you're in, Jeffie," he said. "I'd rather not take chances."

And that was that. Jeff argued that his father's lack of faith in him was insulting. He said that JeffSon had been hailed by *Fortune* magazine as one of the most exciting new companies of the year.

His father bowed his head. "I didn't mean to hurt your feelings, Jeffie. I know you mean well. But I'm too old to gamble."

His father walked him to his car. When Jeff had bought the Lamborghini, he'd debated between red and a neon yellow and finally settled on the yellow, which now looked garish in this drab neighborhood. "Oh my," said his father when he caught sight of the car. "Is that yours?"

"Yes." Even to his own ears, Jeff sounded like a sulky child.

"It certainly is . . . splashy," said his father. Then, instead of his usual handshake, he enveloped his son in an awkward hug. "Beware of Faustian bargains, Jeffie," he said.

NPR was playing Verdi's *Requiem*. The stately lament suited Jeff's mood, and as he drove back to Wrightstown alongside the winding river, he turned up the volume on his car radio. The visit with his father had brought to the surface thoughts that Jeff usually tried to keep buried. Contrary to what he'd told his father, Jeff had been ambivalent about his choice to drop his beloved philosophy courses and go into business administration. And the ambivalence had gotten worse when he'd begun working.

But then there would be a visit home, and he would remember

once again the cramped rooms in the dingy little house. He'd remember the much-dreamed-of trip to Europe that was always postponed for lack of money and the look of longing on his mother's face when a neighbor gave his wife a pair of diamond earrings that Father could never have afforded. And Jeff would go back to the purgatory of his job, determined to become one of those who never had to think twice about buying plane tickets or diamond earrings.

But even with all that, when the opportunity to get into the risky business that was now his had been presented to him, he'd been hesitant. In fact, he probably would have passed it up if he hadn't met that girl at Gwendolyn Wright's birthday party—the girl whose name he did not know.

*Get over your doubts,* she'd said. And he had.

The result had been JeffSon. What would she say if he were to tell her that she was responsible for the creation of one of the country's hottest new businesses? Her energy had been like a life force on that night two years ago, and he could use some of it now. Maybe she could erase from his memory the look on his father's face and the words he'd said: *Beware of Faustian bargains, Jeffie.*

The river straightened as he reached Wrightstown. He checked the time; it was not yet six. His visit to his father had taken two hours longer than he'd thought it would. He could go to the hotel where he'd been camping out while he waited for his house to be built, take a shower, order an early dinner, and call it a day. Or he could go back to the office and see if that call to South America had gone through. He opted for the office and the call.

JEWEL was ready to give up. The parking lot attendant had said that Jeff Henry would be back in three hours, and acting on a hunch, she'd claimed to have a headache and asked Patsy to give her the rest of the day off. After dawdling around the lobby of Jeff's office building for an hour and a half, she'd returned to the parking lot with a magazine and sat on one of the concrete benches near the entrance to wait. But after two and a half hours, the man hadn't shown up. She stood up and was starting toward the parking lot exit when she heard a roar behind her. She turned and saw a yellow car whipping into the parking garage. But this was not any car; this was the kind of car you dreamed about, the kind of car you would kill to drive just once.

JEFF parked in his spot and got out of his car.

"Hey," a feminine voice called out. He turned and there in front of him, miraculously and unbelievably, was the oval face, the blue-black hair, the spectacular eyes, and the smile that he'd been thinking about on the way back to Wrightstown.

"What the hell is your name?" he demanded.

"Jewel," she said. "So, are you rich yet?"

JEWEL made Jeff laugh. She was so pure, so unabashed in her pleasure at the things his money could buy. A gold bangle for her wrist, a dress from Sofia's, a trip to New York in a chartered plane, a night at the Waldorf after seeing the season's biggest Broadway musical—all these things filled her with a childlike delight that made his father's warning about bargains with the devil seem like nothing more than the fears of a tired old man. When he said he wanted a yacht, Jewel saw nothing wrong in it; when he voiced the wish for a private plane, she thought he should have a fleet of them.

She had met most of the men with whom he did business at various parties, and she was a big favorite with them, as well as with their wives and girlfriends. She was so overtly affectionate with him that it probably would have stunned his friends to know that the separate rooms he booked at the Waldorf were not just for show. She slept chastely in hers, and he stayed chaste in his. Because, irony of ironies, Jeff Henry, who had had women throwing themselves at him since he was in his teens, had fallen for a girl who had announced on their third date that she was saving herself for marriage.

After the initial surprise, he found it rather charming. There was something intensely romantic—and exciting—about holding back. Soon, his desire for her was far more intense than any he could remember feeling before.

And yet he couldn't seem to make the next move. He couldn't seem to ask the question that hovered on the tip of his tongue. *Will you marry me, Jewel?*

When he was alone, when she was not in front of him with her spectacular beauty wiping away all rational thought, he wondered whether they really had much in common. He was a reader; she was not. But then he would ask himself how important it was to have what is called "learning." He wanted her and he wanted her for keeps—wasn't that enough?

He took her to Horaceville to meet his father. And he knew as soon as they walked in the door that it had been a mistake.

"You wouldn't believe how that Lamborghini drives, Mr. Henry!" Jewel said as they sat down to have tea. "It was better than flying. You must be so proud of Jeff."

"I'm afraid I don't believe in being proud of another man's accomplishments," Father said stiffly. "Not that I can see anything particularly glorious in the ownership of an automobile."

"But this isn't just any automobile!" Jewel protested with her most sparkling smile. "This is a Lamborghini! It cost six figures!"

Father's eyes were now slits. "Ah," he said, "a chariot for the nouveau riche." He turned to Jeff. "Son, the next time you are in Boston, you must take in the new exhibit at the Gardner. A former colleague writes that it is quite extraordinary." He turned to Jewel. "Do you like Renoir, Miss Fairchild?"

"I don't know anything about it," Jewel said. Then as Jeff tried to think of a way to rescue her, his father launched into a lecture on the Impressionists, only stopping every once in a while to ask Jewel questions that she could not answer. After that, he launched into the fields of literature and music, interspersed with more questions. It was an exercise designed to expose Jewel's ignorance. Fortunately, she didn't seem to notice.

When Jeff suggested that it was time for them to be on their way, Father didn't even bother with the ritual of urging them to stay on. Jewel excused herself to powder her nose, and as soon as she was out of the room, Father began his diatribe. "Jeffie, you cannot be contemplating anything more serious than a fling with that girl. I'll admit she is beautiful. Have your fun, but for God's sake, don't tie yourself down. Because someday you will wish to talk to your mate, and for that you will want a woman who is your equal in intellect, education, and breeding."

Father was doing nothing more than saying out loud exactly what Jeff had been thinking privately, but hearing his own objections coming out of his father's mouth made Jeff realize how incredibly shallow, snobby, mean-spirited, and unimportant they were.

And yet, they had come all the way back to Wrightstown and he still hadn't asked the question they were both waiting for. He pulled up in front of the deli where Jewel lived and leaned over for the good-night kiss that would end with them tangled like teenagers in the front seat of his car. Since Jewel had never asked him to come upstairs to her apartment, and she'd always refused to visit his suite in the hotel, they were left with the front seat of his car. But tonight when he leaned in, Jewel did not turn to him. He sat back.

"You've been awfully quiet," he said.

"Obviously, I don't have a lot to say. Not about the things that are important to you, like artists and writers and all of that."

So she *had* realized what Father was doing. "Hey, don't confuse my old man with me," he said.

She turned to him. "Your father thinks I'm not good enough for you." And before he could protest, she asked, "Would you like to come upstairs tonight?"

And, of course, they both knew what she was really saying, and for a moment the thought ran through his mind, *I won!* But then he looked at her. There was weariness in her eyes, and defeat. And he knew that was not what he wanted. Not at all.

"No," he said gently. "I won't go upstairs with you tonight, Jewel my darling. But I have a question to ask you." And he took her hands in his. *This is right, what I am about to do,* he told himself.

"Jewel Fairchild, will you marry me?" he asked.

He thought the neighbors up and down the block could probably hear her shriek of joy.

Jewel Fairchild, now Jewel Henry, was on her honeymoon! She stood on the terrace outside the mansion-size "cottage" her husband had rented—on a private Caribbean island—and looked out at the beach of sugary white sand below. She still couldn't believe it had actually happened. After that awful visit to Jeff's father—the mean old goat—she'd been sure she'd lost Jeff for good.

Refusing to go to bed with Jeff had been a calculated risk; it could have turned him off so easily. But her instincts told her that underneath the hard-nosed businessman was a dreamy boy, and wooing an innocent virgin would stir him far more than another easy conquest. And she was still a virgin, although she was not exactly an innocent one.

Now Jewel woke each morning to watch the sun rise over a turquoise ocean, and flowers she'd never seen before perfumed the air outside her windows. Still, Jewel couldn't wait to get home. That was when her new life would really begin. Jeff had promised that when they were back in Wrightstown, he'd throw away the blueprints for the home he'd wanted to build and let her start planning one to suit her taste. He was going to spoil her rotten, he said. *If Gwen Wright could see me now,* Jewel thought.

# Chapter 7

The air in Stan's apartment was heavy. It was funny how Gwen always thought of it as his apartment in spite of the fact that it had been her home since she'd married him four years ago. She sat up in their bed. It was late; Stan had already left for work. She looked around the bedroom that had been hers for four years. Had it really been such a long time? She'd lost track. The doctor said that confusion was normal; it was a part of the grieving process. She must give herself time.

Gwen got out of bed and walked to the bedroom window. If she looked directly below, she could see a little piece of the courtyard behind the apartment building. This little patch of anemic grass and concrete was supposed to provide the residents with an outdoor oasis. Their other option for fresh air was the roof, where there were deck chairs in the summertime. Unfortunately, you couldn't get much of a tan on the roof, because across the street was a big office building called the Amber, which blocked the sun for the greater part of the day. Not that Gwen ever went up to the roof. She hadn't done that even before the tragedy.

She closed her eyes. And, as it so often did now, her mind went back. Back to the happy days she and Stan had spent in Paris.

It had seemed so romantic, to be married in Paris. She was the one who had suggested it, and Stan had loved the idea. He had insisted on paying for the trip.

There had been no first-class airline tickets, no VIP lounges, and no palatial hotel once they reached Paris. There weren't any fancy meals or expensive sightseeing trips. But they had the streets and parks of the city, and at night they had each other. They had all the sweetness and the ecstasy that two people who were in love could give each other, and it had been enough to make their hearts sing. Then they had come home.

"This is it," Stan had said, beaming with pride. And he'd showed Gwen the four boxlike rooms that made up his nest.

She'd tried to smile. The apartment was so small! The walls were so thin! She was used to space. And privacy. And while she loved the nearness of her new husband, she knew there would come a time when she would want to read quietly without hearing the sporting event he was watching on television through the thin walls.

After they were settled in, there had been the matter of housekeeping. Gwen quickly discovered she had no talent for domesticity. Cooking was a special nightmare, and there was no one nearby she could ask how to go about it. At times, loneliness would threaten to overtake her, and Stan would find her crying. All he could do was hold her and tell her he understood.

But he didn't understand—especially not about her longing for the outdoors. Stan had never had acres of woodland to tramp over. He'd never had his own refuge under a canopy of trees.

"There's a public park not ten minutes away from here," he told her when they moved in. "Everyone says it's a little bit of country right here in the city." Gwen had tried to go to the park. She'd tried to make herself believe that the overfed pigeons strutting around were a satisfying substitute for the songbirds, chipmunks, and squirrels she'd loved watching. She just couldn't do it.

Then, at the moment when she had started to despair, Cassie had stepped in. When Stan and Gwen came home from France, Cassie had been remarkably restrained. Even after Cassie had toured Gwen's new home, she had not uttered a disapproving word. She had kept her silence for a year. But then she had invited Stan and Gwen out to the house for Sunday brunch.

She had gotten down to business as soon as the omelets had been served. "Stan, I want to buy a house for you and Gwen," Cassie said. The family was sitting in the dining room, where Gwen could see her old refuge through the window. She'd been drinking it in, but when Cassie spoke, she turned in time to see Stan stiffen and she knew what was coming next. So did Cassie.

"Before you say no, hear me out," she went on. "The house I'm proposing to buy is in a new development out here. You probably saw it from the road as you drove by. The construction is ecologically sound, and the prices are reasonable."

"It's very kind, but no thank you," Stan said.

But Gwen was remembering the development. *The houses were small,* she thought, *but they were beautifully designed—rustic and simple. And there was land around each of them. Real land!*

"Gwen and I are planning to buy a house when we have enough saved," Stan said.

"And how close are you to being able to do it?" asked Cassie.

"We would have the money for a down payment right now, but the landlord who owns the building where my shop is decided he wants to sell, and I'm buying it. I have one more installment to go."

"I simply want to give you a gift," Cassie said.

"A very expensive gift, and we can't take it."

*And if we did let her give it to us, I could plant a garden,* Gwen thought.

But Stan was talking again. "Gwen and I are not the first couple who will have to wait until we can afford to buy our home on our own," he said. "We're no better than anyone else in our situation."

"But Gwen isn't in your situation. She has a family that can do this for her. Why should she wait if she doesn't have to? You can't think she's enjoying living in that apartment."

And then Stan turned to her. "What about it, Gwen?" he asked. "Is it so bad living the way we do?"

*Oh, Stan, I love you. So very much. But we could have trees and fresh, clean air, and I could plant roses.* The words were on the tip of her tongue, but then she looked at his face. And she saw how important this was to him. "No, it's not that bad," she said.

But on the way back home in the car, she couldn't help herself. "Why couldn't we take Mother's offer?" she demanded.

"Your mother doesn't like me, and she has no respect for me. How do you think I will feel letting her pay for the roof over my head? Gwen, you can't want that!"

She didn't. She didn't want him to lose his dignity or his self-respect. So she tried to make the best of it. She decided to get a job. It would get her out of the hated apartment, and she would earn a little money to add to the down-payment fund.

WHILE Gwen looked through the Help Wanted section each morning, she sat in the courtyard behind the apartment building, and she discovered that several of the babysitters working for her neighbors brought their charges down there to play. Watching the children, a second hunger—as strong as the need for the country—was born in her.

"Don't you think it's time we thought about having a family?" she asked Stan one night when they were lying next to each other.

"Let's wait until we're in our house first," he'd said.

"That's going to take so long. I don't want to wait."

"Well, I guess there's nothing that says we can't get a head start," he'd said as he reached for her. After that, all practical considerations of timing and budgets were forgotten. And when, after a few months, Gwen discovered she was pregnant, Stan was as overjoyed as she was. And she prepared to be blissful.

She and Stan picked out two names, one for a boy and one for a girl. They selected Michael and Abigail.

Suddenly Gwen was full of energy. She made over the second bedroom into a nursery, painting it a happy, gender-neutral yellow. Cassie had given Gwen a gift certificate to the most exclusive infant shop in town, and Stan didn't say a word when expensive baby paraphernalia started showing up at the apartment. Their child was more important to him than his pride. Gwen couldn't remember when she'd been happier.

Then suddenly everything was wrong. Terribly wrong. She could no longer feel the baby moving inside her. Stan rushed her to the doctor. Tests were run to try to prove that what Gwen knew in her bones and her blood wasn't true, that she was wrong. But she wasn't wrong.

Finally, the word was said. "Stillborn." Their baby daughter—she was a little girl—would never see her yellow nursery or the brightly colored mobile that was hanging over her crib. Stillborn. All the dreams and hopes died with that word.

*I failed you, Abby, and I failed Stan. I failed myself.*

THE room was hot. Gwen opened her eyes and looked at her watch. It was almost noon. She had to get dressed.

"Don't try to push yourself too hard," the doctor had said. "Remember, you need time to grieve. It's only been two weeks."

*I should have given her a garden. I should have seen to it that she had space and fresh air and trees and grass. I knew that was what she needed.* And crazy though it was—and Gwen did know it was crazy—there was part of her that believed her baby would have lived if she and Stan had had their own house with their own land.

They'd done a caesarean when they took the baby, and she had spent two nights in the hospital. When she came home, Stan had dismantled the nursery. He had painted the walls a soft taupe and gotten rid of the furniture from the fancy baby shop. Their nursery was now a guest bedroom.

Stan had stayed home with her after she'd come back from the hospital, and he had tried to talk to her about their loss. But finally, after three days, she told him she was feeling better and he should go back to work. Perhaps it was just her imagination, but she thought he'd been relieved.

Then last night he'd said to her, "Get dressed tomorrow and I'll take you to lunch. You need to get out of the house."

And she had screamed at him, "We don't have a house. We have this damned apartment."

Stan had looked as if she'd shot him.

Gwen knew how much her words had hurt. That was why, this morning, she'd decided to go to his shop at noon and surprise him. She started pulling clothes out of the closet. She had to get dressed sometime.

THE office building known as the Amber sat on the northwest corner of the busiest intersection in Wrightstown. Jeff enjoyed standing at his window, sixteen floors above the street, to watch the pedestrians bustle to and fro. It reminded him of New York, which was probably his favorite city in the States.

He had favorite cities worldwide now, was enough of a regular visitor to London, Buenos Aires, Moscow, Beijing, and Okinawa that there were hotel concierges and headwaiters in all those places who knew which suite was Mr. Henry's favorite and which wine he preferred. JeffSon had continued to grow—as it had had to, to hold off the sharks. Now the little business that had started as a small natural gas company was a conglomerate of gas lines and power plants involved in the transmission and distribution of power around the globe. And JeffSon was poised to involve itself in a new area— the water utility market. Jeff had done his homework as much as he could, but at a certain point, you just had to go for broke.

*Beware of Faustian bargains, Jeffie,* his father had said.

Jeff shook his head to clear it. This was no time to think about his father's antiquated notions. He started to turn away from the window when, down on the street below, he saw Gwen Wright—only her last name was something else now—coming out of her apartment building.

It was his wife, Jewel, who had first told him that the former Miss Wright had married a man who owned some kind of service shop and now lived downtown, across the street from the Amber. For some reason, Jewel always seemed to know what was going on with the Wright family, especially Gwen.

When Jewel had first mentioned Gwen's name, Jeff hadn't been sure who she was talking about. Then he had remembered the party he'd attended at the Wright house and the quiet girl whose birthday it had been. That night—was it four years ago?—he'd thought that there was something a little otherworldly about the party's honoree.

Then one day he'd seen Gwen in the neighborhood. She had walked out of her apartment building and headed in the direction of the old part of town. He soon realized that this morning walk was a regular occurrence. Every morning like clockwork, she left the building at the same time. He found he liked to watch her walk. Even in her condition—he soon realized that she was pregnant—her stride was long and fast and . . . well, "joyful" was the only word for it.

Jeff watched Gwen now as she headed down the street. She hadn't been out of her apartment since she'd lost her baby—this bit of gossip had come to him from Jewel, naturally—and he was glad to see Gwen out and about. But she was moving slowly and wearily.

He turned away from his window. He was leaving in two days to conclude a deal for the water concession in Buenos Aires, and he had reading to do. But the information packet didn't hold his attention. Thinking about Gwen Wright had reminded him of the painting he'd bought from her stepfather, Walter Amburn. He looked up. It was on his wall here in the office, the simple little picture of a little girl sitting on a roof watching the river flow by her house at dusk. Until Jeff had married Jewel, it had hung in the most prominent spot in his home. Even after he moved to the hotel where he and Jewel now lived while they waited for their home to be finished, the painting had hung over the fireplace in his five-room suite. There was something about the isolation of the child, and the endless river, that spoke to him.

However, when Jewel came to live with him in the hotel suite after they were married, she'd asked if it would be all right if they took it down. "It's so gloomy, honey," she'd said. "It gives me the creeps." She'd shivered.

That was his wife. His Jewel. Jeff thought about the changes she'd brought into his life, changes that did not thrill him.

Take the matter of their new home. It was he who had told Jewel to tear up the plans for the sleek modern house he had originally commissioned. The architect had designed it to be light and airy, with clean lines, but Jewel had lobbied instead for a "McMansion." Jeff told himself that it didn't matter that his house was a vulgar attempt to re-create . . . he didn't know what. A mansion in Great Britain? A French château? A Tuscan villa? But when he actually found himself faced with the prospect of living in Jewel's mansion/château/villa, he was embarrassed. He was embarrassed when she wore all her gold bangles—heavy bracelets studded with diamonds that she had wanted and he had purchased—at once.

But his discontent went deeper than embarrassment. He wished just once that his wife would have something interesting to say. It could be about anything, politics or the weather, as long as it wasn't yet more chatter about the latest gossip. When he'd married her, he'd known she didn't read, but he wished she'd take up a hobby or a sport—tennis or bridge or quilting—anything to keep her from touring the shops in the Algonquin Mall in her endless search for more clothes, more objects, more loot. . . .

*Stop that, Jeff,* he told himself sternly. *You have to be patient. She had nothing when she married you, so it's only natural that she would go a little wild with credit cards.*

Besides, hadn't he married her in part because she knew how to spend money? He hadn't been embarrassed by her when she encouraged him to buy the yacht he wanted. But the thing about that was, after she had encouraged him, he hadn't done it. Somehow watching her shop day after day had soured him on it for himself.

Jeff tried again to focus on the documents on his desk, but his mind kept wandering. He stood up and went back to look out the window, and he saw Gwen Wright walking back from wherever she'd gone. Her weariness was even worse now. She stopped at the entrance to her building and seemed to be thinking about something. Then, instead of going inside, she began in the direction of the park at the end of the street. That had to be her destination.

*But there are children playing in that park,* Jeff thought. *That's no place for someone who is suffering from the loss of her own baby.* Without thinking, Jeff ran out of his office toward the elevator.

STAN had not been in the shop. Even though Gwen knew it had nothing to do with her, that he had probably gone out on a job, after her outburst the night before, she'd felt as if he was avoiding her. *I will not let our tragedy destroy us,* she'd thought as she stood in the middle of Stan's empty shop. *The blaming and the anger and the guilt stop here.* And with those thoughts in her head, she'd turned around and started back to the apartment building.

But when Gwen reached her building, she stopped dead in her tracks and wondered, *What would Cassie do now?* The answer came back loud and clear: Cassandra Wright would face down her pain. She would look at it squarely, and she would wrestle it to the ground. Galvanized, Gwen started for the little park at the end of the street—the one where all the kids played.

There were children of all ages playing in the park—boys and girls. The sweet little faces and high, delighted laughter overwhelmed her. She stood at the entrance, unable to breathe. She was about to turn away when a voice at her side said, "Excuse me, aren't you . . . that is, *weren't* you Gwen Wright?" And standing next to her was a man she recognized from the many stories written about him in the newspapers. He was the owner and CEO of the JeffSon Corporation, but she would always think of him as the pirate who had come to her birthday party.

"I've been to your house . . . your mother's house . . . it was about four years ago. But you probably don't remember."

"But I do. How do you do, Mr. Henry?" she said. She held out her hand for him to shake. "I used to be Gwen Wright. Now my name is Gwen Girard." Then, because she couldn't help herself, she added, "Didn't you marry Jewel Fairchild?"

JEFF sat across the table from Gwen and tried to think of something to say. He had invited her to have coffee with him. She had accepted, and they had walked back to his office building, where there was a fancy little place that dispensed lattes. He found himself momentarily at a loss for something to say. Finally he settled on, "Do you go to that park often?"

"I don't like that park very much," she answered. "It's so small and crowded."

He thought of her athletic stride and the feeling he'd had that she should be walking on country roads and open fields. This was the wrong setting for her, he thought. But what had Jewel said about the man she'd married—the one whose name Jeff couldn't remember? Jewel said he was beneath Gwen. A nobody. So probably this was the best they could afford.

"What does your husband do for a living?" he asked.

"Stan has his own electrician's shop," was the answer. An electrician's shop! And her family owned one of the biggest glassworks in the country. Jewel was right; the girl had married beneath her.

"I really should be getting home," Gwen Wright—no, it was Gwen Girard, he remembered—was saying. "Thank you so much for the coffee."

"I'll see you to your building," Jeff said.

"You don't have to do that."

"We're right across the street from each other. We're neighbors."

THE penthouse suite in the glitzy hotel where Jewel and Jeff were camping out consisted of five rooms with views that stretched as far off as the glassworks. Jewel got up out of bed and walked to one of the massive bedroom's floor-to-ceiling windows. She could see the whole city spread out at her feet. And soon her view would be even more grand, when she moved into her new house. The house that would make up for all the early years of desperate wanting.

Jewel turned back to bed, where Jeff was sleeping. He used to love watching her pleasure at the gifts he showered on her. But lately she'd sensed a certain disapproval coming from him, as if there was something distasteful about her squealing with joy over her new diamond earrings or their new Learjet. At such moments, he looked a little too much like his father.

Then she thought of something that Jeff had told her at dinner. He'd seen Gwen Wright that afternoon. He'd been taking a walk to clear his head, and he'd bumped into her, and he'd felt that it was only good manners to invite her to have a cup of coffee with him.

Jewel still couldn't believe that Gwen Wright was living in downtown Wrightstown! In a building that was fine—it was actually rather glamorous—if you were trying to make your way as a paralegal or a dental assistant. But if you were Gwen Wright . . . Could anyone have imagined that this was how things would turn out? That Jewel Henry, born Jewel Fairchild, would one day be able to buy and sell Gwen Wright ten times over if she'd wanted to?

## CHAPTER 8

—⁓—

THOSE who said time heals everything were wrong, Gwen knew. There are certain wounds that never go away—like the one she'd sustained when she learned that Cassie had been lying to her about her birth parents. That hurt was permanent, as were the questions it raised about the man and woman who gave her life.

But the loss of a baby was different. That pain would never go away, either, but you finally did figure out how to absorb it. At first you were convinced that you'd never be happy again; then one morning you woke up and it was autumn, and the trees in the little park at the end of your street were spreading a gold and orange carpet on the ground. And you found that far from avoiding the little room Stan had redone as a guest room, you now enjoyed sitting in there when you read. The soft taupe on the walls was a soothing color, and the light was excellent. That was why you'd chosen to make it the nursery—and when you realized that now you could say that word "nursery" to yourself without tears, you knew that you'd turned a corner.

Stan seemed to feel that she was ready to move on, too. One night he gave her a box wrapped in pink paper with artificial roses in the bow. Inside was a computer.

He smiled his smile that made the skin crinkle at the corners of his eyes. "You always wanted to write, Gwen. Why don't you try?"

So she did. She sat in the guest room and tried to write a children's story about a pigeon who lived in a park. But she couldn't make her mind think like a city pigeon. She tried to write a story about a squirrel who lived on a hill behind a big white house. But she found she'd lost her connection to the squirrels and chipmunks she'd once watched for hours. Finally, she put the computer in the living room, where she and Stan both could use it, and she went back to reading when she sat in the guest room.

But Stan wouldn't give up. "Writing was your dream when I met you," he said. "You say you don't have any stories to tell, but I know one day you'll do it."

She didn't say that she needed space and sky to spin her stories. That was one of the things they didn't talk about.

Once in a while, when she was walking to the park, she and Jeff Henry would run into each other. And he would ask her if she'd like to have coffee with him, and she would say yes, because it was fun to talk to a man who shared her taste for Dickens and Tolstoy, and they both enjoyed their ongoing debate over the merits of his favorite opera composer, Wagner, versus her beloved Puccini.

But gradually, as one does with a good friend, she and Jeff started opening up about less trivial, more personal matters. He told her

about his teenage years as the nerdy son of two pretentious intellectuals, and Gwen talked about her childhood as an odd duck, the
animals she loved, and the stories she made up about them.

So time passed, and the healing continued, and before Gwen
knew it, a year had passed since she'd lost her baby. And that day,
the old fog threatened to descend again. It wasn't the kind of thing
she could say to Stan—he might find something morbid about remembering the date. Still, she wished she could talk to someone.
She thought of Jeff, who listened and would find something to say
that would help. It would be nice if she were to run into him today,
she thought as she left the apartment and headed to the elevators.
She was going out into the neighborhood to pick up Stan's jacket
at the dry cleaner's.

JEFF stood at his window and watched Gwen walk out of her
building. He thought about rushing down to the street to stage another of his "accidental" encounters with her, but instead he looked
back to his desk, where a report waited for him. It had been assembled by his staff at his request some time ago, but he had not
read it yet. Because when he did, he would have to make a decision
that he'd been putting off. It concerned the woman who was now
walking down the street in the direction of the shops that serviced
the neighborhood. Gwen Girard was probably doing some wifely
errand, shopping for some last-minute item at the grocery store or
picking up some shoes that had been repaired. He frowned. He
didn't like to think of her involved in such mundane pursuits, and
yet he knew from a recent conversation they had had that she had
finally found a kind of peace in them. He couldn't help contrasting
her minimal desire with the never-ending grasping of his wife.

Jeff moved back to his desk and sat. For a while now, he'd been
serially and consistently unfaithful to his wife. He was discreet—
when one was away from home as much as he was, that was easy.
Although he wondered if it would have mattered to Jewel if she had
known. Her passion, he had come to understand, had nothing to do
with him and everything to do with what he could provide.

The final blow had come when they had moved into the nightmare of a house she had designed and loved so much—the house that humiliated him. That was when he started noticing how irritating she was. And how noisy. It wasn't just her incessant, mindless chatter. Her sweet voice now grated on his ears, and her laugh, which had once seemed so warm and free to him, had now turned into a loud braying bid for attention. It was no wonder that Gwen Wright, who was so quiet and so intelligent, attracted him.

Jeff picked up the report on his desk and began to read—but then he put it down. The neatly stapled sheaf of papers was the result of the research he'd asked his staff to do on Stanley Girard. The business decision he had to make concerned the husband of the woman he wanted. But in what way did he want her?

He knew Gwen enjoyed his company, and he was pretty sure that he could push their relationship further. The trouble was, there were elements of his arrangement with Jewel that worked. She still looked fabulous on his arm, and as long as the conversation was light social chatter, she could be charming. And if he tried to divorce her, there would be hell to pay. At the moment, there were reasons—serious business reasons—why he could not afford that.

Jeff rubbed his temples, where a headache seemed to be starting. The deal for the water utility concession had gone through about a year ago, but lately there had been some disturbing rumblings coming out of Buenos Aires. The sharp young man Jeff had hired as his second in command—his name was Mark Scotto—had assured Jeff that the solution was to create a separate corporation for the water concession. They would be skating fairly close to the edge with a few FTC regulations, but Jeff had done that before. It all sounded logical, and there was nothing about it that everyone else wasn't doing, so there was no reason for Jeff to suddenly remember his father saying, *Beware of Faustian bargains, Jeffie.* At the same time, he didn't want Jewel's divorce lawyers going through his books right now, as they would be sure to do if he was stupid enough to rock the boat.

Jeff looked down at his desk and the report on Stan Girard. Gwen's husband was a talented guy who was parlaying his shop into an operation that specialized in the installation, maintenance, and repair of some sophisticated electrical systems for major corporate clients. He was a good candidate for what Jeff had in mind.

Jeff walked back to the window and looked down at the street where Gwen had stood a few minutes earlier, waiting for the light to change. She had looked unhappy today. He thought for a moment—wasn't it about this time last year that he had heard she'd lost her baby? Yes, he was sure it was. Suddenly, he wanted to give her something, something that would make the sad look go away.

He picked up the phone on his desk and buzzed his secretary. "Set up a meeting for me with Stanley Girard," he said.

"YOU want to buy Stan's Electronics?" Stan looked at the man sitting across the desk from him in disbelief. He was sitting in a huge office that was decorated with lots of glass and chrome, and Jeff Henry had just offered to buy him out.

"What could you possibly want with my operation?" Stan asked.

"Good question," Jeff Henry said. "You must know the JeffSon Corporation has been expanding all over the country. We purchased that twenty-five-hundred-megawatt plant in upstate New York last year and connected it to the local grid; and we're looking at buying several other plants in the area, which we will connect in a similar way. We'll need centrally located stations from which to install, operate, and maintain these new plants, and your shop is in an ideal location in the center of Wrightstown."

"And I own the building and the land under it."

Jeff Henry nodded. His attitude seemed rather brusque, Stan thought. The man was supposed to be a great negotiator, but it was almost as if he was deliberately being rude.

"So what you want, essentially, is to buy my real estate," he said.

"Not only that," came the answer. "When we purchase a small business, like yours, it isn't a total cash transaction. A piece of your compensation will be in JeffSon stock." The voice now took on a condescending tone. "You'll be a shareholder in one of the biggest and most important new companies in the world. You will also have the same deal on stock options that every JeffSon exec does."

"A JeffSon exec? But I'm not—"

Jeff Henry interrupted. "We would want you to work for us. Overseeing the crews and managing the installation and maintenance of our various operations in this part of the country." He shrugged and smiled. "It's an executive position, although of course what we're buying is your expertise in the field."

"That's very flattering." *But why do I feel that there's something you're not telling me?*

*WHY isn't he jumping at this?* Jeff thought angrily. *Doesn't he realize what I'm offering him? Poor Gwen; she really did marry an idiot.* But there was nothing idiotic about Stanley Girard's eyes. Or the thoughtful way he was studying Jeff.

"Look, Stan . . . I think you know the situation as well as I do. JeffSon is going to be taking over more and more small companies all over the state. And to say it plainly, those we don't buy we'll put out of business.

"Your choice is to continue with a small business that will eventually be obsolete or to sign on now with us and be a part of an expanding organization. Your salary will be commensurate with that of all our top management, and I think you'll find that when you add in your benefits, your JeffSon stock, and stock options, that you'll be doing much better than you could ever do on your own."

"I see." For whatever reason, Stanley Girard was handing him the classic noncommittal response.

"Well, that's our offer in a nutshell," Jeff said. "I have to go out of town for a few days, so think it over."

"Thank you. I'll be in touch," said Stan.

"HOW did you hear about the offer JeffSon made to Stan?" Gwen demanded.

She and her mother were sitting in the food court at the Algonquin Mall. It was not a usual haunt for Cassie, but when she'd called Gwen, she'd said she wanted anonymity, a place where no one would see Cassandra Wright and her daughter sitting and talking in the middle of a workday.

They had purchased their slices of pizza and taken them to a secluded part of the food court next to the coffee stand. Then Cassandra had delivered her bombshell.

"You must keep Stanley from taking JeffSon's offer," she'd said.

The offer had only been made three days ago, so Gwen repeated her question. "Mother, how did you know about this?"

"There is very little that goes on in the business community in this town that I don't know. Besides, this was predictable. JeffSon's gobbling up small companies like Stan's all over the place. Add to that the fact that Stan owns his building free and clear, and it's in a great location on a busy avenue."

"It's not just the shop—they want Stan to work for them. In a management position. Or didn't your spies tell you that?"

Cassandra sighed. "It's even worse than I thought."

"Worse? What do you mean?" Gwen had been proud to hear that a brilliant man like Jeff Henry saw the value in Stan and was offering him a job.

"Gwen, listen to me," Cassie went on urgently. "Stan is doing well with his shop, and I'm very happy for you. He works hard, and he deserves as much success as he can handle. But for him to get himself involved with a company like JeffSon . . ."

"What's wrong with JeffSon?"

"Maybe nothing. But there are things that concern me. They're buying and selling way too much for my taste, creating offshore corporations that are hard to monitor, and just a couple of months ago, they hired a new accounting firm that has a reputation for skating very close to the line. . . ."

"Somehow I think Jeff Henry knows what he's doing."

"Jeff Henry is a Johnny-come-lately who appeared out of nowhere and has made an enormous amount of money very quickly. One has to wonder about that, Gwen."

"Why? Maybe Jeff Henry's just brilliant. Maybe he's a genius."

"Good Lord, why are you defending the man?"

It was a good question. Too good. The answer was, Gwen had been pleased that Jeff had offered her husband a big job, because it meant that she and Jewel were closer to being equals. Because, childish as it was, when she thought about Jewel, it bothered her that Stan hadn't set the world on fire and accumulated a pile of money. "None of what you're saying means that Jeff Henry is doing anything wrong," she said.

"Not necessarily, but it can be a red flag." Cassie drew in a deep breath, and then she said, "The truth is, the people at JeffSon are big-stakes players—highfliers, if you will. And with all due respect to your husband, I don't think he's . . . well, sophisticated enough for that kind of environment."

Gwen couldn't believe it. "Do you have any idea how insulting you're being?" she cried. "You're talking as if Stan were an idiot."

"I never said anything like that. But I do know something about the Jeff Henrys of the world, and I'm giving you some advice I think you need. Tell Stan to stay with his honest business."

And then it burst out. It was the last thing Gwen wanted to say, but she couldn't stop herself. "You're just saying all of this because Jeff is Jewel's husband! You've never forgiven her."

"For heaven's sake, it's not that way at all. The thought never crossed my mind, although it did cross yours, and I must say—"

But whatever it was that she must say didn't get said, because they were interrupted by an enthusiastic voice. "Gwen! Cassandra!" it called out. And there was Jewel, loaded down with packages and waving at them. She hurried over.

"How wonderful to see both of you!" she said. "I can't believe you two are here in the food court, of all places!"

"Hello, Jewel," Cassie said, hoping her voice didn't sound as chilly to everyone else as it did to her.

Gwen followed her lead with a polite "How are you, Jewel?"

"Fine, couldn't be better," Jewel said. "May I sit with you?" She drew out a chair at the table. "I just stopped at the jeweler's to have my bracelets cleaned. They do it so much more thoroughly than anyone else does."

It is an automatic reflex to look at an article someone has just mentioned. Cassie and Gwen both did so.

"Very pretty, Jewel," Cassie said, as she was expected to say.

"Jeff gave them to me for our anniversary. He spoils me rotten. And, of course, he's doing so well, I just can't believe it. He's into so many different businesses. Why, just the other day, I heard him talking to someone on the phone about the water markets in South America—can you imagine?"

Something cold prickled down Cassie's back. She couldn't help trying to get a little more information.

"I certainly appreciate the need for any company to diversify," she said to Jewel. "But it was my understanding that JeffSon is in the business of distributing energy. What could that possibly have to do with water rights?"

Jewel gave her a dismissive wave of her hand. "I'm really not worried about what's going on at JeffSon. That's my husband's department, and believe me, he can take care of himself." Then she turned to Gwen and changed the subject. "I have an idea," she said. "Jeff is out of town, and I'm at loose ends. Why don't you come out to my place? You can follow me in my car, and I'll show you around. We've just finished the house, and I'd love for you to see it."

"It sounds like fun, Mother!" Gwen cried. "We have the time, don't we?"

"It'll only take an hour, I promise," Jewel chimed in.

There really wasn't a graceful way for Cassie to back out.

GWEN waited for her mother's protest to begin. Sure enough, it came as soon as they were in Gwen's car.

"What on earth were you thinking?" Cassie demanded.

Gwen looked at her mother. "Oh, come on. Jewel just wants to show off her house. Let's give her the satisfaction."

"I do not want to give Jewel Henry satisfaction for anything."

"You see? You are still angry at her after all these years!"

"Are you trying to annoy me, Gwendolyn?"

Gwen waited a beat. "No," she said thoughtfully. "I guess I'm just trying to put an old ghost to bed." She looked at the scenery that was passing by them. "It is a lovely ride, isn't it?"

"Charming," Cassie admitted grudgingly. "It's old America out here, all these colonial houses. . . ." Then she stopped short. "And some new ones, " she added grimly as Jewel's car led them through the wrought-iron front gate of an enormous house that sprawled at the head of a long, sloping driveway. Architecturally speaking, the thing was a hodgepodge of styles and periods.

"Is that a pond at the top of the driveway?" Cassie asked.

"You mean where that fountain is spurting? Yes, I think it is a pond. Or possibly a moat."

They ascended the drive. Above them, Jewel got out of her car and waved them onward. They got out of the car, and Jewel bustled up to them. "I can't wait to give you the tour," she burbled as she ushered them through the massive front door of her home.

The inside of the house wasn't any better than the outside. From the great circle of the entrance hall, there radiated corridors—the floor of each had been done in a different kind of exotic wood, Jewel proudly pointed out—and they all led to the varied luxuries of the house: the card room, the billiard room, the bowling alley, the theater, and the spa.

The tour wound up in the foyer, where the windows looked out upon the lawns, the guest cottage, and the pool, which was backed by what looked like a slab of some kind of rock. A touch of a button on a huge electrical panel on the foyer wall turned the slab into a violently rushing waterfall worthy of Niagara. Jewel frantically adjusted levers and switches until the flood was under control. "I'm still not used to working this thing," she said with her wide smile. The nearby tennis courts were soaked. Gwen didn't dare look at her mother for fear that they would both start laughing.

"The designer tried to convince me to put an eternal flame behind the pool, but I said no; I wanted a water feature," Jewel said.

"Well, you certainly got one," said Cassandra.

*THEY'RE LAUGHING AT ME,* Jewel thought. *They think I don't know it, but I'm not dumb. What have they got to laugh about, anyway? My house is bigger than that musty old place that Cassie owns—and as for Gwen living in her little city apartment, she doesn't have the right to turn up her nose at me or anyone else.*

But even as she was thinking these things, Jewel was remembering the way Jeff had reacted when the house was finished. At first he'd seemed stunned, but then that funny look that was halfway between pity and disgust had come into her husband's eyes—it was the same look she was seeing now with Gwen and Cassie.

For the first time in years, Jewel wanted to cry. Because she realized that she hadn't just brought Gwen and Cassie to her house to make them jealous; she'd wanted them to . . . accept her. She had wanted Cassie and Gwen to admit that, at long last, Jewel Fairchild belonged to the exclusive club they'd been members of forever. But now they were letting her know that she'd never belong. No matter what she did, she would always be an outsider. *How I hate them,* she thought as she blinked back tears.

*IS JEWEL going to cry?* Gwen wondered. *What does she have to cry about?* Her home was a travesty, of course, but if you looked past the pool and the ridiculous water feature, you could see beautiful land with trees and wildflowers that Jewel and her landscape designer had not managed to destroy.

More important than that, Jewel's husband, who was brilliant and funny and far too good for her, had given all of it to her. Even if it was not his taste, he loved her enough to want to make her happy. Gwen's husband loved her, too, but he expected her to be patient and wait for the house she needed and wanted so desperately.

Suddenly, Gwen wanted to get away from Jewel and her mansion and the vision of Jeff Henry living in it for Jewel's sake. It was obvious that Cassie wanted to leave, too, because she was looking at her watch. "I think . . ." she was starting to say, when a man's voice in the hallway startled all of them.

"I'll take my bags up to my room, George," said the voice.

And George, whoever he was, answered, "Of course, Mr. Henry. Mrs. Henry is in the living room with guests, sir."

Before the three women could take a breath, Jeff was entering the room with his swaggering stride. Gwen thought she saw his eyes light up when he spotted her. The moment passed in an instant, and Jeff was greeting Cassandra and then giving Jewel a kiss on the cheek and explaining that he'd come home early because one of the guys from Texas had fallen and broken his arm and the whole bunch would be flying up the next day in somebody's private jet.

JEWEL slipped her hand possessively through Jeff's arm. For a second when he'd first walked in the door, she'd thought she'd seen something in the look he gave Gwen—a warmth and a tenderness that he never displayed. But then she realized it had been her imagination. That was what happened when you let people like Gwen and Cassie make you feel inferior. If you didn't watch it, you found yourself imagining that dull, shy Gwen could actually be attractive to your husband. It was ridiculous to even think that Gwen Girard could ever compete with Jewel Fairchild Henry.

# CHAPTER 9

"A PENNY for your thoughts," Gwen said to her uncharacteristically silent mother as they drove back to Wrightstown. The visit to Jewel's house had ended quickly after Jeff's entrance. He'd tried to start a little idle chitchat with Cassandra. "My father taught art history at Wrightstown College," he'd told her. "One of his students, his name is Edward Lawrence, is the curator at the Wright Glass Museum. He was brought on board by your first husband."

Of course, Jeff had no way of knowing that any mention of Bradford Greeley was enough to send Cassandra out of a room. Instead of picking up on the opening, she had murmured that she must look up the man sometime and had hustled herself and Gwen out the door.

"You look angry," Gwen now said as they drove. "Are you?"

"Not angry. Just . . . thinking."

"You're not going to start that stuff about JeffSon again, are you? Because anyone can see from looking at that house that Jeff Henry is in fine shape."

"That's not important." Her mother frowned. "There's something else. I didn't like the way Jeff Henry looked at you when he walked in the room."

"I cannot begin to imagine what you're talking about!" But Gwen could feel her face getting red.

"Oh, Gwen! Yes, you can. You can't tell me you weren't aware of it. Women can always recognize a thing like that."

"Well, I wasn't!" Gwen said. "Because there was nothing to be aware of!" But Gwen felt guilty. And since guilt is one of the least comfortable emotions we can experience, she got angry at Cassie. "And you are wrong about Stan and the JeffSon offer," she said. "I think he should take it, and I'm going to tell him so!"

STAN hadn't expected Gwen to be so strongly in favor of the Jeff-Son deal. Nor had he expected his own reaction to her enthusiasm. He was proud of the small business he'd built from nothing, and it hurt to see how easily his wife could contemplate selling it. On the other hand, he knew that Jeff Henry's offer was an excellent one and most people in his position would jump at it.

Then the letter came. It was addressed to him at his shop. He recognized Cassandra's correct handwriting at once.

*Dear Stan,* she'd written. *I find myself in a difficult position. It is well known that for the sake of family peace, in-laws should not meddle with young people's lives. So I have had a few misgivings about bringing up a subject that is really none of my business. But I've decided to go ahead anyway and risk your displeasure.*

*To put the matter plainly, I understand that you have received an offer to sell your business to JeffSon and, in exchange for various financial considerations, join them. The more I think about this, the more I feel that it is not a good idea. I do not trust the things I hear about JeffSon or the people connected with it. You are a man who works hard, and you are to be commended for that. Let the highfliers at JeffSon do their wheeling and dealing; you stick to what you know.*

Stan showed the letter to Gwen. "Did Cassie talk to you about this?" he asked.

"Yes," she said.

"It's clear she doesn't think I'm up to the challenge."

Gwen took the letter out of his hand and tore it in half. "And I told her that you could hold your own with the people at JeffSon or anywhere else," she said proudly.

And with Gwen looking at him with that mixture of love and defiance and perfect faith in his abilities, there was only one thing he could do. "I guess you're looking at a new JeffSon employee," he said. And when she hugged and kissed him and told him how happy she was, he told himself that he was doing the right thing.

But a nagging little voice in the back of his brain was saying that Cassie Wright was a smart woman. She knew a lot more about high finance than he did. So tomorrow he was going to call and accept the offer, but he had made up his mind—he would not accept any JeffSon stock for his building and land. Jeff Henry would have to pay him in cash, or there would be no deal. He would work for Jeff-Son, but he would keep his money safely tucked away until he was sure that everything was going to be all right.

JEWEL sat on the satin-covered chaise in the bedroom that Jeff had once said was the size of a football field and watched him unpack. She watched as he took the monogrammed leather case in which he kept his watches and cuff links from the suitcase and returned the contents to the bigger case in his walk-in closet. His shirts, custom made of the finest poplin, were rehung on the wooden hangers that had been specially made for the purpose. He looked down on Jewel for her extravagances, but when it came to his own, nothing but the best would do for Jeff Henry! He was like all the rest of the hypocrites who thought they were too good for people like Jewel—hypocrites like Cassandra Wright and dear, dull Gwen.

"She's not the princess you think she is," she told him as she watched him push shoe trees into his handmade Italian loafers.

"What?" He was too busy with the shoes to look at her.

"I know a nasty secret about Gwen Wright Girard."

That got his attention. He came over to stand in front of her. "What are you talking about?" he demanded. And so she leaned back on the satin chaise, and for the second time in her life, she told the story of Gwen Wright's birth parents.

After she had finished, she waited. Jeff didn't say anything for a minute; then he asked, "You did say the mother was from New Orleans, right?"

"Yes. Some barmaid who—" But Jewel never got to finish the sentence, because Jeff had rushed out of the room.

A WEEK later, Jeff called Gwen at home—the first time he'd ever done that—and asked her to meet him at the Wright Glass Museum the next day.

THE Wright Glass Museum had won several architectural awards when it was built in the sixties. The design was as unique as it was beautiful; it was a beige cube constructed of site-cast concrete with many skylights and mammoth windows, giving the interior an airy feel that was a perfect setting for the delicate displays of the glass-blower's artistry. All the work exhibited had come from the Wright Glassworks Studio, where skilled artisans from all over the world had been creating one-of-a-kind figurines, sculptures, vases, bowls, and other decorative works for more than a hundred years.

Gwen was standing in the atrium when a beaming Jeff came toward her.

"There's something I want to show you," he said excitedly. "But first, I believe I told you about my father's student who is the curator at this museum. His name is Edward Lawrence." Jeff paused. "He worked here when your father was running the glassworks."

It took her a moment to digest what he'd said—that he knew about Bradford Greeley being her father.

"Who told you—" she asked, then stopped. "Jewel," she said.

He nodded dismissively. "Yes, but that doesn't matter now." Gwen was about to protest that it did matter very much, but he went on. "I thought I remembered hearing Edward talking once about an entire series of figurines your father asked the Glassworks Studio to create. He called it the New Orleans Group."

"Oh," Gwen whispered.

"Bradford died before he could tell anyone what he wanted done with them. And Cassandra didn't . . ." He trailed off uncertainly.

"She didn't want to have anything to do with them," Gwen said.

Jeff nodded. "They were packed away. But I contacted Edward a couple of days ago and asked if I could take a look at them. Would you like to see them?"

"Yes," Gwen breathed.

"They're in the back storage area."

JEFF ushered Gwen through a door marked EMPLOYEES ONLY and introduced her to Edward Lawrence, who led them to a storage space where a table had been placed directly under a skylight so that a shaft of sunshine shone down on it.

"This is it, Mrs. Girard!" Edward cried. "I have set up the grouping as it might have looked if it had been displayed in the museum."

Gwen gasped with sheer pleasure. In front of her, in exquisite miniature, was a forest scene full of sparkling woodland creatures. The trees were actual branches that had been cut to scale, but the animals were all painstakingly and lovingly made out of glass. Two raccoons foraged for food under the watchful eye of a frog, while squirrels with threads of glass whiskers ate acorns, and two delicate little chipmunks stuffed their cheeks. A rabbit looked up to a tree branch on which sat an array of different songbirds, each feather etched in careful, minute detail.

"Oh," Gwen said. "Oh, it's so beautiful!"

"Yes," Edward said softly. "I think this collection is one of our greatest masterpieces. I always hoped . . ." He stopped himself.

"I wish they could be displayed, too," she said. "Thank you for letting me see them." She turned to Jeff. "And thank you," she said. He didn't say anything until they had left the storage room and were back in the museum.

"I wanted you to see that Bradford wasn't all bad," Jeff said. "When Jewel told me that you were his daughter and the story about your birth mother . . . I could imagine what you must have thought about him."

"I didn't let myself think much, to be honest with you. He was not a subject my mother wanted to discuss, for obvious reasons."

He stood there staring at her. He was very still, as if he was debating with himself about something. And her mother's words echoed in her head: *I don't like the way he looks at you.*

"I should be getting back home," Gwen said. "I still have to shop for dinner." Then she added, "For Stan."

He came out of his trance. "And I have paperwork back at the office." They walked to the entrance of the museum together. He did not offer to drive her back to her apartment. She took the bus.

GWEN didn't mention the museum visit to Stan. In a couple of weeks, her husband would be working for Jeff, and she didn't want the two men to start off on the wrong foot.

But at night, when she lay in bed next to Stan, her mind went back to the little enchanted forest that had been the vision of the man whose DNA she carried, and she wondered, *Which one of my parents loved the woods and the creatures in it the way I do? Was it my father? My mother? I'll never know, but I want to think he did it for her. I want to think they loved each other that much.*

The next morning when Gwen woke up, she went into the taupe-colored guest room and opened the laptop computer Stan had given her. She took out a yellow legal pad and a pile of pencils and set them near the computer so she could make notes on ideas.

When everything was exactly the way she wanted it, she sat in front of the computer. She closed her eyes and let her mind drift back to her tree stump on the hill. Then she opened her eyes and began to type: *Abby the squirrel was the odd duck of the forest.*

When the words appeared on the monitor screen, a voice behind her said softly, "You're finally doing it." And she turned to see Stan leaning over to read the screen. "And you're calling her Abby," he added. Then Stan, who never showed emotion, leaned over to kiss her, and he was smiling with tears in his eyes.

SOMETIMES Stan couldn't believe it had been two years since he'd become a member of the JeffSon family. But then there were other times, like today, when it seemed as if he'd been working at the company forever. This usually happened when he'd had to stay behind his desk for too long. Or when he had to go to meetings. It seemed to him that three quarters of his job consisted of going to meetings.

Stan far preferred being out in the field troubleshooting technical and mechanical problems. He'd done quite a bit of that when he'd first started in his new position, back when there had been big plans for upgrading the existing power plants and buying new ones. But suddenly, all those plans were put on hold. For a couple of days, he'd heard a rumor about a cash flow problem, but the gossip had subsided, and JeffSon was showing huge profits. And the stock was trading higher than ever on the Exchange, as Jeff Henry ran around the country winning awards as Entrepreneur of the Year.

Stan stood up and walked around his office—anything to get the blood flowing again. He stopped in front of a small shelf, which was empty except for a thin book with a painting of a squirrel on the cover. It was an advance copy of the children's book Gwen had written. She'd named it *Abby* after the little squirrel who was the lead character, and it would be in bookstores at the end of the month. Gwen already had several book signings scheduled in nearby towns, and she would be going on a book tour after that. His Gwen on a book tour! Stan still couldn't believe it. And her publisher had just signed on for three more books about Abby and her forest friends. He was so proud of her.

And he was a little proud of himself, too. Because he had had a hand in her success. He took the book back to his desk, leaned back in his chair, and remembered how it had all come about.

Gwen had finished her book at the same time that he had started working at JeffSon. He'd already sold his business to the company, and he was well aware that Cassie was angry because he and Gwen had not taken her advice. Stan had done his best to steer clear of his formidable mother-in-law.

But then he'd read the manuscript for Gwen's book. And he'd known right away that it was special. It wasn't just the story about a little squirrel who was different and shy and learned to accept herself that fascinated him. It was the way Gwen seemed to get inside the heads of the characters she'd created.

"What are you going to do with this?" he'd asked her.

"I hadn't thought about that. I was just glad to finish it."

"Someone should publish it."

"I wouldn't know how to try to get it published," she'd said.

Stan couldn't let the matter rest. The book was good; he knew it was. He had faith in his instincts. He needed to talk to someone who knew more about this kind of thing than he did. He sought out Gwen's stepfather.

Walter read the book and saw immediately what Stan had seen. "The person you need to speak to is Cassie," he told Stan. "She serves on so many charitable boards, including several based in New York, and she knows quite a few bigwigs in publishing."

"My mother-in-law isn't very fond of me right now," Stan said ruefully.

"That's putting it mildly," Walter said. "But you both appreciate a job well done—and this book is very good." He paused. "And, of course, you both love Gwen."

So, armed with a copy of Gwen's manuscript, Stan drove out to the Wright house to take on his mother-in-law. Cassie was working in her garden, and she didn't stop when he walked over to her. But she did look up. "Is Gwen with you?" she asked.

"I came here alone," he said. "I need your help."

She turned back to her roses. "I'd say it's a little late in the day for that. From what I've heard, you've already sold your business."

"This isn't about me," he said, determined to keep his temper. "This is about Gwen." Again, her head snapped up. "She's not sick or anything like that," he assured her hurriedly. "She's done something that's . . . Well, she's written a book."

"A book? Gwen?"

"It's called *Abby*. It's a children's book, and it's really fine, at least I think it is, and . . ." He stopped and eyed the woman who had always thought he was a borderline idiot. "Look at it this way," he said. "If this book of hers is as good as I think it is, then she'll have her own money and a career, and she won't have to depend on me. Wouldn't you like that?"

Cassie removed her gardening gloves and held out her hand for the manuscript. While Stan stood in front of her, she read it. When she looked up, there was a strange expression on her face, equal parts sadness, tenderness, and pride. It only lasted for a second. "I'll keep this, if I may," she said, "and I'll make a few calls."

"Thank you," Stan said, and he turned to go.

"Stan," she called out to him. He turned back. "We all make mistakes," she said. "If you and Gwen are ever in trouble . . . please let me know."

He nodded and left. And six weeks later, she called to say that Gwen had a publisher for her first book.

STAN picked up the copy of Gwen's book and looked at her picture on the back. She was facing the camera head-on, but her thoughtful gaze was fixed somewhere far off. Her intelligence shone through her big brown eyes, and her dreamy, far-off look was typical of her. This was the Gwen he knew and loved, and as far as he was concerned, she'd gotten prettier with the passing years. Not that she would ever be a beauty like Jewel Henry. But he'd take Gwen over that woman any day. He frowned a little at that thought. Because he was sure Jewel's husband shared it.

Stan leaned back in his chair again, and more memories flooded into his mind. The whole thing had begun when he and Gwen had attended their first party at Jeff and Jewel's house. At dinner that evening, they sat at small round tables in the dining room, and Gwen had been placed at Jeff's. Something in it set off warning bells for Stan. It wasn't that Jeff was flirting with Gwen, because he certainly didn't cross the line in any way—but he admired her. That was clear. And she who had thought herself unappealing and odd for so many years was flattered. That was clear, too. But as far as Stan could see, that was it. There was a certain sexual tension when a man and woman were attracted to each other, and Stan didn't get any sense of that. At least not on his wife's part.

Over the next two years, whenever he and Gwen were in Jeff's company, Stan was on his guard. And he became more and more convinced that Jeff Henry had feelings for Gwen that he had no right to have. But there was nothing Stan could do about it.

Stan took the book back to the shelf. He'd learned to live with his suspicions about Jeff Henry—mostly because he trusted his wife's integrity so much.

But he had never really settled in and become gung ho about working at JeffSon. He was probably the only person working at the place who had not taken advantage of his stock-option plan. The money he'd been paid for his business had been socked away in a money market account. He hadn't spent any of it, because he couldn't forget Cassie's warning.

But in the last couple of weeks, he'd decided he was being ridiculous. All around him, his colleagues who had invested in the company were making out like bandits, and his money was earning peanuts. It was time to buy JeffSon stock—and it was time to buy a house for Gwen. He'd told her to start looking, and she'd already found a place she liked. In fact, she was going to meet him today for lunch. He checked his watch. He had two hours before he was supposed to meet her downstairs in the lobby.

On his desk was a preliminary draft for one of the newsletters Jeff-Son released to keep its shareholders—and potential shareholders—informed about the company. Usually Stan skipped reading these things, because he considered them nothing more than puff pieces, but if he was planning to buy JeffSon stock, he told himself he probably should read up on the company.

Twenty minutes later, deeply troubled, he put the newsletter down and turned on his computer. There were some numbers he wanted to check.

As THE small jet circled the airport and prepared to land, Jeff looked out the window at the city below him. He'd always considered Wrightstown his good-luck charm, the place where great things happened to him. So how had everything gone so desperately wrong? How had his company, his brainchild, stopped being a vibrant, growing business with limitless potential and become one that was hemorrhaging red ink? JeffSon was millions of dollars in debt. The New York accounting firm had done all it could to hide the losses, but unless a miracle happened, it was only a question of time before the whole thing imploded. So Jeff had continued to make his speeches touting his dying company while privately unloading his own stock in JeffSon. And just in case, Jeff was putting as much of his assets as he could in Jewel's name.

He'd debated long and hard about turning over so much to Jewel. Fortunately, she was too stupid to understand what he was doing. But for some reason, he hadn't transferred the house to her yet. There was something about handing her the roof over his head that made him feel vulnerable. But he *was* vulnerable. And he had to salvage whatever he could. He pulled out his cell phone, called his lawyer, and told him to prepare the paperwork for the transfer.

"I'll be landing in Wrightstown in half an hour," he said. "Be in my office. I want to get this done."

His head was throbbing. Putting the house in Jewel's name would tie them together for a far longer time than he'd wanted. For a while now, he'd known he wanted to leave Jewel. Because of Gwen. He wanted Gwen as much as he had once wanted his private jet and the Lamborghini. He had dreamed of being a free man for Gwen so he could ask her to free herself, too. But that dream was over. It belonged to a time when he could still make choices.

He closed his burning eyes. He hadn't wanted to make Gwen his mistress, but there was no other way. He had to have her, even if he couldn't free himself for her.

There was a call on his cell phone. His lawyer needed a copy of the deed to the house.

JEWEL had spent the morning in the gym working out. When she was finished, she headed for the bedroom to shower and change. The master suite was in the opposite wing of the house, and as she walked down the halls, they echoed with her footsteps.

She picked up her pace. Sometimes it seemed as if it took forever to get from one part of her home to the other. Once, she would have loved that, but she had changed. So much had changed since she'd built this house.

Jeff was coming home from a business trip this morning, and there had been a time when she would have rushed out to the airport to meet him. He would have been so eager to see her that he wouldn't have been able to keep his hands off her.

But Jeff had been tired of her for a long time now. She'd known for years that he had girls, and there had always been the danger that he'd fall in love with one of them. Now she was afraid that it had happened. The signs were all there. And Jeff being Jeff, he'd want to throw over everything like one of the heroes in those stupid operas he loved so much. He would want a divorce.

It hurt to know that your husband didn't want you anymore—even if you had never been deeply in love with him. And it really hurt to know that he didn't care enough about you to try to pretend otherwise. But she had made her bed, and it was a cushy one, and she wanted to go on lying in it. She'd be damned if she'd let anyone kick her out of it.

She'd finally reached the bedroom. As she stripped off her workout clothes, the phone rang. It was Jeff.

"I need you to bring a copy of the deed to the house to my office this afternoon," he said tersely. "Go into my study. Open the left-hand bottom drawer of my desk, and—"

"Why do you want that?" Jewel blurted out. In an instant, icy prickles ran down her spine. What the hell was he up to?

"I'm planning to put the house in your name—I'll explain when you get here. Now listen while I tell you where the deed is."

She had listened. And she was happier than she had been in months. Because if the house was going in her name, that meant things couldn't be as bad as she'd thought they were. If Jeff was giving her the house, then he wasn't going anywhere.

GWEN wanted to dance around the apartment from sheer happiness. In three days, she'd be giving her first reading of her book. The event was to take place in a library in Langham, a town about forty-five minutes north of Wrightstown. Stan was planning to drive up with her so he could cheer her on, and then they would spend the night in a charming old inn. Stan was so excited for her. In fact, Stan and her mother seemed to have started competing for the title of Loved One Who Is Most Proud of Gwen. When Stan had turned to Cassie for help, that had softened her mother toward him.

"He's got a good heart," she told Gwen. "And he does care about you." It had been high praise, coming from Cassandra Wright.

And then, just when it seemed that things couldn't get any better, Stan had decided it was time to buy a house. Gwen was thrilled.

She picked up the flyer on the house she'd seen that she wanted to show Stan. She had found a place in a suburb called Brookside. It was far enough out of the city for her to see trees and birds, but it was close enough for Stan to have a little hustle and bustle if that was what he wanted. Brookside was perfect. And so was her life.

"THIS is Stan Girard again, and I really need to speak to Mark Scotto," Stan said to the assistant who had answered Scotto's phone. "This is the second time I've called."

"I'm well aware of that, Mr. Girard," came the supercilious reply. "But he's been on the phone all afternoon, and I can't disturb him."

"Okay, when he takes a break, give him this message. I think I've discovered something that could be very serious. There's an error in the figures in the JeffSon newsletter we're sending out this month. We're reporting profits on two of our electrical plants that can't be true. I work with both plants, and I know that for a fact."

"I'll relay your message to Mr. Scotto." The voice on the phone sounded a little rattled now. "I'm sure he'll get back to you soon."

Five minutes later, Stan's phone rang.

"Thank you for bringing this to my attention, Stan," said Scotto after Stan had explained the problem again. "I'll follow up on it personally, and I'll be in touch to let you know what I've found."

FOR three days, Stan waited to hear the results of Mark Scotto's investigation into the inflated figures in the JeffSon newsletter. There was nothing from the man. When Stan tried to call, he was told that Mr. Scotto was in yet another meeting. Which was interesting because Stan himself wasn't going to any meetings. They were still being held—he could hear his colleagues traipsing down the halls to the conference room—but he wasn't asked to join them.

On the fourth day, he was summoned to Jeff Henry's office. His boss looked weary. And angry. He got straight to the point.

"Stan, I understand you've been poking around in some areas of the company that—to be perfectly frank—are way off your turf."

"I just noticed that there was a problem with the newsletter—"

"Get this through your head, Stan, okay? There is no problem. We have one of the best accounting firms in the country. These guys are tops—we're talking MBAs from Harvard and Yale with years of experience at Fortune five hundred companies. Do you really think that you could catch a mistake that slipped by them?"

Stan didn't. Not really. But he didn't like the sneer on Jeff Henry's face. "I know what I saw," he said stubbornly.

"Let me explain a few facts of financial life to you. A company the size of JeffSon depends on its good image. We have worked hard—way too hard—to build the reputation of JeffSon to allow it to be damaged by a disgruntled employee—"

"I asked a question!"

"You didn't know what you were talking about! And now you're too stubborn and arrogant to admit that you were wrong!"

And that was when Stan quit.

"You quit your job?" Gwen cried. "Why, Stan?" She'd been so happy, and now this. "You didn't think it was something you should talk over with me?"

"It was almost as if I didn't have any choice. I think Henry was trying to make me quit."

"Oh, come on!"

"He was insulting me—treating me like something he'd scrape off the bottom of his shoe. He knew I wouldn't put up with it."

She couldn't believe that. Not of Jeff Henry. "You're not making any sense. Why would he want you to quit?"

"Because I started asking questions, and he wanted me gone."

Stan had already told her his suspicions—that there was something going on at JeffSon that was, to use his word, dicey. She definitely couldn't believe that. Obviously, Stan was in over his head. He'd seen something he didn't understand, and he'd gotten all worked up about it.

"Isn't this all a little far-fetched?" Gwen demanded.

"I know what I saw, Gwen. They're cooking the books!"

"I just don't believe Jeff Henry would do something like that! Jeff is a great businessman—a genius. He doesn't have to do things like cook the books, or—"

But now Stan was angry. "Oh yes, I know how you feel about Jeff Henry!"

"What is that supposed to mean?"

"You have a crush on the man."

"That is not fair!" But maybe the reason it stung so much was that it was just a little bit true. "And it's a lousy thing to say."

"Okay, maybe you don't have one on him, but he sure has a thing for you. His tongue hangs out when he looks at you. And what's more, you enjoy it."

"*What?*"

"You know how he feels, Gwen, and you like it. He's Jewel's husband, and you've always been jealous of her."

"Jeff Henry is my friend, all right? I do like him. And what's more, I owe him."

"Because he gave your stupid husband a job?"

"He is my friend because he helped *me!* Not everything in my life revolves around you." And then she told Stan, biting off the words in her anger, about the collection of glass animal figures Jeff had unearthed for her to see. "I wouldn't have started writing if it hadn't been for Jeff," she finished breathlessly. And then she looked at Stan's face. And if she could have, she would have taken it all back. Because Stan, who had been so proud of her writing career, and so proud of his part in it, was deeply wounded. "Stan, I didn't mean it like that."

"Yes, you did," he said softly.

"You said I was jealous of Jewel. I got angry . . . You were the one who got the book published and—"

But he didn't let her finish. "Look, I don't think I'll go with you to Langham tomorrow night." And he turned and walked away.

She wanted to call after him, but she was starting to get angry again. This reading at the library was one of the most important things she'd ever do, and she had been counting on his support. Now he was abandoning her because of a dumb fight. "Fine," she called after him. "It probably would be better if you didn't come."

JEFF rested his forehead on his desk. His head was pounding. It had been ever since the little scene he'd staged yesterday when he'd pushed Stan Girard to quit. If the man hadn't taken the bait, Jeff would have fired him, which would have looked far worse later on if Stan was in court testifying against the officers of JeffSon . . . and its owner.

Jeff looked over his desk. There was a small mountain of paper sitting in front of him, and just the thought of going through it made him tired.

Tonight he was going to play hooky. He had called the publicity department at Gwen's publishing house and learned that this evening she would be giving her first reading at the library in Langham. He was going to be there. The hope of being with Gwen was the only thing he had to look forward to now. He'd already called Jewel to tell her that he wouldn't be coming home tonight, because he had to go out of town. As he'd expected, she hadn't bothered to ask where he was going. It could be a real plus to have a wife who didn't care enough about you to know your whereabouts.

JEWEL was packing her overnight bag. She'd called Jeff's secretary and learned that his mysterious business trip would be taking him to Langham, and she'd decided to drive over there, show up at his hotel—there was only one in the town, an old inn that sounded romantic—and surprise him.

A week ago, she wouldn't have thought about doing such a thing. But three days ago, he'd put the house in her name. And he'd told her that there were other assets that had already been transferred. He wouldn't have done it if the divorce she dreaded was looming. So why not rekindle a few of those sparks that had once burned so brightly? Maybe the marriage wasn't dead after all.

# CHAPTER 10

THE reading at the Langham library had been a success. The children and their parents had listened to Gwen with hushed attention. They had stayed after the reading to ask questions and had lined up so that Gwen could sign their copies of *Abby*. Everyone seemed to be having such a good time. Gwen thought they might have stayed for hours if there hadn't been several claps of thunder, indicating that a storm was on its way. People began bundling up their kids and rushing out to their cars before the rain started.

Gwen now had the evening ahead of her. A very long evening, which she would be spending alone in a hotel room in a town where she knew no one. She headed toward her car, which was parked in front of the library. Suddenly she felt weary—a letdown after the high of the night's successful event. Maybe she should cancel her room at the Langham Inn and just drive home.

"Gwen!" said a voice behind her. She turned to see Jeff coming toward her with an eager smile.

*Oh God,* she thought, and didn't know whether to be pleased or dismayed.

"Brava! You were wonderful!" he said.

"Jeff? What are you doing here?"

"I came for your reading," he said. "Did you think I'd miss it?"

"I never expected . . . I didn't see you."

"I stood in the alcove on the side. I was afraid I'd distract you." He looked around. "You're alone?" But he knew she was. He'd checked her audience from his safe alcove, and he'd seen that her husband hadn't bothered to come.

"Yes, I'm alone," she said.

"Well, we can't have that on your big night!" he sang out brightly. "Let me take you to dinner. I understand the Langham Inn has a great dining room."

"I was thinking of going home . . ." she said tentatively. At that moment, the rain that had been threatening fell from the sky in a downpour.

"You can't drive in this," he shouted over a peal of thunder. "Come on, meet me at the hotel."

She hesitated, but only for a second, because she was getting soaked. "Okay," she said, and she dashed for her car. Jeff waited until he was sure she was headed in the direction of the Langham Inn; then he ran to the Lamborghini.

JEWEL pulled into the parking lot in front of the Langham Inn. She checked out the lot, looking for Jeff's car. The Lamborghini was nowhere to be seen. She parked as far away from the entrance of the hotel as she could so he wouldn't see her and waited for the storm to let up.

A few minutes later, she heard the familiar roar of a finely tuned Italian sports car as Jeff pulled the Lamborghini up to the front of the hotel. She watched her husband get out of his car. She was about to call out to him, but then she saw that he wasn't rushing into the hotel. He was standing next to his car as the rain fell on him, and it was clear that he was waiting for someone. Sure enough, a second car drove into the lot, and the driver pulled into the spot next to Jeff's. Jewel watched her husband step forward, take off the jacket of his five-thousand-dollar custom-made suit, and hold it over the woman's head as they ran into the hotel together.

Jewel's stomach turned to ice. There were two large bay windows at the front of the Langham Inn, and through them one could see everything that was going on in the lobby. Jewel got out of her car, ran to the inn, and fought her way through the boxwood hedge that surrounded the windows. There, in spite of all the demeaning clichéd scenes she'd watched in a hundred bad movies about jealous women, she stood in the mud and spied on her husband.

GWEN'S mind was whirling. It was sweet of Jeff to have come to hear her read her book. But why did it feel like it was too much, like there was something desperate about the way he was smiling and insisting on having dinner with her? He was checking the menu that was posted outside the dining room right now.

"This looks good!" he said enthusiastically. Maybe too enthusiastically. Or was she just imagining things because Stan had accused the man of having feelings for her? Jeff had never done anything to suggest that he wanted to be more than friends.

"Jeff," she said, "I'm grateful to you for coming here, but given what happened between you and Stan, I feel a little awkward. . . ."

For an answer, he grabbed her hands. "Oh, don't," he pleaded. "The fight with Stan was really for the best. I don't think he ever really wanted to work for JeffSon—it was always a bad fit. But you mustn't let that get in the way of us."

He held her hands up to his mouth, and he kissed each of them. And then he looked up at her. And that was when she saw it in his eyes—there was no mistaking it now. Stan had been right about Jeff. And she, Gwen, had been an idiot. She tried, ever so gently, to pull her hands away, but Jeff held on to them.

"What we have is something special, Gwen. I've never felt this . . . kind of friendship . . . with any other woman." Then he paused. "Don't let Stan come between us." She couldn't help shivering. "You're cold," he said softly.

"It's because of the rain . . . I got wet . . . I should probably go upstairs and change."

"That's a good idea. We both should."

And he let go of her hands to push the button for the elevator. "You're on the sixth floor," he said as the elevator doors opened. "So am I."

JEWEL'S face was scratched from the boxwood branches, and her shoes were sinking into the muddy mulch that surrounded the hedge. For once in her life, she didn't give a damn what she looked like. She had watched her husband take Gwen's hands and kiss them. Had he ever looked at Jewel with that kind of tenderness? He had gotten into the elevator with Gwen. The indicator arrow above the elevator registered only one floor. You didn't have to be a genius to know what was going on right now between Jewel's husband and Gwen Wright. Gwen was the woman Jewel had been fearing all these months—the woman Jeff loved, for whom he would uproot his life and get a divorce. Jewel wanted to smash Gwen's face into a wall. She wanted to tear at Gwen's skin with her perfectly manicured nails until the blood ran; she wanted to hit and maim and hurt. She scrambled away from the window of the inn and through the hedge and ran for her car.

THE elevator reached the sixth floor. During the ride, Jeff had chatted about Gwen's reading as if there was nothing else going on.

"I watched your audience tonight," he said. "The kids were enthralled. I predict that *Abby* will take her place someday next to *Winnie the Pooh.*"

"She's just a little squirrel trying to figure out who she is." Gwen tried to shrug away the compliment as the elevator doors opened.

"I don't think I want anything to eat tonight," she said. "I think I'll just turn in and get an early start tomorrow. Thank you again for coming all this way."

"I understand," he said. But when she turned and headed for her room, he was following her. They reached her door. She opened her handbag and fished around for her room key. "Thank you again for coming. It was so nice of you."

Gwen found the key, but it slipped through her fingers and fell to the carpet next to her feet. Before she could bend down, Jeff had scooped it up. He put the key in the lock, opened the door, and was moving into her room.

Later, when she thought about it, it seemed as if she'd watched what happened next but hadn't really been a part of it. She saw herself move to the door to block the path of a man who looked like Jeff but couldn't be Jeff, because Jeff wouldn't do this. She heard this awful new Jeff whisper in her ear as he tried to force his way past her, that she was the only thing that mattered to him now, that he couldn't lose her, too. And she heard someone—a Gwen who was also unrecognizable—say that, please, he mustn't do this. And the Gwen who wasn't really Gwen had pushed hard at the Jeff who wasn't really Jeff until she was off balance, and when he had stepped back, she had fallen to the floor. There was a popping sound as if something had snapped. And then Gwen wasn't watching from a distance anymore. That was when the pain came. It shot through her hand to her wrist and up her arm in a white-hot streak. She had looked up at Jeff as the tears sprang to her eyes. He had to see how badly she hurt. Foolishly, stupidly, she waited for him to help her to her feet.

"You slut!" he spat at her. "You tease a man, you let him think . . . to hell with you! To hell with all of it." He turned on his heel and strode away.

GWEN wasn't sure how long she stayed on the floor. But eventually the first screaming pain died away, and she was able to get to her feet and close the door. Gingerly she tried moving her fingers—she'd heard somewhere that she wouldn't be able to do that if her hand was broken. The test was a success—if agonizing. The fingers were mobile. What she had was nothing more than a nasty sprain. She had some aspirin in her purse, and she swallowed a couple of tablets. Slowly and painfully, she set about the process of gathering her belongings and putting them in her overnight bag. There was no way she was staying in this room tonight.

JEWEL was driving way too fast. She knew it, and she didn't care. She had to get away from Langham, had to get away from the vision of her husband kissing Gwen's hands. Gwen Wright! Cassie Wright's spoiled brat daughter, who always got everything she wanted. Now she had Jewel's husband, and . . . the curve ahead was sharp, and the divider in the middle of the road suddenly loomed up from out of nowhere. Jewel slammed on the brakes and felt the car swerve first to the left and then to the right. The divider was coming nearer. Helpless, Jewel could only wait to see how hard the crash would be when the car smashed into it.

At the last second, the car righted itself and stalled. Miraculously, it had stopped inches away from the divider. Shaken, Jewel started the engine and drove slowly to the nearest exit. She kept on going until she found an all-night diner, where she pulled in between two trucks. Tears started down Jewel's cheeks, coming faster and faster as little animal cries of pain emerged from her throat. With trembling hands, she dug her cell phone out of her purse and dialed Wrightstown information.

STAN was waiting for Gwen to call. By now she'd finished her reading, and she had to know how sorry he was that he hadn't been there with her. She had to know how much he'd want to hear from her. He looked at his watch. He'd give her five more minutes, and then he'd call her. He started for the kitchen to get a drink of water, and the phone rang.

"Gwen!" he said joyously into the phone. "Gwen, darling—"

"If you want to know where your darling wife is, try my husband's room at the Langham Inn," gasped a vaguely familiar voice.

"Jewel? Is that you?"

"Yes," Jewel cried. "He said he was working. I went there to see him."

"Jewel, where are you?"

"He put the damn house in my name!" She choked out the words through sobs. "He put most of his portfolio in my name. A man wouldn't do that if he was going to leave—that's what I thought."

"I don't know what you're talking about."

"Jeff!" she screamed. "And your perfect little wife. They were up there together. I saw them in the parking lot of the hotel, and they went up together in the elevator. I knew he was leaving me for someone. If it had been anyone but her, I could have—"

But she got no further, because Stan cut her off. "I've got to go, Jewel," he said, and hung up the phone. What Jewel had said was absurd. Until that day, he had been the one who was going to Langham with Gwen, so there was no way she'd planned an assignation with a lover. Even if he'd thought Gwen was capable of doing such a thing. Which he didn't. But Jeff Henry was a different matter; he was capable of anything—including following Gwen to her reading and trying to seduce her while she was alone and vulnerable. He ran to grab his car keys off the sideboard. There was the sound of scratching at the front door as if someone was trying to unlock it; then the doorbell rang. He answered it.

Gwen stood in the doorway. Her hair was dripping wet from the rain, and her face looked drained and white. She was carrying her overnight case in her left hand, and there was a large bulky towel wrapped around her right wrist.

"You were right!" she said. "I'm so sorry. You were right!" And she started to cry.

It took a little time for him to get the whole story out of her. He'd threatened to find Jeff Henry and kill him, and she'd begged him to let it go, because it had been partly her fault. Then he had to take her into the bathroom and stand guard while she took a hot shower and dry her off himself and put her to bed and lie down next to her and listen while she told him about the reading and the good part of the night before Jeff had appeared in the parking lot. And sometime after that, she drifted off to sleep with his arm around her—not wanting to disturb her, he fell asleep at her side still fully dressed.

Sometime in the middle of the night, the pain in her wrist woke her, and he got up to bring her an aspirin, after which he undressed. As he was climbing back into bed, he sat up with a jolt. He'd just remembered something that had been gnawing at the back of his mind. He hadn't registered it, because so much else had happened, but now it came back to him. It was something Jewel had said.

THE next morning, Stan awoke while Gwen still slept and dialed his mother-in-law's number. Cassie answered on the second ring.

"I have a problem," Stan said. "I think something's happening at JeffSon." He told Cassie about the numbers that hadn't added up, the way he'd been treated after he'd reported his discovery, and the final scene with Jeff Henry in which he had quit.

"It does sound suspicious," she said thoughtfully. "But it could have been a legitimate mistake."

"I tried to tell myself that, too," Stan said. "But then I heard that Jeff Henry has been moving all his assets into his wife's name."

There was a long silence on the other end of the phone; then Cassandra drew in a breath he could hear. "It's probably better if you don't say anything more about this until I look into it," she said. "And Stan? Do you own any JeffSon stock?"

"No. I never bought any when I had the chance."

"Thank God."

THE collapse of the JeffSon Corporation was like a clap of thunder on a mild afternoon. Soon the shock waves were roiling through the business community. It had started, said the Wall Street pundits, in a little backwater town in New England. Cassandra Wright, the

CEO of Wright Glassworks, had somehow gotten wind of something that didn't smell quite right at JeffSon, and she'd alerted Tommy Rubin, the stock analyst who had a very popular radio talk show dealing with finances. Tommy began poking around, and three weeks later, he was advising the public to unload its JeffSon stock. The house of cards that had been JeffSon came tumbling down soon after, and the rest, as they say, was history. Jeff Henry was one of the most hated men in America.

Inevitably, the investigations followed. And the lawyers. "Get yourself the best; you're going to need them," the head of the New York accounting firm advised Jeff.

In her big mausoleum-like house, Jewel panicked. "What are you telling me?" she screamed. "That they're going to put you in jail?"

Jeff had taken off his jacket and sunk into a chair near the door of the cavernous living room. He rubbed his head as if it ached.

"Haven't I explained it to you at least ten times? For God's sake, what more do you want me to tell you? Calm down!"

There he sat. His legs were sprawled while one hand wiped his forehead. She kept staring at him as if she were trying to recognize and remember some stranger's face and name. Jeff's tie was loosened and lay on his heaving chest.

"I would have been all right," he said. "I could have claimed that I didn't know anything. I didn't pay attention to the day-to-day operations . . . I was innocent . . ." He trailed off. "But she found out. That bitch Cassandra Wright found out I was transferring assets to you—that was what started it all."

And Jewel remembered sitting in her car after she'd nearly run off the road, because she'd just seen her husband kissing Gwen's hands. Jewel remembered the rage that had swept over her. She remembered wanting to make Gwen—lucky, pampered, undeserving Gwen—pay, for once in her life.

So, blinded by jealousy, without thinking of the consequences, Jewel had called Stan Girard to tell him that his wife was no better than her birth mother, who had been a whore. She had also told Stan Girard that her husband had just put the house in her name.

Jewel looked around the room, at the tall window that framed a suddenly frightening vision of an eternal, limitless, empty sky.

She turned back to Jeff. He was a different man now. He was bankrupt. He was going to jail. And overriding everything else was the thought she knew would be with her forever—she had been the one who had done it to him. It had taken one tiny moment of jealous rage to begin the process that had led her husband to the indictments he was now saying he could not beat. One sliver of a second in which Jewel had brought her own world crashing down around her ears. And somewhere in the muddle that filled Jewel's head was an unexplainable, queer kernel of bewildered, awful pity for Jeff, who had once loved her so much.

# CHAPTER 11

—⁓—

THE Lamborghini was worth every dollar it had cost, Jeff thought for the hundredth time. The graceful simplicity of its lines and the bright triumphant glint of its yellow paint, the soft silky leather of the interior—all were so absolutely right. He pressed the accelerator, and the car leaped forward as if he had spoken to it, as if it had understood his mood, the variable mood that he himself could not possibly have described.

He had driven to his father's house, to the neighborhood that was quietly decaying next to the river. He had gone to see the old man for . . . what reason? To obtain absolution? To explain?

"There was nothing I could do, Dad," he had said, as close to tears as he had been since he became an adult. "Everything spiraled out of control."

"Faustian bargains, Jeffie," the old man had said, shaking his head. That had been it; that had been the only comfort his father had offered—*Faustian bargains*.

And so Jeff had walked out of the house where there was no

comfort to be had and started driving his beautiful, triumphant car. Not back to Wrightstown, for there was no comfort there, either. The river appeared at his side; the road ran parallel to it. He thought about the picture that hung in his office, the one of the little girl who was all alone and looking out over this very river. Walter Amburn had painted it. Was that only a few years ago? Jeff had seen the painting and known he had to have it. That was before he'd gone to Gwen Wright's party, before he met Jewel, who encouraged him to make his millions—and his Faustian bargain.

So now go, Jeff. Just go to any place that is different. Not to the next town. Not, most of all, to a city. He had seen the world's cities, and he was tired of them. He was tired of people, too, of their faces, their voices: *Today you should do this. If you do this today, you will get that. If you get that, you will be able to get some more.*

*I don't want any more. But maybe I do. I know I don't want to go back to that house—my house. And I don't want to go back to the woman in that house. The woman I wanted. I don't want to go back to the place where she lives. That I do know.*

The road was following the river into a gap in a low mountain range whose name Jeff couldn't remember. The river sparkled like one of the diamond tennis bracelets he had bought for Jewel back in the days when it still delighted him to see her joy at his presents. Back when he still cared what happened to him.

But God! He didn't want to sit in a cell, like a bear at the zoo. In a cage for years. But the appeal . . . He could afford it, so the lawyers said. Oh, sure! And if it didn't work? It would be two years, two years of courts, of fear, of sick stomach, dry mouth, staring, cold eyes, so curious. People judging him. Two years.

But look ahead—the road is curving up onto the hill. Below it is the sparkling river. All this is so beautiful . . . At the top of the hill, the road stops at a crossroads. To the east is another road. To the west . . . the river will turn, curve, and race away from this place to the real West. The West of beautiful America. Fly to the West with the river, Jeff. Race. Feel the cool wind through the wide-open windows. Let the sweet air flow in. So cool, so fresh. Faster. Faster.

On the turn, the car leaps over the embankment, plunges, and comes to a final stop in the river below, and there it lies. In the silence, in the silent water.

And the car, with all it contains, lies still. Broken, crushed, and still.

JEFF Henry's funeral was mercifully simple. For once, it seemed that Jewel had decided to be restrained.

"I'm glad," Gwen told Stan. "For Jeff's sake." Her husband was silent. "I think about how much Jeff loved music and books . . . the way he'd talk about history and philosophy. He had such a fine mind. And you have to admit that he was generous; look at that shelter he started for homeless families. He endowed it so it can go on for years."

"Good. Maybe some of the people who lost their homes when they discovered their JeffSon stock was worthless can live there." Stan's lips tightened.

"Do you think you'll ever be able to forgive him?" she asked.

Stan brushed his hair out of his eyes and fixed her with a steady look. "I'll work on it. But I can't make any promises."

GWEN thought that was the last of the conversations she would have about Jeff Henry. But one afternoon, there was a knock on her door. She opened it to see Jewel standing in front of her. A changed and different Jewel. Gone were the diamond bracelets and the big dangling earrings. Jewel was dressed in a tweed skirt and cashmere sweater. Her face seemed changed, too. There were circles under her eyes and a hint of a wrinkle on either side of her mouth.

"May I come in?" she asked. Gwen nodded and led her into the living room. "I wanted to say good-bye," Jewel said. "I'm leaving Wrightstown—the house is already sold—and I'm going home. Back where I grew up. Two of my sisters are still living there. Peggy's husband left her after their third baby was born, so I'm going to buy a place, and she and the children will come and live with me."

"That sounds very . . ." Gwen struggled for a word and finally produced one. "Practical," she said.

"I won't be alone anymore," Jewel said. "I realized the other day that I've never really put down any roots in Wrightstown." Then she laughed her big warm laugh. "Hell," she said. "Why do you think I'm here saying good-bye to you? You and Patsy Allen are the only people I know well enough. That's pathetic."

Gwen laughed to keep her company. Then Jewel sobered up.

"Do you think he did it on purpose, Gwen?" she asked softly. "I keep telling myself he wouldn't, that it was an accident, but . . ."

"My mother always used to say 'let sleeping dogs lie,' " Gwen said. "Sometimes that's the only thing we can do. Just live your life and don't look back."

Jewel nodded and turned as if to go. Then she stopped. "Being jealous is a terrible waste, isn't it?"

"Yes," Gwen said. "It is."

Jewel turned again, and Gwen walked with her to the door. "If you're ever up in my neck of the woods," Jewel said, "check out my new shop. I'm opening a branch of Past Times."

# EPILOGUE

CASSIE drove down the quiet street in Brookside. The little town had been one of the first suburbs of Wrightstown, a blue-collar community built for the workers at the glassworks. The streets were laid out on a neat grid, with rows of simple, matching houses. The homes were not new. But the lots on which the houses were built were good-sized, and there was a park with hiking trails nearby.

Cassie reached the house that was her destination. As she always did when she pulled into the driveway, she shook her head and sighed. There were dandelions all over the front lawn, which had gone at least three weeks without being mowed. If it had been

Cassie's place, she would have been on her knees at that moment pulling up the offending vegetation. But the house wasn't hers. It belonged to Gwen and Stan. He did his best, but after three years of home ownership, in his heart he was still a city boy.

She could still remember the day—it had been about six months after the collapse of JeffSon and Jeff Henry's suicide—when Stan had asked if he could come to her office to talk. He'd paced around nervously for several minutes before he'd come to the point.

"There's a house," he said. "Gwen wants it very much. And I'd like it, too, now that we . . ." He stopped himself. "But I'll let Gwen tell you our good news. The fact is, we'd like to buy this house. It's in an old neighborhood, but it's been very well kept up." He drew in a big breath. "But we can't afford it. I'm going to go back into business for myself, and that's going to take all the money I got when I sold my shop. So I was wondering if—"

And she'd broken in happily. "I'd love to give you and Gwen the money to buy whatever house you want, Stan."

"I was hoping you'd let us borrow the money," he said.

She had learned a lot about this man, so she didn't try to argue. It had only taken her a second to say, "Did you want to draw up a formal contract with lawyers or can we just shake hands?"

Cassie stopped the car in the driveway and got out. The front door opened, and a small bullet propelled itself across the front lawn to throw itself into her arms. "Grandma!" shrieked Stanley Wright Girard, age two.

At the same time, Gwen said from the doorway, "We'll just be another minute. Stan has a new camera that he wants to try today, and he's still fussing with it." She disappeared again, and small Stanley began lobbying Cassie for ice cream.

"A cone, Grandma," he said. "A cone!"

"You're incorrigible," Cassie informed him as she knelt to hug him. But Little Stan was not to be deterred. He wriggled out of her grasp. "Ice-cream cone," he said sternly. Cassie started to laugh.

"All right, you win," she said. "We'll get an ice-cream cone."

"Chocolate," Little Stan specified, wreathed in smiles.

"He plays you like a fine violin," said Gwen as she joined them. Behind her, Big Stan, as he was now called, was walking and fiddling with the camera. The three Girards and Cassie headed for Cassie's car.

"Walter will join us at the Glassworks Museum," Cassie told Gwen. "He just finished painting the background diorama, and he was afraid it wouldn't be dry in time for the unveiling of the exhibit. But he called me as I was driving here, and he said it's fine. He and the curator are setting the figurines up in front of it now."

"I loved the sketch he did. It looked exactly like my little refuge on the hill," Gwen said.

"That's what it's meant to be," said Cassie.

Gwen linked her arm through Cassie's. "Thank you for doing this, Mother," she said. "Thank you for exhibiting the New Orleans Group."

"The figurines are beautiful. People should be able to see them," Cassie said. "And it's time for me to grow up."

Little Stan had run ahead of them, and he'd reached the young red maples at the edge of the property. "Honey, that's far enough!" his mother called out to him.

He turned, planted himself where he stood, and fixed his mother with a quizzical gaze as if he was trying to decide if he wished to obey her. There was something in that strong little stance and the determined tilt of the little head that reminded Cassie of her father and her grandfather—never mind that there was no direct blood line connecting them all. She could see Little Stan someday taking his place as the head of the Wright Glassworks and living in the Wright house. Neither of those options would ever be right for his mother—Gwen had found her own way. But this little person standing in front of them all . . . well, he was a very different story.

Little Stan ran to Gwen, who scooped him up in her arms and swung him into the air. The air was filled with the sound of their laughter.

Cassie watched them. *Gwen's come such a long way,* she thought. Looking at her now, it was almost impossible to remember the diffident, unhappy girl who had once been jealous of flashy Jewel Fairchild. In spite of herself, Cassie felt her eyes well up.

"Cassie, stand with them," Stan commanded, his camera at the ready.

Cassie blinked back her tears and smiled as she moved close to the child she had rescued so long ago and that child's child. The two women, with Little Stan in Gwen's arms, stood together in the bright morning sunlight. In front of them was Gwen's house and the husband who was so very right for her. Behind them were the red maples Gwen had planted with loving memories of the gardens and forests of her old home.

There was a mechanical whir as Big Stan began taking pictures, freezing this slice of time into pictures that could be copied onto some tangible substance like paper and saved. Over the years, with all the joys and sorrows that would inevitably come, the pictures would be a reminder of this perfect moment.

But Cassie knew she would never need pictures printed on paper. The laughter, and the sunshine, and the love were already tucked away in her mind—and in her heart.

# Looking Back with
## *Belva Plain*

## Vital Stats

**BORN:** October 9, 1919, New York City

**RESIDENCE:** Essex County, NJ

**FAMILY:** Three children, six grandchildren, and Andy—a small terrier mix

**FAVORITE AUTHOR:** Anthony Trollope

**WOULD TRADE PLACES WITH:** "Winston Churchill, on the day he learned Hitler was dead"

**WEBSITE:** www.BelvaPlain.com

THROUGHOUT the course of her thirty-year writing career, Belva Plain has focused her books on the things that matter most: love, loyalty, and personal integrity. Known for her memorable, emotionally insightful family sagas, she compares fiction with a lengthy road: "There are so many forks, so many highways and winding paths through great, indifferent cities or, then again, small towns—where it is hard to keep hidden the thing that you most want to hide."

Plain says her inspiration comes mostly from the people around her: "You can get the germ of an idea from an overheard conversation on a bus. Someone tells me something; it stays in my head unprocessed; then I take it through the many permutations, and voilà!" The author even admits that she reproduced one particularly interesting overheard conversation from a restaurant where she was having breakfast during a publicity tour in one of her books.

Heritage and history—the legacies that flow down through the generations—play a role in all Plain's books. She enjoys learning about those who have come before us, especially those who have come to the United States from other countries. "Is not every one of us a blending of traits we inherit from people whose very names are unknown to us?" Plain asks. At Barnard College, she majored in history, and she was surrounded by both immigrants and descendants of the Founding Fathers. As a third-generation American, she says she "fell between the extremes and found I could learn something from each of these groups. The courage that most moves me is the courage that led our ancestors to cross that enormous ocean into the unknown."

Plain's road to literary success began in 1978 with the publication of her first novel, *Evergreen,* which topped the *New York Times* bestseller list for forty-one weeks and was subsequently made into a popular television miniseries. Since then, she has written twenty-one more novels, including her most recent, *Cross-*

## Stepping Up

Like *Crossroads*'s Cassandra Wright, there have been several women throughout history who inherited successful businesses from their fathers and turned them into global powerhouses. Marjorie Merriweather Post (1887–1973), seen at right, inherited the Postum Cereal Company and grew it into the giant General Foods Corporation. Donna Wolf Steigerwaldt (1929–2000) achieved much the same result at Jockey International, where she introduced the company's first line of underwear for women. And when Christie Hefner (1952–) became CEO of Playboy Enterprises, she expanded the company into the digital arena, making it the first national magazine on the Web.

*roads.* Her work has been translated into twenty-two languages, and she remains one of America's most popular authors. As she nears her ninetieth birthday, Plain shows no signs of slowing down: "Life is very, very interesting these days," she says, "and the older you are, the more surprising it becomes." ∎

# KAREN ROBARDS

## Guilty

# CHAPTER 1

**August 1994**

"WHERE do you think you're going?"

Just after midnight on a steamy Friday in Baltimore, fifteen-year-old Katrina Kominski was halfway down the fire escape of the run-down brick apartment building where she had lived for the past seven months when the bellow from above froze her in her tracks.

*Busted,* she thought, because what she was

doing was sneaking out after being grounded for the weekend.

Casting a scared glance up, she discovered her foster mother leaning out the fourth-floor window above her, fat cheeks jiggling, pink curlers bobbing. Behind her she could see two of the other girls—Mrs. Coleman took in only girls; right now she had five in the three-bedroom apartment—crowding around.

"Out," Katrina yelled back. The response was pure bravado, because down below, her friends were watching. Inside, where no one could see, her stomach knotted in fear. Her heart pounded.

"Come on, Kat!" Jason Winter—the to-die-for cute boy she was crazy about—yelled up to her. She looked down in indecision. He was at the wheel of his beat-up blue Camaro, which was idling in the alley below. It was crammed with kids; her best friend, Leah Oscar, had her head stuck out the rear window on the driver's side, yelling, "Come on" to her along with Jason. A kid with black curly hair—Mario Castellanos, one of Jason's friends—had his head out the front passenger window as he yelled insults at Mrs. Coleman, who was now raining abuse down on Kat's head.

"Look out!" Leah shrieked, pointing above Kat. Kat looked up again, and her heart leaped into her throat.

Marty Jones, Mrs. Coleman's live-in boyfriend, had taken Mrs. Coleman's place and was halfway out the window. Last time she'd seen him he'd been zonked out on the couch. Now here he came after her. Like Mrs. Coleman, he was maybe in his midforties. Unlike Mrs. Coleman, he didn't even pretend to like the girls she fostered for a living.

Except in a creepy way. Kat hated him. He'd been eyeing her since she had arrived from the group home where she had been sent after the last foster-care placement hadn't worked out. Being a skinny, cute blue-eyed blonde was not a good thing when the world you lived in was full of predatory men like Marty Jones.

"You better get back up here right now!" Almost through the window now, Marty held a baseball bat in one hand. "Right now! You hear me, girl?"

Oh, yeah. She did. And even as the weight of him emerging onto the top of the fire escape made the whole thing shiver, she ran, hanging on to the rail, clattering down the remaining steps to the encouraging screams of her friends.

If he caught her . . .

"Hurry, Kat!"

Kat jumped down the last two steps. Hands reached out of the Camaro's door to drag her inside. She half leaped and half was pulled in on top of a shifting mass of teenage bodies. Tires squealing, the Camaro peeled out.

"That was so cool!"

"Man, he almost caught her! They gonna call the cops?"

"No, they won't call the cops," Kat replied as she wiggled her butt down between Leah and her boyfriend, Roger Friedkin, while Donna Bianco was squashed against the far window. With the four of them wedged into the backseat and Jason and Mario up front, the car was hot despite all the windows being rolled down. "If they did, the social workers would come and take me away, and they don't want that. They need the money."

"You gonna be okay when you go back there, Kitty-cat?" Jason asked with quiet concern. His eyes—blue as the waters of the Chesapeake Bay—looked into hers through the rearview mirror.

She nodded.

"That fat old fart's gonna whup your ass, Kitty-cat," Mario chortled, turning so he could smirk at her. "I bet he's gonna like it, too."

"Shut up." Jason punched his friend in the arm.

"Ow!" Mario, glaring, covered the spot with his hand.

"It's okay," Kat said to Jason. But the thought of what her reception was going to be like when she returned to the apartment was enough to make her want to puke.

"Hey, how about we get us some beer?" Mario yelled. They were on the expressway now, speeding toward D.C., with the wind rushing in through the open windows and the radio blaring.

"Yeah!"

"Beer! Woo-hoo!"

"I could use a beer!"

Kat hated beer, but she said nothing.

The Camaro swerved suddenly, and Kat clutched reflexively at Leah's arm. From the blur outside the window she knew that they were off the expressway and flying down an exit ramp. Jason stomped the brake at the intersection at the bottom of the ramp, and everybody was flung violently forward.

As Jason swung the Camaro out onto a nearly deserted four-lane road, Mario turned to look at them. "Anybody got any *dinero?*"

"I got a dollar and . . . look at that, twenty-two cents."

"I got a buck."

"I . . . don't have any money," Kat said, when all eyes were on her after everyone else in the backseat had turned out their pockets.

"That's okay." Jason looked at her through the mirror again. "I'll spring for yours." And he smiled at her.

The hard little knot in Kat's stomach eased.

That late at night the only things still open were gas stations and convenience stores. A Quik-Pik on the next corner was Jason's destination.

"Does somebody have an ID?" Kat asked, meaning a fake one, as the Camaro bumped into the parking lot and slid to a stop beside one of the gas pumps.

"I do, but it don't matter." Mario grinned at her. "I can pass for twenty-one easy."

Everybody piled out of the car.

"I gotta pee," Leah announced cheerfully, and looked at Kat. "You wanna come to the bathroom with me?"

"Yeah," Kat agreed, and the two of them broke off to head around the side of the building where a battered sign announced RESTROOMS. They had both finished and Kat was washing her hands when they heard a series of staccato sounds from outside.

*Crack! Crack! Crack!*

"What the hell?" Leah gasped.

"It's a gun." Kat knew what gunfire sounded like. Mrs. Coleman's apartment was actually one of the nicer places in which she had lived. The seven years she had spent with her mother were a blur of crack houses and abandoned buildings and the occasional homeless shelter. After that, she'd been passed around among relatives until one day a social worker had taken her away. During that time the sound of gunfire had been a nightly occurrence.

Leah ran for the door. Kat was right behind her. What they saw as they burst around the corner of the building was the rest of the gang bolting toward the Camaro like something bad was chasing them. Jason looked scared to death—and Mario was holding a gun.

Kat's breathing suspended. Her gut clenched.

There was a man between her and Leah and the car. An older man, stocky and gray-haired, in what looked like a blue uniform. He was on his knees with his back to them. Leah flew past him. As Kat ran up behind him, he groaned and toppled over. She saw that he was clutching his chest. She stopped in her tracks.

Bright blood bubbled up between his fingers. In a single glance she saw that there was a badge on his chest, silver, with a plastic name tag below it. She wasn't close enough to read the name.

*He's been shot.* She remembered the gun in Mario's hands, and a chill ran through her.

He saw her. His eyes flickered. "Help . . . me."

*Oh, God.* She dropped to her knees beside him, bent over him, frantic to do something, moving his hands aside so that she could see the wound. She pressed desperately against the hole, trying to stem the flow of blood. It was warm and slimy.

"Hurts," he muttered. And closed his eyes.

"Kat, come on!" The voice—Leah's—shrieked out at her as the Camaro screamed to a stop just a few feet away.

"Come on! Come on!" They were all shouting at her, but she couldn't move. She could feel the man's—his name was David Brady; she could read his name tag now—life slipping away. Then the Camaro sped off with a squeal of rubber, and she was left alone.

Really alone, because David Brady was dead.

She stayed beside him until she heard the sirens. Then she jumped to her feet and fled into the darkness.

# CHAPTER 2

**Thirteen years later**

SOMETHING'S *wrong*. The thought hit Tom Braga with all the explosive force of a bullet to the brain.

His gut clenched as he listened to the silence on the other end of the phone. He didn't know how he knew it, but he did. They were speaking on cell phones, Tom from his unmarked car, which was at that moment slicing through the downpour en route to Philadelphia's Criminal Justice Center, where he was scheduled to be in court at nine—in about three minutes—and his younger brother, Charlie, from wherever he was. They were both cops, he a homicide detective, Charlie a sheriff's deputy. On this rainy Monday morning they were both on duty. And Charlie was in trouble.

"Yo, bro, you still there?" Tom gripped the phone hard, but his voice stayed deceptively casual. They'd been talking about Mom's weekly Sunday dinner, which Tom had missed for the third time in a row yesterday because he was tired of being ragged on all the time about being thirty-five and single and because sometimes his congregated family was enough to drive him nuts. In the middle of rubbing Tom's nose in the glories of the chicken parmigiana, Charlie had grunted as if in surprise, then simply stopped talking. And Tom had started getting this really bad vibe.

"Yeah," Charlie replied, to Tom's instant relief. Until he realized that his excitable brother's voice was absolutely flat and that he could hear Charlie breathing hard. "Um, look, I gotta go."

"Okay, well, you tell your sweet little wife hello for me, hear?" Tom's tone was hearty. Cold sweat prickled to life at his hairline.

"I'll do that," Charlie said, and his phone went dead.

With that answer ringing in his ears, Tom practically ran through the red light he was rushing up on. Slamming on the brakes hard enough to make the department-issue black Taurus fishtail on the wet street, he managed to stop just in time to avoid barreling out into the middle of the busy intersection.

Taking a deep breath, Tom called on years of experience to separate mind from emotion and did what he had been trained to do in emergency situations: what came next.

He punched buttons on his cell phone. An infinity seemed to pass as he listened to the ringing on the other end.

*Pick up, pick up, pick up.*

"Johnson here."

"Tom Braga." Tom identified himself to Charlie's supervisor, Bruce Johnson. Adrenaline rushed through his veins, yet at the same time he felt very focused, very calm. "Where's Charlie?"

"Charlie?" Johnson paused. "Let me check."

He covered the mouthpiece—not well—and yelled, "Anybody know where Charlie Braga is this morning?"

*Hurry,* Tom thought, gritting his teeth.

Seconds later Johnson was back on the line. "He took a witness from the jail over to the Justice Center. Wasn't that long ago, so he should still be there. Any particular reason why you're interested?"

The Justice Center. Tom could see it, a little more than a block away on the right.

The light was green, and the intersection in front of him was clear. He stomped on the gas.

"I was talking to him on the phone right before I called you." Tom was rushing toward the building now. Cars were parallel parked out in front. People hurried along the sidewalk, a sea of umbrellas. From outside the revolving doors he got a glimpse of the security checkpoint, with its guards and metal detectors. There was no sign of trouble. But his gut was telling him otherwise.

"He gave me a signal, like." Even as he scanned the area, Tom continued talking to Johnson. "Something's wrong. You need to get some backup to Charlie's location, stat. And tell them to keep it quiet. No sirens, nothing like that. I just got a real creepy feeling."

"Will do," Johnson said. He was enough of a professional not to take chances when it was a matter of an officer's safety. He covered the mouthpiece again, and Tom could hear him giving the orders.

"Where in the Justice Center?" Tom yelled into the phone. He was in front of the center now, cruising past the row of parked cars. He double-parked beside a big silver Suburban.

"Subbasement," Johnson replied. "Probably."

The subbasement was a badly lit rabbit warren two stories underground. Holding cells for prisoners needed in court that day, administrative offices, the courtroom for arraignments, anterooms for lawyers and court officials—all that and more were located down there. The place teemed with activity from seven a.m. on as the accused, the convicted, the acquitted, and everything and everyone connected with their cases rotated in and out.

Charlie could've found all kinds of trouble down there.

"I'm on the scene," Tom said grimly, and disconnected.

Jumping out, head bent, into the pouring rain that began instantly soaking his short thick black hair and court-ready attire of navy sport jacket, white shirt, red tie, and gray slacks, he slammed the door and took off at a sprint toward the building. As he ran, he reached beneath his jacket to unsnap the safety strap on his Glock.

If he was lucky, he wouldn't need it. But then, he'd never been very lucky.

BEING *a prosecutor is not for sissies,* Kate White thought grimly as the backs of the elegant pumps she had bought on eBay for ten dollars rubbed against her increasingly tender heels with every purposeful step she took. The pay was lousy, the perks were nonexistent, and the people—well, there were a few good apples. Very few.

"Get a move on, would you? If we're late, he'll hang us out to dry," Bryan Chen muttered behind her. A small, compact Asian American, the forty-two-year-old veteran assistant district attorney was definitely one of the good apples. Four months before, he'd taken her under his wing when she had graduated from law school at age twenty-eight and joined the prosecutor's office. It was the first step on a career ladder that she was determined would take her to one of Philadelphia's superfirms. Bryan, on the other hand, had been an assistant DA for going on sixteen years now and seemed perfectly content to make a career of it. Of course, he didn't have a hundred thousand dollars in student loans to pay off and a young son for whom he was the only source of support, either.

She personally wanted more, for herself and for Ben, her sweet-faced nine-year-old, than to live in a tiny leased house on a diet of pasta and peanut butter at the end of every pay period.

Pushing through the heavy mahogany doors of courtroom 207 in the Criminal Justice Center, she was relieved to see that Circuit Court Judge Michael Moran was nowhere in sight, although the courtroom deputy stood in front of the bench with an anticipatory eye on the door that led to the judge's chambers.

*Hurry. Must not get on wrong side of notoriously cranky judge before trial even starts,* she thought as she strode down the aisle. The defense was already in place, and the courtroom galleries were full. The only thing missing was the judge—and the prosecution.

Silvery rivulets of rain streamed down the pair of tall windows that flanked the bench, making the courtroom seem unusually closed off. It had been officially autumn for more than a week, but today's cold rain was the first real indication that the seasons had changed. The downpour was also why they were late—every parking spot near the Justice Center was taken, which meant they'd had to park in a garage on the next block—and why strands of her normally sleek shoulder-length blond hair were escaping from her once-neat bun to wave around her face. She could only hope the mascara she'd hurriedly swiped on was still framing her blue eyes and not making inky rivers down her smooth ivory-pale cheeks.

Juggling umbrella and briefcase, Kate ran her fingers beneath her lower lashes, then brushed down the front of her black skirt suit. At the same time, she absorbed all of it—the high-ceilinged room with its mahogany walls, the heads of the public defender and his client bent together as they conferred, the steady murmur of conversation—with a surge of satisfaction. This was her world, the world she had fashioned for herself out of nothing but her own determination. The knowledge that she belonged in it now, that she was one of the good guys, brought a small smile to her lips. Walking a little taller, she was instantly brought back to earth by the stabbing of the shoes into her heels. The price on the pointy-toed pumps had been right, but they hurt.

*Beggars can't be choosers,* as the last—and least lamented—of her foster mothers used to say. This month she had paid the rent and the utilities and the babysitter and the minimum on her Visa bill and student loans and put gas in the car and bought Ben a new pair of sneakers. Now, with six days to go before the first of October, she was scarily close to dead broke. That was pretty much how it went every month, which meant there was little in the budget for clothes. The thing that made it difficult was that to achieve her goal she had to look like a successful professional. Ergo, she turned to eBay when necessary. But getting the right clothes on the cheap came with a price, and today the price was going to be hamburger heels.

The minute hand on the large round clock that hung on the wall moved incrementally. It was now officially nine o'clock.

"Look out, here he comes." Bryan practically shoved her through the low swinging door that separated the gallery from the well just as the deputy turned to face the crowded courtroom.

"All rise," he boomed as Kate and Bryan scrambled into place behind the counsel table. Everyone was on their feet as the door to chambers was pulled open. "Court is now in session. The Honorable Judge Michael Moran presiding."

While Judge Moran strode out, his black robe flapping around his portly frame, Kate quietly dropped her umbrella to the floor, slid her briefcase onto the table, and shifted her attention sideways to the jury box, which was to her right. It held fourteen people, twelve jurors and two alternates, skewing toward older, white, and female, which was just the way she had wanted it. This was an armed-robbery case, nothing unusual for Philly, but the defendant, Julio "Little Julie" Soto, a twenty-three-year-old street punk, had beaten up the woman behind the convenience-store counter badly enough that she had spent five days in the hospital. That degree of violence, in Kate's estimation, was the mark of a dangerous man. She had refused to plea-bargain. She was asking for a sentence of twenty years.

"Good morning," Judge Moran said to the courtroom in general. His tone was sour. Kate presumed he didn't like rainy Mondays any more than anybody else. To the left of the bench the court reporter, a plump, fiftyish blonde, was seated in front of her computer, recording the judge's greeting.

"Good morning, Your Honor," Kate, Bryan, and opposing counsel chorused in reply.

Judge Moran settled into his tall leather chair and accepted a sheaf of papers handed to him by the deputy. That was everyone else's cue to sit, too, which Kate did with relief, surreptitiously easing her feet a little way out of her shoes.

Pulling her notes from her briefcase, she discreetly checked her reflection in the small mirror she kept clipped to one of the inside pockets. What little makeup she wore seemed to have survived the deluge more or less intact. Her hair was well on its way to working free of its bun, so she quickly pushed the pins holding it in tighter. Otherwise she was good to go. She wasn't gorgeous by any means, but she was attractive, with a square-jawed, high-cheekboned face punctuated by intelligent blue eyes and a wide mouth.

Judge Moran's attention was still focused on the papers in front of him. Beside her Bryan had pulled a legal pad and pen from his own briefcase and was doodling away. This was nominally his case, but she had done all the preparation and would be trying it. After the trial was over, unless she did something horribly wrong, she would be handling cases on her own, no longer under Bryan's wing.

"Mr. Curry?" Moran looked up from the papers at last and frowned in the direction of the defense. "What's this?"

Kate's antennae went up. "Mr. Curry" was the public defender, Ed Curry, who had been opposing counsel on several of the cases Kate had worked. Average height, thin, balding, midforties, Curry wasn't given to springing surprises in court. Straightforward and unimaginative, he did a competent job for his clients in the meager time he was able to allot to each of them.

Curry stood. "Your Honor, I apologize, but our office just received the information on this witness late Friday. Over the weekend I talked to the man in jail, and I found him to be cred—"

"Witness? What witness?" Kate jammed her feet back into the torturous shoes and shot upright. Judge Moran sent her a quelling glance. Curry's gaze shifted her way for a split second, and then he quickly refocused on the judge. He looked uncharacteristically ill at ease. *As well he should,* Kate thought. Springing a surprise witness on the opening day of a trial was one of those no-no's that even newbies like herself knew not to do. A quick check showed her that the jurors had brightened with interest. *Not good.* "Your Honor, permission to approach the bench."

"Permission granted. You, too, Mr. Curry."

Kate whisked out from behind the counsel table and marched toward the bench. Refusing to look at her, Curry walked forward, too. As soon as he joined her in front of the bench, Kate pounced.

"Your Honor, opposing counsel knows very well that it's too late to introduce a new witness. Discovery was closed weeks ago."

"Spare me the lecture, Ms. White." Judge Moran held up his hand. "I'm well aware of the appropriate timetable here."

Kate clamped her jaws shut, crossed her arms over her chest, and glared, presenting a picture of eloquent indignation for the jury.

Moran looked at the public defender. "Mr. Curry, I presume you were about to tell me just why it is that this is the first we've heard about this witness. And I warn you, if I find that you've deliberately withheld information from the prosecution . . ."

Curry shook his head vigorously. "Nothing like that, Your Honor. As I was saying, the witness just got in contact with our office on Friday. He's in custody himself and claims he was unaware of the facts of the case until then. His evidence is compelling, and it provides my client with a full alibi."

"Bull—" Kate caught herself in time and swallowed the inevitable ending. "Your Honor, the evidence against the defendant is overwhelming, as Mr. Curry knows. This witness cannot possibly provide a credible alibi for his client because we already have eye-witnesses, a security videotape, and forensic evidence placing Mr. Soto at the scene. There is no way your client"—and here she shot a hard-eyed look at the public defender—"isn't guilty as sin."

"Ms. White, I realize you're just out of school, so we all have to cut you some slack, but for future reference that's usually up to the jury to decide," Curry said, giving her a snarky smile.

"That's right," Moran said, frowning at her. "Remember, Ms. White, we are here to find out the truth, whatever that may be. Potentially exculpatory testimony cannot be ruled out simply because the timing is inconvenient for the prosecution."

Moran's lecture had the patronizing tone of a professor to a student, and Kate's hackles rose. The defense's tactics were clear: Curry knew he couldn't win today in court, so he was trying to delay. Delay was a defense attorney's best friend. Put a trial off long enough, and anything could happen. Witnesses could move away or die, evidence could be lost, memories could fail, judges could retire. With each day that passes, the case loses priority.

"Mr. Curry, you want to give Ms. White and me an idea of who this witness is and what he is prepared to testify to?" Moran asked.

Curry glanced at her again. Kate could see the craftiness at the backs of his eyes. He knew that there was no way anyone could testify truthfully that Soto was not at the scene of the crime. Her gaze shot to the judge, whose expression was solemnly unctuous.

"My witness—and I don't want to give his name here in open court, for his protection—says Mr. Soto has a cousin who—"

The cheerfully funky notes of the Pussycat Dolls' hit "Don't Cha" blared without warning from somewhere in the room. While Judge Moran stiffened and Curry glanced over his shoulder, Kate froze.

She knew the source of the disruption. It was her cell phone. She had forgotten to turn it off. The mortifyingly unprofessional ringtone only made things worse. Ben and his friend Samantha had been experimenting with her phone yesterday when she had driven Samantha home from a playdate. This had been their favorite ringtone. This was what they had left on her phone. And she hadn't gotten around to changing it back to its usual businesslike chime.

"Whose cell phone is that?" Judge Moran asked.

A glance at Bryan's face told her that he knew the distracting sound was emanating from somewhere around their table.

Her briefcase, to be precise. Nestled against the far leg of the counsel table, there on the floor beside her chair.

"It's mine, Your Honor," she said, doing her best to keep her chin up. Right on cue, the ringtone sounded again.

"Turn it off." Moran's voice was like thunder. His face was taking on color like a quickly ripening tomato. "Now."

"Yes, Your Honor."

Toddling off in the direction of counsel table while doing her best to maintain some semblance of professional cool, she was hideously conscious of being the cynosure of all eyes. Bryan's face was a study in dismay. Except for another exuberant burst of melody from her phone, the silence in that courtroom was absolute.

Teeth clenched, Kate crouched beside the prosecution's table, flipped the clasps open on her briefcase, and thrust her hand into the side pocket to grab her phone.

She found the button and turned off the ringer with a quick, vicious jab even as recognition dawned: The phone number dancing across the little digital display was that of Ben's school.

*Ben.* She had dropped him off at seven thirty, as she did every morning so she could get to work on time. He was part of the school's breakfast group, which was made up of the kids whose parents had to be at work before the official beginning of the school day. This—fourth grade—was Ben's first year at the school, because they'd moved into the district at the beginning of the summer, when she'd been hired on at the DA's office. So far, he had told her, it had been "okay." Which in Ben-speak meant he didn't want to talk about it. Which worried her.

Now the school was calling, and the knowledge made her stomach tighten with anxiety. Was Ben sick? Was he hurt? Whatever it was, she couldn't possibly return the call now.

She stuffed the now silenced phone into her briefcase and rose to her feet.

*Crack! Crack! Crack!*

The sounds, faintly muffled, came out of nowhere.

With her peripheral vision Kate caught a blur of sudden movement: A door—the metal door to the secure corridor where prisoners were kept in holding rooms until their presence was required in court—flew open. Someone in the gallery screamed.

*Those are gunshots* was her instinctive first thought as the courtroom erupted into chaos around her.

To her astonishment Little Julie Soto sprang to his feet and ran around the far end of the defense table, his wiry frame conveying a surprising amount of menace despite its diminutive proportions and the ill-fitting gray suit he wore. His long black hair bounced as he moved, and his narrow face was alight with savage triumph. From somewhere he had acquired a pistol; it was in his hand.

"You ain't putting me back in jail," Soto shouted.

Judge Moran was on his feet, Kate saw, as her disbelieving gaze followed Soto's. The judge raised his hands, palms outward, as if to ward off the threat. His eyes were wide and his mouth was opening, as if he was about to speak, or yell, or something. Whatever he meant to do, she never knew, because she was just in time to watch—*bang!*—as his head was blown to pieces.

# CHAPTER 3

KATE gasped. Her ears rang. A sour taste sprang into her mouth.

*This can't be real.*

Blood splattered the wall behind the bench. The judge's body dropped like a rock, disappearing from view. Kate's knees buckled at the same time. She collapsed into a kneeling position at the far side of the counsel table, eyes huge with disbelief, heart pounding.

*Please, oh please, let this be a bad dream.*

Men—two of them, at least one a prisoner, judging from the orange jumpsuit he wore—burst from the secure corridor. Pistols were in their hands. Soto glanced over his shoulder at them.

"*Vámonos!* Let's go!"

*Crack! Crack!*

More shots rang out, coming from roughly the direction of the jury box. One of the deputies was firing back, Kate thought, although she couldn't see who was shooting because she still couldn't move. At the same time panicked confusion erupted everywhere.

Ducking low, Soto and the newcomers ran toward the front of the courtroom as one of them—the one in the orange jumpsuit—shouted at him, "What the hell did you just do?"

"I killed him, so what?" Soto yelled back.

The three converged, dashing around the side of the bench toward the window, snapping off shots as they ran. Curry hit the ground in front of the bench, his arms flying to cover his head as a bullet smacked into the smooth mahogany not two feet above where he lay. Hands in the air, the court reporter fled shrieking toward the jury box. The deputy nearest the bench screamed and dropped; he'd been shot. Screams and curses and gunfire mingled hideously, exploding off the walls and floor and ceiling.

Kate seemed to be paralyzed, rooted to the smooth, hard terrazzo beneath her bent legs.

*Blood—so much blood. Blood everywhere. . . .*

Icy with horror now, she knew there was nothing she could do to save herself or anyone else as the nightmare unfolded around her.

"Where are they?" the guy in the orange jumpsuit screamed, sharply enough to pierce the noise. "They oughta be here!"

"Get out, get out!" This, from the gallery, was some other, innocent man's yell, rising over the tumult, urging others to flee.

"Mama, where are you?" It was a child's frantic screech.

"God help me," a nearby woman wailed.

These and other disembodied voices reached Kate's ears through the sounds of dozens of people screaming and fighting to escape.

She knew she should move, run, hide, but she couldn't. For the second time in her life, she was frozen to the spot with fear.

Some people in the galleries were hunkered down, doing their best to hide from the bullets as the remaining deputies and the prisoners exchanged fire. Others jumped over the backs of the benches or charged down the center aisle as they tried to escape. A fleeing man was shot in the back. In the jury box, some were on their feet, stampeding toward the door to the jury room. Others dived out of sight behind the box's low wall.

Another deputy, retreating along the courtroom's left wall, shot steadily at the murderous trio now sheltering behind the bench before a barrage of return fire cut him down. The jackhammerlike crack of the shots blasted Kate's eardrums.

"Kate, for God's sake, get under here!"

The urgent summons came from nearby. Something warm and faintly moist grabbed at her leg. She jumped. Even as she recognized Bryan's pudgy fingers sliding away from her ankle, she saw him, hunkered down under the counsel table.

Twisting around, she speed-crawled toward Bryan. Although she knew she really wasn't, she felt safer once the thin slab of mahogany was over her head. Crowding next to Bryan, she strained to look out beneath the overhang. What she could see was limited: briefcases and umbrellas and a scattering of papers that had fallen to the floor from the counsel table, part of the jury box, the lower half of the bench. The only people visible from that angle were the fallen deputy and Curry, who, while still hugging the floor, was moving in a fast commando-style crawl toward the defense table.

"This is bad," Bryan said in her ear, his voice shaky.

"We've got to get out of here." Terror squeezed her throat. For Ben's sake if for no other reason, she had to survive.

"Is that bastard even out there?" Orange Jumpsuit shrieked. "Pack, you see him?"

"Can't see nothing through the rain."

"We gotta chance it. We gotta *go*."

At least two of the trio were scarily close, Kate estimated, judging from the clarity with which she heard their shouted exchange. Their guns sounded like they were being fired directly overhead.

*Please, God, don't let it be my time to die.*

Knowing that the counsel table offered only an illusion of protection, she desperately looked around for the best way out.

"We need to make a break for it," she whispered to Bryan.

Before they could even think about making a move, the last remaining deputy, the one who earlier had been standing nearest to the jury box, popped into view. He was, she saw, middle-aged, his brown hair going gray around the temples, a little paunchy in his uniform. He shot out from behind the jury-box wall in an awkward, crouching run, yelling, "Officer down! Officer down!" into a walkie-talkie even as he fired his weapon multiple times to cover himself. Seconds after she spotted him, he took a bullet in the back. He landed, hard, just a few feet from where she and Bryan cowered. Kate looked with horror at his blinking eyes and at the growing circle of crimson on his dark blue shirt.

Her heart turned over.

"Hang on," she mouthed to the deputy, whose eyes had quit blinking. He was staring at her in a fixed way that she feared meant nothing but bad news. She was nearly positive he wasn't seeing her.

As she looked back at him, two things happened almost simultaneously. First, there was a quick barrage of shots, accompanied by the crash of glass shattering. From the sound of it, the window closest to them had been shot out. Shards rained noisily to the floor, breaking again on the stone. Second, from the opposite end of the room, where the doors to the hall were located, came a mighty bellow loud enough to be heard over the chaos.

"Police! Freeze! Get down, get down!"

*Thank God, we're saved. . . .*

"There's an army of pigs outside!" Orange Jumpsuit shrieked.

"I'm going for it." The voice was high-pitched, hysterical.

"Little Julie, no!"

If there was an answer, Kate didn't hear it, maybe because the words were swallowed up by another bellowed *"I said freeze!"* followed by a burst of gunfire. More shots were being fired outside the building. A muffled scream, abruptly cut off, sent a chill racing down Kate's spine.

"I think they've got the building surrounded," Bryan whispered. "I think that guy jumped from the window, and they shot him."

A bullet smacked into the table leg just inches away from Kate, sending splinters flying. Footsteps pounded nearby.

As she scanned what little she could see beyond the table, her heart thumped wildly. Crouching as low to the floor as she could get, sucking in ragged gulps of air, she became aware that the quality of what she was breathing had changed. It was cooler and smelled of rain, which confirmed her guess that the window almost directly in front of the prosecution table had been blown out. Apparently the prisoners had planned to jump but had been dissuaded—all but Soto, anyway—by some sort of police presence outside. She could hear the rush of the downpour, and, cutting through it, sirens.

*If I can just survive a little longer, it'll all be over.*

"Drop your weapons now!" a police officer yelled from inside the courtroom.

Another quick flurry of running footsteps sent cold chills racing over her body. Suddenly a pair of feet in black sneakers jumped into view. Kate's heart lurched as Orange Jumpsuit crouched in front of the counsel table. A big black pistol was in his hand. Like Soto, this guy appeared to be Hispanic, midtwenties, a street punk. He was sweating, panicky. He was looking over her head, over the table, she thought, probably at the cop or cops at the other end of the room, and his eyes were small and hard and cruel.

Then his gaze lowered, and their eyes locked.

"Throw down your weapon!" a cop roared from the gallery.

Kate's pulse was pounding so hard in her ears now that the voice sounded muffled, as if it were coming from miles away.

Orange Jumpsuit gave no indication that he heard. He never even blinked. He just kept holding her gaze. The realization that she was in all likelihood eyeball to eyeball with her own death broke over Kate like an icy wave.

"Throw down your weapon!" the cop screamed again.

Only then did Kate notice that he was saying "weapon," singular, instead of "weapons," plural, as he had earlier. Did that mean that there was only one gun left for the cops to take out? The one Orange Jumpsuit was holding right in front of her?

"Come on." Orange Jumpsuit grabbed her arm above the elbow, fingers clamping roughly into her flesh. Pointing his gun at her face, he pulled her toward him. She didn't resist; she had no doubt whatsoever that he would shoot her if she did.

Bryan didn't try to help her. He shrank away instead, and for that she couldn't blame him. It was abundantly clear that he would have been shot dead in an instant if he had interfered in any way.

"Please, I've got a little boy," Kate said.

"Shut up." Orange Jumpsuit shifted his grip, pulling her around so that they were facing the same way, then wrapped an arm around her neck so that he had her in a choke hold, all the while keeping his head below the table. "Now we're gonna stand up. Together."

The cold, hard muzzle of his pistol jammed into Kate's cheek. Her heart gave a terrified leap. Her knees trembled and threatened to fold, but Orange Jumpsuit forced her up. Plastered against her back, his surprisingly muscular arm locked around her neck, he felt hot and sweaty and loathsome.

"I'll kill her," he yelled, holding her tight against him as they slowly straightened together. His arm forced her chin up. The pistol ground into her cheek. "Back off, or I'll blow her head off."

*"Hold your fire!"* a man—she thought it was a cop, but her head was tipped up at such an angle that she couldn't see the speaker— yelled in warning to, presumably, his fellow cops. *"Don't shoot!"*

Orange Jumpsuit's grip shifted again, and she was able to lower her chin slightly. Stretched to her full height, Kate found herself staring at a courtroom in which all the remaining civilian occupants—there were maybe ten—were curled into protective balls, hiding among the galleries. A wedge of armed deputies and cops was frozen in place in the back of the courtroom, some sheltered behind galleries and others exposed in the center aisle. All had weapons, and all were pointing them at her. Nobody was moving.

The black-haired, olive-skinned cop in the lead was in plainclothes—a navy jacket, white shirt, and red tie that were soaked with rain. Maybe in his midthirties, he was good-looking enough to have rated a second glance from her under other, better circumstances. He was down on one knee in the aisle, holding his pistol with a two-handed grip. It was aimed straight at Kate.

*No, not at me,* she told herself, trying to slow her racing heart. Like the others, he pointed his gun at the man using her as a human shield. She just happened to be in the way.

Her eyes locked with the cop's. His dark, heavy-lidded eyes were cool, calm, and reassuring. He held her gaze for the briefest of moments before shifting his attention to the man behind her.

"Let her go," the cop said. Like his eyes, his voice was calm. His pistol never wavered.

"Yeah, right." Orange Jumpsuit tightened his arm around her neck and began pulling her to the right, toward the doors to chambers and the secure corridor. "What, do you think I'm stupid? You think I don't know I'm looking at the death penalty here?" He hesitated fractionally, and Kate could feel the too-rapid rise and fall of his chest against her back. "I want a helicopter. Out in front of this building. In fifteen minutes. Otherwise I kill her."

"You kill her, we kill you," the cop said. His tone was the verbal equivalent of a shrug. His lean dark face was expressionless. His eyes never wavered from her captor. His gun tracked them.

"Without that helicopter I'm dead anyway."

They reached the door to the secure corridor.

"Open the door," Orange Jumpsuit said in her ear. When Kate didn't immediately comply, he jabbed the gun viciously against her cheek. Wincing, she gave a choked little cry and reached for the knob, which she could see out of the corner of her eye.

*Don't turn the knob. Try to delay. . . .*

"Look," she said. "Maybe we could work out a deal—"

"Open the damn door. *Now.*"

The gun jabbed her cheek again, grinding painfully into the

hollow below her cheekbone. This time she felt her skin rip. A warm trickle that she knew was blood spilled down her cheek.

Breathing hard, she did as he said. Inch by inch, she eased open the heavy metal door.

"Let her go, and you got years to figure out some way to beat the death penalty," the cop said, still conversational, like he was discussing the weather. Her eyes clung to his face beseechingly. Not by so much as the flicker of an eyelash did he acknowledge her.

"Smart guy like you, that should be a piece of cake," the cop continued. "You know how the system works. On the other hand, if you kill her, I guarantee you won't live out the day."

"You're full of it," Orange Jumpsuit said, and to Kate's horror he used his foot to shove the door the rest of the way open. Then he backed into the secure corridor, pulling Kate in behind him. "I ain't ridin' the needle, *amigo*. No way. You got fifteen minutes to get me that helicopter."

THE door, which closed automatically, clicked shut in Kate's face. She was now alone with Orange Jumpsuit and whoever else might be left in the secure area. It was eerily quiet. A security camera mounted on the wall just above the door was clearly useless, having been shot to smithereens.

"Lock it," Orange Jumpsuit ordered. Glancing down, Kate saw that there was a dead bolt below the knob. He didn't expect or want anyone to join them, and that confirmed her impression that both his buddies were now out of the picture—dead, wounded, or escaped. Despairing, feeling like she was cutting off her last best hope of rescue, Kate did as he told her. The dead bolt clicked into place. The smooth metal door was bulletproof, she knew. It was also, as far as she could tell, soundproof. If anything was happening in the courtroom, she couldn't hear it.

"That's a good little prosecutor."

The venom in his voice as he said "prosecutor" made her certain that whatever happened, he was going to kill her.

"What time is it?" he asked.

Glancing down at her wrist, she saw that it was nine sixteen and told him so.

"You got till nine thirty-one. Walk."

Swinging her around so that she faced the opposite end of the hall, he marched her forward, shifting his grip so that his hand curled into the neck of her jacket and thrusting his gun hard into her spine. She grimaced at the sudden jab but didn't dare protest.

*Stay calm. Think. There has to be a way out of this.*

The corridor was part of a labyrinth of connected passages that led from the subbasement prisoner holding area throughout the building. They allowed deputies to move prisoners about inside the Justice Center in virtual invisibility. In an emergency each section of hallway could be isolated from the others by bulletproof doors. From what she could see, the hallways were all but impregnable.

This particular one was narrow, brightly lit, and painted a depressing shade of gray. The floor was smooth concrete. Two doors, both gray metal, both with small glass-enclosed grilles that allowed deputies in the hallway to check on the prisoners inside, opened through its right wall into holding cells. The left wall was a smooth, unbroken expanse of gray paint. A black telephone hung on the narrow wall at the end of the hall.

All of a sudden the possibility that the cell doors were almost certainly bulletproof, too, occurred to her, bringing with it a ray of hope. If she could somehow break away from Orange Jumpsuit, maybe she could dart inside a holding cell and lock herself in. . . .

"You better be praying for that helicopter," he said, nudging her in the spine with his gun.

She took a deep, steadying breath. "Maybe a helicopter's not the only option. Maybe we could work something else out—like a plea deal." She was proud of how steady her voice sounded. "If you let me walk out of here now, I can guarantee you that I can fix it so you won't face the death penalty."

"Don't give me that." His fingers tightened on the neck of her jacket, and his gun jabbed into her spine. "And if you don't shut your mouth so I can think, I'm going to kill you right now."

*Okay.* So much for trying to talk her way free. She kept walking, her heart thundering as the reality of her situation hit home.

They had just reached the first cell when its doorknob rattled. Jumping a little, eyes widening in surprise, Kate saw a face pressed to the grille in the door. It was a man with deeply tanned skin and a shiny bald head, his features faintly distorted by the glass. What was clear, however, was that he was looking at them as he tried without success to open the door.

Her captor sounded angry. "Open the door."

This was addressed to her, and she did as he told her. There were dead-bolt locks on each cell door, but the latches were on the outside. Of course. The prisoners needed to be locked in. In all likelihood there weren't locks on the inside.

Her stomach knotted as she realized just how close she had come to making a fatal mistake.

She was just registering with some confusion that the dead bolt didn't seem to be engaged after all when the door was thrust open and the newcomer pushed through it. He was, she saw, a little taller than her captor, maybe five eleven or so, with an unnaturally muscular torso that told her he was a fan of steroids and he'd had plenty of time to work out—probably in prison. His orange jumpsuit strained at the shoulders. His biceps bulged. His neck was as thick as a bull's. He had bushy dark brown eyebrows above smallish brown eyes and a neatly trimmed dark brown mustache and goatee.

There was a big black pistol in his hand.

"The hell happened to you? And where's Newton?" her captor growled, pushing her face-first against the wall as he spoke. As the cell door closed right beside her nose, she got a glimpse inside before it clicked shut. Three men sprawled motionless on the floor. She could see only the legs of two. One was wearing an orange jumpsuit. The other was a blue-uniformed deputy. The third man was another deputy. Unnaturally pale, he lay facedown, dead or unconscious, she couldn't be sure which. He had short thick black hair and was thin and looked young.

"Newton's in there, dead. Damned deputy who brought him over from the jail still had a shot left in him. We were on our way out when Newton bought it. I stopped to finish the deputy off, and the door jammed." In contrast to her captor's obvious agitation, this guy sounded untroubled. Kate stayed where she had been shoved, cheek and palms pressed against the smooth, cool wall, heart thundering. Now she had two armed murderers to contend with. "Couldn't believe it. Door wouldn't open for nothing. I was stuck as a duck." His tone changed. "It went to hell, huh?"

"Yeah."

"Pack and Little Julie?"

"Dead, both of 'em. Meltzer never showed with the truck. Maybe he couldn't get through. There was po-po everywhere, all around the building, already there when we shot out the window, like they'd been tipped off or something. Little Julie jumped anyway, and they tore him up. Pack bought it in the courtroom. I grabbed her"—Kate could feel them looking at her—"the hot little pro-se-cu-tor"—he drew the word out mockingly—"and—"

He broke off as the phone at the end of the hall began to ring.

The shrill peals made all three of them start.

"Who's that?" There was an edge to the new guy's voice.

"How should I know? Wait—maybe it's the cops. Maybe they got the helicopter."

A hand closed around Kate's arm. Orange Jumpsuit swung her away from the wall and shoved her toward the phone.

"Move," he said to her as she stumbled in her shoes.

"Helicopter?" the new guy inquired.

"I gave 'em fifteen minutes to get me a helicopter or I pop her." Orange Jumpsuit sounded proud of himself. "Hey, Miss Prosecutor, what time is it now?"

Kate looked at her watch. "Nine twenty."

"They got eleven minutes left, then."

"You think that'll work?"

"How do I know? If they want her alive, it'll work."

The phone was still ringing as they reached it. Kate was first, with Orange Jumpsuit behind her and the new guy behind him.

Orange Jumpsuit shoved her against the wall beside the phone. It rang again just then, setting her teeth on edge.

"Don't you even think about trying nothing," he said to her, letting go of her arm. The gun moved. Cold and hard and terrifying, it nestled against her neck just below her jawline. She closed her eyes as he picked up the receiver, silencing the phone at last.

"Yeah?" he said into it. Then, a moment later, "Don't give me that crap. You ain't getting more time." He listened, then said, "Sure. Talk to her. Long as you remember the clock's ticking."

Orange Jumpsuit pressed the receiver to his chest and glared at Kate. "Says he wants to make sure you're alive," he said, trailing the mouth of the gun across her skin until it nestled below her ear. "Watch yourself, 'cause I'm watching you."

Then he held the receiver to her ear.

"Hello." Wetting her parched lips, she spoke into the phone.

"Kate White?" a man asked in her ear. It was the cop from the courtroom, the one with the calm, reassuring eyes.

"Yes." She didn't know how long she would be allowed to talk, and she wanted to make sure she got the essentials across first. "I have a little boy." Despite her determination to remain cool and calm, her voice was no longer even. It was hoarse and cracked with fear. "I'm a single mother. Please give this man what he wants."

Orange Jumpsuit nodded at her approvingly.

"We're going to do our best to get you out of there in one piece," the cop said. "Are you the only hostage?"

"Yes." She thought of the bodies lying in the holding cell, and the other cell that she hadn't seen the inside of. "I think so."

Orange Jumpsuit frowned. "That's enough."

He pulled the phone away from her. The gun dug in deeper. She could feel her pulse beating frantically against the hard little metal circle.

"You call me back when you get that helicopter," he said into the receiver. "And remember, tick tick."

As he hung up, Kate could hear the cop talking on the other end.

"You ain't going to get that helicopter," the second guy said.

"What do you mean?" Orange Jumpsuit whipped around to face the speaker. His gun went with him. Kate let out a silent breath of relief now that it was no longer pressing into her flesh.

"They're just yankin' your chain. You ain't going to get it."

"They're not yankin' my chain. They know I'll kill her."

"And if you kill her, what good does that do, huh? That doesn't get us out of here."

Tension between the two men electrified the atmosphere.

"They want her alive. They'll give me what I want." But Orange Jumpsuit no longer sounded sure.

"Say you get the helicopter. Where's it gonna be?"

"I told 'em the roof."

"There's a helipad up there." The second guy seemed to be thinking aloud, weighing the possibilities. "But how you gonna get to the roof without them offing you?"

"I'm gonna use her like a shield, that's how. And I'm gonna tell 'em if I even so much as smell a cop, I'll blow her head off."

The second guy shook his head. "Not gonna work. Too far to go. Gotta get to the elevator, go up to the roof, get out, and get across to the helicopter. With her. They'll get you with snipers."

Orange Jumpsuit practically vibrated with rage and frustration. He bounced up and down on the balls of his feet. "You got a better plan? Huh? You got a better plan?"

"Yeah," the second guy said. "Better for me, that is."

Kate never even saw his hand move. There was an ear-splitting crack, and Orange Jumpsuit smacked into the wall right beside her. Screaming, she jumped back, out of the way. Eyes huge, jaw dropping, she watched with disbelief as he slid down the wall as bonelessly as a rag doll. Even before she saw blood spilling from his mouth and down the front of his jumpsuit, she knew he was dead.

Her stunned gaze flew to the second guy's face. He was looking down at Orange Jumpsuit with a twisted smile, still holding the just-fired gun. His eyes rose to lock with hers.

"Hey there, Kitty-cat," he said. "No need to look so scared. What, don't you remember your old buddy Mario?"

# CHAPTER 4

TOM'S hand was rock steady as he picked up the receiver. His breathing was under control, and he wasn't sweating. There was nothing about to give away the sick feeling in his stomach.

They—the small group of cops and sheriff's deputies clustered with him around the bailiff's phone—had just heard the muffled sound of a gun going off inside the secure corridor. Tom thought of Kate White, slim and lovely with her Scandinavian blond hair and wide blue eyes, helpless as a mouse between the paws of a hungry cat, and felt his gut clench. Was she dead?

What about Charlie, whom he hadn't been able to locate yet? Was Charlie dead?

The possibility was making Tom crazy. The dispatcher in the sub-basement had thought, but wasn't sure, that after logging his prisoner in, Charlie had escorted him to the second floor. Instead of taking the labyrinthine secure corridors that his brother had used, Tom had opted for the easier, civilian route to the second floor. He had just leaped off the elevator with a pair of deputies in tow when he'd heard the first shots being fired in courtroom 207. He'd had to battle his way through the stampede of people exiting the courtroom. In the midst of all the carnage he still hadn't found Charlie.

But at the moment his first duty was to Kate White.

"If he won't put her on the phone, we got to assume he probably shot her, right?" Mitch Cooney asked. The deputy was gray-faced. The massacre of so many fellow officers had hit him hard.

"He'd be stupid to kill her. Then he's got nothing. No bargaining power." Police Corporal LaRonda Davis sounded shaken. She was part of the group huddled around the phone.

"I'm calling in now." In his ear Tom could hear the phone in the secure corridor start to ring.

He waited. The suspense was making him jittery. Determined not to let it show, Tom set his teeth.

*Brriing . . .*

Four minutes were left of the fifteen-minute deadline the convict, Nico Rodriguez, had given them. The helicopter—they were getting Rodriguez the helicopter he'd demanded, but he wasn't going to be flying away in it; it was basically bait to lure him into the open—was at least ten minutes out. The SWAT team was on the way: ETA three minutes. So was a hostage negotiator.

All he had to do was keep Kate White alive long enough for the real professionals at this kind of thing to arrive and take over.

If she wasn't already dead.

*Brriing . . .*

The courtroom was chaotic, teeming with cops and medical personnel and civilians and even reporters who had happened to be in the courthouse when the shooting had started. Blood and gore were everywhere. Victims were being treated where they lay. From outside, dozens of sirens screamed through the broken-out window.

*Brriing . . .*

His job, because right now he was the senior cop on the scene, was to keep Rodriguez talking, keep him believing he was going to get what he wanted, keep him from killing Kate White.

Her eyes, clinging to his as if she actually thought he could save her, haunted him. So did her voice, cracking with fear.

*Brri—*

The sound broke off. Somebody was picking up. He tensed.

The others must have been able to see that something was going down from his expression or body language, because they all leaned in a little closer, their eyes on his face.

On the other end of the line nobody said anything. But Tom was sure—almost sure—he could hear somebody breathing.

"Rodriguez?" Tom hazarded a guess.

"No." It was Kate White. He recognized her voice instantly. Only then did relief loosen the death grip fear had on his senses.

"You doing all right?" he asked.

"Yes."

Her breathing was ragged, and he sure couldn't blame her. All things considered, she was hanging tough, being very calm, very aware, and he admired her for that.

"We heard—" he began, but she cut him off.

"A shot," she said. "I know." He could hear her taking a deep breath. Then she stunned him. "I shot him. He's dead."

For a moment Tom wasn't sure he had heard her right. "What?"

"He's dead. It's all over. I'm coming out."

"How did—" Tom began, stupefied, but again she cut him off, this time by hanging up. Just like that.

Tom listened to the hum of the dial tone in his ear for only a few seconds before hanging up himself and then staring down at the phone in bemusement.

"What?" A dozen pairs of questioning eyes were pinned on him.

"She said Rodriguez is dead." Tom couldn't quite bend his mind around it. "She said she shot him. And she's coming out."

"Alone?" Cooney asked.

"I guess." Tom shrugged. Was it a trick? Was Rodriguez setting them up for something?

A pair of deputies rushed to clear the courtroom in case Rodriguez came out shooting or a gunfight should erupt. The rest of them, weapons drawn, took cover behind galleries and chairs and flattened themselves back against the wall, anything to keep out of sight but able to take a shot if necessary.

The door to the secure corridor was surrounded. Whoever emerged would be covered by a host of guns.

Tom stood about ten feet away, facing the door. His Glock was in his hand, but his hand rested unthreateningly at his side.

The door began to open. Tom held his breath as Kate White came into view. She stood just inside the secure corridor, pale as a ghost and fragile-looking as a porcelain doll in her figure-hugging black suit, her blond hair loose now and spilling to her shoulders, her body seemingly unbloodied and in one piece, her face expressionless. Except for her eyes. They were huge with what he presumed was shock.

As far as Tom could tell, she was indeed alone. Her build was too slight to allow Rodriguez or anyone else to hide behind her.

"Kate? Is Rodriguez dead?"

She nodded, then seemed to take a deep breath before she started toward him on slim, unsteady legs.

"Hold your fire," he ordered over his shoulder. "She's alone."

As the door swung closed behind Kate, he holstered his gun and strode to meet her.

She was so white she looked like she was drained of blood. He deliberately made his voice gentle. "Are you okay?"

She nodded again, and stopped walking. As he reached her, Tom saw the ladders in her stockings, the little trickle of dried blood on her cheek, the horror in her eyes.

Then her knees gave way. Tom was just close enough to catch her in his arms before she hit the floor.

"YOU sure you don't want to ride on over to the hospital, get checked out?" the female EMT asked.

"No, thanks."

Kate was sitting on a bench just outside courtroom 207, having been deposited there by the same cop who had scooped her up and yelled for an EMT when Kate's knees betrayed her. Someone had called to him urgently right after he had summoned the EMT, and Kate hadn't seen him since. She didn't even know his name.

Not that it mattered. What mattered was surviving this nightmare the best way she could. She was alive, anyway, when so many others weren't. That was the most important thing.

"I need to go pick my son up at school. He's sick," Kate said. Which was true. While the EMT had been checking Kate's vital signs and applying antibiotic ointment and a Band-Aid to the cut on her cheek, she had remembered the call from Ben's school and asked for her briefcase. An obliging deputy fetched it, and she had fished out her phone and returned the call. As she had known they would be, the shootings were already a media sensation. The school secretary was more than pleased to hear from her.

Ben was terribly afraid that his mother might be caught up in the tragedy, the secretary told her. Kate didn't have the heart to tell her that Ben was right.

The original call had been made because Ben had thrown up in class and was even now lying in the school's sick bay. Kate had promised to come get him as soon as possible.

"The world could be coming to an end and we mothers would still be on the job, wouldn't we?" The EMT shook her head. "I got three of my own, so I know."

Before Kate could reply, the doors to courtroom 207 flew open and were held by a pair of grim-faced deputies as a gurney rolled through them. It was moving fast, which told Kate that the condition of the person on the gurney was grave.

"Hold that elevator!" one of the EMTs yelled to someone Kate couldn't see. The wide hallway with its vaulted ceiling was busy with cops and deputies and heavily armed SWAT officers rushing in and out of various courtrooms, calling to one another and talking on cell phones and two-way radios. Kate assumed the building, which was still being evacuated, was being thoroughly searched.

Kate caught a glimpse of an IV bag swinging on a thin metal pole as it dripped clear liquid down into the arm of the man on the gurney—who, Kate realized, was the young black-haired cop she'd last seen lying on the floor of the cell in the secure corridor.

"He's alive," she said aloud, and realized she was glad. It was a shred of something positive to hold on to on this hellish day.

The gurney trundled noisily toward the elevators, and Kate recognized one of the cops loping behind it: the lean, black-haired man in plainclothes who had been her lifeline throughout the ordeal. From his tense expression and the way he was sticking close to the gurney, she guessed the man on it must be someone important to him. A relative, possibly, because they shared the same raven hair.

With all eyes still craning after the gurney, Kate figured this would be a good time to make her exit. She knew the cops would want to talk to her. She knew she should stay and give a statement, but she couldn't. The shock was too new, too awful, for her to trust herself to be thinking properly. She could not make a mistake. For Ben's sake as well as her own, she had to be very careful in what she said and did next. A mistake could cost them everything.

Accordingly, she curled her fingers around the handle on her briefcase and stood up, ignoring the light-headedness that immediately assailed her. Her knees wobbled, but she ignored that, too. Her despised high heels were under the bench, where she had kicked them off, but she left them where they lay. Their torment was more than she could deal with. She would be better off escaping—because that's what she was doing—in her stockinged feet.

"Thanks," she said to the EMT with a quick, grateful smile.

"You start feeling funny, you give us a call, hear?"

"I will," Kate promised, and started walking toward the stairs. The terrazzo felt cool beneath her feet. Taking the elevators would be quicker, but she was afraid of who she might run into. Witnesses were surely being rounded up and she—by taking the blame, or credit, depending on one's point of view, for the killing of Orange Jumpsuit—had made herself far more than just a witness.

What she needed before all the official stuff kicked in was to buy herself a little time to calm down and think everything through.

Fortunately, she had the perfect excuse: Ben was sick and needed her. Who could blame a mother for rushing to her son?

Hanging on to the banister, she reached the bottom of the enormous curved staircase without attracting any undue attention. But even before she took the first step across the lobby toward the entrance, she saw, through the tall windows and banks of revolving doors, the pandemonium going on in front of the building.

Ambulances and fire trucks and police cruisers jammed the narrow street. Dozens of specialty units, including an armored SWAT vehicle and the bomb-squad truck, filled the lawn. On the sidewalks crowds of onlookers gaped at the action. Reporters talked into cameras from various spots on the steps.

*Oh, no.*

Kate turned and padded quickly across the bustling lobby to the hallway where the restrooms were located. A small smoking room furnished with card tables and chairs had been elbowed in next to the ladies' room. As she had hoped, it was empty. At the far end was a little-used side door. On the stoop outside stood a tall, stocky cop with his back to her, almost certainly stationed there to prevent unauthorized persons from entering. The stoop must have been covered by a roof, because the area where he stood was dry, while around him the rain fell like a gently undulating silver curtain.

She stopped, eyeing his uniformed back uncertainly.

*He's there to keep people out, not in. Just walk past. Keep going.*

Easy to say, but her heart thumped wildly as she approached the heavy glass door. When she pulled it open, the cop glanced around in surprise, then registered her apparent harmlessness before stepping aside to make room for her. As she stepped out onto the stoop, he nodded a greeting, and she nodded back. Shrieking sirens assaulted her eardrums. More cop cars crept into view, lights flashing.

She was glad for the pandemonium. It gave her a legitimate excuse to look anywhere but at the cop. She could feel his gaze on her face. She was shoeless and disheveled, she realized nervously. Maybe she even had blood on her somewhere. Would he notice? And what would he do if he did?

"Terrible thing." With his voice raised to be heard over the commotion, he made small talk with her, shaking his head.

"Terrible," Kate agreed, heart thumping, and kept walking.

Just as easy as that, she moved past him and out into the rain, down the narrow steps to the sidewalk. She was almost instantly soaked, and as the moisture quickly worked its way through her clothes to her skin, she was suddenly freezing.

Turning left, away from the front of the building, and using her briefcase as a shield—ostensibly from the rain but mostly to keep from being recognized—Kate ducked her head and hurried past a stream of newly arriving law-enforcement and crime-scene types rushing down backstreets toward the Justice Center.

Her feet splashed through the freezing shallow stream the rain had turned the sidewalks into. She was glad to leave the insanity behind, glad to turn one corner and then another, before finally emerging onto the busy corner near Benington's Department Store.

From there it was easy to hail a cab. Giving the driver the address of the parking garage next to the DA's office—she'd ridden to the Justice Center with Bryan that morning, leaving her own car at work—Kate slumped in the seat.

Her eyes closed. Instantly images of the carnage in the courtroom began replaying against the screen of her closed lids. Judge Moran, the deputies—they had all gone to work that morning just as she had, and now they were dead. It was unbelievable. Horrible.

*It was almost me.*

Which brought her back to the nightmare she didn't want to face. *What am I going to do?*

Panic clawed at her insides. As the cab progressed through the gridlocked streets, her mind raced, frantically searching for a stratagem, a loophole, any possible means of escape from the nightmare in which she was trapped. Gritting her teeth, clenching her fists, she finally faced the terrible truth: Her past had caught up with her.

SHE had always disliked Mario Castellanos. As a teen, he had been a loudmouthed braggart and a bully. As far as she could tell, he hadn't changed a bit. Except now he was bigger. Badder. Scarier. The street punk had morphed into a hard-core criminal.

Who held her life—and Ben's life—in the palm of his hand.

There had to be some way out, but if there was, she couldn't see it. Right now the best she could come up with was that she was going to have to do exactly what he said.

Claiming that she had shot Orange Jumpsuit was just the first step down a road she didn't want to take. Doing it terrified her. She wouldn't face any legal liability over the killing—if ever there was a case that screamed self-defense, shooting the man who had taken her hostage at gunpoint would have been it—but the lie shook her. Her life wasn't about lies anymore.

"Long time no see," Mario had said, smiling, immediately after murdering Orange Jumpsuit right in front of her eyes.

Her eyes, wide with shock and disbelief, had met Mario's. She could see the swaggering teenage boy she had known thirteen years before in the steroid-pumped man standing in front of her. He would be thirty-one now. The bulk of him, the bald head and deep tan and facial hair, the orange jumpsuit, the sheer unexpectedness of the encounter—all had combined to keep her from recognizing him until he had called her by her old nickname: Kitty-cat. Then she had known him at once.

"I just saved your life," Mario had added when she didn't say anything. "You owe me."

Her heart beat like a drum in her chest. She tried to breathe normally, tried to stay cool. "Thank you," she said.

He laughed, a low sound that sent a chill racing down her spine. "Thank you's not gonna cut it, Kitty-cat." His tone was playful, and he reached out to tug on a strand of her hair.

"I figured." Putting up her chin, she jerked her head back just enough so that her hair was pulled from his grasp. She knew how thugs like him worked. The first rule of survival was don't ever let them see fear. "So, what do you want?"

"Out of jail. And I want you to get me out."

He squatted down and began wiping the gun on the hem of Orange Jumpsuit's pants. The dead man's face was gray now. His eyes were still open but glazed over. Blood trickled from his mouth.

"I can't do that." Her tone was abrupt. No need to pretend they were friends. They never had been.

"Don't give me that."

Satisfied with his cleaning efforts, he let the murder weapon slide to the floor beside Orange Jumpsuit's leg without touching it again. Then he picked up Orange Jumpsuit's dropped gun in its place. He held it negligently, not pointing it at her, but still . . .

"So you're a big-time *prosecutor* now. Hey, girl, I'm proud of you!" Mario smiled at her. "That's good for you, and I'm thinking it's even better for me."

"Are you? How so?"

"I'm looking at some hard time here, twenty to life, for nothing. *Nothing.* Violating probation. Possession of a firearm. Persistent felon." He grimaced. "So when these guys started hatching their little get-out-of-jail-free plan, I told 'em, hell, yeah, count me in. But they were idiots. Nobody was supposed to get killed. Guy on the outside was supposed to drive up under the window with a U-Haul. The plan was to blast out a window, leap down onto the truck, get inside, and haul ass. Once Soto shot that judge, far as I was concerned, it was all over. I aborted the mission. I was unclipping the keys from that deputy's belt so I could get out of this hallway when Rodriguez here came back in with you." He smiled. "I took one look at his little prosecutor friend, and I couldn't believe my—"

*Brriing . . .*

The phone's shrill summons had sliced the tense atmosphere like a knife. Kate had jumped, looking at the phone with horror. It was almost certainly the cop in the courtroom outside. Her lifeline, but also, now, in a new and terrible way, her enemy.

"Bottom line is, I came up with a better plan," he continued, ignoring the ringing phone. "Want to know what it is? You. My old friend Kitty-cat. 'Member that security-guard dude we took down that night in Baltimore?"

*Brriing . . .*

"I had nothing to do with that."

He smirked. "Baby, you were there just like the rest of us. You know the law better than I do. You know that's all it takes. Somebody lets the cat out of the bag, we're looking at Murder One."

*He's right. Oh, God, he's right.*

*Brriing . . .*

"I was a kid! Fifteen. And I didn't even go inside the store."

"Doesn't make you any less guilty."

*Youth is a mitigating circumstance.*

But as she'd learned later, David Brady had been an off-duty cop. Justice tended to come down hard on people who killed cops.

"Don't worry, I'm not going to tell on you. 'Less you don't do what I say, that is." His gaze shifted downward. "Pick up that gun." He nodded to the gun he'd used to kill Orange Jumpsuit.

When Kate hesitated, he said sharply, *"Do it."*

*Brriing . . .*

She did what he said. As she straightened, she saw that the gun in Mario's hand—Orange Jumpsuit's gun—was now pointed straight at her. Her heart skipped a beat. For a moment she didn't understand. Then she did. She was now holding a loaded weapon.

She took a deep breath. "You can't tell on me without telling on yourself," she said.

Their eyes met. He smiled. It was a small, self-satisfied smile.

"But see, that's the beauty of it. Way I see it is, of the two of us, I got a whole lot less to lose."

*Brriing . . .*

"Okay, baby, listen up. Here's how this thing is gonna go down."

# CHAPTER 5

BEN'S school, Greathouse Elementary, was a large, boxy two-story brick rectangle with a tree-lined circular driveway in front and an overhang that sheltered the front steps.

Kate pulled her blue Toyota Camry next to the curb right in front of the overhang. She'd had the heat blasting on high in hopes of drying her wet hair and clothes during the twenty-minute drive from the DA's office to Ben's school in the Northeast Philadelphia suburb where they lived, but she still felt cold and clammy. Twisting her hair up in back and stabbing the resultant knot with a pair of bobby pins, she grabbed her umbrella and got out. As she went up the front steps, she did a quick mental inventory and decided that except for the gray sneakers from the gym bag she kept in the car, which she now wore over bare feet, she looked relatively normal.

Which was important, for Ben's sake.

"Ms. White?"

The secretary greeted her in a pleasant voice. She sat at her desk behind the counter that separated the office from the main hall.

"Yes. Hi. I'm sorry it took me so long. I came as quickly as I could."

"Oh, I understand. With everything that's been going on downtown—well, I'm just glad you called back when you did. Ben was really getting worried. The TV was on back there, but I had to turn it off. They started showing live pictures of what was happening on every channel, and he was just sure you were in the thick of it." The secretary's voice grew hushed. "They're saying that ten people were killed, including a judge."

Kate felt her stomach tighten. *Don't think about it.* She shook her head. "I don't know."

"Well." The woman smiled at her. "Ben's lying down in the back. If you'll just sign him out"—she indicated a clipboard on the counter—"I'll go and get him."

While Kate signed Ben out, loud voices and the sound of running feet made her glance around. The noise was coming from a group of six or so boys who looked to be about Ben's age. They were wearing sneakers and bright blue gym uniforms, and one of the boys was clutching a basketball. Kate smiled at them as they ran past.

"Mom?"

Kate's head whipped around at the sound of Ben's voice. He was emerging through a door to the right of the office, with the secretary right behind him. His backpack hung from one shoulder. Towheaded and shaggy-haired, a handsome boy with Kate's own light blue eyes, fair complexion, and fine features, he was small for his age, and thin. Today he was wearing jeans, a blue-and-green-striped polo, and sneakers.

Considering what had almost happened, what they had almost lost, the sight of him brought tears to her eyes. She smiled at him. "Hi, pumpkin."

Ben grimaced, and immediately Kate knew that she had said the wrong thing. Now that he was in fourth grade, "pumpkin" sounded babyish to him.

Kate stepped forward to relieve Ben of his backpack. As she did, another pack of boys in gym uniforms burst into view at the end of the hall but, upon seeing the school secretary, slowed to a decorous walk. Kate became aware that Ben was sidling behind her, clearly trying to get out of sight.

She frowned.

Kate could sense Ben's shrinking, feel the shape of him close against her back, and her heart contracted. Leaving the tough South Kensington neighborhood where they had lived while she had attended first Drexel University and then Temple Law School had been hard on him, she knew. But she wanted so much more for him than to grow up in an impoverished area. She wanted him to have a happy, ordinary childhood in a normal, middle-class suburb. She wanted him to get a good education in a warm, nurturing school, like this one was reputed to be. She wanted a sense of security to be so much a part of his life that he never even thought about it. In short, she wanted him to have everything she had not had.

The boys sped up again until they reached the stairwell, where they vanished.

"With this weather, playing basketball for gym class is about all Mr. Farris can have them do." The secretary glanced at Ben, who had sidled back into view as the boys disappeared. "Some of those boys are in your class, aren't they, Ben?"

"Yeah," Ben said glumly. He looked up at Kate. "Mom, could we go? I don't feel so good."

"Sure," Kate said.

As the secretary headed back toward her office, she called over her shoulder to Ben, "Hope you feel better tomorrow."

"Thanks," Kate answered when Ben didn't.

He slid into the backseat while she hurried around the front of the car and got in. Kate started the Camry and glanced around at him at the same time.

"So, you want to stop by the pediatrician's office?" Putting the car in gear, she pulled away from the curb. "If you're sick—"

"I'm not that sick."

Kate sighed. "This wouldn't have anything to do with the fact that they're playing basketball in gym today, would it?"

Silence. Which she translated to mean, "Oh, yeah."

She glanced in the rearview mirror at her son. His thin shoulders were hunched, and he was looking gloomily out the rain-drenched window. He looked small and defeated sitting there, and she felt a familiar burst of love and guilt and worry.

"Okay, Ben, let's have it. Tell me the whole thing."

She braked at a stop sign, then turned right onto Maple Avenue. They lived on Beech Court, which was just a little way farther along, within walking distance of the school, in one of the least expensive sections of Fox Chase, an upscale neighborhood that she had to really scrape to afford. She had signed the year's lease on the small house with visions of a smiling Ben and his buddies skipping along the tree-shaded sidewalks to and from school. The reality was that every morning she drove him to school and Suzy Perry, mother of Ben's friend Samantha, picked him up afterward and drove him to her house half a mile away, where he stayed until Kate fetched him after work. The rest of the reality was that Ben didn't seem to have any buddies except Samantha, who was a grade below him, and Ben rarely smiled anymore.

"I suck at basketball." After the briefest of pauses he added, "Nobody wants me on their team."

Kate's heart broke. She almost said, "Sure they do." But the thing about Ben was, he really wasn't very good at basketball, or any other sport. He was good at school, especially language arts and math. He was a whiz with computers. He loved to read, and this tended to endear him to teachers—but to classmates, not so much. Add that to the fact that he was small for his age, shy around strangers, and just getting started in a new school, and it shouldn't be surprising that he was having trouble making friends.

Which didn't mean that it didn't hurt. A lot.

Another quick glance in the rearview mirror told her that he was drawing aimless designs in the condensation on the window.

"We should practice. You and me, kid," Kate said.

"Mom, you suck at basketball. You know you do."

"That doesn't mean we can't practice. We'd both get better."

Ben snorted. "Like that would help. Anyway, I hate basketball."

Kate pressed her lips together as their house came into view on the left. It was a pretty little Cape Cod with gray-painted brick, black shutters, and two picturesque gables. Right now rain pelted the tall pin oak by the sidewalk and rolled off the roof to cascade onto the neat line of bushes that hugged the front of the house.

As they drove up the driveway, Kate pressed the garage-door opener. Of all the things she liked about this house, and there were many, the attached garage had to be right up at the top of the list. Driving into a garage—even a small, cluttered, one-car garage without an overhead light—felt like a real luxury.

She parked in the garage and pressed the button so that the garage door would go down.

"Mom?" asked Ben as she turned off the car. "Who would take care of me if something happened to you?"

The question struck icy terror into her soul.

Because today it was just too close to home.

She knew why he asked, of course. He had seen parts of what had happened at the Criminal Justice Center on TV. No doubt they had talked about the dead judge, the dead deputies. She only hoped he hadn't seen much of it. She was going to have to talk to him about it, to tell him an edited version of how she had been caught up in the horror, because if she didn't, someone at school almost certainly would. But not yet. She just could not face it yet.

"Nothing's going to happen to me," she said firmly, and got out. Ben followed suit, and they went into the house. The garage opened into the cheerful yellow kitchen. On the far side of the refrigerator a door led out into the small fenced backyard. The middle of the room was dominated by a round maple table with four chairs. It was, like most of the rest of her furniture, secondhand.

She flipped on the light. There were dishes in the sink from breakfast. Upstairs, the beds weren't made. A couple of loads of laundry waited to be done in the basement.

So Supermom she wasn't. She was trying.

"You hungry?" she asked as Ben put his backpack on the table.

"No." Then he flashed her a cheeky grin. "I just threw up, remember?"

"I remember." Her tone was dry, and she aimed a not entirely playful swat at his backside. He dodged, grinned at her, then vanished upstairs to his bedroom. She called after him. "No more faking sick, understand?"

*I should probably ground him or something, just so he knows I really mean it.*

But Ben's faking sick was the least of her problems.

Fear twisted inside her. *What am I going to do?*

But she was hideously, horribly afraid she already knew the answer. Ben's question had crystallized the situation for her.

She was going to do just exactly what Mario had told her to do. Dance with the devil, just this once, and get him out of her life.

There simply wasn't any choice. For Ben's sake.

Kate called the office. Her administrative assistant, Mona Morrison, a forty-one-year-old recently divorced mother, answered.

"Oh my God, Kate, where are you? Bryan, the police, a couple of reporters—everybody's been looking for you. Are you all right?"

"I'm fine. Ben got sick at school, so I had to go pick him up."

"What do you mean, you're fine?" Mona screeched. "There's no way. You were taken hostage. You got hold of a gun and killed the guy to get free. The story's all over TV. How can you be fine?"

"I really am," Kate insisted, even as her heart sank at the idea that her lie was already being broadcast all over the city. "And Ben really is home sick. I just need some time to decompress, so I'm taking the rest of the day off. Tell everybody I'll be in tomorrow."

"But—"

Kate didn't give Mona time to protest any further. She hung up and walked into the living room to close the draperies. A large brown and tan couch (courtesy of Goodwill), a gold recliner (consignment store), matching oak coffee and end tables (yard sale), and a TV on a cart beside the fireplace made up the furnishings. Along with a separate dining room, which she had turned into an office so she could work at home, there was a tiny half bath, the entry hall, and the kitchen. That was the entire ground floor of the house.

With the draperies closed, the room was dark. Kate switched on a lamp, then looked at the TV. For a moment she stood there, undecided, then shook her head. Right now she didn't want to know.

Instead, she went upstairs to take a shower.

She came down again some half an hour later, a little warmer and a whole lot drier. Halfway down the stairs she stopped dead. Through the small glass window in her front door she watched a police cruiser pull into her driveway.

Followed a scant moment later by a white TV van.

THE Federal Detention Center was just around the corner from Kate's office. She waited until after lunch the next day, until the in-office brouhaha about her supposed heroism in killing her abductor had died down a little, to walk the few blocks to the tall stone building in the heart of Center City.

*Stay calm. It's your imagination that everyone's looking at you.*

Or not. Stories on the massacre at the Criminal Justice Center had been featured this morning on *Today, Good Morning America,* and *The Early Show.* The story took up the entire front page in all the local dailies. She had little doubt that her own picture would be featured in them somewhere. Luckily her law-school yearbook photo, the one that seemed to be getting the most play, featured her smiling. Today she definitely wasn't smiling.

Just thinking about Mario sent chills down her spine. If she did not meet with him—today, as he had instructed before hoisting himself up into the ventilation shaft and disappearing—he might start making good on his threat to talk about their shared past.

It was a beautiful, crisp fall day, sunny, with white clouds that soared above the jagged edge of the city's skyscrapers. Yesterday's rain had left behind only a few isolated puddles. She was walking fast, hugging the charcoal pin-striped blazer she wore with black slacks and a white T-shirt close because she was freezing, which was, she knew, more the result of emotional distress than of the weather. She breathed deeply, trying to calm her jagged nerves.

Turning the corner onto Arch Street, she glanced up at the stone rectangle of the detention center. The narrow slits that served in place of windows were the only outside indication that some of the most dangerous criminals in the city were housed inside.

As she passed beneath it, the U.S. flag snapped sharply in a gust of wind. Both it and the blue commonwealth flag flapping beside it were at half-mast. For Judge Moran, of course, and for the four deputies and two civilians who had lost their lives yesterday.

If things had worked out differently, she might well be dead now, too. The fact that she was alive was something to be profoundly thankful for, she reminded herself grimly.

*Even if I am caught like a rat in a trap.*

"I saw you on TV this morning," the female guard exclaimed as she processed Kate through security at the entrance. "Honey, after what you went through, you should be home in bed with the covers over your head. What are you doing working today?"

Kate managed a smile and a shrug. "Gotta eat."

By the time she was seated in a cheap plastic chair in one of the grubby, graffiti-scarred cubicles where attorneys meet with prisoners, Kate felt like she had run a gauntlet. Nearly everybody she came into contact with had a question or comment about what had happened yesterday. Fortunately the detention center was having a busy day, which meant nobody had time to indulge in a prolonged chat. The Criminal Justice Center had been closed to the public as part of the ongoing investigation into the shootings. All trials scheduled for the near future were being moved or postponed, which translated into massive confusion as well as extra work for all involved. Kate viewed the chaos as a blessing. It had the double virtue of keeping everybody almost too busy to think as well as scrambling timelines and case files.

It made doing what Mario wanted just that much easier.

Calling up Mario's file on the computer system had been simple. An assistant DA from the felony waiver unit had been assigned to the case, but it didn't look like anything much had been done on it. The file was mostly low-level stuff, a couple of drug busts, petty theft, check kiting. There were two felony convictions, one for aggravated assault and one for dealing. He'd done time—six months for the aggravated assault and nine for dealing. He'd been released on probation eight months ago, picked up again three and a half weeks ago. The possession-of-a-firearm charge counted as another felony, which meant he fell under the guidelines of the "three strikes and you're out" law. As he'd said, he was looking at some serious time.

Personally, she felt there were few people more deserving.

The thing was, she was going to put him back on the streets.

Her stomach knotted at the thought. Besides the crimes that had caused him to be thrown in jail, he was guilty of taking part in yesterday's escape attempt, which had left so many dead. If anyone knew, he would be charged with Murder One. But no one did—except her. And she wasn't in a position to do one thing about it.

*If they find out about David Brady, the first thing they'll do is fire you. Then they'll arrest you and take Ben away. . . .*

Panic was just starting to curl through her insides again when the door to the cubicle opened. Kate looked up through the bulletproof glass wall that rose from the center of the table where she was sitting in time to watch Mario swagger in on the other side.

Dread balled into what felt like a rock in her stomach.

Mario saw her through the barrier. His eyes swept over her. His lips smirked with transparent satisfaction.

She took a deep breath. Deliberately she averted her gaze. Opening her briefcase, she grabbed a pen and a yellow legal pad.

Clearly Mario had managed to rejoin the general population of prisoners being held in the Justice Center yesterday without anyone's suspecting that he had played a role in the botched escape. Otherwise he wouldn't be here. He was dressed once again in the orange jumpsuit that all the prisoners wore, and his bald head gleamed in the harsh fluorescent lighting. For the first time she noticed a tattoo of what looked like a snakelike black dragon curling around his right wrist. Was it some sort of gang symbol?

The deputy escorting him glanced at Kate, nodded once, then withdrew, leaving them alone together. She knew the drill: When she was ready to leave, or if she needed help, all she had to do was press a button on the wall near her elbow. Deputies remained stationed outside in the hall at all times.

Mario slid into his seat. He propped his elbows on the other half of the table and folded his arms, leaning forward, looking at her confidently through the glass.

*I can't do this,* she thought. Not that actually getting him out would pose any real problem. The assistant DA assigned to the case would never even miss it. On an average day each one of them took care of something like forty cases. The DA's office handled about seventy thousand cases a year; the system was drowning under the sheer volume of proceedings. All she had to do was take over his case and then just fail to do anything. Show up in court unprepared, with no witnesses. It would be a slam dunk. Case dismissed.

No one would know. She could get on with her life.

Smiling at her, Mario picked up the telephone that allowed them to communicate. After a pause she did the same, settling the hard plastic receiver against her ear. Her heart raced; her palms grew damp. But she kept her face expressionless.

"Looking good, Kitty-cat," he said through the phone. "Real high-class nowadays. And hot."

"If I'm going to do this . . ." Her voice was cold, abrupt. She couldn't just roll over and play dead for him. There had to be some way out of this, some way to save herself and Ben without giving in to his blackmail. But what? She needed time to think. Thus her immediate strategy became delay, delay, delay.

"Oh, you are," he said. And his smile widened.

Kate fixed him with a steely stare. "*If* I'm going to do this," she repeated icily, "you're going to have to give me something in return. The name of your supplier, maybe. Or the details of some crime you know about and who committed it."

His eyes narrowed, and he lost the smile. "What? Hell, no."

"I don't have any get-out-of-jail-free cards stashed in my pocket. If you want me to spring you, you're going to have to work with me here. Give me something that I can take to a judge."

"You can forget that. I ain't no snitch."

"And I'm not a miracle worker."

His eyes narrowed. "I saved your life yesterday. Don't you forget that. You better get me the hell out of here. I own you, baby."

"You don't own squat. You start shooting off your big mouth, the person who's going down is you. You were the one who was carrying the gun that night. You think twenty years sucks? Try looking at the death penalty."

"Believe me, if I'm looking at it, you'll be looking at it right along with me. And anyway, it wasn't me who pulled the trigger. Keep pushing me, and I'll swear it was you."

*Impasse.* It was time to dial the confrontational tone down.

"Look, Mario. I want to help you, but I've been on the job only a couple of months. I still need my boss to sign off on everything I do. If I'm going to tell him I want to bargain the charges against you down, I'm going to have to give him a reason."

His lips compressed. For the first time he looked uncertain.

"I'm not giving you nothin'."

She shrugged as if to say, "Your call," then pressed the round gray button on the wall that summoned the deputy.

Mario's eyes widened. "What are you doing?"

"Leaving. I've got to get back to work."

"What about getting me out of here?"

"Like I said, I need your help to do that."

"Kat . . ." Alarm and anger mixed in his tone.

"And by the way, calling me that, or anything except Ms. White, is a mistake. Let on that you know me in any way other than as a lawyer, and you're screwed. If any whiff of the fact that we have a previous acquaintance gets out, I'll be yanked from your case."

The door opened. As the deputy stepped into the room, Kate smiled at Mario through the glass.

"I'll be in touch," she said, and hung up the phone.

There was no way he could possibly know her knees were shaking. But she'd bought herself some time. Exactly what good that would do she didn't know. But it was something.

By the time she was back to the office, she was almost calm again.

The Major Trials Unit occupied all of the ninth floor, and it was bustling, Kate saw as the elevator door opened. She waved at Cindy Hartnett, the receptionist, whose semicircular desk faced the elevators. Behind Cindy, a large room full of cubicles was home to the paralegals, who did much of the grunt work on the cases. Several were on their feet, standing and chatting or walking around with files or cell phones in their hands. Kate headed toward her own office, waving to a few of her colleagues whose doors were open. Bryan's door was closed, she saw as she passed it. She had talked to him on the phone last night when he'd called to check on her, but she hadn't seen him all day. Which suited her just fine. As far as she was concerned, the fewer people who wanted to discuss yesterday's events, the better.

*I have to get my act together about this.*

"Oh my God." Mona shot to her feet as Kate hurried past her administrative assistant's office, which was right next door to hers. "Where have you been?"

Kate stopped and forced a smile.

"What's up?" she asked, guiltily aware that it wasn't an answer.

Mona didn't appear to notice anything amiss. With her short flaming-red hair, scarlet-painted lips, and pin-thin body clad in a burnt-orange turtleneck and gold plaid skirt, she resembled nothing so much as a living finger of flame.

"You're not going to believe this," Mona said, "*The View* called. They want you to be a guest on the show. They're calling you the heroine of courtroom two oh seven!"

For a moment Kate was rendered speechless. For her part, Mona practically vibrated with excitement.

"No." Kate turned and continued walking toward her office.

"What do you mean, 'No'?" Mona screeched. She definitely wasn't the shy, retiring type. "Do you realize what a chance this is for you? You'll be famous."

"I don't want to be famous."

"But think what it could mean for your career. You'd get noticed!"

"No buts," Kate said, reaching her door and turning the knob. She looked back at Mona as she pushed the door open. "I don't want to be on *The View* or any other television show, thank you very much."

"You can't just . . ." Mona protested. Whatever else she said was lost as Kate stepped inside her office to find a man already in there.

The black-haired cop who'd been her lifeline in courtroom 207, to be precise.

# CHAPTER 6

"What are you doing in here?"

Kate was so shocked that her tone was a whole lot sharper than it would have been if she'd had even a few seconds' warning to prepare. A cop—even this cop, especially this cop, with whom she discovered she felt a weird kind of connection, like the courtroom thing had linked them in some mysterious way—waiting in her office right on the heels of where she had just been was unnerving.

Mona practically bumped into her before stopping behind her. "Um, that's the other thing I meant to tell you," Mona said. "There's a couple of cops waiting in your office."

"Thanks for the heads-up." Kate's voice was dry.

*A couple of cops . . .*

She spotted the second one as he stepped out from behind the first. Stylishly dressed in a dark blue suit with a pale blue shirt and a yellow tie, he was about five ten, stocky, with close-cropped sandy hair, a ruddy complexion, and a blunt-featured, good-humored face. The cop from the courtroom smiled at her—he really was as good-looking as she remembered, with a hard, angular face, coffee-brown eyes, and a slow smile—and held out his hand.

"Thought I'd stop by to see how you're doing," he said as she took his hand. "I'm Tom Braga, by the way. Detective, Homicide

Division." His eyes touched the small Band-Aid on her cheek. "I'm glad to see you've recovered so fast."

Her heart was beating a mile a minute, and not because he was cute. Probably because he was a cop—a homicide detective, yet—and she felt like a criminal. Like he could somehow tell that what he believed had happened in the secure corridor yesterday was a lie.

*Get a grip, Kate. As far as he knows, you're the victim here.*

She forced a smile to her lips.

"This is Detective Howard Fischback, also from Homicide," Braga added, gesturing at the other man. The second cop stepped forward with his hand out.

"Kate White." She pumped his hand and let it drop.

"And I'm her administrative assistant, Mona Morrison." Mona stepped forward with her hand out. Both men shook it briskly, and Fischback flashed her a dimpled smile, but it was Braga whom she made big eyes at. *Of course.* Mona made no bones about being perpetually on the hunt, and Braga was nothing if not sexy.

"I've seen you around the building, so it's nice to finally meet you," Mona gushed, her gaze targeting Braga like a laser.

"Thanks, Mona," Kate said. Her nerves were raw, and watching Mona flirt was the last thing she wanted to do.

Her administrative assistant flashed her a reproachful look but took the hint. "Well, I'll be in my office if you need anything."

Fischback's gaze followed Mona as she left the room. Braga, on the other hand, was watching her, Kate discovered when their eyes met. The office suddenly felt way too small.

"After yesterday I'm surprised you're at work," Braga said.

"You're working today," Kate pointed out.

"I already used up my sick days for the year."

From the hint of humor in his tone, Kate knew not to take that seriously. She was walking as he spoke, putting some much-needed distance between them by moving around the two men to set her briefcase down on her desk.

*Stay cool. They have no clue.*

"I saw you leaving the Justice Center behind a sheriff's deputy on a stretcher yesterday," she said. "I hope he's doing okay." The best defense was always a good offense, and taking the lead in the conversation was a classic diversion strategy.

Braga shrugged, and a shadow passed over his face. "He's alive, and the doctors say he's going to make it. He's still in ICU, though." His eyes flickered. "He's my brother."

That pierced her wariness a little bit. She nodded with sympathy. "I thought I saw a resemblance. The black hair."

A small smile touched his lips, lightening his expression.

"Which brings me to the other reason why we're here. Do you mind answering a few questions?"

Caught off guard, Kate felt her heart lurch. "I gave my statement yesterday. Some officers came by my house."

God, she'd been so rattled then—could she even remember what she'd said? The TV truck had been only the first of a wave of media that had descended on her house. They had knocked on her door and rung her doorbell incessantly until one of the uniforms who had arrived to take her statement had told them to knock it off. Even as they grudgingly obeyed, her phones had started to ring, both landline and cell. Gritting her teeth, she turned the ringers off. Later she walked through the house, closing all the drapes, checking the doors and windows to make sure they were locked.

She ended up in Ben's room, where he was propped up in bed reading. He took his nose out of his book to look up at her.

"Mom, what were all those people doing outside? Did you really shoot somebody today?" He was wide-eyed with interest.

All the commotion had pulled him to his window. No doubt he'd heard some of the questions shouted at her. Her heart sank.

"No," she said, because she didn't want him to think of his mother and violence in the same breath. Then, because she had to, because somebody might ask him questions, she changed her answer to "Yes."

Then she sat down beside him and told him the whole story. Sort of. With a lot of editing and a few crucial lies.

Just like she was getting ready to do again with these guys. Just like she'd done in her official statement.

"It won't take very long," Braga said. "Mind if we sit down?"

"Of course not. Go ahead," Kate said, like she had any choice. Braga pulled a small flip-top notebook and a pen from his jacket pocket. She sank into her own chair, facing them across her desk, acutely aware that he was reading through scribbled notes.

"After Rodriguez pulled you into the hall, did you see anyone?"

It took everything Kate had to keep her eyes from widening. *They know about Mario.* That was her first thought. Then she remembered Braga's brother, the other fallen deputy, and the other downed prisoner in the holding cell. Of course, Braga meant them.

"There were three men lying on the floor of one of the holding cells. I just got a glimpse. Two of them were deputies—your brother was one, although I didn't know that at the time—and the third was wearing an orange jumpsuit. I . . . I thought at the time that they were all dead."

He nodded and wrote something in his notebook. Fischback, Kate saw, was looking over her desk. A quick, searching flicker of her eyes confirmed that there was nothing incriminating to be seen. Her laptop was open but in sleep mode. The phone, stacks of files, piles of paperwork, a trayful of mail, assorted pencils and pens. There was, she was sure, no trace of Mario to be seen.

"So how did you come to 'just get a glimpse' inside the cell?" Braga asked.

Kate frowned. Here was one of the places where she had lied about what had happened, where she had to lie, because of course the reason she had seen inside that cell was because Mario had come out of it.

"Rodriguez pulled the door open for just a moment, I don't know why. He shoved me against the wall first, and I was in a position to look inside the door when it opened."

"And what did you see?"

"I told you. The three men lying on the floor."

"Did you see any weapons? A gun?"

"No. Except for the one Rodriguez was holding, of course."

"Okay." Braga consulted his notebook again.

"Any idea where Soto got his gun?" Fischback asked.

Kate was on solid ground here. "None. When he jumped to his feet in the courtroom, the gun was just there in his hand."

"And that's the first time you saw it?"

Again she was on solid ground. "Yes."

"So where'd you get the gun you shot Rodriguez with?" Braga asked, his pen poised over the notebook.

Kate felt sweat prickling to life under her clothes.

"It was just there—on the floor."

"It was lying on the floor in the hall?"

"Yes." She had to fight the urge to look away or to lick her lips. "He pushed me down, and I landed, and there the gun was, just lying on the floor next to the wall. I hadn't noticed it earlier."

Silence filled the room as he seemed to be waiting for her to continue. She met his gaze straight on, while her heart pounded and she had the urge to jump up and walk away. But she couldn't; she had to sit there and look calm and lie through her teeth and wait.

"So you saw a gun on the floor against the wall," Braga said finally. "To your right or left?"

Kate tried to visualize the scenario she was creating in her mind. "To my right."

"Okay." He paused to scribble in his notebook. "You said he pushed you down. How did you land? Stomach, back, side . . ."

"On my butt. I landed on my butt and saw the gun. I knew Rodriguez was getting ready to shoot me, so I grabbed it and just pointed it and pulled the trigger. And I shot him."

"Where was he? Rodriguez?"

Kate could feel sweat trickling down her spine.

"Near the wall, where the phone is. He was facing me. He . . . he dropped his gun and bent to pick it up. I didn't think I'd ever get a better chance. So I went for it. The gun on the floor."

Braga wrote something down. Then he looked up at her again.

"So he dropped his gun, and while he was picking it up again, you grabbed the gun you saw on the floor. Had he recovered his gun when you shot him? What position was he in?"

*Forensics. They'll be able to tell what position Rodriguez and I were in from the trajectory of the bullet.*

"He was holding the gun, lifting it. He was standing again. I think . . . I was on my feet by that time. We were both on our feet when I shot him."

"Was the safety on?"

That caught her by surprise, but she hoped she didn't show it. Her eyes didn't widen. Her body didn't stiffen. She stayed perfectly composed. She frowned slightly, as if trying to remember.

She'd fired a gun before, both in her misspent youth and later, at a practice range, with a fifty-dollar special she'd bought for protection, but she didn't know that much about pistols in general. Thinking fast, she came up with what she considered the safest response.

Her frown cleared. "No." Her voice was confident.

He nodded and wrote that down, too. So simple. So easy.

Her phone rang, and she jumped. It was her cell, and it was a normal *brriing.* After yesterday she'd had enough of custom ringtones.

Braga and Fischback were watching her expectantly.

"Excuse me. I have to take this."

It was Ben. She knew it as soon as she retrieved the phone from her briefcase and saw the number on the screen. Ben always called her as soon as he was in Suzy's car so she would know he had been safely picked up from school.

"Hey, Mom. I'm on my way to the Perrys'."

"Did you have a good day?"

"It was okay."

"I'll be there to get you as soon as I can. Probably a little early today. Grab a snack. Have fun. Do your homework."

"Yeah, right."

Kate had to smile. That last had been thrown in there as a kind of parental Hail Mary pass. Homework almost never got done at Suzy's, which was a place for hanging out with Samantha. Homework was for home—and for Mom to help with.

Braga and Fischback were still watching her. Kate became aware of the smile that still lingered around her lips. Hearing Ben's voice, picturing him on the other end of the phone, had both calmed her and given her a renewed sense of purpose. She was going to get them through this, whatever it took.

"Got to go, sweetie," she said into the phone.

"Okay, bye."

Closing the phone, she placed it on her desk. She had her nerve back and her guard up. Placing her hands flat on her desk as if she was getting ready to stand up, she looked at the two detectives with cool inquiry. "If there's nothing else?"

"No." Braga flipped his notebook closed, then stood up. Fischback was a second behind him. "I think that's all."

"If you think of anything else, you know where I am." Her tone was brisk. She held out her hand, first to Braga and then to Fischback, then walked around her desk to escort them to the door.

"I just want you to know, I wasn't sure you were going to make it out of there yesterday," Braga said. "I'd had dealings with Rodriguez before. You took out a real bad dude."

Kate swallowed. "That makes it a little easier," she said, because it was clear that he was trying to ease some of the guilt she might be feeling over having taken a human life. "And by the way, in case I didn't say it, thanks for trying to save my life yesterday."

He smiled a little. "All in a day's work."

Then he walked on out of her office.

Kate closed the door and pressed her back to it. Her heart was still beating too fast. Closing her eyes, regulating her breathing, she fought off the minibreakdown she could feel coming on.

*Stay strong.*


"PRETTY lady." Fish's voice was reflective. They were riding the elevator down, just the two of them in the car.

"Yeah." Tom was leaning back against the wall, his arms folded across his chest. Kate White was pretty, exceptionally pretty, even if she was a little on the skinny side for his tastes.

"You catch an off vibe there?"

"Just a little one."

"So what do you think?"

There was a ping as they reached the ground floor.

"Good question," Tom said.

There were maybe a dozen people milling around the lobby, so the conversation was suspended until they were out on the side-walk. Tom's Taurus was parked at the curb to the right, in front of a NO PARKING ANYTIME sign, but something, either good timing or the police tag Tom had hung from his rearview mirror, had kept them from getting a ticket.

As Tom rounded the front of the car, a gust of wind spiraling down the street caught him. It set his jacket flapping. He started to button it in self-defense, only to have the top button pop off. It sailed through the air, hit the pavement, and rolled.

With a quick glance down, he retrieved the button from beside the left-front wheel, got into the car, and dropped the button into the cup holder between the seats.

"What's that?" Fish asked as the engine turned over.

"Button popped off." Tom pulled out into traffic.

"Your jacket?" Fish looked at the threads that marked where the button had been. "Hallelujah. Maybe now you'll buy a new one."

The corners of Tom's mouth curved upward.

"Tom, you need to go shopping. That jacket deserves to be re-tired. Get a new one. Hell, get a whole new wardrobe. Live a little."

"Hey, Fish? Shut up." It was said without heat. They both knew where Fish was coming from. They'd been friends since they'd played high school football together in South Philly. Fish had joined the Philadelphia Police Department the year after Tom had, and had been his partner for the last four years. Fish knew his history, knew it all, about the divorce and everything else, knew that since then Tom had done his best to allow nothing permanent in his life, renting an apartment rather than buying a house, seeing a string of women, not keeping any pets. Tom kept a low profile, did his job, and saved his money. Why everyone, from his family to Fish, was starting to have a problem with that he couldn't begin to fathom.

"Fine." Fish was clearly exasperated. "Be that way. Wear your crummy old clothes. Work all the time. Don't have any fun. See who gets all the women."

Tom grinned. So did Fish, reluctantly. They both knew who was number one when it came to women, and who tried harder. Though Fish, having worked for it, usually did all right.

"You don't think she planted the gun, do you?" Fish asked after a moment, referring back to their earlier subject.

"Kate White?" Tom had been there in that courtroom. He had seen firsthand her terror when Rodriguez grabbed her. If she'd been faking any of that, he would turn in his badge. "No."

Where Soto got the gun he killed Judge Moran with was, in the detectives' judgment, the key to unraveling the conspiracy. They were only one of several teams working on different angles of the crime. The thing was, all the known perps—Rodriguez, Soto, Lonnie Pack, and Chili Newton—were dead, which was blunting the fury of the investigation. No arrest, no prosecution, no death penalties were possible, although the law-enforcement community was foaming at the mouth to exact retribution.

The bottom line was, the killers had to have had help, and that was where their investigation was presently focused. Tom was almost sure that the weapons had been planted either in courtroom 207 itself or in the holding cells or the secure corridor associated with that particular courtroom. Which pointed to an inside job.

Tom hung a left, toward the police administration building, aka the Roundhouse because of its distinctive shape.

"Something was off about her. She was nervous," Fish said.

Tom was aware. She had tried hard to hide it, but there had been too many subtle signals to ignore. But something, perhaps the memory of terrified blue eyes clinging to his like he was the only hope she had in the world when Rodriguez took her captive, made him feel unexpectedly protective toward her. Whatever was making her nervous, he didn't think she had planted any weapons or helped with the escape attempt.

"Maybe it was seeing me. Maybe I brought up bad memories from yesterday or something for her."

"Possible," Fish said.

The Roundhouse came into view. It was a large multistory oval-shaped building. Right now there were TV trucks out front, and uniforms were controlling access.

"Hell, maybe she's just a high-strung type," Tom said.

Fish made a noncommittal sound. "You buying what she's selling about finding Charlie's gun just lying there on the floor?"

Forensics had already determined that Rodriguez had been shot with Charlie Braga's service revolver. Determining how it had gotten into Kate White's hands had been one of the primary reasons for their visit to her office.

"I don't see any reason not to believe it, for now." Tom paused to pull into the parking lot. "The safety was off, she said, which means somebody was getting ready to fire it before she got her hands on it. Maybe there was a struggle and Charlie dropped his weapon."

"And maybe she's lying through her straight little white teeth."

Tom's lips tightened. Truth to tell, that suspicion was worming through his thought processes, too. "Why would she?"

"Because she has something to hide."

Tom didn't reply.

Fish gave him a long, appraising look as Tom slowly circled the lot, searching for an open spot. "Turns you on, does she?"

*"What?"* It took Tom a second, but then the truth of it hit him, and he wondered why he hadn't realized it before. Because he hadn't wanted to, of course. It complicated things. But the truth was that the instant he'd seen her, willowy, blond, and more than pretty, wide-eyed with fear yet fiercely brave in Rodriguez's murderous grip, he'd felt an intense reaction that went far beyond the typical cop/victim-in-need-of-saving relationship. Not that he meant to admit it. "You're nuts."

"Stay objective, that's all I'm saying." Fish released his seat belt as Tom parked and cut the engine. "Just because she looks like an angel doesn't mean she is one."

THE Duty Room of the PPD homicide unit was located on the first floor. Tom pushed through the glass doors first, with Fish behind him. The chaos and activity level and noise were cranked up. Multiple murders were nothing new to Philly, but multiple murders by prisoners, of deputies and a judge—well, that was new. It was also embarrassing. A black eye for the whole Philly law-enforcement community.

A chorus of voices greeted them as they entered and separated, each heading to his own desk. Tom waved by way of reply and was just dropping into his own desk chair when Sergeant Ike Stella, the shift supervisor, stopped by his desk. Stella was a big man, six foot three and a good three hundred pounds, most of which he carried in his gut. He was fifty-five years old, with walnut-colored skin, rugged features, and a gruff, no-nonsense demeanor.

"Any inkling where they got the weapons?" Stella asked, turning his habitual scowl on Tom.

"Working on it."

"Work faster," Stella said. "Inquiring minds want to know."

He moved away, and Tom got to work, spending the next hour or so at his desk, writing up the interview with Kate White, answering phone calls, going through witness statements, trying to get a handle on all the paperwork piling up in connection with this case. The problem wasn't that they didn't have enough information. It was that they had too much, reams of it. And they were just getting started. He had little doubt that the truth was in there somewhere, buried in the mountains of paper that would just keep piling higher until the case was resolved. The problem was, finding it was going to be akin to finding a specific grain of sand on the beach.

Quitting time, five o'clock, found Tom on the phone with the medical examiner, Dr. Mary Hardy, who confirmed that the shots that had wounded Charlie and killed Deputy Dino Russo had come from Russo's department-issue weapon, which had been found near Chili Newton's body. Newton's fingerprints were on it.

Hanging up, Tom went back over his notes, pondering. It was fairly obvious that the weapon had been taken from Russo either pre- or postmortem, and thus the origin of one of the murder weapons was accounted for. The Sig that Soto had used, however, which had killed the judge and a deputy, was not department issue, nor was it immediately traceable, as all identifying features had been filed off. The other two pistols—each had killed a deputy and a civilian—were a PSM and a non-department-issue Glock, likewise minus identifying features, almost certainly smuggled in from the street. The mystery was how and by whom.

"You planning on pulling an all-nighter?" Fish asked. Tom looked up from his notes to find his partner standing beside his desk. Tom was, he realized, dead tired. The previous night he had stayed all night at the hospital with Charlie, alternating between spending fifteen minutes every couple of hours with his unconscious brother (all that the ICU would allow) and the rest of the time hanging out in the waiting room with his mother, sisters, sister-in-law, and the flocks of other assorted relatives.

"Nah." He put down his pencil, stood up, and shrugged into his jacket. "I'm out of here."

"I checked with forensics. The distance checks out," Fish said in a grudging tone as they headed out of the building. "And her prints are all over the murder weapon. It's looking like your smokin' little assistant DA could have shot Rodriguez the way she says she did."

By calling Kate White *his* smokin' little assistant DA, Fish was deliberately needling him. Tom knew it and so ignored the effort.

"Good to know," he said mildly.

They pushed out the door, pausing on the sidewalk. Fish's car was in the lot behind the building, so that was the point where their paths diverged.

"You wanna get dinner?" Fish asked.

Tom shook his head. "I'm going on over to the hospital."

"Want company?" Fish had come by the hospital last night, too, but the demands of the investigation had pulled him away.

"My whole family's there. Last night there were cousins I've never seen in my life. At the hospital, I *got* company."

"Still, I'll probably stop by later."

Tom nodded, then lifted a hand in farewell as they both started walking toward their respective vehicles.

HALF AN HOUR LATER, TOM walked into the waiting room outside the ICU and found himself, as he had known he would be, engulfed in relatives.

"Tommy." His mother stood up from the red vinyl couch where she'd been sitting with her sister Miriam and his middle sister, thirty-year-old Vicky, to embrace him. "Charlie's better, praise God." She made the sign of the cross. "Have you eaten?"

"I grabbed a burger on the way over," he lied as his mother stepped back to look him over critically.

"You've lost a button on your coat." Her disapproving gaze focused on the telltale dangling threads. She looked up at him, shaking her head. "You need somebody to take care of things like that for you. A wife. A man doesn't think of such things."

It was all Tom could do not to roll his eyes. She'd been on this Tom-needs-a-wife kick for almost the last year.

"So what's going on with Charlie?" He figured the way to get their mother's attention off himself was to focus it on his brother.

"They've taken him off the ventilator. Terry's with him."

ICU rules allowed only one person with a patient at a time.

"That's good. I think I'll just go look in on him. Maybe Terry wants a break."

When Tom opened the door of the ICU ward, his sister-in-law, Terry, a short, athletically built, freckle-faced redhead, looked around. Seeing him, she smiled, then rose from the chair she'd been sitting in and came over to him.

"I'm glad you're here," she said quietly, after they had exchanged hugs. "Go to him."

She came out, and he walked inside the ICU. Charlie lay at the far end of the four-bed ward.

It was cold in the ICU, Tom thought as he stopped at the foot of his brother's bed, and eerily quiet. Except for the sounds of various lifesaving machines, there was nothing: no voices, no telephones or TVs, no footsteps. It was like the patients were in limbo.

A curtain separated his brother from whoever was in the bed next door. Tom registered the machines beeping around the bed, the IV pole and myriad tubes attached to his brother's body, and felt his gut tighten. It could so easily have gone the other way.

He looked at his brother's face—something he'd been putting off, because seeing Charlie so still and pale bothered him more than he liked to admit—to find that Charlie was looking back at him.

# CHAPTER 7

"I MUST'VE got your genes," Ben said glumly as he watched Kate's shot smack into the brick above the garage a yard to the left of the hoop, then go bouncing away. Bugs swooped around the light fixture that illuminated a fuzzy circle at the top of the driveway.

"You say that like it's a bad thing," Kate panted, running into the dark front yard to retrieve the ball. Trying to maintain her outward good humor at a little after eight thirty p.m. on the day after she'd seen roughly half a dozen people murdered before her eyes and her life had gone to hell wasn't easy. Supper and homework were over, and she was trying to help her unenthusiastic son practice basketball.

That was the thing about having a kid, Kate thought as she jogged across the yard in pursuit of the ball. No matter what disasters were happening in your own life, your kid's regimen kept on.

She spotted the ball in the bushes and bent to scoop it up. She was hot, sweaty, and so tired she was drooping.

"Was my dad any good at sports?" Ben asked wistfully as Kate, carrying the ball, walked back into the light. They'd been out there for maybe fifteen minutes, shooting hoops and missing a good ninety percent of the shots between them, and she was getting a stitch in her side. But Ben was afraid that he was going to be the worst player in the class, and she was prepared to do whatever it took to make sure it didn't happen. Not that he had expressed his fears in so many words. But she knew. When he had told her about the upcoming basketball week in gym, she'd been able to read between the lines. He'd been thinking of missing school for a week. She'd been thinking, *Not possible.* And so here they were. And now he was breaking her heart anew with questions about his father.

"Yes, he was," she lied. As far as she knew, Ben's father, Chaz White, whom she had married at eighteen and who had deserted her at nineteen, two months after Ben's birth, had never played any kind of organized sport in his life. She'd met him in Atlantic City, where she'd fled after David Brady's death. Chaz had been a handsome street tough who'd worked as a bouncer in the casino where she'd been a waitress. In the year that she'd known him, she'd learned that along with abundant charm he had a nose for trouble. Less than a month after their split, he had died in a drive-by shooting. She had grabbed Ben and run again, this time to Philly, where she had been working ever since to give her son a better life. Not that she meant to tell Ben any of that, at least not for many years.

"He was good at lots of things. But he told me that he wasn't very athletic until he got to high school. He had to grow into it."

She bounced the ball to Ben as a way of distracting him from asking more questions about his father. Over the years she had fudged the facts to create a kinder, gentler father who had loved Ben devotedly but had died in a car accident shortly after his birth. At some point she might tell him more, but she was never, ever going to tell him that Chaz had freaked when their screaming, colicky baby had come home from the hospital and then left them flat.

That Ben never needed to know.

"Just shoot the thing, would you please?" she said.

"This is lame." Ben groaned but obediently heaved the ball at the goal. This time it actually hit the rim before bouncing off.

"Good job. That was close," Kate encouraged as the ball went rolling toward the big oak by the sidewalk. "Your rebound."

Ben trudged off after the ball, which had disappeared in the inky shadows at the base of the tree. His shoulders slumped, and his movements were dispirited.

A car drove slowly past, its headlights catching Ben for an instant and throwing his shadow against the big oak's rough gray bark. He had almost reached the basketball, which was nestled in the roots. Kate was relieved that the car kept going. There had been a knot of reporters waiting in front of her house when she'd pulled in from picking up Ben, and once more she'd had reason to be grateful for the attached garage and automatic opener. Driving right inside and closing the door, she'd managed to avoid them. She had stayed inside with the curtains drawn, refusing to come out or answer the phone, and as dark had fallen, they had finally gone away. She exhaled and shifted her gaze back to Ben.

She was seriously considering sending a note to school on Monday saying that Ben had twisted his ankle and couldn't play basketball next week when she saw a figure slide around the oak and approach Ben, who was bending over to pick up the ball.

Her eyes widened. Her breath caught.

Although she was too far away to hear it, the person must have said something to Ben, because, holding the ball in both hands now, he straightened way too quickly to look at whoever it was.

The hair stood up on the back of Kate's neck. All she could tell through the darkness was that whoever was standing there was an adult. A large adult.

It was probably a neighbor. But something felt wrong.

"Ben!" She shot across the few yards separating them.

"Mom." Holding the basketball against his chest, Ben was backing toward her as she reached him. Her hands closed protectively over his thin shoulders. She looked at the man standing only a few feet away.

"Kate . . . White," he said before she could speak, pronouncing her name like a judgment. His voice was deep, with a rough West Philly accent. A knit cap was pulled down over his eyes, and a dark jacket or shirt was zipped up to his throat. He was about six feet tall, with a muscular build. But the night obscured the details of his features.

"Go in the house," she said fiercely to Ben.

"Mom . . ." There was fear in his voice.

"Do what I tell you!"

Still clutching the basketball, he headed at a trot toward the closed garage door and the opener that waited in the grass by the pavement. The front door was locked. They had come out through the garage, and it was the only way back in. No matter how fast they were, this guy was almost certain to be faster. And the garage door took a long time to rise, and then an equally long time to close.

She planted herself in front of the man. "Who are you?" she asked sharply.

"I got a message for you," he said. "Mario says you owe him."

Horrified, Kate sucked in air. The groan of the garage door lifting up rumbled in the background, and she was conscious of Ben joggling anxiously from foot to foot as he waited and watched her through the dark. As she stood rooted to the spot, more headlights cut through the blackness at the top of the street, coming toward them. Just when the beams would have illuminated the stranger's face, he stepped back out of their path.

The voice turned ugly. "He says you better not screw him over."

Kate felt a wave of dizziness. Terror blossomed in her anew. The headlights caught Kate in their glare, and she turned to glance at the oncoming car. To her surprise, instead of sweeping past, the headlights arced across her yard. This car was pulling into her driveway. She looked toward the stranger again. But he was gone.

*Oh my God.*

Her eyes cut to the car, now parking in her driveway. Its headlights illuminated Ben, who had turned to look at the car as it pulled in, and the slowly rising garage door behind him. Ben was wide-eyed and pale in the bright beams, obviously scared.

Sick at the fear in Ben's face, she jogged across the yard toward him. Whoever this was, friend, neighbor, reporter, anyone, she could only be thankful that they'd come when they had.

The driver's door opened. She reached Ben just as a man got out and straightened to his full height. Detective Braga.

As she recognized him, he said, "Ms. White?"

"Who is he, Mom?" Ben's voice was urgent.

"It's all right," Kate told him as relief washed over her. "I know him. He's a police officer. He's safe."

"Is something wrong?" Braga came toward them.

Unable to help herself, Kate compulsively glanced toward the oak. Was Mario's emissary still there? Was he watching?

"Kate?" Braga's gaze followed hers to probe the darkness.

*Get a grip. Downplay this.*

"It's nothing. Just . . . oh, come inside, would you, please?"

He was looking at her now, a frown still in place.

"Thanks."

Kate didn't wait for more. Instead she turned away and headed inside. She pulled Ben with her through the dark garage.

Braga was right behind them.

She felt hideously vulnerable, even with a presumably armed homicide detective just a step behind them. She realized that gradually, over the past eight and a half years, ever since she'd run from Atlantic City with Ben, she had forgotten what it was like to be afraid. Now she remembered.

"Close the garage door, please," she said to Ben as they reached the door that led into the house. He obediently pushed the button on the remote, and the grinding sound of the garage door going down followed them into the kitchen.

Inside, warmth and bright light greeted them.

"Who was that man, Mom?" Ben asked as she closed and locked the kitchen door, then turned back into the kitchen. She folded her arms over her chest to ward off the sudden chill that beset her. Braga was watching her. Hoping to hide her agitation, she forced a smile for Ben. Her little boy's small mouth was tight with anxiety.

"I don't know." Shaking her head, she took the garage-door opener from him and put it on the counter by the door.

"So, you want to tell me what's going on?"

Braga's eyes were on her face. They were almost black in the unforgiving light, and narrowed with speculation. He looked tired, she thought, and on edge.

"There was a man outside," Ben said before Kate could reply. Unlike her, her son had no reason to lie. "He was scary."

"Just now? When I pulled up?"

"He left," Kate said. "It really wasn't anything."

"What did he do?"

"He came out from behind the tree and said, 'Are you Ben?' " Ben told him. "And then my mom came."

The idea that the stranger had known she had a son named Ben took Kate's breath away.

Braga frowned. "Who was it? Did you know him?"

Kate shook her head. "No."

"I thought he was going to kill us." Ben looked up at Braga. "So did my mom." He glanced at her for confirmation, and when she didn't say anything, he added, "You know you did. I could tell."

Braga's gaze fixed once again on her face.

"It was a little unnerving," she admitted. "I think it scared us so much because it was dark and . . . he just appeared out of the blue." She followed up with a small smile. "It was kind of bizarre."

Braga moved purposefully toward the door.

"Where are you going?"

"Outside to look around. In case this joker's still close by."

He picked up the garage-door opener from the counter and left the kitchen. While Kate listened to the muffled growl of the garage door rising, she said a little prayer that the thug was long gone. She didn't want this veteran detective grilling any acquaintance of Mario's about anything.

"Are you okay, Mom?" Ben asked. "You look really upset."

"I am upset," she admitted. "But I'm getting over it." She moved toward him and wrapped her arms around his thin body, hugging him tight. "You were so brave out there. You did exactly what I told you to do, too. Good job."

They heard the rattle of the garage door closing a split second before the kitchen door opened. Ben was pulling out of Kate's arms as Braga walked in.

"Nobody," he said in response to Kate's questioning look. "I have a black-and-white looking around the neighborhood, though, just in case." He glanced at Ben, then smiled and held out his hand. "I'm Tom Braga, by the way."

"Ben White." Ben shook hands, looking and sounding so grown up suddenly that Kate felt a tightness in her throat. She felt she was being given a glimpse of the man her son would someday become.

"What are you doing here, anyway?" She frowned at Braga. It was just now occurring to her that his opportune arrival couldn't simply be chalked up to good fortune.

"I wanted to talk to you. Nothing that important. Just a few details about what you told my partner and me earlier."

Kate's heart lurched. She wondered if he was acting like it was no big deal for Ben's benefit, and decided he was.

"I'm surprised it couldn't wait until tomorrow."

He shrugged.

"So, are you a friend of my mom's or what?" Ben's question came out of nowhere, bristling with sudden protectiveness.

"I'm a friend," Braga said. With a quick glance at Kate, who nodded confirmation, Ben relaxed. Braga's gaze shifted to Kate. "You wouldn't happen to have any coffee available, would you?"

Her eyes narrowed at him. She appreciated the fact that he had scared away Mario's henchman and reassured Ben just now, but she completely recognized his present show of relaxed affability for what it was—a show.

"Detective, would you like a cup of coffee?" A healthy dose of irony underlay the question.

"Thank you. That would be great," he responded with aplomb. "And please call me Tom." There was the tiniest of pauses. "Kate."

*So we're Tom and Kate now, are we? Just so you know, that doesn't fool me into thinking we're friends.*

Braga turned to Ben. "Maybe you and I could go sit down somewhere and you could tell me exactly what happened outside again. Just to make sure I've got it straight."

"Okay." Ben took off his hoodie. "You want to come in the living room?" Uncertain, he glanced at Kate. "It's all right, isn't it?"

Kate just barely managed not to purse her lips. She suspected that Braga thought that without her presence he could get more information out of Ben. Which was probably true.

"Sure." She glanced at the clock on the wall. It was eight fifty. "You'd better talk fast, though. Tomorrow's a school day."

Ben groaned. "I hate school," he said glumly, and headed toward the living room with Braga following.

IN THE living room, which was just off the kitchen, close enough so Tom could hear Kate as she made coffee, Ben settled into a gold plush rocker-recliner. Tom sank down on the couch.

Probably not going home and crashing before tackling Kate White had been a mistake, but what Charlie had told him had disturbed him to the point where he knew he wasn't going to be able to sleep until he had at least made a stab at clearing it up. According to Charlie, who had been lapsing in and out of consciousness as he lay in the holding cell after being shot, when everybody else was gone and just before he'd been rescued, there had been two men and a woman alive and on their feet in the secure corridor. Two men, not one, both wearing prisoners' orange jumpsuits.

"So, what do you want to know?" Ben asked.

Tom looked at the kid. Like his mother he was thin and fine-boned, with a shock of white-blond hair and big, vividly blue eyes. He guessed him to be about seven or, at most, eight years old.

"Let's start at the beginning. What were you doing outside?"

Ben grimaced. "Practicing basketball."

"You don't like basketball?"

Ben shook his head.

"So why were you outside practicing it? After dark?"

"Because I suck. And we're having this tournament next week."

Tom nodded. "So you were outside practicing. Then what?"

"The ball rolled away and I went to get it and that man just came out from behind the tree and asked me if I was Ben."

"What did you say?"

"I didn't say anything. I was too scared."

"Where was your mom?"

"She was out there the whole time. She was helping me practice." His voice turned confidential. "Don't tell her I said this, but she really isn't much help. She sucks at basketball, too."

"Your dad's not around?"

Ben shook his head. "He died in a car crash when I was a baby."

"I'm sorry to hear that." Tom felt bad for bringing it up. "My dad died when I was a kid, too. I was nine."

"That's how old I am."

"Oh yeah?" The kid was small for his age.

Ben nodded. "I don't know why people like basketball anyway."

"Sometimes it can be fun. Once you get the hang of it." Tom looked at Ben's huddled form and felt a twinge of sympathy. He remembered what it was like growing up without a dad.

"Did you ever play basketball?"

"I was pretty good in high school. I made the team, but I had to quit after freshman year. I had to get a job to help out my family. There were five of us kids, so it took a lot to keep us going." He turned the subject back to the topic at hand. "Look, Ben, have you noticed anybody hanging around your house or yard lately?"

Ben shook his head.

"Your mom have any old boyfriends who might be mad at her?"

Ben shook his head again. "She doesn't have boyfriends. She's pretty busy all the time."

Tom let that pass without comment, although he figured that it was nearly impossible that a looker like Kate White didn't have a boyfriend or two in the wings.

"Did you see which way the guy went when he left?"

Once more with the head shake. "I was over by the garage by then. Mom told me to go inside and pushed me away."

Tom frowned. "She stayed?"

Ben nodded.

"Did you hear what the guy said to her?"

"No. I was trying to get in the house to call the police. Then you came." Then, before Tom could ask anything else, Ben added in a small voice, "Is somebody trying to hurt my mom?"

"What?" Tom's attention was caught. "Why do you ask that?"

Ben's brow wrinkled. "There was that thing yesterday where she works. Somebody at school said she was almost killed. Then that man came to our house tonight. And you're a cop, and you're here, too. And . . . and . . ." His eyes held Tom's. "I think she's scared."

*Smart kid.* Tom almost said it aloud, because that was the vibe he was picking up from Kate. She was afraid. Not just tonight but earlier today as well, in her office. But then he heard rattling sounds approaching—the lady of the house heading their way with coffee.

"Nine o'clock," she said crisply to Ben as she handed Tom a mug and set a saucer and napkins down on the coffee table. The saucer, he saw at a glance, held a few chocolate-chip cookies.

"Thanks," he said, and reached for a cookie.

"You're welcome." Her gaze shifted to Ben. "Bath and bed."

Ben groaned but slid to his feet without argument.

"Say good night to Detective Braga," Kate directed.

Ben flicked a sideways look at him. Tom could tell that Ben was silently charging him not to repeat what he had been told.

"Good night."

"Night, Ben," Tom replied.

"Call me when you're ready," Kate said to her son. Ben nodded. Then Tom lost track of him as Kate, steaming mug in hand, sat down in the gold chair the kid had just vacated.

With her hair pulled back in a ponytail that allowed just a few wavy blond tendrils to frame her face, she looked more like a teenager than a prosecutor. Her rounded forehead, high cheekbones, and square jawline made him wonder if maybe she had Vikings in her family tree. Her blue eyes were unmistakably wary.

*She's hiding something.* He was almost certain.

"Thank you for coming to my rescue again."

He smiled at her. "That's what us police officers do. By the way, you got a great kid there."

"Thank you." Her smile didn't touch the wariness in her eyes. It was becoming clear: Something was up with her. He found himself suddenly hoping that it wasn't what he was beginning to fear—that she was, in some way, part of yesterday's murderous plot.

"Must have been hard for you, raising him on your own."

"We've managed." This time she didn't even attempt to mitigate the coldness. "So, Detective, what can I do for you?"

"Tom," he corrected.

"Tom."

"You can tell me what you're afraid of, to begin with." It was a shot in the dark, but it hit home. Her eyes widened, flickered. He knew then, without a doubt, that he was on the right track. But as quickly as her expression changed, it changed back, closing down.

"What in the world are you talking about?"

"What really happened yesterday, Kate?" His eyes never left her face. His voice was almost tender.

She met his gaze.

"I told you what happened. I gave a sworn statement."

"Who was the man in the corridor with you and Rodriguez?"

She didn't move, didn't flinch. There was no flicker, nothing.

"We've been over this. Your brother and another deputy and a prisoner were lying on the floor of one of the holding cells. Other than that, there was no one."

If she was lying, she'd just gotten better at it. Maybe Charlie was wrong. Maybe there hadn't been another prisoner besides Rodriguez in the corridor. Hell, maybe Charlie had been hallucinating.

"Who else do you think was back there, Detective?"

Forget calling him Tom. She was hostile now.

"Look, Kate. We have a whole lot of people, including a judge and a number of deputies, dead. It's my job to get to the bottom of what happened."

"And you think I had something to do with it?"

The incredulity in her voice struck him as sincere. Tom narrowed his eyes. It almost—*almost*—made him believe in her innocence.

But if she was innocent, what was she afraid of?

"Mom! I'm ready!"

Kate's eyes bored into Tom's. Then she rose. "I'm coming," she called. Her gaze shifted back to him. Her expression was stony. "I always tuck Ben in and read to him before he falls asleep. So . . ."

It was obvious that she was asking him to leave.

Tom smiled. "Would you mind if I wait here until you're finished? If you could come back down, that would be great. I still have a few more questions to ask. Of course, if you'd rather, we could do it tomorrow. At the Roundhouse."

It was clear from her expression that she understood the implied threat. If she didn't cooperate, he could show up at her office and take her down to police headquarters for additional questioning. But he was betting that she wouldn't want that to happen.

She glared at him. "Are you trying to intimidate me?"

"Absolutely not."

"Mom!"

"I'm coming!" she called. Then she looked back at Tom. "Fine. I'll be upstairs for about half an hour. Make yourself at home."

Sarcasm practically dripped from that last sentence.

"Thank you," Tom said gently. Then he watched as she stalked up the stairs, her back rigid and her head held high.

# CHAPTER 8

PANIC tasted sour and vinegary in the mouth, as Kate had already discovered. Some forty minutes after she had left Braga waiting downstairs, she was in the small, utilitarian bathroom off her small, utilitarian bedroom, brushing her teeth to rid herself of the taste.

How had Braga known there was a second man in the secure corridor? The security camera above the door had been shot to hell. She remembered it clearly. Could there have been another one that she had missed? At the thought of the cops possessing a tape of everything that had happened in that corridor, she started to sweat.

*If Mario had been caught on tape, you wouldn't have been visiting him in the detention center because he would have been taken into custody so fast smoke would've been coming out the windows.*

*Okay. Deep breath.*

Which left another possibility. She wasn't the only person who had made it out of that corridor alive. Charlie Braga had survived, too. Maybe he had seen her with Mario. But he couldn't have seen Mario shoot Rodriguez and then force her to take the gun. He couldn't have overheard anything she and Mario had said. Given Charlie Braga's position on the floor of the cell, it was impossible.

Therefore, Tom Braga couldn't know anything, not for sure. If he did, he'd already have put her under arrest. He might be scarily on target with his accusations, but he could be bluffing, trying to rattle her into making some kind of damaging admission.

The bottom line was, Braga clearly didn't *know* anything, and unless and until he did, she could still hold everything together if she just kept her cool.

That conclusion should have made her feel better. But it didn't. She still felt guilty.

Conscious of her heart knocking against her ribs, she headed down the stairs. Halfway down, part of the coffee table and the couch came into view.

Kate found herself looking at a pair of long, unmistakably masculine legs in navy pants that ended in boat-sized feet in black wingtips, with sturdy ankles in black socks. The ankles were crossed; the feet were propped up on her coffee table.

She frowned. She didn't like that. Except that it gave her something to yell at him about, putting him on the defensive.

She proceeded down the stairs, only to discover as she reached the bottom that Braga had fallen asleep on her couch.

The discovery took her aback. What was she supposed to do?

She moved toward him, meaning to wake him, then stopped. Unwillingly, she registered it: Even asleep, he looked sexy.

Kate thought about waking him up. But if she did, she would have to answer his questions. Her gaze slid to the cable box on top of the TV. The time was 10:06. If she left him alone for an hour, and then woke him, she could immediately send him on his way, pleading the late hour and her own need for sleep.

Okay, she had work to do anyway. With one last careful look at the man on her couch, she quietly turned off the lamp, then went into her office, which, since it was the former dining room, was connected to the living room by a glass-paned door. Her briefcase waited unopened on the desk.

*So get to work.*

A sudden, vivid memory of Mario's friend appearing in her dark yard earlier popped into her mind, and she glanced quickly toward the window, relieved when the plain white fall of the curtains blocked her view of the night beyond. Still, she felt exposed. It was almost as if she could sense a presence beyond the curtains, beyond the glass. Was someone out there?

Turning away from the window required a real effort of will, but she did it. The open doorway to the kitchen was dark; beyond it, the kitchen itself was thick with shadows. The house was silent. Spookily so. Kate was conscious of a kind of sneaky gladness that she and Ben were not alone.

Sitting down in the blue-upholstered office chair, Kate got busy, clicking on the small lamp on her desk, opening her briefcase, and plunging into her upcoming cases. Even with all the chaos the attack at the Justice Center had thrown into the system, legal life had to go on. Motions still had to be heard, charges filed, pleas negotiated, cases tried. She had to prepare.

But with the best will in the world, finally she had to admit it just wasn't happening. After reading the same witness statement three times before she realized that it was the same, she acknowledged defeat. She was doing no one any good by sitting there staring at pieces of paper that weren't registering while her mind wrestled fearfully with her own situation. She would be better off heading up to bed and starting fresh in the morning.

Closing the file she was working on, she slid it and the others she would need for tomorrow back into her briefcase, then looked through the glass door. Braga was still asleep. In the same position.

Frowning, she glanced at the small clock on her desk and registered the time with surprise: eleven fifty-seven.

Standing up, stretching, she turned off the lamp on her desk, picked up her briefcase, and padded into the kitchen, wanting to put off waking Braga for as long as possible. There was something reassuring about being under the same roof as a cop with a gun, even if said cop was not exactly her best friend.

She didn't turn on the kitchen light. Moonlight filtering through the window in the top half of the back door provided plenty of illumination when all she was doing was dropping off her briefcase on the counter by the garage door and grabbing a couple of Tylenol. Her headache was back, her mouth was dry, and her eyes felt grainy. And she was exhausted, the kind of fatigue that probably had as much to do with anxiety as lack of sleep.

Shaking a couple of Tylenol into her palm from the bottle she kept in the cabinet beside the stove, she turned to the refrigerator for a glass of milk to wash it down. It was midnight, and she had run out of excuses not to wake Braga.

*I'll tell him he was sleeping so soundly I couldn't bear to—*

That was the thought running through her mind when it was interrupted by a sound. A small, metallic sound. It was the scritch of the doorknob turning.

Kate recognized it with horror even as her head slewed in its direction. It was coming from the door to the backyard. For a moment her gaze was riveted on the brass knob. It was turning back and forth impatiently.

*Someone's trying to break into the house.*

Her heart leaped into her throat. Then she realized that she could no longer see the night sky through the window in the door. And the reason she couldn't see it was that a huge black shape—a man; she could make out the outline of his head, his shoulders, his arms—was standing on the other side of the door blocking out the stars, trying to get into her kitchen, trying to get to *her.*

KATE screamed, bolting for the living room.

"Kate!" Braga met her in the doorway. "What the hell—"

"A man, just now . . . *there.*" She pointed at the back door.

"Stay here."

Braga leaped toward the door, pulling his gun from his shoulder holster as he moved. She could hear the door being jerked open, followed by Braga's footsteps on the small wooden deck and a rush of cool air.

*It has to be Mario. He's sending people to break into my house now. To deliver another message? So I know he means business?*

Her knees gave way without warning at the thought of what might have happened had she and Ben been alone, and she sank down abruptly to sit cross-legged on the hardwood floor.

*This can't go on.* She tried to consider the possibility that maybe this had nothing to do with Mario—maybe it was just a garden-variety burglar or psycho intent on committing a random crime, without success. But the timing was too pat. She realized her teeth were chattering and clenched them to stop it.

*I've got to find a way to make this go away.*

Braga came back inside, closing the door behind him. He stood looking down at her. "Nobody there."

She met his gaze. "Somehow I knew that."

"Are you sure . . ." His voice trailed off.

"That there was a man trying to get in the back door? Oh, yeah."

"Did you recognize him? Was it the same guy who was out in the yard earlier?"

"No, I didn't recognize him. And since I never got a good look at the other guy, I don't know. It could have been."

"I fell asleep," he said. "Why didn't you wake me?"

She shrugged. "You seemed tired."

"I was." Braga pulled out his cell phone.

"What are you doing?"

"Calling it in. Somebody will—"

"Please don't." Her voice was sharp.

"What?" He stopped pushing buttons and looked at her. "Why?"

"Because it won't do any good. They won't find anybody. And I just can't face any more right now. Please. Let it go. As a favor."

Braga looked at her a moment longer without saying anything, then closed his phone with a snap. "We need to talk."

"You keep saying that. I still haven't figured out why, exactly."

He grunted by way of a reply, then reached a hand down to help her to her feet. "Come on. Upsy-daisy."

Kate gripped that hand and felt its warm strength close around her own clammy palm. Then he was hauling her up and she was almost upright. Her knees sagged, and she stumbled.

"Hey."

His arms came around her as she lurched into him, and for just a moment her hands flattened against his shoulders and she rested against him. He was tall and solid and his arms were hard and strong around her waist. She was conscious of a sudden strong urge to stay where she was for a very long time. *To have somebody else to lean on.*

"You okay?" His voice broke the spell.

"Fine." Reluctantly she pushed away.

"You always fall into someone's arms when you're fine?"

"It's been a rough couple of days."

"Tell me about it." His voice was dry. His hands rode the sides of her waist, light but protective, as if he wasn't entirely sure she wasn't going to collapse on the floor again.

Which, frankly, neither was she.

His grip on her waist tightened fractionally. She could feel the size and strength of his hands through the layers of her sweatshirt and T-shirt all the way to her skin. His eyes, black in the gloom, moved over her face. There was suddenly—what? A flicker of heat, a kind of chemistry?—sizzling in the air between them.

It hit her: She was attracted to him. And he was attracted back. *Oh, no. No, no, no.*

"So, you want to tell me what's going on here?"

He spoke before she could even begin to process all the reasons why developing a thing for Braga was such a bad idea. Whatever might have been struggling to life between them, his question— asked in an impersonal, cop kind of voice—killed it stone-cold dead.

She stiffened. "We've been over this." She turned away from him and padded toward the living room. "It's late. I want to go to bed. Do you mind?"

He was behind her. "You're not worried about your visitor—oh, sorry, one of your visitors—coming back?"

Okay, he had her there. Yes, she was.

"I have a gun." Unloaded, in a gun safe in a drawer in her room. With the bullets stored separately. "And I know how to use it."

"Believe me, I'm well aware." There was a dry note to his voice. It took Kate a second before she remembered she was supposed to have shot and killed Rodriguez.

She was striding across the living room now, heading for the front door, meaning to show him out and be done with this.

"Mom." Ben's sleepy voice calling from the top of the stairs stopped her in her tracks. "Is everything all right?"

"Everything's fine, sweetie." Regaining her composure, she walked to the foot of the stairs and looked up at him. This was her baby, her little boy, and her heart swelled with fierce love for him. Whatever it took to keep him safe, she would do.

"I thought I heard you scream."

Kate's blood ran cold at the thought that if Braga hadn't been there, Ben might have gotten up to find her at the mercy of whoever had been trying to break into the house.

"It must have been a bad dream," Kate said. "Go back to bed."

Ben yawned. "Okay."

He turned and went back into his room. Kate looked at Braga. Their eyes met.

"How about I stay the night? It's already after midnight. By the time I get home, it'll be closer to one a.m. I could sack out on your couch, go home in time to shave and change for work."

A beat passed in which they stared measuringly at each other.

"Why would you want to do that?" she asked at last.

"I don't like the idea of leaving you and the kid alone." His lips tightened. "That's twice in one night somebody's tried to get you."

Kate didn't say anything for a moment. Much as she hated to admit it, she didn't like that idea, either. "It's nice of you to offer," she said at last, grudgingly.

"You're welcome." His eyes slid over her. "You look beat. If you'll toss me down a blanket and a pillow after you get upstairs, we can both get some sleep."

Kate hesitated. Letting him sleep on her couch just felt like a really bad idea. But she was so tired, and so scared, and having him in the house would make all the difference. Maybe if she got some decent sleep, tomorrow her head would be clear enough to allow her to figure some way out of this. Still she hesitated.

"There were reporters out in front of the house this morning from about seven on, waiting for me to come out and head for work. If they show up tomorrow . . ."

"I'll be out of here long before seven, don't worry."

"All right, then. I'll just go get some things for the couch."

DESPITE everything Kate slept like the dead. If she had dreams, she couldn't remember them. When her alarm went off at six, she felt like she was swimming through deep water before she finally surfaced, heard the shrill beeping, and silenced it. It was only then, as she lay there, that she remembered Braga.

Then she was out of bed like a shot.

It took her less than five minutes to do everything she needed to do. Barefoot and wrapped in her ratty blue terry robe, she headed downstairs. Her mission: Make sure he was up and on his way out before anyone knew he'd been there.

The smell of coffee greeted her as she neared the bottom of the stairs. Clearly Braga was up. The couch was empty; the sheets were folded along with the blankets. The pillow was stacked on top. A light was on in the kitchen. She headed toward it.

The coffeemaker was on, and one of her thick white mugs waited beside the coffeemaker. But there was no sign of Braga.

Kate turned back toward the dark living room just as the door to the powder room under the stairs opened and Braga walked out. He was wearing his pants and was rubbing his face with a towel. His chest was bare.

It was a very masculine chest, a classic V shape, wide and broad-shouldered on top, then tapering to a narrow waist and hips. His leanness when dressed was deceptive. Shirtless, he was surprisingly muscular and tanned.

Her eyes jerked up and away at just about the time he emerged from beneath the towel.

"Morning," he said, sounding surprised to see her. "Sleep well?" He dropped the towel on the coffee table and picked up his shirt, glancing at her over his shoulder.

"Pretty well." If he could do casual, so could she. She tightened the belt on her wraparound robe, which covered her from neck to knees, and adjusted the neckline. Beneath it she wore a pink midthigh-length T-shirt that said KISS ME above a picture of a frog. Luckily there was no way he could know that. "How about you?"

"Good." He shrugged his shirt on and proceeded to button it. Kate tried not to watch. "That's a comfortable couch."

"Thanks." The conversation felt ridiculous and stilted.

"I'm just going to grab a cup of coffee," she said as it occurred to her that standing there watching him get dressed was probably a really stupid thing to do.

"I already put a pot on."

"I smelled it coming downstairs."

Padding into the kitchen, she filled his cup. Then she poured herself one as well. Her gaze was drawn inexorably to the window in the door. This morning there was nothing to see except the soft gray dawn as it crept over the backyard. She shuddered, remembering the intruder.

*Who's going to protect Ben and me tonight?*

When Braga walked in, she was leaning against the counter in front of the sink. He was now fully dressed, down to the shoes.

"Did I miss anything during the night?" she asked, thrusting the cup she'd filled at him as he came toward her.

"Nope." He accepted it. "Except maybe me snoring."

She smiled involuntarily. "Um, too much information?"

A glimmer of an answering smile appeared in his eyes. Then it vanished as he took a quick chug of coffee, set his mug down on the counter, and started walking away.

"I'm out of here," he said. "Come lock the door behind me."

Setting her own mug down, she followed him through the kitchen and across the shadowy living room. He paused with a hand on the knob to look warily out the small window in the door, then opened it. A rush of crisp air, fragrant with the scent of fall, hit her. Moving to the door to close it behind him as he stepped out onto the small front porch, she looked past him to see that his car was still in the dark driveway and pink fingers of dawn were just beginning to climb the sky. Nothing stirred. No one was in view.

"Hey," she said to him. Stepping off the porch, he glanced back at her inquiringly. "Thanks for staying."

"You're welcome." His eyes slid down her body, and he grinned suddenly. "Nice frog."

Kate frowned in incomprehension before suddenly stopping to look down at herself. Sure enough, the lapels of her robe had parted. A section of her pink nightshirt, including a big green head topped by googly eyes and the words KISS ME, was clearly visible.

She felt her face growing warm with embarrassment. The sound of a car door closing caused her to look up. Braga was already in his car, she saw. Seconds later the headlights came on and his car started backing out.

She stepped inside, quickly shutting and locking the door. As the shadowy stillness of her now quiet house enveloped her, she was conscious of fear closing like a fist around her stomach.

Braga suspected there had been a second man in the security corridor. And Mario was sending goons to threaten her. As the new realities of her life came crashing down, her heart started to pound.

And the sad thing was, the day was only beginning.

TOM knew he had trouble even before he got the call back from Wade Bowling in forensics.

Located in the lab in the Roundhouse's basement, forensics was conducting tests on the various guns used in the shootings, trying to ascertain which victim had been shot by which weapon and which perp had been responsible for firing said weapon. Tom had called

Bowling for an update as soon as he'd gotten to work that morning. After that, he'd been so busy that the call to forensics had almost slipped his mind.

Which, when it wasn't wrestling with trying to determine how the original guns had gotten into the inmates' hands, was continually being infiltrated by thoughts of Kate White. By staying the night at her house, he had overstepped the boundaries of professional distance. Still, playing overnight protector to a scared woman and her kid was not actually against any rules. She was not officially suspected of anything. And he had slept on the couch.

The problem was, he was attracted to her.

When she wasn't scared to death, it turned out that she was funny, smart, and assertive, and from everything he'd been able to observe, a hell of a good mom. And her boy seemed like a nice kid.

Under different circumstances he would turn tail and run from the pair of them.

Unfortunately that didn't look like it was going to be possible.

Like any careful investigator would, he had spent a portion of the morning doing a background check on a person of interest in the case whose story wasn't quite adding up. That person was Kate.

First things first: She had no criminal record in the state, which was a relief. Then he'd worked his way back through her life. What he had found had both increased his admiration of her and raised a number of red flags. Hired at the DA's office at age twenty-eight, she had spent the three previous years funded by student loans and scholarships at Temple Law School, where she had excelled despite what one source referred to as "the pressures of being a single mother." Before that, she had earned a degree in psychology from Drexel University. In addition to receiving financial aid she had supported herself and her son by working nights as a waitress.

Before that, the picture started to get a little murky, but he traced her back to Atlantic City, New Jersey. There, her son had been born—she'd been nineteen at the time; one Chaz White was listed on the birth certificate as the father, and she, Katrina Dawn Kominski, had married Charles Edward White, age twenty-four, seven months before. Other records—notably, White's obituary—listed his occupation as a bouncer at Harrah's Casino. He was twenty-five at the time of his death, which was called "sudden," though no cause was given.

Tom remembered Ben saying that his father had perished in a car accident not long after his birth.

The marriage license also named Kate's parents and place of birth: Baltimore, Maryland. Both parents had criminal records, the mother for drugs and a variety of other nonviolent crimes, the father for drugs and a list of offenses, some violent, some not, as long as Tom's arm. Both were now deceased.

It was in Maryland that the trail got really interesting. Kate had a juvenile record, which he couldn't access. From the age of nine she'd bounced around the foster-care system, and at age fifteen she had apparently disappeared without a trace, not to resurface until she'd filed for a marriage license three years later in Atlantic City.

He was still pondering what that meant for the investigation when Bowling in forensics finally called him back.

"So, what'd he say?" Fish asked, referring to Bowling, after Tom hung up.

Tom was seated behind his cluttered desk, a cup of coffee at his elbow. They were in the Duty Room at the Roundhouse, it was past lunchtime, and Fish was kicked back in the chair across from Tom's desk, waiting for them to head out on their usual midday run to Margee's for cheesesteaks. Tom was tired—the truth was, he hadn't slept worth a damn on Kate's couch—and slightly distracted by an inconvenient attraction to a woman lawyer with a juvie record and a murky past who might or might not be a player in the crime he was investigating.

Then Bowling called, and that was when Tom knew he had it bad. Because right after he hung up the phone and Fish asked what Bowling had said, his first impulse had been to lie to his partner and say, "Nothing new."

Instead he hesitated, frowning at Fish across the desk.

"What?" Fish sat up a little straighter.

"The usual. What we knew. Except whoever shot Rodriguez was probably left-handed."

Fish's eyes widened. "Is the pretty prosecutor left-handed?"

"I don't know. But I mean to find out."

"So—" Fish began, but was cut off by Ike Stella's looming presence behind him.

"Glad you two are still here." The sergeant looked about as cheerful as Tom felt. "A call just came in. Two bodies found in a burned-out U-Haul in Montgomery County. Looks like they might be our guys."

"The ones who were supposed to drive the getaway vehicle?" Fish's voice quickened with interest. He surged to his feet.

Tom rose, too. "We'll check it out."

"WHAT do you mean, the charges were dropped?" Kate yelled into her cell phone. One hand covered her free ear in an effort to block the street noise. "The charges couldn't have been dropped."

"Let me check again," the woman on the other end of the phone said, and there was a click. She had been put on hold.

These were the first moments Kate had had to herself during a very hectic day. She had been working flat out since she stepped onto the ninth floor at eight that morning. Rescheduling everything was a backbreaker that had the entire criminal justice system scrambling. The first funerals were scheduled for the next day, and re-working timetables around them was creating even more of a snarl. Finally telling Mona she needed a breath of fresh air to clear her head, she had at last managed to get away.

Now, at just a few minutes shy of five p.m., she was striding purposefully toward the detention center.

"I'm sorry." The woman on the phone was back. "But our records show that all charges against Mr. Castellanos have been dropped and he was released from custody about an hour ago."

Dumbfounded, Kate stopped dead. "Who signed the release order?" she demanded.

It was too late. The woman had hung up. For a long moment

Kate stared blindly at the busy intersection in front of her and the news slowly sank in.

*Mario's out on the street.*

Her stomach knotted and her heart began to pound as she gripped her cell phone—which she had been using to arrange for another meeting with Mario, in which she had meant to threaten to trump up enough charges to see to it that he was put away for life if any of his goon pals ever came within spitting distance of her or Ben again.

She had even been prepared to promise that she would get him out—whatever it took to keep him and his pals away from Ben.

*Oh my God, maybe Mario thinks I did what he asked. Maybe he thinks I got him out. Maybe he'll be satisfied and leave me alone.*

Kate savored that thought for a calming second before reality hit.

*Yeah, and maybe there's a tooth fairy, too.*

She lowered her phone, snapping it shut, stowing it away in her pocket. She now had no reason to go to the detention center. She reversed course, heading back toward the office.

*Mario's free.* Little curls of panic spiraled to life inside her at the thought. *What do I do now?*

She was just realizing that she didn't have an answer for that when, out of nowhere, someone grabbed her arm.

# CHAPTER 9

KATE jumped. Her head snapped around to see who had grabbed her.

"Did I startle you? Sorry 'bout that." Bryan grinned at her. It was his hand curled around her upper arm. Her galloping heart slowed. "You heading anywhere interesting?"

"Depends on what you call interesting. I'm on my way back to work." Kate dredged up a smile. She had seen Bryan only in passing since Rodriguez had dragged her out from under the counsel table in courtroom 207. He looked unchanged by the ordeal. His round face was cheerful. "How about you?"

"Actually I'm just on my way back from a meeting with the mayor." Bryan fell into step beside her. His tone was nonchalant, but Kate could tell how proud he was of that. "Or should I say, *we're* just on our way back from a meeting with the mayor."

Bryan wasn't alone. The tall, portly, white-haired figure on Bryan's other side was Sylvester Buchanan—the district attorney himself, Kate's boss of bosses. Her eyes widened. She had met him only once before, for a few brief moments at a reception, when she'd been on the job for just over a month. She doubted he remembered.

"We were just talking about you," Bryan said. "And I'm happy to be the one to give you some good news. The mayor wants to honor you with a Shining Star award. And he wants to present it to you personally next Friday night at the fund-raiser for Jim Wolff."

From his tone it was clear that he expected her to be overwhelmed. Which she was, but not with excitement. James Arvin Wolff IV was the front-running Republican candidate for president. And a Shining Star award was part of the mayor's new crime-fighting initiative: It recognized citizens who had played a significant role in the citywide effort to combat violent crime.

"It's a very exclusive event, you know," Buchanan confided. "Black tie. All the local movers and shakers. Good for you. Good for all of us at the DA's office."

Kate fumbled for a response that would get her off the hook. "I . . . I really don't think I deserve an award."

What she truly wanted to say was, "No way, José."

"I told you she's modest," Bryan said to Buchanan as they reached the imposing stone edifice that housed the DA's offices. Getting to the door nearest them first, Bryan pulled it open for her.

Kate groaned inwardly as she walked past Bryan into the spacious lobby, only to hear a stampede of footsteps on the marble floor. Half a dozen reporters converged on them, complete with a phalanx of cameras. Kate veered toward the elevator banks with Bryan and Buchanan moving fast behind her.

"Mrs. White, how does it feel to know you've been selected to receive a Shining Star award?"

"Mrs. White, are you a supporter of Jim Wolff?"

"Can you talk about what happened in courtroom two oh seven?"

"No comment," Kate said. She jabbed at the elevator button.

"Ms. White is both honored to be chosen and deeply deserving of a Shining Star award," Buchanan said in a deep, authoritative voice as a ping announced the arrival of the elevator. Kate slid inside. Bryan and Buchanan followed with alacrity.

"Kate, will you be at Judge Moran's funeral tomorrow?"

"Mr. Buchanan, do you have any idea about the timetable for appointing a replacement judge?"

"Kate, do you think you—"

The doors slid shut. Kate slumped against the sidewall in relief.

"How did they get in here?" Buchanan shook his head in annoyance as Bryan shrugged. "Kate . . . may I call you Kate?" She nodded assent. "Would you press four, please?"

Kate wordlessly pressed the button for the fourth floor.

"And where the devil do they get their information? The mayor hasn't made any kind of announcement about that award yet."

The elevator rocked to a stop.

"Well, I guess I'll let the mayor sort this one out." Buchanan patted her arm. "See you next Friday." He exited the elevator.

"You don't seem too thrilled about getting an award," Bryan observed as they got under way again. "It's a good thing. It could raise your profile around here. Get you on the fast track to the top."

Once upon a time that would have been music to her ears.

"I don't have anything to wear," she said faintly.

Bryan chuckled. "I'm sure you can find something."

The elevator pinged on nine, and as she followed Bryan through the opening doors onto their floor, Kate decided to give it up for the moment. She had more than a week to come up with a good reason why she would not be attending the fund-raiser. If worst came to worst, she could always plead illness. Anyway, at the moment she had more pressing concerns. Like Mario. He could show up at any time, and the thought made her sick with dread.

Waving absentmindedly back at Cindy, the receptionist, who was talking on the phone as she wiggled her manicured fingers at them in greeting, Kate fell into step beside Bryan as he headed down the hall toward their offices. The ninth floor was, as usual, a beehive of activity. Phones rang with discordant insistence, copy machines whirred, and a hodgepodge of simultaneous conversations raised the background noise level to a near roar.

"How are you doing?" They had almost reached his office when Bryan glanced at her. "I mean, are you holding up all right? Lord knows what happened Monday was traumatic as hell."

"Working helps," Kate said. "I try not to dwell on it, you know?"

"That's probably good." Brian paused and cut his eyes at her again. "There are counselors available. If you need one, I mean."

"I'll keep it in mind," she promised. But since she couldn't tell the truth about her experience, she didn't think counseling would be of much use. "How are you doing?"

Bryan gave her a quick sheepish grin. "I've already seen a counselor. And it helped. But keep that on the down-low, would you?"

"You got it." Since they were talking about Monday, there was something she realized she badly needed to know.

"Let me ask you a question," she said. "Is there a gang that uses a dragon as a symbol, or a dragon tattoo?"

Bryan frowned. "Why do you want to know?" They had reached his office. He gestured at her to precede him inside.

"I've heard some things," she said vaguely, and plopped down in one of the chrome and leather chairs in front of his desk.

"There's the Black Dragons." Setting his briefcase down, he settled in his chair. "They came in here about four years ago from Baltimore and D.C. At first we didn't really pay much attention, but then they started turning up in relation to some pretty heinous crimes. Remember that tenement fire last year that killed sixteen people? That was the Dragons, in retaliation for a drug deal gone bad. They're vicious and have ties to organized crime."

*Not reassuring. And if that's so, how did Mario get out of jail?*

"You prosecuting a case involving a Dragon?"

Kate shook her head. "I was curious. I saw a dragon tattoo on an inmate at the detention center the other day, and I thought it looked like something that might be gang-related."

"You were right." Bryan started to say something more, but then his phone rang. After a quick "Sorry" to her, he picked it up, and she stood to leave. He waved good-bye. Closing his door behind her, she headed toward her office, only to have her steps falter as she spotted Mona. Her assistant stood half in the hall and half inside Kate's open door, talking to someone inside Kate's office.

Mona glanced her way just then, and her face lit up as she saw Kate. Kate distinctly heard her say, "Here she comes now" to the person waiting in her office. Then Mona stepped into the hall and moved quickly toward her.

"Who is it?" Kate whispered when Mona was close enough.

Widening her eyes theatrically, Mona mimed fanning herself as if she were dying of heatstroke. "The hot cop," she mouthed.

Then, as Kate walked by her, she added in a voice meant for public consumption, "Detective Braga is here to see you."

Kate shot her a look over her shoulder. Walking backward now, Mona grinned and gave her two thumbs up.

Then Kate reached her office.

Braga stood in front of the window, facing the door. His head was bent as if he were studying something on the floor in front of him; his hands seemed to be clasped behind his back. He looked up as she entered, and she instantly felt a little pang of gladness upon seeing him. As if he were a friend. Which he definitely was not.

"Hey," Braga said in greeting. "Busy day?"

Her eyes narrowed at him. "Is this a social call?" she asked as she set her briefcase down. Standing behind her desk, she braced herself for whatever he was about to throw at her. "Because if it is, I don't have the time."

"This'll only take a minute." His hands came out from behind his back. He was holding a thin white plastic grocery bag that bulged with whatever was in it. "I brought you something."

"You brought me something?" Not what she had been expecting. Kate reached out to take the bag, mystified.

"Actually it's for Ben. A basketball. I happened to run across one that has hands printed on it to show him the correct shooting position. I thought it might help."

Kate peeked in the bag. There was a basketball in there, all right. Orange leather, with small magenta hands tooled into it.

Her eyes met his. "Thank you," she said, and meant it. Because it was for Ben, because he'd thought of Ben and the problem her son must have told him he was having in gym, the gift touched her.

He nodded brusquely in response. His feet were braced slightly apart, his expression was inscrutable as he met her gaze.

"Is there anything else?"

"Yeah, there is." He crossed the room in two quick strides and closed the door, then came to stand in front of her desk. "I need you to clarify something for me. About how you shot Rodriguez. Go over that one more time for me, would you, please?"

Her heart started thudding like a kettledrum. "I don't want to talk about it anymore. Talking about it upsets me."

Placing his hands flat on her desk, he leaned toward her. "You're going to have to talk about it with somebody sooner or later. If I were you, I'd choose me. Now."

She lifted her chin. "I don't have to say a word. It's my legal right not to answer your questions, or anybody else's."

"That's right, it is. Are you exercising it?"

They both knew that an assistant DA such as herself refusing to answer the legitimate questions of a homicide detective investigating a case she was involved in would raise all kinds of red flags.

"No." It was all she could do not to sound sulky. "What do you want to know?"

"How you shot Rodriguez."

What, exactly, did he know? Was this about the second man in the security corridor again? Or something different?

She tried to concentrate on recalling the story she had told exactly the way she had told it. Consistency, that was the key.

"He pushed me down. I saw a gun on the floor. He dropped his gun. I grabbed the gun on the floor and jumped up and shot him."

Kate gave a very real shudder at the very real memory of Rodriguez being shot. She was almost positive she had the sequence of supposed events right. She even remembered claiming that the safety had been off. Was that what this was about?

"Which hand were you holding the gun in when you fired it?"

For Kate, for a split second, everything stopped. This was what he was after. This was the discrepancy. Because as vividly as she had ever recalled anything in her life, she suddenly recalled that Mario had held the gun in his left hand when he shot Rodriguez.

"My left."

"You're right-handed, aren't you?"

Something about the surety with which he said it made her frown. Then it hit her. *Of course.* The basketball—he had handed her the bag. And she'd taken it with her right hand. Automatically.

He had done it deliberately, as a test.

She glared at him, pointed at the door. "That's it. Get out."

He straightened. "You haven't answered the question."

"And I'm not going to. This conversation is over."

Because she'd been touched at his gift, because she'd thought for a moment that maybe they were friends, because she had allowed herself to imagine that he cared in some small way for Ben and for her, because she'd been wrong and tricked, it hurt worse than she had ever guessed it could. Stepping out from behind her desk, she stalked toward the door. But he caught her arm as she went past, swinging her around to face him.

"You're right-handed, Kate."

"Keep your hands off me. Get out of my office."

"If there's an explanation for why a right-handed woman would shoot a man with her left hand, I'd like to hear it."

Fuming, she resumed her march toward the door. "Then I guess I'd have to say you're out of luck, Detective, because I'm not answering any more of your questions." Reaching the door, she flung it open. "Get out!"

His face was hard. "I'm not the only one who'll be asking."

"I said, *get out!*"

Mona popped out of her office, her eyes wide. Behind her a couple of paralegals turned to look, too.

"Is something wrong?" Mona said.

"The detective was just leaving." Ice dripped from Kate's voice.

His eyes swept her face. Leaning into her, his mouth brushing her ear, he whispered, "Just for the record, you're a lousy liar."

Then, as she sucked in an infuriated breath, he left.

SHE was too shaken up to get anything done. She'd meant to call the detention center back and have someone check to see who had signed the release order on Mario. She'd meant to call a couple of key witnesses who'd been slated to appear in court tomorrow to make sure they knew the trials had been postponed. She'd meant to . . .

To hell with it. She was going home. A glance at her watch confirmed it: She wouldn't even be leaving early. It was just a few minutes before six o'clock.

She picked up her briefcase. The bag containing the basketball was on the floor behind her desk. She glanced at it, hesitating. Hating the fact that the reason it had been given to her still bothered her, she picked that up, too. Then she headed out. Mona had left. Bryan's light was still on, which meant he was still working.

At the end of the hall Kate got an unpleasant surprise.

Cindy, the receptionist, was still at her desk, laughing and making fluttering eyes at the man standing on the other side of it, who didn't see Kate approaching because he had his back to her. Braga.

*What's he still doing here?*

With a quick, silent wave for Cindy, Kate hung a sharp left toward the elevator banks, where about a dozen employees waited. With luck, she calculated, Braga would never even look around.

Unfortunately luck didn't seem to be on her side.

"Feel like talking yet?" A moment later Braga had sidled up behind her, asking the question in a quiet voice that she was pretty sure only she could hear.

Conscious of the potentially listening ears of her coworkers, Kate didn't respond. Instead she stared fixedly at the elevator doors in front of her. Which, unfortunately, were brass. And reflective. So that she could see him behind her.

Their eyes met through the brass. She glared at him.

"Nope," he concluded.

An elevator arrived just then. Kate and everybody else crowded on. Once again Braga was behind her.

When the elevator reached the ground floor, Kate filed out with everyone else. Heading toward the door closest to the underground parking garage, she was annoyed to find Braga right behind her.

"Go away," she said over her shoulder as she pushed through the door, with Braga still following.

His reply was mild. "My car's parked in here, too."

Without replying, Kate walked briskly down a short stairwell into the cavernous parking garage. It was six levels deep, a vast, echoing concrete vault that smelled of gas fumes and rubber and was lit by small white lights recessed in the ceiling. A few people were in sight, heading along the uppermost level toward their parked cars. It looked to be about half full. It was even colder in the garage than it was outside, and Kate shivered a little as she headed toward the nearby elevator.

"You want to talk to me, Kate." Braga was right behind her. "Believe it or not, I'm on your side."

"Oh, right." She jabbed the elevator button. "Does that work on many people? Because I have to tell you, it didn't convince me."

The elevator arrived. It was a small, dingy metal box. As the doors cranked slowly open, she stepped inside. Braga did, too.

"Maybe you're ambidextrous," Braga said. "You know, I never thought of that."

At his baiting, Kate saw red. "Go to hell." She turned on him, her voice fierce. "And take your damned ball with you."

She thrust the bag containing the ball at him. Surprised, he took it. Then she stepped back through the narrow fissure in the closing doors. The opening was now way too small for him to follow—she hoped. He lunged for the elevator button. The doors closed. *Hah.*

Her last glimpse of him found him jabbing at the button and looking after her in frustration.

Just to make sure he didn't catch up with her, she ran down two flights of stairs to the third level, where she had left her car. The place was so silent now, her footsteps echoed in her ears.

As she power-walked to her car, it occurred to her that Braga might come looking for her, but since—presumably—he had no idea where she had parked, he was unlikely to find her before she could get in her car and drive away. And if he had the gall to show up at her house later, she would order him to leave.

Still fuming, she clicked the UNLOCK button, opened the door, chucked her briefcase onto the floor in front of the passenger seat as she got in, then started the engine and backed out of the space. Changing direction, heading toward the ramp that led up and out, she sensed—not saw but sensed—movement in the backseat.

Glancing over her shoulder, she almost jumped out of her skin when she saw Mario levering himself up off the floor.

# CHAPTER 10

KATE squeaked. It would have been a scream, but she caught herself before the full force of the shriek that instinctively burst from her lungs could get out.

"Don't stop," he said. "Just keep on driving."

*Oh my God, what should I do?*

Kate did a lightning-fast mental assessment of the chances of getting away. She had not yet put on her seat belt, so getting out of the vehicle fast was doable. The problem was, this level of the parking garage was nearly deserted. Better to hang tough for now and see how things went. But she bitterly regretted ditching Braga in that elevator. And she kept her seat belt off.

"What the hell do you think you're doing hiding in my car?" Her voice was tough, angry. Heading toward the exit ramp, she gave no indication that inside she was quaking.

"Waiting for you, baby." Mario's voice was silky smooth.

Asking him how he'd gotten into her car was pointless. The Marios of the world never had any trouble doing things like that.

"What do you want?" Reaching the ramp, she turned onto it and started heading up toward the street level. Whatever happened, she figured she would have a better chance of responding to it once she was out of the garage.

"You didn't come through for me. I'm pissed."

Okay, so he knew she'd had nothing to do with getting him out. She could feel herself starting to sweat.

"I was working on it. You're out, aren't you?"

"No thanks to you."

"So why are you here?"

"I got some friends I want you to meet."

Kate remembered Mario's friend who'd showed up at her house, and she shuddered inwardly.

Mario scooted forward so that he was pressed up close to the space between the front bucket seats. He was wearing black sweatpants and a black hoodie, she saw through the rearview mirror, and had a diamond stud in his left ear. She felt something tap her left shoulder and glanced toward it.

A gun. With him being left-handed, the pistol was between her and the driver's-side door.

Her mouth went dry. So much for making a quick exit.

From somewhere she managed to summon the necessary bravado. "What, are you going to shoot me now?"

"Nah." He rubbed the side of her neck with the barrel of the gun. "Not unless you make me. I always did like you, Kitty-cat."

*Lucky me.*

"Then get the gun away from me. I don't like it."

"No can do." The gun stayed where it was.

By now the Camry had nosed its way to the surface. The parking-garage attendant's hut was empty, as was usual at this time of night. The turnstile arm lifted, and they were through.

"Head for the Vine Street Expressway," Mario directed.

The parking garage exited into a dark alley. The alley ran parallel to Arch Street, ending at Thirteenth. She could turn right there, drive two blocks, and then hit the on-ramp for the expressway. If she were to miss the ramp "accidentally," she calculated, Thirteenth led straight through one of the seediest sections of downtown. It was crowded with adult bookstores, strip clubs, and bars. If she were to drive that way and somehow manage to bolt from the car without getting shot, at least she'd be running down a highly populated street. Whether or not anyone would help her if Mario gave chase was debatable, though, especially if he was flashing the gun.

Still it was probably the best chance she was going to get. Once on the expressway, she would have no chance to jump.

"The way things are going, you ought to thank your lucky stars that you have a friend like me in the prosecutor's office," Kate tried. She was trying to pretend to be his friend, because at the moment the "old friend" card was the only one she had to play. "You in touch with any of the old group? Jason, or Leah?"

He laughed. "They're dead. All of 'em. Car crash, about three months after you left us. I probably would've been with them, except I was in jail at the time." He leaned closer. "And just for the record, it was your boyfriend who shot that security guard, not me."

*Liar. It was never Jason; it was you.* Kate screamed the words at him in her mind as she reeled inwardly at the news. All of them— her friends, Jason with the blue eyes—dead.

"Turn right up here at Thirteenth. And don't miss the expressway turn-off. I won't like that."

They reached the end of the alley, and she stopped to look both ways before merging onto Thirteenth. Brightly lit and busy, with heavy traffic and a fair number of pedestrians, this next block and a half or so was probably her best chance of escape. The gun on her shoulder was the biggest obstacle.

Would he shoot her if she tried to open the door and run? He was close enough, so close that she could feel the heat of his arm behind her head.

"You got any money?" Mario asked. "I bet prosecutors make a lot of money."

"Not much."

She had exactly six dollars tucked away in her briefcase, which rested in the passenger-seat footwell.

Headlights shining in the alley behind them caught her attention as she turned right onto Thirteenth, carefully wedging in between a white pickup in front and a small red car behind. Glancing back, she saw a black Taurus waiting in the mouth of the alley for its chance to join the stream of traffic, and her heart skipped a beat.

She was almost positive that was Braga's car.

"How much?" Mario growled.

"A hundred bucks," she lied. "Give or take a couple of dollars." She braked for the red light at the intersection before the one leading to the expressway ramp. Now, while the light was red and the car was stopped, was the best chance she was going to get, she knew. "It's in my briefcase. Why?"

" 'Cause I want it." Mario looked down at her briefcase, then shifted himself, reaching between the seats for it.

The gun moved when he did. Suddenly, it was no longer there.

Kate's heart lurched. *This is it.*

Grabbing the door handle, she shoved the door open, throwing herself from the car. She landed hard on her hands and knees.

Mario yelled as the car lurched forward. She caught a terrifying glimpse of him snapping upright and turning toward her, but she was already on her feet, running screaming down the center line between the stopped rows of traffic. She glanced fearfully back over her shoulder. The driver's door was still open, but the Camry wasn't moving. No sign of Mario—or the gun. Around her the street pulsed with life. A few heads turned in her direction. But Kate's focus was on the black Taurus that was maybe six cars back.

Even as she reached it, Tom jumped out, drawing his gun.

"Kate!"

"Tom! Tom, help!"

She ran straight into his arms. Gun and all, they closed around her, holding her tightly.

*Oh, God, I'm safe.*

Clinging, burrowing her face into his coat, she was aware that he was cursing and asking her what had happened. Then the light must have changed, because suddenly all around them traffic began to move and the cars behind the Taurus began to honk their horns.

With a quick glance over her shoulder, Kate could see that her Camry was gone with the rest of the traffic ahead of them.

*Mario stole my car.* That was her first, instinctive reaction. Then, *I made it. I got out.*

Holstering his gun, wrapping his arm tightly around her, Tom hustled her around to the passenger seat of the Taurus and bundled her inside. Then he loped around the front of the car, slid back behind the wheel, and drove off. He glanced her way.

"What just happened here? Were you carjacked?"

She was going to have to lie to him again. The thought made her sick. For Ben's sake, she had to be strong, had to think fast.

*If you're going to lie, stick as close to the truth as possible.*

"There was a man in the backseat when I got in my car." Her voice was unsteady. "He had a gun."

Curses fell from Tom's mouth. "Did he hurt you?" he asked as he pulled the Taurus over to the curb and parked.

"No." She shook her head.

"Anybody you know? The guy from last night, maybe?"

He had his cell phone in his hand and was punching numbers into it, clearly to report her car stolen. She couldn't ask him not to; he would immediately become suspicious.

He was already talking to somebody on the phone. She gave him the license-plate number and a slightly wrong description of the perpetrator, claiming she hadn't really gotten all that good a look at him, thanks to the dark, shock, etc. All the while she prayed that Mario wouldn't be caught, because if he was, he might talk.

"They're putting out an APB on your car. Somebody'll come by your house to take your statement," Tom said when he was finished. Then he restarted the car and pulled into traffic. "Where to?"

"I have to pick up Ben." She gave him the address.

He nodded. She borrowed his phone to call Suzy and explain about being late, without telling her precisely what had happened, because she didn't want Ben worrying. When she disconnected, they drove in silence for a while. They crossed the bridge over the Delaware. Philly's glittering skyline receded into the distance.

"So, you still hell-bent on stonewalling me?" he asked. They weren't too far from the West Oak exit, the one she took to get Ben.

"I don't know what you mea—" she began, but he cut her off.

"Let's see. A right-handed woman uses her left hand to shoot and kill a vicious punk with a rap sheet as long as my arm. Then she's harassed at home by another punk who just happens to know her kid's name. Later that same night a man—Same punk? Different punk? Who knows?—tries to break into her house. The following night an armed man is hiding in her car when she gets into it, and she barely manages to escape." He slanted a hard-eyed look at her. "So what do you think, Counselor, in your professional opinion? Is our girl having a run of rotten luck, or is she involved up to her pretty neck in something she's not coming clean about?"

By the time he finished, Kate was glaring at him.

"You know what? I don't appreciate your attitude."

"Well, gee, I don't appreciate being jerked around."

"You know what else I don't appreciate? You trying to trick me. Why didn't you just ask me outright whether or not I'm right-handed? Instead of pretending that you had a gift for Ben so I would reach for it?" That still stung.

A beat passed. "I did have a gift for Ben. The basketball is a gift. Handing it to you—okay, maybe I had an ulterior motive."

"Maybe?" Scorn dripped from the word. But at the idea that the gift itself possibly wasn't part of the trick, she felt a little better.

"Get off here," she added. The West Oak exit was just ahead.

"You want to talk about ulterior motives, seems to me like you might have an ulterior motive in the way you just changed the subject," he said as he guided the Taurus off the expressway. "Like dodging an explanation for the run of bad luck I mentioned."

"Okay." Her voice was tart. "Did it ever occur to you that maybe all the publicity I've gotten has brought these creeps out of the woodwork? And that maybe a right-handed woman shot a man with her left hand because I grabbed the gun with my left and didn't have time to switch it to my right before I fired it?"

"That's your story?"

She bristled. "No, that's not my story. That's what happened." She glanced out at the passing streets. "You want to turn right up here at Pine."

He complied. "So you think this guy who was hiding in your car targeted you because you've been on TV?"

The skepticism in his voice was too much. She was lying, he suspected she was lying, and she knew it. The thing was, she hated telling lie upon lie, especially to him.

"I don't know." Her voice wobbled with helplessness. "I don't know, okay? All I know is he was in my car and he had a gun."

Something, either her obvious emotion or the thought of what might have happened to her had she not escaped, shut him up.

Kate took a deep breath, trying to get herself under control, and glanced around. The yards were bigger here where the Perrys lived, and the houses were farther apart. The Perrys' rambling ranch was set far back on its lot. Big trees dotted the yard, most of them nearly leafless now.

"Next driveway," she said.

"You know, there's just one problem." He pulled into the long unpaved driveway. "None of what you said explains why you've been scared to death ever since I first walked into your office. The hostage situation had been resolved by then. You were safe. But you were still scared. You *are* still scared."

She wanted to tell him the truth then. She really did. But she had to play the game as if her lies were the truth.

"If I said you were wrong, you wouldn't believe me."

The car was even with the walkway now. He braked and stopped.

"I'm not wrong."

"See?" She gave a brittle little laugh. "Listen, I appreciate all your help, but I wish you'd leave now. I'll get one of the Perrys to give Ben and me a lift home."

He turned off the ignition. The headlights shut off automatically. The interior of the car went dark. He turned to look at her.

"I think you're forgetting something. The guy who took your car has your keys. I assume your house key was on the same key ring?"

Kate hadn't thought of that. Now Mario and company wouldn't even have to break in.

"I'll drive you two home, and I'll sleep on the couch again. To-morrow you can have the locks changed and get a security system put in." His voice hardened. "After that, you're on your own."

Kate wanted to refuse, but the idea that Mario could now walk in on them at will was absolutely terrifying.

"Fine," she snapped, and opened her door and got out. He got out, too, and was coming toward her.

"You don't have to come in with me," she said when they converged in front of the Taurus.

"I just want you to answer one question for me." He caught her upper arm. He was close, standing right in front of her.

"What?"

"Did you have anything to do with helping that escape attempt?"

Her eyes widened. "No! I didn't. I swear it."

"That's what I needed to hear," he said.

Then his free hand slid around the back of her neck, and he bent his head and kissed her.

HIS lips were warm, and as soon as he touched them to hers, she went weak at the knees. It had nothing to do with him, personally, she assured herself. It was simply that it had been years since she'd been kissed, years since she'd been with a man. The woman in her was responding to the man in him. Nothing personal at all.

At least that's what she told herself as his arms came around her, pressing her even closer against him.

She rose on tiptoe and strained against him. His arms were so tight around her that she couldn't have broken away if she'd wanted to. Which she didn't. Not in a million years.

"Tom." Kate shivered as her head fell back against his shoulder.

*I love this,* she thought hazily, and then his lips were on hers again, and she kissed him back. Hungrily. Feverishly.

"Kate, is that you?"

The voice, calling from some little distance away, blasted them apart like a bomb. Suzy stood on her front porch, peering at them.

"Yes, it's me," Kate called back. "I'm just on my way in."

A quick glance around confirmed that where they stood was deep in shadow. She didn't think Suzy could have seen a thing. But still she couldn't keep her face from heating as she glanced self-consciously at Tom. Electricity still hung in the air between them.

"I'll wait in the car for you," he said, and turned away.

She took a deep breath. I'll think this through later, she promised herself, and started walking toward the house.

SHE wasn't gone five minutes. But that was long enough for Tom to get himself back under control. By the time Ben came trudging down the sidewalk toward him, dragging a backpack behind him, Tom had finished kicking himself and had his game face on. It was the adrenaline rush he was operating on that had caused him to go off the rails like that, he concluded. Frustration at the runaround she was giving him and fear for her safety had combined with lack of sleep into that debacle of a kiss. Even before he'd gone by her office, he'd already had a hell of an afternoon.

Those two charred corpses in the burned-out U-Haul both had criminal records, were known associates of Rodriguez and Soto, and were almost certainly the guys they'd been seeking. Now they were dead, killed with one neat bullet hole between the eyes each before the U-Haul was set on fire. By someone else involved in the escape? Maybe. The guy who had stolen Kate's car? Another maybe. Still, those blackened corpses had been the first thing he'd thought of when she had told him what had happened to her. Seeing her running toward him between those parked cars looking as terrified as if the devil himself were after her had awoken his protective instincts. He wouldn't like it if she were to get hurt. And that was bad. It meant his emotions were involved. He never let himself get emotionally involved with women anymore.

Was she in danger? Was she dangerous? Or both? That's what he was trying to decide. As a cop he had good reason to keep close tabs on her. But keeping close tabs on her wasn't really what he was doing. At least it wasn't all he was doing.

As someone under suspicion she should have been strictly off-limits. Kissing her was the stupidest thing he could have done.

Despite her denials he didn't trust her, but that didn't stop him from thinking about her much more than he should. Like there was a connection between them. Like she had become his responsibility.

He even liked her kid. Who was opening the rear door and sliding into the car behind him even as he had the thought.

"Hi," Ben said. "Are you here 'cause my mom's car got stolen?"

Tom glanced at him through the rearview mirror. "Yeah."

Ben closed the door. "So what really happened with that?"

It was such an adult question, uttered in such an adult tone, that Tom turned around in the seat to look at him. Blue eyes regarded him unblinkingly from beneath fans of thick dark lashes.

"You need to ask your mom that."

Ben grimaced. "She won't tell me. She always tries to protect me from stuff she thinks I'm too young to know."

The passenger-side door opened, and Kate slid in. Her cheeks were rosy, he saw, and her lips were rosy, too, and fuller than usual. The swift little glance she sent him as she settled in was almost furtive, almost shy, and it ignited all that tamped-down heat inside him.

Tom gritted his teeth and started the car.

SHE didn't want to like him. That was the thought that popped into her mind as she watched him with her son.

After Kate walked to her front door with the officers who had come to take the report on her stolen car, after the police yelled good-bye to Tom and got into their car and drove away, she continued to stand in the open doorway, her attention caught by the sight of Ben and Tom playing basketball in the fuzzy glow cast by the light over the garage. It disturbed her in a way she couldn't quite put her finger on. Tired and worried as she was, she was caught by the sight of her son's easy interaction with this man who seemed to be assuming outsize importance in both their lives. As she gazed on the pair of them, Ben took a shot, missed, and Tom caught the rebound. Then he demonstrated for Ben the correct stance, showing him how to hold the ball—they were using the beginner ball, Kate saw—and stepping back out of the way. Ben shot—and made it. As Ben ran to retrieve the ball, Tom applauded. And Kate saw Ben grin and watched his face flush with pride.

Unnoticed by either of them, Kate smiled. And she knew: The way to her heart was through her son.

It was a sneaky wormhole in the defenses she'd established over the years. Letting herself fall for Tom Braga would be just about the stupidest thing she could possibly do. Even if she wasn't doing a high-wire act with the truth, even if her past wasn't a ticking time bomb that threatened to blow her life apart at any moment, she had Ben to raise. A career to ace. And no room in her life for anything—or anyone—else.

Squaring her shoulders, no longer smiling, she turned back into the house. "Ben," she called over her shoulder. "Homework."

The bouncing sound of the ball followed her inside.

"Mo-*om*."

"Now," she said, and headed for the kitchen.

Ben came in a few minutes later, flushed and perspiring, the new ball clutched in his hands. "Look what Tom gave me."

He held up the ball for her inspection. He looked bright-eyed and pink-cheeked and, yes, happy. Despite her misgivings—Ben sounded frighteningly comfortable calling this near stranger "Tom"—she found she couldn't rain on her child's parade.

"Wow," she said, and smiled at him.

"I think it's really helping."

"That's good. Think you could put it down now so we could get this homework out of the way?"

"I hate homework." But Ben obediently put the ball down on the counter and sat at the kitchen table, pulling his math notebook toward him. Sighing, he opened it, picked up a pencil, and looked up at her with a frown. "What are we going to do without a car?"

She had told him only that her car had been stolen, without mentioning that she had been in it at the time, so he found the whole thing more exciting than anything else. It was possible he was concerned about how they were going to get around, but Kate recognized a delaying tactic when she came eyeball to eyeball with one.

"The insurance company is getting me a loaner tomorrow. Do your math."

"I hate math."

"I know. Do it anyway."

The whole time they were doing homework—and it took almost an hour, right up until Ben's scheduled nine p.m. bedtime—Kate was conscious that the two of them were not alone. The house felt smaller with Tom in it, even though he stayed in the living room, out of their way. But she could hear him moving around, hear him flipping through channels, hear him making calls on his cell phone. They weren't particularly intrusive sounds—even the volume on the TV was turned low—but they unsettled her in some vague way.

When Ben finally finished, he hopped up and started for the living room. Eagerly.

"Bedtime." Kate rose, too, and followed him, her chest tightening. Since that kiss she felt wary of Tom in an all new kind of way.

In the living room Tom sat sprawled on the couch, his head resting back against the upholstery, his stockinged feet on her coffee table, the remote in one hand, looking totally at home.

And it was then that it struck her. She knew why having him in the house unsettled her so—it felt like they were a family.

And that was somewhere she just wasn't going to go.

# CHAPTER 11

BY THE time she had finished reading to Ben and he had fallen asleep, Kate was dead on her feet. With the loss of her briefcase and its contents, which included her laptop and phone, she couldn't do any work. So with Ben asleep and Tom on guard she was free to do what she was dying to do: go to bed. Only she couldn't. Because she had to go back downstairs and deal with the problem that was Tom.

He wasn't in the living room, although the TV and lamps were on. As Kate glanced around, she heard faint sounds from the kitchen. Holding fast to her resolution, she headed that way.

She discovered him wedging one of her kitchen chairs beneath the knob on the back door.

"What are you doing?"

"Taking precautions."

She had to smile. "If you weren't here, that's what I would have done. Only I would have figured it was pretty useless."

"And you would have been right. Thing is, somebody's got your house key, so a minute ago they could've walked right in. Now they have to break something first, and theoretically I'll hear it."

He was smiling wryly, looking tall and dark and sexy, and her heart was beating fast.

Then she couldn't help it: She caught herself remembering that blistering kiss. And the whole thing scared her so badly that her stomach cramped. Her grin died like somebody had shot it.

"What?" His eyebrows lifted at her.

"We need to talk." Turning on her heel, she headed for the living room.

"Now you're starting to sound like me."

He followed her, and when she reached the coffee table, she turned around to face him again. He stood a few feet away.

"First, I want to thank you for giving Ben that basketball and playing with him out there tonight."

He shrugged. "I like Ben."

"I'm glad, because Ben likes you, too. That's the problem."

"There's a problem?"

"Look, about what happened tonight, when we k-kissed . . ." She was stuttering now. How pathetic was that? "The thing is, I don't do that. I don't kiss people. I don't get involved. I don't date."

"Meaning?"

"Meaning I'm really grateful you're staying here tonight, and I appreciate everything else you've done, but . . . but after tonight, I don't think we should see each other anymore."

"I didn't realize we were seeing each other."

She made an impatient sound. "You know what I mean. I know you have to do your job, and I'm willing to answer questions, but I want things between us to be strictly professional. No more—"

Her voice broke off as she searched for the best way to put it.

"Kissing?" he suggested.

Her chin came up. "Yes. Exactly."

"Okay," he said. "You got it."

His easy acquiescence left her without anything else to say.

"Okay. Good." Feeling ridiculously uncomfortable with him now, she cast a quick glance at the couch. "Um . . . the sheets and things you used last night are in the dryer—"

"I'll get them," he interrupted. "I know where the dryer is, and I can find anything else I need. Go on up to bed. Get some sleep."

"I'm going," she said, and headed toward the stairs. She could feel his gaze on her. She glanced at him. "Good night," she said.

He simply nodded in reply.

FOR the next two days Philadelphia was a sea of blue. Thousands of police officers from across the Northeast lined up along the streets to pay their respects during the funeral processions for Judge Moran and the slain deputies. The citizens of Philadelphia turned out en masse. Flags flew at half-mast. Bells tolled. At the huge cathedral basilica of Saints Peter and Paul, Judge Moran's and Deputy Russo's funeral masses were celebrated within hours of each other. Kate attended all the funerals, usually sitting between Mona and Bryan. The services were emotionally wrenching; witnessing the grief of the bereaved families was terrible, especially when Kate couldn't shake the thought that she could so easily have been among the dead, with Ben left to cry useless tears for her.

She glimpsed Tom at a distance several times, always in the company of police officers. His mouth tight, his expression somber, he looked so handsome that Mona was poking her in the ribs and sighing over his good looks. But Mona pined alone, because Kate wasn't in the mood to sigh over them herself.

Despite the little speech she'd given him, he ended up spending Thursday night on her couch. Why? Because after they had delivered Ben to school Thursday morning and he had driven her to work, where the insurance company had arranged to drop off a rental car for her use, he had dropped a bombshell on her.

"You want to be extra careful today." As they had driven over the bridge into the city, Tom had glanced at her. "Yesterday afternoon we found two adult male bodies in a torched U-Haul. Looks like they were supposed to be the getaway drivers Rodriguez and his pals were waiting for. Which means there's somebody else out there who killed them. And given the run of bad luck you've been having lately"—here a touch of sarcasm colored his voice—"I'd say it's not impossible that you might encounter this somebody."

Kate's blood ran cold. *Mario.*

It was then that she had a stunning epiphany: With the deaths of the others who'd been present that night, just like Mario was the only one who knew she'd been there when David Brady had been killed, she was the only one who knew the same about him. She also knew that he had shot Rodriguez. And had been party to the escape attempt that had left Judge Moran and the others dead.

She was even more of a danger to him than he was to her.

If Mario was killing witnesses to his crimes, she had to be number one on his hit list.

"Why didn't you tell me this last night?" she asked when she could trust herself to speak.

"I didn't see any point in worrying you. I was there, and I knew you were safe. Today's a different story."

When she didn't respond, he continued. "Look, I called in some favors with some first-rate people I know. By the time you get home tonight, your locks will be changed and you'll have a security system installed. But nothing's foolproof. If there's something going on with you that's putting you in danger, you need to tell me before you—and maybe Ben with you—wind up dead."

*Oh, God.* It was her worst fear. Should she tell Tom everything and thereby at least make sure Ben would be safe? Physically safe but with his mother in custody and his life destroyed?

Or should she try to come up with another alternative? Like abandoning her job and grabbing Ben and running for it, maybe? But she was broke. And anyway Mario might come after her or have someone come after her. He wouldn't feel safe while she lived. She would be forever at risk.

How about making sure Ben was kept safe while she tried to deal with Mario on her own?

Tom glanced at her again, waiting for her reply.

"I keep telling you," Kate said. "There's nothing."

They were across the bridge now, cutting through Chinatown. Looking out at the crowded streets without really seeing anything, Kate came to a decision.

The first thing she had to do was make sure nothing happened to Ben while she made further plans. Keeping Tom as their protector until she could get Ben out of harm's way was only smart.

She turned to look at Tom. "I have a favor to ask."

"What?"

"Do you think you could spend the night with us again tonight?" The glance he sent her way was unreadable. "Yeah."

"But no . . ." Stupid as it was, she still couldn't put it into words.

"Kissing?" His mouth twisted. "You don't have to worry. I won't touch you again."

By the time Tom let her out in front of her office, a plan was taking shape inside her head. The first thing to do was to make arrangements for Ben to spend Friday night at the Perrys'. The second was to tell Tom they were going out of town. Then, with her son safely out of the way and Tom no longer hovering protectively, she was going to confront Mario. It had occurred to her that Mario had her cell phone, which gave her a way to get in touch with him. She would set up a meeting at her house to supposedly talk things over, and if Mario showed up, she would shoot him and claim he was a burglar. Given the way the law was written, if he was inside her house when she pulled the trigger, she wouldn't even be charged with a crime.

It was a terrible solution. But now that she realized she was truly fighting for her and Ben's lives, she was prepared to do whatever she had to do.

Which was why on Friday she was alone in a rented Civic as she pulled into her driveway. Tom thought she was picking up Ben at the Perrys' and then going to a hotel for the night. What she planned to tell him, if Mario showed up and everything went as planned, was that she had changed her mind, deciding that she just wanted to be alone for the night to decompress. Tom might have his suspicions, but with Mario dead, there would be no way for him, or anyone else, to uncover anything that could hurt her or Ben.

They would be safe forevermore. They could go on with their lives as if this whole nightmare had never happened.

All she had to do was kill a man first.

Yesterday she had called her cell phone and left a message: Call me. When Mario called back, she told him she wanted to talk and asked him to meet her at her house at midnight Friday. He had agreed.

It was almost seven by the time she stopped in her driveway. The remote to the garage had been lost along with everything else in her car, but, courtesy of Tom's connections, she had a new one, along with a new garage-door system complete with an automatic light.

It was full night as she pressed the button to open the garage door. A lamp was on in the living room—she'd deliberately left it on that morning—and the soft glow visible through the curtains should have been comforting. It wasn't. She was too nervous.

Her heart was thudding as the garage door finally opened all the way. Given the new locks and the new security system, it was unlikely that Mario could already be inside the house waiting. But she had felt hideously vulnerable sitting in her driveway, and she felt hideously vulnerable now as she drove inside the garage and sat waiting in her locked car for the door to close again.

She was so busy watching out the rearview mirror in case anyone—read: Mario—should duck under the door as she waited for the thing to close that she almost missed it. Or, rather, him.

Mario. He was already there, in her garage.

KATE gasped. He was in the corner, partially hidden by some boxes of dishes and things she hadn't yet unpacked. From what she could tell, he sat on the concrete floor with his legs splayed out in front of him and his head slumped toward his shoulder.

And unless her eyes were playing tricks on her, there was a bullet hole in the middle of his forehead.

*Oh, God. Oh, God. Oh, God.*

Terror sluiced like ice water through her veins as, all at the same time, it occurred to her that if Mario had been murdered, someone had to have been in her garage, and they might still be somewhere nearby. She looked wildly around, making sure the car doors were still locked and that no one was hidden in the shadows. At the same time she jabbed at the garage-door opener so that the door would open back up and she could get out of there.

With glacial slowness the garage door rose.

*Call 911. Call Tom.*

She had just replaced her cell phone the day before, and she grabbed it. Punching Tom's number, she listened to the call connecting and at the same time shifted into reverse with one hand while the garage door continued to rise.

"Tom Braga." Tom's voice in her ear was the most welcome sound she had ever heard.

"Tom. You need to come." Even as she gasped the words out, she was reminding herself that she didn't know who this man in her garage was. To her, supposedly, he was a dead stranger. "There's a dead man in my garage. Please hurry."

"*What?* Is anyone else there? Are you in danger?"

"I . . . don't think so." The garage door was finally high enough. She hit the gas and zoomed backward down the driveway toward the street. "I don't know."

He was swearing a blue streak. He said something in reply to something that was said to him by whomever he was with, but she didn't really catch what it was he said. The Civic careened into the street just as another car went past that she nearly hit, but it honked and went on its way, so she shifted into forward and took off, heading back the way she had come. The one thought in her head was to get as far away as she could from the scene.

"Kate! There's a patrol car close by. It'll be at your house in a few minutes. I'm on my way."

"Okay." Kate was at the top of the street, braking for the stop sign, when she saw the flashing lights coming toward her. "I see it."

"That's good." He said something indistinguishable, presumably to whoever was with him, and then the patrol car was in full view, speeding toward her, and her pulse was quieting a little because it was starting to seem like she was safe now. If Mario was dead . . .

The patrol car bore down on her street, and she knew that when it passed, an innocent person would follow it back to her house, open the garage door for the officers, let them see Mario, answer their questions. . . .

Then it hit her. She was an innocent person. At least about this. She hadn't killed Mario.

THE investigation hadn't been assigned to him and Fish, which suited Tom perfectly. He knew Kate too well now to be satisfied with her responses, although he was keeping his opinions to himself and letting the detectives on the case, Jeff Kirchoff and Tim Stone, take the lead. In her living room he stayed out of the way, watching and listening as Kirchoff, who was young and easily dazzled, gently led Kate through her discovery of the body one more time.

Still wearing the conservative navy blue skirt suit she'd worn to work, she sat on the couch with her slender knees and calves pressed tightly together. With her hair pulled back into a loose bun so that her beautiful bone structure was on full display and her big blue eyes on Kirchoff's face, she looked sexy and fragile and the very picture of innocence. Kirchoff didn't stand a chance. He was so convinced that he was dealing with an innocent victim that he wasn't even bothering to write things down.

Tom, on the other hand, was drawing an entirely different conclusion. Those flickering lashes, the quick downward glances, the tight clasping of her hands—he'd seen them all before. His smokin' little prosecutor was lying through her pretty white teeth again.

And the thing that was really getting to him about it was the knowledge that he had no intention in the world of calling her on it. At least not where anyone else could hear.

Finally he couldn't take it any longer.

"Is she free to go?" he asked.

"Yeah." Kirchoff looked at Kate. "Sorry to keep you so long."

"That's all right." She smiled at him, a brave little smile that had Kirchoff practically melting in the chair.

The medical examiner's office was still busy in the garage, and behind Tom, flashes were popping as investigators finished photographing the premises. They'd already searched the house, dusted for prints, etc. It was after ten now, and things were winding up.

"Go pack a bag," he said. "I'm taking you home with me."

She stood, looking up at him in mute surprise.

"You got any better offers?"

She shook her head. Then Kate was heading for the stairs, presumably to pack a bag.

Tom cursed himself for three kinds of a fool as he watched her go. At least Fish, in whose car they had arrived, was already gone.

Otherwise he'd be getting an earful. An earful of hard truths and common sense that he was too far gone to hear.

"We'll have to take your car," he said when they were outside. "Fish drove."

She nodded, pausing for a moment on the porch to look around. Yellow crime-scene tape cordoned off the front of the house just beyond the sidewalk, although it had not yet been extended to the driveway, which was still full of vehicles.

"How long do you think they'll be here?" Kate asked over her shoulder as she stepped off the porch and onto the walkway.

"Few more hours. You can probably come back tomorrow night, if you want."

He followed her down the walk, opened the door for her, tossed her suitcase in the back. Then he walked around the trunk of the car to get to the driver's seat. The night was clear. The moon looked like a Ping-Pong ball sailing high overhead.

What he was getting ready to do—take Kate home with him— was probably one of the stupider things he'd ever done in his life. And the sad thing was, he knew it and was going to do it anyway.

He got in. "Keys?"

She passed them over, and he started the car. As he negotiated the streets of her neighborhood, neither of them spoke.

"So," Tom said as they pulled onto the expressway. "That was the guy who carjacked you?" He'd heard her tell Kirchoff so.

"I think so."

"Who do you think shot him?"

"I have no idea."

"Must have given you a turn to see him like that in your garage."

"It did."

"Thought you were going out of town."

"I changed my mind."

"So you parked Ben with his babysitter so you could spend the night in your house alone."

"That's right."

"Correct me if I'm wrong, but wasn't it just last night that I slept

on your couch, at your request, because you were scared to death?"
In a clearly useless attempt to keep from getting dragged deeper
into the ongoing debacle that was his relationship with her, he had
not arrived until after eleven, when she'd already been in bed.

"I was worried about Ben." Her tone was getting snappish.

"Not about yourself."

"That's right."

He digested that, sent her a look. "Remember that day I told you
you're a lousy liar? Just for the record, that still applies."

She sat bolt upright in the seat. Her eyes spat fire at him.

"That's it. I've had it. I'm sick of being questioned every minute
I'm with you. You turn this car around right now and—"

"Forget it." He interrupted her in full tirade. "It's not happening,
Katrina Dawn Kominski."

That shut her up. She sat there gaping at him like he'd slapped
her face. It was a full minute before she said anything else.

"You've been investigating me."

"I'm an investigator. That's what we do."

"So you know all about me, huh?"

"I know you had a tough childhood, that your husband died, that
you've done an admirable job of pulling yourself and Ben up by
your bootstraps." They were on the exit ramp now, whizzing down
toward South Philly. His place was just blocks away. He glanced at
her, his voice gentling. "Why don't you tell me the rest?"

"What are you, the good cop without the bad cop?"

"I'm not being a cop now, Kate. I'm just asking."

"Oh, right. You've been trying to catch me in a lie ever since you
and your partner first showed up in my office. You were there in the
courtroom that day. You saw how it all went down. How can you
possibly imagine that I had anything to do with that?"

"I don't think you did have anything to do with that." He turned
onto Seventh. His place—the end segment of a triple row house—
was just up the block, close to the busy Italian Market.

"Then what's the point of this?"

"I think something else is up with you. You're lying about something, you're scared of something, and way too many evildoers seem to be popping up in your life for it to be a coincidence." He shot her a quick glance as his parking space, protected by a sawhorse with a sign that said RESERVED FOR POLICE, came up on the right. Double-parking beside the car next to it, he got out, picked up the sawhorse, set it on the sidewalk, and then got back into the car. She was sitting there with her arms crossed over her chest.

"Leave the keys in the ignition," she said as he eased the Civic into the space. "As soon as you get out, I'm leaving."

"Oh yeah?" He turned off the car, pulled the keys out of the ignition, and handed them to her. "Where are you going to go that comes complete with police protection? Because you probably want to keep in mind that *somebody* killed that dude in your garage."

Then he got out of the car. She still hadn't moved when he made it around to her door, so he opened it for her. She got out without a word. He retrieved her suitcase and tucked his sawhorse under one arm, and they proceeded up the steps that led to his front door.

Then he stepped back to let her precede him inside. By the time he had the door locked again and the sawhorse stowed away in its usual spot, she was in his living room, which—because she was in it—he saw through fresh eyes. With an inner wince.

Unlike her he hadn't tried to make a home. This shotgun-style town house was where he slept, did laundry, and cooked when he got tired of eating out. Otherwise he was never in it.

Kate was standing near the fireplace, looking around. He walked past her into the dining room—the rooms opened into each other, three to a floor—and went into the kitchen, where he opened the refrigerator and snagged a beer.

"You hungry?" he bellowed in her direction, popping the top. "You want something to drink?"

"No," she called back.

Taking a chug, he headed back toward the living room.

Having her in his house was making him uncomfortable, he discovered. Like he was heading somewhere he didn't want to go.

Accordingly, when he stopped in the living-room doorway and

discovered that she was picking up pictures from the mantel and looking at them, he scowled at her.

"Want to fill me in on your juvenile record?" He took another swallow of beer. "It's sealed. I can get a court order to open it if I need to, but it'd be easier if you just told me about it."

He watched her shoulders square. "I shoplifted, okay? And I stole twenty dollars from a foster family I was living with. And I hit a boy in the head with a soda bottle."

"That was in Baltimore," he said. It wasn't a question, because he knew he was right. "So how'd you end up in Atlantic City?"

Her eyes darkened. "You know what? I'm not answering any more questions. It's your turn. The only thing I know about you is that you're a homicide detective with a suspicious nature and a brother. Do you have other family?"

He leaned a shoulder against the doorjamb and eyed her contemplatively. "I have a mother, three married sisters, my brother, who's also married, and so many nieces and nephews I've lost count. They all live in Philly, so we see each other fairly often."

"Are your brothers and sisters older? Or younger?"

"I'm the oldest."

Her lips curved into a slight smile. "I should have guessed."

"Why's that?"

"Bossy. Controlling." She was looking at the pictures on the mantel. "Is this a nephew?" She held up the silver-framed picture she was clutching so that he could see it. It was a plump baby boy in blue corduroy overalls. He held a rattle in one hand. His eyes were big and brown, he had a mop of black hair, and he was grinning a huge grin.

Tom's heart began to slam in his chest. "That's my son."

Her eyes went wide. "Your *son*?"

"He was killed in a boating accident with his mother, my ex-wife. Josh—his name was Joshua—was ten months old."

"Oh my God." Kate stared at him, then put the picture back on the mantel and came toward him. "I'm so sorry. I had no idea."

She touched his arm. Despite his best efforts he could feel a familiar tightening at the back of his throat.

"It happened eleven years ago, so it's not like it's some fresh tragedy." Her eyes were full of sympathy. He tried to make light of his feelings, tried to keep his voice even. "Michelle and I had just gotten divorced about two weeks before, and she and Josh were out on the Delaware River with her new boyfriend in his boat when another boat crashed into them. Everybody had been drinking. Nobody was wearing life jackets. Not that it would have mattered for Josh. He was killed on impact."

The stark recitation gave no clue about the agonies he had endured, about the nightmares he'd suffered for years afterward.

"That is so . . . sad." The catch in her voice made his gut tighten. She was holding on to his arm now, her slender fingers pale as they curled into his jacket. "I'm so very, very sorry, Tom."

Tears were puddling in her eyes as she looked up at him.

"Are you crying?" His voice was harsh. "For me?"

"Yes. Yes, I am. Is there some reason why I shouldn't?"

That was it. He couldn't stand it. The pain for him he saw in her face was absolutely tearing him apart. His hands slid around her upper arms, and he pulled her up against him, hard.

She didn't resist. Instead she melted against him. He could feel the soft warmth of her with every nerve ending he possessed. It was a mistake, he knew it was a mistake, and he did it anyway.

He covered her mouth with his.

# CHAPTER 12

OF COURSE they ended up not getting much sleep at all, even though they did spend the night together in his big, rumpled bed. They made love and talked and dozed off. She told him about her early life, about how she had met Ben's father when they had both worked at the same casino, about falling crazily in love with him and getting pregnant with Ben only to discover that the last thing

Chaz White wanted was a family. She told him how Chaz died and about finding herself broke and alone with baby Ben; about Chaz's associates coming around looking for money he'd owed them and demanding she pay it back. She told him about packing up her old car and driving away with baby Ben and their few possessions, about ending up in Philly, where she'd gone on welfare at first to survive, where she'd started college, where she'd become Kate.

What she didn't tell him was how she'd come to leave Baltimore, or about David Brady.

They must have fallen asleep at last, because when Kate finally opened her eyes, light was streaming in around the drawn curtains. There was a weird buzzing sound that she couldn't place, so she lifted her head to look for the source. The sound was coming from his phone, which was vibrating away on the bedside table. Tom opened an eye, then stretched a long arm out to pick it up.

"Tom Braga," he said into the phone a moment later as Kate blinked at the clock beside the bedside lamp—7:42 a.m.

With an inner groan she dropped her head back down on Tom's chest. His arm tightened around her shoulders.

"You need a ride to work or what?" Kate could hear the other man's voice coming over the phone perfectly.

"I'm taking a personal day," Tom said.

"A personal day? You haven't missed work in ten years."

" 'Bout time then, wouldn't you say?"

"This wouldn't have anything to do with the red Civic that's parked in your parking space, would it?"

Tom frowned. "Where are you?"

"Circling the block. Your car's at the Roundhouse, remember? I was going to give you a ride in?"

"Oh, yeah. Sorry, I forgot. Thanks for coming by."

"She got you, didn't she? The smokin' little prosecutor got you."

Tom slanted a glance down at her. "Her name's Kate, Fish."

"Damn it, Tom—"

But whatever else Fish had been going to say was lost, because Tom disconnected. Then he punched a number and told the woman who answered that he was taking a personal day. By the time he finished that call, Kate was making twisty little curls out of the hair on his chest.

" 'Smokin' little prosecutor,' hmm?" She lifted her head.

He grinned at her. "I wondered if you could hear that. And I would say definitely smokin'."

He was grinning at her, with one arm tucked behind his head and the other wrapped around her shoulders. "By the way, you look beautiful first thing in the morning," he said, and rolled her so that she was on her back and he was looming above her on his elbows.

Kate traced a teasing finger down the middle of his chest.

"So do you," she informed him, because it was the truth, and then, because it was obvious where this was going, she added, "I need to pick Ben up at noon."

"Not a problem," he said, and kissed her.

So MAYBE he was stupid, Tom thought later that day as he found himself at a bowling alley not far from Kate's house, where Ben had been invited to a birthday party. Kate had offered to let him off the hook while she took care of the party. But Tom was having none of it, both because he was afraid that, with her penchant for finding trouble, things might go south fast if he wasn't there to keep an eye out and because he wanted to see how he handled the family thing. The last-minute invitation involved rushing around for a present, waiting in the Civic as Kate walked Ben in, and then, two hours later, going in with her to pick Ben up. Ben, excited, had asked them to bowl with him and his friend Samantha. Kate had looked alarmed—once he'd seen her bowl, Tom understood, because she was lousy at it, gutter ball after gutter ball. He, on the other hand, was good, earning Ben's admiration, racking up strike after strike.

He even had fun. Which, he recognized, was because Kate was there with him having fun, laughing at herself, applauding him, applauding Ben, interacting with the other adults with cheerful ease, more relaxed and carefree than he had ever seen her.

It was sometime between bowling and dinner, which the three of them had together at a little Italian restaurant, that he accepted the fact that there was no maybe about it: He *was* stupid. He'd fallen hard for this woman, and her kid as well, which meant his heart was hanging out there, vulnerable, just like he'd sworn he would never let it be again.

Afterward they piled into the Civic, which they were driving since Tom had not yet had a chance to retrieve his car from the Roundhouse.

Tom pulled out of the parking lot and headed for Kate's house, where, he and Kate had agreed before they picked up Ben, they would spend the night. Another part of the agreement had involved their behavior around Ben—no kissing, no overt displays of affection, no sleeping together while Ben was under the same roof.

Kate hadn't been back to her house since he had taken her out of there the night before, and Tom could tell she was a little uneasy as they turned onto her street. He parked in her driveway. No need to use the garage until he'd done a visual inspection to make sure that the crime scene had been completely cleaned up.

Just to be on the safe side, Tom went in first, turning on the lights and conducting a quick search of the house. It was clean.

He and Ben shot a little ball—the kid was getting better, although he remained gloomy about his prospects for the following week in gym—and then the three of them settled in to watch a movie on TV, with him and Ben side by side on the couch and Kate sitting primly all by herself in the gold chair. Tom didn't realize he'd dozed off until the phone in his jeans pocket started vibrating. His eyes popped open, and he reached for his pocket.

The caller was Fish.

"Just want to let you know that they found your girlfriend's car." That woke him up. He sat up, blinking. "What? Where?"

"About a block from her house. Mulberry Street. They towed it in. It's at the impound lot."

"Oh yeah?" Hoping to keep Ben from overhearing things, Kate was already shooing the kid toward the stairs. Tom stood up and walked into the dark kitchen. "Anything I should know?"

"Dead guy's fingerprints are all over it. I'd say it's a sure bet that he drove it over there. Probably walked the rest of the way to her house. How he got into the garage, though, is still up in the air."

"Maybe he was able to activate the garage-door opener." *Or*—and Tom hated the fact that the thought even ran through his mind—*maybe somebody let him in.* "Any leads on who shot him?"

"Not yet."

Kate came into the kitchen then. The light from the living room backlit her blond hair and slender shape.

*Think she's told you everything? Not a chance.*

"I'll call you if I hear anything else," Fish said.

"Yeah. Thanks." Tom disconnected, stuck the phone back in his pocket, and said to Kate, "They found your car."

She stopped in front of him. "Where?"

"A few streets over." With the kitchen dark and the light behind her, he couldn't read her expression.

"Are my things still in there? My briefcase? My phone?"

"Fish didn't say. If they were, it'll probably be a few days before you can get them back."

"I really need my briefcase. I was able to get duplicates of the case files, but I need my notes."

"I'll see what I can do to speed things up. Where's Ben?"

"Taking a bath."

She might be playing him. He prayed she was not. But the niggling doubt was enough to make him just a little rougher than he needed to be when he put a hand behind her neck and kissed her hard. She wrapped her arms around his neck and kissed him back for all she was worth.

"Mom!"

She pulled her mouth from his. Reluctantly he let her go. She made an apologetic face at him as she went to read Ben to sleep.

Such were the realities of life with a kid. With that, he could deal.

Sunday passed quietly. On Monday, Tom and Kate dropped Ben off at school, and Tom dropped her off in front of her office. This was another agreement they had going: no more half-empty parking garages for her for the time being. He drove on to the Roundhouse, where he arranged to have the Civic picked up by the rental car agency and Kate's car released from the pound. There were a thousand things needing his attention, and he methodically tried to work through the pile. He was checking out known associates of the two men in the burned-out U-Haul, having confirmed their identities earlier, when Kirchoff, blond and preppy, stopped by his desk.

"I just wanted to let you know that we've got an ID on that dead guy in Mrs. White's garage."

"Oh yeah?"

"It's all right here. Have a look." Kirchoff handed over the manila folder he was carrying. Tom flipped it open.

"Guy's name was Mario Castellanos," Kirchoff continued. "Just got out of the detention center a few days ago. Rap sheet a mile long. So far, no idea what he was doing in that garage."

Tom had no idea, either, not even when he finished checking the guy out. But he did have lots of ideas about lots of other things.

Like some of the things Kate had been lying to him about.

WHEN Tom walked through the door to her office, Kate had just returned from a makeshift courtroom in City Hall—the Justice Center was still closed—where she had argued that a motion to suppress evidence in an upcoming armed-robbery trial was unjustified, and won. Kate was at that moment on the phone, relaying this news to Bryan, whose case it technically was. Bryan had just called to ask about its resolution, interrupting Mona, who had dropped by to offer Kate what she promised was a totally to-die-for slinky black evening gown to wear to the upcoming fund-raiser for Jim Wolff, the very thought of which was enough to make Kate groan.

". . . look fantastic," Mona mouthed over her shoulder as she headed out the door.

Then Tom walked in. He didn't look any too happy. In fact, he looked downright grim.

Kate began to feel the first stirring of unease. Finishing up with Bryan, she hung up the phone.

"What?" she asked without preamble.

"Come for a walk with me." There was absolutely no intonation to Tom's voice. His eyes were his cop eyes. Kate glanced at the clock. It was thirteen minutes until five.

Puzzled, she fetched her coat from the rack and put it on, looping a long gray crocheted scarf around her neck.

"What is it?" she asked again as she joined him. He started walking toward the door. "I don't want to talk about this here," he said.

So they didn't talk, not one word, at least not to each other. Kate told Mona, whose head popped out of her office as they passed, that she had to run an errand. She waved at Cindy and exchanged a few remarks with other people she knew on the way out of the building. But Tom, beside her, remained silent as a sphinx.

Finally they were on the sidewalk, moving at a brisk pace away from the building. Two blocks later they were in the paved center courtyard of the Masonic Temple. Only steps away from the busy street, the parklike square was all but deserted.

Tom stopped walking near the base of a large bronze statue of a man on horseback. "Does the name Mario Castellanos mean anything to you?"

Kate felt a sudden constriction of panic in her chest. "Why?"

"That's the name of the man who was found in your garage."

Kate didn't say anything. She couldn't. She couldn't bear to lie anymore. But she couldn't tell the truth, either.

"I checked him out," Tom continued when she didn't answer. "He's got a rap sheet stretching all the way back to when he was a kid in Baltimore. You know what's funny about that? He lived in Baltimore at the same time you did. Same general area, too."

Kate said nothing.

"Okay, how about we go for another coincidence? He was in the Criminal Justice Center Monday to testify in a trial. They lost track of him in the confusion, but when they were evacuating the building, they found him in a holding cell all by his lonesome on the second floor." He smiled at her, but it wasn't a nice smile. "Oh, and you want to hear something else? Castellanos was left-handed."

Kate suddenly found it impossible to breathe. She felt like she'd just taken a blow to the stomach. Mutely she looked at Tom.

"Say something, damn it." He reached out and caught her by her upper arms. His eyes blazed angrily. "Did you know Castellanos?"

Being a lawyer had taught her one important rule: When the going gets tough, keep your mouth shut.

"Get your hands off me." She tried to pull her arms free, but he only tightened his grip.

"Castellanos was the second man Charlie saw back there in the secure corridor, wasn't he? You knew him, he was back there in that corridor with you, and I'm willing to bet he's the one who shot Rodriguez." Kate felt the color leaching out of her face. Tom's voice turned harsh with anger. "Damn it, Kate, tell me you didn't have anything to do with getting those guns in there or setting up that escape attempt."

"I already told you that."

"Yeah, and I believed you, too, like the fool I am. Look, do you think I'm the only one who's going to be asking you these questions? I just put it together quicker than anybody else because I have access to the files. And I know something about your background. But I can't keep it a secret."

"So why did you bring me out here? To warn me?"

"I was hoping I was wrong. I was hoping there was an explanation. But I can see I'm right. Did you shoot Castellanos?"

That was so unexpected she was startled into replying, *"No."*

"Ah," Tom said. "So we've finally got a *no.*"

"Go to hell." Furious at herself, Kate turned and started walking toward the street.

She half expected him to come after her, but he didn't. He let her walk away without another word. Which was a good thing, Kate thought fiercely. She should never have allowed herself to get involved with any man, much less a cop.

She could feel tears starting at the back of her eyes. She blinked them back. *I'll be damned if I'm going to cry over him.*

Knowing that what they'd had was over hurt so much, though,

416 | Karen Robards

that she had trouble pushing it aside to focus on the rest of her problem: what Tom knew. If he managed to put a few more pieces together, she was likely to find herself in legal jeopardy very soon. The thing was, though, he didn't know about David Brady, and with Mario dead there was no way for him or anyone else to find out. That was the charge that would ruin her. Because it was true.

Of all the rest, she was innocent.

But that still wouldn't bring Tom, or what they'd had this past weekend, back.

She was crying. Right in the crowded middle of Kennedy Boulevard. Glancing around self-consciously, she swiped at the tears with her knuckles.

Ducking into the nearest alley, she turned her back to the street and scrubbed at her cheeks. She couldn't go back to work like—

The thought was interrupted as a big black SUV nosed into the alley beside her. She glanced at it in surprise at about the same time that something hard slammed into the back of her head. She crumpled without a sound.

# CHAPTER 13

BY THE time Tom reached the street, Kate was nowhere in sight. He was still furious, still calling himself an idiot for getting involved with her. But her life might still be in danger, and until he knew for sure what was what, he was going to follow Kate around like a puppy dog whether she liked it or not.

That Castellanos was the other man Charlie had seen in the secure corridor had been Tom's guess. Castellanos as Rodriguez's killer made a lot more sense than Kate in the role. But he still didn't have proof—except for Kate's face. Watching it as he spelled his theory out for her was better than a stack of sworn affidavits. Her eyes had flickered, and then she had gone white as a ghost. Bingo.

It was possible that, if he had forensics double-check Charlie's gun, the one with which Kate supposedly had killed Rodriguez, they would find a partial print, some DNA, something belonging to Castellanos on it, and there would be the physical proof he needed. He should be on the phone right now, calling for those tests. But he wasn't. He was out on the street doing his best to pry secrets out of a woman whom he should be hauling off to jail about now.

By keeping what he knew to himself, he was compromising his integrity, compromising the investigation, compromising his job. He made himself party to whatever she was involved in.

That he was ready to blow all that for Kate both appalled and infuriated him. But he was. Because he'd been stupid enough to let himself fall in love with her.

"MS. WHITE?" The man's voice was soft and raspy, with a menacing undertone that made Kate shiver as she regained consciousness. "Can you hear me? Ms. White?"

Something cold touching the back of her neck made her jump. It shocked her to full awareness. Her eyes popped open—to total blackness. She could see nothing, absolutely nothing at all. The cold thing was withdrawn. It had felt hard and metallic, like a gun.

"You're awake." There was satisfaction in the voice.

Something—a cloth—was covering her eyes. My God, had there been an accident? Was her head bandaged? She reached up instinctively, meaning to push the bandage out of the way, only to discover that her hands were handcuffed behind her back.

"Who's there?" The question was meant to be sharp. Instead, it came out wobbly. At the same time she became aware that she was sitting on a cushiony leather or vinyl seat. There were people seated on either side of her, their bodies crowding against her. But the voice talking to her was in front of her. She was conscious of being in motion, of certain sounds—a humming, a whooshing—and realized that she was in a vehicle of some sort. Seated in the rear. The speaker, she felt, was in the front passenger seat.

"Let's just say we're friends of Mario's."

*Oh my God.* "What do you want?"

"Before I get to that, there's something you should know. Mario was a big talker. We know all about you and how you shot that cop at that convenience store in Baltimore."

*Oh, no.* Her pulse raced. A denial rose to her lips, but she choked it back. Even a denial confirmed that she knew what they were talking about, which could be a mistake. Best to say nothing.

"There's something else, too."

She heard a small metallic sound and instinctively flinched. But the weapon they were threatening her with wasn't a gun. It was a tape recorder.

Kate listened with a sense of shock. It was the phone conversation she had had with Mario. The one where she'd asked him to meet her at her house on the night he was killed.

"We also have the gun that was used to kill Mario," he said. "It has your fingerprints all over it. We made sure of it while you were unconscious just now. You're a prosecutor. You do the math."

"Is there a point to this?" Her voice was surprisingly steady.

"Yeah, there's a point: Mario doesn't own you anymore. We do. And we want you to do us a favor."

Kate's breath caught. "What favor?"

"We'll let you know. For now, just remember we're around."

The vehicle stopped. What was happening now? Why were they stopping? The man on her right pushed her forward roughly, then reached behind her and unlocked the handcuffs.

"Tell anybody about this, and you're dead," the voice said. Then the handcuffs were pulled away, the blindfold was ripped off, and Kate was shoved out the door. She hit the ground on her hands and knees, hard. Tires squealed as the vehicle took off. It was the black SUV, but that was all she got. The license plate was impossible to read in the dark.

Because she *was* in the dark. While she'd been in the SUV, night had fallen. They had pushed her out into the alley between her office and the parking garage where she usually left her car. Only today she hadn't. Someone had been going to drive it over from the impound lot and drop the keys off with security. The deal had been that Tom would meet her in her office at six, then walk her out to her car and follow her home.

It made her cold all over to think that the thugs in the SUV knew where she parked her car. And it made her cold in a different way to know that Tom wouldn't have been there anyway. They were over. He was too much the cop. And she had too much to hide.

Her whole life had blown up on her one more time. But she still had Ben to pick up. She still needed to get home.

Ignoring her aching head and stinging knees, she went inside to security and got the keys and location of her car. Since it was already almost six thirty and the place had pretty much emptied out, he offered to walk her to her car, which was on the second level of the garage. She accepted.

As soon as the elevator doors opened and she and her big, burly bodyguard—Bob, by name—stepped out onto the second level, she saw Tom. He was pacing in front of her Camry, clearly agitated, talking on his cell phone. Then he turned, saw her, and stopped dead. Watching her walk toward him, he said something into the phone, then snapped it shut. His eyes stayed glued on her, his expression savage.

"Is this gentleman a problem, Ms. White?" Bob asked, reaching for the two-way radio clipped to his belt.

"No."

"Are you sure? Because he looks—"

"Where the hell have you been?" Tom burst out.

"Hey, buddy—" Bob began. Tom flashed his badge.

"It's okay," Kate told Bob. "I know him. Thanks for walking me to my car."

Looking unhappy, Bob faded away.

"Where'd you go?" Tom was breathing fire at her. "It was like you dropped off the face of the earth."

The good thing about Tom being so worked up was that any signs she might be exhibiting of her recent ordeal went right over his head. When she continued walking past him, he caught her arm.

"Wait a minute. I've been going out of my mind, and you're not even going to tell me where you've been?"

"It's none of your business." Kate pulled her arm free, slid into her car, and power-locked the doors.

"Damn it, Kate." Glaring at her through the windshield, he slammed a hand down on her hood in frustration. Then, as she put the transmission into drive, he got out of the way. *Smart man.*

He followed her all the way to the Perrys'. By the time she reached Ben's babysitter's, she had a plan. She was going to take Ben and run. She didn't know exactly who those goons in the SUV were. What she did know was they scared her. Worse than Mario ever had. There was a deadlier feel to them. Like they were professionals. Like they were mob.

She and Ben couldn't go tonight, because she didn't have any money. If they were going to head for California—or maybe Oregon or Washington, somewhere as far away as she could get—she needed every dime she could scrape together. She could clean out her bank account, her 401(k). There were things she could pawn. It wouldn't be a lot, but it would have to do.

At this point, if she left, she didn't think the goons would come looking for her. She was no threat to them, not like she had been to Mario. If she lit out now, before she got in any deeper, she didn't see any reason why they wouldn't just let her go.

So that was the plan.

Even if every time she thought about it she felt like she was bleeding to death inside.

It was hard putting on a happy face for the Perrys, for Ben, apologizing for being late and pretending all was well.

"You okay, Mom?" Ben asked as they pulled into the driveway.

Pressing the button for the garage door, she looked over at him. "I'm fine. Why?"

"Because I told you I made a basket in gym and all you said was, 'Mm-hmm.' "

"You made a basket? *Wow.*" Despite everything, Kate's face lit up. He nodded and grinned at her.

"It was a fluke, though. I just kind of threw it up there, and it hit the edge of the backboard and rolled in."

"That works. What did the rest of—" The door was up, and she was just getting ready to pull forward when Ben interrupted her.

"I got to tell Tom." He opened the door and burst out of the car.

Looking in the rearview mirror, Kate saw the Taurus behind her.

She drove into the garage and parked. As she got out, she saw Tom standing beside his car in the driveway and Ben telling him all about the basket he'd made. Tom was smiling down at Ben.

Kate's heart clenched. Her stomach turned over.

The hardest thing about leaving was going to be Tom.

"Sweetie, why don't you run on in?" she said to Ben. Tom looked at her over Ben's head. His smile was gone. The drive had apparently cooled his temper, but there was a glint in his eyes that told her the underlying anger was still there.

Ben made a face at her, glanced at Tom, and then obediently headed through the garage for the house.

"I want you to leave," Kate said without preamble when Ben disappeared inside the house. "We had fun, but it's over."

Tom leaned a hip against his car. His expression was grim.

"Look, I know you've been lying to me," he said. "I admit, I don't have a handle on what you're hiding, but I will figure it out, unless you want to make this easier on both of us and just tell me."

She turned away. "Good-bye, Tom."

"They're professional hits, Kate. The two guys in the U-Haul and Castellanos in your garage. I'm willing to stake my badge on it. What's scaring the life out of me here is the thought that you could be next. Think about it. Everybody we know of who was in any way involved in that escape attempt is now dead—except you."

That stopped her in her tracks. An icy finger of fear ran down her spine. "I keep telling you, I wasn't involved in it."

"And I take your word for that." He straightened away from the car. "You don't want to continue our personal relationship? That's fine. Consider it over. But I don't like the idea of you and Ben being alone here at night. Even with the new locks and the alarm system, you're too easy a target, especially for a professional."

Kate felt her throat dry up. She had never thought of it that way before. She wished she wasn't thinking of it that way now.

"Okay, fine. You can stay." Her tone was less than gracious. A moment later she added, almost gruffly, "Thank you."

His eyes were dark as they met hers. "You're welcome."

Turning away again, she headed for the house. Having him stay over until she could get things together and take off with Ben was only smart. It just might keep them alive.

Tom followed her in without another word.

Two days later Kate acknowledged the truth: She was stalling. Even while she was making preparations to run, she kept putting off actually leaving. During the day she continued to handle her normal workload while also postponing and handing off what she could without rousing suspicion. She amassed as much cash as she could. She packed suitcases in secret and stored them in the Camry's trunk. If her heart ached when Bryan called her for an update on a case or when Mona brought in her long black dress and sparkly earrings and insisted Kate try them on, well, she could deal.

She was having a much harder time with the idea of leaving Tom.

He met her at work and followed her home; he ate supper with them; he played ball with Ben; he watched TV and slept on the couch. He didn't ask her any questions and spoke to her very little. Their relationship was polite but guarded. He was there as a protector only, and she did her best to stay out of his way. She had the feeling he was doing the same with her.

The thing was, though, she loved having him in the house. More than ever now, she didn't want to leave.

Midmorning Thursday, she got the wake-up call she needed. She went to the ladies' room during a break in an evidentiary hearing at the Criminal Justice Center, which was again open for business. The restroom was empty when she went in, and she ducked into a stall. She was actually sitting on the toilet when something made her glance to her right.

There, just visible beneath the wall of the stall next door, was a man's leg. She could see black trousers and a black wingtip shoe.

"Hello, Ms. White." Her heart leaped. "It's almost time for you to do us that favor. Answer if you can hear me."

She went cold all over. "I can hear you," she said.

"Good. Tomorrow night, you're going to a fund-raiser for Jim Wolff at the Trocadero Theatre. We'll call you while you're there with further instructions. Do what we tell you then, and we're square. We leave you alone. You screw up or tell anybody about this, and we kill you."

There was the sound of the stall door opening, a quick footfall, and then he was gone.

Kate, on the other hand, sat there shivering.

What could they possibly want her to do? Maybe she was supposed to deliver a message. Or steal something. Or rob someone.

The possibilities took on hellishly sinister overtones the more she thought about them. Jim Wolff was a highly controversial figure. A former vice president. The clear front-runner for his party's nomination for president. He had heavy security around him at all times. Access to the fund-raiser was tightly controlled. Already she'd had to turn in the name of her planned escort for the evening—Tom— to be vetted by the FBI.

The thought hit her—was it an assassination attempt?

But then, it wasn't going to happen. Nothing was going to happen. Because she wasn't going to be there.

*Time's up. We have to go.*

With that in mind, she made sure to keep the rest of the day as normal-seeming as she could. Luckily, the highlight of the afternoon was a deposition, which she could do in her sleep. Then she put her office in order and got her coat. She wanted to say good-bye to Mona, Bryan, and Cindy. She'd been so proud to be one of them. But in the end she didn't say a word to anyone, because she couldn't. The whole key was to make this look like any other day. Forty-five minutes early—early enough to avoid Tom—she walked out of the building for the last time.

She had a huge lump in her throat as she drove away.

The plan was to meet Tom at the back door at six. When he figured out that she had left without him, he would be livid.

Once she had Ben, she would call him and let him know she was leaving. Although, of course, she couldn't tell him why.

Dangerous as it probably was, she made one final swing by her house. Her heart was in her throat as she ran inside, but there were still a few last things she couldn't leave behind. Ben's teddy bear, the book he was reading. The damned beginner basketball.

That was what finally made her cry.

As she left her house for the last time, tears were streaming down her face. Forever after, every time she looked at that stupid basketball, she would think of Tom. And her heart would break.

Getting Ben was quick. Of course, not knowing that he would never see them again, he left the Perrys with a nonchalant "Bye."

When he got in the car, she had a bad moment, because there was no way he was going to miss the stuff piled in the front seat.

"What's all that?" he asked, right on schedule.

"Oh, just some things I picked up today." She had been debating when to tell him the truth for most of the afternoon, but she wanted to hold off for as long as she could. "How did school go?"

He told her, and she nodded. She turned toward the expressway. Stopping at the stop sign just before the ramp, she saw that it was ten minutes past six. Tom would be getting impatient by now.

Oh, God, she didn't want to leave. Her heart felt like a giant hand was squeezing it dry.

"Who's that?" Ben gasped, startling her out of her reverie.

It was the only warning she received before the window behind her smashed. Little beads of glass hit her in the back of the head.

"Mom!" Ben screamed in terror.

With a glance she saw that his window had been broken out and someone—a man dressed in black, black gloves, black coat—had an arm in the opening, reaching down to open his door.

"No!" she screamed.

A car squealed to a halt in front of her, blocking them in. A man jumped out. Behind her a second vehicle slammed on its brakes, stopping her from going in reverse. Screaming, shoving the transmission into park, Kate surged partway through the opening between the front seats to grab her son, to fight off the man who had wrenched the door open and was yanking Ben out.

"Let him go!"

"Mom!"

"Ben!" she shrieked as he was pulled from her grasp. She catapulted from the car through the driver's door. "Help! Help!"

But they were alone at the stop sign, and it was almost dark, and there wasn't anyone nearby.

"Mom! *Mom!*"

"Let him go!"

As she threw herself after him, something slammed hard into the back of her head. The pain was blinding. Kate dropped to her knees. Her eyes never left him. Kicking and fighting, Ben was being carried away toward the white van that was blocking the Camry from behind, in the grip of a man in black with a ski mask over his face.

"Ben!" she cried as she struggled to get to her feet.

She didn't even see the man who punched her in the stomach until the blow landed. Folding forward, her breath exploding from her body, she collapsed to her knees again. Then he was behind her, grabbing her around the neck.

"You shouldn't've tried to run," he said as he yanked her upright. It was the voice from the restroom and the SUV.

Hauled to her feet, shaking, her knees barely able to support her weight, Kate gagged and choked and fought as Ben, screaming, was thrust into the back of the van. The door rattled shut. The van reversed and then, with a squeal of tires, shot forward, disappearing into the dark.

"Ms. White, you need to listen closely," the man holding her said. "You didn't do what we told you once already, and now, see, you've put your son in danger. Tonight and tomorrow you act normal, like nothing's wrong. Tomorrow night you go to that fund-raiser and you wait for us to call you and you do what we say. You do that, you get your son back. You go to the cops or anybody with this, or you don't answer the phone, or you don't do what we tell you when we call, and your boy's dead."

# CHAPTER 14

THEY would kill him. The fear filled Kate with an icy dread during the short drive back to her house.

*Stop,* she ordered herself fiercely as her mind reeled from visions of her terrified little boy being hurt, being . . .

Shuddering, she had to force the hideous images away. If Ben was to have any chance at all, she had to get and keep a clear head.

*Dear God, please keep him safe.*

She pulled into her garage. Quickly she went through the downstairs, closing the curtains, turning on lights. Then she called Tom.

"Where are you?" he exploded at her over the phone.

"Tom, listen."

He must have heard the distress in her voice. "What's wrong?"

She took a deep breath. The idea that they were watching, listening, unnerved her. "Something's happened."

She heard him inhale. "I'm on my way."

"No! No. Don't come to the house. Go to the corner of Spruce and Mulberry"—two blocks away—"and wait for me there."

"What the hell is going on?"

"I'll tell you when I see you," she said, and disconnected.

She was already wearing her black pantsuit and flats, to blend into the night. She put on her black coat, buttoning it up to her neck, and wrapped the gray wool scarf around her head to hide her bright hair. She turned on the TV in the living room, just to make it look even more like she was home. Then she went into the kitchen, turned off the light, opened the door, and slipped out into the dark.

Keeping to the shadows, she made her way to the intersection. Tom pulled up a few minutes after she got there. Before he had time to park, she ran across the sidewalk and slipped into his car.

"What's going on with you?"

"Drive. Get us out of this neighborhood."

He did as she said. The car turned the corner, heading toward the entrance to the subdivision.

"Oh my God, Tom. They took Ben."

"*What?* Who? Who took Ben?" His face had gone hard. But his voice had gone the other way, maximum calm and cool.

"I don't know. Mob, I think. Or maybe—I don't know. Everything you suspected about me, it's true. I have been lying. About all of it. I . . . They said they'd kill him if I went to the police or anybody. But I think they'll kill him anyway."

"Okay." She heard him exhale. "When did they take Ben?"

"Half an hour ago, maybe."

"Where did this happen?"

"At the entrance to the Perrys' subdivision. I was at a stop sign, and . . . they dragged him out of my car. Two men—they were wearing ski masks. One hit me, one grabbed Ben. There had to be more, though, in the van and the car."

Tom swore under his breath. "Can you give me a description of the vehicles? I'm putting out an APB."

"You can't. They told me not to call the police. They told me to go home and act like nothing had happened." She took a deep breath. "They want me to do something for them. Tomorrow night at that fund-raiser for Jim Wolff. They said they would call once I was there and tell me what it is."

"Kate, listen. I need to put an APB out on those vehicles."

"No. You can't. They've been following me. They know things about me. What if they're listening to police scanners to see if I called the police? What if one of them's a cop?"

Tom was silent for a beat. "All right. We're going to my place, and you're going to tell me the whole thing, and then we'll decide what's best to do."

A few minutes later they were on the expressway. Fifteen minutes after that, they were walking into his living room, having parked on a side street and entered through the back door. In case someone was watching his place, too.

"Are you hurt?" he said when he flipped on the light and got his first good look at her.

Kate had no idea what she looked like, but it was easy to guess that it was bad. "It doesn't matter." Her voice shook. "I'm so scared they'll hurt Ben."

Tom pulled her into his arms. Kate pressed her face into his chest. He was so solid, so strong, and she trusted him absolutely. But she allowed herself only a moment of weakness before she pulled out of his embrace.

She sank down on the couch and told him the whole story: her history with Mario; David Brady's murder; Mario's recognition of her in the secure corridor and his subsequent shooting of Rodriguez and attempt to blackmail her into getting him out of jail; the visits to her house by Mario's henchmen; that it was Mario in the back of her car and that he had been taking her to meet his "friends" when she escaped; about her decision to kill Mario and how she had called Mario to set up a meeting at her house and how he had wound up dead in her garage, courtesy of someone else. Then she told Tom about being snatched off the street by Mario's friends, and how they had threatened her and told her she was going to do them a favor or else.

By the time she finished, tears brimmed in her eyes.

"Hey," he said. "Don't cry. It's going to be okay."

"It doesn't matter about me." Her voice was fierce as she buried her face in his shoulder and sobbed and shook and let her tears soak into his jacket. "It's Ben. We've got to find Ben."

"We'll find him. It sounds like we've got some time. Whoever took him would be stupid to hurt him before they've got what they want out of you."

"Do you think if I do what they tell me tomorrow night they'll let him go?"

"No."

*Okay.* At least he was honest. She didn't think so, either.

"We have to find out who took him. Mario was a Black Dragon. They're a gang . . ."

"I know all about Castellanos and the Black Dragons. Did you forge the judge's signature on the release order that got Castellanos sprung from jail?"

Kate sat up. "Somebody forged the release order? It wasn't me."

"There's a security tape showing the order being filed. I haven't looked at it yet. I wasn't sure I wanted to know."

"I swear I didn't," she said. "I'm finished telling lies. I promise."

The slight inclination of his head accepted that.

"Somebody did. I'd say identifying that somebody is our first step, because it seems pretty clear to me that Castellanos was signed out of jail to take you to his friends. I'm thinking he was killed so whoever this is would have sole control over you." He pulled his cell phone out of his jacket pocket.

"Tom . . ." The sight of it alarmed her.

"I need to call Rick Stuart with Major Cases. They've got the expertise in kidnapping. And Mac Willets with the FBI. And I want to bring Fish in on this. We need help, and I know those guys personally and I trust them."

He walked away from her and placed the calls. By the time he returned, Kate was shaking again.

"They're on their way," he told her. "Willets thinks like you do, that this may be part of a conspiracy to murder Jim Wolff. If so, this is big. Even if it turns out to be wrong, it still gives us enough leverage to swing a deal."

"What kind of deal?"

"In return for your full cooperation we can offer immunity from prosecution for any crimes you may have committed, including the murder of that security guard."

Kate took a deep breath. The idea of no longer having that hanging over her head was dazzling. "Just as long as I get Ben back."

"We'll save Ben, too. Why don't you go wash your face while I make some coffee? It's going to be a long night."

The rest of the night and most of the following day went by in a blur. The reinforcements Tom had summoned arrived, and after that, things seemed to happen at warp speed. Certain moments stood out, such as when Kate sat with Tom and Fish in the kitchen, watching on a monitor Fish brought the replay of the security tape showing a Caucasian male in maybe his late thirties wearing a gray business suit handing Mario's release order across the counter to the clerk. The angle was never right to get a view of the subject's face. Kate was struck by the niggling sense that he was somehow familiar.

Their next hope for uncovering his identity was running a fingerprint and DNA check on the document itself, which was ordinarily a process that could take several weeks. A favor was called in, and the results were promised for the next day.

Before dawn it was agreed that Kate needed to go back to her house, so that she could leave from it the next day as if she had spent the night there. She would go to work, trying to behave as normally as possible. Then she would go home again, where Tom would pick her up at seven for the fund-raiser.

Tom took her home at about five a.m., walking her through the dark backyards, sneaking into her kitchen with her. The house was just as she had left it, with some lights on and the curtains drawn. She took a shower, changed, drank coffee, and took a single bite of the toast Tom had made.

At shortly after seven, when it was time for her to leave for work, he walked her to her car in the dark garage.

"A car will follow you in," he told her. "You may not see them, but there'll be somebody on you all day."

They had agreed that it would be best if he stayed away from her until he picked her up that night.

"Okay." Kate opened her door. The car's dome light flashed on.

"What's all that?" Tom was looking at the pile of Ben's possessions that was still heaped in the passenger seat. The sight of Ben's teddy bear alone was enough to make Kate's throat close up.

"Ben's things." Her reply was as brief as she could make it, because it hurt so much to talk about. "Stuff I couldn't leave behind."

"Were you really going to just leave without a word?" There was something in his voice that made her focus on his face.

"At the time, it didn't seem like I had any choice."

"You would've broken my heart, you know." The smallest of wry smiles curved his mouth, but his eyes were dark and serious as they held hers. "Just for the record, I think you ought to know that I'm crazy in love with you."

Kate stood there absorbing the look in his eyes.

"I'm in love with you, too," she told him.

His smile widened. "I thought you might be," he said, and kissed her. Then he vanished back into the house while she punched the button to open the garage door.

The next fourteen hours were the longest of Kate's life. By nine o'clock Friday night, as she left the stage in Mona's slinky black dress and rhinestone earrings, clutching the Shining Star award (a gold-colored plastic trophy in the shape of a star on a pedestal) that the mayor had just presented to her, it was all she could do not to give in to blind terror. No word had been heard from the kidnappers. Jim Wolff had left the building. After making nice with some big donors, he had been whisked away by his security detail, which had been notified of the possible assassination attempt. The team working to save Ben had substituted a ringer—a man in a business suit with the same general height, build, and coloring—who was now supposedly in a back-room meeting with more donors.

She rejoined Tom—so handsome in his tux—at their table just as his phone rang. The sound startled her so much she almost fell out of her chair.

He excused himself to answer, and she excused herself to follow. It had to be about Ben. Had Ben been found? Had . . .

He disconnected and looked at her. They were standing in a little hall along the east side of the building by this time. Inside the main event room she could just glimpse the stage, where the mayor was introducing someone else.

"We got an ID on the man on the security tape," Tom said. "Edward Curry. He was the public defender in courtroom two oh seven that day. It looks like he forged the judge's name and filed the order himself. One of his fingerprints matches one on the gun Soto used to kill Judge Moran, so we got him on planting the weapons, too."

Ed Curry. Kate was momentarily staggered. "Have they picked him up? Has he said anything?"

Tom shook his head. "They don't want to pick him up yet. In case that should somehow tip off whoever's got Ben."

"Oh my God. What happens if—"

Her phone began to ring. Casting a petrified look at Tom, Kate snatched it out of her evening bag. "Hello."

"Hello, Ms. White." *It was him.* Kate nodded wildly at Tom, who stiffened and picked up the two-way radio he had clipped to his belt, then moved away as he started talking quickly into it.

"Where's my son?" Kate demanded. Her hands shook.

"I'll tell you—as soon as you do that favor for us." He was on a cell phone, she thought, because there seemed to be a lot of static. She could hear a low hum punctuated by a faint click-click-click sound. "I want you to go into the ladies' restroom in the hallway near the kitchen and unlock the window." *Hum. Click-click-click.*

*So someone could enter through it? A gunman, perhaps?*

Tom was back beside her. He had his cop face on. He made a motion with his hand that meant she should keep the conversation going. They were, she knew, trying to trace the call.

"Did you hear me?" the voice asked.

"I want to speak to Ben first," Kate said, as she had been instructed to do. "I'm not doing anything until I talk to my son."

"Ms. White . . ." *Hum. Click-click-click.*

"I mean it. I want to talk to Ben. I won't do it until I talk to Ben."

It must have convinced him, because he said, "Wait." Kate could hear muffled voices in the background.

A moment later Ben said, "Mom?"

"Ben?" Kate's heart lurched. She nearly crumpled to the floor with relief. "Are you all right?"

" 'Member when I had that nightmare about the tyrannosaurus?"

Ben's voice was shaky, but there was a note in it that made her brows contract. "I had another one last night."

There was a scuffling sound and a muffled *"Ow"* from Ben.

"Ben," Kate said desperately. *"Ben."*

Except for the static, there was nothing on the other end.

"Go unlock the window, Ms. White." The man was back.

"Did you hurt him?" Her voice shook with fear and anger. "If you hurt him—"

She broke off because he disconnected. Her eyes flew to Tom.

Tom spoke into the two-way. "Did you get it?"

Kate knew he was talking to whoever was trying to trace the call. He shook his head in response to her pleading look as a squad of police and FBI agents converged on them, including the female agent in the blond wig and slinky black dress who was to take her place in carrying out the caller's request.

Kate grabbed Tom's arm. "I think I know where he is."

"What?" Tom lowered the radio to stare at her.

"Last summer I took him to the navy yard to look at the ships. There was a billboard with a picture of a tyrannosaurus attacking another dinosaur on it. It was advertising a museum exhibit. He had a nightmare about it that night. On the phone just now he said, ' 'Member when I had that nightmare about the tyrannosaurus? I had another one last night.' He's somewhere where he can see that billboard. He was trying to tell me where he is."

THE Philadelphia Navy Yard was located at the end of South Broad Street, with the dark waters of the Delaware Bay stretching beyond. Strung out along the waterfront were miles of floating docks. Dozens of gray and blue metal warehouses lined up in rows behind the docks. Huge metal shipping containers waited beside the warehouses to be moved either into the warehouses or onto ships. Big halogen lights lit the area near the docks, although farther out, the shipyard, which covered hundreds of acres, was dark.

Six cars, moving in single file, pulled slowly onto one of the roads in the middle of the shipyard. Two of them were police cruisers, black-and-whites, with the sirens off. Two more were unmarked cars. The final two belonged to the FBI. Altogether there were twenty law-enforcement officers in the six cars.

"This place is going to be a bitch to search." Fish sounded grim. He was in the backseat of Tom's car. Tom was driving, and Kate was in the front passenger seat. She was looking out at a billboard just beyond the northern edge of the property. Positioned so that it could be seen from the nearby expressway, it was the tyrannosaurus sign. It could be seen from everywhere in the shipyard.

Her stomach dropped as she realized the enormous scale of the task before them. They needed some way to zero in on a specific location within view of that sign. Fearfully she scanned the area.

*Ben, where are you?*

"Why do you think nothing's happened at the fund-raiser yet?" Kate asked. Tom had just gotten off the phone with one of the cops who had remained behind. The female agent had unlocked the window, as Kate had been instructed to do, and a contingent of FBI agents were standing by.

"The plan was for Wolff to exit through the hall that goes past that restroom," Tom said. "Maybe whatever they're planning is supposed to happen as he leaves. And he was scheduled to leave at ten, which is in about twenty minutes."

"They're still trying to get a lock on the cell phone that called yours," Fish said.

What he didn't say was that such a search would take time. And time, Kate feared, was exactly what they didn't have.

The cars in front of them were stopping. Tom parked the Taurus, and they got out. The night was cold, and Kate was glad to have her coat, which she had worn over the evening dress.

"Whatever happens, you stay with me," Tom said to her as Willets and his partner, who, as Feds, were nominally in charge of the operation, divided the area into grids and, with the rest of the federal agents and Fish, began searching it systematically, warehouse by warehouse. Only she and Tom were left by the cars.

"Can we at least walk around?" Shivering, Kate thrust her hands deep into her pockets. If she was wrong, if Ben wasn't here . . .

Tom glanced around. The searchers had fanned out from their location in the middle of the shipyard. From where he and Kate stood by the cars they could see dark figures slipping into narrow side doors and brief bursts of light as flashlights were employed.

"Come on." Tom slid a hand around her elbow, and together they walked down the line of parked cars, the narrow ends of the three-story warehouses on either side. The idea that her son might be imprisoned inside one made Kate want to run among them, shrieking his name. Only the thought that if his captors were alerted to their presence they might kill him on the spot kept her quiet. By ten o'clock, though, whoever was holding Ben was going to know that something had gone wrong. Time was running out.

Kate stopped and clenched her fists and closed her eyes.

*Please, God, keep Ben safe.*

"What?" Tom's voice was low.

"Shh. I just want to see if I can feel him." Maybe it was stupid; maybe it wasn't. But her whole life since his birth had been about Ben. She loved him with every fiber of her being, and he loved her back. She could almost feel the bond between them like an invisible cable stretching out through the darkness, connecting her to him.

*Ben. Where are you, Ben?*

There was something—something tugging at the edges of her mind. Obeying her instincts, she turned to the left, down the path between the long sides of two warehouses. Drawn by *something*.

*Ben. Are you there?*

They reached the end of that row of warehouses, crossed another of the narrow roads, and walked between more warehouses. The farther they got from the lights, the darker it grew, and Kate could feel Tom growing restive beside her. He had drawn his gun.

Then she heard it. *Hum. Click-click-click.*

It was the sound she'd heard over the phone.

Her heart leaped. The sound seemed to be coming from inside the warehouse to her left, which had a sliding, garage-size door in its side. The door was open about three feet, revealing a glimpse of blackness inside. Except for a dull silver gleam a few feet beyond the entrance: a car's bumper.

A black SUV's bumper, to be precise.

"Tom." She grabbed his arm to alert him. He started to say something. Then his gaze moved beyond her, and he froze.

"Mom."

Ben stood just inside the open warehouse door. Somebody off to one side was shining a flashlight on his face, as well as on the black-clad arm around his neck and the gun pressed to his temple.

She felt the color drain out of her face. *"Ben."*

"Don't move. Don't make a sound. Or the kid's dead." The voice spoke out of the darkness just behind Tom. Someone—the man on the phone, the man in the ladies' room, the man who'd done all the talking in the SUV, the man who'd punched her, it was his voice—had crept up behind them, with a gun pointed straight at them.

"Ike?" There was no mistaking the disbelief in Tom's voice. This was someone he knew. A cop? Had her instincts been right?

"Put the gun down, Tom. Nice and slow."

"We got twenty people within a hundred yards," Tom said. "Plus a perimeter set up around the property. There's no way you're getting out of here."

"You underestimate the value of being a police sergeant. We could shoot you all right now, and nobody would question it. Now put your gun down. Don't make me off the kid."

Ben made a little sound of distress.

*"Ben."* Kate's stomach turned inside out. She wanted to rush to him, but there was still a gun to his head.

Tom bent and put his gun on the ground.

"Now back off," Ike said.

Tom stepped toward Kate. Ike scooped up Tom's gun.

"Why?" Tom asked.

"Some of us need to supplement our income." Ike's tone was the verbal equivalent of a shrug. "I've been on Genovese's"—Kate recognized the name as that of an organized-crime boss—"payroll for a while. Wolff pissed him off, and Genovese put a million-dollar price tag on his head. We had a guy going in the window dressed like a waiter. Wolff always drinks a cup of hot tea at the end of these things. Our guy was going to put poison in it."

"Poison?" Kate asked before she could stop herself.

"It takes a little longer to act, and it's not so easy to trace."

"Ed Curry?" Tom asked. "Is he on Genovese's payroll, too?"

"Nah. He's just somebody we had something on, like Ms. White here. He does what we tell him. When we tell him."

"Not anymore. He's being picked up as we speak. But it's not too late for you to make a deal," Tom said. "Go state's evidence against Genovese."

"I don't think so. Pissing Genovese off is not smart." Ike gestured with his gun. "No more talk. Walk into the warehouse."

Kate's eyes found her son's face. He looked pale and small and tired and scared to death. The man holding him pulled him back out of the way as she stepped through the door.

"Mom," Ben whimpered as she neared him.

"It's going to be okay, sweetie," she lied. Kate would have gone straight to him then, but someone grabbed her arm, yanking her the rest of the way inside, causing her to stumble, twisting her arm up behind her back so that she cried out in pain. By the shifting beam of the flashlight her captor held in his other hand—he was clearly the one who had been shining the light on Ben—Kate saw that she was in a cavernous space. Tall stacks of wooden crates formed a wall about twenty feet in. Farther than that she could not see. Closer at hand were two plastic lawn chairs, a sleeping bag, and a kerosene heater. As soon as Kate saw the heater, she knew that this was the source of the sound she had heard: the steady hum of its operation and the click-click-click as it oscillated back and forth.

She saw, too, that the man holding Ben had loosened his grip and no longer had a gun to Ben's head. Ben's terrified eyes were on her.

Despite the fact that she was sweating bullets and her arm was breaking and she was so frightened she felt like the blood was draining from her head, she smiled at him.

Then Tom walked through the opening, hands up, closely followed by Ike. Kate was sure that they were going to die, all three of them. Tom knew them, and Ben and she could identify them. There was no way any of them was going to be left alive.

"Damn it, Ike, are you going to kill a woman and a little kid?" Tom demanded as the flashlight swung toward him.

The man holding Ben screamed.

"Ow! He bit me! The little brat bit me!"

Unbelievably, Ben was free, exploding toward the opening, screaming like a fire engine.

"Run, Ben!" As her captor's grip on her arm slackened with surprise, Kate slammed her heel back into his knee. He yelped, and she was able to jerk free. But the doorway was blocked, so all she could do was scream and dodge her captor, who came after her with a roar. Then she realized that it was Tom in the doorway, Tom struggling with Ike and the man who'd been holding Ben, keeping them from going after her son. Blows were falling thick and fast. As Kate, with her captor in pursuit, glanced back in horror, Tom doubled over as if he'd taken a fist to the stomach.

*Crack. Crack.*

"Ahh!"

The cry was hoarse, pain-filled. Someone had been shot—was it Tom? Her heart exploded with fear for him, her pulse leaped into overdrive, and for a moment the world seemed to slow down.

Then she heard the most welcome sound she had ever heard: Willets's voice shouting, "Freeze, FBI!"

Moments later, when the lights had been turned on and the bad guys had been cuffed and Kate was standing next to Tom, who wasn't wounded but had managed to wrest away Ike's gun and put a bullet into his leg to boot, Ben came trotting in with Fish. He ran to her. Kate wrapped her arms around him, and they hugged as if they would never let go.

EIGHT months later Tom stood in the front of Our Lady of the Sorrows Church and watched his bride walk up the aisle toward him. Charlie, his best man, stood at his side. Fish and Tom's brothers-in-law were beside Charlie. Already having walked down the aisle in front of Kate, his sisters and sister-in-law plus Mona wore lavender dresses and were lined up on the other side of the altar.

His mother was blotting her eyes and beaming at him from the front pew.

The church was filled to overflowing with every relative, friend, acquaintance, or associate of all of the above, approximately five hundred strong.

All he and Kate had wanted was a civil ceremony. Second wedding for both and all that. Go to the courthouse, get married. No fuss, no frills. And this was how it had worked out.

Not that, right at the moment, he minded.

Because Kate, looking beautiful in a long white dress, was smiling at him. And Ben, who was walking her up the aisle and looking surprisingly grown-up in a black tux, was grinning at him, too.

In about half an hour, give or take a long speech or two by the priest, whom he had known all his life, they would be a family.

Every once in a while you just get lucky.

# A Conversation with
## *Karen Robards*

## Vital Stats

**BORN:** August 24, 1954
**FAMILY:** Husband, Doug, and three
  sons—Peter (23), Chris (17),
  and Jack (12)
**MEMBER OF:** Mensa, the group for
  people with a high IQ
**LITTLE-KNOWN TALENT:** Putting
  braces on teeth, a skill learned
  from her orthodontist father
**PETS:** Three cats and three dogs
**WEBSITE:** www.KarenRobards.com

THE author of thirty-five novels and a novella, Karen Robards still lives in her hometown of Louisville, Kentucky. She wrote her first novel, *Island Flame* (1981), while attending law school, which she left after the book was accepted for publication. Now a regular on the *New York Times* and *USA Today* bestseller lists, Robards publishes at least one novel—and sometimes two—every year. She spoke recently with a reporter about *Guilty,* her latest work of romantic suspense.

**Q:** In *Guilty,* Kate White is a prosecutor in the Philadelphia D.A.'s office and a single mother with a secret in her past. What sparked the idea for this book?

**A:** I love the idea that people are malleable, that they can and do remake themselves. Kate has a difficult childhood, makes some wrong choices—then decides she doesn't like the person she's becoming and does something about it. I enjoyed creating the complex, flawed, but struggling person that she is. Actually, she's one of my favorite characters.

**Q:** One of the novel's first scenes is a shooting in a courtroom. Do you draw on events in the media for your books?

**A:** A courtroom shooting in Atlanta originally inspired that scene. As I did more research, I discovered that courtrooms are uniquely vulnerable to violence. Unless and until they are convicted, defendants are presumed innocent and almost always appear in court unrestrained. Some of them are desperate to escape punishment by whatever means they need to use. It's a credit to the security measures in place that there is not more violence in courtrooms across the country.

**Q:** How do you keep coming up with fresh plot and character ideas? Does it become harder with each book?

**A:** Usually I'll start with a character. Just as every person has a story, every character has a story. Setting, secondary characters, even the love interest—those are determined by the primary char-

acter and are the flavorings that make the whole thing come alive. As for whether or not it gets harder—no. Like the truth, stories are out there.  ∎

## Groovy, Man!

When Karen Robards was a teenager, she submitted a humorous story to *Reader's Digest* magazine. To her delight, the piece was accepted and published in the December 1973 issue. We reprint it below for your enjoyment.

"Ever since the youth kick came in, my mother has been after my father to give himself a new image. Finally, after repeated pestering, he agreed to let her 'make him over' during our Florida vacation, as a sort of trial run. So he let his curly hair grow a little, and she decked him out in a bright-yellow silk shirt and a pair of flowered, bell-bottomed pants and sent him and my brother off to the beach on minibikes.

"They returned shortly—my father furious and my brother about to die of suppressed laughter. It seems that while he and Dad were racing down the beach past a crowd of boys, one of them called, 'Go to it, Big Mamma!' "

# HANNAH'S DREAM

## A NOVEL

### DIANE HAMMOND

# 1

SAMSON Brown loved exactly two things in this world: his wife and his elephant. He *nearly* loved lots of others, of course, and had loved dearly some who were now dead and gone—his folks; his twin brother, Jimmy; an old blue dog he'd had once—but real love, in the here-and-now, he reserved for Corinna and Hannah. He knew it, and he made sure they knew it, too. Loving that hard and exclusive didn't make up for the things he couldn't give them—and there were lots of things he couldn't give them—but it went a ways. To a man like Sam, a realistic man, that was something.

The hot-poker truth about the limitations of love was something they'd learned from the dead baby girl Corinna had delivered forty-three years ago, a perfect child with hands as small and tight as fiddle-heads. The grief had nearly killed them, grief as solid and mean and unyielding as an anvil that they'd carried with them everywhere until they were shaking from the weight of it and had no choice but to put it down. The doctor had told them there was nothing they could have done to bring their baby out alive; things like that just happened, he said, and sometimes no one knew why. Whatever the reason, the loss of that baby had changed them forever, especially Corinna, a woman who'd wanted only three things out of life: Sam, a child to raise, and a reasonably good relationship with the Lord. She'd gotten Sam all these years. Her relationship with the Lord was another thing.

Still, at sixty-five Corinna was solid as an old tree, someone you could get a purchase on even in a high wind. Many a time she'd kept him going, this big, beautiful brown woman with skin like milk chocolate who always had time when people came to talk or asked her thoughts about something. And Lord God, but Corinna did have her thoughts. *I've got opinions I'll give away for free to anybody who wants them,* she was fond of saying. *Sam's already heard them all, and God stopped listening a long time ago.* And she'd laugh a laugh that was like warm syrup pouring from a jug.

SAM turned at the corner of Powers and Luke Street and then into the Dunkin' Donuts drive-through.

"Hey," he greeted Rayette at the window.

"Hey, sugar," she said. Rayette was a nice-looking young woman who wore her hair in a million tiny braids Corinna did for her once a month. "You want Bavarian cream today? They just came out."

"Nah. She doesn't like them as much as she used to. How about two custards and a jelly?"

"Sure thing, hon." Rayette ducked inside.

She'd been selling him donuts for years. When she fetched up at the window again, holding his bag of donuts and some coffee, he asked her, "How long have you been doing Dunkin' Donuts? Ten years, maybe?"

"More like fourteen, honey. Where've you been?" Rayette frowned. "We're getting old."

"Don't I know it," Sam said, shaking his head. Rayette passed him the donut bag and a cup of coffee hot enough to scald a rhino. Sam breathed in the scent of donuts. He'd had to give them up a year ago, when he was diagnosed with the diabetes.

"Corinna said you were thinking about retirement again," Rayette said, leaning out the drive-through window on her elbows.

"When the time's right for Hannah, I'll go."

Rayette just shook her head. "She'd get over it, honey. God makes His creatures strong. I swear, the things you've done for her all these years."

"Yeah. Well, I got to go," Sam said. He would brook no negative comments about Hannah, never had. "I'll see you."

"I guess you will," Rayette said.

Sam steered his old Dodge Dart back into morning traffic, making sure the coffee and the bag of donuts were secure. He was a careful man, and it paid off. At sixty-eight, even by his own lights, he looked damned good. He stood upright and proud, no gut whatsoever, not even a little one people would have forgiven him for, at his age. A little snowfall on the top of his head, just a light dusting. Seeing him from the back, you might think he was twenty, but when he turned around, his face gave him away. It was deeply lined, like a road map starting someplace far away—Cincinnati, maybe, where he was born; or Yakima, Washington, where his daddy had had a truck farm; then Korea, where Sam had served in the war; and ending right here in Bladenham, Washington.

He drove the last mile to the Max L. Biedelman Zoo fighting a powerful urge to take a bite of one of the donuts. He wasn't a drinking man or a smoker, never had been, but he did miss his Dunkin' Donuts.

IN THE PACIFIC NORTHWEST, eccentrics are as thick as fleas, but even so, Max L. Biedelman had stood apart. For starters, Max was a woman—Maxine Leona Biedelman, born in 1873 in Seattle, Washington, the only living offspring of timber magnate Arthur Biedelman and his wife, Ruby. Both Ruby and Arthur came from solid, respectable San Francisco families, a fact about which Arthur didn't care a fig but Ruby clung to like a life raft. By the time Max was born, Arthur had already made his fortune, and he spent his time indulging his lust for travel. The child was just six when he took her and Ruby on the first of many extended safaris in Kenya. Ruby, a fainthearted woman at best, would later claim that her prized auburn hair turned white within a week of their arrival in Africa, fearful as she was of everything that moved and much that didn't—rhinos, camp cooking, bugs, Mount Kilimanjaro, Masai men, thunder, and every fresh food either bought or gathered. It was undeniable that her nerves were in a terrible state by the end of the trip. She took to her bed the moment they returned home and stayed there for the next nineteen years, although Max would always maintain that her mother sprang out of bed with a full social calendar the minute she and Arthur embarked on their next trip.

Max herself was made of sterner stuff. She loved being on safari and showed no fear. When she was fourteen, she and Arthur traveled to Burma and made the acquaintance of elephant keepers—mahouts—who had earned their living for generations cutting teak in the Burmese forests. Max was so taken with what they'd seen that she made the elephant her personal totem and would return to Burma many times in later years, always staying among the mahouts and their animals.

Her father's untimely death of fever in 1898, and Ruby's subsequent return to her family in San Francisco, left Max, at twenty-five, in possession of a sizable inheritance that included Havenside, her parents' three-hundred-acre estate in the small agricultural town of Bladenham, Washington. Their land included rolling hills and woodlands that, in the summer, smelled like hay and apples. In the winter, when the wind turned, it carried in the saltwater smell of Puget Sound.

Arthur had designed the fifty-room Victorian mansion in the tradition of the great houses of Newport, Rhode Island. After his death, Max opened Havenside to the public once each year without fail. She stood at her wrought-iron gate and greeted each person individually, a strapping, long-legged, long-toothed, silver-haired woman, a committed cross-dresser who wore men's bush clothing and carried a shooting stick or riding crop wherever she went. The only exceptions were the flowing Turkish robes she sometimes donned on cool winter evenings. Her neighbors considered her quite dashing, if odd.

By the mid-1950s, she had turned nearly half of Havenside's grounds into yards and outbuildings for a growing collection of wild and exotic species. Conical thatched huts, small barns, and whimsical pavilions provided shelter for those animals in need of it. Max's most prized possessions were two female elephants from Burma, retired from their work in the teak forests and given to Max as gifts by her mahout friends. She talked about "my girls" at length and brought them baklava every afternoon at teatime.

In 1953, the first of her beloved elephants succumbed to old age, and to replace her, Max purchased Hannah, a small, two-year-old female that had been partially blinded. At eighty years old, Max had already begun negotiations with Bladenham's city council to turn her entire property and animal collection over to the city upon her death, with the understanding that her animals would never want for anything.

At the time, it had been a promise sincerely made.

IN THE fall of 1995, the elephant barn was a shabby place despite a fresh interior coat of yellow paint. A lack of insulation made the damp a perpetual intruder, and the high ceiling and soaring hayloft gave the place a hollow feel. It was also outfitted with a small kitchen; a tiny office; an open space furnished like a living room with a couple of inexpensive armchairs and a big-screen television; and

Hannah's confinement area at the back. "Hey, baby girl," Sam said softly when he reached the back of the barn. "How's my sugar?"

Hannah lifted her trunk and rumbled a greeting, the same greeting she'd given him almost every day for the last forty-one years.

"How was your night? You hear that thunderstorm come through? Mama nearly jumped out of bed it scared her so bad. Here, look what Papa brought you."

Sam took the donuts from the Dunkin' Donuts bag and lined them up lovingly on the windowsill. Hannah investigated each one, inhaling delicately, exhaling small puffs of powdered sugar. "Go ahead, sugar. They're those custards you like. Plus a strawberry jelly. I swear, it was all I could do to keep my fingers out of that bag. I'd have done it, too, if I didn't think Mama would catch me." Sam chuckled. "But she always does. When the Lord made that woman, he must have given her supernatural powers."

While Hannah ate her donuts, Sam eased down beside her left front foot and unhooked the heavy chain from its shackle. The anklet had worn away the skin underneath, and sometimes there were open sores. Not today.

"Let Papa have a look at that foot, sugar." Hannah lifted her foot. Max Biedelman had told him an elephant's toenails should be smooth and the cuticle soft and close-fitting, but two of Hannah's bulged, foul-smelling from sores underneath; another had a split that Sam had been watching for signs of trouble. His girl had started getting arthritic ten years ago or more, from never having anything soft to stand on, and the more arthritic she got, the more she walked funny, and the funnier she walked, the more unevenly she wore down her foot pads, which put uneven pressure on her toenails, which busted. Sam spent so much time caring for Hannah's feet that he told Corinna sometimes he might hire himself out as a pedicurist at the Beauty Spot, Corinna's beauty salon.

Now he dug in his pocket and pulled out a small plastic jar of salve. "Let's try this, sugar." Sam had a bad foot, too, with a diabetic ulcer along one side of his heel, so Corinna was always whipping up some new healing concoction in the kitchen. If it yielded any improvement, Sam would bring it in the next day and slather some on Hannah's poor feet. Sam used a tongue depressor like a paddle to apply the ointment. Hannah flinched but stayed put, like she always did. It nearly broke his heart. He patted her on the shoulder.

"Okay, shug, that's done—you can put your foot down. You ready to go outside on this fine sunny day?" It was early September, when Bladenham smelled of apple orchards and harvested fields. "You bringing your tire with you?" Hannah picked up an old, bald car tire she liked to keep nearby, especially when she was alone. Corinna said it was no different than those shreds of baby blankets that some kids kept with them for comfort, and Sam guessed she was right. He watched Hannah amble outside, blinking in the sudden sunshine after the barn's dim interior, before he climbed up into the hayloft and pitchforked some fresh hay down into the yard. Hannah shambled over, propping her tire against the barn wall in the exact same spot she always did, and began to eat. He loved to watch the way she pinched up a switch of hay with her trunk, tucked it inside her mouth, and chewed as slow and deliberate as if her thoughts were a million miles away. In Burma maybe, in those teak forests Max Biedelman had used to tell him about.

MAX Biedelman had hired him after he came home from Korea in 1955, a black veteran with nothing to show for his service time except a wicked case of shingles and an aversion to mess hall food. His first job was as a groundskeeper, which he thought of as temporary, not being overly fond of mowing grass and raking dead leaves. He'd been hired by a foreman, and though he knew Max Biedelman by reputation, he didn't meet her until he'd been on the job for six days. He'd been in the orchard pruning apple trees when he heard her call to him. She strode toward him in a tweed hat, houndstooth jacket, and high leather boots.

"Mr. Brown," she said, approaching with her hand outstretched, "I don't believe we've had the pleasure. I'm Max Biedelman."

Dumbstruck, Sam grasped the old woman's hand and found it as dry and light as an old corn husk.

"I understand you've been working here for several days already. Please accept my apology for not having greeted you sooner. I've been unwell."

"Yes, ma'am."

She frowned. "Please don't call me ma'am, Mr. Brown. I answer to Max or to Miss Biedelman."

"Yes, ma'am," Sam said before he'd thought it through, but the old woman only chuckled and patted his arm. "Never mind," she said. "I make you nervous. I seem to have that effect on people." She started to walk away but then turned back, calling to him, "If you feel very strongly about your manners, Mr. Brown, you may call me sir."

Havenside's second old elephant, Reyna, died less than a year later. Sam heard that Max Biedelman stayed with the elephant until she quietly slipped away with her trunk in the old woman's lap. Sam kept a lookout for her for two days, until he finally saw her walking in the farthest part of the property, where wildflowers grew.

He approached her with his heart beating hard. "Me and my wife, we want to extend our condolences, sir," he said.

She managed a smile. "Thank you, Mr. Brown. It has been difficult. Do you have a moment—yes? Then walk with me."

Sam fell into step beside her. She matched him stride for stride. "I understand that you and your wife lost a child."

"Yes, sir."

"Then you know how hard it is to part with a loved one."

"Yes, sir, I do."

She looked at him closely, as though she were trying to decide something. "You were a farm boy, weren't you, Mr. Brown?"

"Yes, sir. My daddy raised vegetables for the family, grew hops, wheat, and alfalfa to sell. Had a few milk cows, goats, a couple of sheep." Sam wiped his palms on his pants.

"Tell me what you think of my Hannah, Mr. Brown."

"Hannah?"

"Hannah is my elephant. My last elephant. Unless I'm mistaken, you often watch her during your breaks and at lunchtime. I thought you might have some observations."

Sam was sweating freely, trying to figure out where she was headed with this conversation. "I've never seen anything like her before," he ventured.

"Well, let me tell you about her, then. Hannah's actually quite small for her age, probably from malnutrition when she was still in Burma. Life in the wild is not always bountiful, Mr. Brown. In 1952, she was found on a rubber plantation near her mother, who had been shot and killed for trespassing. Hannah was probably just two years old at the time, and she'd been wounded, but she was lucky. The plantation worker who found her had a brother who was a mahout— an elephant keeper. The brother saw that Hannah would be useless for work because of her partial blindness, but he also realized that simply releasing her would be a death sentence, so he agreed to take the elephant and care for her until a buyer could be found. I was well-known to the mahouts by then, and they contacted me and asked if I'd like her—as of course I did. It's quite a story, isn't it?"

"Yes, sir."

"Hannah is quite healthy now, Mr. Brown, and she has a long future. She may be sixty years old before she dies. But there are no other elephants here, and in all likelihood there never will be again." The old woman stopped walking and turned to face him. "I'm going to ask you to do something, Mr. Brown. I'd like you to be Hannah's keeper."

"Keeper?"

"I'd like you to take care of her from now on."

"Isn't there somebody already doing that, sir?"

"Not someone I trust, Mr. Brown, and trust is very important to me. Please understand that you'll be well paid for your work."

Sam was struck dumb. This old woman was asking him to take responsibility for an animal the likes of which he had never even seen, except in pictures, until he came to Havenside. And yet, when he watched Hannah, he felt he was in the presence of a sharp mind and a gentle heart. Before he had a chance to change his mind, he said, "I believe I could do that, sir, but who's going to teach me how?"

Max Biedelman clapped him on the back and crowed, "Hannah, Mr. Brown! Hannah will teach you."

And so she had.

IN THE little kitchen in the barn, Sam quartered apples, sundered yams, halved bananas and carrots and melons. Corinna used to tease him about being Hannah's personal chef, and damned if it wasn't true. He didn't mind, though. Hannah's food meant a lot to her.

Now, he strapped around his waist a canvas pouch filled with fruit, and went out into the elephant yard. "You want to go for a walk, baby girl?" he asked her as she reached for the pouch with her trunk.

Sam imagined the Lord must have been in an odd frame of mind the day He created the Asian elephant. When he first met her, Hannah had reminded him of nothing so much as a worn-out, hip-shot, low-slung, dog-ugly, poorly dressed old floozy in bad shoes. And what about that tail, scrawny thing with a little hairy fly whisk on the end; looked like something picked up late on the last day of a church sale. And yet there was a soul, a thing of pure beauty, behind those eyes. Samson Brown saw it shining there every day.

"Come on, sugar," he said, handing Hannah half a banana as she went through the gate leading out of the elephant yard and into the visitor area. She wore no harness or restraint of any kind, and she never had. Sam carried an elephant hook, a short stick with a blunt metal hook on the end, that had once belonged to Max Biedelman. He brought it along more out of habit than anything else. Hannah was like a big, placid dog padding along beside him on her poor feet. They walked at least once a day when the weather was fine and often when it wasn't, because Sam thought it did her good to walk on grass or even the asphalt paths when she could—anything softer than concrete. And it gave her a change of scene.

Surprised zoo visitors cut wide paths around them as they walked up the hill past the rhino, around the tapirs, and past the monkeys and the marmosets, before heading back down to the elephant barn, which was nestled in a small depression at the bottom of the hill. Sam stayed on Hannah's right side—her seeing side—so she'd know that he was there, watching out for her. She might be big, but she was timid even after all these years.

He heard someone call, "How come you're walking that elephant, mister?" A boy appeared at his elbow, a small but good-looking kid about eleven years old.

"How come you're walking around the zoo?" Sam asked.

The boy shrugged, falling into step beside Sam. "To see stuff."

"Guess you answered your own question, then," Sam said. He handed Hannah a yam. "What's your name?" he asked the boy.

"Reginald."

"Reginald. That's a pretty big name for a small fry."

"I'm not small," the boy said, puffing up a little.

"Your daddy a big man?" Sam asked him.

"He's big." The boy's eyes got shifty: no daddy.

"You got any questions about Hannah you want to ask me?"

The boy looked around Sam at Hannah chewing placidly on a cantaloupe half. "How come her chin's all wobbly?" the boy asked.

"That's not her chin; it's her lip," Sam said, slipping Hannah a couple of apple quarters. "She can make that lip work just like a funnel. You ever seen someone pour oil into a car engine using a funnel? Same thing—she doesn't lose any food or drink that way. You grow up in a hot jungle, you don't want to miss even a drop of that cool stream."

"Give her one of those cantaloupes," Reginald said.

"You want to give it to her?"

"Yeah, I'll give it to her," the boy said, voice shaking a little.

Sam put a cantaloupe half in Reginald's hand. "Come closer to her, now, but move slow. Girl doesn't like being startled."

The boy went to stand behind Sam.

"Go on, now," he said. "You've got to hold it out to her, or she won't know to take it. Shug's real polite that way."

Reginald held the melon out to her, and Hannah picked it off the boy's palm with great delicacy.

"You see that?" he crowed. "You see her take that right out of my hand? She likes me, I bet."

"Reginald!" A shrill female voice called out from behind them on the path. "Lord, boy, you scared me half to death wandering off like that."

"That your mama?" Sam asked.

"Nah, she's my aunt. I live with her."

"Where's your mama, son?"

The boy shrugged.

"All right, go on. Don't make her chase you, now."

Reginald started off, turned back. "I'll see you, mister."

"Yeah, I expect you will. Next time you come here, you ask for Sam Brown."

As he and Hannah moved on, Sam could hear the boy calling excitedly to his aunt, "Hey, I fed that elephant. I fed her right off my hand!"

Sam reached up and patted Hannah's shoulder. "You were real good with that boy, sugar. That was a nice thing you did for him."

## 2

THERE were many days when, if Max Biedelman was watching over her zoo from the hereafter, she'd be appalled. Most of the exquisite landscaping had been replaced by asphalt and concrete. Nocturnal animals like the slow lorises, difficult to see by daytime visitors, were no longer replaced when they died. One by one their areas were converted into snack or trinket kiosks. The zebra yard had been turned into a petting zoo of common goats, sheep, and a large, bad-tempered sow named Hilda. By 1995, what had once been one of the country's foremost private exotic animal collections had become a seedy third-rate zoo.

Harriet Saul had been hired five months earlier to change all that.

In middle age she was stocky, shrewd, and focused: Fifty-two years of plainness had tempered her like hand-forged steel. She knew by then that it was her lot to fall in love with institutions instead of men. Her previous love affairs had been with a regional science museum and a dairy cooperative. Now, when she closed her eyes at night, she dreamt about the Max L. Biedelman Zoo.

The zoo's offices were on the ground floor of Havenside, the old Biedelman mansion, long past its glory. After Max Biedelman's death, maintenance fell woefully behind. The second floor had been closed off, and what had once been a large library on the first floor was now divided into Harriet's office and a half-dozen cubicles.

This Monday morning, she yelled through her office doorway, "Has Geneva Wilson showed up yet?"

Truman Levy, her director of operations, sat in a cubicle no more than ten feet from her office door. He glanced up from his paperwork. "It's only five past eight," he said.

"Well, *I'm* here," she said. "You're here."

Truman took four steps to the doorway of Harriet's office and said, "It's her first day, and she doesn't know the area yet. She might have gotten caught in traffic or forgotten the way."

"I don't care," Harriet intoned. "I'm not pleased."

TRUMAN withdrew to the relative asylum of his cubicle, where he chewed his first antacid of the day, reflecting gloomily that it was the earliest he'd taken one yet, beating by ten minutes his previous record. Ever since he'd gone to work for Harriet Saul, he'd been buying Tums in bulk from Costco. There had been a time when he would have argued that appearances—especially appearances as unprepossessing as hers—shouldn't matter. Several years ago Truman's ex-wife Rhonda, a sculptor, had challenged that opinion. She'd said, *Let me tell you something, Truman. You know the only people who really believe appearances shouldn't matter? Ugly people.*

She'd been right, of course, about this and many other things. Last year, when she left him and their eleven-year-old son Winslow, she'd accused him of being the least memorable person she had ever known. *And it's not just me,* she'd said. *You're the least memorable person* anybody's *ever known.*

It was true. People sitting directly across a dinner table from him for an entire meal consistently failed to recognize him the next time they met. This had happened not just once, but time after time. He seemed simply to disappear from people's memories.

Rhonda had asked him once if he thought she was destined to accomplish great things, and he'd said probably not. He'd only meant that the statistical probabilities were against her, but she'd thrown an expensive dried flower arrangement at him and stalked out of the house; a prelude, as it turned out, to leaving them for good. Truman had appealed to her to stay, if only for Winslow's sake. The boy was then ten years old; he needed his mother. Rhonda had sighed, *He's your son, Truman. He takes after you. You'll know what to do with him.*

Winslow was, indeed, Truman's son. He could sit perfectly still for an hour or more, roaming the galaxy inside his own mind. He kept his room spotless, his socks neatly paired in his designated sock drawer and his closet organized by color. He'd driven Rhonda to frenzy. She used to scream at him, *You're a child! You're supposed to be messy!*

At no time since Rhonda had left them just over a year ago had Winslow commented on her absence except factually and in passing. He seemed perfectly satisfied with the way things were, and for that, as much as for anything else, Truman loved him fiercely.

Neva Wilson arrived at last, forty-two minutes late. She was slight and tensile, red-haired and freckled, with the thin, smart face of a fox. Truman winced as she stepped into the minefield that was Harriet's office.

"Am I late?" he heard Neva say.

Dead silence. Harriet would be looking pointedly at her watch.

"I'm sorry," he heard Neva say, clearing her throat. "I made a wrong turn, and by the time I figured it out, I was ten miles out of town."

"Well," Harriet said; and then, no doubt having made her point, her voice lightened beneficently. "When did you get to town? Are you all settled in?"

"Yesterday. And settling in is never a problem. Everything I own fits in my car."

Truman quietly approached Harriet's doorway with a stack of uniform shirts and paperwork. "Excuse me," he said. He handed the clothes and papers to Neva. "You can fill these out anytime today. Just leave them with me before five. You'll have a locker at the elephant barn. Shall I take you down there?"

"I can find my way."

"I don't mind." Truman ignored a disapproving look from Harriet. She was not beyond docking an employee fifteen minutes of pay, claiming she saw him or her malingering someplace on the grounds or in one of the outlying zookeeper workrooms.

"I'm sorry, but I don't think we've met," Neva said, holding out her hand once they'd emerged into the watery fall sunlight. Truman took it.

"I was on your interview panel," he said.

"God, I'm sorry." Neva clapped her hand to her forehead.

Truman smiled sadly. "It happens all the time."

"No, it's me. I do this. And here's the weird thing: I can remember the face of every animal I've ever worked with. But I never remember people. I think it's some kind of learning disability."

Truman smiled again as Neva gabbled a little at a passing peacock, a moth-eaten specimen fanning his ratty tail beside the path.

"So tell me about Harriet Saul," she said.

"Ah," Truman said. "She can be a bully, but her heart's in the right place. She was brought in by the city to turn the zoo around. We have some financial challenges."

"You've got a charismatic mega-vertebrate, though."

"I beg your pardon?"

"Charismatic mega-vertebrates," Neva repeated. "Whales, dolphins, elephants. They're the money animals. They're what people come to see. Of course, you've only got one, and she has some problems."

"Her feet, you mean."

"For starters." Neva looked at him and smiled. "You're probably thinking it's no big deal. But foot problems are one of the primary causes of death for a lot of elephants at older zoos like this one."

*"Death?"*

Neva nodded. "Mother Nature didn't take concrete into account when she designed the elephant. A three- or four-ton animal is going to break its feet down if there's nothing soft to stand on. And if you're kept indoors all night, which Hannah is, you're standing in a toilet, which leads to infections and blood poisoning. Which leads to death."

"Good God."

They completed the walk in silence. Truman thought that walking beside Neva Wilson was like walking beside a high-voltage electrical transformer. He could almost hear the hum, feel the heat.

Just as he pulled open the door to the elephant barn, the wall phone rang. He saw Harriet's extension flashing on the console, and picked up the receiver.

"You need to come back," she said.

"Yes, I was just ready to."

"She could have found her own way, Truman."

Truman sighed. It was only two minutes after nine, and it was Monday.

SAM was in the elephant yard, looking at Hannah's bad foot in the sunlight. Even through the ointment he'd slathered on, he could see that the foot was worse. "Okay, baby girl," he murmured, patting her foot down gently. "Guess Papa's going to have to find something different to try." He stood beside her, reaching up to stroke the back of her ear. She touched his face with her trunk, blowing lightly.

"Good morning." Neva Wilson came out of the barn and into the yard, wearing a zoo sweatshirt so new it still had fold marks.

"Morning, miss. I didn't hear you come in. Hey, baby girl," he said softly to Hannah. "Look who's here."

"Please don't call me miss," Neva said, flushing. "I hate formality."

"All right, miss."

Neva sighed. "Is that getting worse?" She nodded at Hannah's foot.

"Yeah, a little bit. Nothing new about it, though. Seems like she always has some foot problem. Shug's worse than an old woman with bunions."

Neva looked at the shattered nails and underlying abscesses. "What medication's she on for this?"

"Right now, nothing. We tried everything the zoo doc recommended, but it seemed like none of it made any difference. So me and Mama—that's my wife, Corinna—we've tried some homeopathic cures, you know? They haven't helped much this time, though."

"Homeopathic cures? Like what?"

"Well, Mama could tell you more about that than me, but let's see." Sam leaned against Hannah, thinking. The elephant wrapped her trunk around his head affectionately. "Right off the top of my head, there was witch hazel and ribwort, calendula, comfrey, and that's about all I can remember."

"Has the vet ever given her footbaths of peroxide, betadyne, and chlorhexidine?"

Sam frowned, raking his fingernails up and down Hannah's side. She made a low, contented rumble and put her trunk into the canvas treat bag Sam wore strapped around his waist, fetching up two chunks of apple and popping them in her mouth like candy. "Not those, miss, but we've tried Epsom salts," Sam said as he pushed her trunk away. "Warm water and salts a couple times a day. It didn't seem to do anything besides make her sleepy. By the time the ten minutes was done, why she'd be sawing logs." Sam chuckled gently. "Breaks my heart, seeing the girl in pain."

"Does she limp?"

"Not much. I believe she has a touch of rheumatism in the joints, though—she takes after me that way. Seems like she stands still more than she used to. Except for our walks, of course."

"You walk her?"

"Sure," Sam said. "It does her good, gives her a chance to see some things, stretch out a little, let her poor feet touch some grass. Plus you meet people. Yesterday we met a real nice boy, lives with an aunt. Too many kids out there are bringing themselves up these days. My folks never did have a lot, but there was plenty of love to go around. My mama used to say to us kids, *You help yourself to a hug whenever you want one, sugar. They're warm, and they're free.*"

Neva smiled. "So how does Hannah show pain?"

"She doesn't show it; she just comes right out and says it. She's a talky thing, talks all day long." His voice faded. "I love my girl, miss. Me and Hannah, we've been together forty-one years. Miss Biedelman trusted me to take good care of her, and I've done the best job I could. It's about time for me to be retiring, been time for a couple of years already, but I can't do it unless I know my baby's in good hands. You show me you've got those hands, and I'll do anything I can to make the rest easy on you."

Neva folded her arms and regarded him for a minute. "If you could give Hannah anything in the world, what would it be?"

"That's easy. I'd give her a good place to live and someone who'd never leave her."

"But she could easily live for another twenty years. No keeper's going to commit to being in one place that long."

"Didn't say anything about keepers, miss. I meant other elephants."

Neva sighed. "Well, given what I know about this zoo, that would take a miracle."

"I dream about it sometimes," Sam said before he could think better of it.

"Sure. We all dream about having more money and better living conditions for our animals."

Sam nodded, but it wasn't what he'd meant.

UNLIKE any of the dozens of backup keepers Sam Brown had been given over the years, Neva Wilson had not washed up on the unpromising shores of the Max L. Biedelman Zoo because of diminished circumstances. She had worked at some of the best zoos in the country and trained under some of the finest senior elephant keepers in the world. But lately she'd begun to believe that she needed something more; some sort of purpose. She'd decided that she would become an elephant-care ambassador, bringing what she knew to one of the country's many mediocre, backwater, needy facilities. When the Max L. Biedelman Zoo had advertised for an elephant keeper, Neva had never heard of the place. A week later her interview with Harriet Saul and the zoo's top management convinced her that the zoo's leadership was clueless, arrogant, misguided, and blind. It sounded perfect. When she was offered the job at a salary that was not quite half what she had been earning, she accepted on the spot.

At the end of her first day, she pulled into her driveway and climbed out of the beat-up tin can that was her current car. Instead of an apartment, she'd rented a detached, converted garage in Bladenham's historic neighborhood. It was just her kind of place: carpeting laid directly over the concrete slab, tiny kitchenette, tinier bathroom, dirt-cheap rent. She pulled into the driveway just as her landlord, Johnson Johnson, came out the back door of his house and approached her across the narrow lawn that separated her apartment from his house, a 1920s craftsman bungalow with a deep front porch and leaded windows. He was in his late thirties, tall, balding, and impossibly thin, with a sweet, vague air about him.

He lifted his hand uncertainly and said, "Hi."

Neva pulled a stack of Biedelman Zoo uniform shirts out of her car.

"You work at the zoo?"

"My first day."

"I like the zoo. They have animals."

She waited for more, but evidently he was done. "Well," she said, "what is it that you do?"

Johnson Johnson looked at his feet. "I make things."

"What kinds of things?"

He shrugged.

She was beginning to run out of patience, which had never

been a strong quality of hers. "Is your real name Johnson Johnson?"

"Yes."

"I can't imagine anybody actually naming a baby Johnson Johnson." She kicked her car door shut with her foot.

Johnson Johnson flushed with pride.

"Okay," Neva explained. "I have to go in now."

"Oh."

And so she did. As she took the key from the lock and closed her door, she could still see Johnson Johnson standing in place, his hand finally lifted in farewell.

The interior of her tiny house was cheerful, with bright yellow doors, orange walls, and fiery red baseboards. Somebody in its past had had color-courage. She put her things away and dumped canned chicken noodle soup into a pot, encouraging the front burner of her little Pullman stove to choose life. Chances were excellent that she would stand right there and eat it directly from the pot once it was heated. For years she had resisted her mother's efforts to teach her to cook. *You can only eat tuna casserole so many times, Neva. Sooner or later the body will rebel.*

In the end it hadn't been the body but Neva's ex-husband Howard who had rebelled, not against her tuna casserole but Neva's refusal to choose a different career path. He'd wanted to know how she could be passionate about jobs that listed shoveling manure as one of their major duties.

As she ate her soup, Neva thought about Samson Brown. She'd never met a keeper with so little training. He knew nothing about operant conditioning or environmental enrichment, or any of the other cornerstones of modern animal husbandry. Still, his work with Hannah showed flawless instincts. By taking her for walks, he gave her feet some relief from the unyielding concrete in her barn. It also gave her a change of scene, a relief from the sameness of her exhibit. Her diet was good, and her attitude seemed positive, even in light of the poverty of her surroundings and her nearly lifelong isolation from other elephants.

And Hannah's feet weren't nearly as bad as some she'd seen.

Maybe there was something to Sam's wife's homeopathic remedies. They had certainly done the animal no harm.

"TRUMAN, come here for a minute," Harriet called from her office as Truman tried to slip past her door to go home. He stopped with a sigh: She seemed to take a perverse pleasure in preventing him from leaving on time. Nevertheless, he stepped into her office and shut the door partway, raising his eyebrows at Harriet: *Close it?* She nodded, and he pulled it to. Outside the door, Brenda, the receptionist, would be all ears.

He stood in front of Harriet's desk, or in front of what he assumed was Harriet's desk if only he could see it beneath the mounds of paper. The office was squalid with half-filled coffee mugs and partially eaten nachos teetering dangerously atop shifting dunes of paper. Mess notwithstanding, she seemed to know the exact location and content of every single memo, report, spreadsheet, and phone message, right down to the bare wood.

Harriet nodded toward a visitor's chair that was relatively clear of debris. "I've been looking at this," she said, holding out a financial statement he had prepared for her earlier in the day. "Are you sure about the numbers?"

"Very sure," he said. "A number of school groups cancelled last month."

"Do we know why?"

"Evidently the Pumpkin Patch had a corn maze."

"We're losing business to a *farm stand?*"

"Apparently so."

In disgust, Harriet tossed the sheet of paper on top of a half-eaten grilled cheese sandwich.

"Look," Truman said. "I'd like to ask my father to review the old city files pertaining to the zoo." Matthew Levy was a retired federal court judge and lifelong Bladenham resident. "Maybe there's money we're entitled to that no one remembers anymore. Special funds of some kind, or maybe a small endowment. It's a long-shot, but I think it's worth looking into."

"Well, I can't pay him," Harriet said.

"No, that's just fine."

"Tell him to go ahead, then."

Truman stood up. "I'm sorry, Harriet, but I've got to go pick up Winslow from his piano lesson. You're leaving soon, too, I hope?"

"Eventually," she said, already mining her desk for a buried document. She didn't seem to have much of a home life. He gathered that she lived alone and kept birds—finches, as he remembered.

Winslow was in the front window of his piano teacher's house, watching for him. Truman could see the boy's pale moon face, framed by curtains, sweeten with relief as he saw Truman's car pull into the driveway.

"Hey," Truman greeted the boy as Winslow climbed into the car. "How was Mrs. Leahey? How was the lesson?"

"It was okay. She gave me a new piece."

"Still Mozart?"

"Yeah." Winslow nodded. "It's hard."

"Well, she warned us," Truman said.

Shortly after Rhonda left them, Mrs. Leahey had called him at work and said, *He's very musical, Mr. Levy. With your permission, I'd like to push him, see what he's capable of.* Truman had agreed, of course, and on the wings of Mozart, Winslow had risen and soared. The boy might have the demeanor of an accountant, but he had an artist's soul. Truman often sat just outside the den while he practiced, listening. In Winslow's playing, the boy was all brilliant hues and soft, rich shadows. Truman wondered sometimes whether, if the two of them had been outwardly vivid people, Rhonda would have stayed with them. But he was not a colorful man. Winslow was not a colorful boy. Their riches were subterranean.

Once home, Truman sent Winslow upstairs to begin his homework while he thawed a Tupperware container full of spaghetti sauce he'd prepared over the weekend. His freezer was neatly stocked with chili, stew, chicken tetrazzini, beef stroganoff, all meticulously labeled and dated. He liked to cook and got a quiet satisfaction from maintaining order and readiness in the household. If he had been a caveman, he would have been the one awake late into the night, taking inventory of the spear-points and stone axes.

*Order is for mediocre minds, Truman,* Rhonda had often told him. She mocked the way Truman and Winslow arranged the books alphabetically, stored CDs by musical genre and composer. Rhonda was not an easy woman to survive.

When the pasta was ready, Truman called Winslow, and while they ate in companionable silence, Winslow patted his foot on an imaginary piano pedal, keeping time to some piece of music shining in his head.

THAT night, for Sam, was a dream night. As always, he found himself in a meadow full of high grass and rolling hills, with a pond deep enough for an elephant to belly down in. It smelled like summer. Like always, he found himself there with a joyful heart. Not that he was himself. No, he moved in a herky-jerky sort of way, so that even when he was going forward, he was also swaying from side to side. It was like being on a hayride, way up high, but there was no hay, no wagon. When he looked down, he saw perfect feet, healthy feet. Elephant feet.

And as always, he ambled around the dream-meadow smelling everything, feeling the warm sun on his head and the cool earth underfoot. When he was done, he wallowed in the pond, pinching up gobs of good thick mud that he flung over every part of himself. And then he heard a trumpeting, a rumbling, the low thrumming of elephants; first one, then a second and a third. As they ran toward him, he could feel the very ground shake. His heart filled to nearly overflowing, every beat sending out a prayer of thanks.

Next morning, like all the mornings after the dreams, he felt the way he always did after a sickness, heavy and slow and filled with the unyielding knowledge of all the things he couldn't do, couldn't give; knowing, too, that he would go back to the zoo to find his sugar chained to the wall in her little barn at the zoo, waiting patiently for him to come back to her one more day. It was on those mornings, not being able to bear showing up empty-handed, that he brought his baby donuts.

## 3

WHEN Sam arrived at work the next day, he saw that Neva Wilson had gotten there before him. She waved gaily from the elephant yard as he pulled in. He didn't see his baby, though. Hurrying into the barn, he found her still standing in her overnight mess and shackled to the wall, rocking back and forth in great agitation. And her tire was gone.

He laid hands on, murmured quietly, "Hey, sugar. How's Papa's girl this fine morning?" He leaned down and unclipped the heavy chain from her shackle as she continued to rock beside him, swaying back and forth rhythmically like some kind of broken thing. The skin under the metal anklet was rubbed raw again after a month of healing. Sam was steaming. "What in hell was that woman thinking, leaving you chained up in here when she's out there all sunny and smiling like some damn Florida orange juice commercial?"

"Good morning!" Neva sang from the door leading out to the yard.

"No, it's not," Sam snapped. "What in the name of God were you thinking, miss, leaving Hannah in here in her own filth? The girl's been in here all by herself since six o'clock last night."

Neva winked at him. *Winked.* "Can you keep her busy for about five more minutes? I'm just about ready."

And damned if she didn't sail out to the yard again, leaving Sam muttering things it was good that no one but Hannah could hear. He forked down a flake of hay from the loft and was about to start getting the day's fruits and vegetables ready when Neva called from out in the yard. "Okay. Go ahead and bring her out!"

"C'mon, sugar. Let's get you out of this mess and into some fresh air," Sam said to Hannah, clucking a little to encourage her. They both blinked as they stepped into sunshine as powerful as a search-light after the fetid gloom of the barn.

Neva was solidly planted next to the door with her arms folded across her chest, grinning like a fool. She put a finger to her lips to shush him. He was about to let his words fly when she motioned for him to turn around quick. When he did, he stopped dead in his tracks.

Hannah was rushing around the yard. Bewildered, he looked at Neva, who just smiled and said in a low voice, "Watch. Just watch! She's already figured it out. She's a smart girl, your elephant."

So Sam watched as Hannah lumbered over to one of the trees and found her tire in the highest notch in the branches. She ran her trunk around the outside of it, and then around the inside—with-drawing a banana, which she neatly ate. Then she went back to the outside of the tire again, working on something Sam couldn't see.

"Peanut butter," Neva said, clapping her hands. "She's found the peanut butter. Wait until she starts finding the pumpkins. There are eleven of them, and I filled them all with raisins and jelly beans."

"A scavenger hunt," Sam said in wonder.

Neva grinned. "It's one of my all-time favorite things. The ani-mals light up just like it's Christmas."

Hannah was hustling around pulling bananas from branches, a pumpkin from inside a hollow log, squashes from the little wallow Sam kept for her. "What time did you get here to do all of this?"

Neva shrugged. "Six, six-thirty."

"Lord. Guess I owe you an apology, miss."

"No you don't," Neva said. "How could you have known?"

BY NOON Hannah was dozing peacefully in the sun, sated with treats and happiness and hay. Neva hoisted herself onto a counter in the tiny office inside the elephant barn. It was a small room, more like a glorified closet, and it was furnished with a rickety old desk and a rolling wooden chair that tilted dangerously to the right.

She'd had furniture just like it for years—had it and abandoned it in four cities and three states. Howard had laid claim to most of their good things when they split—the washstand with the Delft tile backsplash, a rocking chair with beautiful acanthus-leaf arms. Neva's mother had been appalled, but as far as Neva was concerned, Howard had been welcome to it all.

She unwrapped a Milky Way bar. "Want some?" She held out the candy to Sam. "I can split it."

"Can't, miss—diabetes. Found out last year. It's a damned shame, too. I sure do miss my sweets. Me and Hannah, we could go through a bag of Hershey's Kisses in a day. Baby Ruths, too. And Paydays." Sam's eyes took on a dreamy, faraway look. "I haven't seen Hannah playful like this morning in an awful long time, kittenish that way."

Neva smiled.

"But she gets real upset if somebody gets here in the morning and they don't unchain her. She starts rocking, and once she's rocking, it's hard to get her to stop. She can keep it up for days. When she does, that metal anklet of hers just digs up her leg something awful. Took three months to heal, last time."

"Has she always done that?"

"Long as I've known her. When she first came over from Burma, I guess the only thing that calmed her down was old Reyna, the elephant Hannah was supposed to keep company. Course, Hannah was nothing but a little tiny thing then. Reyna was a big old cow, and she'd stand right up against Hannah, not enough room between them for a flea to pass. Guess it made Hannah feel secure, having old Reyna plastered on her like that. She quit rocking after a while. It was awful bad for her when old Reyna died. Shug didn't stop rocking for two weeks."

Neva sighed. "How does Hannah do when you go away for a few days? Is there anyone else she trusts?"

"Hasn't been anyone who stuck around long enough for her to get to know. Anyway, I don't take much time off. Longest time was when I was in the hospital last year. That's when we found out about the diabetes. It took me nearly a month to get back on my feet. Sometime in through there, somebody left shug chained up in the barn for three days straight. Like I was saying, she gets real spooked now being in that barn too long, especially when someone besides me comes around and doesn't unchain her."

"And that's why she was rocking this morning?" Neva said.

"Uh-huh."

"*Damn* it."

"Next time you want to do some game, just let me know ahead of time, and I'll come in early and keep Hannah company."

"You're very good to her," Neva said.

"Well," said Sam, "I had a good teacher."

"Miss Biedelman? So who was *Mr.* Biedelman?"

Sam grinned. "Wasn't one. Maxine Leona Biedelman's the whole name, except she never used the Leona part except as an initial. It sure made her mad when someone called her Maxine. *Real* mad. She was a fine old lady."

"Haven't you ever wanted to work with other elephants besides Hannah?"

"Nah. Miss Biedelman asked me to take care of Hannah for her, and that's what I've done."

"But don't you want variety? Don't you want to see what's out there beyond the zoo?"

"I did that, miss. Before you were born, I was in Korea. I saw that. Don't need to see any more."

Neva touched him on the shoulder lightly. "You're a very good man," she said, and she meant it. This morning she had been arrogant enough to plan on teaching him all she knew about elephant care. Now she understood that it wasn't going to be like that at all.

FOR Winslow's eleventh birthday, Truman Levy had agreed to get him a pig. He hadn't been able to come up with a credible reason to say no, so he'd said yes, despite the fact that he knew nothing about pigs in general or potbellied miniature pigs in particular; and despite the certainty that he would come to regret this decision in ways he couldn't even begin to imagine.

Sunday afternoon, in a light drizzle, he and Winslow had driven to a run-down farm, squished through the muck, and surveyed the squealing piglets. Truman paid one hundred and twenty-five dollars in crisp new bills, and they became the owners of a twelve-pound potbellied piglet named Miles. Miles was black and white, had tiny, wicked black eyes and a nose like a tin can hit head-on by a truck. His coat felt like something between human whiskers and tooth-brush bristles, and he rode home beside Winslow in a cat carrier.

On the boy's other side was nearly a hundred and fifty dollars' worth of essential pig-nursery items. These included a sack of feed, a hoof trimmer, an untippable food dish and water bowl, a dog bed with fleecy liner, a collar and harness, a litter box, rubber balls in an assortment of sizes, rawhide chew treats, a selection of stuffed toys, and a book called *Miniature Pigs and You: A New Owner's Guide to Love and Happiness.*

Yesterday they had created a pen with wire fencing that would be Miles's outdoor domain, reached from the den through a dog door. Now, while Winslow kept the piglet busy out back, Truman closely consulted the *Guide to Love and Happiness* and arranged a cozy living space for Miles in the den. He artfully strewed old towels around for Miles to root through, this evidently being a pig behavior as elemental as eating. If the pig was allowed to become bored, Truman read, he could be expected to tear up carpeting, eat drywall and baseboards, tip over and root through potted plants, and generally destroy any luckless object upon which he chose to lavish his attention. And, the book made clear, it would be the owner's fault for his lack of imagination in keeping the pig's superior intellect more productively engaged.

Filled with dread, Truman opened the sliding glass door into the backyard and summoned Winslow and Miles. The boy came in first, followed closely by the pig, which emitted a steady stream of old-mannish grunts and snorts.

"I think he likes me," Winslow said.

The pig approached a pile of towels, buried his nose, and began sorting through and rearranging them.

"What's he doing?" Winslow said.

"Rooting. Either rooting or wallowing." Truman thumbed through the guide. "Yes. This would be rooting."

"Why?"

Truman sighed deeply. "Because he's a pig. We can't always expect to understand these things, Winslow."

"So what's wallowing?"

"Technically, rolling in mud and filth. According to this, though, an indoor pig will be satisfied wallowing in blankets and towels."

"Maybe we should have gotten a dog," Winslow said.

"Let's give him time, Winnie. Let's just give him some time."

HARRIET Saul had recently commissioned a marketing study that would help her revitalize the zoo. She intended to double attendance and triple income within the next two years. It was ambitious, but Harriet had turned far less promising organizations around. At least the zoo had animals, and animals brought people.

Sitting at her desk on Sunday morning, she reviewed the marketing firm's preliminary report. It told her what she had already assumed: Hannah was by far the zoo's biggest draw. Parents brought their children to the zoo, but children brought their parents to see Hannah. An incredible one out of every three children under the age of twelve in the greater Bladenham area had visited Hannah, and hers was the only animal's name the majority could remember. Twenty-eight percent of all monetary donations to the Biedelman Zoo were made directly or indirectly to Hannah. The elephant *was* the Max L. Biedelman Zoo.

Harriet intended to put Hannah's picture on billboards, mugs, hats, T-shirts, posters, balloons—the works. She intended to make Hannah the most famous elephant on the West Coast. She'd already selected a Seattle ad agency that she would ask to execute an ad campaign pro bono.

Closing the report summary, she pulled on a baggy Biedelman Zoo cardigan and left the office—a walk would do her good. It was a glorious October day. Harriet had always seen the waning days of autumn as times of hope and renewal. School was back in session, and winter clothes hid her hefty figure. Her Aunt Maude, with whom Harriet had lived from her ninth birthday until she was eighteen, used to tell her to cover up, for God's sake, as though the dumpy figure she'd inherited from her father's side of the family were her fault. Harriet would often hear Maude looking through wastebaskets for wrappers that would prove Harriet was sneaking candy bars—which she was, although Maude never caught her because Harriet put the wrappers between the pages of her textbooks and threw them out at school.

Maude had made no secret of her displeasure at being stuck with Harriet after her mother, Maude's sister, died of a brain aneurysm. She disliked children, especially large, messy girls. As a senior in high school, Harriet had saved her money for months to have a beauty makeover at Nordstrom's. At the end of the hour, Harriet had spent one hundred and thirty-two dollars on a pore minimizer, six complementary shades of eye shadow, and two complementary lipsticks. When she got home, Maude's single comment was, *Dear God. I assume you intend to demand your money back.*

Now, as Harriet walked down the path past the elephant barn, en route to the employee parking lot, she saw the new girl, Neva Wilson, out shoveling a thick layer of sand onto the concrete pad of the elephant yard. When she looked up, Harriet lifted her hand in greeting and called, "How's our elephant this morning?"

"Actually, the abscess is a little better," Neva called back. "Plus this sand should give her a softer substrate."

"Excellent! Anything to keep our star happy!"

"How about another elephant?"

Harriet pretended Neva had said something amusing and walked on. The girl was far too intense for Harriet's taste. Neva had come with an excellent background and the most glowing references, but Harriet was still reserving final judgment. If Geneva Wilson turned out to be a drinker or drug abuser, Harriet wouldn't hesitate to let her go. She'd already explained this to Truman, who seemed unnecessarily attentive to her—and on zoo time. Harriet was paying her people a fair living wage, and she expected them to earn it. They could socialize on their own time.

Back in her office, Harriet stood at her window, pink-cheeked and too full of energy to settle down. On a sudden impulse, she grabbed her bundle of keys, including the heavy old skeleton key that supposedly unlocked any door in the house, and headed up the grand staircase to the second floor. She'd been saving this exploration for just the right day.

The first three rooms seemed to be bedrooms, but a fourth door led into a room furnished with huge old oak file cabinets and a map case that held sixty or seventy old maps. Harriet glanced at maps of southern Africa, India, Thailand, Burma, Indonesia. In the filing cabinets, she found hundreds and hundreds of photographs—old sepia prints, gorgeous black-and-white studio shots, and more modern color snapshots.

She dragged over a heavy oak desk chair and, one drawer at a time, brought the photographs out into the light. Early pictures showed a sturdy little girl standing outside a canvas tent or near a camp table. In some she wore the clothing of a Victorian schoolgirl, but in others—the most striking ones, Harriet thought—the girl wore a pith helmet and boy's safari costume: baggy shorts, low sturdy boots, a khaki shirt, and incongruous hair ribbons, indifferently tied.

The girl was in the habit of looking straight and intensely into the camera lens, her light eyes as clear as rainwater. Many of the pictures also included a man whom Harriet assumed was the girl's father—an exceedingly handsome man, hard and fit-looking and very much at his ease, with the same light eyes as the child's. Harriet lingered on those photos that showed Maxine's father. Sometimes her heart ached for a man like this one. Her own father had been killed in a car wreck two days before her seventh birthday.

Harriet put away the first set of pictures, reached into the next drawer. Maxine had grown into a tall, vigorous young woman with the same pale eyes, still amused, still youthful. These pictures were taken in jungles and on plantations in Burma, India, Indonesia, and

Thailand. Maxine was often riding or standing beside Asian elephants, or towering over dark-skinned men carrying short sticks with metal hooks on one end.

The next drawer of photographs had been taken during the first fifteen years of the new century. A middle-aged Maxine now wore men's tweeds. In the next several decades, the pictures often showed the zoo and the growing animal population, including the two old elephants to which Maxine had apparently been so devoted. In these photographs she was often pitching hay or hauling piles of dirt as the property grew every which way into sheds and animal yards. Harriet recognized much of it, even in its current, run-down condition. For the first time, she understood the full extent of Maxine Biedelman's accomplishment.

Harriet flipped through the pictures with growing excitement. Here was a life she could use.

In the very early hours of Monday morning, Truman dozed uncomfortably in an armchair in the den as Miles snuffled at his feet, ceaselessly rearranging his towels. Truman recognized the absurdity of his situation, but he hadn't been able to relax in bed, listening for sounds of crashing furniture or piggy bereavement. In the end it seemed more bearable to doze upright in a chair than to lie wide-awake in bed, contemplating loneliness beneath his roof. The *Guide to Love and Happiness* had been quite stern about not giving your pig more attention at the start than it would get later on: The pig would never understand what had gone wrong. Truman had been a pig owner for less than twenty-four hours, and he was already making bad choices.

Indefatigable, the pig was still working on the towels beneath his chair. Miles. Truman could see Rhonda rolling her eyes at the name he and Winslow had deliberated over for so long. *It's a pig, not a banker. Why not name it Sir Francis Bacon, something clever?* But Truman and Winslow weren't clever, not in the ways Rhonda had expected.

Truman reached down and touched the animal's side. The pig instantly dropped to the floor in bliss. Absently, Truman scratched the sparsely haired belly while Miles subsided into soft piggy grunts and then snores. Outside it was still pitch dark, the domain of the abandoned and the loveless.

ON MONDAY morning, Sam found himself walking past the Biedelman mansion. Poor place needed a new coat of paint for its trim in the worst way; that, and to have its drive re-graveled. Max Biedelman would have died, seeing it this way. She'd been proud of her house, showed him paintings and statues and furniture she'd brought home from all over the world. The place had looked just like a museum.

He and Corinna had been invited there to supper now and then. The first time wasn't more than a few months after Hannah had been given to Sam to take care of. Miss Biedelman had set that huge dark table with a fine white tablecloth, china and crystal and silver, looked just like some movie. They'd sat way up at one end, but you could have fed a baseball team at that table and still had room to spare.

Sam had been self-conscious of his manners, but Corinna settled in like visiting royalty. Miss Biedelman asked her all sorts of questions about her grandmother and grandfather coming out from Chicago and settling a claim out near Bladenham, so poor they'd had to make their clothes from hides one year just like the Indians. They'd been too embarrassed to be seen like that, so they lived off the land until Corinna's grandmother had spun and woven enough cloth to make Corinna's granddaddy a proper suit of clothes.

Corinna had talked on and on, sitting up so straight and fine, her face glowing just like a polished chestnut. She had a smooth, rich voice, and she could spin a story as well as anyone he'd ever heard. Sam had been so proud of her. Even now, it was a memory that sustained him sometimes when he was feeling low.

Halfway back to the elephant yard, Sam felt a tug on the back of his shirt. "Mister? Hey, mister."

He turned around and saw Reginald Poole, the boy who'd come along for a walk with him and Hannah.

"I came back like you asked me to. You remember me?"

"Of course I do. You treating your aunt right?"

"Yeah, I'm treating her good."

"Glad to hear it, son. Treating women right's one of the most important jobs a man's got, seeing as how they give birth to us and all. It's the least we can do in return."

"Yeah. So are you going to walk that elephant again sometime?" Reginald walked with a big-man, basketball walk, bouncing up on the balls of his feet.

"Guess we could. You got any fruit in your pockets, a banana or two, maybe, or a couple of apples?"

"Nah."

"Then you'll have to just come back to the elephant barn with me and cut some for us. Your aunt know you're here?"

"Yeah, she knows. She's going to come back for me later, maybe in a couple of hours."

"Well, we've got some time, then. Tell you what. I've got some chores to do before we can go off with Hannah, but you can come along and give me a hand, as long as you don't get in the way and don't rile Hannah. Say that back to me."

"I can come along if I don't get in the way and don't rile Hannah. That means don't piss her off, right, mister?"

"Yeah, just a prettier way of saying it." Sam opened the gate leading to the barn and ushered Reginald in ahead of him. It wouldn't hurt to show him the ropes a little bit. It would be best not to tell Harriet Saul about it, though.

"How come it's so cold in here?" the boy asked as they went into the food prep room. "Feels like the damn North Pole."

Sam shot him a look that said, *Your language, son,* and Reginald looked away. "It's not that cold," Sam said. "Course, I shouldn't say that, seeing as how I've never been to the North Pole myself. You been there, a great traveler like you?"

"Naw. I just imagine it."

"Imagining is good. You know some grown-ups go through their entire lives without using their imagination a single time? Now, I call that a waste." Sam set apples and bananas and carrots on the counter. "All right, son, you take these apples and bananas, and you cut the apples in quarters, the bananas in halves, and the carrots you can leave alone because they're just little ones anyway. Think you can do that? That knife's real sharp, so you've got to be careful, got to keep your mind on your work."

"Yeah, I can do that. That's not hard."

"Well you must be experienced, then. Me, I found it real hard at first—kept having to fetch my mind back every two minutes because it kept wanting to fly away like some big lazy bird. I nearly cut my finger off one time. See that scar?"

"Uh-huh."

"Happened when I was cutting a melon for my girl and forgot what I was doing for a minute. Next thing I know, I've got blood all over the place—took six stitches to get it to stop."

"I got stitches once, in my head."

"Is that right? You have a scar from it?"

"Right here."

"Uh-huh. I see that. You're lucky your brains didn't escape right out of there before you got it patched up. Brains like to go their own way sometimes. I had an uncle who got a cut no bigger than yours, and next thing we knew, he couldn't even talk right. It was about the saddest thing I ever saw. Only thing he could do after that was shuck corn. He was a champion corn-shucker, but where's that going to get you?"

Reginald shrugged.

"See there?" Sam waggled the knife at him. "That's why you've got to start out your life with all your wits protected. You never know when you might lose a few, and you want to always have extra if you can. Now Hannah, she got extra wits right from the get-go, and not only because she's bigger. She's just plain smart. You, now, I bet you're pretty smart. And I bet your aunt is, too."

"Naw. She's good at yelling, though. She can yell real loud when she wants to get on you about something."

"Well, yelling real loud, that's an important skill to have, too. You never know when you might walk right in front of a train and her yelling's all that stands between you and eternity. But for that yell, you'd be flat, and there's nothing worse than a flat boy, just kind of ruins the day for everyone."

Reginald started giggling. "You tell a pretty good story, mister."

"Me? Naw. I'm just an old man who's seen a lot of things in my time. One day you're going to be just like me, except better looking."

NEVA Wilson spent nearly her entire day off chasing down necessities: paper towels, toilet paper, dishwashing detergent, sponges, canned goods, shampoo, conditioner, and soap. This was the part she hated most about moving. You went to make a sandwich, and damn it, you'd left your mustard in New York. Or you knew exactly which cupboard had the honey, but that was in San Diego. By six o'clock in the evening, she was in a foul mood. Grabbing a baseball cap off the top of her TV set, she stuffed her not-quite-clean hair underneath, got back in the car, and headed for the zoo.

To her surprise, she saw flickering lights in the elephant barn when she pulled up. She looked in the window as she approached, and of all things, she saw Hannah watching *Star Wars* on the barn's wide-screen TV. Sam was sitting in one of the armchairs with his foot up on an overturned steel bucket, while a big, beautiful woman removed a gauze dressing. As Neva pulled the barn door open, both of them jumped.

"I'm sorry—am I interrupting?" she said.

The wound on Sam's foot looked old and serious. The woman moved to block Neva's view, quickly finished applying ointment and a fresh dressing. "Mama was just fixing up a cut I got the other day," Sam said, pulling his sock up over the bandage. "Just me being clumsy, miss. How come you're here so late?"

"I didn't want to be at my apartment anymore, so I thought I'd keep Hannah company for a little while."

"Well, pull up a chair," Sam said. "This is my wife, Corinna. Sugar, this is Miss Wilson."

Corinna held out a warm, soft hand. "Sam's told me all the good things you've done for the baby."

"We're just getting started," Neva said, smiling.

Hannah wandered over, stood behind Corinna's chair, and put her trunk over Corinna's shoulder, sniffed beneath Corinna's ear. When Corinna held up her hand, Hannah blew a soft breath or two into her palm. "Aren't you the sweetest thing," Corinna crooned.

Neva smiled. "Do you do this often?" She indicated the television.

"Two, three times a week, maybe," Sam said. "We've been doing it for years now. Down at the video store, they've got a little display, 'Hannah's Pick.' She gets new releases, whatever she wants, for free. She likes action pictures." Hannah shuffled and made low rumbles in her throat. "You're sure welcome to join us, if you want to."

So Neva rolled out the office desk chair and settled in. Corinna took Sam's hand while Hannah watched the screen with her good eye, her trunk draped gently over Corinna's shoulder, chuffing now and then. Neva thought there was something surreal about the scene, if soothing.

"My father was diabetic, too," Neva said when the movie was over. "He lost a foot from an ulcer like yours."

Sam and Corinna exchanged a look. "Anyways, it doesn't hurt," Sam said.

"He can't even feel that foot anymore," Corinna said. "That's why it doesn't hurt."

"Neuropathy," Neva said.

"Uh-huh," Corinna said. "Doctor's told him he could lose that foot if it doesn't start getting better. And it's not going to get better as long as he's got it rubbing around inside a shoe. Man's a mule, though."

"You find me someone for Hannah, and I'll be done tomorrow," Sam said to Neva, then jerked his head toward Corinna. "She knows that."

After that, there was nothing left to say. Neva helped Corinna shut off the TV and roll it back to its place along the wall, while Sam led Hannah to the back of the barn and the windowless stall where she spent the night. Neva could hear the clanking of the chain and shackle as Sam secured her, turned on a night-light, gave her one last yam, and tuned a radio to an easy-listening station.

"You be good now, sugar," he said in the gloom. "Morning'll come soon."

It was the one thing she'd ever heard him say that wasn't true.

# 4

By Tuesday morning Harriet had almost finished assembling her kit. She'd ordered a safari hat, safari boots, four pairs of khaki pants, four big-game-hunter shirts, a whistle, and a lanyard from a safari outfitter. She'd even found Max's riding crop and shooting stick in a huge armoire in one of the bedrooms. She was so excited she was trembling. When Truman arrived, she leapt out of her chair and pulled him into her office by the arm.

"Truman, I've had the most brilliant idea!" she cried, solicitously pushing a pile of papers from the visitor's chair onto the floor to make room for him. "I want to show you something."

Truman nodded in bleary agreement. It had been another long night with Miles, and Winslow had woken up with an ominous cough.

Harriet was trembling with excitement as she handed him a stack of Max Biedelman's photographs, which he looked through with faint enthusiasm. "They're very striking. Thank you for showing them to me." Truman rose.

"No, no!" she said. "I haven't even started yet. Sit!"

Truman sat.

"I got the preliminary marketing report on Saturday, and of course Hannah's the big draw, no surprise there. I'd already decided to have an agency do a big ad campaign featuring her. But—*but!*—I came up with something else." She paused for dramatic effect. "I will *be* Maxine Biedelman."

"What?"

Harriet unveiled her plan: She would incorporate living history into the zoo by impersonating Max Biedelman and reenacting her experience with elephants—Hannah, in particular. She would give lectures, make informal appearances around the facility, the works. And the program would be supported by an exhibit of the pictures and maps she'd found upstairs. "Those pictures can go on coffee cups, refrigerator magnets, greeting cards, T-shirts, you name it! Don't you think it's brilliant?"

"It certainly has merit. The educational possibilities—"

"You don't like it," Harriet said flatly.

"Yes, I do, Harriet. I do."

Brenda, the receptionist, knocked on the doorjamb and said, "Truman, Winslow just called from school. He says he doesn't feel well and can you pick him up in the nurse's office."

"Go," Harriet said coolly, dismissing him.

As Truman drove to Winslow's school, he found himself wondering if there were such a thing as anti-luck, because if there was, he was suffering a string of it. Not only was Harriet preparing to launch a megalomaniacal marketing campaign balanced on the back of an ailing elephant, but last night had been Truman's third night in a row of pig-sitting. *Pigs that are poorly bonded with their owners are too often turned into pork,* the *Guide to Love and Happiness* intoned, *and who is at fault? Surely not Piggy.* Truman took limited comfort from the fact that the pig appeared to be in fine fettle, perky and bright-eyed and hellishly busy. During his first two days in residence, Miles had rooted up a whole section of lawn to form a shallow, pig-shaped pit in which to snooze. Teenage boys ate less. Worse, whenever he caught sight of Truman, the animal trotted toward him with piggish declarations of love. He slept at Truman's feet—*when* he slept—pressed up hard against his calves and snoring like a wino.

Truman found Winslow sitting forlornly on a cot in the school nurse's office, coughing dryly and staring at his shoes.

"Hey, buddy," Truman said. "Feeling crummy, huh?"

"Kind of."

Truman signed him out and brought him back to the zoo. He kept him in his cubicle for an hour, but when Winslow got restless and asked if he could take a walk, Truman said yes. A little fresh air wouldn't do the boy any harm; in fact might do him good, and he wasn't coughing all that much.

"All right," he told Winslow. "But wear my sweatshirt, and keep the hood up. And be back in an hour, please."

WINSLOW wandered down the path to the elephant barn. A lot of the kids said he was lucky having a dad who worked at the zoo because he probably got to do neat stuff no one else did, like feed bugs to the aardvark. They also thought it was cool that he had a pig, but the only cool thing Miles had done so far was suck a piece of Kleenex up his nose, and Winslow was pretty sure that hadn't been on purpose.

When he reached the elephant yard, he stood outside the fence, watching Hannah fling mud over her back. A woman he didn't recognize was with her, hosing the wallow to keep the mud gloppy. Winslow admired the elephant's ability to shape and then pinch up a precise gob of mud in a bend in her trunk. It was like watching someone knit using only their elbows—it didn't look like it should work.

The woman noticed him. "Hi. Can I help you?"

"No, thank you," Winslow said. "I just like to watch her sometimes. I like her trunk."

"One hundred thousand muscles, all perfectly coordinated. She can shell a peanut. A single peanut."

"Yeah," Winslow said appreciatively.

She looked him over. "Do you work here?" She indicated the zoo sweatshirt he was wearing.

"No, just my dad. His name's Truman Levy."

The woman turned off the water, came to the fence, and stuck part of her hand through the chain links. "I'm Neva," she said.

Winslow shook the fingers solemnly. "My name's Winslow. My mom named me after Winslow Homer, the painter."

"Are you an artist?"

"No," Winslow said. "She wanted me to be, though."

"Well, we can't always be what other people want." Neva turned the water back on, brought the hose around Hannah, and blasted a jet of water straight into her open mouth. "So how come you're here on a school day?"

"I didn't feel well, so I left early."

"Well, that's okay, right?" Neva said, training the hose at Hannah's flanks. "Kind of like getting a snow day."

"Yeah, but I was supposed to have a piano lesson this afternoon, and now I won't."

"And that's a bad thing?"

Winslow shrugged. "I wanted to play something for my teacher."

"What were you going to play?"

"Mozart's *Fantasia in D Minor.*"

"Whoa," Neva said. "How long have you been playing?"

"I started when I was six. So, five years."

Hannah approached the fence carrying her tire. When she got close enough, she set down her tire, extended her trunk straight at Winslow through the chain-link fence, and blew a breath of air at him. He took a cautious step back.

Neva patted Hannah's leg. "She's just trying to get your attention. Here." Neva fished around for something in her pants pocket. "Hold out your hand."

Obediently Winslow held out his hand. Neva dropped in a red jelly bean, a green jelly bean, a white jelly bean, and four raisins. "Get ready," she said. Hannah's trunk was already snaking through the fence. Winslow trembled slightly but held his ground as Hannah daintily picked off the jelly beans and then the raisins, popping them into her mouth one by one. When she was done, she reclaimed her tire and moved off, blowing bits of hay around the yard.

"Good job," Neva told Winslow. She coiled the hose and hung

it on a hook on the barn. "Your dad seems like a pretty nice guy."

"Yeah," Winslow said. "He worries a lot."

"About you?"

"Uh-huh. He wants me to have other interests besides music. He gave me a pig for my birthday. Miles."

Neva grinned. *"Miles?"*

"My dad named him. He's a Vietnamese potbelly. He doesn't sleep."

"Ever?"

Winslow shrugged. "Not so far. We've had him for three days."

"Do you like him?"

Winslow shrugged. "He's okay. He likes to listen when I practice piano. Kids just say they're bored or cover their ears and stuff."

"Well, they'll regret it when you play Carnegie Hall."

"Yeah."

"Your mom must be proud of you."

Winslow shrugged. "She used to get mad at me because I didn't have playdates. She used to say if there was no one left in the whole world but me and one other kid, I still wouldn't invite him over."

Neva laughed. "Well, blessed are the self-reliant. Doesn't she say it anymore?"

"No. She lives in Colorado now. There's an artist colony there. She makes sculpture out of nails and rusty cans and barbed wire and stuff."

Winslow watched Hannah across the yard, where she was methodically breaking up a pumpkin shell by hitting it on a rock.

"Look," Neva said, "can you keep a secret?"

"Usually."

"Well, see if your dad can bring you here tomorrow at three-thirty. We're going to try something with Hannah, but it's a big secret." Neva lowered her voice to just above a whisper. "We're going to teach her to paint."

"You mean like buildings and stuff?"

"No, like pictures."

"Why?"

"Because it's something new. We're trying to find things to keep her from getting bored."

"How are you going to teach her?"

"Come back tomorrow and see. You can tell your dad, but you can't tell anybody else. And your dad can't, either. Swear?"

"Swear," Winslow said. "I probably better go." He turned to leave and then turned back. "It was nice to meet you and everything."

"It was nice to meet you, too, Winslow. Oh, and listen. Pigs are very smart, so don't let yours boss you around."

"I won't," Winslow said, and then he trotted up the path in the direction of the Biedelman house.

THE next afternoon, in thin, brilliant sunshine, Neva set up a sturdy wooden easel outside the barn and clamped a pre-stretched canvas to it, then squeezed blobs of acrylic paint in primary colors onto an oversized artist's palette and took a big new brush out of its cellophane wrapper. Winslow and Truman stood outside the fence, watching as Neva gave Sam the go-ahead to bring Hannah over. The elephant brought her tire along, carefully setting it at her feet as Neva dipped the brush into red paint, made a bold swipe at the canvas, and then held out the brush.

Hannah grasped its handle in her trunk and waved it around.

"Put it on the canvas, shug!" Sam encouraged.

Hannah swiped at the canvas with the brush, crossing the mark Neva had made.

"Good girl!" Neva and Sam cried in unison. Neva took the brush back and loaded it with yellow paint this time. Hannah brought it from the upper left corner of the canvas to the lower right, and then made a series of jabs and swipes.

"I'll be damned," Truman said softly to Winslow.

"Just look at her," Sam said.

"What made you think of doing this?" Truman asked Neva.

"It's been done at other zoos. It gives the elephants something fun to do, and the zoos can sell the paintings to raise money."

"I never would have guessed she'd be so dexterous," Truman said.

"They have one hundred thousand muscles in their trunk," Winslow said. "They can take the shell off a peanut."

Neva smiled. The canvas was filling up with strokes and splashes of color. It could have been art, or it could have been accident. Either was okay with her.

Winslow sneezed. "Fifty-nine."

"Fifty-nine?" Neva said.

"That's how many times he's sneezed today," Truman said.

"My dad bought me some of that Kleenex that has lotion or something in it. It's supposed to keep your nose from getting chapped, but it's not working. Plus I have a cold sore." Winslow opened his mouth and turned his cheek inside out for Neva's inspection. "See?"

Neva peered out through the fence. "Ow. So I'm guessing no school again today, huh?"

"Nope. I'm missing a social studies quiz."

"He'll probably be well enough to go back tomorrow," Truman said. "Anyway, here's hoping. Come on, Winnie. Time to go."

"Well, you two take care." To Winslow, Neva said, "I bet you get to eighty-six. No. Eighty-two. I bet you get to eighty-two sneezes by the end of the day."

"A hundred and seven," Winslow called over his shoulder as he and Truman started up the hill. "Bet you a buck!"

"You're on!"

As the two turned to leave, Neva heard Truman say, "Well, you're as thick as thieves."

"Yeah," Winslow said. "She's nice."

NEVA rinsed out the paintbrushes with the elephant yard hose. Sam had gathered up the easel and canvas. "Why don't you take the painting home?" she told him. "You can have it framed and then hang it in the living room or someplace. It's colorful. And it's her first."

"Nah. It's zoo property and all."

"If you don't take it, you can bet Harriet will. You know I'm right."

"Well, it would look real pretty in the kitchen. Imagine, me having a shug original on my wall."

Neva was glad their experiment had gone so well, and not just for Hannah's sake. She'd gotten up this morning in a melancholy mood. At first she hadn't known why, but then she'd seen the wall calendar in the elephant barn. The boy turned twelve today. His hair, Neva was sure, was dark red like hers, thick like hers; it had been when he was born. She'd been twenty-four when she had been pregnant. It had been an awful time. She and Howard had fought about everything—her choice of career, his misery at a dead-end job selling athletic shoes, their crappy little apartment above a crappy little bar.

*We don't have the money,* he'd said to her over and over. In the end, the free health clinic had referred her to a private adoption attorney who represented an infertile couple willing to pay all Neva's prenatal and delivery expenses in return for a closed adoption—no contact between biological mother and son, ever. The baby had been whisked away within minutes of his birth. Neva and Howard hadn't officially divorced for another two years, but the outcome hadn't been in doubt, only the timing.

*Fifty-nine sneezes.* She picked up the phone in the tiny office, dialed Truman's extension, and asked for Winslow.

"Sixty-eight," she said when he came on the line.

"Seventy-one. But my dad made me take a decongestant, so I'm never going to win now," the boy said disconsolately. "I haven't sneezed in half an hour."

"Bummer," Neva said. "You're probably a lot more comfortable, though."

"Yeah."

"Look, let's do this. After you're better, we'll just bet on something else."

"Like what?"

"I don't know. Number of farts?"

"No way!" he said in the tone of someone who considers himself to be in the presence of greatness. "In a day?"

"In a day. Pig-farts, not boy-farts."

"Awesome!"

She could hear him telling Truman all about it as he hung up the phone.

THE Beauty Spot hair salon was in the half-basement of Sam and Corinna Brown's small white clapboard house. Corinna had fixed it up with gingham curtains and a pink salon chair and big mirrors on the walls that had little etched doodads in their corners. Her customers' protective smocks were black with pink musical notes spilled all over them like someone had had an accident with a tune. She'd never figured out if the notes went to a real song.

Corinna's new customer had given her name over the phone as Maxine. Corinna hadn't thought much about it until she saw Harriet Saul stumping through her beauty shop door.

"Ms. Saul," Corinna said. "I thought you said Maxine over the phone."

"I did." Harriet rummaged around in a bulging leather briefcase and took out a stack of photos of Max Biedelman, which she handed over to Corinna. "I want you to make me look like her," she said. "Can you do it?"

Corinna frowned. "Well, first we're going to need to turn your hair white, and that's going to take a bunch of chemicals."

"Do whatever you have to," Harriet said.

Corinna shook out a smock. The musical notes looked small all bunched up in Harriet's lap that way.

"Won't I make a good Maxine Biedelman?"

"Well, she was one of a kind," Corinna said doubtfully. "But we can sure give it a try."

AN HOUR and a half later, Harriet Saul took one last look at herself in the beauty salon mirror. Her new hairstyle was as near to

Max Biedelman's as she could have asked for. And she looked good with white hair—it gave her a dignity she otherwise lacked.

Thus armed, she called Howard Bolton, mayor of Bladenham, and made an appointment to talk. It was time to get things started.

## 5

NEXT morning, Harriet set aside two hours to get ready for her debut as Maxine Biedelman. She didn't own a full-length mirror—the last one had broken several months ago, when she slammed the door on her reflection. She didn't need a mirror to know what she looked like. What she looked like was fat. She'd been fat and was getting fatter at the rate of almost twenty pounds a year. If she still had a mirror, she knew exactly what she'd see—the Tweedledee belly, heavy arms, thick waist, legs that fit better in a pair of men's suit trousers than the detested panty hose that were always too short and too narrow.

Standing in front of the medicine cabinet mirror on a cold and gloomy morning, she dressed in her new safari things and arranged her hair to look as much as possible like the pictures of Maxine. To her surprise, her new look suited her—the white hair flattered her dark eyes and energetic smile, and the loose-cut men's safari shirts minimized her breasts. From what she could see—and, granted, it was only from the waist up—she cut a surprisingly dashing figure. Here was a woman who was confident, leaderly, and strong.

At the zoo offices, Truman did a double take when he saw her. "Wow," he said. "You look—"

She prepared herself.

"—like Max Biedelman." And he said it like he meant it.

There could have been no higher compliment.

Truman drove them to City Hall. Mayor Howard Bolton was waiting for them. He was a big, florid man with the over-hearty manner of a small-town politician. Shaking Harriet's hand, he said, "Good to see you, Harriet. And you are—?"

Truman held out his hand. "Truman Levy."

"For heaven's sake, Howard!" Harriet said. "You've met him half a dozen times. He's my business manager."

Truman gave a small, embarrassed smile.

The mayor gave Harriet a once-over and said, "So what's with the getup, there, Harriet?"

"I'm going to save the zoo."

"You moving it to Africa?" Howard cracked himself up, punching Truman lightly in the arm to share the joke.

Harriet gave him a withering look. "What's our ad budget, Howard?"

"Off the top of my head—? Ten thousand. Maybe."

"For the quarter?"

"Yeah, right. For the year."

Harriet and Truman exchanged glances. "Find more," Harriet said.

"Beg your pardon?"

"Find more. Ten thousand, at least," Harriet said. "If you want me to save this zoo, you'd better give me the tools to do it." She hauled a stack of photographs and a neatly bound proposal out of her briefcase. "Now, listen. It's all going to be about the elephant."

TWO days before Thanksgiving, 1956, Sam had sought out Miss Biedelman about something that had been on his and Corinna's minds. It was late morning, and cold; in the fields, wisps of ground fog were still caught in the corn stubble, and the air smelled like animals and loam. Sam found the old woman moving painfully across the front lawn. Her arthritis had been worse lately—he could see it in her face as well as her walk. He'd taken a strengthening breath and approached her. "Excuse me, sir."

"Good morning, Mr. Brown," she said.

"I wonder if I could ask you a question."

"Of course. You may walk with me. Let me take your arm." Sam held out his elbow, and she slipped her arm through his; and though she gave him most of her weight, it was surprisingly little— she was as light and dry as cured tobacco.

"Sir, you remember that reincarnation you were telling me about?"

Max Biedelman nodded. "I remember."

"Me and Corinna have been talking about it, and we wanted to know, can a person come back as an animal?"

"According to the Hindu faith, it happens all the time. Why?"

Sam was perspiring lightly despite the chill. He breathed in, breathed out for nerve. "We think Hannah's our baby girl."

Max Biedelman pressed Sam's arm; they'd stopped walking without his noticing. Then they started again. "Yes?" she said. "And why is that?"

"Well, sir, from the very first time I set eyes on shug, I thought there was something familiar about her. That's why you used to see me watching her at lunch and all. And Corinna, she took one look into shug's eye and started crying, and Hannah, she wrapped her trunk around Mama's head and started making this low sound, this humming, you know how she does. And Corinna says to me, *She's talking to us, honey.* She meant *her*—that she'd lived after all, only she was doing it as Hannah. We figure her soul must have passed from one of them to the other, like you can pass along a flame from candle to candle. Call us damn fools, but we both saw it as clear as if God Himself came down and shined His heavenly light."

"Well, Mr. Brown," Max Biedelman said, "I can't speak for God, of course, but I believe you've already answered your question."

"Yes, sir. I guess I did."

They had reached the house. Max Biedelman had withdrawn her arm from his and pressed his hand warmly. "Mr. Brown. If the truth be told, I'm envious. I've been all around the world, but I have had precious few revelations. And to think one was right here all the time."

HARRIET CLEARED A SPACE ON the desk between herself and Truman and laid out a half-dozen receipts. "She's spending money like water," she said. "Look at these! Art supplies. *Art* supplies for forty-seven dollars and thirteen cents."

"I authorized it. She wanted to surprise you."

"Well, she did," Harriet said. "And frankly, you've surprised me, too."

"If I may finish," Truman said quietly, "she wanted to surprise you once she and Hannah were ready."

"Ready for what, unveiling some kind of mural?"

"She's taught Hannah to paint."

"What do you mean?"

Truman smiled faintly. "Hannah paints pictures."

"That's ridiculous. Get her on the phone."

"I can try, but they usually work outside until late morning."

"Truman."

Truman sighed, lifted the phone receiver, and entered the extension for the elephant barn. The phone rang into an empty building, as he had known it would. He switched to the phone's speaker so Harriet could hear it for herself. Three times. Four times, and then to voice mail. Harriet picked up the receiver and dropped it down again to disconnect the call, leaving no message. Then she folded her hands in front of her.

"Truman, I've been in the workforce much longer than you," she said. "And one thing I've learned is that workplace relationships rarely work out."

"Relationships?"

"You seem to know a lot about her," Harriet said.

"I know nothing about her. She's had some entirely appropriate questions, and I've tried to give her answers. Period."

"I'm just saying," said Harriet.

"Look, would you like me to set something up so you can see Hannah paint?"

"I think that would be appropriate," Harriet said, straightening in her chair. "Don't you?"

Neva set up Hannah's easel in the sunny part of the elephant yard. Sam pulled several peppermints from his trouser pocket and unwrapped the cellophane, luring Hannah to the other side of the yard. Sam made sure he kept her back to Neva so she couldn't see the preparations, and once she'd eaten her peppermints, he rubbed her tongue, which made her go piggy-eyed with bliss. Finally he heard Truman and Harriet coming into the yard.

"Looks like it's showtime, baby girl," he said to Hannah.

Neva was telling Truman and Harriet, "I'd prefer that you stay over by the barn wall. Hannah's very excited, and we don't want to give her too many distractions."

"But you can't see from over there," Harriet said.

"You can see well enough," Neva said. "Please."

Sam saw the muscles flex in Harriet's jaw—two strong women in a struggle to dominate.

Sam led Hannah to Neva. "Do you remember this?" She held up a brush loaded with blue paint. Hannah took it in her trunk and without hesitation laid down a track of blue from the upper left to the lower right-hand corner of the canvas. Truman shifted a few feet along the barn wall to get a better view. Harriet strode directly across the yard until she was standing right beside Neva. Hannah's eye rolled nervously.

"It's much safer if you don't stand right here," Neva said in a low, quiet voice. "She's very excited."

Harriet folded her arms in defiance.

Sam saw Truman catch Neva's eye and make the slightest gesture: *Unless she's about to be killed, let her be.* Neva collected herself and turned back to the elephant, saying, "All right, Hannah. You're doing a great job. Do you want more paint?" She offered the palette, and Hannah dabbed her brush and made a tornado of red at the bottom of her canvas. Zoo visitors were piling up along the fence, including a young man who was frantically scribbling notes in a small reporter's spiral notebook.

Hannah switched to orange paint and then black. The canvas was filling with strokes and color, swoops and dots and vortexes. The

young man with the notepad took several pictures of Hannah painting, and of Harriet and Neva watching. Then it was over. Hannah
returned the paintbrush to Neva and walked off to her mud wallow without a backward glance.

The visitors applauded.

Neva unclamped the canvas, handed it to Harriet without a
word, and began to clean up.

HARRIET walked out of the elephant yard without a word. She
was furious. She wouldn't stand for it. These two employees were
completely out of hand. Harriet had been so involved with her own
projects that she'd allowed Sam and Neva too much freedom, and
this was what it had led to: insubordination. She expected—no, she
demanded—respect for her office if not for herself. Without that,
Harriet could never move the zoo into the future she envisioned, a
brilliant gem in Washington's tourism crown.

When she arrived at the office, she found the young man from
outside the elephant exhibit talking to Brenda at the reception desk.
He was trying to take notes while juggling a great deal of camera
gear.

"Hello," Harriet said coolly, cutting Brenda off in midsentence.
To the young man, she said, "I am the zoo's director. May I help
you with something?"

The young man looked up. "Oh! Sorry. My name is Martin
Choi." He held out his hand. "I'm a reporter with the *Bladenham
News-Gazette*."

Harriet grasped his hand and smiled. "It's a pleasure."

"Sure." The reporter looked with confusion at Harriet's badge.
"Maxine Biedelman?"

"My real name is Harriet Saul."

"So who's Maxine Biedelman? She his daughter or something?"

"Whose daughter?"

"Max Biedelman's."

"Max *was* Maxine," Harriet said. "It's what she called herself."

"No kidding? I thought it was a guy." Martin scribbled a note.

"Look." Harriet pulled several photographs out of her pocket. "Meet Maxine Biedelman."

Martin looked through the pictures. "Not a very good-looking old broad, was she? No wonder she called herself Max."

Harriet reached for the photos, snatching them out of his hand. "Let's start again. I'm Harriet Saul, the director of this zoo. I'm re-enacting the role of Maxine Biedelman as part of a brand-new living history program. This is the first day, in fact. I'll be giving daily lectures so our visitors can get a better feel for the zoo's roots. We have colorful beginnings."

"Yeah?"

"Why don't we go into my office?"

Harriet led the way. Inside her office door, Martin stopped, surveying the wreckage. "Whoa! This looks like my apartment. No kidding. You should fire your janitor."

Harriet swept the visitor's chair clear. "We're a nonprofit organization. We don't have a janitor."

"No kidding."

A small vein pulsed in Harriet's temple. She sat down behind her desk, took a fortifying breath, and outlined the history of the Max L. Biedelman Zoo in extreme, even numbing, detail. When she finally stopped at somewhere between forty-five minutes and eternity, Martin Choi squinted at her and said, "Well, hey, you've given me lots of great information. I have to talk to my editor, but maybe we'll be able to run a feature story. I'd love to get some pictures, maybe some of you with the elephant. That painting, that was some cool stuff. Would you have a few minutes to go back down there with me now?"

"Of course," said Harriet. She continued to brief him as they walked. Her twice-daily interpretive performance as Maxine Biedelman was to be called *My Walks on the Wild Side,* which she believed was sexy enough to draw at least a small crowd to her impromptu stage on Havenside's marble steps at ten every morning and three every afternoon. She would give a dramatic recitation of Max Biedelman's travels in Burma, using as props Max Biedelman's own elephant hook, shooting stick, and old Haaselblad camera. Though she was by no means a professional performer, she thought zoo guests would find the result moving.

The elephant yard was quiet when they arrived. Hannah appeared to be dozing against the fence, her eyes closed and trunk moving only now and then to check on the tire leaning against her ankle. They never even saw Sam or Neva.

When her work with Martin Choi was finished, Harriet sat at her computer and composed a memo for all employees.

> Today, as part of our recent focus on revitalizing the Max L. Biedelman Zoo, we will begin offering a living history program that will feature the life and accomplishments of our founder, Maxine L. Biedelman. Please be advised that in support of this new effort, I, Harriet Saul, will be costumed as Maxine Biedelman, and during zoo hours am to be addressed exclusively by her name. You may also be called upon to improvise in a supporting role from time to time as Maxine moves through the zoo in character. Your cooperation is appreciated.
>
> *Signed, Maxine Biedelman, née Harriet Saul*

That done, Harriet put on the pith helmet, tipped it to a jaunty angle, and walked outside. A family of four was coming toward her along the path. Harriet grinned broadly and extended her hand.

"Good afternoon!" she cried. "I am Maxine Biedelman. Welcome to my zoo."

WHEN Neva got out of her car at home that evening, she smelled something miraculous in the air. Cookies. Sweet, sweet chocolate chip cookies. Her landlord, Johnson Johnson, was baking.

A foil-covered plate sat on the stoop of her garage-cum-apartment. It was the third time she'd received cookies since moving in. With trepidation she walked up to Johnson Johnson's door. He answered her knock at the exact moment that she had decided to turn and run. Spectrally thin in battered jeans and a T-shirt that said JESUS IS COMING: LOOK BUSY, he appeared at the door holding a spatula.

"Hey!" he said. "Did you get the cookies? Did you taste one?"

"No, I just got home, but I wanted to thank you."

"Sure." A timer went off inside the kitchen, and Johnson Johnson began windmilling with his arm. "Come in."

"No, no—"

But he was already across the kitchen. She followed and found, to her astonishment, that the kitchen was painted, even saturated, in the colors of a Mexican fiesta: brilliant yellows, reds, oranges, and greens. In place of baseboards, a seven-inch band of black-and-white checkerboard wrapped all the way around the room, and above that ran what appeared to be a poem. No—Neva recognized it as the opening lines of Lewis Carroll's *Jabberwocky:* TWAS BRILLIG, AND THE SLITHY TOVES DID GYRE AND GIMBLE IN THE WABE. . . . The wood floor had been painted brick red, with a compass dial beneath the kitchen table.

"It's so I know where North is," Johnson Johnson said, sliding hot cookies onto a cooling rack.

"Why do you need to know?"

He looked up at her. "Well, you're supposed to."

"You are?"

"Course."

It was best not to expect clarity from the fun house that was Johnson Johnson's mind. "So did you do all this yourself?"

"Yeah," he said modestly. "I don't like white." He spaded gobs of cookie dough out of a mixing bowl and onto the cookie sheet. "So, you want a glass of milk with your cookies?" he said. "I even have"—he waited a reverential beat—"strawberry milk."

"No, no. I just wanted to say thank you. Your cookies were the best things that happened all day."

"Hey! If you're hungry we could get a pizza, maybe."

Neva immediately put her hand on the doorknob. "Look, I'm sorry. All I can think of is a shower and then bed. I'm beat."

"You do, like, smell of something."

"Elephant." The subject was getting a little too personal. Neva backed out the door. "Okay. So thanks again, okay?"

"Okay," said Johnson Johnson.

# 6

MILES and Truman had bonded.

It was not what Truman had had in mind.

The little pig followed him everywhere, and when Truman went beyond the baby gate that limited Miles to the kitchen and den, the pig cried, making little snuffling sounds. It was heartbreaking. He showed no such devotion to Winslow. Happily, the boy didn't seem to mind, taking only the faintest interest in the animal he'd once so desperately wanted.

Truman heaved himself up from the depths of the sofa Rhonda had insisted he keep because she knew he hated it. Why weren't more women like Neva Wilson? He didn't know her, really, but she seemed balanced, reasonable. She even had a sense of humor. He wondered what she would think of Harriet's ad campaign.

Harriet had shown him storyboards. There was a three-quarter profile of Hannah and, ghosted behind her, a picture of Harriet as Maxine Biedelman, squinting heroically into the jungle interior as suggested by a few ghosted palm fronds. Truman hadn't given her much of a reaction, saying he would prefer to give the matter a night's thought before offering his opinion. Of course, this amounted to feet of clay, since he knew that tomorrow he'd advise her to use a picture of the real Max Biedelman instead. He wondered how much unemployment he might be able to collect if he found himself suddenly out of work.

Winslow shuffled into the kitchen as Truman assembled chopped meat, an egg, fresh breadcrumbs, and ketchup in a mixing bowl and, shuddering, plunged his hands in. The combined feel of cold animal fat and raw egg was almost more than he could bear. He squished the stuff through his fingers.

"Hand me that pan, would you, Winnie?"

Winslow handed him a glass baking dish, and Truman dumped the meat loaf out of the bowl. "You want to shape it, or no?"

"You can."

Truman slapped the clammy stuff into a tidy loaf, iced it with ketchup, and, with infinite relief, slid it into the oven. He set down the bowl for Miles to lick. The pig pushed it around the floor, running it into the baseboards, cupboard doors, and Truman's feet.

"So tell me about your day."

Winslow shrugged. "It was okay."

"Okay, like you couldn't wait for it to end, or okay, like there were some bright spots?"

"I don't know. We got to draw in art class. Mr. Warner put some crushed cans, a fern, and two marbles on a table, and we were supposed to draw it."

"Yes, it's called a still life. And did you?"

"Yeah, but I was the only one. Jeremy Ireland called me a kiss-ass."

"I'm sure that Vincent van Gogh's classmates called him names, too."

Truman drizzled halved baby red potatoes with olive oil and rosemary and slid the potatoes into the oven with the meat loaf. He fished lettuce, carrots, cauliflower, and radishes out of the vegetable bin. He didn't feel that Winslow got enough vegetables, so he insisted on making a salad for them every night, a chore he detested. As additional penance, he refused to use prewashed and bagged lettuces, struggling with messy heads of red leaf and romaine, vigilant for the omnipresent aphids.

"Have you talked to your mother lately?"

"Nah."

"Why don't you give her a call while dinner's cooking?"

"That's okay."

Truman decided to let it go. Winslow's reluctance might be simple dislike of talking to Rhonda on the phone, an experience Truman himself likened to a jousting match where only one person had a lance and that person wasn't you.

"Then go do piano until dinner's ready." Truman tripped over

Miles snuffling around under the open dishwasher door. "And Winnie? Take Miles with you."

"He doesn't want to come."

"Yes he does; he just doesn't know it."


ONE morning in early fall, 1956, Sam had found a note taped to the door of the elephant barn, asking him to come up to the house. He'd gotten Hannah squared away in a hurry and headed up the hill. Miss Biedelman wasn't strong, and her rheumatism was bothering her more and more. He was relieved when the old woman herself answered the door, her quick old eyes dancing with excitement.

"Mr. Brown! It's a pleasure to see you. Come in for just a moment while I get my coat." She hurried out of the front room and came back wearing a man's heavy canvas barn coat and brandishing one of her walking sticks. "Come, Mr. Brown." She urged him out the door with a hand on his back. "I'll explain as we go." She led the way back to the barn, hobbling along at a remarkably fast clip.

"Looks like you're feeling better today," Sam said.

"Yes, yes, I feel quite myself, Mr. Brown. Slow as the dickens, of course, but never mind. At my age it's best to lower one's standards." She chuckled to herself as they got near the elephant barn. "Now here's my plan. We're going to take Hannah for a walk."

Sam frowned. "We don't have a lead or a halter."

"We don't need one, Mr. Brown! Could you restrain her even if we had? No, the mahouts work their elephants without restraints of any kind, and so shall we. Do you have an elephant hook? I know we did at one time. Go and see, Mr. Brown."

Sam went inside and rummaged around in a closet. He finally found the tool beneath a pile of old feed sacks. The stick was about a foot and a half long, not quite as stout as an axe handle, and with a blunt metal hook coming out of one end.

"Yes, that's it!" Max cried when Sam reappeared with it. "Yes, yes! Come on, then." She took the stick from him, tucking it beneath one arm.

Sam regarded it doubtfully. "Looks like a mean thing, sir, with that hook and all."

"No, no. It's used to suggest, Mr. Brown, not to punish. I'll show you. Why don't you bring her to the gate?"

Hannah was chewing her hay contemplatively when Sam approached her and said, "Guess what, sugar? Me and Miss Biedelman are going to take you out, give you a look at some things."

Hannah sucked on her trunk apprehensively. Sam looked at Max Biedelman. "It about breaks my heart seeing her fearful, a big girl like her."

Max patted Hannah's shoulder. "She'll be fine, Mr. Brown. You'll see. Go and load your pockets with fruit. Fill this, too, please." She dug a string bag out of a trouser pocket and handed it to Sam.

"All right, sir, only take me a minute—I've got food cut up already from before I went home last night." Sam hurried into the barn and filled his canvas pouch, then Max Biedelman's string bag, with yams, gourds, squashes, and apples. When he was done, he found Max Biedelman patting Hannah and talking to her quietly. The elephant browsed around the old woman's feet, occasionally lifting her trunk to sniff her pockets.

"We're all set now, sir."

"Good, good." The old woman attached her bulging string bag to her sturdy leather belt, and Sam slung a leather pouch over his shoulder.

"Come along, Hannah," she said. With the twin lures of apples and yams, Hannah took small steps forward until she was out of the yard, but there she stopped, lifting her head nervously.

"We're going to have an adventure," Sam soothed. "We're taking you places you've never been before." He handed her another yam, and, evidently resigned, she started walking again.

"Worlds will open up to her, Mr. Brown, once she's regained her confidence," Max Biedelman said. "Small worlds, I'll grant you, but new ones just the same."

"Think she remembers walking free?" Sam asked.

"It's possible—even quite likely."

"Makes me sad, thinking about that."

"Yes, I can see why you might say so, but you must remember that in the wild she was starving. No one was cutting up canta-loupes for her, were they, Mr. Brown? Nature is never so simple as we like to think."

"Yes, sir," Sam said, but he still felt the way he felt.

They had reached the edge of Havenside's lawns, where a sketchy trail led into the woods. Hannah rolled her eye nervously, first look-ing to Sam, then Max Biedelman. The old woman reached out and gently touched Hannah's right knee with the hook. "Come along, Hannah. There's a good girl." Slowly, Hannah walked into the woods. Max Biedelman continued to coax with the elephant hook, and Sam kept a firm hand on her for reassurance. She trumpeted once and tossed her head a time or two, but out of a growing ex-citement rather than nervousness. Finally she began browsing among the leaves and ferns on the forest floor.

"Hannah has done very well, indeed," Max said. "I think this is as far as we'll take her today, Mr. Brown. It would be best if we just let her root and get comfortable."

Sam crossed his arms over his chest and watched Hannah bend several small alder trees with her trunk to strip off and sample the leaves. When he took a step or two away from her, she lifted her head, but Sam said, "I'm right here, sugar."

"May I ask you a question, Mr. Brown?" Max Biedelman said.

"You go right ahead."

"When you were a small boy, what did you dream of?"

"Well, now, that's a hard question. I don't know that I had any dreams. I always figured I'd have to help my daddy on the farm."

"I don't mean practical considerations, Mr. Brown. I mean if you could have been anything, what would you have chosen?"

Sam shifted, patting Hannah. "You've got to understand that my kind of people, sir, we don't always have dreams, at least not in the way you're thinking. It's better not to, sometimes."

Max Biedelman looked at him keenly. "Why is it better? One should always dream, Mr. Brown."

"Well, maybe that's so, sir, but I'd rather appreciate what I've got. I've got Corinna, got my sugar, got you to talk to sometimes, got this beautiful place to come to every day."

Max Biedelman smiled a little smile. "You're a fortunate man, Mr. Brown, to want so little."

"*No,* sir. It's not little at all."

"Well, perhaps not."

"Corinna, now, she's something different. She wants a way to get back at God. There isn't a way to get back at God, never has been, never will be. But Corinna, she just goes on taunting Him and being disappointed when He doesn't care." Sam shook his head sadly. "It's a hard thing to dream about what you can't have."

"I don't believe that we have any choice about our dreams, Mr. Brown. I believe they simply come to us, like head colds and bad habits."

"Maybe so," Sam said. "Maybe so. I had a brother Emmanuel who always wanted to be white, or at least light-skinned. Sad fact was, he was the darkest of us kids. He'd wear hats and long sleeves on the farm all summer long to keep from getting any darker, damn near killed himself with heatstroke more than once."

Max Biedelman smiled. "And did he stay on the farm?"

"Nah. He got killed in a bar in Yakima, trying to break up a fight between a couple of white men. Emmanuel got between them, and they turned on him faster than a prayer reaches heaven. Shot him three times in the chest. Man didn't stand a chance."

"That's a terrible story."

Sam shrugged. "Yes, sir, I guess it is. But Emmanuel would have probably found something else to get killed over, if those white men hadn't been there in that bar. Mama used to say, *That boy has a strange look about him, always has. We gonna lose him young.* And we did."

"And yet, you're not bitter," the old woman said. "Why aren't you bitter, Mr. Brown?"

"Bitter? No point in it. Emmanuel died because he was stupid and the Lord called him home out of pity for what else would happen to him if He let the boy stay any longer."

Max Biedelman laughed. A small breeze had sprung up, and she pulled her coat collar up around her ears. "I think our little experiment has been a success," she said. "Wouldn't you agree?"

"Yes, sir," Sam said. "But I guess it's time to go home, just the same."

NOW Sam sat in his chair in the living room, listening to Corinna washing up the dinner things. He had his recliner back and heaved his bad leg up beside the good one like a rotten old fish, burning from the inside out like he had fire for veins. Neuropathy, it was called; he'd read about it in the diabetes pamphlets Corinna had collected for him. Nerve death. There was going to come a day when he wouldn't have that foot to use anymore, wouldn't be able to stand beside Hannah and tell her everything was all right. And deep in his heart he knew that day was coming just as surely as nightfall.

He'd been having visions of the past more and more lately. He wondered if diabetes could make you crazy. Half the time he didn't know if he was coming or going anymore, what with dreaming the same damn dream almost every night. Every morning when he woke up, he felt like he'd climbed a mountain or been worked over with a meat tenderizer like his mother used for tough old farm animals that had been butchered late in life.

Corinna was right: He was going to have to do something—talk to Neva Wilson, maybe, or get hypnotized like people did to quit smoking, so he could get some rest.

WHEN Truman woke Winslow the next morning, he found the boy running a low-grade fever all over again. Rather than leave him home with Miles, Truman rounded up two boxes of apple juice, a fresh box of Kleenex, a couple of decongestants, and a few good books and brought him to work.

Later that morning when Winslow asked if he could go outside,

Truman let the boy go. Winslow liked going to work with Truman. It was a lot more fun than when his father had worked for Allstate Insurance, where the best thing about it was a coffee mug full of free Allstate pens that skipped when you wrote with them. Whenever Winslow cleaned his room, another pen or two still appeared along with the lint balls. It was like they had legs and wandered freely through the halls and closets when no one was home.

Winslow had gotten as far as the dik-dik exhibit when a boy about his own age fell into step with him.

"You work here?" he asked Winslow, seeing Truman's sweatshirt.

"Nah. I'm sick, so my dad brought me to work for a while."

The boy looked him over. "You don't look sick."

"Well, that's because I'm not *sick*-sick. Just sick. How come you're here? Isn't it school?"

The boy shrugged. "I faked a note saying I was supposed to go to the dentist. I have a friend here I come see sometimes." He puffed up a little. "His name's Samson Brown. He's in charge of Hannah. She's the elephant here."

"I know that."

"Yeah? Well, me and Mr. Brown, we take her for walks sometimes. You want to come?"

"Sure." They headed off down the hill together toward the barn. "What's your name?" Winslow asked.

"Reginald Poole. What's yours?"

"Winslow Levy."

They found Sam in the elephant yard, lashing a hose to a tree.

"Hey, mister!" Reginald called from outside the fence.

Sam turned around. "Well, what are you doing here, boy?"

"I got excused from school this morning."

"How come?"

Reginald shrugged. "I'm ahead of everybody else."

Sam frowned at him. "I don't much like to be lied to."

Reginald looked down at his feet.

"And what's your excuse for being here, Winslow?" Sam asked. "You too smart to be in school, too?"

"No, sir. I'm sick."

"Don't look sick to me."

Winslow groaned. "Not *sick*-sick. Just a *little* sick."

"Hey, mister, what are you going to do with that hose?" Reginald asked Sam. "You going to give Hannah a bath?"

"Did you hear something, maybe a little bug buzzing around my ear?" Sam asked.

"Aw, *you* ask him," Reginald said, poking Winslow in the side.

"What's the hose for?" Winslow said.

"Watch." Sam walked back to the barn and turned on the spigot. A perfect arc of water bloomed and fell fifteen feet away. Hannah lifted her head and trumpeted nervously.

"Go on, baby girl, you show that water who's boss." Sam adjusted the hose to make the arc land closer to Hannah. Then he got a push broom, soaked it under the hose, and then brought it over and touched Hannah's side with the wet bristles until, little by little and with the added enticement of peppermints, he coaxed her toward the arcing water until she was finally standing directly under the stream.

"Baby's got it now!" Sam crowed, watching her turn every which way under the hose and then scoop up a big gob of mud with her trunk and toss it onto her back. "Shug looks like a pig in heaven."

"We have a pig," Winslow said through the fence. "Me and my dad. His name is Miles."

"That's a fine name for a pig," Sam said.

"You going to walk Hannah today, mister?" Reginald asked.

"Not with you I'm not, *no* sir," Sam said. "No way some child too sneaky to be in school is going anywhere with me and Hannah. I can't have her around someone who doesn't believe school's important. It might be a bad influence on her."

"Aw, come on, mister."

"Nope, I don't even want to see your face. You bring me some schoolwork with a good grade on it, and then we'll talk."

Reginald shuffled off, and Winslow followed. Hannah was still flinging mud.

"He's pretty strict," Winslow said.

"Yeah," Reginald said with admiration.

They hiked up toward the zoo gates and administrative offices. Winslow stopped outside the Biedelman house. "Well, I better go."

"Okay, Windermere."

*"Winslow,"* said Winslow. "Maybe if you come to see Mr. Brown this weekend, I could meet you here."

"Yeah?"

"Yeah."

"Okay. I'll see you Saturday," said Reginald.

"Okay," said Winslow.


NEVA was leaning against the barn door with her arms folded, smiling at Hannah and Sam. "She sure is a good girl," she said.

Sam beamed with pride. "See that? You're already getting partial. I bet you talk to her, too, tell her stuff."

"Yeah," Neva said. She looked at Sam closely. "What do you think of Harriet Saul's pretending she's Max Biedelman?"

"I think it's a damn stupid idea. Disrespectful, too."

"What do you think Max Biedelman would think?"

"She'd be cussing up a blue streak is what she'd be doing. Miss Biedelman sure could cuss, too, when she put her mind to it."

Hannah bumped Sam with exquisite gentleness. "Hannah doesn't think much of that Harriet Saul, either, do you, sugar?" Hannah wrapped her trunk around Sam's head. "You sure are in a lovey mood this morning," Sam told her.

"Listen, if she's in such a good mood, let's take a closer look at her foot," Neva said.

"Yeah?" Sam turned to Hannah. "Foot, shug."

Hannah lifted her foot. Neva probed gently, and Hannah flinched. "Can you see?" she asked Sam. "Damn."

"Yeah," Sam said quietly. "It's worse. You got any ideas?"

"I do, actually." Neva said. She patted Hannah's knee, and the elephant lowered her foot. "Last night I talked to a friend who works at the Pachyderm Sanctuary outside Redding. She told me to soak the foot in apple cider vinegar twice a day."

"Apple cider vinegar?"

"Bacteria doesn't like the acidity of vinegar. I know it sounds far-fetched, but it certainly can't do her any harm."

Sam nodded. "What's that sanctuary, miss?"

"The Pachyderm Sanctuary. It's a wonderful place, seven hundred fenced acres. Alice McNeary started it with one old circus elephant. Since then she's taken three other circus elephants and a couple more that were in bad situations."

"What's it look like? The land and all."

"I've only been there once, but it was beautiful. Mostly rolling fields and woods. The elephants can go wherever they want."

"I think I've been there, miss," Sam whispered.

Neva looked at him. "I don't understand."

"What kind of bad situations were those other elephants in?"

Neva frowned, trying to remember. "Well, one was at some tire dealership in Texas that was closing down, and no one wanted her because she was too old. The second one had been by herself for twenty-eight years at some godforsaken zoo in Alabama."

"Was that why the place took her—because she was alone?"

Neva frowned. "How long has Hannah been alone here?"

"Forty-one years, miss," Sam said softly.

Neva's eyes locked onto Sam's. "This might be a good time to start calling me Neva."

## 7

Neva had just started pulling odds and ends from her refrigerator for dinner—deli turkey, a bowl of grapes, a whole-wheat roll—when the phone rang. Piped through the answering machine was a nervous sigh and sounds of distressed throat-clearing.

"Neva? This is Truman Levy. Listen, I need your advice. It's about Winslow's pig—"

Neva picked up the phone. "Truman?"

"Oh, thank God."

"Are you all right?"

"Yes, I'm all right, but something's wrong with Miles, Winslow's pig. He's congested, and he feels warm."

"Have you taken his temperature?"

"Do you think that's necessary?"

"Animal care is not for the faint of heart, Truman," Neva said. "Coat a thermometer well with Vaseline and insert it in his rectum for two minutes. Do you want me to stay on the line?"

"Yes, yes. Please don't hang up," Truman said, and she could hear him shudder. "What's a pig's normal temperature?"

"I don't know, but I'll find out by the time you've finished taking it." Neva set the receiver down and pulled one of her veterinary books out of a cardboard box. She picked up the receiver just as Truman was coming back on the line, breathing hard.

"His temperature's one hundred and four point two."

"Well, it should be between a hundred and two and a hundred and three point six."

"He's snorting and gurgling. Listen. It's heartbreaking." Neva heard loud congested snuffles being breathed directly into the receiver.

"Wasn't your son sick recently?"

"Winslow? Yes, all the kids were. There was some bug going around. It happens every fall."

"Are you familiar with the term *zoonosis?*"

"Is it serious?"

Neva smiled. "No, no, it means disease transmission between animals and humans. I think there's a good chance that Miles caught Winslow's cold."

"His cold. Pigs can have colds?"

"Well, the porcine equivalent, anyway. You might want to take him to see a vet tomorrow. For tonight I'd cover him with a blanket if he'll let you. And you could run a vaporizer for him, if you make sure it isn't in a place where he can get at it and scald himself."

The line fell silent.

"Truman?"

She could hear him sigh heavily. "My parents are attorneys. I hold advanced degrees in business and English literature. I have never pictured myself as a swineherd."

"A whole new future may await you in animal care," Neva said cheerfully.

"I'd sooner eat flies."

TRUMAN stayed up most of the night, checking on the pig's breathing, topping off the vaporizer, and tucking Miles's little blanket up around his shoulders, if pigs could be said to have shoulders. He tried and failed to remember the cut of pork that would roughly correspond. Eventually, he concluded that he'd be better off just pulling up stakes and sleeping in a sleeping bag beside the damned pig. He and Rhonda had been less intimate in the last years of their marriage.

Either through nature's resiliency or the palliative effect of Truman's presence, Miles began breathing more easily and by five in the morning had fallen into a peaceful sleep, tucked into the hollow of Truman's arm. By seven, the pig's fever peaked, and Truman had wracking pains through his entire body. He called Harriet's extension and left a message that he would be staying home, rallied just long enough to see Winslow off to school, and then crawled to the couch in the den. When the phone rang at nine o'clock, Truman steeled himself for Harriet's voice, but instead it was Neva's.

"So?" she said. "What's his temperature?"

"A hundred and two, same as mine."

He could hear Neva snort into the receiver. "Look, would you like me to check on you both at lunch? I can bring along some soup from the Oat Maiden." The Oat Maiden was a café several blocks from the zoo. It specialized in dishes made with husks, stems, hulls, rinds, and pith. Truman was too sick to care. He gave her directions to his house and hung up, ruminating over the novelty of imagining that someone cared. Truman was not a good patient, but given to whimpering and elaborate descriptions of the fresh hells of illness.

He let Miles outside, swallowed acetaminophen, and made a steaming mug of tea to breathe over. Then he wrapped himself tightly in an afghan and fell into an interminable fever dream. He didn't wake up until Neva appeared in the doorway of his den.

"Six-bean soup with veggie garlic sausage," she said cheerfully, pulling a cardboard container from a brown paper bag.

"Why do they call it health food?" Truman said petulantly. "It's not. No one healthy would eat this."

"Go on, it'll be good for you. Now where's Miles?"

"In the backyard."

In fact, Miles had his snout pressed pathetically against the sliding glass door. Neva let him in, and when she crouched beside him, he made brazenly seductive noises and fell like the dead at her feet. She listened to him breathe and ran her hand over his sparse coat. "He feels cool, and his eyes are bright. Is he eating well?"

"I haven't fed him yet," Truman said, stricken. He told Neva where the pig kibble was and how much to put in his dish. Miles set to like he hadn't been fed in days, and then, sated, circled twice and fell heavily into his basket beneath the piano.

"What a good pig," Neva crooned.

"He's actually quite musical," Truman said. "He especially likes Mozart. Winslow's working on several pieces right now, and Miles stays right there under the piano until he's done, no matter how long he practices."

"Clearly a pig with discriminating tastes." Neva bent down to pet Miles's head.

Truman watched as the pig snuffled with pleasure. "Truthfully," he said, "I'd never envisioned pigs as being so—"

"Responsive?"

"Flatulent."

Neva started laughing. "Well, he's a pig. Pigs and gas go together."

"I just wish someone had told me," Truman said sadly, and pulled his afghan closer around his shoulders.

For the last nine days, Harriet had driven an extra eight miles on her way to work so she could admire her new billboard with its prominent pictures of Hannah beside herself as Maxine Biedelman. Since the billboard had gone up, zoo attendance had increased twenty percent—and in mid-November, to boot. Her one-woman performances were attracting larger audiences each day.

Harriet loved her new persona. As Maxine, she was courageous and accomplished, a woman of sophistication equally at home in Cannes or on the Indian subcontinent. As Maxine, she didn't walk; she strode. The very air she breathed was bracing. There had been some awkward moments, of course, with disrespectful employees who continued to address her as Harriet, but as Maxine, she had discovered magnanimity: She merely smiled and reminded them of her policy.

From the scribbled captions on the backs of Maxine's childhood photographs, she had sometimes been called Brave Boy, which Harriet thought was a wonderful name. Harriet's own childhood nickname had been Bucket, a reference to her appetite for fried chicken.

But all of that was in the past. Harriet Saul—clumsy, unliked, unlikable—had dropped away, leaving Maxine. As Maxine, she was strong, successful, capable, and adored.

That morning *Bladenham News-Gazette* reporter Martin Choi arrived for his appointment clanking with gear. Harriet glided from her office with her hand extended to clasp his.

"Good to see you, Martin. You did a nice job on your article about the zoo. Is there something else you'd like to work on?"

"I'm thinking I might be able to put something together about"—he gestured at her safari gear—"you know. This. You."

"Do you mean Maxine Biedelman?"

"Yeah. The one who's dead and you pretend you're her."

Harriet's smile became somewhat fixed. "I take on her persona, yes. Living history is a popular, proven educational technique."

"Yeah, well, how about we do an interview with you, and then I'll take some pictures of you dressed, you know, in your safari outfit."

"That would be fine."

She motioned him into her office and for the next half hour laid out the marvel that was Maxine—her travels, her family, her experiences in Thailand and Burma, in Borneo and Sumatra. She talked for exactly half an hour and then, at ten o'clock sharp, brought him outside with her. Several groups of schoolchildren and their adult chaperones waited at the foot of the porch, fidgeting in the late autumn chill. Harriet doffed her pith helmet and gave them all a hearty greeting. Martin Choi began shooting pictures.

"Good morning to you all," Harriet called. The gathering got quiet. "I am Maxine Biedelman. Welcome to my zoo!"

Her performance lasted forty-five minutes, followed by a brief question-and-answer period, after which she bade her visitors farewell with a lifted hand. Martin Choi took picture after picture.

"Hey, what you just did, now that was really something," he said admiringly when it was over. "You were great—no kidding."

Harriet studied him closely for a minute or two and then said, "I like you, Martin. You're a promising young journalist. Let me offer you something."

"Yeah?"

"Depending on your article and how you portray me—me, Maxine Biedelman—I'll contact you first when things of interest happen here at the zoo."

"Hey, I've got to report the truth, black and white, as I see it."

"Of course," Harriet said. "You're obviously a man of principle who's dedicated to your profession. I understood that about you the first time we met."

Martin Choi puffed up. "So, good."

"We'll talk soon," Harriet said.

They would talk soon and frequently. It wasn't every day that you were handed a gift like Martin Choi, and Harriet was shrewd enough to know it.

"HOW'RE you doing, girl?" Corinna cried, holding open the door to the Beauty Spot for Neva Wilson. "Come on in. Is it raining?

When did that start?" She folded Neva into a quick one-armed hug against her substantial bosom.

"A couple of hours ago."

"Really? My head must be in the clouds today." Corinna settled Neva in her chair and gently fastened one of her salon drapes around the girl's shoulders. "I hope you know you can come chew the fat over here anytime, without having to go and get your hair involved," she said.

Neva shook her head, pulling her hair out from under the smock and letting it spill down her back. "Come on. Who else am I going to trust with my finest asset?"

She was being flippant, but Corinna couldn't help thinking she was also right; the girl had thick, glossy, dark red hair most African-American girls would cut off their right arm for. Corinna could relax, moisturize, condition, weave, and braid until the cows came home, but no beautician on earth could give a black girl what Neva Wilson got for free, and that was all there was to it.

"So what are we doing, sugar?" she asked Neva.

"Just trim it, please—I've been doing it myself, and you can see what a bad idea that is."

Corinna clucked and brushed. "You sure you don't want a nice bob, maybe something a little different?"

"Cornrows would be nice," Neva said. "With lots of beads."

"You got four hours? Because that's what it's going to take with all this hair you've got."

Neva sighed. "I guess I'll have to do that on a day off."

"Let's just clean you up for now. We can save the fancy stuff for next time." Corinna got to work. "So how's my Hannah today? Baby in a good mood?"

"She's in a great mood. We cut twenty-four honeydew melons in half, filled them with frozen raspberries, put them back together, and hid them in the branches of trees all over the zoo. Sam took her for a walk, and it was just like an Easter egg hunt, only in November."

Corinna smiled broadly. "You've done wonderful things for shug, girl. She's got that old sparkle back in her eye, like we haven't seen for a long time. A mighty long time." Corinna snipped, thoughtful. "You think she ever waits for Miss Biedelman to come down those steps? Hannah and Sam, they used to go up to the house for Miss Biedelman when the weather was fine so she could come along on their walks. But then her poor hips got bad—it was a damned shame." She clucked gently. "Sam used to worry about Miss Biedelman all the time."

"He's told me about their walks in the woods," Neva said. "I wish the city hadn't put up that fence along the property line. We can't go there anymore."

Corinna smiled, remembering. "Baby would pad along next to Miss Biedelman just as easy as an old dog and every bit that affectionate. You know the way a dog will look at his owner, just head over heels in love."

"She looks at Sam that way all the time," Neva smiled. "She thinks he hung the moon."

"Sam ever tell you about Hannah's dream?" Corinna asked.

"What dream?"

"There's this dream he has, been having it for years—close your eyes now," Corinna said as she began trimming Neva's bangs. "He dreams he's an elephant in a wide open place with other elephants. Go ahead and open again." Corinna leaned down and blew hair clippings from Neva's forehead.

"Is there a pond?" Neva said.

"Why did you ask that?"

"He said something about a meadow and a pond."

"Yeah. He used to have that dream maybe a couple of times a month, but lately he's dreaming it four, five nights a week. He says it's Hannah's dream, and he doesn't know what to do with it except to bring her more Dunkin' Donuts, and donuts don't make up for things beyond a point, though."

The women's eyes met in the mirror. "The funny thing is," Neva said, "when he described it to me, it sounded like a real place in California. It's called the Pachyderm Sanctuary. They take circus elephants that can't perform anymore, and zoo animals who are just too old for anyone to want them anymore. The sanctuary makes a commitment that the elephants that come to them will stay there and be taken care of for the rest of their lives. The elephants live within a herd, with as little human interference as possible."

"Oh, honey. You think they'd take shug?"

"I don't know. I honestly don't know—"

"Girl, I've been waiting for an apology from Jesus for years, for what He did to Sam and me with our baby and all," she said. "But if He can just make this happen, this *one thing,* I'll forgive Him for everything, I swear. I'll be singing hymns to the rafters, be praising His goodness so loud they're going to have to turn down the volume in heaven, if He'd let Hannah go there so Sam can retire."

"Whoa—whoa! It's not that simple," Neva said. "The sanctuary won't take an animal before an endowment has been raised for its care—and that's *if* they agree to take Hannah at all."

Corinna looked at Neva. "I don't believe they'd turn my baby away if they got to know her."

Neva sighed. "Look. I'll probably go straight to hell for even saying this, but I know the director down there. I've been thinking about approaching her. You've got to promise to keep this a secret."

Corinna took Neva's hands in hers and pressed so hard it hurt. "Girl, you've got my word. You can count on Sam, too."

Neva nodded.

"You do this thing, and I'll take care of your hair for free for life. It's not much, but it's what I've got to offer."

"Even cornrows?" Neva said.

"Amen, baby." Corinna grinned. "Even cornrows."


JOHNSON Johnson lay on his back in bed, in the dark, admiring the constellation of stars on his ceiling. It was a work in progress, applied a single star at a time with glow-in-the-dark paint and the finest brush he could find. He figured he'd painted something like ten thousand stars already, plus a bunch of planets, plotted out according to a celestial map he'd found in an issue of *National Geo-*

*graphic.* So far, the project had taken seven years. He figured he'd be done in another two if he kept up his current rate.

Right now he had another project in mind. He had come up with the idea of making Neva's elephant a musical instrument. He could buy several steel drums and hammer out their tops, maybe make them so they had different tonal ranges—a low drum, a high drum, like that. The elephant could play them using a rubber mallet. He'd go to Home Depot in the morning.

Johnson Johnson loved Home Depot. He'd gotten some of his best ideas there. You didn't know when good ideas were going to come to you until you were right in the middle of them, so it was best to always be ready. He pulled his covers up to his chin, basking in the faint light of the stars above his head and thinking with unfathomable wonder about how good the world was.

NEVA was outside hosing down the elephant when Truman and Winslow approached on the path to Hannah's barn. Neva smiled and saluted with the hose. Truman admired the way the sunlight set her hair on fire, like a Japanese maple in autumn.

"Have you seen a boy named Reginald around anywhere?" Truman asked. "He and Winslow cooked up a plan to meet here this afternoon."

"He's with Sam in the barn." She opened the gate for them. Hannah stood in the yard, dripping with water, her eyes squeezed shut with pleasure. Neva turned on the water again, set the nozzle to the hardest stream possible, and pointed it straight into Hannah's open mouth. Hannah moved her tongue back and forth and let the spray hit the back of her throat at full strength. "She loves this," Neva said. "Go on in. I'm just finishing up."

They found Sam and Reginald in the food preparation room, cutting apples. The boy lit up when he saw Winslow. "Hey, you remembered!"

"Course," Winslow said.

"Well, we're going to walk the elephant pretty soon," Reginald said.

"Soon as she's done with her bath." Sam handed a second knife to Winslow. "If you're going to hang around here, you've got to work, though. Hannah doesn't like slackers."

Truman watched Winslow belly up to the counter beside Reginald and grab a couple of apples from a plastic washtub. He shook Sam's hand. "Thank you for letting the boys spend time with you. Next time we'll be sure to give you some notice before we show up."

Sam clasped his hand. "We don't need any notice. They're good kids, plus shug's always happy to have a new face to look at, especially a child's."

"Winslow, stay out of the way, now, and do what Mr. Brown tells you," Truman said. "I'll be back in an hour and a half."

Neva was just stowing the hose when Truman left the barn. She smiled. "So how's Miles?"

Truman hung his head. Just that morning the piglet had chewed the bottom out of a plastic wastebasket in Winslow's bathroom, but why go into it?

"Listen, can I ask you a question?" she said, walking with him to the gate.

"Sure."

"How much does it cost a year for Hannah's care and upkeep?"

Truman frowned. "I'd have to look at the budget, but ballpark, it's around a hundred, hundred and twenty-five thousand dollars, if you include staff salaries and benefits. Maybe a little more. There's actually a separate trust Max Biedelman established so that Hannah would always be given the proper care. It's something I didn't know about until recently. My father only unearthed it a couple of days ago. The money wasn't a surprise, but the fact that it was in a discretionary fund was."

Neva squinted in the sunlight. "Hypothetically, if Hannah were to leave the zoo for any reason, would the trust go with her?"

Truman looked at her, surprised. "I have no idea. Why?"

Neva shrugged, but there was clearly more going on behind her eyes. "No reason."

"Ah."

"Listen, would you have lunch with me sometime?"

"I'd like that. Not at the Oat Maiden, though." Truman shuddered. "Anywhere but the Oat Maiden."

Neva smiled. "All right. You can choose the place. How about Monday, then?"

"That would be fine. Harriet is a bit odd about employee fraternization, so it might be best if we make this our little secret."


FROM time to time, as they walked through the zoo, Hannah tucked her trunk under Sam's arm.

"How come she does that, mister?" Reginald said. "Put her trunk in there like that?"

"Because she can't hold my hand."

"What do you mean?"

"Watch her," Sam said. "She usually does it when something makes her feel nervous. Too many people around, especially on her blind side, or maybe she hears a noise she doesn't recognize."

"She's *scared?*" Reginald laughed. "She gets scared? Hell, she's bigger than anything I've ever seen."

"Don't be disrespectful, boy," Sam said sternly. "If you're going to be disrespectful, you can just walk home right now."

Reginald ducked his head. "Sorry, mister. I didn't mean anything."

Winslow spoke. "Is she scared of us—of me and Reginald, I mean?"

"Nah, at least not right now. You're not doing anything but walking, and she's good about people walking on her seeing side, at least as long as they're people she knows. Now, see that man right there, the one walking toward us real fast?"

The boys watched. The man passed close by her blind side, and Hannah tucked her trunk into Sam's armpit. "Baby doesn't like people coming at her fast like that when she can't see them," he explained.

The boys walked along thoughtfully.

"What are you afraid of?" Sam asked Reginald.

"Nothin'."

"Now, that's not true. Everybody's afraid of something."

"I'm afraid of my aunt when she gets mad," Reginald said. "She starts talking and talking, and the spit just *flies.*"

"What does she talk about?" Winslow asked.

"How I'll end up in the gutter if I don't try extra hard, how it's in my blood. I don't think so, though."

"She probably just wants you to make something of yourself," Sam said. "Woman is looking out for you, son. You remember that."

"Yeah."

Sam fished a small gourd out of his canvas pouch and handed it up to Hannah. "Either of you suck your thumb when you were little?" he asked.

"I did," Winslow admitted.

"Well, Hannah sucks her trunk sometimes, if she's feeling spooky, especially at night. Girl doesn't like the dark."

The boys smiled at the thought.

NEVA waited until she was at home that evening before making her call to Alice McNeary, the director of the Pachyderm Sanctuary, to talk about Hannah. Alice was a gravel-voiced, tough-as-leather old circus trainer who'd been on the circuit for twenty-five years before giving it up to found the sanctuary. Neva gave her an overview of Hannah's circumstances.

"Which zoo is it?" Alice asked.

"The Max L. Biedelman. In Bladenham, Washington."

"What the hell are you doing in a place like that?" Alice said.

"It's a long story."

"I didn't know they even had an elephant."

"Give it another couple of weeks, and everyone will know. The director's launching a big marketing campaign about Hannah and Maxine Biedelman."

"Isn't she dead?"

Neva sighed. "Yes. It's hard to explain. The zoo director is actually billing herself as Maxine Biedelman, walking around in period clothes, giving talks, stuff like that."

"How does she feel about the prospect of giving up the zoo's main attraction?"

"That's the thing—she doesn't know anything about it. She's a controlling harridan. We're going to have to get such overwhelming grassroots support that by the time she gets wind of it, there won't be any way out. Even if we can pull that off, it will probably get ugly by the end. You need to know that up front."

Alice laughed. "And when has that ever stopped me? You know I love a good fight. But, honey, you can't do this alone. You're tough, but you're not *that* tough."

"No, it won't be me, alone. There are several of us already. The trick will be to keep it away from the zoo until we're ready to go public."

"Look, here's what we'll do. I'll brief my executive committee and go ahead and put her on a wait-list. There are four animals ahead of her, though, and I only have room for two. And my board's very tough on this. Any animal coming here has to bring two hundred fifty thousand dollars along as an endowment for their care. Those are the terms. No money, no dice."

"Well, all right, then," said Neva. "I guess I'd better go out and find me some rich people."

On Monday, Truman picked Neva up just outside the zoo gates and drove them to a place on the far side of town called Teriyaki Time, where he was relatively sure no one from the zoo would see them. The restaurant was one of Winslow's favorites, a place they often resorted to after work when Truman lacked culinary inspiration. The owner greeted him enthusiastically.

"Hey, Truman! How's it going?" He shook Truman's hand and looked admiringly at Neva.

"Hello, Thomas. Neva, meet Thomas Kubota. This is his restaurant. Thomas, this is Geneva Wilson. She's an elephant keeper at the zoo."

"I'll be damned." Thomas shook Neva's hand admiringly. "You're pretty small to be bossing a big animal around."

"It's all in the wrist."

Thomas handed Neva a menu. "Take this with you. He won't need one."

"Home away from home?" Neva asked Truman when they'd found a table at the very back of the restaurant.

"More often than I care to admit. Winslow puts up with my cooking, but there are times when neither one of us can summon the necessary forbearance."

"So you come here."

"So we come here."

While Neva examined the menu, Truman allowed himself to take her in. He had a nearly overwhelming desire to touch her. He imagined it would be like touching a lightly charged wire, that he would feel the hum and the heat. He was startled to realize that she was blushing. "Was I staring?" he said.

"Yes."

"I'm sorry. It's a novelty to be here with anyone older than eleven. Not to mention nice-looking."

"Winslow's nice-looking."

"Even so."

A waiter arrived to take their order. Once he was gone, Neva appeared to marshal herself and said, "Look, I'd like to talk to you about something."

"Uh-oh."

"The thing is, it's got to be held in the strictest confidence." Neva took a deep breath. "Is there any chance at all that the zoo might get another Asian elephant to keep Hannah company?"

Truman looked startled. "I don't see how. The zoo's revenues haven't met operating expenses in years. Why?"

Neva clasped her hands in front of her and said quietly, "Okay, then here's the thing. I'm going to try to get Hannah relocated to an elephant sanctuary in northern California. I can't believe I'm saying this to you."

"What? Why?"

"Because she'll die if she has to stay here after Sam Brown retires."

"*What?* Has something happened? Is he retiring?"

Neva poked at the ice cubes in her water glass with her fork. "Look, I'm not very good at this. No, nothing's happened. Yet. But Sam's sixty-eight years old, and he's got diabetes. I don't think he's going to be able to work that much longer, and once he's gone, you might as well put a gun to Hannah's head."

"I don't understand."

"Well you see, Truman, the thing is, elephants are extremely social. They live in herds dominated by a single leader—usually a female, but in Hannah's case Sam is her leader. Take that away, and what she's left with is a yard that's way too small, a barn that's a hell-hole, chronically infected feet, and advancing arthritis. Her entire world will shrink to about three thousand square feet of concrete and up to fourteen hours a day chained to a wall."

"Good God."

"Look. I'm not anti-captivity, and I don't have a bleeding heart. But I also believe in doing what's right for the animals. We need to get Hannah out. And I'd like your help."

THAT evening, Truman stood at the stove stirring a pan of spaghetti sauce while Miles and Winslow played nose hockey across the kitchen floor with a plastic puck. He didn't know who was more delighted, the pig or the boy.

When it was ready, Truman set a plate of spaghetti on the round oak table for Winslow, and a second one for himself. On a place mat in the corner, Miles received his own small dish of pasta, which he consumed in four gulps and a burp. Truman was discovering a certain charm in the little pig. His utter lack of guile, his naked and cheerful dedication to his appetites—food, warmth, and affection—were not so different from Winslow's or Truman's. By some obscure Darwinian chance eons ago, humans cared for pigs and not the other way around. But surely it could have gone differently. Admittedly Truman overcompensated. Miles ate cereal for his breakfast just as Winslow did, down to the brand name and the milk. At the end of each meal, his dishes were washed and stored in a cupboard. He had his own polar fleece throw in the den.

"Winslow, I'd like your opinion about something."

The boy looked up, strands of spaghetti arrested mid-suck.

Truman smiled. "Tell me about Hannah. What's she like?"

The boy shrugged. "I don't know. She's big, but she's real gentle. *She* gets scared sometimes."

"Does she?"

Winslow nodded solemnly. "Sam says when he used to take her for walks in the woods she'd get upset if he got too far away. You can tell she likes Sam. She hugs his head with her trunk. He keeps a hand on her when we take her for walks."

"I wouldn't think that would keep her from running away."

"She'd never run away, Dad. Sam does it to keep her from getting spooked. Me and Reginald asked if we could take her for a walk by ourselves sometime, but he said she wouldn't go unless he was with her."

"Ah."

"She's real smart, though. Like, Sam says she can tell when he has a headache. He gets these real bad headaches, and she'll just stand over him like she's guarding him until he feels better." Winslow twirled a huge forkful of spaghetti and continued talking through his food. "Sometimes she'll give him stuff, too. Like if it's a real bad day, she'll bring him her tire. You know, that car tire she sleeps with at night."

"She sleeps with a tire?"

"Sam says she uses it to keep her company when she's chained up by herself all night."

Truman wondered if he could bear to hear more. "What do you think would happen to her if Sam couldn't take care of her anymore?"

"That'd never happen, Dad."

"But if it did?"

"She'd die."

Truman stared. "Why do you say that?"

Winslow shrugged. "Because she would."

Truman let Winslow finish his meal and clear the table. Then he picked up the telephone and called Neva Wilson.

## 8

HARRIET fussed over her finches, wondering if they knew how beautiful they were. They were no more substantial than a dandelion blown into the wind; their songs were heavier than their bones. So ponderous in motion herself, she had always wondered what it would be like to take wing, to no more than wish yourself airborne to *be* airborne. She'd built a large aviary in her home, devoting two whole rooms to her birds so they could fly. In the last several weeks, she had sat inside the aviary often, feeling the breath of their flight on her face as they passed. Now, late on a dark Thursday evening, she confronted squarely the fact that Truman Levy had abandoned her.

For months he had shared her deep devotion to the zoo. They had talked at length, familiarly; sometimes he even put his feet up on her second visitor's chair, crossing one neat ankle over the other, his brown leather loafers as spruce as he was. Several times she had invited him out to lunch, and he had always accepted. He was only five or six years younger than she was; she had once or twice caught herself wondering if a more intimate relationship might be possible.

But that had all changed when Neva Wilson came to the zoo. Harriet had expected his enthusiastic support for the new advertising campaign, but instead she detected a degree of discomfort. Their shared commitment to the zoo—which was to say, to each other—was clearly eroding.

Harriet was never sure at what age she had recognized that she would probably never marry. By the time she was in her late twenties, the list of social opportunities that she had never experienced was already long: high school proms, homecoming dances, double dates, drive-in movies, sorority pledges. Instead there had been an endless string of weddings, of cousins, colleagues, neighbors. She had spent money she didn't have on silver plate and cheap crystal for the gifts. She began to decline the endless string of baby showers that had replaced the wedding invitations, using the saved gift money to buy finches instead, and then to build an aviary in the small house she had bought for herself on her thirtieth birthday.

In all those years, there'd never even been a serious boyfriend. There had been men from time to time, more or less interchangeably. They phoned, proposing movie dates or dinner at inexpensive ethnic restaurants. Then the calls would come less and less frequently until finally they failed to come at all. She'd thought that Truman was different, but clearly she'd been wrong.

ACROSS town in her apartment, Neva was in a less philosophical frame of mind. Another gale had blown in off Puget Sound, the third in a week. The windows rattled as sudden hail clattered against the glass like BBs. Sam had told her he and Corinna spent evenings like these in the barn because storms made Hannah anxious, and there were a lot of storms in this part of the Northwest. Neva sometimes found their devotion unnerving. He and Corinna were also childless; if she remembered right, there had been something about a baby many years ago, some tragedy. Sitting in her Goodwill armchair in her one-room apartment, Neva contemplated the nature of loss. Six months ago, she had been in the waiting room of a dental office in Yonkers, New York, when across the room a boy reading a book went off in her mind like a bomb. He had a long, slender face and hair that blazed like autumn. He might have been her, twenty-five years earlier.

Or he might have been her son.

She'd left the office with a pounding heart. In putting her baby up for adoption, she had agreed that she would never try to find the child. But she went to a nearby Barnes & Noble and bought a book about dragons that the clerk assured her would suit an eleven-year-old boy. Then she returned to the dental office.

"I just noticed this book in my backpack," she said, lying to the receptionist. "I must have picked it up by accident—it belongs to the boy who was here this morning, and I'd like to return it to him. Can you tell me his name or an address where I can drop it off?"

"You can just leave it with me, and I can call for you," the girl had said brightly.

Neva had slid the book into an envelope, put a card inside that simply said, "I've heard this is a great book," and sealed it up. No signature, no phone number. No harm. She might as well have seen a ghost in that waiting room.

Harriet had been sitting in her aviary for several hours with a bottle of wine, and now she poured out the last glass. Somewhere around the middle of the bottle she had gone to her bedroom to change into her Maxine Biedelman clothes. She couldn't say why; no one was going to see her tonight. But she felt better in them, much better. Maxine Biedelman went her own way, shining the dual beams of her strength and independence far ahead into the darkness. No one would have dared to call her Bucket. Maxine was a force to be reckoned with.

Harriet took a yellow legal tablet from a little Indonesian teak table she'd bought recently and fished a pen out of her breast pocket. She had had reading lenses made for a pince-nez she'd found among Maxine's things in the attic, and now she clipped these on her nose as she consulted her notes.

She was developing a budget for renovating Havenside. The house had once been a place of glory. There had been painted skies on the ceilings, with birds and scudding clouds; ornate moldings and gothic arched windows and claw-foot bathtubs with taps in the shape of griffon heads. It would cost between seven hundred and fifty thousand and one million dollars to return the house to its original splendor. Restoring Havenside's paths and gardens would cost another twelve thousand dollars.

It wasn't that much. Harriet estimated that she could raise the money through an aggressive capital campaign in less than two years. She would have Martin Choi run periodic articles keeping the citizens of Bladenham informed, fueling their civic pride. As Maxine, Harriet was also ripe for television coverage, including regional and even national programs like *60 Minutes.* National Public Radio was another must-have. She made a note to investigate the cost of commissioning theme music—a signature piece, something robust and memorable that could be used in future zoo ads.

And then, while sipping the last of the wine and paging idly through a stack of old photographs she had brought home from the zoo, Harriet Saul experienced an epiphany. Skipping over animal images, she studied for a long time a picture of Maxine Biedelman at the turn of the century on the Serengeti Plain in Africa. No girl now, but a woman standing tanned and clear-eyed, Maxine regarded the camera with a straight back and a faint smile, solidly grounded in her heavy brown boots. An energy beat from the paper like a drum, not civilized but primal, elemental, a throbbing in the gut, in the belly like an oath. *I am, I am, I am.*

For the first time in her life, Harriet understood what her spirit had known for some time: She was in love.


SAM sat on a hassock in his living room, gently rubbing Corinna's poor flat feet and swollen ankles. "You're getting too old to stand up all day, Mama," he said.

Corinna dismissed his remark with a wave of the hand. "That apple cider vinegar footbath helping the baby at all?"

"Not much. But I'm hoping," Sam said.

"You think it's really going to happen?" Corinna asked.

"What?"

"Moving the baby."

"Don't know, Mama, but it's the right thing to do, taking shug to that place."

"I never thought of her living just with elephants."

"You mean I've been dreaming it all these years and you never saw it?"

"No," Corinna said. "I don't know why, exactly. But the baby's people. I never thought of other elephants as people, not like shug."

"They are, though," Sam said, frowning. "At least, they're *her* people."

"Think she'll know what to say to them?" Corinna asked.

"If she doesn't, she'll learn. She must have known how to do it over there in Burma."

"That was a long time ago."

"I know that, Mama," Sam said quietly. "But she's going to be all right. I can feel it." He stopped rubbing, holding Corinna's feet quietly in the palms of his hands.

"What are you thinking about?" she asked.

"Don't know who I'll be, without the girl."

"I've thought that, too," Corinna said softly.

"I guess we'll find out, when the time comes," Sam said. He lowered Corinna's feet into her slippers, arranged her skirt over her ample lap, and kissed her hand.

"Well." Corinna heaved herself out of her chair and patted his cheek. "I think I'd better see about supper."

"Something I can do?"

"Nah, you just put your legs up."

Sam stood until she was gone, then lowered himself into his own chair with gratitude. His legs were on fire from the knees down, and the ulcer was moving down onto the sole of his foot. He didn't know how much longer he could hold on, though he'd never tell that to Corinna. She worried too much as it was.

He parked his eyes on the far wall and found himself thinking about the baby they'd lost. At first Corinna had gone so far away in her mind, Sam had thought he might lose her, too. But except for her everlasting feud with God, she'd healed. Maybe not completely, maybe not perfectly, but mostly you couldn't see the scar, not even when you knew where to look.

But since Neva Wilson had started talking about moving Hannah to the sanctuary, Corinna had been suffering; Sam, too. Neither of them had much experience with travel. They'd pretend they were planning to visit that place, but they'd never do it. They'd grieve. Hannah would go, and they would not, and that was just the way it had to be.

JOHNSON Johnson paced in his kitchen, waiting and waiting. Finally there was a knock on his door.

"What surprise?" Neva said, holding the note he'd taped to her front door. He breathed in the smell of animal dung and musk and fruit and hay that wafted around her like a fine perfume.

"I made something," he said. "Come on." He was out of the room and headed upstairs before Neva had even closed the outside door. He could feel her following warily. She'd be pleased, though, once she saw what he'd done.

"Here," he said. Three steel drums sat on the wide landing outside his bathroom, where he'd been working on them under his yellow lightbulb. He used the yellow light when he needed to hear as well as see something he was making. He didn't know why it worked that way, just that he'd always been able to hear better when it was turned on.

Neva inhaled sharply, running her hands over the drums. Johnson Johnson had cut them at different heights and hammered their tops into different shapes. Around the outsides he'd painted friezes of elephants. From a rivet on the side of each drum he'd hung a rubber mallet with foam tape wrapped around the wooden handle as a grip.

"I thought, you know. For your elephant," he explained.

"My god, they're *beautiful,*" Neva breathed. "Can you play them?"

"You can."

Neva gonged one of the drums tentatively. It returned a perfect C major. "You've calibrated the entire drum to play true tones?"

Johnson Johnson blinked anxiously. "Well, it's supposed to be for music."

"You're amazing."

"You think maybe she'll like them?"

"How could she not like them?"

"Well, I mean, she's an elephant," he pointed out.

"Listen. Let's take them down to the zoo together," Neva said.

"Me?"

"Sure. Don't you want to see her play them?"

"Okay. But first come see this," he said, pulling her into his bedroom by the arm. She looked alarmed and tried to pull away. He quickly closed the door behind them to make the room dark.

"No, let me—"

"Look up," he said, letting go of her arm. He pointed to the stars.

Neva looked up and did a double take. "You did this, too?"

"It's not done yet, though." They both stood still, heads back, mouths slightly open, watching the evening stars. Then he opened the door and switched on the light again in case she was afraid of the dark.

Neva looked at Johnson Johnson, paused momentarily for effect, and said, "What would you think about getting a pizza?"

"*Pizza?*" Johnson Johnson breathed, unsure of what else to say in the face of such an unexpected gift.

"Pizza," Neva confirmed. "I'll order it. There's someone I'd like you to meet, and I'd like to do it here, if you don't mind, so he can see your work."

"Okay."

"Can I ask him to come over now? Would that be okay?"

"Okay. He can have pizza."

NEVA went down to the kitchen and called Truman, who promised to be there as soon as he and Winslow had eaten dinner. She told him not to bother; they'd have food waiting for them. Then she called another number from a magnet on Johnson Johnson's refrigerator and ordered an extra-large pizza with everything.

Half an hour later—five minutes behind the pizza delivery guy—Truman and Winslow knocked on Johnson Johnson's door. Neva introduced them all around, passing out paper plates. Johnson Johnson extended the pizza box to them with the utmost dignity.

Neva tore through her own slice. "I can't wait to show you these drums Johnson's made for Hannah." She caught the look Truman gave her. "I know. Just wait until you see them. Let's show you now. It won't take long, and then we can finish eating." She turned to Johnson Johnson. "Is that okay with you?"

"Okay," he said.

Neva led the way upstairs. Johnson Johnson trailed behind. When they reached the landing, Neva put her hands over Truman's eyes until he was in position, then pulled her hands away. "Ta-dah!"

Truman looked, tapped, gonged. "These are extraordinary. Really—they're *beautiful.*"

Johnson Johnson flushed with pleasure.

Truman turned to Neva. "You know, folk art has really come into its own in the last decade or so."

"Any idea what they might sell for?"

Truman frowned. "Well, if people knew they were to benefit Hannah—or, say, an anonymous but needy elephant—I'd bet a set like this could sell for two thousand, twenty-five-hundred dollars. Maybe more."

"Look," Neva said. "Why don't we get dinner over with and bring the drums to Hannah? I want Johnson to see what she does with them. Harriet won't be there this late, will she?"

Truman consulted his watch. "Probably not," he said. "Though with her, you can never be sure."

Neva called Sam and Corinna's house. She let the phone ring eight times, but no one answered. Then she dialed the elephant barn. After four rings, Sam picked up.

"Sam? Is Corinna there, too?"

"Uh-huh. We're watching Laurel and Hardy."

"Well, stay there. We're bringing something for Hannah."

"We?"

"Just wait. You'll never guess," Neva said, and hung up.

JOHNSON Johnson followed Neva down to the elephant yard. Neva carried one drum, and Johnson Johnson carried two. Truman and Winslow had headed off to the mansion to make sure Harriet Saul wasn't there.

"You're sure Hannah won't ruin them if she hits them too hard?" Neva asked as they set the drums down while she unlocked the gate.

"Well, if she retunes them, it'd probably be so she can play her own songs better. Maybe elephant music doesn't sound like people music."

Sam met them at the barn door and helped them bring the three drums inside. Once they were safely through, Neva introduced him and Corinna to Johnson Johnson.

"It's a pleasure to meet you," Sam said, shaking hands and then turning to inspect the drums. "Just look at these," he said. "Shug, come over here and see what this man's made for you. Music!"

Hannah shambled over from the television, cradling a small rock in the crook of her trunk. Neva patted her. "Johnson, meet Hannah. Hannah, this is Johnson Johnson."

Johnson Johnson held out his hand to shake, Hannah put down her rock to stretch her trunk, and they met someplace in the middle. Then Hannah walked her trunk up Johnson Johnson's arm, sniffing.

"She's big," he said.

"Well, she's an elephant."

"Uh-huh."

Truman and Winslow slipped in the door. "We're all clear," Truman said.

Done assessing Johnson Johnson, Hannah stretched her trunk toward Sam, nosing around his pocket. "No treats left in there, shug," he said. "Here's your treat, right here."

Sam gave Hannah one of the mallets, and she wrapped her trunk around it and swung aimlessly.

"You've got to try banging it on Mr. Johnson's drum like this." Sam brought the second mallet down on one of the drums, producing a ringing G major. Hannah opened her eyes wide and lifted her trunk in great excitement. Sam slapped her shoulder supportively. "You can do it, too, shug. Go on, now."

Hannah hit the drum once, and then again, and soon there was a halting chain of notes, all perfectly pitched. Johnson Johnson rose up on his toes and bounced. Sam turned to him and grinned. "You've done something awful nice, Mr. Johnson. Sugar's never made music before."

"Well, you know." Johnson Johnson tucked his chin in embarrassment and pride. Sam clapped him on the back reassuringly.

Hannah played a riff between the two drums. It might have been music. Even if it wasn't, the notes were pleasing.

"I think we might want to talk about something," Neva said.

All eyes turned.

"I think we need to talk about money. We need two hundred and fifty thousand dollars for the sanctuary to take Hannah. Plus whatever it'll cost to transport her."

Truman cleared his throat. "Let's wait before we have this conversation. It's getting late, and I've asked my father to do a little snooping. I don't want to say anything more at this point, because it's too soon to get our hopes up."

Hannah had wandered off to find her tire, and everyone else began yawning and searching for jackets and car keys. Sam shackled Hannah to the wall for the night, whispering reassuring words Neva couldn't make out.

As Neva let the door swing shut behind her, she looked back at Hannah, alone and chained to the wall in the gloom. The elephant was already rocking slowly from side to side, silently and relentlessly. By morning, Neva knew, her ankle would be bleeding beneath the shackle, as someone might cut bright, secret wounds with a razor blade.

MARTIN Choi had a plan, and that plan did not include covering a beat for the *Bladenham News-Gazette* for the rest of his life. He was going places, and to do that, he needed page-one bylines, unexpected story angles, scoops. He felt that his newfound access to the inner workings of the Max L. Biedelman Zoo might help him get there. Harriet Saul had made it clear that he would be on the inside of breaking news. That didn't mean he was going to sell out and become her boy, though. He would use his investigative skills, look around, develop inside sources.

He shifted on the uncomfortable plastic chair in the zoo's waiting room. Martin had been here for half an hour. He promised himself he'd wait just fifteen more minutes. He had his limits.

The phone rang, and the receptionist picked it up, nodded at it, and put it down. "She'll see you now."

Martin lifted and stood in stages: first his camera bag and accessories, then his cameras and several lenses, finally his bandoleer of film canisters. It took a while. The office door opened, and Harriet appeared looking impatient.

"Hey, yeah, great to see you again," Martin said, freeing a hand and extending it. "I appreciate your taking the time, you know, on so little notice."

"It's fine." She led him into the surprisingly grimy inner sanctum of her office, showed him to a chair, and sat down herself like royalty behind her desk. "What story are you working on?"

"Tell me about the drums," he said.

"Drums?"

"Yeah. The elephant was playing a couple of steel drums, real fancy. Drew a big crowd and everything."

"When?"

536 | Diane Hammond

"Now. This morning."

Harriet's left eye twitched. "Why don't we just go down there and see?" she said ominously.

Clanking like Marley's ghost, he set off after Harriet, who was steaming ahead so fast that Martin lost her in the crowd when they got to the elephant exhibit. By the time he found her, she was talking through the fence to a woman employee inside the exhibit. "And when did you think you'd let me know about this?"

"Look, it was strictly spur-of-the-moment," the woman said. "The man who made the drums is my landlord. I didn't even know he was working on them until he gave them to me last night."

"Did anyone else know about this?"

"No."

"I'll bet. I'm going to have Truman put a letter in your personnel file, documenting that you're now on probation."

"You've got to be kidding!"

Harriet turned her back and walked away.

"So do you care to make any comments about the drums?" Martin said, trotting up beside her.

Harriet gave him a withering look. "I think you can see for yourself that Hannah's received a set of drums, which she's using. It's all part of our environmental enrichment program."

Martin watched as Harriet's sizable khaki haunches receded from the exhibit and up the hill to her office.

TRUMAN sat at his desk, looking at a memo Harriet had tossed there with instructions that it was to be placed in Neva's personnel file immediately. It was an ugly thing, closing with, *I, Harriet Saul, recommend immediate termination if or when this employee acts without prior authorization in the future.*

Truman slipped the memo into the file, locked the drawer, and called the elephant barn. Neva answered.

"Hey," Truman said.

Neva said, "Hi. How's life up there in the gulag?"

"Scary. Would you have dinner with me tonight?"

Neva sighed. "I don't think I'd be very good company."

"Please say yes."

"All right, as long as I don't have to be perky. I'm definitely not up for being perky."

"I'm not feeling all that perky myself. How about meeting me at Teriyaki Time at six-fifteen?"

"Okay."

Truman hung up the phone and pressed the heels of his hands hard against his eyes. It was only 10:05, and he could feel a pounding headache coming on.

SAM removed his zoo ball cap and said to the receptionist, "Miss Saul wanted to see me."

Harriet called out through her open office door, "Come in, Sam."

Sam walked in slowly and stood in front of her desk, cap in hand. "Yes, ma'am."

"Were you here last night when Neva Wilson brought in the drums?"

"Yes, ma'am."

"She lied, then. She said no one else knew about it."

"I didn't know, ma'am—I was already here."

"Why?"

Sam ducked his head. "Me and Mrs. Brown come in the evenings sometimes to keep Hannah company."

Harriet frowned. "I wasn't aware of that. How often?"

"Not often, ma'am," Sam said, alarmed. "Maybe once a week, sometimes twice. It does Hannah good to—"

Harriet was shaking her head. "I can't have that, Sam."

Stunned, Sam said, "Why?"

"You're an hourly employee. I can't have you here working hours I'm unprepared to pay you for. There are liability issues."

"I don't do it to get paid, ma'am. I'm just giving Hannah a little extra company. She gets lonely chained to that—"

"I'm sorry." Harriet's attention was already moving on. She began sifting through a pile of papers. "Please let Geneva know, also. You may not be on the premises except during your regular hours."

"But, ma'am," Sam protested with growing alarm. "Hannah's already alone in that barn for twelve, fourteen hours a day sometimes."

"That's all, Sam. Thank you."

"Miss Saul, you're doing the wrong thing, the *wrong* damn thing for that elephant," Sam said bitterly.

"I don't appreciate being sworn at, Sam. And I really must insist that you call me Maxine." Harriet began to write notes in the margins of a document on her desk. "Maxine Biedelman."

TERIYAKI Time was packed when Truman got there, but Thomas had saved a table for them. Truman stood until Neva had slipped into the booth, a gesture of respect his parents had drilled into him early. He thought Neva looked strained. Even her hair seemed at odds, pulled into a messy bun from which strands kept escaping.

"What?" Neva said, blushing. She attempted a smile, but it failed before it even reached the corners of her mouth.

"Nothing. You look tired. Tired and discouraged."

"How do you do it?" she asked.

"Do what?"

"I've known rhinos with better dispositions. And I hate rhinos." Truman conceded the point.

"So where's Winslow?"

"Ah. He's with his mother. She got into town last night. He'll be with her through Thanksgiving."

"How long have you been divorced?"

"Just about a year."

"Why?"

"Why did we divorce?" Truman blew out a ruminative breath. "I guess you could say we had trouble synchronizing. You know that carnival ride where two cages swing in opposite directions, going higher and higher until they go over the top? That was us. We never stopped in the same place until it was time to get off the ride."

"So that doesn't sound good," Neva said.

"No."

"How is Winslow dealing with it?"

"Mostly okay—frankly, I think he's relieved that she's not around very much. She tends to take up a lot of space."

Neva looked at him for a long moment, weighing something. Then she said, "I have a son Winslow's age. I gave the baby up for adoption. I was twenty-five. He deserved to live with someone more suitable than me."

"Do you know where he is?"

"No. I thought I saw him once in New York, but that's not likely. I lived in San Diego when he was born."

"Have you ever been married?"

"A couple of years."

Truman raised his eyebrows encouragingly.

"Howard's dream was to become a securities analyst. My dream was to *shovel manure,* as he liked to put it. Manure and securities don't mix."

"So you got out," Truman said.

"So I got out. It was all very amicable. He remarried a few years ago, and she was a good choice for him. I think they're happy."

Truman suddenly stood and beckoned with one raised hand to Sam and Corinna, who had just arrived.

"Now I know why you had Thomas put us at a big table," Neva said. "How nice!"

Truman helped Corinna into a seat. "Thanks, baby," she said, and then to Neva, "How are you, honey? Sam said it was a bad, bad day."

"Yeah, it was," Neva said.

"Well, I have some news that might help," Truman said. Three faces turned to him as one.

"Spill it, honey," Corinna said. "I think we could all use something good."

Truman crossed his hands on the tabletop. "My father's a retired judge. You probably know that the zoo's financial situation isn't the best, so a few weeks ago I asked him to go through some old city records to see if there might be a long-forgotten fund or an endowment that could help make up the zoo's shortfall. He found something interesting. Sam, when Max Biedelman passed away, did anyone say anything to you about Hannah?"

"No, sir. Not that I remember."

"Well, they should have. Before she died, Max Biedelman set up a trust that would be used for Hannah's upkeep. It was to be overseen by a trustee who was—is—empowered to make decisions about anything that involves Hannah's welfare."

"I never heard anything about that," Sam said.

"You should have. Because it's you. You're the trustee!" Truman grinned. "How d'ya like *them* apples?"

"But what does it mean?" Corinna asked.

"It means that Sam is Hannah's legal guardian," Truman said. "It means if he feels Hannah's at risk in any way, he can ask the zoo to make whatever changes he feels are necessary. The zoo has to comply, or it loses roughly seventy-five thousand dollars a year. Which, let me tell you, it cannot afford to do."

"Are you saying that the trust owns her?" Neva said.

"No. On the surface of it, the zoo owns her. *But*—and here's where it gets fun—what if Sam deems that the *zoo itself* does not and cannot meet Hannah's needs? Does he have the legal right to move her to a facility that can?"

"Like the Pachyderm Sanctuary," Neva said.

"Like the Pachyderm Sanctuary. My father needs a little more time to look into this before he gives us his final opinion. But the bottom line is, things are going to get better for Hannah. Sam has the power to make that happen."

"Someone going to tell that to Harriet Saul?" Sam asked.

"My father's offered to talk with her. And he'll meet with Sam and Neva before work tomorrow morning."

TRUMAN and Neva sat in Truman's car watching the rain outside Teriyaki Time long after Sam and Corinna had driven away. "I don't understand why no one ever told Sam he was the trustee," Neva said. "That makes no sense."

Truman smiled and said, "I'd never have guessed it—you're naïve!"

"Me? Naïve?"

"Think about it. Sam was a black man in 1958 when Max Biedelman died. The town leaders weren't going to put him in charge of seventy-five thousand dollars a year."

"Seventy-five thousand, is that how much the zoo gets? That's less than a third of what we'd need for the sanctuary to take her."

"No, no. That's just the annual earnings," Truman said. "The trust itself is worth more than half a million."

"God, I *love* you," she crowed, and then she folded herself over the emergency brake and the gearshift column and kissed him in a way he hadn't been kissed in years or maybe longer; maybe ever.

AT SEVEN a.m., Truman, Sam, and Neva sat at a table farthest from the door of the Oat Maiden, nervously fidgeting with thick, mismatched mugs of coffee. It was the first time either Truman or Sam had been inside—and most likely would be the last, at least as far as Truman was concerned. The café's walls were painted navy blue, and all the tables and chairs apparently came from mothballed public high school classrooms. Cheerful little notes were taped to the walls: TRY THE ORGANIC HAND-PRESSED CIDER! and WE CHEERFULLY SUBSTITUTE SOY MILK. Only Neva seemed at ease.

Truman's father, Matthew, arrived with a heavy briefcase and a broad smile. Matthew Levy had the build of a boy and the large, agile brain of a man perfectly suited to receiving and processing information. He shook Neva's hand, and then Sam's. "It's a pleasure to meet you, Mr. Brown," Matthew said. "I've heard a lot about you."

"Don't know what there'd be to say about me, sir. But me and Hannah and my wife are real grateful to you for helping like this. You can call me Sam."

"All right then, Sam," Matthew said pleasantly.

He spread documents across the tabletop and described to Sam and Neva what each one established, and what he felt was the best plan for opening up a discussion with Harriet Saul.

"Sam, you and I have a meeting with Harriet Saul scheduled for ten o'clock this morning. I thought it might be best for me to open with an overview of the changed situation in which we suddenly find ourselves. We need to establish that you, as Hannah's legal guardian, have the right and responsibility to ensure that her care is of the highest quality. Is this all right with you so far, Sam?"

"Yes, sir," Sam said gravely.

"After that, you may say whatever you feel needs to be said—for instance, that you and your wife will continue to provide company for Hannah in the evenings as often as you see fit."

"I hate to be stirring things up, sir," Sam said, "but shug just doesn't do well when she's alone too much."

"You don't need to justify yourself to me, Sam. Truman has described the situation, and I believe you are every bit within your moral as well as your legal rights to act as you have done." He pressed Sam's forearm reassuringly. "We're going to need a governmental permit in order to legally move Hannah. The process will take weeks, at best."

Sam looked alarmed. "You going to tell her about us taking the girl to the sanctuary?"

"For now we think it would be best not to talk about moving Hannah. We have a little more legal work to do before we're comfortable scaling that wall."

"Yes, sir," Sam said, visibly relieved.

"You don't expect me to take your word for any of this, do you?" Harriet Saul said after Matthew had finished his presentation. Sam hunched in his seat at the conference room table.

"Of course not," Matthew soothed. "You'd be wise to talk with the city's legal counsel. In the meantime, however, I trust we've been clear that Mr. Brown will be on the premises whenever he feels it's necessary, day or night, but that he does not intend to request compensation beyond his usual and customary wages. And if you consult the zoo's insurance carrier, I'm sure the liability issues will be easy to resolve."

Harriet stared at him hostilely. Matthew continued, "Let me remind you that Mr. Brown's wages are not paid by the zoo itself, but by the trust. Technically, Mr. Brown wouldn't require your authorization for overtime compensation. But never mind—we're acting in good faith, and we're confident that you'll proceed in the same spirit."

Harriet turned and stalked out of the room without a word, slamming the door behind her.

"What happens now, sir?" Sam asked.

"A rebuttal from the zoo, I would imagine, challenging the validity of the trust. I want you to call if you have any concerns or questions, Sam, or if Ms. Saul takes any action that you're uncomfortable with."

"Like what?" Sam said.

"Oh, there are a number of things she can do to make things difficult for you," Matthew said. "Taking away your keys to the facility. Attempting to fire you. Denying you access to the zoo property. You get the idea."

Alarmed, Sam said, "You think she's going to do any of those things?"

"Ah—that I don't know," Matthew said. "But I'd say she's capable of it."

## 10

AFTER work that day—the day before Thanksgiving—Truman found a message from Winslow on the answering machine. Winslow said that he and Rhonda were going to have Thanksgiving dinner at the Ramada Inn, and asked if he could come home right afterwards. The boy had been whispering, as though he hadn't wanted his mother to hear him. The original plan had been for Winslow to stay with Rhonda until sometime Friday afternoon. Truman called her cell phone with a sinking heart.

"He says he wants homemade pies," Rhonda said grimly when Truman reached her. "I can't imagine what he's thinking. I am not Betty Crocker."

"He knows you're not Betty Crocker."

"Have I ever baked a pie—have I ever even *once* expressed an interest in baking a pie?"

"I bake. He's probably just forgetting."

"That child has never forgotten a thing in his life. He's unnatural. We were in a Walgreen's, and he remembered the brand of moisturizing cream I use. It's not normal for a child, a *boy* child, to commit his mother's toiletries to memory."

"Is he there? Can he hear you?"

"No. He's in the tub," Rhonda said ominously. "He's bathing."

"Bathing is okay."

"It's the second bath he's taken, Truman. He's eleven. He's supposed to like dirty socks and his hair sticking up."

"Well, he never has before, so I can't think why he'd start now."

Rhonda blew out a breath and said, "Let it be on your head."

"What?"

"His emasculation. Let it be on your head."

"Yes, all right. Would you ask him to call me when he's out of the tub? He left me a message saying he'd like me to pick him up tomorrow after your Thanksgiving dinner. That's fine with me, if it's all right with you."

Rhonda's tone was frosty. "He gets more like you every day."

Almost as soon as Truman hung up, the phone rang again. It was Neva, calling to say that she, Sam, and Corinna would be at the elephant barn for Thanksgiving dinner, and they'd like him to come, too. "I guess they spend every Thanksgiving and Christmas there," Neva told him. "Hannah gets two of her own pumpkin pies, plus one banana cream. Anyway, they've asked us and your mom and dad to join them. Bring mashed potatoes, if you can."

"I wouldn't miss it," Truman said. "What did my folks say?"

"Exactly the same thing."

CORINNA had dressed for the occasion with a Thanksgiving holiday apron and Indian corn fingernail decals. Sam wore a sweater, khaki wash pants, and suspenders. Matthew, Truman's father, had dressed down in a sport coat and tie; Truman's elegant mother, Lavinia, wore her pearls, a cashmere twin set, and a Pendleton wool skirt. Neva had on jeans because she always wore jeans, plus a thick, soft chenille sweater the color of tangerines; she wore her hair down, falling softly around her face. Truman's heart ached when he looked at her. Truman himself had chosen a tie with embroidered turkeys all over it that Winslow had given him as a gift the year before. Winslow, fresh from Rhonda's loving arms, had chosen to dress in his sweater vest, oxford cloth button-down shirt, and sharp-creased slacks. Truman could only imagine—and with a wicked little smile—the wrath his clothes had probably incurred at Rhonda's. All in all, they were a festive group, perched around the inside of the barn on lawn chairs, sharing TV tables. Hannah stood in their midst, rolling pebbles in the crook of her trunk while she watched Corinna take foil off the tops of several pies.

"Baby sure loves these," Corinna said. "The first year we tried mincemeat, too, but she didn't take to that one so much. Whipped cream, though, that's a whole other thing. She's a whipped cream kind of girl—whipped cream and banana cream pie."

Lavinia stretched out her hand toward Hannah but hesitated. "May I touch her, Sam? Will I startle her?"

"Naw, she likes being touched. Just give her a good, firm pat—or you can just leave your hand on her, let her know you're friendly. She likes that, too."

Lavinia reached up and thumped Hannah smartly on her side. Hannah stretched her trunk toward the older woman, zeroing in on her pearls and twin set en route to her face and neck. Lavinia held very still as the questing trunk made its way around her.

"She's telling you she likes you, putting her trunk by your ear like that," Sam said. "Baby always was one for bath powder and perfume. If you've got either of those on, she'll be stuck to you like glue."

Matthew smiled. "Your elephant has good taste, Sam. Lavinia wears nothing but Chanel Number Five."

Sam went over to Hannah's probing trunk and headed her away. "It isn't good manners to smell a lady for too long, shug, even when you're doing it out of admiration."

Corinna was making the rounds with what was left of the pumpkin pie when there was a knock at the barn door. Everyone else looked concerned, but Neva said, "It's okay," and jumped up as though she'd expected it. "I'm glad you're here," she said, pushing the door open. "Come on in." Behind her, Johnson Johnson dipped his head self-consciously and worked the hem of his coat between a thumb and forefinger. His hair was plastered down with something, and he wore a strange, nubbly brown sports coat over a brilliant tie-dyed T-shirt.

"Matthew, Lavinia, this is Johnson Johnson," Neva said. "He's my landlord, Hannah's patron, and a folk artist extraordinaire. Johnson, I think you know everyone else here."

"He's the one who made those drums for the girl. I've never seen anything so beautiful. You just come on in, sugar," Corinna said, taking Johnson Johnson's arm and leading him to a chair beside her own. "We got pumpkin and banana cream. Which one do you want to start with?"

Johnson Johnson looked up at her. "Pumpkin," he said and then, flushing, "Pumpkin, *please.*"

Matthew stood and held up his paper cup of cider. "A toast," he said, and everyone turned to him. "To Hannah, to her trustee, and, most of all, to safe journeys."

No one made a sound; no one even breathed.

Matthew grinned and raised his cup high. "The trust is fully transferable."

ACROSS THE ZOO PROPERTY, Harriet Saul sat in her office in the dark, sipping her fourth plastic cup of wine. It was a cheap bottle of Merlot from an unknown Argentinean vineyard, something she had found in the grocery store closeout bin. Outside her office, in the now-deserted reception area, an electric Christmas wreath blinked red, green, red, endlessly like a conflicted heart. *Stop! Go! Stop!*

She had seen lights on at the elephant barn when she came in, heard faint laughter as she crossed the parking lot to her office. They had betrayed her, all of them, and she couldn't understand it, knew she'd never understand it, except to realize that once again she had misplaced her trust. In the end, the mistake had been hers.

Harriet tapped out the last drop of wine, hid the bottle among others in her office closet, and re-enabled the security system. As she pulled the outside door to, a fresh volley of laughter rang out from the elephant barn, mocking her; mocking everything she was and ever would be.

FOR Martin Choi, Friday morning came late and brought with it one hell of a hangover. That's what he got for spending Thanksgiving at No Place Special, the *Bladenham News-Gazette*'s bar of choice. He had won nearly fifty dollars at darts, but after that, things got fuzzy. He woke up in his clothes, lying on top of his bed with one shoe on.

The phone on his desk rang. Closing his eyes so that the assault would be limited to just one of his senses, he lifted the receiver and mumbled something that was meant to resemble his name.

"Yes, good morning," a well-modulated male voice said. "Are you the reporter who has written several features about the Biedelman Zoo recently? If you are, I believe I have a story for you."

Martin straightened up: Hell yes, he was that reporter.

The caller identified himself as Matthew Levy. Martin knew the name—Matthew Levy was something of a legend around Bladenham, one of the youngest judges ever appointed.

"You may be interested to know that a forty-one-year-old document has surfaced at the city of Bladenham archives that establishes that Hannah—of course you are familiar with Hannah, the elephant—has a trustee, a guardian, if you will; and that he, not the zoo, has the responsibility of overseeing her care and monitoring her health. Would this story be of interest to you?"

"Hell, yes!"

On his way to the judge's house, Martin dry-shaved and picked up and bolted a desperately needed double shot of espresso from the Java Hut. It was a good thing he did, too, because the Levy sunporch was agonizingly white, with white walls and white wicker.

"Please sit down, Martin," Matthew said, gesturing to a chair. "You've already met my wife, Lavinia, of course." Indeed he had: Lavinia had met him at the door, wearing so much solid gold Martin figured her net worth, just sitting there beside him, was probably twice the value of Martin's car. Martin smiled and nodded.

Lavinia poured a cup of coffee from a carafe into a thin china cup and handed it to him.

Matthew began. "As it turns out, Martin—and this knowledge is brand-new, fresh news—Mr. Brown, Hannah's keeper, is also her legal guardian and has been since 1958, though no one informed him of that until now." Matthew explained the trust fund and how some money flowed into the zoo's operating budget each year. And how, now that there was a trustee involved, the zoo would spend the trust money at the trustee's behest—possibly even reallocating it, "if he finds that the zoo's facilities are inadequate."

Martin squinted. "So *are* there inadequacies? Is she treated right? I mean, she always looks kind of depressed when you go down there, now that I think about it. She's usually just standing around with this crummy old tire. Except when she's painting or something. Playing the drums."

"All of those are excellent observations, Martin. There is also something else, but I can't share it with you without an absolute guarantee of anonymity," Matthew said.

"Yeah, hey, no problem," Martin agreed. Sometimes people wouldn't say the really ugly stuff except anonymously. Martin was okay with that.

"Then I would like to tell you something about Harriet Saul that she would never tell you herself—might even deny if you confronted her with it." Matthew took a deep breath, lowered his voice, leaned forward, and said, "Harriet Saul is personally spearheading an effort to move Hannah to the Pachyderm Sanctuary. *Personally,* Martin. She's committing an act of keen integrity, I might even say courage. I'm sure you understand fully how much more difficult her job as the zoo's managerial and financial overseer will become without Hannah."

Martin squinted suspiciously.

"Harriet Saul's not doing this to draw attention to herself, Martin; she isn't doing this for self-aggrandizement or even basic recognition. She's doing it for Hannah, *because it's right*. Because it's right. Pure and simple."

"Well, sure," Martin said. "Sure! Picture being the head of an operation like the Biedelman Zoo, and knowing that the one animal you need most to put you on the map is the one who needs *you* to let it go? How are you going to explain that? You're not!"

"So you understand," Matthew said gravely.

"Damn right."

"Martin."

"Huh?"

"Report it, son. Report it."

"THAT was masterful," Lavinia told Matthew after she saw Martin to his car.

Matthew shrugged disparagingly. "It's what we call 'seizing the higher ground.' Especially about Harriet Saul's goodness."

A FRONT-PAGE, above-the-fold headline in forty-point type in the *Bladenham News-Gazette* proclaimed, TROUBLE AT THE ZOO? FAVORITE ELEPHANT HAS NEW BOSS. It was bylined Martin Choi.

Harriet crackled with fury as she huddled with Mayor Howard Bolton and city of Bladenham counsel Bob Medford at City Hall. "I'm not going to accept this—you can't possibly expect me to accept this. It's ridiculous, Howard. Without that elephant, the zoo's nothing but a collection of hoofed stock, barnyard animals, and a couple of ratty primates."

Howard turned to his legal counsel. "Bob, in your experience, if we contest this thing, would we win?"

"Probably not. The documents establishing the trust and setting its provisions are very straightforward."

"Oh, we'll contest it," Harriet said in a low, dangerous voice.

"Now, Harriet," Howard said. "We don't want to get into any expensive, drawn-out legal battle. Especially one we're likely to lose."

"I assume the candidate who ran against you was a moron," Harriet said bitterly. "Because why else they elected you I can't imagine."

SAM was the first one at work on Saturday morning, bearing a sack of pumpkin crème donuts. Juggling the bag, a leftover turkey sandwich, and cranberry sauce in a mayonnaise jar, he fumbled for his keys and tried the gate. The key wouldn't work. He looked at his key, looked at the gate, reinserted the key. Nothing. While he was trying to figure out what was going on, a relief zookeeper Sam had only seen once or twice before came out of the barn. They saw each other in the same instant. The zookeeper, a pasty-faced man in his twenties, looked uncomfortable.

"My key won't work," Sam said. "You break this lock?"

"Nah. She had security change the locks this morning."

"Why'd she do that?" Sam said.

"Look, dude, all I know is she told me to come in and feed the elephant, so that's what I'm doing."

Sam tried to stay calm. "You unchain the girl yet?"

"I'm supposed to leave her chained up for now. I gave her some hay, though."

"Let me in," Sam said.

"No can do, bud. I'm really sorry."

"Just unchain the girl. You can do that."

The zookeeper headed around the barn. "Sorry, man, but I don't want to piss off the boss."

Sam called as loud as he could, "You hold on, shug! Papa's going to be right back, and then we'll get you out of that place. Just hold on, sugar."

He tore up the hill and straight into the house. Before he even came into the office suite, he could hear loud voices: Truman and that Harriet.

"For God's sake, Harriet," Truman was saying. "You can't lock them out."

"Oh? And why not?"

"He has twenty-four-hour access. Legally."

Sam stood outside the door.

"And I'm not contesting that," Harriet said. "But the zoo is my domain. I can deny access to anyone I feel might be a destructive presence."

"Oh, come on, Harriet," Truman said. "What are you going to gain? You have no legal basis for keeping him from her. Or Neva."

Sam could tell Harriet was smiling, one of those mean, pinched little smiles. "I do, as a matter of fact. Neva Wilson no longer works here."

Sam couldn't stand by for that. He pushed through into the office suite. Truman was standing in the door to Harriet's office, his back to Sam. "You're kidding," he was saying.

"She's been trouble since the first day she got here."

Sam could see muscles tighten in Truman's back. "Harriet, as the director of this zoo, your first obligation is to the animals. You can't keep that elephant chained up."

Harriet's voice got tight and shrill. "Oh, so you're an animal expert now? Don't you *dare* get sanctimonious with me, Truman. You've taken her side ever since she got here, and I won't have it."

Truman turned around and saw Sam. "Go back to the barn and

wait for me there," he said in a low voice. "I'll call my father and see what we can do. We'll get you in."

"Shug's going to hurt herself if she's left in there. She doesn't understand."

"I know," Truman said. "We'll fix this."

NEVA was waiting at the elephant yard fence when Sam got back. Truman must have called and warned her. She trotted to meet him.

"Sam, I'm going to call down to the sanctuary and ask Alice to get emergency clearance from her board so we can bring Hannah down as soon as we can get the permit through the USDA."

"How long's that going to take?"

"I don't know. A week. Maybe a little longer."

"Shug ain't got a week."

Truman pulled into the parking lot by the barn, and he and Winslow hopped out of his car.

"Shug's going to hurt herself if she's left in there," Sam said to him again. "You hear that noise, sounds like a hammer on an anvil? That's shug tearing up her leg. She doesn't understand."

Truman bowed his head. "I know, Sam."

"It's going to be okay," Neva said with as much confidence as she could muster. She walked away to her car and pulled out her cell phone.

SAM, Truman, and Winslow settled down behind a hedge outside the fence line to formulate a plan and keep an eye on the relief zookeeper. As soon as he left, locking the gate after him, Sam gave Winslow a nudge, and the boy dashed to the twelve-foot-high chain-link fence, climbed over the top, and dropped into the elephant yard. He came back to open the gate from the inside. Sam rushed into the barn and to Hannah's side. Blood was running down her ankle and had made a sticky pool beneath her feet. Sam unfastened the shackle and started petting and talking as reassuringly as he could manage with his own heart nearly broken. "It's okay now, sugar; Papa's here. You're going to be just fine."

Winslow came over. "Is she okay? She's sure bleeding a lot." He pointed to her ankle.

"She'll be better once we get her out of here," Sam said.

It was 2:58—two minutes before Harriet's afternoon performance. Truman backed his car up to the gate to the elephant yard, and Neva pulled up behind him. She hopped out of her car and disappeared inside; a minute later the hayloft door opened, and she pushed out four bales of hay. Truman loaded two in his trunk, then two in Neva's car. While he was doing that, Neva reappeared with two huge plastic totes full of uncut produce. Truman loaded these in the backseat of his car.

"Go," Neva told Sam. "Go! We'll see you there."

"Let's go now, shug," Sam said quietly. "We're going on a little adventure."

Reginald Poole appeared at the top of the hill. "Hey, wait up, you guys!" he shouted, running down as fast as he could. "You going on a walk?"

"Yeah, we are, but we got to make some tracks today. No dawdling. And no sassing, either. I'm not in the mood for any sassing."

"Where are we going?" Reginald said.

"You just give the girl a yam now and then and be patient," Sam said. "You'll see." And that was all he would say.

Harriet put on her pith helmet with grim determination. Her zoo was hemorrhaging like a leaking dike, spewing money, personnel, control. It couldn't go on. But first she had a performance to give. She gave her clothes a grim little tug and walked onto the front porch. Several hundred visitors were gathered at the foot of the stairs.

She raised the microphone. "Good morning, friends!" she called. "I am Maxine Biedelman. Welcome to my zoo!"

Light applause broke out. Martin Choi, clanking with his usual excessive gear, pushed forward through the crowd, which parted to let him up onto the stairs with Harriet. He seized the microphone. "Ladies and gentlemen, let me introduce you to Harriet Saul, the director of this terrific zoo of ours."

Harriet hissed, "Martin, for God's sake."

He kept right on going. "Let me tell you about this woman," he said into the mike.

*"What?"* Harriet said. She tried to grab the microphone away, but Martin lifted it high over his head and spun away, out of her reach.

"This is a wonderful woman, ladies and gentlemen. A *brave* woman. Do you all know Hannah, our elephant?"

Sounds of concurrence rose from the crowd.

"Well, this woman is going to save Hannah's life. That's right. Hannah lives alone and in lousy conditions—nobody's fault, just the truth, and Harriet Saul knows it. So here it is: She's working to relocate Hannah to someplace better, someplace where she can get healthy and live with other elephants."

A general gasp rose from the crowd. Martin went on. "Friends, you are looking at a woman who's putting it all on the line to make sure Hannah can go to an elephant sanctuary. It's where Hannah should be, not here, and this woman"—and here he actually *grasped Harriet's hand*—"is big enough to see it. That's integrity! That's courage! Folks, you are looking at a hero. A hero."

Harriet struggled to free her hand, but Martin kept it in an iron grasp. "She's a woman who's doing something not because it is easy, not because it's popular, but because it is *right.* Right, ladies and gentlemen! And I, for one, am proud to stand here beside her!"

And to her astonishment, he lifted her sweating hand high overhead in a victory salute.

SAM walked beside Winslow, with Hannah on his other side; and beyond that, Reginald. Hannah carried her tire, and she moved faster than she had in a long time. The Lord only knew where she thought she was going. She hadn't come this way, up the far side of the zoo property, in thirty years or more.

Sam asked Winslow, "You got the fruit like I asked you to bring?"

Winslow held up a gallon-sized ziplock bag of yams and carrots. Sam knew the boy had it; he was just talking to calm his nerves.

"You bring some for me, too?" Reginald called. "I didn't have time to cut anything, what with you all being so secretive."

"When we get there," Winslow said.

"Get *where?* What's the big damn secret?"

"You watch your mouth, boy," Sam warned, and Reginald subsided.

"Do you think someone's going to come after us, Sam?" Winslow asked.

"Nah. They probably won't even notice we're gone for a little while yet." He hoped he sounded more convinced than he felt.

They arrived at a chain-link fence. Sam brought wire cutters out of his jacket pocket and, working fast, cut the links until he'd freed a section of fence wide enough for Hannah to fit through. They walked on, into the woods now, farther than either Winslow or Reginald had ever been.

"Is this okay?" Reginald called from Hannah's far side. "I didn't think we were supposed to come here."

"Today is different," Sam said. "Today it's okay."

Hannah padded ahead of them now, following the same route she'd often walked so many years before.

"Do you like living with your daddy?" Sam asked Winslow, to keep his mind off worrying.

"Yeah. Miles does, too."

"The pig."

"Yup."

"Wouldn't normally picture your daddy with a pig," Sam said.

"Miles likes him, though."

"Pigs have a good sense of people. Old Hilda, she's the sow here; she doesn't like kids, but that's because she's afraid they'll sneak up and throw something at her."

"Why would she think that?"

"Someone tossed a firecracker in with her once. It scared her so bad she didn't come out of her shed for a week."

"That was mean," Winslow said.

"People are, sometimes."

"My dad told me Hannah's not going to live at the zoo anymore," Winslow said.

"Yup. Shug's going to go to a retirement home for elephants."

"Do you think she'll be okay down there?"

"Yeah, I do. Course, she's going to miss us at first, like we're going to miss her. But she'll get her feet nice and healed up, get to roam around where there's grass and a pond and other elephants. I expect she's going to think she landed in the Garden of Eden."

Reginald came around. "It's lonely over there," he said. "What are you guys talking about?"

"Heaven," Sam said. "You boys want to switch sides? Winslow, take shug's blind side for a little while and let Reginald come over here. Remember to keep your hand on her, so she knows you're there."

Winslow crossed over, and Reginald took his place.

"So tell me something about yourself I don't already know," Sam said.

"Like what?"

"I don't know. Tell me about your daddy."

Reginald's shoulders hunched up a little bit. "I haven't seen him for a while."

"That right?"

Reginald seemed to reach a decision. "He's in prison. He broke into a liquor store in Bothell. Said he didn't mean to hurt anything, just needed a little something to take the edge off a bad headache. Why would you break into a liquor store for that? He should have broken into a drugstore."

"Sometimes people do wrong things, son. Bet he'd take it back if he could. He's probably real sorry he isn't around to watch you grow up."

"Yeah," Reginald said without conviction.

"People can do all manner of stupid things. Doesn't mean they're bad people, necessarily. We get up some days and do something we shouldn't, and we can't even explain why. That's human nature. Maybe that's the way it was with your daddy."

They walked along quietly, listening to the sound of Hannah snapping twigs underfoot. Sam said, "You know, sometimes the folks we're given at the beginning don't end up being the ones who raise us. Someone loves you, why, then they're raising you. You got your aunt. Hannah, she found Miss Biedelman, and then she found me and Corinna. She's been lucky that way. And now she's got you, too."

That perked Reginald up. "You think she knows me?"

"Of course she knows you, son. She might have a buggered-up eye, but she's not blind. You're the man with the treats. Plus she trusts you. There's something about you she just likes."

"Yeah?"

"Sure."

"How about Winslow?" Reginald asked.

"Not so much," Sam said in a voice too low for Winslow to hear. "At least, not yet. But he's got Miles, so there's that—Hannah doesn't necessarily like to share."

"So she chose me."

"Yep."

The boy spread his chest, walked a little higher on his toes.

"Hey, you guys!" Winslow called. "It's getting creepy in here." Dusk was well underway. "Can I come over there with you?"

"Yeah, just tell shug where you're going and keep your hand on her when you cross behind her, so she doesn't startle," Sam said.

Winslow circled around and joined them. "Either of you ever have nightmares?" Sam asked.

"I do," Winslow said. "I dream my mom's mad at me. She was always mad about something."

"How about you?" Sam asked Reginald.

"Nah."

"Hannah, she dreams," Sam told them.

Reginald rolled his eyes. "Aw, you don't know that."

"Sure I do," Sam said. "If you look in her eyes, you can see it there as plain as day. Shug dreams about grass. Grass and elephants."

HARRIET closed herself in her office with a pounding headache. The Trojan Horse had wrought less havoc than Martin Choi's declaration on Havenside's front stairs. Within an hour of completing her show, she had declined interviews with the Associated Press, the *Tacoma News-Tribune,* Northwest Cable News, the *Seattle Post-Intelligencer,* the *Seattle Times,* and Reuters. She had had the receptionist tell them all she would return their calls after four p.m. She figured by then she'd either be dead from a stroke or her blood pressure and pulse would have returned to a sustainable range.

She paced the perimeter of her office. For the first time in her adult life, she didn't know what to do. Her experience centered on rejection, not courtship. She'd been sabotaged by praise.

Her security radio crackled, and then one of the security guards said, "Security to Ms. Biedelman-Saul. Ma'am, there's no elephant down here. Over."

"What do you mean? How can there not be an elephant?"

"I don't know, ma'am. Over."

"Well, are you saying she escaped?"

"No, ma'am, I don't see any sign of that. Over."

"Oh, for God's sake."

"Yes, ma'am. Over and out."

JUST when Sam's flashlight batteries began to die, they broke from the woods into a meadow. "Hey!" Winslow said. "Now I know where we are! This is my grandpa's farm." Then he saw the barn, golden light flooding through two small windows. "We're going to keep Hannah here, aren't we?"

"Smart boy!" Sam said, clapping Winslow on the back. "Shug's going to stay the night, give us a chance to sort some things out."

Matthew came out the back door of the house as they neared the barn. Winslow ran to meet him.

"Look who we've got!" he called.

Matthew gave the boy a hug and walked with him toward the barn, where Sam, Reginald, and Hannah were standing. Matthew slid open the barn door. The barn was a clean, dry, open place with hay strewn over the dirt floor. Matthew hung several Coleman lanterns to boost the golden light of the overhead bulbs. Hot white lantern light threw shadows into the corners.

"Think this'll do, Sam?"

"Yes, sir. I think this should be about perfect."

A car crunched up the gravel drive and stopped in front of the barn.

"Ah!" Matthew said. "Here's my son."

Truman joined them in the barn, closely followed by Miles. Miles snuffled his way in while Hannah watched him with rolling eyes, reached toward him tentatively with her trunk. The little pig twitched his tail and gamely turned in a circle so Hannah could sniff all of him. Truman took the wheelbarrow to the car and came back with his two bales of hay.

Reginald poked Winslow hard in the ribs. "That your pig?"

"Yeah. He farts a lot."

Reginald snorted appreciatively, looking around. "This is real nice. You get to come over here often?"

"Yeah," Winslow said. "Sometimes I get to drive the tractor."

"Yeah? I visit my grandpa sometimes, too. He lets me do whatever I want. One time I ate twenty-two Eskimo Pies in a row."

"You're lying," Winslow said.

"Nuh-uh," said Reginald.

"So where does he live?"

"Here."

"Where's here?"

"Bladenham."

"Yeah, but what street?"

"I don't know. I never paid attention."

"I bet you don't even have a grandpa."

Reginald kicked Winslow hard on the shin, and then they were scuffling in the hay.

"Boys!" Truman called. "Knock it off."

"He's telling all these lies," Winslow said.

"Then he probably has a good reason," Truman said. "Find something else to talk about."

Sam was telling Matthew, "Shug must think she's died and gone to heaven with all this nice hay and pretty barn."

"Did she get through the day without too much harm?" Truman asked. He looked down at Hannah's bloody ankle and winced.

"She got a little upset earlier, but she'll be okay," Sam said.

Truman's gaze went from Hannah's leg to Sam's. "Sam—good god!" The cuff of Sam's khaki pants was wet with blood. "What happened?"

"Just a nasty sore I've got. Bleeds sometimes, but the doctor's got me on a new medicine that should fix it right up—that and getting off my feet for a while once shug's settled."

"I hope so," Truman said, and then car tires crunched over the gravel again. Neva pulled up and jumped out.

Sam, Truman, Winslow, Reginald, and Matthew all turned.

"I just heard from Alice. They'll take her as soon as we can have her ready!"

A whoop rang out.

"Details!" Truman said. "We want details!"

Neva said, "Well, evidently this lockout was the final straw. When Alice told the board chairman, he called the executive committee together, and I guess they just about set the room on fire. Apparently, they drew up a motion to accept Hannah on the spot, and the full board passed it by a phone vote without a single dissension." She turned and said quietly, "Congratulations, Sam."

Sam shook his head. "Don't know what to say." Hannah wrapped her trunk around his head, explored his ear. He reached up and patted her. "It's all right, baby doll. It's all right now."

Off to the side, Matthew was saying to Winslow, "Come with me, my boy." The two of them trotted off.

"What on earth?" Neva asked Truman, but he just shook his head.

"Could I borrow your phone?" Sam asked him. "I'd like to call Mama and tell her the news. She's going to be on the moon." Truman extended his cell phone, and Sam walked deeper into the barn.

Matthew came back into the barn with Lavinia and Winslow. Winslow carried two cream sodas; Matthew had a bottle of wine and a bouquet of glasses.

"You know we're going to have to tell Harriet," Truman said to Neva.

"I thought I would do that myself in a little while. Unless you'd rather do it, of course," Matthew said to Sam, who'd come back with Truman's phone.

"No, sir," said Sam, returning Truman's cell phone.

"Is Corinna all right?"

"Woman's beside herself. I never heard her stuck for words before."

"Then I believe a toast is in order." Matthew uncorked the wine and had Winslow pass around the filled wineglasses, and cream sodas for the boys.

"To Hannah!" Matthew called.

"To Hannah!" they all echoed.

SAM pulled Reginald aside and pointed to his watch: five-fifteen. "I forgot all about your aunt. When was she picking you up?"

"Five. It's okay, though. She won't care."

"Course she'll care. She's probably worried sick. You ask Mister Levy over there if you can use his cell phone, and then you tell her we'll drive you home."

"Aw, man," Reginald said, and shuffled over to Matthew.

"He seems like a nice boy," Matthew said to Sam, watching Reginald shuffle away, punching a number into Matthew's cell phone.

"Yeah, he just needs some attention."

"I gather his father's in jail," Matthew said.

"Yeah," Sam said. "It about killed him to tell me that."

Reginald headed back looking dejected as they both watched. "She's real mad," he said when he reached them.

"She should be, you promising her something and then breaking your word. Your word is the only thing a man's got, so don't you go wasting it." Sam put his hand on the boy's back. "I think we got some things to talk about, you and me."

"Yeah? Like what?"

"Like what you want more, a future or a past."

"What's that supposed to mean?" Reginald said.

"Looks like I'm going to have a little time on my hands pretty soon, so you stick with me, and I'll show you."

NEVA hauled an air mattress, sleeping bag, pillow, and toilet kit out of her car and into the barn. She told Matthew, "I'm taking first watch, if that's okay with you."

Matthew nodded. "You know best. Just come into the house anytime you need to. Walk right in. I'll set some towels out for you, and Lavinia's preparing supper."

Sam said to her, "You sure you don't want me to be the one to stay over? Mama could bring me a sweater and some blankets, and I'd be fine."

"Nope. Your turn will come," Neva assured him.

"Uh-oh," said Winslow, pointing across the lawn.

Approaching from across the lawn were Lavinia and Harriet Saul. Matthew stepped forward to greet her. "Hello, Harriet. What a pleasure."

Harriet nodded at him curtly, and then at the others. "Sam. Neva. Truman."

"Ma'am," Sam said, stepping between Harriet and Hannah.

"Martin Choi has publicly declared me Saint Francis of Assisi. If I'm going to be beatified, I'd better at least understand why."

Neva said to Sam, "Let me talk. She's already fired me."

"That might have been a bit hasty," Harriet said.

"Oh, probably not."

"Look, I need to know. Is it absolutely necessary for Hannah to leave?" Harriet asked. "You know what it'll do to the zoo."

"She'll die if we don't move her," Neva said.

"And you agree?" Harriet asked Sam.

"Yes, ma'am."

"I assume you have someplace lined up to take her."

"The Pachyderm Sanctuary has agreed to take her as soon as she can be moved," Neva said. "It's an excellent facility near Sacramento."

"No doubt," Harriet said dryly. "And what will you do, Sam?"

"I'll be retiring," Sam said. "I've got some medical things I need to take care of."

"Medical things?" Harriet said.

"Diabetes, ma'am. I've got diabetes."

"You never said anything about this."

"No, ma'am."

"Believe it or not, I do care about these things."

"Yes, ma'am," Sam said. "I didn't know."

"And I assume you have a plan for moving her."

"Yes, ma'am, we do," Sam said.

"All right, then," she said. "I'm listening."

Matthew brought a glass of wine and a folding chair for her, and the others dragged over boxes and a bench. Harriet pulled her barn coat around her more tightly, and they began.

At ten o'clock that night, Truman and Neva were sitting on wooden crates at an upturned industrial spool they were using as a table. The remnants of a late spaghetti dinner had been loaded into black trash bags nearby, and in one of the stalls, Miles blinked in porcine contentment, bedded down in fresh straw. Winslow lay on a straw bed one stall over, cozy in his down sleeping bag; Hannah stood near Neva and Truman, dozing over her tire.

"I admire your dedication," Truman was saying.

"It's just selfishness—I love what I do. I can't imagine doing anything else."

"You're lucky. Most of us don't feel that way. Lives of quiet desperation and all that."

"Are you desperate?"

"Me? No. There have been moments, but no—I have choices. Actually, I've been thinking about going to law school." He smiled ruefully. "Imagine being a student again at thirty-six."

From his stall, Miles heaved a mighty sigh. Truman smiled at Neva, who smiled back. Who would have ever thought he'd be here minding an elephant in a barn on a late fall evening, side by side with a woman with whom he believed he was falling in love.

"What will you do, once Hannah's gone?" Harriet had reinstated her to the ranks of a zoo employee, but only until Hannah was moved.

"Oh, there are lots of places I can go," Neva said. "I've been in the business a long time, and I have a good reputation. It's a small pond out there where man and elephant meet, and I'm a pretty good-sized fish. I've had some offers."

Truman drew a fortifying breath. "Well, here's an idea Winslow and I have come up with. We think what Bladenham needs is a top-drawer miniature pig breeder and trainer. No, now, wait, hear me out. Pigs are cute when they're young. I know this from experience. And by the time they grow up, they're someone else's problem."

Neva laughed. "Me, a pig breeder?"

"*And* trainer. Winslow and I will teach you everything we know."

"That wouldn't take long."

"It might," Truman said. "It depends on how quickly we reveal our secrets."

"Do you have secrets?"

"Not many, but we could string them out. Think about staying. Please."

"We'll see," said Neva. "But in the meantime, listen: If you climb into my sleeping bag tonight, I won't kick you out."

"Ah," said Truman. "I should warn you that Miles may try to get in with me."

"And that," said Neva, "is where I set my limits."

As HER last customer drove away, Corinna saw Sam just pulling into the driveway. As they often did, the two of them closed up the shop together, Sam sweeping up hair clippings while Corinna emptied bowls of old disinfectant and poured in new. Sam seemed like he was in a pensive mood. "Now that shug's going, I don't know what I'm going to do with myself, Mama."

"We'll figure it out," Corinna said. "Like we always do."

"Don't know that I want to figure it out."

"Sure you do, honey. I guess we've got some mourning to do first, but once that's over, we'll still be right here, together."

Sam stowed his broom in the closet and came over to put his arms around her. "We're a fine pair," he said softly.

Corinna looked up at him, her eyes brimming. "Yeah, we are." She raised her hand to his face, his cheek as familiar to her as her own. "Aw, sugar man," she whispered, "now we get to be old."

HARRIET wondered why the expression stopped at a glass half empty. It could be a lot emptier than that, and she was in a position to know. She'd been drinking a bottle of Merlot that was definitely more than half empty.

She wandered out of the aviary with the wine bottle in one hand and her empty glass in the other, moving from room to room to visit the framed photographs she had hung everywhere—photographs of Brave Boy and Arthur, of Maxine in the company of mahouts in the jungles of Burma. Maxine, who was now mocking her: *You can look, but you may not have.* Harriet had been betrayed by her employees, by family, by love in general—and now, unkindest of all, she was being betrayed by Maxine Biedelman herself, Harriet's angel and savior, her beloved. The elephant would not be staying.

From her night table, Harriet pulled a thick stack of unframed pictures and fingered them like rosary beads. She left on top a close-up of the face of a young elephant, its left eye mangled and swollen shut, the eyelid pulpy and weeping blood. Under the picture was written in faint pencil, OUR DEAR GIRL. The photograph was of Hannah, freshly orphaned: Hannah, Maxine's crowning achievement, the object of her final passion. A big, awkward, wounded creature who was lucky enough to be loved by a woman who saw beauty where there wasn't any.

Harriet regarded the next photograph, a picture of Maxine in safari-wear, striding up the path of her property, neatly thatched huts on one side—a balloon-animal kiosk stood there now—and, on the other, an open yard with two gentle-eyed dik-diks and a zebra.

And just like that, from the ashes heaped around her, Harriet found her salvation. She was not, never had been, and never would be Maxine—Max—Biedelman. But she could be her agent, could keep the flame of Max's legacy alive by restoring Havenside, all of it. The whimsical gazebos and pavilions, the lush grounds, the grand home, the lifetime of photographs; and yes, gradually, the animals. She would tell Max's story to anyone who would hear her, and with the money she raised, she would rebuild the zoo. All of it.

And maybe one day there could be elephants again.

# 11

PEOPLE lined the streets of Bladenham two and three deep despite the drizzle. From inside the closed cab of the transport truck, Sam watched them cheering and holding up homemade signs and balloons to say good-bye to Hannah. His shug had been loved.

He hated that she was riding in an open cage like she was, even with the wooden windbreak on three sides. It was cold out, and it nearly broke his heart, seeing her chained to the transport cage by one front foot and one back foot so she couldn't turn around. It kept her safe, but he hated it anyway, his sugar being driven out of town like a criminal, like something wild and dangerous. What was she thinking, all by herself in those chains, with no idea where she was going? Sam wasn't allowed to ride back there with her.

Satellite trucks were broadcasting Hannah's departure live throughout the Pacific Northwest and feeding news services around the world. Harriet Saul had been giving interviews continuously since *Good Morning America* powered up at three a.m. It was now nine. Neva was ahead of them someplace, driving her run-down little car. She'd meet the transport truck at designated rest stops on I–5 heading south—two in Oregon, three or four in California. It would probably take them twelve hours to reach the sanctuary.

The truck driver didn't have a lot to say, and that was all right with Sam. His heart was too sore for company, all his feelings riding high and tight in his throat. If Max Biedelman was watching, he hoped she'd be proud—proud of Hannah, and proud of him, too. Sam thought about Corinna, about last night, when Corinna had said her good-byes to Hannah. She had been composed, at least mostly. Sam had stood back while she'd let Hannah's trunk explore her hands one last time. Hannah had moved close and rumbled deep down in her throat, as though she knew.

"Honey girl," Corinna had said, "you've been the best thing that's ever happened to Papa and me, and I think you know that. We love you, and that won't ever change, no matter how far away you are."

With her trunk, Hannah nudged Corinna gently to one side and wrapped her ear around the woman, holding her close. Sam had never seen the girl do something like that before. "Lord, but I'm going to miss you," Corinna broke down. "It's all right, baby— they're tears of joy. You're finally going to have the life the good Lord intended all along. And if that's not a joyful thing, I don't know what is."

"You been driving elephants for long?" Sam asked the driver, mostly to keep himself from entertaining sad thoughts. The driver was a big man—big belly, big face, stubbly cheeks. He had nasty, wet-sounding lungs, a cough full of junk.

"A few years," the driver said, resting a meaty forearm on the wheel. "I done 'em all—elephants, tigers, lions, giraffes. Walrus, one time; a killer whale one time, too. Big box of water sure made a mess when you stopped, slopping all over the place."

"You worry about them, when you're driving?"

"Nah," the driver said. "I figure that's someone else's job. Yours, today. I just keep us on the road and steer."

FORTY-ONE years ago, Max Biedelman had taught Sam how to ask Hannah for things: lie down, lift a foot, rise.

"When you ask her to do something, Mr. Brown, you must ask her nicely, and in a normal speaking tone," the old woman had said. "She is every bit as civilized as we are; indeed, more than some people I've known." She'd smiled to herself when she said that. "Hannah will understand you perfectly. Never underestimate her intelligence, or her desire to please you, once you've earned her trust. Trust is the glue that will bind her to you. Trust and respect."

Sam had never stood beside something so big before, or so soulful. The old woman had stood back, arms crossed, watching him, watching Hannah.

"Come, Hannah," he'd said.

The elephant had just stood there.

"Try again, Mr. Brown."

"Come, Hannah."

The elephant had stood there.

Max Biedelman's eyes twinkled. "You're unsure, Mr. Brown. If you're unsure, she will be, too, and it's in an elephant's nature to want to be sure of things before doing them."

Sam took a deep breath. In a low, quiet voice, he said, "Come on now, sugar. You and me got places to go."

And from that moment on, they had.

"HOW LONG YOU BEEN WITH this one?" The truck driver jerked his thumb over his shoulder.

"Forty-one years."

"Wow."

BY YREKA, California, Hannah's legs were raw from the constant friction of the shackles. Neva stood beside Sam, handing him strips of foam tape to wrap the leather in. Not that it would help much.

"Sam," she said softly, closing her hand around his wrist, and that's how he knew he was crying.

MAX Biedelman had called Sam to the house to help her move boxes. "What does one do with all the detritus of one's life?" she asked as he was pulling a trunk from a closet for her. "In the end it means so little to anyone."

"You're lucky to have had the life you did, sir—done so many things, been so many places."

Max Biedelman stood silhouetted in the parlor window, silent. Finally she said, "Do you know what I've been thinking lately? I've been thinking that we're animals, like any others—we senesce; we sink into decrepitude just as they do. But I've wondered if it isn't our special hell that we are able to register the swift passage of time, the lightning speed of it all, and the absoluteness with which it is gone. I feel my age, Mr. Brown; I feel every bit of it, and yet I can recall so very clearly what it was like to be young. It torments me. I should like, just one more time, to feel the winds of Africa, to feel the heat of the Indonesian jungle. The world is a fine place when one sees it from the back of an elephant." Her voice sank to a whisper. "You cannot know how hard it is, saying good-bye to it all. There are moments when it is unendurable."

"You're alive," Sam said. "You still got life all around you, so God isn't ready to bring you home yet. When He's ready, you'll be ready, too."

Max Biedelman wiped at her face with her shirt cuff and looked at him. "I hope so, Sam. I do hope so."

"Yes, ma'am," Sam said softly.

Maxine Leona Biedelman died in her room one week later.

And that night, for the very first time, Sam dreamed Hannah's dream.

"LOOKS like this is the place," the truck driver said, startling Sam, who must have dozed off. When they drove past a wooden sign saying PACHYDERM SANCTUARY, his heart began to pound.

Out the window he watched as the gravel road led them through woods and clearings, then into a huge meadow that disappeared over the top of rolling hills.

He had already seen it, right down to the rocks and hillocks.

They pulled up to a big white barn. A tall, long-legged, weathered woman signaled the driver where to park the truck. Neva shot by in her car and stopped alongside the barn, hopping out to embrace the woman. When Sam got out of the cab, Neva brought the tall woman over. "Sam, this is Alice McNeary."

"Nice to meet you, Sam. Neva's told me a lot about you."

Sam shook her hand. "Ma'am."

And then he'd turned and walked away.

Alice put her arm around Neva's shoulders and hugged her reassuringly. "It's always tough," she said quietly. "And they're always fine."

"The keepers or the elephant?"

"Both."

"God," Neva said, wiping her nose.

"You sure you won't stay with us?"

"I'm sure. I promised someone I'd come back, at least for a little while."

Alice gave her a quick hug and then strode to the truck, where Sam was fumbling with the cage's locking mechanism.

"Neva's told me Hannah is a good animal, Sam. One of the best."

"Yes, ma'am, she is."

"Has she had much to eat?"

"No, ma'am. Just some Dunkin' Donuts."

Alice cracked a smile. Sam smiled back.

"So she's spoiled, is she?"

"Yes, ma'am, she is."

Neva had put a ramp in place against the side of the cage and slid back the gate. All that was keeping Hannah inside were the chains and shackles.

"Hey, sugar," Sam said softly, climbing into the open gate of the cage. "How's my baby girl?"

Alice had been standing to one side, watching. Now she handed him a wrench. "Whenever you feel she's ready, Sam, you can do the honors."

Sam looked at her, not understanding.

"You can take off the shackles."

"Yes, ma'am," he said. "Me and shug have a couple things to talk over first, though, if that's all right with you."

"Of course. Take all the time you need. There's no hurry."

Neva started toward him, but Alice caught her by the arm and shook her head.

Sam reached into his pocket and pulled out the last donut, wrapped in a napkin. He held it out to Hannah on the palm of his hand. "I suppose that's the last Dunkin' Donut you're going to get for a while, baby girl."

Hannah nudged his hip anxiously with her trunk. He leaned into her and said, "Let me get through this, sugar. You're going to be with elephants now. You won't need me and Mama anymore." Sam turned the wrench over and over in his hand. "But no matter what, you can count on me thinking about you up there at home, so if you feel a little breeze or smell a donut smell sometimes, why, you know it's just my thoughts passing through. I won't leave you, is what I'm saying."

Hannah wrapped her trunk around Sam's head gently, whistled in his ear. "That's all, shug. That's what I got to say." He took a deep breath. "Foot, baby girl."

Hannah lifted her front foot. Sam unwrapped enough of the shackle to get at the fitting, and then the steel clattered onto the bed of the truck. He walked around behind her, and she lifted her foot before he'd even asked. The second shackle came undone like a well-oiled lock. Sam caught it before it could fall, staring at it in his hand. Then, still holding the shackle tightly, he turned and walked down the ramp. Hannah followed him the way she'd followed him so many times before, over so many years.

At the bottom of the ramp, he stopped and looked around. Cresting the hill Sam knew better than his own backyard, he saw four elephants. How many times had he seen them in his sleep—six hundred? A thousand?

He felt Hannah see them, too. She pulled up short like she'd been touched with something electric. One of the elephants trumpeted, and then the others trumpeted, too.

Sam could feel what she was feeling: that it had been so long.

He pushed her gently, willing her to leave him. His had been a long and solitary vigil, but it was over.

"We're going to be all right now, shug," he said. "This is how we begin."

# All About
## *Diane Hammond*

DIANE Hammond was in college when she realized she could write in James Joyce's stream-of-consciousness style fluently and for long periods of time without breaking a sweat. "That was also the very first time I dabbled in fiction," the author says on her website, "though I wasn't aware of it at the time, only that I was having fun."

Hammond began her professional life at a department store in Honolulu, Hawaii, in 1977, "but I was fired," she says, "so who cares about that job." She badly wanted to be an advertising copywriter, but no one would hire her, so instead she became an editorial assistant for a publisher of building industry tabloids. "At the first office Christmas party the executives exchanged, with a lot of fanfare and as tokens of their highest mutual regard, a decommissioned and presumably disarmed land

## Vital Stats

**BORN:** Queens, NY
**RESIDENCE:** Tacoma, WA
**FAMILY:** Husband, Nolan; daughter, Kerry
**EDUCATION:** Middlebury College, VT
**PETS:** Five very large cats and a Pembroke Welsh corgi
**BOOKS:** *Going to Bend* (2004), *Homesick Creek* (2005)
**WEBSITE:** www.DianeHammond.com

mine and a surplus torpedo. It was an interesting place to work."

Hammond moved to Washington, DC, in 1980. There, at a trade association and then a women's college, she had her first experiences with editing ("I like it, but I'm not very good at it") and public relations ("I'm good at it, but I don't like it"). She also began writing fiction, "cutting my teeth on short stories, attending classes and workshops in Glen Echo, Maryland, and joining a number of writing groups." Her first two short stories were published in *Woman's World,* followed by others in *Mademoiselle, Yankee,* and the *Washington Review.*

Four years later, Hammond moved to tiny Newport, Oregon (pop. 9,000), on the central Oregon coast, a writer's paradise with its relative isolation, constant winter storms, and harsh beauty. "I began maturing artistically there, discovering themes and settings that have resonated in my writing ever since." At the same time, she worked for the local electric utility. "I wrote an in-house newsletter that featured the reimagining of everyday workplace events as folk tales, melding creative writing with employee morale-boosting. God only knows if anyone but me ever got the point, but I was humored."

After leaving the utility, Hammond headed up communications efforts for the Oregon Coast Aquarium, which owned the facility built for Keiko, the killer-whale star of the hit movie *Free Willy.* She then worked for the Free Willy-Keiko Foundation, which owned the whale but not the facility, mirroring Samson Brown's official relationship with the Biedelman Zoo in *Hannah's Dream.* Hammond also wrote half of her first book, *Going to Bend,* at this time, but she

## The Real Sam

In 2001, Diane Hammond stumbled on television footage of a man named Solomon James, Jr. (pictured at right), unshackling Shirley, the Asian elephant he had taken care of for 22 years, for the last time. He had just transported her from the Louisiana Purchase Gardens and Zoo to the Elephant Sanctuary in Hohenwald, Tennessee. "It was clear that theirs had been a long and complex journey," Hammond says. That moment, along with her experience with the Keiko project, inspired the story of Samson Brown and Hannah.

## The Facts Behind the Fiction

The U.S. organizations that keep elephants vary widely. Some zoos have expansive, state-of-the-art facilities that more than meet their resident elephants' needs. Others, like the fictional Max L. Biedelman Zoo, are old, inadequate, and lacking the enormous resources necessary to upgrade their elephant exhibits.

There is a growing movement among animal welfare organizations to pressure zoos into letting their elephants go to sanctuaries, where they will have companionship, more room, and healthier living conditions. "I have enormous respect for the Elephant Sanctuary in Hohenwald, Tennessee, and other facilities where circus elephants as  well as zoo animals can find a lush haven," author Diane Hammond says." These facilities are terrifically expensive and can't serve all the elephants in need, but for the animals lucky enough to find new homes there, they mean a whole new life."

"got tangled up in craft and plot issues and put the whole thing aside for eight years."

In 1998, when Keiko was moved to Iceland, Hammond and her husband moved to Bend in the high desert of central Oregon and established Web-Wrights, their website-design company. "One snowy day when I didn't feel like doing whatever I was supposed to be doing, I resurrected the *Going to Bend* half-manuscript and read the thing over. Lo! I saw exactly where I'd been headed, if only I'd known it. I finished the book in six months, and it found a home with Doubleday.

The day the book was accepted was rivaled only by the days I got married and gave birth to my daughter, Kerry."

*Going to Bend* was well received, especially in the Pacific Northwest, although "it took confidence-bolstering hypnotherapy and the constant support of my family to get me through that first book tour, but get through it I did." Hammond wrote *Homesick Creek,* her second novel, on the road between Bend and Tacoma while her family made endless trips back and forth to find and ready a home there, where they now live, "hopefully for good." ∎

# ACKNOWLEDGMENTS

Page 167: Robert Azmitia. Pages 5, 168, 441, and 575: iStockphoto.com. Page 286: © Jan Press/Photomedia. Page 440: © Sigrid Estrada. Pages 440–441: Bookreporter.com. Page 573: Studio 404 Photography. Page 574: Margaret Croft/*The News Star*.

The volumes in this series are issued every two to three months.
The typical volume contains four outstanding books in condensed form.
None of the selections in any volume has appeared in *Reader's Digest* itself.
Any reader may receive this service by writing
The Reader's Digest Association, Inc., Pleasantville, NY 10570
or by calling 1-800-481-1454.
In Canada write to:
The Reader's Digest Association (Canada) Ltd.,
1125 Stanley Street, Montreal, Quebec H3B 5H5
or call 1-800-465-0780.

Some of the titles in this volume are also available in a large-print format.
For information about Select Editions Large Type call 1-800-877-5293.

**Visit us on the Web at:**
**rd.com**
**readersdigest.ca (in Canada)**